# hapa japan

VOLUME ONE  History

EDITED BY  Duncan Ryūken Williams

ITO CENTER EDITIONS
AN IMPRINT OF KAYA PRESS

17 18 19 20 4 3 2 1

First Edition
For information about permission to reproduce selections from this
book, please write to: kaya@kaya.com.

Printed in Korea
Distributed by D.A.P./Distributed Art Publishers
155 Avenue of the Americas, 2nd Floor, New York, NY 10013
800.338.BOOK www.artbook.com

HAPA JAPAN: HISTORY (Volume 1)
Edited by Duncan Ryūken Williams
ISBN 978-1-885030-53-5;
Library of Congress Control Number: 2016961884

HAPA JAPAN: IDENTITIES & REPRESENTATIONS (Volume 2)
Edited by Duncan Ryūken Williams
ISBN 978-1-885030-54-2;
Library of Congress Control Number: 2016961884

*This publication is made possible by support from: the Japan Foundation; the Shinnyo-en Buddhist order; the Andrew W. Mellon Foundation; the USC Dana and David Dornsife College of Arts, Letters, and Sciences; the USC Department of American Studies and Ethnicity; and the USC Asian American Studies Program. Special thanks to the Choi Chang Soo Foundation for their support of this work. Additional funding was provided by the generous contributions of: Amna Akbar, Jade Chang, Lisa Chen & Andy Hsiao, Floyd & Sheri Cheung, Prince Kahmolvat Gomolvilas, Jean Ho, Huy Hong, Helen Heran Kim, Juliana S. Koo, Pritsana Kootint-Hadiatmodjo, Ed Lin, Viet Nguyen, Chez Bryan Ong, Whakyung & Hong Yung Lee, Amarnath Ravva, Duncan Williams, Mikoto Yoshida, Anita Wu & James Spicer, and others. Kaya Press is also supported, in part, by: the National Endowment for the Arts; the Los Angeles County Board of Supervisors through the Los Angeles County Arts Commission; the Community of Literary Magazines and Presses; and the City of Los Angeles Department of Cultural Affairs.*

# TABLE OF CONTENTS

# Global Hapa Japanese Histories: Migration, Empires, and Postcoloniality

# World War II and Its Aftermath

# Developments in the Post-war Mixed Race Japanese American Community

*indicates that the chapter is a reprint of a previously published article*

# ACKNOWLEDGEMENTS & STYLISTIC CONVENTIONS

This two-volume collection is the result of a five-year process of editing the best papers delivered at the Hapa Japan Festivals of 2011 (hosted by the UC Berkeley Center for Japanese Studies) and 2013 (hosted by the USC Shinso Ito Center for Japanese Religions and Culture) as well as compiling and soliciting as reprints classic articles and cutting-edge research published elsewhere. The funding for the academic conferences and this publication came from the Hapa Japan Database Project, which in turn, received the generous financial support from the Japan Foundation, the Shinnyo-en Buddhist order, the Japan Society for the Promotion of Science, the Andrew W. Mellon Foundation, and Kyoto University's "A Japan-based Global Study of Racial Representations (Grant-in-Aid for Scientific Research (S))" project headed by Professor Yasuko Takezawa. The staff at the two Japan studies centers at UC Berkeley and USC respectively—Kana Sugita, Kumi Hadler, Alyssa Yoneyama, Mieko Araki, and Shannon Takushi—also played a major role in the production of the two academic conferences and this publication.

I would also like to acknowledge the Academic Advisory Committee of the Hapa Japan Database Project, whose members include Cynthia Nakashima, Stephen Murphy-Shigematsu, Lily Anne Yumi Welty Tamai, and Jane H. Yamashiro. Their guidance was invaluable throughout the editorial process. Dave Harris and Vanessa Haugh also contributed in many ways to refining the final version of the manuscript. For their thoughtful design and production of this collection, my gratitude goes to Bryan Ong and his team at Spoon+Fork Studio and Sunyoung Lee and her staff at Kaya Press.

Among the stylistic conventions used in this collection, for Japanese terms, we have italicized words that have not entered colloquial English (the exceptions include Nikkei, Issei, and Nisei). The romanization of Japanese terms is standard except with the term ハーフ which we have romanized as *hafu* instead of *haafu*. The convention for Japanese name order follows the "family name, first name" order for those who lived prior to 1868 and the "first name, family name" order for those who have lived primarily in the modern or contemporary periods.

I

For English-language conventions, we have opted to capitalize Black and White (or Blackness and Whiteness) as racial groupings or categories except when used adjectivally. Hyphenation for terms like Irish American or Japanese American is also only used when employed adjectivally as is the phrase "mixed race." These conventions are disregarded when an author is directly quoting from a text that uses a different approach. Please note that the bibliographic references for both volumes one and two are located at the end of volume two.

# INTRODUCTION

DUNCAN RYŪKEN WILLIAMS

This two-volume project is an attempt to document the diversity of mixed-roots and mixed-race Japanese not only in the Japanese archipelago, but in its global spread, across regions such as Australia, North America, Europe, Brazil, Taiwan, Pakistan, or the Philippines. This collection aims not only to showcase the global reach of Japanese of mixed ancestry, but to provide the historical context of identity formations and representations of such peoples, so as to inform discussions of Japan and its diaspora's futures as increasingly polycultural and multiethnic societies.

It is widely recognized that in the course of Japan's modernization process, a rhetoric of the "purity" and monoethnicity of the island nation's peoples took hold, with several waves—such as the early seventeenth century, the turn of the century (nineteen into twentieth), and the post-World War II periods—as particularly key moments when these notions came to the fore. This is despite the much longer history of mixing among those who came to inhabit the Japanese archipelago from other transpacific oceanic cultures, from various continental Asian regions, or from territories to the north. Indeed, global trade, migration, and conflict engender new polycultural and multiethnic formations, even in regions that have historically been resistant to mixedness. The rhetoric of purity has obscured the importance of such multi-ethnicity in Japan's past and present. And Japan's current demographic shifts portend an even more diverse future for Japan.

With one of the world's lowest fertility rates and highest longevity rates, Japan's population has been rapidly decreasing while becoming top heavy in the demographic pyramid. The Japanese government has projected that its nation's population will fall from its peak of 128 million in 2007 to roughly 87 million people in 2060, with half of the population at that time over 65 years of age.[1] The October 2015 appointment of ex-Finance Ministry bureaucrat, Katsunobu Katō, by the Abe administration, to the new post of Minister of State for Measures for Declining Birthrate, dedicated to stabilizing the falling birthrate to a population of 100 million by 2050, reflects the heightened attention the problem of Japan's low birth rate (*shōshika mondai*) and the "graying of society" (*kōreika shakai*).

But there is another story revealed in the government statistics that is hardly ever discussed. Government statistics from 2014 revealed that one out of 29 babies born in Japan had one parent who was a non-Japanese national, a dramatic rise even from 2010 data that showed one out of 49 babies having mixed-roots parentage.[2] Although the current Japanese government has rejected the possibility of a more open immigration policy as a primary approach to addressing its declining population, we should expect that these numbers will only increase.

Of course, these trends are not limited to Japan, both in terms of the general shift to racial mixing and the more specific shift within the Japanese diasporic population, especially in Brazil, Canada, and the United States. For example, in the United States, where a mixed-race President proudly proclaimed himself the first "Pacific" President of America, the latest decennial U.S. Census showed that as of 2010, there were 4.2 million multiracial children (an increase of nearly 50 percent from the 2000 Census findings), out of a total multiracial American population of 9 million. Although these 9 million Americans only make up 2.9% of the overall population, the dynamic growth among younger populations portends a much greater role for multiracial Americans in the future, much like in Japan.

In a surprise to many demographers, the 2010 U.S. Census also revealed Asians are the fastest growing racial group in America and that the number of multiracial Asians grew at a faster rate than the number of monoracial individuals (a near 60-percent growth since 2000), and that the combination "Black and Asian" grew the fastest among multiple-minority race groups of 10,000 or more individuals.[3]

Among Asian Americans, Japanese Americans historically have had the highest rates of out-marriage. This has led to a situation where the 2010 Census data showed that out of 1.3 million Japanese Americans, more than 460,000 identified themselves as multiracial, a number growing at such a pace that by the next Census count (in 2020) a majority of the Japanese American community will be multiracial if current trends continue. While every American ethnic and racial group is experiencing these trends of increased mixedness, the Japanese American case stands out because it will be the first Asian American community to become majority multiracial.[4]

With these demographic shifts, both the visible and invisible aspects of national representation and belonging come into relief as they are challenged by the new generation. In the case of Japan, while it is unlikely that a visibly mixed-roots person will be elected head of state in the near future, having mixed roots is not the barrier it once was. Denny Tamaki (born in Uruma, Okinawa to a Okinawan mother and a father from the United States) represents a shift as the first visibly mixed-race legislator from Okinawa elected to the National Diet. Another politician, Renhō Murata (often known simply as Renhō), born in Tokyo to a Japanese mother and Taiwanese father, who phenotypically doesn't read as mixed race, is a Diet member, former Minister of Administrative Reforms and State Minister of Government Revitalization, and elected as the leader of the opposition Democratic Party in fall 2016. Her election as the leader of a major opposition party came despite considerable political and media discussion about her dual citizenship that questioned her loyalties.

In terms of national representation, two of the three most prominent figures presenting Tokyo's bid to host the 2020 Summer Olympics, were of mixed heritage. In addition to Prime Minister Shinzō Abe, the two "faces" of Japan on the international stage were Christel Takigawa, a well-known television announcer and news presenter of Japanese-French heritage, who delivered the bid's main presentation in English and French and representing the Japanese athletes, Koji Murofuji, the Olympic Gold medalist and former World Champion in the hammer throw, who was born in Shizuoka Prefecture to a Japanese father and a Romanian mother.

Indeed, 2015-2016 was a banner season for mixed-race Japanese as representatives of the nation in the realm of sports. During the summer, the 16-year sprinter Abdul Hakim Sani Brown, with a Japanese mother and a Ghanaian father, won both the 100 and 200 meters at the IAAF World Junior Championship in Cali, Columbia beating Usain Bolt's previous championship record in the 200 meter race. This earned him a spot on the Japanese senior national team for the World Athletics Championship in Beijing. Further, in the media spotlight during the National High School Championship (Summer Koshien) baseball tournament—one of Japan's most popular sports events—was Rui Okoye, an 18-year-old outfielder for Kantō Daiichi High School, born to a Japanese mother and a Nigerian father, who led his team to the semi-finals. Also during the summer, tennis player Taro Daniel, born to a Japanese mother and an American father, became the first mixed-race Japanese to have played at all the Grand Slams including The Championships at Wimbledon and, more significantly, clinched the decisive point against Columbia while representing Japan at the Davis Cup that allowed Japan to advance to the World Group. Not to be outdone, his colleague on the women's tour, the Japanese-Haitian Naomi Osaka reached the third rounds of both the Australian Open and the U.S. Open. And half-Japanese and half-Nigerian high school volleyball sensation, Airi Miyabe, helped Japan qualify for the summer FIVB Volleyball World Grand Prix as a new selection on the national team.

But it would be during the Fall that Japan was riveted with the shocking play of the national team at the 2015 Rugby World Cup. Indeed, the Japanese public set a new world record for the biggest domestic audience to ever watch a televised rugby game when 25 million Japanese, nearly a quarter of the country's population, watched the "Brave Blossoms" defeat Samoa only a few days after causing the biggest upset in the history of rugby when they defeated two-time champions, South Africa's Springboks. Japan's multiethnic national team was led by head coach Eddie Jones, born to a Japanese mother and Australian father, along with other *hafu* national team members like utility back and try scorer Kotaro Matsushima, who was born in South Africa to a Japanese mother and a Zimbawean father.

Another reflection of the changing "face" of Japan was the selection of the 2015 Japanese representative for the Miss Universe pageant, Ariane Miyamoto, who was born in Sasebo, Nagasaki Prefecture to a Japanese mother and an African American father. Her selection as Miss Universe Japan was met with some controversy that she was not "Japanese enough," revealing the persistent notion of Japanese racial purity, against which Miyamoto has used her victory to campaign for raising awareness of difficulties faced by fellow *hafu* Japanese nationals in Japan. In her interview with the *New York Times*, she claimed, "Even today, I am usually seen not as a Japanese but as a foreigner. ... I want to challenge the definition of being Japanese."[5] Miyamoto's ground-breaking selection as a representative for Japan was followed in 2016 with the half-Japanese and half-Indian Priyanka Yoshikawa chosen as Japan's representative for the Miss World pageant.

These recent developments, however, should not be viewed as complete novel, given the long history of mixedness in Japan and its diasporic networks around the globe. In this collection, we attempt to reveal the complex history of mixedness in Japan and in its diasporic worlds—both the mixed past, and the complexity of the current mixed experience. To explore the many individuals and communities described in this volume, I would recommend the Hapa Japan Database Project's website: www.hapajapan.com.

In the two volumes, we use the term "hapa Japanese" to refer to these mixed-roots and mixed-race persons in a variety of historical and spatial contexts. The term "hapa" has its origins in Hawai'i, where in Hawaiian Creole English (or Pidgin), it originally referred to something that is "half" or "part" of something else. Historically, the most common usage of the term was for a person of mixed Hawaiian and white heritage, or a hapa haole. Residents of Hawai'i also began to use hapa to refer to other people of mixed Hawaiian and non-Hawaiian heritage, such as hapa pake (part Chinese), hapa kepani (part Japanese), or hapa popolo (part Black). More recently, the term hapa has been adopted outside of Hawai'i, its meaning expanded to refer to any person of partial Asian or Pacific Islander heritage, a cause of some controversy and concern around the ethics of appropriation. Here, we use the term in its broadest sense to refer not only to those who are literally "half" Hawaiian and Japanese, but to all in Japan and its diaspora, whose heritage mixes Japanese roots with any other source. *Hafu* is more commonly used in Japan to refer to persons of mixed roots and mixed race Japanese heritage. Like hapa, the Japanese term *hafu* is derived from the English term "half," and increasingly is used in a much broader manner than the earlier strict reference to a person having one Japanese national as a parent. The Japanese term has also not been without its detractors, some of whom would prefer other Japanized English terms like *daburu* ("double") to refer to the doubling effect of having parents with multiple heritages or point to the term *hafu*'s early history as excluding those who were neither half White nor phenotypically interpreted by most Japanese as mixed. But these days, the term *hafu* as well as the more recent term *mikkusu rūtsu* (mixed roots) have gained a broader currency in Japan that is more inclusive than exclusive and includes persons of so-called "invisible race," typically individuals of East Asian heritage whose mixed heritage is not visibly apparent, such as Japanese-Koreans or Japanese-Chinese. Thus, for purposes of this collection, the terms "hapa Japanese," "*hafu*," or "mixed-roots Japanese," appear frequently and sometimes interchangeably to encompass persons with some partial Japanese mixed-roots and mixed-race heritage, all the while acknowledging the socially constructed nature of racial and ethnic categories.

We begin these two volumes in the eighth century with historian Nadia Kanagawa's chapter on migration to the Japanese archipelago from the Asian continent and migrant integration during the Nara (710-794) and Heian (794-1185) periods. Through a study of legal codes of the period and other historical documents, Kanagawa focuses on the creation and definition of identities during that period, including those named "*karako*" in one of Japan's official histories, the *Nihon shoki*, who were "children born when people of Nihon marry foreign women." As Kanagawa's exploration of Japan's imperial family reveals, mixedness was a feature of the very center of power in classical Japanese history and more specifically, the famous emperor who oversaw two shifts in the location of the imperial capital, Kammu Tennō (737-806), who is recorded as being descended from King Muryong of Paekche (kingdom in southwest Korea) through his mother Takano no Niigasa. Such evidence belies the myth of a racially pure Japanese people in a classical past, especially given that official records of the genealogies of 1,180 royally recognized lineages of the central provinces issued in the year 815 reveal that approximately a third of the imperial court was originally from families of foreign origin. Kanagawa's Chapter 1 reveals just how closely connected the

Japanese archipelago was with neighboring lands and cultures. What the study of early Japanese history helps us see is that for most of the archipelago's history, it was a chain of islands that connected, rather than cut off, linkages to other oceanic islands as well as continental Asian regions.

The island's connection to the West through the opening of trade with Europeans marks yet another stage in the history of hapa Japanese peoples. Historian Gary Leupp covers a critical period in Japan's encounter with Europeans, from the first arrival of the Portuguese in 1543 until the opening of the so-called "treaty ports" in 1859. In Chapter 2, Leupp tells of how commerce in the sixteenth and early seventeenth centuries resulted in mixed communities, including the Japanese-Siamese community in Ayutthaya, a Japanese-Vietnamese community in Hoi An, a mixed Japanese-Filipino community in Dilao in Luzon, and intermarriages throughout many regions of Southeast Asia, but with a primary focus on European-Japanese persons. Highlighting the very different notions of the ethnic or racial "other" found in European and Japanese categories of peoples, Leupp describes the wide range of intimacies between Japanese women and European men in the Kyushu port towns of Hirado, Nagasaki, and Hakata that resulted in mixed-race persons prior to the so-called "closed country" (sakoku) policies, which severely restricted encounters, commercial or intimate, between Japanese and Europeans with the exception of the Dutch. The chapter describes several instances when, as part of the expulsion orders, mixed-race Japanese Europeans were deported to places like Macao or Batavia as "barbarians" along with their parents. Leupp shows how shifting political and economic structures of the early modern period played a critical role in whether those of mixed heritage could "belong" to any one community represented by either parent or possibly even hold multiple allegiances and identities—a theme that is repeated in many of the essays in these two volumes.

In Chapter 3, Brian Burke-Gaffney extends Leupp's discussion by focusing on the intimate encounters on Nagasaki's artificial island of Dejima, where the Dutch were stationed, and the Chinese Quarters in the port city. By examining the period after the so-called "closed country" policies went into effect, when the Japanese permitted only the Dutch and Chinese restricted access to the island nation, Burke-Gaffney highlights the importance of Nagasaki and the fascinating accounts of mixed-race Japanese people like the brief life of Michitomi Jōkichi (1806-1823), the son of Dutch East India Company factor Hendrik Doeff and a Japanese courtesan named Uriuno. Burke-Gaffney uses the long history of the port city to paint a vivid picture of its thoroughly international character, including during the so-called foreign settlement period that began with the establishment of the ports of Nagasaki, Yokohama, and Hakodate as commercial zones for trade in 1859. Burke-Gaffney also focuses on the son of Scottish merchant Thomas B. Glover and his Japanese mother, Kaga Maki. Known in Japanese circles as Kuraba Tomisaburō (1871-1945) and T.A. Glover when engaged in business and social affairs within the Nagasaki foreign settlement, he was also a part of a truly international Japanese couple in the port city after he married Nakano Waka, a British-Japanese native of Yokohama. Burke-Gaffney outlines the impact Kuraba/Glover had on the economic development of Nagasaki, including his leadership of the Steamship Fisheries Co., a company that introduced Japan's first steam trawlers and modernized the Japanese fishing industry.

Another Nagasaki-born European hapa Japanese, Kusumoto Ine (1827-1903), daughter of Philipp Franz von Siebold, a physician of German origin, and, Kusumoto Taki, her Japanese mother, is the subject of Ellen Nakamura's study in Chapter 4 of the first woman in Japan to practice Western-style medicine. Through new sources, Nakamura reveals the complex textures of Ine's life, placing her in the context of the history of medicine in Japan, as she rose from humble beginnings to serve Date Munenari, the *daimyo* of Uwajima, and later the Imperial Palace, even being in attendance in 1873 of the birth of the Meiji Emperor's child.

In Chapter 5, Lane Earns continues the focus on Nagasaki, but with special attention to North Americans in the Nagasaki foreign settlement. Decades of research on the history of Nagasaki is brought to bear on Earns's account of the (mis)adventures of an American sailor-turned-merchant named George Lake and his various children, including a son claimed to have been born from a relationship with Takashino, a woman from a Nagasaki house of prostitution, who helped manage his successful provisions company in the port city. He relates how the Lake affair may have influenced the famous novel *Madame Chrysanthème* (1887), written by French seaman Viaud, as well as the immensely popular Puccini opera *Madama Butterfly*, set in Nagasaki featuring the American Lt. Pinkerton, the young Nagasaki courtesan Cio Cio San, and their mixed-race son, Trouble. Many other American-Japanese families appear in Earns's account of Nagasaki's bustling international zone prior to the rise of Japanese militarism that brought an end to the social acceptance of interracial relationships and biracial children: as war approached, such individuals became suspect. His study of these families demonstrates the importance of a transpacific, rather than national, approach to the history of hapa Japanese. Earns relates the stories of many of the children of Nagasaki, not all of whom were destined to life in Japan. For example, the three children of Irish-born American merchant John Breen— two, Henry and Catherine, with Shie Tomonaga, and a daughter,

Margaret, with Yoka Miyahara—while educated in Nagasaki, left the city after their father's death, and a number of their offspring eventually made their way to the United States. And Ai Yamaguchi (born 1864), the only daughter of the U.S. Consul John Walsh and Rin Yamaguchi, married a Japanese man, and her many descendants, some of whom married Westerners and others Japanese, spread across Japan, the United States, and Europe, continue to communicate with each other despite the distances. The story of Nagasaki hotelier John F. Jefferson, the son of African American bartender J.J. Jefferson and his Japanese mother Naka Morita, is unusual in that there were so few black-Japanese families in this early period. And, perhaps most notably, there is the example of Masa Nakayama (Masa Powers), the daughter of Naka Iida and American merchant R.H. Powers, who in 1960 became Japan's Welfare Minister, the first woman—mixed-race or not—to hold a cabinet position in Japan.

The sociologist Itsuko Kamoto, in Chapter 6, helps us understand the shifting social and legal structures that governed the standing of mixed families in the transition from early modern to modern Japan. Arguing that the concept of an "international marriage" (kokusai kekkon) could only exist when legal frameworks gave legitimacy to binding relationships between individuals from two differing nation states, Kamoto's work reveals the complexity of the questions of nationality for hapa Japanese. She examines legal cases about such issues, both before and after the promulgation of Edict 103 (otherwise known as Regulations on Japanese-Foreigner Marriage of 1873; the first Japanese law to regulate international marriage). In a fascinating account of the legal case of King Kiku Kingdon, the son of Nicholas Philip Kingdon, a British resident of Yokohama, and Utagawa Mura of the renowned Utagawa family of ukiyoe woodblock print artists, Kamoto explores how British and Japanese law and customs were variously interpreted by numerous British officials as well as by the Japanese Ministry of Justice, Ministry of Foreign Affairs, and Ministry of Home Affairs. Ultimately, after a lengthy legal battle, including nearly six years of indecision by the modern nation states as they debated how "international marriages" would be regulated, Kingdon was able to have his Japanese nationality reinstated. In describing the changes in Japan's legal standards of national belonging, which were motivated by the need to contend with the Western powers that had created an imbalanced relationship with Japan under the so-called "unequal treaties," Kamoto explores how Japanese imperial ambitions affected persons in the newly incorporated colonial territories. Chapter 6 also delineates the ways in which real distinctions were made between "inner-territory" Japan and the "outer-territory" colonies and how naisen kekkon (Japanese-Korean mixed marriages) in particular were legally structured.

In chapter 7, historian Jennifer Robertson explores how the concept of a family-state (*kazoku kokka*) system was developed to frame this newly emergent "nation" of Japan and how national membership would become linked to a "bloodline" (*kettō*). Triangulated between premodern notions of blood and family and new Western notions about blood, race, and eugenics, Robertson discusses the "new Japanese" that would be formed through a eugenic modernity. While notions of authentic Japaneseness as linked to "pure blood" began circulating in public discourse by the 1880s, Robertson also notes how interchangeably the new ideas of *jinshu* (race) and *minzoku* (ethnic nation) operated in the context of race betterment and empire building. Resonating with debates around hybrid vigor and hybrid degeneration, Robertson demonstrates how in the Japanese context discussions of the pros and cons of "mixing blood," struggled with these issues. On the one hand, there were those like the veteran politician and chancellor of the Tokyo Imperial University, Hiroyuki Katō, who would publish scathing critiques of mixed marriage including his 1886 publication that miscegenation would result in diluting the pure blood—or racial and cultural essence—of the Japanese, with special vitriol aimed at intermarriage with white Europeans, which he claimed would ensure the "complete defeat" (*zenpai*) of Japan by Westerners. On the other hand, advocates of miscegenation included political theorist Susumu Ijichi, who in 1939, advocated intermarriage of Japanese males and "carefully selected" Manchurian females as a form of "racial blood transfusion" (*minzoku yūketsu*) to produce "hybrid offspring who would mature as natural political leaders."

In Chapter 8, historian Paul Barclay examines how such kinds of debates on miscegenation figured into colonial policy, especially in Taiwan under Japanese colonial rule. His study highlights the political and commercial functions of interethnic marriage between Aboriginal Atayal women and male Japanese colonists, encouraged by the example set in the late Ming Chinese immigration to Taiwan, where children of Sinophone husbands and Aboriginal wives served as intermediaries between the migrants and the local population. One of Barclay's subjects, Hajime Shimoyama, the son of Japanese army veteran Jihei Shimoyama and daughter of the headman of the Malepa region, Pixo Doleh, noted how his Aboriginal mother became fluent in Japanese and like many in such positions, became interpreters and intermediaries for the Japanese during the colonial period.

Of course, the late nineteenth and early twentieth centuries were not only periods of Japanese colonial expansion, but a period of mass migration out of Japan wherein a new generation of mixed-roots Japanese people emerged in many regions beyond the empire. In Chapter 9, Duncan Ryūken Williams identifies several key moments in the history of Japanese community formation in Hawai'i and the continental United States, from the initial migration of 1868 until the end of the Pacific War in 1945. Williams begins his chapter noting that several of the first Japanese settlers to Hawai'i in 1868, such as Matsugorō Kuwata, Tokujirō Satō, and Toyokichi Fukumura, married and had children with local Hawaiian women. Williams highlights how multiraciality was a common feature of the Japanese American community even in its earliest phases, as for example, with the first Japanese settlers in California and Oregon, who were members of mixed-race families. But with the rise of anti-miscegenation laws in the American West that mimicked laws originally enacted in the American South to prevent racial mixing of black and native America with white America, and which specifically added "Mongolians," "Chinese," and "Japanese" to the list of those prohibited from marrying white Americans, hapa Japanese Americans would find their very existence "illegal," as their parents were barred from legally-recognized marriage, and thus were forced to go to states that did not prohibit these interracial marriages or even to Mexico to get married. Mirroring Japan's obsession with "pure blood" and national belonging, the notion of a white and Christian America that could not be sullied by the introduction of "Oriental" blood and "heathen" religions increasingly became a dominant framework for national belonging in North America. Thus hapa Japanese American individuals like William Knight (a decorated U.S. Navy veteran, who had a white father and a half-Japanese and half-Chinese mother) and Japanese-Scottish Jō Makino (the older brother of Fred Makino, founder of the influential *Hawaii Hochi* newspaper in Honolulu) fought and failed in the courts to obtain U.S. citizenship. These failures portended the better-known 1922 U.S. Supreme Court case, *United States v. Ozawa*, which made it clear that those with even partial Japanese heritage were going to be excluded from the national polity. The most extreme manifestation of these exclusionary policies was in the World War II mass incarceration of Japanese Americans, wherein one of the architects of the exclusion policy, Colonel Karl Bendetsen famously stated in 1942, "I am determined that if they have one drop of Japanese blood in them, they must go to camp." Williams contrasts these exclusionary policies of the U.S. government with the valiant service by hapa Japanese American volunteers in the segregated 100th Battalion and 442nd Regimental Combat Team as well as those mixed-race individuals who served in the Pacific in the U.S. Military Intelligence Service to demonstrate their loyalty, their identity, and their sense of belonging to the United States even at a time when racially discriminatory government policies placed both monoracial and multiracial Japanese Americans on the West Coast behind barbed wire.

Despite these difficult circumstances, hapa Japanese Americans continued to flourish. In Chapter 10, historian Greg Robinson offers up portraits of a panoply of hapa Japanese American individuals in the artistic and creative fields, including in regions beyond the traditional enclaves of Japanese America on the West Coast and Hawai'i. Robinson chronicles the lives of Sadakichi Hartmann (1867-1944), the Dejima-born and New York City-based "King of Bohemia"; the Chicago-born novelist Kathleen Tamagawa [Eldridge] (1893-1979); the Racine, Wisconsin-born mystery writer Milton K. Ozaki (1913-1989), and perhaps the most famous hapa Japanese American artist, sculptor-designer-architect Isamu Noguchi (1904-1988), among others. Robinson's chapter highlights many untold aspects of the community, showcasing the hitherto hidden contributions of those of mixed heritage to Japanese American history.

Australian and Indigenous studies scholar, Yuriko Yamanouchi, highlights another little known story from the Japanese diaspora of hapa Japanese individuals in Chapter 11. She relates the history of those of mixed Australian aboriginal and Japanese heritage in the Broome (North Western Australia) region. Chronicling the history of Japanese in that region who worked in the pearl shell industry—one of the few industries exempted from the immigration restrictions of the White Australia Policy—Yamanouchi not only documents the history of Broome, but shows the more general issue of how the social meanings of "being mixed" are locally and historically specific. In particular, she notes how the polyethnic history of Broome provides a very different context of mixedness than other regions of Australia. Despite the black versus white binaries of the contemporary Australian government categories for Aboriginal policies, those of Japanese-Indigenous Australian mixed heritage have been resisting all-too-simple racial boundaries imposed on them by those from outside a region that has traditionally been polyethnic.

In documenting these histories of mixedness, perhaps it is in times of war and its aftermath that the contrast between self-understandings and state-imposed understandings of race and mixed race become most stark. In a reprint of a classic essay, historian Paul Spickard in Chapter 12, drawing from hundreds of pages of U.S. government archival materials, describes the ways in which the various government agencies developed policies for how to deal with those of mixed Japanese heritage during the World War II mass incarceration of nearly 120,000 Japanese and Japanese Americans on the West Coast. He notes how memos like the 1942 one written by Major Herman P. Goebel, Jr. about "Mixed Marriage Leave Clearances," made assumptions based on gender as to the relative threat to national security mixed families posed. By assuming that fathers would dominate the culture and loyalties of their households, they favored releasing or exempting mixed families with a white father, but not those with a Japanese father. Spickard chronicles the reactions of various civilian officials to this policy, including the First Lady, Eleanor Roosevelt, who made her strong feelings known to the Secretary of War Henry Stimson that a certain Theresa Takeyashi should be allowed to rejoin her family in Seattle because of her loyalty and her partial non-Japaneseness. Eventually, mixed Japanese American families would be the first to receive exemptions to the exclusion policies which lay the foundation for the eventual return of the Japanese American community to the West Coast from camps. The U.S. Army even felt confident enough about popular opinion to make public in December 1943 for the first time the fact that they had been letting some intermarried Japanese Americans reside on the West Coast all along. Despite some of these early releases, Spickard documents a wide variation in the experiences of hapa Japanese Americans, from those whose families were split, with some of the family in camp and the rest outside, to the many families who languished in camps for the duration of the war, but who were nonetheless sometimes, harassed by fellow Japanese American detainees for being mixed.

The wartime and immediate postwar experiences of another hapa Japanese community is taken up by cultural anthropologist and historian of World War II, Eveline Buchheim. She looks at the region of the world formerly known as the Dutch East Indies. Here, Buchheim examines the racial and mixed-race hierarchies in the context of the shift in colonial regimes (from Dutch to Japanese) during the Pacific War. By March 1942, the Japanese had advanced through Kalimantan, Sulawesi, the Moluccas, and finally into former Dutch colonial center of power, Java. Under its military rule, the Japanese authorities interned all Dutch males (and females who wanted to stay with husbands and other family members), but the Japanese presumed that people of Dutch and local mixed descent, called *Indisch*, would sympathize with the Japanese ideal of a Greater East Asia Co-Prosperity Sphere, and so did not intern them. But Buchheim's findings show that the Japanese presumptions were wrong as most Indisch identified with the Dutch colonial elite and underplayed their Eurasian identity. However, in the context of war and being free from internment because of their mixed race, Chapter 13 is a study in "fraternization" between Indisch (and a few monoracial Dutch) women and Japanese men, told through oral histories provided by the children of such encounters as well as archival records kept in the immediate post-war environment by the Dutch, documenting cases of sexual aggression by Japanese men towards Dutch women. Because these relationships were often viewed negatively, Buchheim's findings about mixed Indisch/Dutch-Japanese persons, some of whom remained in the region, but many of whom followed their mothers to the Netherlands or, in rare cases, accompanied their Japanese father and Dutch mothers to Japan, represents an amazing piece of scholarship about a group that many would prefer to forget in the fogs of war.

In Chapter 14, journalist Walter Hamilton explores the community of mixed Japanese-Australian *konketsuji* in Kure, Hiroshima, where the British Commonwealth Occupation Force (BCOF) was based. Although the BCOF enforced a policy of non-fraternization right through the Occupation, in February 1956, an Australian Army sergeant went public with the claim that 200-300 *konketsuji* were living in Kure in miserable circumstances. With even more restrictive immigration policies than the U.S.—the White Australia policy restricted migration to those who could prove that they were at least three-quarters European—not only were many children classified as illegitimate, Australia's Immigration Minister, Alexander Downer Sr., announced in 1958 that: "The illegitimate children of servicemen in Japan are not generally eligible for admission to Australia." Thus, growing up in Kure, Hamilton's interviewees, such as Mayumi Kosugi, noted that "Many mixed-blood children like us were bullied." And Australian-Japanese, Joji Tsutsumi, recognized that people like him had "the faces of those who, not so long ago, were dropping bombs. The faces, by themselves, provoked animosity. ... I guess it was natural to feel hatred when they saw miniatures of their enemy hanging around." Hamilton's study of these "miniatures of their enemy" draws from many oral histories he conducted as well as from an Australian International Social Service longitudinal study called the ISS Kure Project, that ran from 1959 until 1977 documenting their education, employment, and family life. These studies contradict the oft-repeated image, as Hamilton notes, "that all *konketsuji* were corralled into institutions or sent abroad, or denied an education and confined to menial jobs, or could never marry and lived only miserable lives."

The complex life story of one such mixed-race person, Kaoru Morioka (who later adopted the name Karl Lippincott), is the subject of historian Lily Anne Welty Tamai's Chapter 15. While chronicling the tremendous hardship that he experienced because of his mixed racial background, Welty Tamai reveals through the lens of one individual's story, the ways in which many individuals from that period persevered on both sides of the Pacific. While phenotypically appearing White, he found he could not pass as a "foreigner" (*gaijin*) during his early upbringing in Kyoto because he only spoke Japanese, and thus he was identified as mixed race. Welty Tamai documents how he negotiated both his early years in Japan and his teen years and thereafter in the eastern U.S., giving a rich understanding of his experience in contrast to the often simplistic narratives surrounding such individuals of either the tragedy-filled accounts of unwanted children or the motif of the rarer mixed-race individual who "made it big" in Japan's entertainment industry. Karl Lippincott resides in New

Hampshire today and though an American citizen of partial Japanese ancestry, does not fit the traditional, narrowly-constructed notion of a "Japanese American."

Indeed, the history of Japanese America has often shied away from including those of mixed heritage, preferring instead to speak of generations (Issei, Nisei, Sansei, Yonsei, etc.) of Japanese Americans as if it were monolithic and homogenous. Sociologist Rebecca Chiyoko King-O'Riain examines these structures of the exclusion of persons of mixed Japanese American heritage, not from white America, but from Japanese America. Analyzing Japanese American beauty pageants from 1935-2010, King-O'Riain compares racial eligibility rules in the four cities of Los Angeles, San Francisco, Seattle, and Honolulu and in what circumstances persons of mixed heritage might be eligible to participate in an event that is a symbol of the Japanese American community. Combining historical research with interviews and even conducting participant-observation by serving as a member of the San Francisco Cherry Blossom Queen Pageant Committee, Chapter 16 examines notions of cultural authenticity, race and beauty, and how hapa Japanese Americans have challenged the equation between cultural authenticity and "natural" or bodily inscriptions of such authenticity as read through one's appearance.

Questions of whether mixed-race individuals have agency or "choice" in ethnic identity, how factors such as the ethnic composition of one's neighborhood, the extent of knowledge about Japanese or black American culture, phenotype, and levels of acceptance by various minority communities, all feature in sociologist Christine Iijima Hall's classic essay about attitudes among a group of half black and half Japanese individuals during the 1970s. This essay, reprinted as Chapter 17, was one of the early pieces of research that revealed just how complex identify formations of mixed-race individuals were. While just over half of those studied closely identified with Blackness, many individuals saw themselves as not fitting into a simple category (the majority of these individuals identified specifically as "Black-Japanese"), while others chose to identify as "Japanese" or refused to identify with any racial category. These findings, in a controlled quantitative study, while focused on Americans of black and Japanese mixed heritage, has broad implications for how mixed-roots individuals make ethnic identification decisions. These include strategies such as the tendency to identify more closely with one heritage over another (foundationalist identity), to identify sometimes with one heritage and at other times with the other (situationalist identity), to identify as a combination of the multiple heritages (integrationalist identity), or to identify as something other than one heritage (transcendentalist identity).

Iijima Hall's study also represents an important contribution to the study of mixed Americans of black-Japanese heritage and how they position themselves vis-à-vis Japanese America. In Chapter 18, Cynthia Nakashima brings the story of hapa Japanese Americans up to the present. Nakashima begins her analysis by studying the debates that raged in the Japanese American ethnic press during the late 1970s and 1980s about the visibly growing presence of hapa Japanese Americans in ethnic sports leagues and beauty pageants that provoked pieces in publications such as the national JACL newspaper, the *Pacific Citizen*, that argued that the community faced a "major ethnic disaster" with the growing number of multiracial families, using rather hyperbolic language that "intermarriage" represented a threat far worse to Japanese America as one "hundred million Manzanars, Tule Lakes, or Pearl Harbors."

Nakashima's apt summary of the articles and letters to the editors written by newspaper columnists, community members, academics, both monoracial and multiracial, and her chronicle of the role of hapa Japanese Americans in creating organizations and movements beyond the confines of the ethnic press to advocate for mixed-race persons, provides a historical context for the emergence of many of the scholars featured in this collection such as the critical scholarship of Christine Iijima Hall, Stephen Murphy-Shigematsu, and Velina Hasu Houston. Furthermore, she describes the role played by activists and scholars in such movements as I-Pride, the first organization for interracial families and people, founded in 1979 by George Kitahara Kich, or the Hapa Issues Forum (HIF) founded by three UC Berkeley hapa Japanese American students—Greg Mayeda, Steve Masami Ropp, and Eric Tate—in 1992. Though primarily a history, Nakashima's chapter concludes with reflections on the current state of not only Japanese America, but Japanese Canada and Nikkei in South America, as national boundaries are becoming challenged by a "New Nikkei" consciousness that can be found not only among monoracial persons, but hapa Japanese across the American continent.

Volume 2 begins with these questions of identity and category formation among various hapa Japanese communities in the more contemporary moment. The psychologist and pioneering scholar of persons of mixed-race Asian heritage, Stephen Murphy-Shigematsu helps set the frame for understanding identity formations that are rapidly shifting and being reconfigured in the twenty-first century. Murphy-Shigematsu's study of individuals who navigate Japan's border worlds, including the increasingly blurred boundaries of so-called minority groups within Japan, includes Emiko Gushiken from Okinawa who struggles with identity terms such as *hafu*, *shima hafu*, or *daburu*; Young Sook Kim who regards herself as Korean despite her mother being Japanese; Kaori Nakamura, who variously used Kaori Lee or Yong Mi Lee as her name before concluding she was "Japanese" after spending time away from Japan in the United States; Hideki Johnson, whose experiences in the Japanese public educational system and international schools affects his embrace or rejection of his African American father; Kevin O'Hara, who as a dual national of Japan and the United States faces both opportunities and challenges in his decision about where to base himself; and Masumi Takahashi, who feels neither fully Japanese nor Korean, with a Japanese mother who provided a certain kind of upbringing in Japan and a Korean father, from whom he derives his Korean nationality. Murphy-Shigematsu's approach in Chapter 19 is similar to his 2012 publication, *When Half is Whole: Multiethnic Asian American Identities*, which also attempts to avoid a stereotypical depiction of a monolithic group of multiethnic people by showcasing nuanced portraits of the lives of individuals.

This diversity in positionality in regards to ethnic identity markers is also evident in sociologist Jane H. Yamashiro's study of "mixed" Japanese Americans of various ages, generations, and Japanese language abilities and how they identify themselves in the context of Japanese society. Chapter 20 is a part of a larger study of Japanese Americans who for reasons of education or employment found themselves in Japan. While monoracial Japanese Americans are often initially perceived of as Japanese in Japan because of phenotypical resemblance, the "mixed" Japanese Americans in Yamashiro's study often encounter the category of *hafu* as they attempt to describe themselves in ways that are intelligible in Japan. Yamashiro argues that transnational mixed Japanese-American migrants reconstruct their identities based on social interaction in Japan. In the back-and-forth of shifting social categorizations and identity assertions, the subjects of her study negotiate internalized notions of themselves with Japanese societal notions of inside/outside, race and ethnicity, and Japanese and "foreigner." Unlike monoracial Japanese Americans who can claim or become labeled as Nikkei, "mixed" Japanese Americans in this study grapple with the ever-evolving terms hapa in the U.S. and *hafu* in Japan. Her findings show that whilst in Japan some reject identification as *hafu* and continue to identify in U.S. terms, others use *hafu* as a strategic identity, to be more recognizable in Japanese terms, or to assert their connection to Japan and not be seen as a complete foreigner. What Yamashiro's case study of Americans of Japanese mixed ancestry suggests is that just as they migrate between mixed-race categories in Japan and the United States, the study of transnational mixed people reveal the complexities of categorizing complex racial formation processes.

In a similar vein, historian Frédéric Roustan takes up the case of mixed-roots Japanese-Filipinos who contend with the broader category *hafu* in Japan as well as other terms such as *Japino* or *Nippikokusaiji*, often abbreviated to its English acronym, JFC (Japanese Filipino Children);

the related JFY (Japanese Filipino Youth), which became popularized in the Philippines; *Shin Nikkeifiripinjin* (New Nikkei Filipino/a); or *Firipinkei Nipponjin shōnen* (Filipino-Japanese Youth). In Chapter 21, Roustan outlines the historical context of migration histories between the Philippines and Japan from which these terms emerged as well as the complex issue of nationality claims by individuals whose Japanese fathers did not formally register them in Japan. Roustan also notes how these categories are linked to scholarly studies of this community of mixed-roots individuals as well as specific organizational histories, such as Philippines-based NGOs such as Development Action for Women Network (DAWN) or the Japan-based Lawyers' Association for Japanese Filipino Children (*JFC Bengodan*) and The Citizen's Network for Japanese-Filipino Children (*JFC o kangaeru nettowāku*). His findings show how terms that well-meaning parents or activists create may or may not resonate with the mixed-roots individuals themselves, who in recent years are developing their own networks, including online communities through social media.

In Chapter 22, cultural anthropologist Masako Kudo adds further complexity to this discussion of identity when religious affiliation and belonging are thrown into the mix. Her study of the category *hafu* as it relates to individuals of mixed Japanese and Pakistani heritage, sometimes living transnational lives between Japan and Pakistan, is a portrait of a mixed-roots community that has emerged from the late 1980s onward. Focusing on the Japanese-Pakistani youth and their experiences in the educational systems of Japan and Pakistan, Kudo notes how for this subgroup of mixed individuals religion plays a significant role in complicating a sense of belonging, given that the religious marriage contract (*nikah nama*) required by Pakistan has a built-in expectation of Islamic law that male Muslims are obligated to marry a fellow Muslim or "people of the Book" (mainly Christians and Jews), which means that most families (starting with the Japanese mother) have converted to Islam, and this marker of difference in Japan, where the majority population is Buddhist/Shinto, heightens whatever racial difference is perceived by the majority Japanese population with religious difference as well. Her longitudinal research shows that most youth embrace the term *hafu* to describe themselves, perhaps as a method to associate with the desirable "Other" promoted by media images of *hafu* and as a counterpoint to whatever undesirable Otherness is associated with Pakistan or Islam. And yet, it would be with a caveat, not only because the term *hafu* has in previous decades had an association with Japanese-white mixed individuals, but because they would note how being a Japanese-Pakistani girl, for example, was a multiply "Othering" experience. The feelings of exclusion came because they would not be considered fully Japanese, nor considered fully "foreign" (*gaijin*), but also not quite comfortable with the media-generated image of *hafu*, such as models on fashion magazine covers, because of expectations of covering and modest dress that came from their (and their family's) religious convictions. Kudo notes one subject who discussed how her particular mixedness differentiated her from other *hafu* at her school, like those with a Japanese father and Filipino mother, because those other *hafu* could "pass" as Japanese phenotypically and had a Japanese family name. Thus, the two conflicting forces of assimilation and Otherization were found by Kudo to be very significant in the experiences of *hafu* of Japanese-Pakistani parentage living in Japan.

Examining a group of the same age as Kudo's respondents, linguist Tim Greer examines how students at one of the private international schools in Japan, who associated with the category *hafu*, talk about identity. As a linguist, Greer in Chapter 23, focuses not on social forces, religion, or media images as much as ways in which language itself both reflects and forms identity. Using conversation analysis and membership categorization analysis, Greer examines code-switching and identity ascription through "talking" derived from analyses of bits of unscripted conversations among mixed-race students at an international school in Japan. Greer proposes that a parsing of language usage reveals that individuals tend to occupy a middle ground that defies and at times obscures fixed societal binaries of *Nihonjin-Gaijin* ("Japanese-Outsider") and how the sometimes strategic and sometimes unconscious use of certain terms and phrases invoke kind of ethnification towards "Japanization" or "Gaijinization."

Conducting her research in another school context is Akemi Johnson, whose study of the AmerAsian School in Ginowan, Okinawa, begins a section of the collection on Okinawa. In Chapter 24, Johnson, who spent time as a volunteer teacher at the AmerAsian School, the only K-9 school established specifically as a bilingual, bicultural institution for biracial American-Okinawan students, focuses on the issues faced by the majority of the students, who are mixed-race children of Okinawans and American military personnel stationed on the island. Established in 1998 by five Okinawan mothers who felt that neither the local public schools nor the Department of Defense Dependents Schools on base were properly accommodating the needs of their biracial children, they chose to capitalize both "Amer" and "Asian" to lend equal weight to both of the children's heritages. Johnson's study of the school not only provides the history of this educational institution, but an analysis of the school's mission of providing bilingual education—or more specifically English-language education for students whose first language is Japanese—as a way to succeed in Okinawan society, in the words of the school principal, not as a "half'" person but as a two-language-and-culture "double." The challenges of being mixed race in Okinawa, being so closely associated with the highly visible presence of U.S. military bases, is different from the Japanese mainland. The term *shima hafu* (literally "island half") as used for Amerasians is reflective of the conditions of this "island," where, Johnson argues, "individuals with identifiable biracial features often evoke the controversial issues regarding the presence of American military bases," and are often stereotyped as monolingual and monocultural, with a single Japanese mother. She also argues that the tropes of the mother either having been forcibly assaulted by a U.S. military personnel or conversely, all too willingly having had sexual relations with them, equally stigmatize *shima hafu* in Okinawan society. It is in this context of wanting to avoid the label of "an illegitimate base child" as someone abandoned by their American father that Johnson proposes we understand the emphasis on bilinguality and English-language ability at the AmerAsian School. In contrast to the image of a *shima hafu*, the school purports to provide a "double" (*daburu*) education that would give pride to students in becoming bilingual and bicultural. Johnson also notes however laudable this vision, it can sometimes create unrealistic expectations for American-Okinawans that paradoxically demeans those who are unable to attain fluency in multiple languages or have dual racial and cultural identities. The ultimate goal of education for American-Okinawans, Johnson proposes, should not be to make all biracial people "double," but to create a society wherein everyone feels free to form their own unique identities.

Annmaria Shimabuku also highlights the distinctive context of Okinawa as a place where mixed-race people inevitably encounter, in her words a "transpacific colonialism," where race is seen through the lens of "the U.S. military basing project in Okinawa with the backing of the mighty Japanese yen." Her piece in Chapter 25 highlights the precarious position of mixed-race persons in such a militarized context as both a paramount symbol of Okinawa's anti-base movement (where miscegenation would be viewed in its most violent expression as rape) as well as a symbol of Okinawa's love of the U.S. military (where miscegenation would be interpreted in its more romantic expression of international marriage). These complexities compel Shimabuku to offer a cautionary note about recent trends that overly celebrate the lure of hybridity without calling into question the militarized and colonial practices that underlie representations of the mixed-race subject in Okinawa. In addition to the colonizer/colonized framework that structures the relationships between U.S. military men and Okinawan women and their children, Shimabuku also provides a gender analysis of both the colonizing male (U.S. military personnel) and colonized male (Okinawan men) vis-à-vis Okinawan women and the children born of miscegenation. Ultimately, Shimabuku highlights the vulnerability of the mixed-race person in Okinawa as being used to justify positive effects of global militarization.

In a similar vein, Mitzi Uehara Carter explores the dynamic and shifting multiplicities of identity for Okinawan-Americans that tend to get homogenized, especially in media interviews and representations. Critical of the singular narrative often found in the news media, Carter explores hybrid communicative practices as an anthropologist, who also maintains a personal blog from her Black Okinawan-American perspective, eager to reveal the variety of mixed-race experiences within multiple dislocations in militarized Okinawa. In Chapter 26, Carter explores the complex subject positions of people like Byron Fija, an *Amerika-Uchinanchu* advocate of Okinawan language and culture; Lisa Akamine, a Black Okinawan woman whose educational experience in the base town of Koza, among many others, all with the aim of discovering ways of telling life stories that are not automatically hijacked and recontextualized into a pro/ against U.S. base binary. Efforts like Carter's bilingual community engagement event described in the chapter build a more complex body of knowledge about mixed Okinawans.

In the final chapter in the Okinawa section, artist, scholar, and co-founder of the Critical Mixed Race Studies Association, Laura Kina, reflects on her own family's transpacific journeys. As a self-described *yonsei, hapa-Uchinanchu* American artist, Kina uses five of her portrait paintings—*Issei, Nisei, Sansei, Yonsei,* and *Gosei*—to examine the lives of five generations of *Uchinanchu* (persons of Okinawan heritage) as lived in Hawai'i and North America. Unlike some of the other chapters in this collection, which focus on representative individuals of a community or provide micro-histories through a detailed view of one individual, Chapter 27 manages to narrate a history of Okinawan Americans in multiple diasporic contexts through a longitudinal study of one family—her own—and through commentary on artistic representations produced by someone in the fourth-generation (*yonsei*) of this history.

Kina's artistic self-representation can be contrasted with the creative productions of novels, memoirs, graphic novels, and cinematic films where hapa Japanese are centrally or peripherally featured. In Chapter 28, Zelideth María Rivas examines the shifting portrayal of mixed-race Japanese Brazilians both in prewar historical documents as well as in contemporary short stories by Japanese immigrants to Brazil, such as Sekiko Shimizu's "Shōnen to sofu" (*The Boy and the Grandfather*, 1993) and Isamu Endō's "Kuroi mago" (*Black Grandchild*, 1980), as well as Chikako Hironaka's memoirs, *Inochi oriori*, (*Moments of My Life*, 1994). She argues that these depictions of race and mixed race arise from the tension of the writers' racial categories that the writers brought with them from Japan meeting Brazil's racial framework, which had traditionally been built on a triangulation of three races—

African (Black), Indigenous (Brown), and European (White)—and that the ambiguous position of Japanese and mixed Japanese in Brazil requires us to develop a more nuanced understanding of Brazilian history.

Rivas explores some fascinating new sources from prewar Brazil, such as the work of Bruno Lobo, a professor at the Rio de Janeiro medical school in the 1930s and an advocate for Japanese immigration, who encouraged the permanent settlement of the Japanese into Brazilian society through interracial marriages with Brazilians and by having biracial children. And within Japanese society, she brings to light a 1934 publication by the Centro Nipônico de Cultura that featured photographs of interracial Japanese and Brazilian families. Rivas curiously juxtaposes these prewar texts with contemporary literary works, analyzing Sekiko Shimizu's character Hirō Sakada from the short story *Shōnen to sofu* (1993). Hirō, the *mestiço* son of a Japanese father (Kazuo) and a Brazilian mother (Luiza), is figured as a "racial shadow" within the Japanese community in the *colonias* who problematizes the nostalgic maintenance of a homogeneous Japanese racial construction. Her analysis of Hirō as having to forge his identity rooted in biracialness, embracing others' perceptions of him as a *mestiço*, plays into a notion of distancing him from the immigrant "alien" grandfather and the simultaneous integration into a broader Brazilian societal frame of mixedness. Indeed, Rivas suggests that the prewar project of people like Bruno Lobo to include biracial children in the Brazilian national imaginary is directly linked to this kind of narrative of the mixed person. But, by contrasting Shimizu's work with Isamu Endō's *Kuroi mago* (1980), she also points out the difference in these stories regarding mixing Japaneseness into Whiteness versus Blackness of Brazil. *Kuroi mago* is the story of two second-generation Japanese Brazilians, Kazuo and Akira, their respective marriages to a white Brazilian and a *morena* (dark skinned—typically also mixed race), and the difficulties faced by Augusto, son of the latter couple, whose acceptance by the Japanese immigrant generation as well as the mixed-race child's "pure" Japanese nephew was initially met with resistance. Ultimately, the Japanese matriarch embraces her sons' interracial marriages and her mixed-race grandchildren, and the characters become symbols of the first generations' acceptance of the family's Brazilianness.

In Chapter 29, LeiLani Nishime takes on another complex narrative, this one presented in a hybrid media created by the use of both texts and images, namely, the comic or graphic novel. She argues that in the form itself can be found a "hybrid aesthetic that reveals the influence of both U.S. and Japanese cartoon styles" as well as in the specific ways in which the two texts under study—*Drawing from Memory* by Allen Say and *Johnny Hiro: Half Asian, All Hero* by Fred

Chao—deal with time, space, and face, which Nishime identifies as the three most common cultural preoccupations with mixed-race Asians. The texts deliver "an articulate and complex response to the frustratingly simplistic stories we usually tell about mixed race." Like other chapters that have problematized the stereotypical and all-too-well worn tropes of either a tragic mixed-race individual doomed to fail to cross racial divides or a heroic mixed-race individual or celebrity who augurs an optimistic and enlightened future by the very fact of their multiracial bodies, Nishime details how these graphic novels undermine "the binary logic of Asian/Other and domestic/foreign" that is commonly shared by both tropes. Furthermore, because of the visual nature of these texts, this research delves into how race and mixed race are represented when the characters defy simplistic visual categorizations, especially by employing methods of inter-textual references to manga and anime rather than older U.S. cartoon traditions. Nishime points out how these graphic representations "mine the possibilities of formal conventions such as rapid shifts in perspective, the occasional breaking of the frame, and a self-conscious emphasis on the hand of the artist to lend readers a critical distance from stereotyped images."

Shifting focus from the context of the U.S. to that of Japan, Sayuri Arai explores the representations of mixed-race children in the well-known film *Kiku to Isamu* (1959) by film director Tadashi Imai. Unlike Nishime, who argues that the graphic novels of her study provide possibilities for new narratives for representations of mixed race, Arai in Chapter 30 notes the distinct limitations in this early cinematic representation of mixed race. Analyzing various scenes from the film, Arai notes that the young Black American-Japanese protagonists and siblings, Kiku and Isamu, are never represented as both Japanese and Black, but inevitably within a limiting binary epistemology of Japanese or Black. Her argument is that this was not some personal failure of the film director, who was known to be sympathetic to oppressed groups in Japan, to imagine the possibility of hybridity, but that anti-Blackness as a part of the social milieu of that period in Japan did not permit liminal or third spaces that embraced identities that could be seen as being in opposition. Given that the narrative premise of the film was that the two siblings had two different absent black G.I. fathers and their Japanese mother, who had died from illness, the trope of abandoned mixed-race children as the Black Other despite the children's having been born and raised solely in Japan, dominates the film's representation of mixed race as exclusively non-Japanese, Arai's study of the film in terms of Japan's history of representations of Blackness and Japaneseness provides a critical lens to one of the first major films produced in Japan about mixed race as a "social problem."

In Chapter 31, Velina Hasu Houston explores another black-

Japanese character, the computer expert Jingo Asakuma, from the 1993 movie *Rising Sun*, who is in a romantic relationship with the police detective played by star Sean Connery. She serves as a cultural broker for him and his African American colleague (played by Wesley Snipes) who are investigating a murder of a Euro-American woman in the headquarters of Nakamoto Corporation just as that Japanese company is in the midst of acquiring the U.S.-owned Microcomm. Set in the period of Japan's rapid economic rise in the 1980s, the film dramatizes notions of competing economic nationalisms as played out by U.S. and Japanese corporations and the racial identities of the film's main characters. In addition to providing a historical overview of how race and nationalism came to be interlinked, Houston also examines how mixed-race individuals like Jingo Asakuma are represented as simultaneously capable of taking advantage of two cultures, races, and nationalisms—Jingo's bilingualism allows her to crack open the murder case by determining that the Japanese firm tampered with the footage of the crime—while also being abnormal, even crippled, as she has a deformed left hand. Houston suggests, "Deformity is deployed in the film to represent society's inability to accept the mixed-race identity as a normative identity, an inability grounded in historical views about miscegenation, particularly the plantation mentality and the legacy of European American racial ideology." Houston refers to this type of representation as the "Other's Other," where physical and societal "deformity" as a mixed-race individual make it impossible for such persons to be situated in competing nationalisms. And yet, by the end of the film, Asakuma seems to embrace multidimensional mixed-race identity that Houston suggests augurs a more promising future: one that allows mixed-race people to combine their multiple identities fluidly and ultimately transcend boundaries of nation, continent, race, and ethnicity.

In Chapter 32, race and media studies expert, Kent Ono analyzes *Come See the Paradise* (1990), another film from that period. Ono argues that the film, which features a study of the character Mini, the child born of Japanese American Lily Kawamura and Irish American Jack McGurn, is best understood as a genre in Hollywood films that feature white protagonists that get portrayed as antiracist heroes in a former time of virulent white racism. The mixed-race Mini serves as a character whose very existence "serves as the salve that helps heal the wounding divide between Japanese America and white society, by the end of the film marking the possibility of a successful cross-racial white-Japanese American relationship." Though made in the era of the economic rise of Japan, the film is set in the prewar and World War II incarceration period. Mini, while having been incarcerated herself, is portrayed as neither having the racist baggage of white America nor the baggage of the history of injustice directed toward

Japanese America. Ono suggests that by not overly developing her character, the film renders her a perfect conceit as a blankness where her Whiteness, Irish Americanness, Japanese Americanness, or Asian Americanness are ignored in favor of a "mixed raceness." The film's narration is structured on Mini simply listening to her mother recount flashbacks of the family's experience in the prewar period to incarceration during World War II, a "structured absence" aimed to draw an empathetic viewership into the film's "message" that actually features the character of her father Jack (played by Dennis Quaid) who is the antiracist white hero. Ono critiques the way this film sidelines the mixed-race character and expects the audience to ignore "contemporary racial oppression" and take comfort in some generic liberal postracist future.

Moving from representations in films to representations in print media, especially fashion magazines, Brazilian studies scholar Tamaki Watarai, focuses on mixed-race Japanese Brazilians who live in Japan and work in the fashion industry in Chapter 33. Highlighting the extensive role played by so-called *hafu moderu* (fashion models identified as *hafu*) in Japan's modeling industry—especially in magazines advertising fashion, jewelry, and weddings—Watarai analyzes the ways in which mixed-race Japanese Brazilian models both handle their migration experience (many originally having come to Japan to work as a labor migrant [*dekasegi*] or as a child of migrant parents) and negotiate the differences between the mixed-race categories of Brazil (*mestiça*) and Japan (*hafu*). These negotiations of mixed-race identities, Watarai emphasizes, occur not only within an individual or within a family context, but in the relationship these individuals forge with their employers, namely, the various modeling agencies and fashion magazines. Here, she makes the point that racial identity formation is closely linked to class and gender as these female models take up modeling as a mechanism for social and economic mobility both in the transition from Brazil to Japan as a migrant and in the adoption of a new mixed-race identity in the putative transition from *mestiça* to *hafu* for the sake of employment.

Unlike the Brazilian-Japanese mixed-race subjects of Watarai's study, the subject of cultural anthropologist Paul Christensen's research, while sharing the trope of migrating for employment opportunities, certainly cannot be seen as having transformed his identity due to economic hardship. Chapter 34 brings the discussion of mixed-race into "a wider conversation on the role and purpose of celebrity, particularly when understood as the source of culturally significant symbols for systems of advanced capitalism." Before the 2012 baseball season, the Texas Rangers posted a bid of $51.7 million dollars for the opportunity to bring Japanese-Iranian baseball pitcher, Yu Darvish, from the Nippon Ham Fighters to Major League Baseball

(MLB) and then signed a $60-million-dollar agreement with him to entice the star pitcher to Texas. Christensen reveals how Darvish's recruitment to MLB cannot be seen simply as yet another example of the league's pull of dominant Japanese players such as Hideo Nomo, Ichiro Suzuki, Hideki Matsui, Daisuke Matsuzaka, and Masahiro Tanaka into the U.S. orbit, but a transpacific story that is complicated by a fascination with his mixed-race identity that conflates existing racial, cultural, athletic, and nationalistic categories that usually frame Asian athletes that migrate to the U.S. to compete. Darvish is variously represented by different groups, and Christensen explores these variations. In the Japanese media, Darvish is typically presented in one of two ways: sometimes his *hafu* identity is emphasized to explain his "bad boy" streak or his athletic ability, and sometimes he is presented in his "Japanese" identity as "as a dutiful son and hard-working Japanese pitcher now trying to succeed in America." Darvish himself has generally presented himself in a manner generally consistent with the Japanese media's "hard-working Japanese" representation. Unlike the Japanese media, which sometimes emphasizes Darvish's *hafu* identity, the U.S. media has typically represented Darvish following the simple narrative mentioned above as just one in a line of Asian players posted to MLB. In the media presentations, he is "exotic"—in Japan as *hafu*; in the U.S. as Japanese—and so he is presented in Japan as an Iranian-Japanese (*hafu*) superstar pitcher, and in the U.S. as a high-priced Japanese MLB talent. In sorting through these different representations, Christensen sees Darvish as an international celebrity, whose marketable identity is rooted in global capitalistic flows of sports, entertainment, endorsement, and social media campaigns, wherein his mixed-race identity permits a flexible and multiple appropriation of his various identities for marketing. For example, in Texas, in addition to the more obvious connection to Japan and its related draw of Japanese media, corporate sponsors, and fans, Darvish has found that Iranian-Americans have begun embracing him as a way to "humanize" their community in Texas. Thus, as Christensen shows, Darvish's personal reality and understandings of identity as *hafu* and Japanese become supplemented or even superseded by a hyperreality of representations generated by media and fans of "Yu Darvish, the brand."

In the final chapter of the collection, musicologist Kevin Fellezs studies a celebrity who, unlike Darvish, has engendered meaningful discussions of race and mixed race, namely, the *enka* superstar Jero (aka Jerome Charles White, Jr.). Born in Pittsburgh, the grandson of a Japanese woman, Takiko Kondō, and Leonard Tabb, an African American naval officer, he learned about the Japanese musical genre of *enka* from his grandmother, while also absorbing the musical culture of his surroundings: he was a hip hop dancer in high school and college. Almost immediately after his professional debut in Japan, he won Best New Artist at the Japan Record Awards in 2008 and his hit single "Umiyuki" shot up Japan's singles charts to number four—the highest ever position for a first time *enka* release in Japanese music history. The hybrid character of his musical styles—his music video often combines hip hop elements with traditional *enka* singing—as well as the fluency of his Japanese language abilities despite his phenotypically appearing Black has certainly provoked discussions of race and mixed race in Japan, especially in *enka*'s more conservative circles. In Chapter 35, Fellezs uses Vijay Prashad's concept of "polyculturalism"—the ability of people to live coherent lives that are made up of a host of lineages, rather than the white/black paradigm of normative U.S. race relations—to better understand Jero's unlikely emergence as an *enka* star in Japan. While Jero embodies and lives a polycultural life, Fellezs is also cognizant of the long Japanese history of both celebrating and denigrating Blackness as well as Japan's general willful non-recognition of its internal racial hierarchy. Jero who is enthusiastically embraced by fans in a music genre that is thought to be quintessentially "Japanese," seems to have surmounted these obstacles. Fellezs' analysis ultimately explores what he calls the "unmarked territories of the racial imaginary" that Jero occupies "by transforming the songs his grandmother taught him into a polycultural *enka*, a music formed out of the confluences between sound and skin."

This volume has attempted to showcase some of the best scholarship on hapa Japanese, including a few selected reprints of classic essays that give a snapshot of emerging scholarship of an earlier era as well as recently published innovative work. By presenting both historical and theoretical analyses from a range of scholars with very diverse disciplinary training, it has been my hope to represent the multifaceted scholarly perspective appropriate for the study of hapa Japanese, both in Japan and across the globe. While the story of hapa Japanese is complex and varied, as the chapters of this volume will show, the histories and analyses reflect and resonate with each other. Whether the reader chooses to focus on particular sections or to read the entire work, it is hoped that the perspectives of hapa Japanese presented here will inform discussions of an increasingly polycultural and multiethnic world.

# CHAPTER ONE

## APPROACH AND BE TRANSFORMED: IMMIGRANTS IN THE NARA AND HEIAN STATE

NADIA KANAGAWA

In December 2001, on the occasion of his sixty-eighth birthday, Emperor Akihito was asked about his feelings towards Korea in advance of the World Cup, which was to be co-hosted by Korea and Japan.[6] In his response, he spoke of the long history of interaction between Korea and Japan, and said that he felt "a certain kinship with Korea" because the mother of one of his distant ancestors, Kammu Tennō (r. 781-806), was descended from King Muryŏng (r. 501-523) of Paekche, an early state on the Korean peninsula.[7] His answer may have come as a surprise to those who think of monarchs past and present as inherently and purely Japanese, the "symbol of the State and the unity of the people,"[8] according to the Japanese constitution of 1946. In fact, however, Kammu Tennō's foreign ancestry is clearly and deliberately recorded in the official histories of the time. His mother, Takano no Niigasa, was a member of the Yamato no Fuhito family who were said to be descended from Paekche immigrants. Not only does the official history of the time specifically describe Takano no Niigasa and her family as being descended from King Muryŏng, but Kammu Tennō also famously issued an edict referring to another important Paekche family as "my maternal relatives" (*chin no gaiseki*).[9] There can be no question but that Kammu Tennō understood and portrayed himself as being related to people from the Korean peninsula.

However, Kammu is also known for ordering the compilation of a new genealogical record that divided the major court families into three categories: descendants of the *tennō*'s line (*kōbetsu*), descendants of the gods (*shinbetsu*), and those of foreign origin (*shoban*).[10] Based on the preface of this text, some scholars have argued that Kammu initiated this project to reinstate clear distinctions between "foreign" and "native" people and to limit foreigner access to high-level positions at court.[11] To even begin to understand how Kammu could both draw attention to his connections to foreign families and institute policies that sought to distinguish those of foreign origin from the other members of the realm, it is necessary to put Kammu Tennō's reign in the context of the formation of the early Japanese state.

In recent years, the number of scholars who have written about the critical contributions made to the early state by immigrants and their descendants has steadily increased. Even so, we have yet to fully recognize that the Yamato court took form in a period characterized by the movement of people to, from, and within the Japanese archipelago.[12] In exploring the changing place of immigrants and their descendants in the early state, my goal will be to draw attention to the complexity of the early state's population and to argue that we cannot be content to view it in terms of "native" and "immigrant" people. To view the early state in terms of a dichotomy between "native" and "immigrant" is to assume that there could at some point have been and ur-population made up only of those born in the Japanese archipelago, and that those who came into the archipelago could always be meaningfully (or objectively) distinguished from this original population. However, Kammu Tennō is only one of many examples of the ways in which the reductive dichotomy between "native" and "immigrant" people simply does not hold. It is important to recognize that "native" and "immigrant" were socially constructed categories, and that the degree to which they mattered to the early rulers of Yamato differed appreciably throughout time.

Indeed, Fumio Tanaka has argued that the trajectory of the sixth-through ninth century-Yamato state policies on integrating external people can be divided into three broad stages. First, in the period before the legal codes were issued, talent and ability were prioritized over exclusive affiliation to a particular ruler or state. Second, with the formation of the *ritsuryō* state in the seventh century, rulers sought greater control over the population of their realm and both rulers and subjects negotiated a series of overlapping systems of status and rank. Finally, the early Heian Period was marked by the increasing rigidity of state attitudes towards immigrants and their descendants, as well as the appearance of new categories of outsiders—shipwrecked people and merchants—whose presence was assumed to be temporary and thus lacking the possibility of integration into the state. During the Heian Period, the ruler and elites of the *ritsuryō* state turned increasingly inward even as the volume and frequency of trade with merchants from Silla and other regional states increased.[13] As the title of this chapter suggests, the idea that external people should "approach and be transformed" into subjects of the realm lay at the core of the relationship between Yamato state formation and immigrant integration. In this chapter, we will examine both the overarching framework for the *ritsuryō* state and the ambiguous place occupied by people of mixed origin, whose in-between status presented an ongoing challenge to early rulers.

One way to understand how early Yamato rulers saw and sought to categorize, configure, and control the varied peoples of their realm is to examine the legal codes that formed the basis of the Yamato state. The worldview embedded in these codes shaped both the process by which external people were integrated into the realm and the understanding of why such a process was necessary to establishing the legitimacy of the ruler. Following promulgation of the laws themselves, the six official histories of the Nara and Heian periods (known collectively as the *Rikkokushi*) give a sense of how various laws were (or were not) implemented over time. Examining a selection of case studies in the official histories will expose many significant gaps between legal ideals and the complex realities of creating and maintaining the Yamato state.

## *Ritsuryō* Law on Immigration and Integration

The Yamato state is often called the "*ritsuryō* state" after the penal (*ritsu*) and administrative (*ryō*) codes that structured it. Several different versions of these codes were promulgated over the late seventh and eighth centuries—the first is thought to have been the Kiyomihara Code of 689, then the Taihō Codes of 702, and the Yōrō Codes, compiled from 717 and promulgated later in 757. While the penal and administrative codes formed the foundation of the early state, the classic *ritsuryō* system also included *kyaku* (supplementary regulations issued as individual decrees), and *shiki* (protocols). Along with the two major compilations of legal commentary, the *Ryō no gige* (an official commentary on the administrative code, 833) and *Ryō no shūge* (collected private commentaries on the administrative code, 859-876), these four types of regulations form the basis for studies of the Yamato legal system.[14]

As critical as these codes were to the formation of the Yamato state, they were not original to it. The *ritsuryō* (or *lü ling*) codes are often identified as one of the critical elements of an East Asian world.[15] The earliest combined penal and administrative codes were compiled on the continent in the third century, and Japanese historians like Jun'ichi Enomoto have been working to trace the complex paths by which the codes were transmitted to Yamato via various continental and peninsular states.[16] Nevertheless it is to the subsequent Tang-dynasty codes that the Taihō and Yōrō codes are most often compared. Importing and adopting these codes was a way for Yamato sovereigns and elites to establish their realm as legitimate in the dynamic and rapidly changing East Asian region.

At the foundation of the political system inscribed in these codes was a mono-centric worldview in which the virtue of a universal sovereign (the Son of Heaven) was thought to transform and civilize the people of the realm. Meanwhile, the realm was surrounded by people to whom the ruler's virtue had not yet extended. Thus the two most fundamental categories of people found in the codes are those who were within the transformative influence of the monarch (*kenai* 化内) and those who were outside of the transformative influence of the monarch (*kegai* 化外). As concepts, *kenai* and *kegai* existed both in terms of the physical space within the borders of the realm, and in terms of affiliation with the state and ruler.[17] Because the sovereign was seen to be a universal ruler, people who were outside of the realm could choose to approach and submit to the ruler and thereby be transformed into civilized subjects. This was both a symbolic process of transformation and a concrete process of integration into the realm, both of which were described and regulated by various sections of the codes. The process of moving between these categories was known as *kika* (帰化), literally "approaching of one's own volition and being transformed."[18] The continental framework of *kenai* and *kegai* as well as the *kika* process can be seen in the extant portions of the Taihō and Yōrō codes.

The process of *kika* as it appears in the *ritsuryō* codes is fairly straightforward. First, the *Kushikiryō* (the Laws on Official Documentation) stipulate that when a foreign person arrived and wanted to submit and be transformed (in other words, to go through the *kika* process), the individual was to be installed in an official lodge and given clothing and provisions. The same protocol also cautioned that these people should not be allowed to come and go as they please.[19] According to the *Koryō* (Law on Residence Units), the step after arranging appropriate grants of clothing and food was for district officials to send an express messenger to inform the throne of the arrival of such a person. The newly arrived individual was then to be moved from temporary lodgings and installed permanently in a wealthy province. Once there, the individual was to be added to the registries of the population, and was again to be given provisions.[20] Finally, the *Buyakuryō* (Law on Taxes) states that people who submitted to the civilizing influence were to be granted ten years of exemption from all taxes.[21] As far as the *ritsuryō* codes are concerned, at this point the process of transformation was complete.

*Ritsuryō* sovereigns were doubly invested in this *kika* process. On one hand, it offered clear and concrete incentives for foreign people to enter and become members of the realm. The benefits of attracting talented people bringing new goods and technologies to the realm would have been obvious. On the other hand, the *kika* process was an important way in which rulers performed their benevolence, and foreign people who had become members of the realm became symbols of the legitimacy and universality of the monarch's rulership. If we also consider that leaving the realm was an act of treason and one of the eight great crimes listed in the penal code, it is clear that managing and maintaining the population was a central concern of *ritsuryō* government. In this regard, Fumio Tanaka, among others, has argued that what made the early *ritsuryō* state fundamentally different from earlier polities on the archipelago was its effort to extend its control down to the level of the individual. In this sense, it was the creation of the registries of residence units (*koseki*) that was truly ground breaking.[22] Thus the process of *kika*, in which people from outside of the realm were welcomed, reported to the center, settled, and added to the registries, was a critical means of asserting the existence and control of the *ritsuryō* government. The ability to attract people from outside of the realm and transform them was also a hallmark of the *ritsuryō* sovereign.

## Putting the *Ritsuryō* in Context

The *ritsuryō* codes were neither created nor implemented in a vacuum, and as important as it is to understand the principles and processes inscribed in the codes, it is equally important to get a sense of the society to which the codes were applied. Here, I will focus on a few episodes from the *Nihon shoki*, the well-known official history of Yamato completed in 720. My strategy is to read these passages from the *Nihon shoki* against the provisions in the *ritsuryō* codes to explore what they reveal about the world into which the codes were introduced. As an official record, the *Nihon shoki* was fundamentally shaped by the political and ideological context in which it was created. It is also primarily focused on the activities and concerns of the central elites. By the same token, the narratives in the *Nihon shoki* reflect the worldview and mindset of the court officials who compiled it. These episodes offer us a valuable opportunity to identify gaps between the ideals of the *ritsuryō* codes and the way rulers and elites represented their world.

Records of interactions with the Korean peninsular states and peoples can be found throughout the *Nihon shoki*. Since the postwar period, historians have increasingly emphasized the importance of these interactions, and at this point, there can hardly be any dispute that the successive waves of people who crossed over from the peninsula brought technology, culture, and knowledge critical to the process of state formation on the Japanese archipelago. Buddhism is a classic example of the kind of knowledge that came to Yamato with people from the Korean peninsula, and the narrative of a particular Buddhist master serves to demonstrate how such individuals were welcomed into the realm and some ways in which a sovereign could adjust application of the *ritsuryō* codes to suit various needs.

The *Nihon shoki* records the arrival of the Buddhist monk Eji from the Korean peninsula state of Koguryō in the third year of Suiko's reign (595). The text very clearly states that Eji went through the *kika* process and then became the tutor to a royal prince. This was not just any royal prince, but the prince known most famously as Prince Shōtoku.[23] Along with another monk who arrived from the Korean peninsula state of Paekche in the same year, Eji is described as "a Master of the Three Jewels," referring to the three central principles of Buddhism: the Buddha, the Dharma, and the Sangha. Two years after their arrival, the monks were installed in the newly completed Hōkōji Temple (Asukadera). Eji is said to have maintained a close relationship with Prince Shōtoku throughout his life. It is therefore somewhat unexpected when the *Nihon shoki* notes without explanation or comment that after twenty years in Yamato, Eji returned to his home, the state of Koguryō.[24] Nevertheless, in his final appearance in the *Nihon shoki*, Eji's bond with Prince Shōtoku is said to have extended beyond death, with Eji mourning the news of the prince's death and vowing to meet him again in the Pure Land.[25]

The use of the word *kika* in Eji's instance cannot serve as evidence that this *ritsuryō* process existed and was functioning at the end of the sixth century, but it can reveal something about the understanding of the term held by the early eighth-century compilers of the *Nihon Shoki* text. These entries suggest that the use of the word *kika* was not indiscriminate—it is used for Eji but not for the other monk who arrived the same year (in the second case, the text simply states he came to Yamato). But this makes the total lack of explanation for Eji's return to a home that clearly is not Yamato difficult to understand. The *kika* process as described in the *ritsuryō* codes assumes a clear divide between those who were and those who were not part of the realm, and the process was by no means meant to be reversible. Once transformed into a civilized member of the realm and added to the registers of the population, there was presumably no way to go back.[26] The account of Eji's life in the *Nihon shoki*, however, suggests a more flexible situation, in which Eji's permanent affiliation with the state was not of paramount importance. Instead of emphasizing that he had been transformed into a subject of the Yamato court, the compilers of the *Nihon shoki* emphasized his knowledge, service to the state, and lasting bond with an individual ruler. This emphasis is characteristic of the pre-*ritsuryō* period, which was one of relative fluidity that allowed for the possibility of affiliation with multiple realms.[27]

Even though affiliation in the pre-*ritsuryō* period was relatively flexible, the following episode from the *Nihon shoki* suggests that ambiguous affiliation could still be problematic, and even dangerous. In 530, an envoy from Mimana on the Korean peninsula is said to have arrived at the Yamato court and complained to the then ruler, Great King Keitai, about the incompetence of a Yamato official named Kena no Omi, who was stationed in Mimana (Kr. Imna). One of the failings of Kena no Omi was that he had been unable to resolve the many conflicts between Yamato and Mimana people over their children. According to the report, he was particularly fond of using a trial by ordeal that involved plunging one hand of each of the claimants into a cauldron of boiling water to judge whose claim was just. Those in the right would emerge from this ordeal unscathed while those who were in the wrong would certainly be scalded, he claimed. The envoy reported that the use of this method had resulted in no solutions and the deaths of many people. In particular, Kena no Omi had killed two children identified as Kibi no karako Natari and Shifuri. In a note, the compilers of the *Nihon shoki* define the term *karako* (韓子) as follows: "Children born when people of Yamato marry foreign women are *karako*."[28] The story goes on to follow the exploits of the offending official in a complicated conflict involving Mimana, Paekche, and Yamato, but there is unfortunately no further discussion of *karako* people and their situation.

It would be unwise to speculate too much about what the term *karako* might imply about the status of "mixed" children in the thinking of officials of the eighth century, as this is the only time the term is used in this way—in fact, it is not used in any later official histories either.[29] Nevertheless, the passage suggests that at the time of the compilation of the *Nihon shoki*, there may have been a vocabulary for speaking about children born to couples of mixed affiliation. The awareness of the ambiguity of *karako* status is not reflected in the *ritsuryō* codes, and there was no legally recognized way for a person to be half in and half out of the *tenno*'s realm.

Whether the level of violence described in this story was a reflection of the seriousness of the question, or of the incompetence of the official, is unclear. In either case the episode from the *Nihon shoki* suggests that the ambiguous status of these children put them in a vulnerable position.

The appearance of a number of people with "mixed" names and titles in diplomatic interactions between Yamato and Paekche gives us another glimpse into how the compilers of the *Nihon shoki* identified individuals as being between states or belonging to multiple states. In the second year of Kinmei's reign (541), the *Nihon shoki* describes a group of officials dispatched by King Sŏng (Jpn. Seiō) of Paekche first to Mimana and then to the Yamato court to report about the situation in Mimana.[30] Among the three officials whose names are given as envoys is one by the name of Ki no Omi Nasol Mimasa. This name is striking in that it combines a name and title typical of Yamato officials—Ki no Omi—and a Paekche official rank—Nasol.[31] The *Nihon shoki* includes an explanatory note on the name: "Ki no Omi Nasol is perhaps the son of a Ki no Omi who took a woman of the Korean peninsula (*karamenoko*) as a wife, had a child, and thus remained in Paekche where he was made Nasol. Nothing is known about this father. Others all follow this example."[32]

Here, the simple fact that the compilers include this note demonstrates that Ki no Omi Nasol Mimasa was an unusual designation that they felt required an explanation. That the explanation appears to be largely speculation based on the "mixed" name, title, and rank gives the impression that there was not an established system for distinguishing people born to parents of differing affiliation (or at the very least, that no such system was still functioning or commonly known at the beginning of the eighth century). At the same time, the reference to other cases that follow the same pattern is borne out by a number of later entries from Kinmei's reign that describe Ki no Omi Nasol traveling back and forth between Paekche and Yamato accompanied at various times by other officials with "mixed" names and titles: Kose no Nasol Kama, Mononobe no Nasol Kai, and Mononobe no Muraji Nasol Yōkata.[33] As in the case of the *karako* children, the compilers recognized the possibility of marriages between people of different realms and that such a marriage would result in children of ambiguous status. It further suggests that the compilers of the *Nihon shoki* thought it possible for a person of Yamato to travel to Paekche, marry and settle there, and receive a title from the ruler of that realm. References to people with "mixed" names and titles are concentrated in the reign of King Sŏng and appear primarily in descriptions of interactions with Yamato. Unlike the earlier passage on Kena no Omi, the descriptions of Ki no Omi Nasol suggest that there may have been ways that the ambiguous status of "mixed" people was seen as an advantage and used strategically in diplomatic interactions with other states. The entries on Ki no Omi Nasol and others like him also demonstrate that the compilers of the *Nihon shoki* saw names and titles as an important way to identify and distinguish people who were of "mixed parentage."

The sixth and seventh centuries were a particularly dynamic period across East Asia, and as people moved about the region, those with talent and knowledge might be welcomed by more than one ruler over the course of their lives. In the early stage of state formation on the Japanese archipelago, talent and ability were critical resources, need for which often superseded concerns about an individual's permanent or exclusive affiliation with the realm. At the same time, the *Nihon Shoki* describes this as a period of rapid change and escalating tension in the region, and in this environment, the ambiguous status and allegiance of people who were born to parents from two different realms could become either an asset or a liability.

**The Ritsuryō State in Practice**

The creation of the *ritsuryō* state brought with it a shift in the state's policies and attitudes towards incorporating external people. Where the pre-*ritsuryō* period was relatively flexible, one of the major goals of creating a *ritsuryō* code-based realm may well have been to solve the problem of multiple allegiances. The practice of registering the population, in which the name and age of each subject of the realm were recorded and then reported to the *tennō*, marked the end of tolerating multiple allegiances.[34] Creating a state in the *ritsuryō* model allowed Yamato rulers to establish their realm as legitimate, both to other East Asian states and to their own subjects. The more that they could visibly fulfill the ideals of the *ritsuryō* codes, the more they proved themselves to be true Chinese-style universal sovereigns. At the same time, the implementation of the *ritsuryō* codes did not negate existing systems of status and rank, and, as we shall see in considering episodes from the six official histories that record events up to the early tenth century, both rulers and subjects tried to negotiate this multi-layered system to their advantage.

There are many articles in the six official histories that demonstrate that the *kika* process as described in the codes was actually implemented, and that people moving into the state received concrete benefits. The sources describe both individuals and groups of people arriving in Yamato, being settled in various provinces across the realm, and receiving tax exemptions. As far as the *ritsuryō* codes were concerned the process of integrating people into the realm ended after the ten-year tax exemption expired, but in reality, the official histories make it clear that process continued long beyond this point. Tracing the life and career of one individual, Takakura no Fukushin, through the official histories demonstrates how far this process of integration might extend, and what possibilities were open to people who went through the *kika* process and their descendants. Fukushin's story also reveals some of the ways in which state attitudes towards external people had changed, and how the *ritsuryō* system intersected with other systems of status and rank.

Takakura no Fukushin (709-789) was born Sena no Fukushin in the Koma district of Musashi Province in Yamato. His grandfather fled the Tang invasion of Koguryō and came to Yamato, where he went through the *kika* process and was settled in Musashi Province.[35] In his youth, Fukushin traveled to the capital, where his remarkable talent as a sumo wrestler brought him to the attention of the court. He started serving at court as a page, rose to palace guard, then to official of the crown prince's household, and finally to concurrent positions of minister of palace construction and governor of Musashi and Ōmi provinces. By the time of his death at age 81, Fukushin had risen from the outer fifth rank lower to the lower third rank. To rise to the third rank was a truly remarkable achievement—only a handful of elite officials attained this rank. Fukushin's career also spanned the reigns of five sovereigns and two dynasties, making it difficult to argue that he was promoted primarily as part of any one ruler's favor or agenda.[36]

Notably, over the course of his career, Fukushin's name and title changed three times. First, in 747, he received the noble title of *konikishi*. The *kabane* system of ranked noble titles granted by the ruler pre-dated the *ritsuryō* state, but it had been expanded and revised by Tenmu (r. 672-686) in the late seventh century.[37] However, the noble title that Fukushin and his family received—*konikishi*—was not one of the titles in Temmu's system. Rather, it was a title granted to only three groups of people, all understood to be from the Korean peninsula. The three groups were: the Kudara no Konikishi, the Koma no Konikishi, and the Sena no Konikishi. The reading "konikishi" or "kokishi" is said to be based on the Korean word for king, and is written with the character 王.[38] We cannot assume that these people actually were members of royal families, but granting this special title allowed the Yamato ruler to imply that the royal families of three fallen Korean states had submitted and been transformed into subjects of the realm of Yamato. This was particularly useful as large-scale immigration declined dramatically with the stabilization of Silla and the Tang empires. Creating and granting titles like *konikishi* brought new attention to an act of approaching the sovereign and being transformed that had, in the case of Fukushin's family, taken place almost a century before. The use of the *konikishi* title in particular asserted Yamato's superior place in the hierarchy of East Asian states.

Three years later, in 750, Fukushin received both a new surname—Koma—and a new title—*ason*—making him Koma no Ason Fukushin. *Ason* was the second highest of the titles in the Tenmu system, and it was usually reserved for those powerful families that had blood ties to the ruling family. The name Koma (高麗) is written with the characters usually used to refer to Koguryō.[39] This second grant of name and noble title to Fukushin is puzzling. The change from the foreigner-only *konikishi* title to the title of *ason* suggests that Fukushin's family had been further integrated into the status rank system of the court. Receiving such a high ranked title was a considerable honor. However, the name "Koma," the name of a former Korean state, emphasized Fukushin's foreign origin.[40]

In 779, Fukushin asked the court to change his surname again, this time from Koma to Takakura. The text quotes his petition, in which he argues that it had been many years since he had approached and submitted to the wisdom of the ruler, and that while he was grateful for receiving the honor of the *ason* title, the name Koma was based on "old customs" (*kyūzoku*) and needed revision. Even though Fukushin was born in Yamato and his grandfather went through the *kika* process over 100 years earlier, he still describes himself in his petition as having gone through the *kika* process. Fukushin's description of himself indicates that he understood the symbolic value of being a subject who had submitted and transformed. Fukushin argues that he should be able to leave the name Koma and the "old customs" it represents behind. It is not clear exactly what Fukushin meant when he refers to "old customs." He may be referring to the process by which the name Koma was chosen as being based on "old customs," but it is also possible that this name indicated that Fukushin and his family were still marked by the "old customs" of their former state of Koguryō. In either case, Fukushin argues that he has served the court long enough to deserve a new name of his own choosing. Fukushin's request for the name Takakura suggests that this name may have represented a higher level of assimilation into the Yamato court, which he was eager to attain. Given that Fukushin clearly did not need to have this name in order to rise in official rank and office, it is not entirely clear what meaning the name held for him or for the court. Nevertheless, Fukushin's declaration that he had left old customs behind and his request for a new name was approved by the *tennō*.[41]

There are many other examples of individuals and groups requesting and receiving new names and titles in the six official histories. Suk Soon Park has argued that these requests prove that people who had been accepted through the *kika* process did not automatically become subjects of the realm (ōmin, literally people of the king), but had to earn this recognition from the sovereign.[42] Just as Fukushin referred to "old customs" in his appeal to the court, earlier edicts make it clear that earning recognition and new names and titles from the sovereign was closely related to the idea of "customs" (*zoku*). In one instance, Kōken Tennō[43] (r. 749-758, 764-770) issued an edict in 757 declaring that people from Paekche, Koguryō, and Silla had gone through the *kika* process long before, and because they had assimilated to Yamato customs, their requests for new names and titles should all be granted.[44] This edict makes it clear that it was assimilation to Yamato customs that allowed people to earn the recognition of the sovereign and receive new names and titles. Park argues this form of recognition was yet another way for rulers to perform and prove their power to transform and civilize subjects. In other words, a true *ritsuryō* sovereign not only transformed external people into subjects, but also into fully assimilated members of the realm with Yamato names and titles. This 757 edict must be seen as an assertion of Kōken Tennō's power and legitimacy as a *ritsuryō* sovereign.

Following Kōken's edict almost two thousand people requested and received new names and titles. This created a major conundrum for the *ritsuryō* rulers of the late Nara period. It was necessary for a *ritsuryō* sovereign to attract and incorporate external people to show that theirs was a universal and legitimate realm, but the number of people arriving to the archipelago was much less than it had been after the fall of Paekche and Koguryō. For the first several generations, *ritsuryō* sovereigns were able use the system of names and titles to mark people as being foreign, and thereby maintain the necessary diversity of their universal realm. However, this system broke down over time as rulers granted requests for Yamato-style names and title. Thus, without a significant flow of people coming into Yamato, it would have been impossible to maintain the claim to legitimate *ritsuryō* rule, as such rule required continuous transfomation of newcomers.

It was Kammu Tennō who found a solution to the conundrum.

Specifically, in 799, he issued a royal decree deploring the state of the genealogical records in the Bureau of Books and Drawings. The edict declared that numerous changes in noble titles had made it difficult to follow the main and branch lines of many families. All of the various provinces of the realm were ordered to submit genealogical records including founding members and branch families for each family.[45] The collected documents were to be used in the compilation of the new genealogical record that would divide the genealogies of the court families into three categories. Although compilation of this text, known as the "Newly Compiled Record of Names and Titles" (*Shinsen shōjiroku*) began in Kanmu's reign, it continued beyond his death, through the reign of his son and heir Heizei (r. 806-809), and into the reign of Heizei's brother and heir, Saga (r. 809-823). Along the way, the scope of the project was adjusted from a realm-wide project to one that included only the capital district and the five provinces around the capital. In its final form as presented to Saga Tennō in 815, the text contained entries for 1,180 royally recognized lineages of the central provinces. While the families who were recorded as being descended from the *tennō*'s line and from the gods represent the majority, approximately thirty percent of the families in the text are recorded as being of foreign origin. By creating a genealogical record of the foreigners present in the immediate domain of the court, the *ritsuryō* sovereigns found a permanent way to preserve the necessary foreign presence at court without the need to continue to incorporate new people from outside the realm.[46] Given this, Kammu Tennō may have been attempting to clarify which families were of foreign origin, but his reason for doing so was not necessarily to discriminate against or exclude those of foreign origin from participation in the state.

As the *ritsuryō* state was established, tolerance of multiple affiliations diminished and emphasis on the symbolic value of bringing new people into the state through the *kika* process increased even as the number of people actually entering the state decreased. Furthermore, in implementing the *ritsuryō* codes and in managing existing status-rank systems, the sovereigns' mandate was to visibly demonstrate themselves to be universal *ritsuryō* sovereigns, thereby demonstrating their legitimacy. But as fewer and fewer external people arrived in Yamato, the sovereigns had to find new ways of maintaining the universality of their realm that did not depend on the incorporation of new people from the outside.

## The Development of the *Ritsuryō* System in the Early Heian Period

The problem of how to deal with foreigners did not entirely disappear with the creation of the "Newly Compiled Record of Names and

Titles," at the new capital of Heian-kyō in 815. Though large-scale immigration had come to an end with the stabilization of the Tang Empire and Silla, there were still people arriving from both the Korean peninsula and the continent. Some people continued to go through the *kika* process as prescribed by the codes, but many others met with a mixed welcome—they received provisions and temporary accommodations in the official lodge but no permanent settlement in the provinces, and no entry in the registries. While the *ritsuryō* codes did not change, the *ritsuryō* system continued to develop through the promulgation of supplementary legislation and protocols that were issued throughout the Nara and Heian period. These supplementary materials were collected collected into a series of texts beginning in Saga's reign.[47] The regulations, ordinances, and edicts compiled in these collections provide a record of how central government policy changed over time, and they also reveal the increasing rigidity of official attitudes towards immigrants and their descendants. The new categories of outsiders that emerged during this time—shipwrecked people and merchants—indicate that early Heian-period rulers had lost interest in formally integrating people from outside the realm. At the same time, however, the actual movement of people in the region did not necessarily decrease—in fact, central elites' interest in acquiring goods from Silla and the Tang Empire increased dramatically. Merchants arriving from Silla became so numerous that their presence was cause for concern and debate at court. An edict from the "Supplementary Legislation of the Three Eras"[48] offers a glimpse of some of the debates over how to deal with this new kind of outsider.

Specifically, in 842 CE, an edict of the Council of State describes a debate over how to deal with people from Silla. Fujiwara no Ason Mamoru, a Dazaifu official, sent a report to the Council declaring that people from Silla who came to Yamato were only using commerce as a pretext, and were actually coming to spy. He demanded that they be banned outright from entering the realm. In the Council's response, the Minister of the Right began by reiterating the basic principles of the *kika* process. He stated that because the virtue of the sovereign extended to faraway lands and had the power to transform and civilize the people of those lands, forbidding foreigners from entering the realm and barring them from access to the influence of the ruler would be inhumane—a major transgression against good government. He went on to outline the policy for dealing with Silla people arriving in Yamato. Shipwrecked people would be sent home with the appropriate provisions. On the other hand, merchants would be allowed to sell their goods to the population and make a profit, and then they too would be sent home. Merchants were not to be given accommodations at the official lodge, nor were they entitled to official provisions of clothing or food.[49]

In this edict, even as the Council of State explicitly reiterated and upheld the principles of the *kika* process, it acknowledged only two categories of people arriving in Yamato: shipwrecked people and merchants. The presence of both of these groups was clearly understood to be temporary, and the edict specifically notes that they were to be sent home. And while this edict deals specifically with people from Silla, similar attitudes were shown to people from other states. In fact, in the sources it is quite difficult to determine exactly where merchants arriving in Yamato came from, and there was significant (and probably deliberate) confusion about their origins. Furthermore Ishii Masatoshi has suggested the possibility that references in the sources to "Silla merchants" may actually refer to merchants who were bringing goods from Silla, and not to the birthplace of the merchant or the realm with which they were affiliated.[50] In any case, the early Heian Period marked a turning point. Though interaction with external people undoubtedly continued to be important to the ruler and central elites as their demand for foreign goods increased, the central government of the tennō was no longer interested in formally incorporating external people and making them visible in the official records.

## Conclusion

In 872, one of the official histories records an epidemic that swept the capital of Heian, killing many people. The record states that the people of the realm were saying that guests from Parhae (a state on the Korean peninsula) had brought a poisonous air or miasma from the foreign land.[51] Here it is clear that over time, ideas of impurity or defilement (*kegare*) began to be associated with foreign peoples in the mid- to late-Heian period. By this point, the *ritsuryō* state and the worldview it expressed was changing dynamically. In particular, the benevolence and universality of a *ritsuryō* sovereign became less important as other centers of power were established—first the Fujiwara regents, then the retired sovereigns, and eventually the various warrior governments. Although the categories of people inscribed in the *ritsuryō* system were not actually abolished until the promulgation of the Meiji Constitution in 1890, each iteration of the Japanese realm had its own categories that it sought to impose on the people of the realm and its own reasons for choosing who to include or exclude and how to do so.

In this chapter it has only been possible to introduce a few of the categories that were relevant to early Yamato rulers while presenting a broad overview of how the state's policies for incorporating external people into the realm changed over the first several centuries of its history. We began with the pre-*ritsuryō* period of relatively flexibility and prioritization of talent and technology over exclusive allegiances, and found that episodes in the early eighth century official histories acknowledge both the potential benefits and the potential dangers of being born to parents from different realms. The establishment of the *ritsuryō* state meant both that multiple affiliations were problematized, and also that integrating new people into the realm gained significance as a way for rulers to demonstrate their benevolence and strengthen the legitimacy of their realm. When large-scale immigration ceased and *ritsuryō* sovereigns faced a challenge in maintaining the universality of their reigns, they turned to genealogical records of court lineages to create a permanently "universal" realm that no longer required external people to be legitimized. Finally, in the early Heian period, even as interest in foreign goods and trade increased, the rulers and central elites lost interest in formally incorporating external people.

It is important to recognize that even at the earliest stages of the formation of the state, any idea of an individual or group as either "native" or "immigrant" was already socially constructed. Centuries of interaction with people from the continent and peninsula meant that that there was never a purely Japanese, or purely "native" population. Rather than assuming that there was some kind of pure *ur*-population of the Japanese archipelago, we should instead start with the assumption of diversity and change and try to understand when and how in the ongoing process of state formation various categories of people came to be identified. The problem of how to delineate the people of the early realm of Yamato and maintain these delineations was fundamental to the *ritsuryō* government just as it is to any polity today. As the various examples discussed above have shown, what the rulers chose to see did not necessarily depend on what actually existed. They found ways to "see" a universal or cosmopolitan realm regardless of the number and type of people coming into the domain. Japan was in this sense always hybrid and multiple, but the ways in which rulers and the court chose to see the diversity of the population varied over time as conditions in the region and the realm changed.

## CHAPTER TWO

# "PLACED ON PAR WITH ALL OTHER JAPANESE": HAPA JAPANESE IN JAPAN AND THE WORLD, 1543-1859

GARY LEUPP

During the sixteenth century, Europeans fatefully entered East Asian waters. Their galleons, crewed by a mix of Europeans, Africans, and Asians, brought New World silver that quickened commercial expansion throughout the region, American food crops that transformed cuisine, tobacco that quickly addicted high and low alike, muskets that transformed warfare, and Christianity that altered minds.

The Europeans also brought their genes. In the second half of the century European traders and adventurers fathered children in newly-founded port-towns such as Batavia in Java, Macao in China, Manila in the Philippines, and Hirado in Japan.[52] They were followed from 1600 by Dutch and English merchants and explorers; a Dutch governor of Taiwan even predicted in 1627 that Hirado would soon "have as many Dutch mestizos as thorough Japanese for inhabitants."[53] Hirado never did in fact ever become half-"Dutch mestizo," but there were certainly as of that time thousands of part-Europeans living in ports from Southeast Asia to Japan. One can say that the history of part-Japanese, part-European *hapa* begins here.[54]

In this chapter, I will confine my topic to Japanese-Europeans from the first arrival of Portuguese in Japan in 1543 and ending with the opening of the treaty ports in 1859. But one must acknowledge that there is a much larger story of Japanese ethnic mixing in this period. From around 1580 to the 1630s, tens of thousands of Japanese seamen, merchants, adventurers, and Christian converts driven into exile settled in "Japan Towns" (*Nihonmachi*) throughout Southeast Asia.[55] They generated a mixed Japanese-Siamese community in Ayutthaya, a mixed Japanese-Vietnamese community in Hoi An, and a mixed Japanese-Filipino community in Dilao in Luzon. Japanese intermarried with Javanese in Dutch-held Batavia and Cambodians in Phnom Penh. This was a period of unprecedented Japanese contact with the outside world that peaked in the 1630s, just before the shogunate made a series of decisions that drastically curtailed that contact.[56] Five edicts issued between 1633 and 1639 reiterated the existing ban on Christianity; expelled all traders from Catholic lands; confined the Dutchmen allowed to remain in the country on a tiny, artificially constructed isle connected to the port town of Nagasaki by a bridge; and banned all Japanese from travelling abroad on pain of death should they return.[57] Thus the Japanese in the Nihonmachi disappeared into local gene pools.[58]

But we should not assume that ethnic mixing only began in the early modern period of accelerated international contact.[59] Most scholars agree that the Japanese are for the most part descended from a people called the Yayoi, of clear northeastern Asian and "Mongoloid" origin, who began entering the archipelago by sea from the fourth century BCE.[60] They encountered an indigenous people, the Jōmon, of unknown origin who had been there from around 12,000 BCE.[61] Given the long duration of the period and the great variety of local Jōmon cultures extending from Hokkaido to the Ryukyus it seems likely that people of various origins had reached Japan by sea and made their own contributions to the islands' gene pool during that period.

The Yayoi and Jōmon were conspicuously different ethnic groups, the Yayoi were, on average, some eight centimeters taller than the latter and had less body hair. To some extent, the Yayoi interbred with the natives.[62] Even while conceding that both groups were "Japanese" by virtue of their habitation of the archipelago, their interactions surely produced people with some sense of dual identity. And there were occasional, significant infusions of new blood in pre-modern times, even before the arrival of Europeans.

The geographical remoteness of Japan worked against international contact; the islands are five times as distant from the Korean Peninsula as England is from continental Europe and were not successfully invaded until the twentieth century. They were close enough to the Asian continent to receive ongoing exposure to several foreign cultures, principally, of course, Chinese; but still distanced sufficiently to evolve a highly independent, distinctive culture. While the Celts on the British isles on the other side of Eurasia were obliged to accept waves of migrants and invaders, all of whom contributed to the gene pool—Romans, Angles, Saxons, Vikings, Danes, Normans etc.—the people of Japan evolved in relative isolation.

Still, a substantial community of half-Japanese, half-Koreans appeared in the fifth and sixth centuries, when about one million Koreans emigrated to Japan. According to the *Shoku Nihongi*, one in ten residents of the Nara basin claimed descent from Paekche.[63] A genealogical register compiled in 815 indicates that over one-quarter of the 1,182 noble families at the court in Heian (Kyoto) were of part-Korean or part-Chinese ancestry.[64] From 1592, tens of thousands of Koreans were brought to Japan as captives in the course of Hideyoshi's invasion of the peninsula. Many of these people intermarried with Japanese.[65]

### The First Europeans in Japan (1543)

But let us return to the Europeans. According to the *Teppō-ki* (Chronicle of the Musket) written in 1607, the first two or three Europeans (who were Portuguese) reached Japan in 1543 on board a junk with an ethnically mixed crew. Arriving at Tanegashima, a small island south of Kyushu, they were spotted on the beach by local people. The headman of the nearest village asked a Chinese sailor arriving aboard the same ship: "Why do they look so different?"[66] The seaman answered:

> They are traders from among the south-western barbarians. They know something of the etiquette of monarchs and ministers, but they do not know that polite attitudes are part of etiquette. Thus, when they drink, they do not use cups. When they eat, they do not use chopsticks. They know how to gratify their appetites but they cannot state their reasons in writing. These traders visit the same places in the hope of exchanging what they have for what they do not have. There is nothing suspicious about them."[67]

The term "South-western barbarians" (*Seinanbanjin*) referred to the fact that the Europeans had arrived from the southwest by way of the Indian Ocean. It seems a demeaning term on the face of it, but it did not necessarily at this point convey disparagement.[68]

Japanese perceptions of the world had long been influenced by the concept of *sankoku* or "the three countries"—the three *civilizations*, really, since all other lands were presumed to be "barbarian." Japan was of course preeminent among the three. China was naturally included among them; it was impossible to deny Japan's cultural indebtedness to the Middle Kingdom, or the prestige that China commanded throughout the known world. This "China" was understood to include the Chinese tribute zone nations (Korea, Annam, the Ryūkyū Kingdom, etc.). The third civilized country was Tenjiku (India). There were no direct trading ties nor ongoing cultural contacts between Japan and south Asia, but India was known to be the homeland of the Buddha, a land of wise men with a rich culture. While they did not use the Chinese characters, normally viewed as a key indicator of cultural attainment, the Indians had their own writing system on which the earliest Buddhist texts had been written. They were plainly very sophisticated and admirable.

According the Portuguese adventurer Fernão Mendes Pinto, the Japanese also referred to Portuguese as *Chenchikogens* (surely a corruption of *Tenjikujin*, a Sino-Japanese term for people from India).[69] This assumption that the Portuguese were Indians reflected the fact that the Portuguese did in fact arrive via the settlement of Goa, already a thriving port city, on India's Malabar Coast. When the first Jesuit evangelizers arrived in 1549, it was natural for Japanese to perceive them as a new wave of Buddhist missionaries from the land of the Buddha.[70]

**European Concepts of Race: Japanese as "White"**
If the Japanese divided humankind into the peoples of the Three Countries plus miscellaneous barbarians, westerners divided it into the progeny of the sons of Noah: Japheth, Shem, and Ham.[71] By the sixteenth century, these were widely viewed as the progenitors of the European, Semitic, and black African "races" respectively, and arranged in a hierarchy based on color with the whitest on the top. From the outset, Europeans regarded Japanese as *White*: The first Jesuit in Japan, Francesco Xavier, declared the Japanese "the best race yet discovered and I do not think you will find their match among pagan nations."[72] "The people are white and cultured," wrote Father Alessandro Valignano in the late sixteenth century,

> [and] even the common folk and peasants are well brought up and are so remarkably polite that they give the impression that they were trained at court. In this respect they are superior to other Eastern peoples but also to Europeans as well. They are very capable and intelligent; and the children are quick to grasp our lessons and instructions. They learn to read and write our language far more quickly and easily than children in Europe. The lower classes are not so coarse

and ignorant as those in Europe; on the contrary, they are generally intelligent, well brought up and quick to learn.[73]

"In their culture, deportment and manners," wrote the Portuguese missionary Luis Frois around 1590, the Japanese excelled Europeans "in so many ways that one is ashamed to tell about it."[74] The Genoan Jesuit Organtino Gnecchi wrote in 1577:

It must be understood these people are in no way barbarous. Excluding the advantage of religion, we ourselves in comparison to them are most barbarous. I learn something from the Japanese every day and I am sure that in the whole of the universe there is no people so gifted by Nature.[75]

In 1585, during the highly publicized visit to the Vatican of young Japanese noblemen converted to Christianity (a visit designed to advertise the expansion of Roman Catholicism into the "newly discovered lands"), the Portuguese Jesuit Gaspare Gonsalves declared that Japan stood "before all the countries of the East," and could be compared to "the West, in its size, the number of its cities, and its warlike and cultured people."[76]

Valignano's matter-of-fact observation that "the people are White" was echoed by nearly all Europeans visiting Japan.[77] At a time when Europeans conflated Whiteness with moral virtues, the Japanese were credited with this attribute.[78] And the women were *especially* White. "The women have mostly white complexions and are very beautiful," wrote the Spanish nobleman García de Escalante Alvarado in the 1550s.[79] His countryman the merchant Avila Gíron concurred: "The women are white and generally of good appearance; indeed, many are comely and graceful...[T]hey are very polite and have less defects than any other persons I have met...they are the most upright and faithful women in the whole world." The Spaniard added that whereas Spanish ladies were apt to use "filthy things" such as "jugs of cosmetics" to improve their appearances, "they do not have a better complexion than the Japanese woman who merely washes her face in water from any pond."[80]

Just as the Japanese were unsure of how to locate the Westerners within their ethnological framework, so Europeans struggled to understand Japanese ethnic affinities. The Japanese were definitely different from the Chinese. How did they relate to the progeny of Noah? Kaempfer, Charlevoix, and Thunberg all suggested that

Japanese were descended from Shem, father of the Semitic peoples.[81] Europeans looked at Japanese as ethnic kin, comparing them (in their martial valor) to the ancient Spartans and Romans; likening their language to German, their women to Spanish senoritas. They were, in any case, white people.

### A Shotgun Wedding

The first known intimate union between a European man and a Japanese woman involved one of the Portuguese men arriving in that Chinese junk in 1543. The strangers possessed muskets, a weapon entirely new to the local people, and immediately impressed the local baron (*daimyo*) with its military potential. He instructed his swordsmith, Yasuita Kinbei Kiyosada, to learn the art of producing the arquebus. The craftsman requested instruction from one of the Portuguese, but was obliged to pay for the lessons--with his teenage daughter. "He thought that she would only be bound [to the foreigner] for a short time," his descendants recorded. "But she became his wife [*yome*]." It is not known if they had any children.[82] According to the *Yasuita-shi Kiyosada ichiryū no keizu* (Geneology of the Yaita Kiyosada Family), her name was Wakasa, and she became the stuff of legend during the Tokugawa and modern periods. Lidin cites "local tradition" for the assertion that Wakasa "lived the most miserable life that was ever lived."[83]

Soon Portuguese merchants were establishing relations with local women in part to facilitate their trading activities. According to Engelbert Kaempfer, a physician in the service of the Dutch East India Company (VOC) from 1690 to 1692, the earliest Portuguese merchants over a century earlier had "married the daughters of the richest inhabitants, and dispos'd of their goods to the best advantage."[84] But wives were not only valued as help-mates in commercial activities in Japan; many Portuguese brought their consorts out of the country after concluding their operations, and by the 1620s the Portuguese settlers in Chinese Macao had "largely intermarried with Japanese wives."[85]

### Japanese Women—For All Foreign Merchants and Sailors

We know little about the experience of Portuguese in Japan for the first half-century of their presence. Starting in 1550, Portuguese vessels arrived at the ports of Hakata and Hirado on the northwestern corner of Kyushu, although they withdrew from Hirado after fourteen of their men were killed in a quarrel over silk prices. In 1561, they relocated to nearby Yokoseura, in the domain of a Christian convert, Ōmura Sumitada, until the port was burned down by a rival of the daimyo. In 1570, Nagasaki, another port in the same domain, was opened under Portuguese supervision and leased to the Jesuit missionaries ten years later. In 1580, the Italian Jesuit Alessandro Valignano wrote that "to secure Nagasaki ... as many married Portuguese are to be settled there as will find accommodations within the town." The missionaries urged Portuguese Christians married to Japanese women to settle in the port to secure Christian control.[86]

Nagasaki was visited each year by several ships from Macao. In Hirado, Yokoseura, and Nagasaki, the Portuguese established piers and docking facilities, residences, warehouses, market spaces, even military fortifications. Hosting daimyos profiting from the trade were happy to provide the merchants with every domestic comfort during their stay in Japan. I have not found clear references to prostitutes being offered to the Europeans before the 1590s but it is safe to assume this occurred to some extent from the 1550s. The missionaries' depictions of Portuguese merchants' and seamen's behavior suggest that, while in the early decades these Catholic laymen were inclined to humbly submit to religious guidance, their conduct gradually become "scandalous" in defiance of the orders of the *religieux*.[87] The French ecclesiastical historian Pierre François Xavier de Charlevoix (1682-1761) noted in work published 1715 that by the time of Hideyoshi's edict against Christianity in 1587, the Jesuits believed some Portuguese ships were favoring the ports of non-Christian daimyo so as to enjoy their brothel districts. "It was remarked that they were eager to anchor only in the ports of the infidel princes, and it was not doubted but it was fear of having the missionaries as witnesses of their libertinage that had produced this change."[88]

But prostitutes were available in Nagasaki too, after Hideyoshi seized direct control (from the Jesuits) in 1587. Like the daimyo hoping to lure the Portuguese ships to their shores with abundant hospitality, Hideyoshi instructed the town leaders of Nagasaki in the 1580s to attend to foreign traders' sexual needs. He ordered them "show kindness" to Chinese merchants and supply them with "Japanese brides [yome]."[89] By the 1590s there is clear evidence that arriving Europeans also were quickly offered local women for their pleasure.

Francesco Carletti, a Florentine merchant who visited Nagasaki in 1597, described the process:

As soon as ever these Portuguese arrive and
disembark, the pimps who control this traffic in women

call on them in the houses where they are quartered
for the time of their stay, and enquire whether they
would like to purchase, or acquire in any other method
they please, a girl, for the period of their sojourn, or to
keep her for so many months, or for a day, or for an
hour, a contract being fist made with these brokers,
or an agreement entered into with the girl's relations,
and the money paid down. And if they prefer it they will
take them to the girl's house, in order that they may
see her first, or else they may take them to see her on
their own premises, which are usually situated in certain
hamlets or villages outside the city. And many of the
Portuguese, upon whose testimony I am relying, fall
into this custom as the fancy takes them, driving the
best bargain for a few pence. And it so often happens
that they will get hold of a pretty little girl of fourteen
or fifteen years of age, for three or four *scudi,* or a little
more or less, according to the time at which they wish
to have her at their disposal, with no other responsibility
beyond that of sending her back home when done with.

He added that a half-year relationship with a European did not
"in any way interfere with a [Japanese] girl's chances for marriage"
to a Japanese thereafter, and noted that some women had "acquired
a dowry, by accumulating 30 or 40 scudi, given to them from time to
time by these Portuguese."[90] As we will see, Westerners, often with
apparent amazement, into the late nineteenth century repeated
this assertion that sexual intimacies with European men did not
affect subsequent prospects for women to marry Japanese men.

In Hakata, another Kyushu port town prosperous from medieval
times, a brothel called the Ebisuya catered to foreign men as of the
1590s. (It was later relocated to Nagasaki where there were more
foreigners, specifically to the Murayama brothel ward where it
supplied prostitutes to the Dutch.)[91] The very first half-Japanese,
half-European children of these unions must have been born in the
mid-sixteenth century.

Alongside the casual relationships, "for so many months, or for
a day, or for an hour," there were also unions of Portuguese men
and Japanese women recognized as Christian marriages by the
Roman Catholic Church. Portuguese men co-resided with women
in Brazil, Africa, and various parts of Asia, procreating with local
women wherever they settled.[92] But although they rarely regarded
the societies into which they intermarried as equal to their own,

sixteenth-century Portuguese and other Europeans often saw in the Japanese a kindred "race" with a highly advanced culture. These perceptions surely helped shape their relations with Japanese women.

Some of the Europeans acquired partners for lifetime terms through outright purchase. In 1590, the warlord Hideyoshi, having reunited Japan under his rule, banned the purchase and sale of human beings.[93] But before and after his edict, foreign men bought women in Japan, including Koreans forced to settle in Kyushu during the Japanese invasion of the peninsula (1592-98). Even the servants and slaves of the Portuguese (Gujaratis, Javanese, black Africans) did so. A Jesuit reported in 1598 that "the very lascars [south Asian sailors] and scullions of the Portuguese purchase and carry [Japanese or Korean] slaves away" to Macao, while "Kaffirs and negroes of the Portuguese ... give a scandalous example by living in debauchery with the girls they have bought, and whom some of them introduce into their cabins on the passage to Macao."[94]

## Japanese-European Children

The historical records (missionary reports, merchants' reports and journals, Japanese official documents) do not tell us much about these early hapa. But they do give us some basic details about a few people. For example, we know that one Beatrix da Costa was born in Japan to a Portuguese man and a Japanese woman around 1590 and married a Portuguese named Antonio da Silva around 1610. They had a daughter, Marie, who left with her mother for Macao in 1634.[95] A Portuguese in Nagasaki named Domingos Jorge married a Japanese woman with the Christian name Isabelle before 1620; they had three children by 1622. A Portuguese surnamed Marquez had a son, Francisco, by a Japanese woman in 1611; he studied in Macao, entered the Society of Jesus and returned to Japan in 1642 as a missionary.[96]

We only know about these people because they are listed among the Christian martyrs and victims of persecution reported by the Jesuit mission active from 1549. Domingos Jorge was the first foreign Christian layman martyred in Japan, perishing with his wife and children in 1622. The half-Japanese Marquez was caught and executed in 1642. Beatrix and Marie were imprisoned and tortured in 1631 before they were exiled from the country. [97]

According to Kaempfer, a "Captain Moro" was executed in 1637 for sending "traitorous Letters to the King of Portugal" apprehended by the Dutch on board a captured Portuguese ship. He was considered "chief of the Portuguese in Japan, himself a

Japanese by birth, and a great zealot for the Christian religion,"[98] from which it would appear that a man with a Japanese mother played a key role in leading the Portuguese Catholic community at the height of persecution.

Attitudes towards Europeans were plainly affected by evolving official policies towards the Roman Catholic religion. In 1587, when the mainly Portuguese-staffed Jesuit mission claimed to have converted around 200,000 Japanese to Christianity, Hideyoshi expelled all missionaries from Japan and banned the faith. There was in fact no serious persecution until 1597, the year before his death; Christianity continued to flourish underground, and even aboveground in some domains, during the early years of the Tokugawa shogunate (1603-1868).

Meanwhile, a new type of barbarian--Protestant Europeans— arrived in Japan.[99] The Dutch East India Company (VOC) established itself in Hirado in 1609, breaking the Portuguese and Spanish monopoly. The English East India Company (initially, the London Merchants Company) arrived four years later. These men looked sufficiently different from the earlier *Seinanbanjin* that they were given their own designation: *Kōmō* (Red-Hairs). By all indications they related to local women much as the other Europeans did.

The English records contain many references to company merchants' relationships with these women. In these records, as Alison Games notes, "the merchants conveyed their perception of the legitimacy of these unions by referring to women as 'wives.' Other words might suffice—traders commonly used woman, whore, and wench. But instead these merchants dignified these relationships with the legal status and permanent connection conveyed by *wife*."[100] There are many references also to the children. The English reported to one another in written notes about the births and deaths of these children, and exchanged gifts with the offspring. Thus we know that in May 1616 Richard Wickham sent fellow merchant William Eaton's daughter two summer kimonos that had been commissioned by Eaton, along with a present for the "woman" of company director Richard Cocks. Cocks distributed gifts to the children of the famous William Adams, who worked for both the company and the shogunate.

In 1621 Cocks recorded that Henry Smith, the purser of the *Royal James*, had had a son by a Japanese woman. Arther Hatch, chaplain of the *Palgrove*, christened the baby, naming him Henry after his father. William Eaton and another English merchant, Joseph Cockram, served as godfathers while the companion of William Sayers (a Japanese woman named Mateyasu or Maria) served as godmother.[101]

### Expulsion of Mixed-Race Children

The repeated edicts banning Christianity naturally impacted the resident foreign community and many children of mixed blood. In 1624, all Spaniards were expelled after authorities concluded that the galleons from the Philippines were smuggling in the banned clerics. As noted above, all Portuguese were soon forced out for the same reason. The anti-Christian campaign targeted most part-Japanese. In 1636, 287 people (Portuguese men married to Japanese wives, their wives and children) were deported to Macao (which already had a significant population of Japanese Christian refugees).[102] The expulsion order stated:

> No offspring of Southern Barbarians [Nanbanjin] will be allowed to remain. Anyone violating this order will be killed, and all relatives punished according to the gravity of the offense. If any Japanese have adopted the offspring of Southern Barbarians they deserve to die. Nevertheless, such adopted children and their foster-parents will be handed over to the Southern Barbarians for deportation.[103]

Still, the part-Portuguese children were targeted less for their Lusitanian genes than for suspected Christian loyalties and beliefs.

This at least is suggested by the fact that *some* Portuguese—priests who had renounced Christianity—were actually pressured by the authorities to marry Japanese women. Christovão Ferreira (1580-1650) was a leading figure in the Jesuit mission from about 1610 until he apostatized under torture in 1633. Spending forty of his seventy years in Japan, he was, according to one Japanese account, "originally a foreigner but was naturalized in Japan ... so gifted he could read *Taiheiki*."[104] Thereafter he apparently lived comfortably enough. Accorded the Japanese name Sawano Chūan, he served as a Japanese-Portuguese interpreter for the shogunate, translated a European astronomical text into Romanized Japanese, composed or helped compose an anti-Christian tract, and assisted in the interrogation of Christians.[105] Authorities in Nagasaki pressured him to marry, and according to a report of Portuguese merchants who visited his home in 1635, he, "now lives with a Japanese woman in Nagasaki." According to another report, the following year Ferreira was "in no way" distinguishable from Japanese natives, and had been forced to marry the widow of a Chinese man who had been executed but "they did not live happily together."[106] Ferreira claimed he only employed her as his maid and denied sleeping with her.[107]

Nevertheless, Japanese records make it clear Ferreira had a son Chūjirō, who died in 1651 and whose ashes were interred with his father's at the same Zen temple in Nagasaki.[108] A Portuguese merchant (who happened to have been married to a Japanese woman) visited his house in 1636 and "saw no woman there, but only one poor little boy."[109] This may have been Chūjirō. A credible source dated 1726 described him year earlier as having become a "skillful pilot."[110] Ferreira is also recorded as having two daughters, including the wife of Sugimoto Chūkei (1618-89), whose descendants served as physicians to the shoguns into the nineteenth century.[111] If these were indeed Ferreira's biological children, it would prove that people of Catholic European patrimony were sometimes accepted in Japanese society.

It has been suggested that the children may have been his by adoption, those of the Chinese merchant. But the Sugimoto family, for its part, traces its ancestry to Ferreira. After the destruction of the family tomb in Nagasaki in 1941, the family erected a monument on the grounds of a Zen temple in Tokyo. It traces the family line to Chūan-jōkō.[112] And Ferreira was not the only Portuguese deliberately paired with a Japanese woman. Francisco Cassola, a Jesuit, was arrested on a small island off Kyushu in 1643. After renouncing Christianity, he was provided with a Japanese wife and quartered on the grounds of a daimyo's mansion.[113] The Italian Jesuit Giuseppe Chiara (1610-85), who was arrested and tortured with Cassola, was given the name and swords of an executed samurai and married to the wife of (an apparently different) executed man.[114] His tomb at a temple in Edo does not indicate any children, nor do we know whether Cassola had any, but it does not appear that the shogunate as of the mid-1630s was bent upon deporting all part-Europeans.

In the eighth month of 1639, however, the Council of Elders (rōjū) in Edo ordered the expulsion of more remaining Europeans including Dutchmen and Englishmen married to Japanese, along with their wives and children. The issue was no longer religion; the Dutchmen had indeed shown their willingness to trample on Roman Catholic religious images to assure their hosts that they were not Christians (at least, of the proselytizing kind). The elders issued a decree making a specifically *ethnic* argument; it posited the possibility that a part-European might somehow gain power in the land of the *kami* and declared that "Japanese desire no such admixture of races, and will not incur the danger that, in the course of time, any one of such descent will rule over [us]."[115]

In October 1639, a Dutch ship carried six Japanese wives of Dutchmen or Englishmen, and 32 mixed-race children from Hirado to Batavia. The passengers included the Dutchman Melchior van Santvoort, who had lived in Japan since 1600 and received favors from Tokugawa Ieyasu, along with his Japanese wife Isabella, his daughter Susannah, his Dutch son-on-law, and a grandson.[116]

But even at this point some exceptions were made. François Caron, head of the Dutch mission, was allowed to remain in the country with his Japanese wife (daughter of one Eguchi Jūzaemon) and five children. Born in Flanders around 1600, Caron had arrived in Japan in 1619 as a cook's assistant. But he became an interpreter and, due in part to his mastery of the Japanese language, finally *opperhoofd* (supreme head) of the VOC in Japan. According to another member of the mission, "the Japanese ... always spoke of him with the greatest respect, both during his residence in the country and after he had left it."[117] In 1641, he averted a crisis produced by the Japanese discovery that the numbers on the foundation stones of VOC warehouses in Hirado represented years in the Christian calendar. He ordered the buildings demolished to affirm that the Dutch were not Christian missionaries. The *bakufu* ordered the Dutch out of Hirado to the tiny, artificially constructed isle of Dejima, which was connected by a bridge to Nagasaki. From this point on, all westerners arriving in Japan were, under normal circumstances, to be confined to Dejima.

### The Children of François Caron, Pieter Hartsinck (1637-80), Oharu of Djakarta (from 1639), and Horiya Fumi (from 1825)

In February 1641, the Caron family left for the Dutch colony of Batavia. The family remained there, where there was a considerable community of Japanese, while Caron returned to the Europe he had left twenty-three years earlier. Many Japanese had intermarried with Dutchmen in the Java colony. Dutch Reformed Church records list 17 church marriages in Batavia involving Japanese or part-Japanese women and European men, and 45 involving Japanese men and Javanese women between 1619 and 1655.[118]

Upon his return to Batavia, Caron found, to his "excessive sorrow," that his Japanese wife had died.[119] To secure the futures of his children, he petitioned the Dutch authorities to "wash out the stain of their birth" resulting from a relationship that had not "been solemnized according to the rites and ceremonies of the Christian church" and to thus entitle them "to all the honours, states and dignities, as well as all lawful and proper inheritances."[120] The petition was accepted and the children seem to have flourished. The eldest son Daniel (1622-58?), studied theology at Leiden University from 1643, returned to Batavia in 1649, and spent the next decade doing missionary work in Taiwan.[121] A second son, Tobias, was living in Batavia in 1653, but nothing else is known of him. The third son, François, also attended Leiden, enrolling a week after his fellow half-Japanese Pieter Hartsinck.[122] He returned to Batavia after graduating in the late 1660s, and worked as a Protestant Christian missionary in the Moluccas, composing religious works in a Malay tongue. He returned to Holland in 1676 and died there in 1705, leaving two daughters who married Dutchmen.[123]

The brothers were not the only half-Japanese attending European universities at this time. A William Eaton, son of an officer of the English East India Company by the same name and a Japanese woman named Kamezō, had left Japan with his father in 1623.[124] In 1639, he was made a denizen of England (i.e., a foreigner with full English rights) and in 1640 was enrolled in Trinity College, Cambridge University. He described himself as "borne in Japaon one of the remotest parts of the East Indyes" and "in his younge yeares brought into England where the charitable dispocion of some and by like well disposed people hath hitherto bene maintained in [Your Majesty's] Colledge in Cambridge."[125]

Pieter Hartsinck was another half-Japanese studying at Leiden from 1654. Born in Hirado in 1637, he was one of two sons of Carel Hartsinck, a Rhineland merchant in the service of the VOC. He was four when the family left Japan, first for Taiwan then Batavia, where his mother died in 1642. Carel brought the boys to his ancestral town of Moers, then under Dutch rule, and raised them to 1651 when he set sail for the East Indies with a new Dutch wife.

In 1654, Pieter enrolled as a philosophy student at Leiden University as Petrus Hartsing Japonesis (Pieter Harsink of Japan), receiving a degree in medicine. But he had wide interests. Studying under the brilliant mathematician Franz von Schooten, he assisted him in translating Descartes's *Geometry* into Latin (from the original French). In the preface of the work Schooten acknowledged "Petrus Hartzingus, a most excellent and in many ways most intelligent, young Japanese who has hitherto been my most apt student in studying mathematics."[126] In 1672, Pieter was hired by Duke Johann Friedrich of Braunschweig-Lüneberg to oversee the mines and mint of his domain. No less a figure than Gottfried Leibniz coveted the post, but Hartsinck held it to his death in 1680.

Wealthy at his death, unmarried and without heirs, Hartsinck willed his property to the *Latinschule* in Moers (where it continues to fund scholarships to this day). There is an impressive memorial tablet to him in St. Jakobi's Church in Osterode, Lower Saxony in what was once Duke Johann Friedrich's domain. It contains this self-composed epigraph:

> India bore my mother and I, Europe my father. My destiny varied from the beginning. I saw countries in Asia and Africa, and the ocean's infinite meridian I have crossed twice. I left my homeland early in life to find my father's country. But I could not find my true home. And so I wandered the three parts of the world, but at last I have found my heavenly repose.[127]

A woman often referred to as "Oharu of Djakarta" is one of the few European-Japanese women of this period for whom we have some biographical details. Born the daughter of an Italian merchant in Hirado in 1625, she escaped the mass deportation of 1636. Her father had died, placing her in the care of one Rizaemon, either her grandfather, a rich merchant, or both. At some point she moved (or was forced to move) to Nagasaki. There is a report from a ward elder in Nagasaki in 1639 of a Japanese woman named Maria—presumably Oharu's mother—widow of an Italian with two children and living with an Englishman.[128] All, including Oharu's older sister Magdalena, who at 18 had her own son, were expelled in that year. In Batavia, Oharu married Simon Simonsen, an employee of the VOC, and bore fours sons and three daughters. She outlived her husband and lived in comfort surrounded by servants and slaves whom she emancipated upon her death in 1698 at age 73. The only reason we know about Oharu is that she wrote at least one letter to friends and family in Nagasaki that has been preserved, though in altered form.[129] Written communications continued to pass between Japan, Macao, Batavia, and Europe; after 1656, foreign mail was admitted into Japan so long as it carried no references to Christianity. There are references to at least 24 such communications between Japanese or part-Japanese in Batavia and relatives in Japan during the period; one woman named Okiyara sent letters (in Dutch, requiring translation in Nagasaki) up until 1707.[130]

## Part-Japanese in Spain, New Spain, and Southeast Asia

If much of the population of Macao was part-Japanese by the mid-seventeenth century, and there were thousands of Japanese and part-Japanese throughout Southeast Asia, there were half-Japanese in some other surprising venues by the early seventeenth century. In 1617, six Japanese men settled down in the small town of Corio del Rio, in the center of Andalusia, near Seville. These were members of the mission from the powerful domain of Sendai to New Spain and Europe from 1613-17.[131] There were around 180 on the mission, including 40 Portuguese and Spaniards; 120 Japanese merchants, sailors, and servants; 10 samurai sent by the shogun; and 12 Sendai samurai. Some 650 of Coria del Rio's population (24,000) today bear the surname Japón and proudly claim part-Japanese ancestry.[132]

A few Japanese settled in New Spain, as well, starting about 1610. Arriving on Spanish vessels, such as the *San Buenaventura*, built in Japan at the shogun's request in that year and dispatched on a trade mission to the New World, Japanese merchants married local women. For example, a man surnamed Fukuchi, born in Japan around 1595, arrived in Mexico around 1620. Assuming the name Luis de Encio, he married a local woman named Catalina de Silva. They had a daughter, Margarita. By 1634, Luis and Catalina were living in Guadalajara, their daughter married to another expatriate Japanese, Osaka-born "Juan de Páez." Juan and Margarita had nine children, only four of whom (all daughters) outlived their father when he died in 1675 at age 69. Juan was the godfather of many "children of the church" (orphans in the care of Guadalajara Cathedral). He rented a house from the church and cultivated close ties with the clergy. He also owned many black and mulatto slaves, especially women. After his death, Juan's half-Japanese widow, Margarita, maintained the Guadalajara estate, presiding over 25 family members, servants, and slaves. Her three-quarter Japanese daughter Juana inherited the estate, maintaining control until her death in 1704, when she was survived by four children.[133]

The life of Maria Guyomar de Pinha (1664 - after 1719) is perhaps the best documented of the lives of part-Japanese in seventeenth century Siam. Born in 1664 in the Nihonmachi, she was the daughter of one Yamada Ursula, whose Christian ancestors had fled Japan to escape persecution.[134] Ursula had married and had a son by an ex-Jesuit before marrying a "Master Phanick" with the surname Guyomar de Pinha. This man, Maria's father, was from the Portuguese colony of Goa. He himself was only one-quarter European: his father was Portuguese-Bengali and mother Japanese. In any case the Guyomar house was "one of the finest in the Portuguese settlement" in Ayutthaya.[135] In 1682, at age 18, Maria married Constantine Phaulkon, a Greek who had left service in the English East India Co. to become a high official in the court of King Narai (r. 1656-88). Four years later Maria—who was six-eighths Japanese, one eighth Portuguese, and one eighth Bengali—was described as possessing the "complexion, appearance and manners of a pretty European woman, who was gentle."[136]

Phaulkon had lived in England, where he had embraced the Anglican faith, but he converted to Catholicism to satisfy Maria. The couple was fabulously wealthy and involved in philanthropy, including the establishment of girls' schools under Maria's direction. They were deeply involved in steering Siamese foreign policy, notably the establishment of an alliance with France. Maria was even given a French noble title.

In 1688, King Narai was overthrown in a revolution led by opponents of his Western ties and tolerance of Catholic missions, and Phaulkon was executed. Maria took refuge with French troops in Ayutthaya, but they were obliged to turn her over to Siamese authorities who sentenced her to a life of serving in the royal kitchen. Her conditions do not appear to have been very oppressive: in 1719 she was visited by Alexander Hamilton, a representative of the English East India Company, who reported that she was "much respected both in the court and city, for her prudence and humanity to natives and strangers."[137] To this day she is famous for creating a number of popular Thai dishes. Her sons George and Constantine both served as officials at court, one supervising the Christian community, as well as designing a pipe organ for King Barromakot (r. 1733-58).[138]

Cornelia van Nieurwoode (1630-92) was another half-Japanese woman living in Southeast Asia in this period. The daughter of a Japanese woman and Cornelis van Nieurwoode, the head (*opperhoofd*) of the Dutch trading mission in Japan from 1623 to 1631, she was sent with a sister to Batavia by her father in 1632. There she eventually married Pieter Cnoll, the Dutch director-general of the colony. There is a famous oil painting of her with her husband and children, made in 1665 and on display in the Rijksmuseum in Amsterdam. The painting shows a proud, wealthy Eurasian family in Java, and all but Pieter have conspicuously Asian features, while a daughter sports a Japanese folding fan.

In 1672, Cnoll died, leaving his fortune to his wife who remarried several years later at age 46. Her unfortunate choice was a 38-year-old gold-digging Englishman named John Bitter. He soon boasted to friends that he was "firmly established in a magnificent house" and possessed "money like shells" as a result of the marriage. But it was a horrible marriage for Cornelia, as Bitter in violation of the marriage contract blocked her business deals, used her money without permission, beat and insulted her. Cornelia obtained a separation and established her independent identity by traveling around the town in a carriage emblazoned by her Japanese family crest. She died in Holland in 1692 while still enmeshed in divorce proceedings.[139]

Thus among seventeenth century *hapa* Japanese outside Japan we have Caron's half-Flemish sons studying at Leiden and working as Calvinist missionaries in Java and Taiwan; half-English William Eaton studying at Cambridge; half-German Pieter Hartsinck studying at Leiden, translating Descartes and overseeing the mines and mint of a German duchy; half-Dutch Oharu linking Nagasaki and Batavia through her letters; half-Dutch Cornelia marrying well in Batavia, but badly the second time, able to litigate for a divorce at the Hague.

## Part-Japanese in Japan after 1641

Did any hapa remain in Japan after 1641? It seems likely they did. The numbers sent into exile to Macao and Batavia seem too small to include the children of all Japanese-Europeans alive as of the late 1630s. An English India Company report from Bantam in 1671 states there are "some Scotch, Irish, etc. there at Firando [Hirado], although we do not know by what occasion." Quite likely they were part-Japanese.[140] One wonders particularly about Joseph Adams and his sister Susannah, children of the English pilot William Adams, a celebrated figure in early seventeenth century Japanese history.

Adams' career is too substantial and well known to recount beyond the bare details. He was a skilled shipbuilder and mariner, a veteran of the English defense against the Spanish Armada in 1588. In 1598 he was hired by a Dutch company (later to become the VOC) to pilot a fleet of ships from Holland to Japan using captured nautical charts. Leaving Rotterdam in June, the five-vessel, 110-man crew mission to break the Catholic monopoly on European trade with Japan met with multiple disasters before just one surviving ship with 24 crew members aboard (six of whom soon died) arrived in Kyushu in April, 1600. Local Jesuits, shocked that Protestants had gained access to Japan, urged that they be executed (as pirates). But Tokugawa Ieyasu, then head of a regency council and soon to become shogun, instead treated the Dutchmen kindly and befriended Adams, who gave him lessons in geography and astronomy and broadened his awareness of conflicts among the European powers. Ieyasu awarded him an estate of about 100 peasants on the Miura Peninsula near Edo (Tokyo), a mansion in Edo, and the two swords of a samurai. No European had ever risen to such honors in Japan.

Adams lived in Japan from 1600 to 1619, from age 38 to his death at 55. He apparently mastered the language, readily adapted to the culture, and admired the emerging institutions of the Tokugawa shogunate. He wrote to Dutch merchants in Bantam in 1612, "The people of this Land of Japan are good of nature, courteous above measure, and valiant in war; their justice is severely executed without any partiality upon transgressors of the law. They are governed in great civility. I mean, not a land better governed in the world by civil policy." When other Englishmen finally met him in 1613, they were startled by his appearance (*chonmage* haircut, samurai outfit, swords, and intimidating Japanese retainer entourage). According to the English merchant John Saris, Adams on first meeting fellow Englishmen after 15 years made "so admirable and affectionated commendaytons of the Counterye as it is generally thought emongst vs he is a naturalized Japanner."[141]

Adams had an English wife and two children back home in England, but he married a Japanese woman around 1605. Details of the relationship are unclear; a late nineteenth century account purports to give her name (Oyuki) and lineage but is not reliable. But it is very clear that the woman referred to as "Mrs. Adams" or "Adams' wife" in English company documents from 1613 was respected by Adams' associates and (with her father and sister) acquired a major stake in his business activities. English documents also indicate that Adams had two children by his Japanese wife, Joseph and Susannah, whom his colleagues treated with affection. Richard Cocks, head of the English trade mission from 1615-22, recorded giving puppets to the children and in 1616 noted receipt of a letter from Joseph with a gift of bread, cooking oil, and powdered beef. In the same year he reports that young Joseph had been confirmed as heir of his father's estate.

In 1621, two years after his father's death, Joseph received his father's swords from Cocks, which Adams had deposited with Cocks as he died in Hirado. "I delivered the two Katana and wakidashi [long and short swords] of Capt Adams left per will to his son, Joseph," recorded Cocks. "There were tears shed at delivery."[142] Joseph was at most 16 at the time. The following year Cocks records a gift to Joseph's "schoolmaster." From 1624 to 1635 (throughout his twenties), Joseph used his inherited license to pilot "vermilion seal" (officially authorized) trading vessels and piloted voyages to Southeast Asia at least five times. In 1636 he and his sister Susannah erected a memorial tablet to their parents at the Kashima Shrine in the village of Hemi, Joseph's inherited fief. Two tombs constructed in Hemi at this time are thought to be those of Adams and Oyuki, or of Joseph and his mother.[143] Such acts of filial piety, expressed in Shinto-Buddhist fashion, are hard to reconcile with Christian belief and may indicate that the children overtly renounced Christianity at this time. (There is evidence that Adams's wife's family were Roman Catholic converts.[144] Adams himself seems to have been a sincere Protestant and it is likely the children had some Christian upbringing.) We do not know when they died, but there is no record of them being martyred or disgraced, and the Edo ward where Adams' mansion had been located continued to be called Anjin-chō (The Pilot's Ward) into the twentieth century.[145]

In Nagasaki, brothels catering to foreigners existed, concentrated in the Maruyama licensed district, even before the Dutch were forced to move to Dejima in 1641. In 1666, an edict from the Nagasaki commissioner specified that only registered courtesans (yūjo) could enter the island compound and have intimate relations with the Dutch. It is not clear what happened in the interim. After a Dutchman was executed in 1640 for the crime of adultery (with a married Japanese woman), a new edict banned relations between Dutchmen and both married and unmarried women. But it is likely that some system of providing prostitutes to the foreigners existed even during this time.[146]

Japanese patriarchal society had always been hospitable to the Westerners, in terms of meeting their perceived basic needs: victuals and female companionship. The fact that the supply of both foodstuffs and prostitutes to the Dutch was handled by the same commissioner (bugyō) indicates that the deeply-rooted cultural inclination towards hospitality to foreigners—especially those bringing new goods and wealth—along with the unproblematic acceptance of sexual pleasure as a good in itself, overrode any hesitation on the part of officials (and brothel owners) to assign prostitutes to "barbarians".[147]

By the end of the century, city officials had established a division of labor, whereby some women trained to socialize with Dutchmen and imbibe such delicacies as chocolate and coffee, referred to as Oranda-yuki ("Holland bound"), were routinely dispatched to Dejima, while other women, called Kara-yuki ("China bound"), were sent to wait on the Chinese merchants.[148] Christopher Fryke, surgeon for the English India Company mission that entered Nagasaki Harbor in 1683 in an unsuccessful bid to reopen trade between Japan and England, describes the aggressiveness of pimps at dockside. "When we began to unlade," he wrote, "a parcel of Japaneses came to us to offer us some Women, and asked us, if we would not have some of them while we stayed there. But no body hearkened to their proposal but the Master, and the Book-Keeper."[149]

The supposed sexual antics of the Dutchmen attracted attention far beyond the port; the great Osaka writer Ihara Saikaku, for example, wrote in the 1680s about Dutchmen "who consume aphrodisiacs everyday and night" in order to enhance their performances with women leading "lives without freedom."[150] *Ukiyo-e* woodblock print artists delighted in depicting scenes of Dutchmen disporting themselves with Maruyama prostitutes, some very explicit.[151]

Within twenty years of the isolation edicts and their confinement to Dejima, the VOC employees had established some semblance of family life on the island. On October 16, 1661, Hendrick Indijck, the VOC chief, wrote that members of the company had on that day both "held a wedding-party" and even "a baptismal meal with merriment" in the presence of a Japanese official (*otona*) and interpreters on Dejima.[152] (Indijk, who had arrived in Japan in 1660, brought a son and daughter by a woman of Mon ethnicity with whom he had lived in Siam.)[153] He was even allowed to take his son, who could not have been more than six years old, with him on the annual audience with the shogun in Edo in 1663.

Some figures on annual visitations of Maruyama women to Dejima have been preserved. In 1722, there were 20,738 to the *Tōjin yashiki*, the walled compound housing hundreds of Chinese; and 270 to the approximately dozen Dutchmen on Dejima. In 1737, the figures were, 16,1913 to the Chinese, 620 to the Dutch.[154] Thus in the latter year the average VOC employee was receiving a visit from Maruyama about once every week.[155] By the late eighteenth century, if we can believe the physician and geographer Furukawa Koshōkoen (1726-1797) who visited Nagasaki in the 1780s, the Dutchmen had caught up with the Chinese in patronizing the brothel district: "Every day, seventy prostitutes leave [Maruyama], thirty-five of them for the Chinese establishment, the others to the Dutch." Furukawa reports that, "Most of the prostitutes dislike going to the Dutch, thinking it tarnishes their reputations. But those who really want to will go and entertain for high fees; it is said that the comely ones who go out and service foreigners always make good money, and some volunteer for the job."[156]

Europeans' sexual activity was not confined to Dejima. Starting in the 1690s, the Dutchmen were allowed to visit brothels in downtown Nagasaki twice a year. There is ample evidence for such visits, and even Dutchmen's visits to a brothel in Osaka--midway between Nagasaki and Edo on the annual journey—"year after year" as of 1788.[157] The rules governing interactions between Western men and the Japanese women organized to service them obviously became more relaxed over time following the initial confinement of the Dutch to Dejima.

It was sometimes rumored among the Dutch that half-Dutch babies, or at least the boys, would be killed at birth.[158] But there was no apparent effort to prevent the birth of half-European children or to suppress them from public view. Indeed, a 1715 law specified that foreigners could not take half-Japanese children with them when they departed the country.[159] Prostitutes servicing foreign men were instructed to report any pregnancy or birth to authorities. If a child was born while the foreign man was away, it would be raised in her lodgings but could be handed over to the father upon his return to Japan and application to the authorities. The foreign men could raise the children in their lodgings while in Japan, and had to provide funds for the education and professional placement of such children. But they were the property of Japan and could not leave.[160]

This assertion of sovereignty over the bodies of hapa indicates that the children were, from the point of view Nagasaki officials, fully Japanese. According to a member of the Dutch factory, J. F. Van Overmeer Fischer, in Japan from 1822, half-Dutch "children are placed on a par with all other Japanese and on no account are exceptions made in regard to them."[161] One must wonder whether Fischer had sufficient interaction with these children to determine that they indeed grew up without confronting discrimination. But his observation is consistent with those of Europeans from the time of Carletti in the 1590s.

In the mid-seventeenth century the visits of prostitutes to the Dutch were limited to one-night stays. But by the end of the century three-day stays were common, and by the late 1700s, five days the norm.[162] Even indefinite stays became common. The Swede Carl Thunberg, who had served with the Dutch mission in Japan in 1775-76, wrote that, "One of these female companions cannot be kept for less than three days, but she may be kept as long as one pleases, a year, or even several years together."[163] He added, "[D]uring my stay in the country I saw a girl of about 6 years of age, who very much resembled her father, a European, and remained with him on our small island the whole year through."[164]

Hendrik Doeff (*ooperhoofd* from 1803-17) reported that during his tenure on Dejima the Japanese mothers of Europeans' children were "allowed to nurse their infants in the houses of the fathers" on the isle, adding however that from "a very early age" the children are subjected to restrictions, in their intercourse with their fathers, similar to those imposed upon the intercourse of all natives with foreigners; and the only indulgence granted to the paternal feelings of the Dutch, consists of permission to receive a few specified visits from their offspring at certain intervals (whether this permission extends to their daughters is not stated) and provide for their education and support through life. The fathers are frequently allowed, if not required, to purchase for their sons some office under government, at Nagasaki or elsewhere.[165]

Fischer also noted that, while considered Japanese, the children were allowed contact with their fathers under some circumstances. He wrote, "it is considered a special grace if [half-Dutch] children are allowed to come to the island [Dejima] during their youth to be taken care of thanks to [their fathers'] buying certain favors through intervention and assent to the Japanese government."[166]

Whereas the Dutch had once wondered whether their offspring were systematically eliminated at birth, they were now not only enjoined to pay for their support but allowed regulated contact with them on the island. This could extend over a decade. Thus there were half-European children in Nagasaki who had contact with their fathers and the latter's colleagues, exposure to the Dutch language, and, one must assume, a sense of identity differing from that of most children in the city.

The expanded "hospitality" reflects changing Japanese views of the Dutchmen, their culture and even their physical bodies. Starting in 1720, the year that the shogunate lifted the ban on the importation of western books that had accompanied the anti-foreign edicts of the 1630s, the Dutchman came to be seen as the representative of a world far more scientifically advanced than China. Scholars called *Rangakusha* (scholars of "Dutch Studies") learned how to read Dutch well enough to translate numerous scientific works, including an anatomy text with detailed illustrations sharply differing from the Chinese depictions. A dissection viewed by doctors with the text on hand in 1771 confirmed the accuracy of Western medical science and made it clear that Japanese and European bodies were indeed the same.[167] Dutch Studies soared as daimyo competed to establish Rangaku academies. The VOC delegations to the shogun's court were treated with mounting courtesy, not teased with trivial questions and performance requests from tittering court ladies, but questions about scientific developments and world affairs.[168]

It became less popular to allege that Dutchmen had hooves rather than human feet and penises shaped like those of dogs, urinated with one leg raised, and were inhumanly hairy.[169] Such rumors may have circulated among the least sophisticated members of society, but even the highly creative philosopher and physician Andō Shōeki (1703-62) opined that physical differences precluded the successful production of mixed children: "It may happen," he wrote, "that a Dutch man and a Japanese woman have intercourse and beget a child, but this cannot live long. When it is about ten years old it will surely die." He explained this by suggesting that the *ki* of metal found in the west does not harmonize with the *ki* of wood found in Japan. Nevertheless he was aware that "longevity *may* be possible" for such children. This admission of the possibility of a long-lived exception suggests that he might have known such a child, but this is only speculation. "Hence it is clear," he wrote more optimistically, "that all human beings under Heaven are one."[170]

The physicians employed by the VOC were treated with particular respect by the Japanese, including physicians eager to learn about Western medicine. It is perhaps fitting that they figure prominently among the Dutchmen known to have had long-term relationships with Nagasaki prostitutes in the early eighteenth century as *Rangaku* emerged. Hendrik van Haaster, who worked as a physician for the VOC from 1734 to 1738, had at least one child with a Wakamatsu of the Tanbaya brothel; his successor, Filipp Pieter Musculus (in Japan, 1738-46) also had at least one child with a Michishio from the Nagatoya brothel.[171]

Hendrik Doeff, mentioned above, had a son, Jōkichi, with a Maruyama courtesan named Uryūno from the Miyakoya brothel, and a daughter, Omon, with Sono'o of the Hiketaya brothel. Doeff arranged, upon his departure in 1817, for his son to be appointed as an expert on foreign goods in Nagasaki. Unfortunately, Jōkichi died seven years later at age 17.[172] Isaac Titsingh, *opperhoofd* from 1779 to 1784, had a child with the fifteen-year-old courtesan Ukine. Since she was of *tayū* rank (the highest in the hierarchy of courtesans) we must assume she was not only beautiful but had musical talent and conversational skills as well as sexual abilities. We must also assume that she was expensive to procure, and it is worth remembering, too, that a man obtaining a *tayū* from a brothel could only do so with her consent. While one can question whether the consensual nature of any union between a fifteen year old and a much older man, Timon Screech suggests that Titsingh courted and won her. Titsingh "spoke fluent Japanese and perhaps because of that became the first European to successfully woo a woman of *tayū* rank."[173] Although it is possible that the some top-ranked courtesans were among the Dejima "volunteers" mentioned by Furukawa, it seems likely that Titsingh met the woman in a brothel in Maruyama.

On his departure for Batavia in 1784, Titsingh seems to have entrusted Ukine to the care of his friend Johan Frederik van Reede, who became *opperhoofd* a year later. "Oekinisan [Ukine-san] is sitting right next to me," van Reede wrote to Titsingh in 1786, "on the canapé playing the samisen, which is her usual amusement and occupation while I am working, and to which I have grown so accustomed, that her music doesn't disturb me the least."[174] Titsingh sent occasional gifts to Ukine, such as a ring and calico cloth, and upon his death in Paris in 1812 left his large fortune and collections to "an only child of his, by an Eastern woman, by whom the fortune was soon spent."[175]

The *opperhoofd* Jan Cock Blomhoff—who became famous for bringing his wife to Japan in 1817 in defiance of the long-standing law banning foreign women from entering the country—had earlier sired a son with the Maruyama prostitute Itohagi.[176] The VOC clerk J. F. Van Overmeer Fischer (1820-29) had a son with a mistress named Shō, who died at the age of nine months.[177] The German medical doctor and botanist Philipp Franz von Siebold, hired by the VOC to serve as company physician from 1823, also fathered a child by a Japanese consort, but as Siebold and his family are discussed at length in Ellen Nakamura's chapter in this volume, we will say no more about him.

### The "Opening of Japan"
Commodore Matthew C. Perry famously "opened" Japan through gunboat diplomacy in 1854, when the shogunate agreed to end over two centuries of isolation and open up several ports to U.S. visits, and to negotiate a trade agreement. The latter, signed in Shimoda and in force from 1859, was rapidly followed by treaties with other Western nations and the residence of foreign merchants and sailors in Yokohama, Hakodate, Kobe, Osaka, Niigata, and, of course, Nagasaki. Since the residence of foreign women was initially banned, the foreign men generally co-resided with a Japanese "temporary wife"/maid, often procured through the same agent that arranged the rental of lodgings in the port. This is, of course, the world depicted in the John Luther Long-David Belasco stage play "Madame Butterfly" of 1900, which inspired the 1904 Puccini opera of the same name.[178]

Even before the treaty ports opened to trade, Shimoda officials designated three teahouses in the port as brothels for Western men. After Nagasaki was opened to Russian visits, town officials established a "resthouse" (*kyūsokujo*) specifically for the Russian "matelots."[179] The Gankiro, a brothel for foreigners, opened in Yokohama in 1861. Commissioned by the shogun, and built by a company experienced in brothel construction, this establishment flourished well into the Meiji era, when the phenomenon of treaty port "temporary marriages" disappeared. Foreign men continued to marvel at the fact that the women who sexually serviced them bore no subsequent onus in Japanese society. The English tourist Albert Tracy wrote in 1892 that since "the relation, in Japanese eyes, is a sort of wedlock, [the woman's] reputation is in no way injured, nor her chances diminished of making another marriage. Everywhere in and about the European quarter [of Yokohama] I came upon children of the mixed race, some of them exceedingly good-looking."[180]

Meanwhile a host of Western dignitaries and government employees, such as architect Josiah Conder, British seismologist John Milne, Italian sculptor Vicenzo Ragusa, German medical doctor and personal physician to Emperor Meiji, Erwin von Baelz (in Japan 1876-1905), the Anglo-Irish journalist Frank Brinkley in Japan from 1881, and many others formally married Japanese women in the late nineteenth century. In 1897, the renowned English poet and journalist Sir Edwin Arnold married Kurokawa Tama of Sendai in a Shinto ceremony. She became the first Japanese woman to bear a British noble title (as Lady Arnold).[181]

## Conclusion

One is struck by the repeated Western references to the fact that neither the women who had spent time with Europeans nor their offspring faced discrimination in Japanese society. From Carletti's observation in 1597 that a half-year relationship with a Portuguese did not "in any way interfere in a girl's changes for marriage [to a Japanese];" to Thunberg's statement in the 1770s that after years servicing Dutchmen, a prostitute could make a "very advantageous" marriage; to Dr. Willis's assertion in the 1860s that such women were "not looked upon as having forfeited all claim to respectability," we find Westerners reaffirming this belief. The example of Otaki, remarrying a year after von Siebold's departure to "a very good" Japanese husband who was fond of von Siebold's daughter Oine, supports this view.

The 1715 edict forbidding foreign men to take their children out of the country indicates that the latter were considered Japanese, subject to the law against departure issued eighty years earlier. By law the children's upkeep and education had to be paid for by the foreign father. This suggests official interest in their well-being (and perhaps an appreciation of their value in facilitating foreign trade; recall Doeff's son Jōkichi, whom the former had arranged to install as a trade official in Nagasaki when he left Japan in 1817). Quite likely, half-Europeans were valued for their physiques (somewhat larger than the Japanese norm), and half-European men may have been in demand as attendants of the elite. (High-ranking samurai delighted in surrounding themselves with attractive attendants. A palanquin born by two hapa might have attracted precisely the sort of interest a *daimyo* wanted.)[182]

As noted earlier, Fischer declared in 1822 that half-Dutch "children are placed on a par with all other Japanese and on no account are exceptions made in regard to them." But surely this positive picture is incomplete. The Dutch were, as we have seen, often ridiculed in popular culture, and this must have affected the experiences and identities of persons who looked different from (other) Japanese and who were known to have a Western parent or some Dutch blood. But the status of the Dutchmen, who had always been treated with courtesy, rose with the popularity of *Rangaku* and the realization, at least among a stratum of the population, that the Dutch were a scientifically and technologically advanced people, whose bodies were not in fact monstrous in any way. On the other hand, the rise of xenophobic nationalism in the early nineteenth century produced tracts that reached new heights of anti-foreign rhetoric, denouncing Western countries for violating Japanese waters and demanding the opening of the country. As of the early nineteenth century there was surely a wide range of views in Japan about Westerners and everything associated with them.

But just as many non-Japanese in contemporary Japan and indeed today's hapa in Japan are acutely aware of their otherness— annoyed by the chorus of "*Harro! Harro!*" from the kids on passing school bus, or the stranger on the subway wanting to suddenly practice English—so it is likely that these early hapa experienced unwanted attention evoked by their different appearances.[183] They were perhaps accustomed to strangers calling out the Japanese for Dutch people, *Orandajin!* —whether disparagingly or in imagined good humor—cracking jokes about their bodies and sexuality, harassing them with unwelcome curiosity.

Northwestern Kyushu however was a unique part of Japan. The hapa here were originally concentrated in Hirado, and appeared in nearby Nagasaki from 1641. While they did not necessarily live out their lives in this small area, it is likely that they did. They would thus have comprised a small but visible population in Nagasaki, a town numbering tens of thousands.[184] Among these, as many as one-third of town may have been Chinese or part-Chinese.[185] This was the most (and only) cosmopolitan place in Japan; even ships from Annam and Siam, present-day Vietnam and Thailand, traded in the port well into the eighteenth century.[186] Foreigners, including part-Europeans, would have been a familiar sight here, and the crude myths about Dutchmen and their bodies would have had little credibility.[187] Did the hapa here experience unwanted attention and rejection, struggle with issues of identity, and form social networks for mutual comfort and support? Future research may shed more light on such questions, but little has been done so far and sources are few.

As for the hapa outside Japan in this period, it is equally difficult to reconstruct their way of seeing the world. Though Pieter Hartsinck saw success in his life in Europe, including receiving a fine education in Leiden, becoming famed as a mathematician and engineer, and obtaining a lucrative post in Saxony in preference to the great Leibniz himself, and although he was—despite being described in Leiden University records and in Schooten's appreciative remarks as a "Japanese"—placed "on a par" with all other Europeans, his epitaph, self-penned in 1680, points to a lifelong alienation: *But I could not find my true home*.

## CHAPTER THREE

# THE HOTCHPOTCH CULTURE OF NAGASAKI: MAGNANIMITY OR IMMORALITY?

BRIAN BURKE-GAFFNEY

The modern history of Nagasaki is a record of international exchange, beginning with the "Christian century" and continuing into the Edo period when Chinese and Dutch residents enjoyed exclusive trading privileges in Japan. The Ansei Five-Power Treaty of 1858 nullified the monopoly, but Nagasaki continued to thrive as the site of a foreign settlement and the country's closest link to China. The prosperity of the international port reached a peak around the turn of the 20th century, but it rapidly declined after the Russo-Japanese War (1904-05) when industrial and military priorities eclipsed trade. The foreign population dwindled, and Nagasaki began its long march to the atomic bombing. This chapter presents an overview of the unique "hotchpotch" culture that grew from the centuries of international contact in Nagasaki, the historical processes that informed it, and its relevance today.

### The Portuguese Period

Portuguese missionaries and adventurers first sailed into Nagasaki Harbor in 1567, searching for a stable foothold on the western fringe of the still little-known Japanese archipelago. The fishing village they found there was similar to other hamlets tucked away in the folds of the ragged shoreline of Kyushu, but the Europeans could tell without even leaving their ship that they were bobbing on one of the best natural harbors in the world. Enclosed by hills on three sides, it bottlenecked at the entrance and enjoyed both the protection of a cluster of well-defined islands on the approach and the convenience of a shoreline sheer enough to allow large ships to pull right up to the rocks. The most distinctive feature was a slender promontory—the *nagasaki* ("long cape") of the name—that protruded into the harbor like a finger pointing to the world's oceans and predicting the role that the port would soon play in international affairs.

The Portuguese entered into negotiations with local authorities and received permission to open the port for foreign trade and missionary activity. As a result, the village turned into a boom town, with aspiring merchants and laborers pouring in from other parts of Japan and buildings shooting up like bamboo sprouts on the promontory and waterfront. In 1580, Ōmura Sumitada, ruler of the region including Nagasaki and a Christian convert, took the unprecedented measure of transferring jurisdiction of the port and environs to the Society of Jesus, establishing the only example—aside from the post-World War II Allied Occupation—of foreign rule over Japanese territory.[188]

The Nagasaki community of the period was multinational but not quite multicultural: the Portuguese burned temples and shrines and drove out Buddhist monks and Shinto priests before building their churches. Christianity so predominated that the Chinese, who received official permission to engage in trade around the year 1600, had to establish their place of worship and burial ground on the opposite side of Nagasaki Harbor. But the fact that the Portuguese lived without hindrance among their Japanese neighbors—as opposed to a segregated quarter or concession as in later centuries — accelerated the assimilation of their language, cuisine and customs into local culture. Hundreds of Portuguese words found their way into the Japanese vernacular and became so thoroughly naturalized that modern people seldom recognize them as imports from abroad, like *kappa*, *juban* and *miira* derived from *capa* (cape), *gibaō* (undergarment) and *mirra* (mummy) respectively. Familiar Japanese foods such as *pan* (bread), *tempura* (deep-fried food), *konpeitō* (candy) and *kasutera* (sponge cake) are also rooted in the foods introduced by the Europeans. The influence of the Portuguese indeed penetrated into every corner of life in Nagasaki, creating a cultural trend, referred to as *namban bunka*, that spilled over the borders of the town and went on to affect lifestyles and ways of thinking throughout Japan.

Sexual contact was another aspect of the Portuguese-Japanese interface. The European visitors, invariably male, engaged in liaisons with Japanese women, everything from marriages sanctified in churches to brief encounters in the brothels operated openly in town. Nagasaki historian Jūjirō Koga asserts that many of the traders hired Japanese women to serve as wife-servants during the interim of their stay in port, often for periods of several months, and that the women received generous wages and various other favors from their employers.[189] A 17th-century Spanish commentator named Domingo Fernandez Navarette confirms the fact in a report from China, although he conveys the information with a tone of disapproval that is notably absent in Koga's account: "What the people of Macau did in Japan is well known, and they ingenuously confess it; they own'd it to me in that City, and F. Gouvea told it to me at Canton. It was, that till the ships return'd, they publickly without any shame keep common Women in their houses. A good help toward the Conversion of those people!"[190]

After consolidating its power and establishing a *bakufu* (shogunate) in Edo (Tokyo) in 1603, the Tokugawa regime accepted the stubborn presence of the Catholic priests and their Japanese congregations as an unavoidable condition for continuation of the profitable foreign trade. But in 1614 it imposed a complete and final ban on Christianity and ordered the destruction of all churches, the expulsion of priests, and the registration of every last Japanese citizen as a member of one of the principal Buddhist sects. Anyone refusing to comply faced the horror of torture and death. It was as though the Shinto and Buddhist idols driven from Nagasaki by the Portuguese half a century earlier had come back with a vengeance to take their rightful place in the streets and hearts of the city.

In 1634, the Tokugawa Shogunate ordered a group of Nagasaki merchants to build an artificial island called Dejima (sometimes rendered as Decima or Deshima) in Nagasaki Harbor and to erect buildings for the confinement of Portuguese residents. By isolating the Portuguese from the rest of the Nagasaki populace, the authorities hoped to maintain commercial interaction while keeping the banned religion at bay. But the Shimabara Rebellion of 1637-38, a peasant revolt viewed by nervous officials in Edo as a Christian insurrection, convinced the Tokugawa Shogunate to expel the Portuguese from Japan and to curtail all trade with the Catholic countries. Subsequently, the Shogunate placed Nagasaki under its own direct control and dispatched a magistrate from Edo to supervise local affairs. To revive the foreign trade, the Shogunate granted special permission to the Buddhist Chinese and the Protestant Dutch to continue a modicum of strictly regulated trade in the port of Nagasaki on the condition that they eschew all activities related to Christianity.

### The Dutch and Chinese Period
The departure of the Portuguese in 1639 gave Chinese residents the lion's share of the prosperous foreign trade, which included the

import of sugar, raw silk and porcelain and the export of copper, grain and marine products. Unlike the Dutch, confined from the outset to the island of Dejima, the Chinese were free to seek accommodation in Japanese homes and any other venue available in the town. What resulted was a rapid flowering of Chinese culture facilitated by the hugely profitable trade and mediated by the scores of Chinese traders, Zen priests and men-of-letters coming ashore.

The *peiron* (dragon boat) races, Ming-style temple architecture, rituals like the dragon dance and *shōrōnagashi* (spirit-boat procession at the Buddhist Bon Festival), techniques of Chinese painting and doctrines of Chinese Zen took root in Nagasaki culture, a process aided, as in the Portuguese period, by the absence of physical and political barriers between Japanese and Chinese segments of the population. One of the most salient examples is *shippoku* cuisine, a combination of Japanese and Chinese dishes—with a smattering of Portuguese influences—enjoyed at a round table in the Chinese fashion. *Shippoku* is often cited as a symbol of Nagasaki's cosmopolitan culture because of its eclectic ingredients and diverse cooking methods. As Hisayo Koba points out, however, the round table, which by its very shape eliminated Japan's rigid traditional seating order, better reflects the city's egalitarian relationships based on free trade (see Figure 3.1).[191]

At the peak of the Chinese trade in 1688, an astonishing 194 Chinese junks lowered their sails in Nagasaki Harbor, as opposed to only three Dutch ships the same year.[192] The Chinese trade was so successful, and problems such as smuggling so rampant, that the Tokugawa Shogunate decided to impose restrictions and to confine Chinese merchants and sailors in a walled-off compound similar to Dejima. Completed in 1689, the *tōjinyashiki* (Chinese Quarter) sprawled over an area of about seven acres in the suburban neighborhood of Jūzenji and included stores, offices, Chinese shrines, and rows of two-story barracks (*nagaya*). The residential facilities provided accommodations for some 2,000 Chinese residents (see Figure 3.2), many times the number of Dutchmen living full-time on Dejima.[193]

The penetration of Chinese culture into early seventeenth-century Nagasaki is remarkable in that it came right on the heels of the Portuguese period, when Japanese residents were almost entirely Christian and supposedly reeling in pain from the persecution of their religion. A certain number of Christians indeed defended their faith and chose either death or a life of hiding in secluded villages near Nagasaki.[194] But it is clear that the majority of Japanese residents stayed in the city and changed colors as

Figure 3.1 *Shippoku* combines elements of Japanese, Chinese and European cuisine served at a round table, a style that enhances communication and eliminates differences of status among participants. (Courtesy of Hisayo Koba)

quickly as the flags flying on foreign ships sailing into Nagasaki Harbor. The abrupt turnaround is attributable to various factors, such as the shifting clouds of political power, the new potential for financial gain, and the fact that most residents hailed from elsewhere and had no strong sense of affiliation, as though, to borrow Saul Bellow's analogy about Los Angeles, western Japan had been tilted and everything not tightly screwed down had slid into Nagasaki. But whatever the cause, the infidelity contributed

Figure 3.2 An 18th-century woodblock print depicts a wealthy Chinese merchant relaxing with his Japanese consort in the Nagasaki Chinese Quarter. The Nagasaki *hanga* conveyed images and information about foreign culture. (Brian Burke-Gaffney Collection)

to an air of decadence that would variously beguile and disgust later visitors to the international port.

In 1641, the Tokugawa Shogunate ordered the Dutch East India Company to move its factory (trading post) from Hirado to Dejima, vacated two years earlier by the Portuguese. As a result the Dutch employees began a more than two century-long career as the only Europeans allowed to reside in Japan (see Figure 3.3). The fan-shaped island was circumscribed by walls and connected to the shore of the town by a heavily guarded bridge. The dozen or so employees lived on the island with their Indonesian servants, waiting for the arrival of a few trade ships that reached Japan every year from the company headquarters in Batavia (modern-day Jakarta). Daily life on Dejima was so monotonous and restrictions on the movements of the Dutchmen so severe that assignment to Japan was tantamount to a prison term on the farthest edge of the earth. For these reasons, the Dutch sojourn fell far short of that of the Portuguese in terms of cultural impact, even though it was later in history and more than twice as long. The Nagasaki example underlines the fact that unrestricted and cooperative cohabitation is a prerequisite for cultural amalgamation.

Another measure taken by the Shogunate in the wake of the Christian period was the establishment of licensed brothel quarters in major urban centers. Promulgated in Nagasaki in 1642, the edict resulted in the closure of brothels scattered previously throughout the town and their reopening under government supervision in the Maruyama neighborhood, a tract of land across a canal from the town center. The two or three-story wooden buildings of the *yūkaku* (brothels) were often larger and more opulently furnished than any house in town. The women working there were called *yūjo*, a word meaning "play woman" or perhaps "loose woman" (loose in the sense of unattached) usually translated as "courtesan." In almost all cases they were daughters of destitute parents sold to the brothel as children. They worked under a system called *yūjobōkō* ("courtesan service"), which

Figure 3.3 Michitomi Jōkichi, son of Dutch factor Hendrik Doeff and his Japanese consort, died in Nagasaki in 1824 at the age of 17. The stone vase in front of the gravestone is inscribed with the letters "HD" (his father's initials) in lieu of a traditional Japanese family crest. (Photograph by Brian Burke-Gaffney)

amounted to temporary slavery because the debt incurred by their parents left them no alternative but to bow to the wishes of the brothel owner.

Engelbert Kaempfer (1651-1716), who served as physician at the Dutch East India Company factory on Dejima from 1690 to 1692, was the first European scientist to publish impressions of Japan. In his monumental work *The History of Japan*, he provides a detailed description of the Nagasaki brothel quarter:

> My next step shall be, according to the custom of the country, from the Temples over to the Bawdy Houses, the concourse of people being as great at the latter, as it is at the former. That part of the Town, where they stand, is call'd kesiematz, that is, the Bawdy House quarters. It lies to the South, on a rising hill, call'd Maria [Maruyama]. It consists, according to the Japanese, of two streets, which an European would be apt to mistake for more, and which contain the handsomest private buildings of the whole Town, all inhabited by Bawds. ... The place accordingly is extraordinarily well furnish'd, and after that of Miaco [Kyoto] the most famous of the whole Empire, the Trade being much more profitable here than it is any where else, not only because of the great number of foreigners, Nagasaki being the only place they have leave to come to, but also on account of the inhabitants themselves, who are said to be the greatest debauchers and lewdest people in the Empire.[195]

Kaempfer reports that, once they had completed their duties, the courtesans could go on to become wives and mothers in mainstream society and that they suffered little denigration or discrimination from their fellow citizens. It should be noted, nevertheless, that the justification of prostitution and the many assertions that the courtesans suffered no discrimination come from male writers, both Japanese and foreign. If the courtesans themselves had been asked how they felt about their lost childhood and youth, a different story might have emerged. In any case, it is clear that the Dutch East India Company employees assigned to Dejima encountered a set of moral values altogether different from the one they had left behind in Europe.

In 1645, the Shogunate granted permission for the brothel

owners of Maruyama to send courtesans to the Dutch East India Company factory on Dejima. The home-delivery system was unique to Nagasaki—in Edo (Tokyo), Kyoto and Osaka the courtesans were invariably forbidden to leave the boundaries of the brothel quarters— and it issued from an eagerness on the part of the Shogunate to encourage the Dutch and Chinese to spend money by the boat-loads without leaving their quarters or mingling unnecessarily with the native population.

Charles Peter Thunberg, who served as resident physician on Dejima from 1775 to 1776, later wrote about the Nagasaki courtesans and their visits to the Dutch East India Company factory:

> If any one desires a companion in his retirement, he makes it known to a certain man, who goes to the island every day for this purpose. This fellow before the evening procures a girl, that is attended by a little maid-servant, generally known under the denomination of *Kabro*, who fetches daily from the town all her mistress's victuals and drink, dresses her victuals, makes tea, &c. keeps everything clean and in order, and runs on errands. One of these female companions cannot be kept less than three days, but she may be kept as long as one pleases, a year, or even several years together.[196]

Thunberg also mentions the offspring of the international relationships on Dejima:

> It very seldom happens that one of these ladies proves pregnant by any of the Europeans; but if such a thing happens, it was supposed that the child, especially if it were a boy, would be murdered. Others again assured me, that such children were narrowly watched until the age of fifteen, and then were sent with the ships to Batavia; but I cannot believe the Japanese inhuman enough for the former procedure, nor is there any instance of the latter taking place. During my stay in this country, I saw a girl of about six years of age, who very much resembled her father, an European, and remained with him on our small island the whole year through.[197]

Thunberg's observation is interesting because it indicates that some of the Dutch East India Company employees stayed willingly beyond their usual term of one or two years and that the relationships with courtesans had all the characteristics of marriage, aside from permanence. The Dutchmen's attachment is hardly surprising, though, because the courtesans, their maids and the children mentioned by Thunberg were the only Japanese citizens other than a few officials, merchants and interpreters allowed regular contact with foreigners. The all-male cast of official characters participated with the Dutch in business negotiations and occasional social affairs, but, however invisible they may be in history books, it was the courtesans who became their intimate companions and probably helped the interpreters when they faltered on some obscure expression in the Dutch language.

As mentioned earlier, the Chinese merchants of Nagasaki made a far greater contribution to the city's economy than their Dutch counterparts and exerted a much more significant impact on local culture. The lack of attention to Chinese contributions is attributable in part to the modern Japanese habit of raising antennas higher to Europeans than to fellow Asian countries. But another reason is that, while the Dejima physicians and factors published one account after another of their adventures in mysterious Japan, few of their Chinese counterparts seem to have considered the task worth the effort. One notable exception is the artist and man-of-letters Wang Peng, who visited Nagasaki in 1764 and penned a description of the town's sights, sounds and flavors, including a colorful portrait of the Maruyama courtesans.[198] Reports Wang: "There are many intelligent women among the courtesans. They speak vivaciously and are skilled in conversation. They are good at making themselves up, and their dazzling apparel matches their beautiful faces...They serve their patrons elegantly and attend to every little need. From meals to financial accounts, their consideration is such that they seem to be cherishing a lifelong companion. When they are with the Chinese, they act no differently than they would with a beloved husband." Wang goes on to chirp that few of his compatriots could "transcend the sea of love and desire" and that because of this they spent money like "fountains." Finally he turns to poetry for a last word on the young women who arrived at the Chinese Quarter from Maruyama:

Row upon row of hair-ties amid the mist-like rain,
Sweeping back their raven tresses, the girls answer the
call to enter.

Their Szechwan silk is beyond reproach, yet its flower
brocade is crude;
On departing, the gold coins they clutch embroider
their silken waistcoats.[199]

Figure 3.4 The Nagasaki Foreign Settlement circa 1865, with the house of Thomas B.
Glover visible in the upper left corner. The buildings of the settlement amalgamated
Japanese construction methods and materials with colonial European architectural styles.
(Glover Garden)

As Wang points out, many of the residents of the Chinese
Quarter, like the Dutchmen on Dejima, engaged in genuine, loving
affiliations with Japanese women. They also fathered children
and established households. But however closely the relationship
between a foreigner and his consort approximated marriage, the
day was bound to come when the man boarded a ship and sailed
away, never to return.

One of the mixed-blood children left behind by their fathers
after a period of bliss in Nagasaki was Michitomi Jōkichi, the
product of a liaison between the Dutch East India Company factor
Hendrik Doeff and a courtesan named Uriuno (see Figure 3.4).[200]

Figure 3.5  American sailors cavort with Japanese women in a Nagasaki photograph
studio circa 1895. (Brian Burke-Gaffney Collection)

Although the factor's term of office was usually one or two years, Doeff served for 14 years from 1803 to 1817 because of the suspension of trade during the Napoleonic Wars in Europe and the annexation of Holland by France. During his tenure, Dejima was the only place on earth still flying the Dutch flag, and he endeared himself to his Japanese hosts by fending off the advances of British ships and by assisting in the compilation of dictionaries. A Dutch ship eventually appeared in Nagasaki Harbor carrying the next factor and the news that Holland had regained its independence. Doeff was compelled to pack up his belongings and bid farewell to Japan. History books proclaim that upon departure he received an award of 50 silver pieces from the Tokugawa Shogunate, but the only information about his undoubtedly tearful separation from Uriuno and the then 11 year-old Jōkichi is a footnote saying that he left a large sum of money for the boy's upbringing and asked the Nagasaki officials to provide for his later employment.

Despite the fatherly gestures and the efforts of Doeff's Nagasaki friends to fulfill his wishes, Michitomi Jōkichi died six years later at the age of 17. His gravestone stands today on the hillside above the Nagasaki temple district, a typical Buddhist obelisk stained dark by nearly two centuries of exposure and forgotten among weeds and drooping tree branches. A small stone incense burner and two stone vases stand in front of the gravestone. One of the vases is embellished with a bas relief showing the initials "HD" (for "Hendrik Doeff") enclosed in a circle, a unique substitute for a traditional family crest. The other vase is inscribed with the *agehachō* ("butterfly with raised wings") crest used commonly by courtesans, geisha and other Japanese women who did not engage in conventional marriages.


**The Foreign Settlement Period**
During Japan's more than two-century long period of national isolation (1641-1859), world news trickled into Japan via the Dutch and Chinese in Nagasaki (and the Koreans who engaged in trade with the residents of Tsushima in present-day Nagasaki Prefecture), but by the 1830s the reports of international upheaval were beginning to issue from sources alarmingly close. In 1842, British forces vanquished the Chinese in the first Opium War and the Qing government signed the Treaty of Nanjing, a set of unilateral demands including the payment of a crushing indemnity, cession of the island of Hong Kong, and the opening five coastal towns including Shanghai, only a day and a night by ship from Nagasaki.

In 1858, the Shogunate signed full-fledged commercial treaties with the United States, Russia, Britain, France and the Netherlands and opened—effective July 1, 1859—the three ports of Nagasaki, Yokohama, and Hakodate, thereby bringing an irrevocable end to its long disengagement from the global network of economic and political relationships. No warfare or outright force was involved in the forging of the treaties, but Japan's huge military and economic disadvantage left it little choice but to agree to the tariffs fixed by the foreign countries, to grant extraterritorial rights to foreign residents, and to allow the construction of foreign settlements or "concessions" in each treaty port (see Figure 3.5). Yokohama was close to the seat of the Shogunate in Edo and would soon grow into the largest of the foreign settlements, but in 1859 Nagasaki was still the most important port, not only because it was the closest to Shanghai, but also because it was still the only place in Japan with an infrastructure geared to trade and a population accustomed to dealing with foreigners. Merchant adventurers and missionaries of various nationalities arrived and began the work of building a community on the blueprints of the foreign concessions in China.

One of the earliest foreign visitors to record his impressions of Nagasaki during this new period was Henry Arthur Tilley, a Briton serving as a language instructor on the Russian corvette *Rynda* which anchored here in June 1859, shortly before the official opening of the ports for trade on July 1. Tilley devotes an entire chapter of his travel journal to Nagasaki, including descriptions of the Japanese officials who came aboard the ship after its arrival, of the Russian navy officers and crew billeted at Goshinji Temple, and of the people and customs of a sleepy port on the verge of momentous change. Like Kaempfer, Thunberg, and his other predecessors, Tilley took special interest in the Maruyama brothels:

> The tea-houses are situated in the upper part of the town, and confined to one or two streets. Some few are placed in gardens, laid out in Japanese style, with rocks, pools of water, mountains in miniature, dwarf cedars, and large shrubs of Camelia [sic] Japonica. The entrance to them is generally through a large gateway, inside which the first thing seen is the kitchen; on either side of this are raised platforms covered with mats, which form the saloons by day, and the chambers by night of the different inmates. At night the whole space is partitioned off by small folding screens, five or six feet high; or, as often may be seen, the different couples lie stretched on their mattresses promiscuously

over the floor, half concealed only by a coarse green mosquito curtain. The second story is generally reserved for the better sort of visitors, and lately, since the buildings have been open to Europeans, for their use.[201]

Figure 3.6  Front page of the Russian newspaper Volya published in Nagasaki from April 1906 to March 1907. (Brian Burke-Gaffney Collection)

The huge increase in the number of foreign ships visiting Nagasaki precipitated a burst of economic prosperity, but there were some Japanese who lost patience with the foreign incursion, particularly samurai from the domains of southwestern Japan who were bitterly opposed to the opening of Japan's doors and who, on several occasions during the 1860s, attacked foreigners when they passed along poorly lit side streets or lay drunk on the street in the brothel quarter. The outside forces were rankled by the cosmopolitan activity of the city and the contamination they thought it implied, but few Nagasaki citizens ever resorted to violence because for them, as always, the intermingling with foreigners was the lifeblood of the city.

Except for a few hours of shore leave, the sailors visiting Nagasaki stayed on board ship and followed a strict schedule of duties and drills. By contrast, the officers on the same warships made arrangements to rent houses and enjoy prolonged encounters with Japanese women during their stay in Nagasaki, like the Dutch and Chinese residents of the Edo period (see Figure 3.6). In his 1859 report, Henry Arthur Tilley mentions that some of the Russian officers had "formed liaisons with some pretty Japanese women, and had their own menage in the town."[202] The women who associated with foreigners under the new system came to be called *rashamen*, a term derived from the Portuguese *raxa*, an archaic term meaning "woolen cloth."

In his magnum opus on the history of the Maruyama brothel quarter, Koga Jūjirō claims that many young women were not only willing to engage in freelance affiliations with foreigners but in fact welcomed them as Cinderella opportunities:

> The ones among them who were beautiful enough became the mistresses of Russian officers. They threw off the traditional garments of a courtesan, tied their hair up in the fashion of Caucasian women and whitened their faces with European makeup. Reeking of European perfume, they adopted Western-style dress, wore rings of gold and jewels on their fingers, kept handkerchiefs in their sleeves and held fancy parasols over their shoulders. And when they appeared on the streets of Nagasaki with all these alluring accouterments, they incited the envy of the daughter of every poor family in the city.[203]

Koga nevertheless points out that the prostitutes were regularly heckled and hit by stones thrown from the street-side, indicating that the jealousy had an undercoat of contempt. But, as always, economic benefits overruled the indignation. A cottage industry sprang up around the sex trade monopolized previously by the brothel owners in the licensed Maruyama quarter. Now any parent willing to peddle a teenage daughter's sexual charm could profit from the business, and the custom of engaging a prostitute as a living companion was practiced so openly that it came to be known among foreigners as "Japanese marriage."[204]

Missionaries and other observers, including British and American naval authorities horrified by the debilitating effects of venereal disease, continued to label the city a den of debauchery and to demand improvements to facilities for sailors visiting the port. However, Nagasaki persisted in its tolerant if dissolute ways and won fame for the very immorality condemned by sticklers, especially after publication of the bestselling travelogue *Madame Chrysanthème* by French writer and naval officer Pierre Loti.[205] The young woman of the title emerged from the faceless ranks of *rashamen*, and her backstreet world came under the spotlight of literature, transformed from the murky unknown of an Oriental port into a realm of poetic beauty paraded in the arts of Europe. Soon the world would know her, whitewashed and fictionalized, as "Madame Butterfly."[206]

In 1894, Japan finally succeeded in negotiating the abolition of the Ansei Five-Power Treaties and replacing them with trade pacts similar to those concluded among European countries. The new agreements came into effect in July 1899, abolishing the

Figure 3.7 Thomas B. Glover (center) poses with his son Tomisaburō Kuraba and daughter-in-law Waka in the Japanese garden below the Glover house circa 1908. (Glover Garden)

foreign settlements as legal entities and abrogating the privilege of extraterritoriality enjoyed by foreigners. The Nagasaki Foreign Settlement ceased to exist as an official entity, but the great prosperity of the port around the turn of the century, caused in part by the military and economic activity related to the Sino-Japanese War, the Spanish-American War, and the Boxer Rebellion, assured its continuation as an unofficial institution retaining its multinational community. The foreign population of Nagasaki peaked the following year, a total of 1,918 people of 19 different nationalities calling the port home, including 1,258 Chinese, 141 Russian, 126 American and 110 British residents.[207]

Everything was fine in Nagasaki until war erupted between Japan and Russia in early 1904 (see Figure 3.7). The Russian consul P.A. Gagarine paid a courtesy call on the governor of Nagasaki Prefecture to express regret and to announce his departure. On February 15, he closed the Russian Consulate and Russian Hospital on the Minamiyamate hillside and, with more than 90 other Russian residents in tow, boarded boats at the Ōura waterfront and disappeared onto a merchant steamer for the voyage to Shanghai. Governor Arakawa and Mayor Yokoyama came out to the waterfront to see the Russians off, bidding farewell not only to a section of the Nagasaki mosaic but also to a peaceful chapter in the city history.[208]

The economy of Nagasaki fell into a sharp slump as a result of the suspension of commercial shipping between Japan and the continent, but after the war the city ironically experienced an increase in the number of Russian visitors, among them revolutionaries and refugees from the Vladivostok mutiny who chose the port, not as a tourist or business destination, but as a base to distribute populist propaganda and to stir up anti-tsarist feelings among their compatriots. The freedom of expression they enjoyed in Nagasaki was obviously a feature of the local community, especially the former foreign settlement.

Among the new arrivals was a charismatic physician, linguist and political activist named Nicolas Russel (original name Nicholai Sudzilovski) who had practiced medicine in various parts of Europe, worked as a government physician in Hawai'i, established a successful coffee plantation, and even served as president of the first territorial legislature after the annexation of Hawai'i by the United States in 1898.[209] In April 1906, Russel and his colleagues gathered donations from sympathizers and launched a newspaper called *Volya* ("Will"). Japan's first Russian-language newspaper, it was produced by Tōyūsha, a Japanese printer with experience in publishing Russian pamphlets and advertisements.[210] The liberal atmosphere of Nagasaki, the frequency of visits by Russian ships, and the surge in the number of Russian visitors in 1906 provided ideal conditions for the newspaper. The experiment, however, proved short: *Volya* ceased publication in March 1907 and most of the members of the "Nagasaki commune" returned to Russia. Nicolas Russel died in the arms of his Japanese wife in Tientsin, China in 1930, aged 79.

Another prominent but temporary foreign resident of Nagasaki was British entrepreneur Robert N. Walker, a former steamship captain who contributed to the early development of the Mitsubishi Company and Nippon Yūsen Kaisha (NYK) but retired after the ship under his command foundered and sank off the coast of Tsushima in 1894.[211] Walker returned to his hometown of Maryport, England with his Japanese wife Sato and nine children, but Sato died of a sudden illness at the age of 36, and the former master mariner pulled up roots again, moving back to Nagasaki and founding the ship Chandling firm R.N. Walker & Co.

Walker's children attended mission schools and joined in the various social events of the foreign settlement. In an article on a concert held in 1906, the editor of the local English-language newspaper mentions that Kitty, Walker's third daughter, participated as a violinist and chorus member and tells readers that: "The chorus was composed of young Japanese ladies, the one exception being Miss K. Walker who rendered the solo parts very pleasingly."[212] The editor seems to be saying that Kitty was the single foreigner in the chorus, but he was not quite correct in that depiction. The fact was that she was neither officially British, because Robert N. Walker had not registered the births of Kitty or her siblings, nor Japanese, because her mother had relinquished Japanese citizenship by marrying a foreigner. Although it may be attributable simply to the former master mariner's reluctance to acknowledge his children's autonomy, Walker's procrastination in clarifying their nationality is suggestive of the neither-here-nor-there culture of the foreign settlement and of the position of long-term residents, particularly those who had been born there, who felt little allegiance to any country. All of the children except one eventually gained British or American citizenship and left Japan. Only Robert Walker Jr., Robert N. Walker's second son and heir apparent to the family company, remained in the limbo of no nationality or, better stated, the comfortable gray-zone of the Nagasaki Foreign Settlement.

### Mixed-race Offspring: The Case of Kuraba Tomisaburō

The children emerging from the meeting of races in the foreign settlement period constituted a unique minority in Nagasaki and other treaty ports. Some assumed the nationality of the foreign parent (usually father) and eventually left Japan; others, often ignored or abandoned by their fathers, took the name of maternal relatives and blended into Japanese society. A small few, like Robert Walker Jr., tried to stay on the fence but found it hard to keep their balance as gusts of nationalism and xenophobia buffeted Japan before and during World War II. The following is a biography of Kuraba Tomisaburō (see Figure 3.8), the son of Scottish entrepreneur Thomas B. Glover and a Japanese mother and a member of the tiny third category whose story illustrates the disintegration of Nagasaki's multinational community in the shadow of war and the predicament faced by residents of mixed race.

Thomas B. Glover (1838-1911) arrived in Nagasaki soon after the opening of Japan's doors in 1859 and went on to make important contributions to the modernization of the country in the fields of trade and industry. On December 8, 1870, he fathered the boy who would grow to be Kuraba Tomisaburō (1870-1945). Household registers preserved at Nagasaki City Hall identify the mother as Kaga Maki, a native of Nagasaki who engaged in a temporary relationship with the Scottish merchant.

Glover took the boy under his wing in 1876, around the time that he left Nagasaki for Tokyo and settled into a permanent — albeit common-law—relationship with Awajiya Tsuru, a former geisha who gave birth to his daughter Hana the same year. Tomisaburō attended Chinzei Gakuin, a Methodist mission school in Nagasaki, and Gakushuin (Peers School) in Tokyo. In 1888 he enrolled at Ohio Wesleyan University, probably through Methodist connections in Nagasaki. Two years later he transferred to the University of Pennsylvania where his friend and mentor, Iwasaki Hisaya (later third generation president of Mitsubishi Company) had also been studying.

The First Sino-Japanese War erupted in August 1894, catapulting Nagasaki into a period of prosperity as the closest port to China. Tomisaburō returned to Nagasaki the same year and joined the staff of Holme, Ringer & Co., a business enterprise established by British merchant Frederick Ringer (1838-1907). The Nagasaki native acquired Japanese citizenship soon after settling in his hometown, identifying himself as "Kuraba Tomisaburō" in a *koseki* (official household register) submitted to Nagasaki City Hall. "Kuraba" is a combination of two ideographs meaning "warehouse place" and is feasible as a Japanese family name, but its rarity and phonetic resemblance to "Glover" leave little doubt that it was fabricated to simulate the English name.

In June 1899, Tomisaburō married Nakano Waka, a British-Japanese native of Yokohama. Waka's facial features revealed her Caucasian roots, but she invariably wore kimono and kept her hair up in the Japanese fashion. The two became an inseparable couple, sharing interests and social connections and finding a comfortable niche in the port of Nagasaki with its multinational community and deep residues of international contact.

Tomisaburō's ability to surpass linguistic and cultural barriers endeared him to both foreign and Japanese friends. In Japanese circles he went by his legal name Kuraba Tomisaburō; in the foreign settlement he participated in business and social affairs as T.A. Glover. His foreign and Japanese friends called him Tommy and Tomi-san respectively, unfazed by the dual identity.

One of Tomisaburō's most notable achievements was stewardship of the Steamship Fisheries Co., a subsidiary of Holme, Ringer & Co. that introduced Japan's first steam trawlers and modernized the Japanese fishing industry in the early 20th century. He also made efforts to promote his hometown as a business center and tourist destination. He was a key figure in the establishment of the Nagasaki International Club in 1899 and the advancement of Unzen as a tourist resort and national park.

However, Nagasaki did not regain its former prosperity or international color after the lull in business caused by the Russo-Japanese War. The foreign population rapidly decreased, and shipbuilding and other Mitsubishi industries rushed to the forefront of the local economy. Military authorities stationed a battalion of the Sasebo Fortress Artillery Regiment in the Takenokubo neighborhood of the city under the name *Nagasaki yōsai shireibu* (Nagasaki Fortress Headquarters), irrevocably transforming Japan's former "window to the world" into a strategic gun port.

In the summer of 1928, Robert Walker Jr. adopted Japanese citizenship and changed his legal name from Robert Walker to "Uokā Robāto," the surname and given name reversed in the Japanese fashion and rendered in the *katakana* syllabary. He followed in the footsteps of Kuraba Tomisaburō and other children of mixed marriages who chose Japan as their permanent home, but he opted for the phonetic katakana script used to render foreign names and words. The use of katakana instead of ideographs in an official family register was, and remains, an extremely unusual case. Despite the change in legal status, Robert obviously continued to think of himself as a citizen, not of Japan, but of the foreign settlement.

After the outbreak of war with China in 1932, the Japanese government began to impose restrictions on the lifestyle of ordinary citizens. Military authorities attempted to remove all traces of Nagasaki's deep connections with the enemy, canceling the annual *peiron* (dragon boat) races and banning the use of firecrackers during the Buddhist Lantern Festival in August 1937. A civilian defense corps was established in Nagasaki City Hall to prepare for possible air raids and to organize blackout simulations and anti-air raid drills, and the Japanese government promulgated the "national spiritual mobilization movement" to enhance unity among the Japanese people and to galvanize wartime attitudes. Foreigners meanwhile found it increasingly difficult to engage in normal business and social activities.

In 1938, unbeknownst to the people of Nagasaki, the Imperial Japanese Navy ordered the Mitsubishi Nagasaki Shipyard to build the 70,000-ton battleship *Musashi*, sister ship of the *Yamato* slated for construction at the naval shipyard in Kure, Hiroshima Prefecture. Mitsubishi employees swore an oath of secrecy, the military police rolled out a tight blanket of security in the harbor and surrounding neighborhoods, and the foreign community shrank to a few missionaries, elderly men with Japanese wives, and employees of companies like Holme, Ringer & Co. and Great Northern Telegraph (Denmark) who ignored the many promptings to leave Japan.

Tomisaburō agreed to sell the Glover house at No.3 Minamiyamate to the Mitsubishi Nagasaki Shipyard in a contract dated April 11, 1939, apparently bowing to the wishes of the military and trying to fall in line with his Japanese friends.[213] The transaction abruptly severed the family link to the fabled house and signaled the demise of international cooperation in Nagasaki.

While the *Musashi* took shape behind curtains at the shipyard, Kuraba Tomisaburō and Waka moved to a house low enough on the hillside to preclude suspicion of espionage. Robert Walker Jr. remained with his wife Mabel and three children in their house at No.28 Minamiyamate, which luckily did not enjoy a view over the shipyard.[214] As Japanese citizens, the Kuraba and Walker families were free from the threat of arrest, but their foreign links made them the target of relentless surveillance by military police and civilian authorities. Waka died in 1943 at the age of 68, leaving Tomisaburō alone in the Minamiyamate house and mostly severed from Nagasaki society.

On August 9, 1945, an atomic bomb exploded over the northern part of Nagasaki, killing or injuring more than two-thirds of the city population, and Emperor Hirohito declared Japan's surrender the following week. The end of the war should have brought a sigh of relief to Kuraba Tomisaburō, but the Nagasaki native hung himself to death a few days later. No suicide note was found and so only conjecture is possible, but Tomisaburō may have chosen death, not just because of the desperate situation in Nagasaki and his terrible solitude, but also because he feared that his adoption of Japanese citizenship would be construed as an act of treason by the British and American forces about to land. He was a man of two cultures, and the prospect of having to reject one in favor of the other was simply too hard to bear.

## Conclusion

Since 1567 when the first Portuguese ship sailed into its lake-like harbor, Nagasaki served as a venue for international trade, religious activity and cultural exchange. The local population swelled with newcomers from various parts of Japan hoping to participate in the lucrative trade and to obtain the latest information from abroad. As outsiders they were naturally accommodating and tolerant toward outsiders from overseas, and they adapted to changing times and different political situations with an alacrity that bordered on unprincipled opportunism. In each period of Nagasaki's colorful history, common commercial interests glued the disparate Japanese and foreign groups together, built ladders over barriers of race and language, and contributed to the development of an eclectic regional culture unknown in other parts of Japan.

The historical facts suggest that a strong sense of religious or national affiliation leads to confrontation, while the lack thereof, as in Nagasaki, tends to promote peaceful multiethnic coexistence, however prone it may be to condemnation as spineless and immoral.

Belligerent external forces repeatedly spoiled the party in Nagasaki, demonstrating once again the intimate correlation between peace and multinational coexistence. First it was the Christian persecutions that rocked the city in the early 17th century, then the troubles at the end of the Edo Period when *rōnin* angered by the opening of Japan's doors slipped into the city and roamed the streets looking for foreign scapegoats, and the Russo-Japanese War of 1904-05 that disrupted shipping and irrevocably altered Nagasaki's economic and social underpinnings. As the shadow of war crept across Japan in the 1930s, civilian authorities bent to national policy and suppressed the cosmopolitan atmosphere of Nagasaki. Caught in the conflict and xenophobia, foreigners found it difficult to maintain business and social connections, and people of mixed race like Kuraba Tomisaburō and Robert Walker Jr. had to cope with discrimination and groundless accusations of duplicity.

Another person of mixed race trapped in the vice of war was the writer Ōizumi Kokuseki. The illegitimate son of a Japanese mother and Russian father born in Nagasaki in 1893, Ōizumi had won commercial success and national acclaim for *Boku no Jijoden*, *Ningen Kaigyō* and other semi-autobiographical novels conveying his eccentric worldviews and experiences as a so-called *kokusaiteki no isōrō* (international freeloader).[215] He steadfastly refused to toe the line of militarism in the 1930s and as a result found himself ostracized by his contemporaries and reduced to writing articles on remote hot-spring resorts. However, the following haiku poem, penned during the war, shows that Ōizumi Kokuseki managed to maintain his optimism and Nagasaki *esprit* despite the tribulations:

*Kirawarete*     Disliked by plucking fingers
*Hananinarikeri*  The wild parsley
*Noserikana*     Flourishes and blooms[216]

# WORKING THE SIEBOLD NETWORK: KUSUMOTO INE (1827-1903) AND WESTERN LEARNING IN NINETEENTH-CENTURY JAPAN[217]

ELLEN NAKAMURA

Kusumoto Ine (1827-1903) was the daughter of Philipp Franz von Siebold, a physician of German origin who visited Japan in the early nineteenth century, and Kusumoto Taki, his Japanese concubine.[218] She became one of the first women in Japan to practise Western-style medicine in the Edo period by learning alongside men, attending dissections, studying the Dutch language, and maintaining a practice both in general medicine and in obstetrics. Ine was not merely valued for her experience, as traditional midwives were, but for her training as a doctor and an obstetrician in the Western-style. It was a path that eventually led her —a woman of humble birth—to great heights: she attended the birth of the Meiji Emperor's child in 1873.

Ine's life history is usually studied either as a simple biography or placed within a trajectory of modernisation that connects her to the female doctors who followed her in the Meiji period.[219] She was certainly seen as a pioneer by later women. For example, Ogino Ginko (1851-1913), Japan's first licensed female doctor of Western medicine, pointed to the importance of Ine as a medical predecessor in her essay, *The Past and Future of Women Doctors in Japan*, which she published in 1893 to argue for the need for women doctors.[220]

To place Ine's history narrowly within the story of the rise of female medical practitioners, however, is problematic. Firstly, Ine lived her life surrounded almost entirely by men, and not enough attention has yet been paid to her scholarly relationships with them, particularly in terms of what she learned and what she did with her knowledge.

Secondly, Ine's career is particularly emblematic of the wide "gap" between the study of Western medicine in the Edo period and in the Meiji period. Unlike the women who trained in the Meiji period, Ine never obtained a medical licence, and technically speaking, was registered only as a midwife. Although it is useful to compare her to the women of the Meiji period who trained under the new system and went on to become female doctors or "new midwives", the comparison necessarily highlights this generational difference. Even in later in life, Ine appears to have had little contact with the younger generation of women doctors. It is important to note that many of the male scholars of Western learning (*rangakusha*) with whom Ine shared her personal and working life did not obtain modern medical licences either.

The following study, therefore, will explore Ine's life through her interactions with *rangakusha* and doctors of Western style medicine, in particular, those associated with her father Siebold. It introduces new sources which shed light on her life, her medical career, and the networks of men who supported her amongst the political turmoil of the *bakumatsu* period (1853-1868), and on into the Meiji period when the medical world was turned upside down.

## Sources

Ine's life story is relatively well-known, and has frequently been romanticized. Previous studies in Japanese may be divided into two broad genres: firstly, fictional or semi-fictional works which romanticize her life and play upon her otherness, for example, Akira Yoshimura's epic novel *Von Shiiboruto no musume*, (1978); and more serious (albeit brief) historical studies, for example, the account in *Nihon Joishi*, published by the Japanese Society of Women Doctors (*Nihon Joikai*) in 1962, or articles published by the Siebold Memorial Musuem.[221] In English, Plutschow has recently published the most comprehensive account of Ine's life to date, based primarily on secondary sources in Japanese.[222]

Due to the limitations of materials authored by Ine herself, many previous studies are based on an oral testimony by her daughter Takako (Tada) Yamawaki, made during interviews with the Nagasaki historian Jūichirō Koga in 1924 when she was seventy-three years of age.[223] Takako's testimony is vivid and is partly the source of the romanticized view of Ine's life that is so prominent in writings about her. Her subjective interpretation of her mother's life is an invaluable source, and it provides significant personal information that is not ascertainable by other means. It does not, however, tell an objective "Truth" about Ine, but is one of the many "truths of experience, history, and perceptions embodied in personal narratives."[224]

The present study is based on letters and other primary materials, and Takako's narrative is used to supplement these. Ine's own writings are limited, but they include a handful of letters, and significantly, a résumé that she submitted to the authorities to gain her midwifery licence in November 1884.[225] Thanks to the work of local historians in Uwajima, several significant new sources of information have come to light in recent years.[226] These are introduced here, along with the scattered writings of the men who knew and admired Ine's father Siebold. They reveal unexpected details of her medical activities, as well as highlighting their own collaboration with her. (see Figure 4.1)

### Ine's Résumé of 1884

In Nagasaki in November 1884, at the age of fifty-seven, Ine wrote a letter to the Nagasaki ward chief, appending her résumé and a supporting letter from a local doctor in order to apply for a midwifery licence (*sanba menkyo*). This important document provides the broad outline of her career and training that is known to historians today.[227] On the one hand, the résumé symbolises Ine's achievements and her incorporation into the modern medical system of the Meiji era. On the other, however, it is a revocation of the freedom to practise medicine that she had enjoyed in the Edo period. Although she had been specialising in obstetrics for much of her career, she chose to register as a midwife, rather than as a doctor. Perhaps it is not insignificant that two months previously, in September 1884, Ogino Ginko had become the first woman to sit and pass the first part of the examinations in Western medicine. They were difficult examinations grounded in modern Western science that presumably Ine had little chance of passing without further study.[228]

The first regulations for medical practice (called the *isei*) were introduced in 1874. They were progressive laws designed to set up sanitary institutions, to regulate medical education, to establish a licensing system for doctors, and to control pharmacists and the sale of medicines.[229] It was recognised, however, that it would take some time for the laws to be properly implemented, and a gentle approach was taken at first. Midwifery, too, became the subject of increasing control, and from the 1870s and 1880s, several regions produced their own midwifery regulations. By the late 1880s, almost all regions had introduced them.[230] Substantial national laws were not made until 1899, with the promulgation of the Midwives' Ordinance. This required midwives to sit examinations, obtain licenses, and register with central authorities. According to these laws, midwives were prohibited from using obstetric instruments, from performing surgery, and from prescribing medicines. They were also obliged to call a doctor whenever they sensed that something was wrong with a birth.[231] In 1884, however, Ine applied only for a license under the old system, that is, as a previously practicing "old midwife". She was required only to submit a résumé, with a letter of support.[232]

Figure 4.1 Kusumoto Ine (Ozu City Museum)

Although Ine had a wealth of medical experience, and she had studied with some of the most highly respected foreign doctors in Japan, in the new world of modern medical discourse she qualified neither as a "new midwife" nor as an obstetric-gynaecologist trained under the new system.[233] Jirō Numata has argued that the study of Western knowledge in the Edo period was haphazard, and that there was a large gap between what was learned in the Edo period, and the new knowledge that was brought in after 1868.[234] Ine's career is a prime example both of this haphazardness and generational gap. Most established doctors did not make the transition to modern medicine themselves, but rather, were replaced by a new, younger generation. The gradual way in which the medical regulations were implemented assisted this process by allowing doctors to continue to practice in the old style until they were replaced. These men, who were doctors of Chinese medicine as well as improperly trained doctors of Western medicine, were given "temporary" licences and continued to practise as before. It was never suggested that they were anything less than "doctors". Why, then, did Ine choose to register as a midwife? How did her training differ from her male contemporaries? The following discussion will trace the development of Ine's career and the importance of networks of *rangaku* scholars in enabling her studies.

### Early Life, Medical Training, and Supporters

Ine was born in Nagasaki on the sixth day of the fifth month, 1827. Her father Philipp Franz von Siebold was a promising young physician and scholar who played an important role in teaching Western medical techniques to the Japanese and eventually became famous for providing important information about Japan to Europe in the nineteenth-century. Her mother Taki was an *orandayuki yūjo* (literally a "Dutch-going" prostitute) in the employ of a brothel called Hiketaya in the Maruyama district of Nagasaki. At the age of sixteen, she had been engaged as Siebold's special companion on Dejima, not long after he arrived to work at the Dutch factory in 1823.[235] Ine spent her earliest years with her mother and Siebold on Dejima.[236] Ine was little more than a baby, however, when Siebold received orders to make preparations to leave Japan. In events that have come to be known as the Siebold Affair, he came under official investigation for his activities, including his secret communications with the Japanese scholar Takahashi Kageyasu, and his collection of several prohibited items. After being found guilty of breaking the law, he was banished in 1829 and ordered never to return to Japan. Taki and Ine were not permitted to go with him.[237]

The circumstances of Ine's birth were undoubtedly unusual. Much attention has been paid to the fact that Ine was only half-Japanese and the discrimination that she must have suffered.[238] Here, it is argued, however, that the financial support that Siebold provided, as well as the emotional and academic support provided by his students, had a significant positive impact on Ine's life.

Before he departed, Siebold arranged to provide for Taki and Ine by leaving them a stockpile of sugar. He also arranged for a number of his associates to look after them after his departure.[239] Siebold encouraged his daughter's studies by sending a book of Dutch grammar (although at the time, she was probably far too young to make use of it).[240] Little more is known about her early education, but it is clear that her medical studies were supported particularly by two of Siebold's students: Ishii Sōken (1796-1861), of Mimasaka Province, near Okayama, and Ninomiya Keisaku (1804-1862), of Uwajima Domain, on the island of Shikoku.

In the small town of Unomachi, near Uwajima, the story is told of how Ine ran away from home at the age of about fourteen or fifteen to study medicine with Keisaku, who had been one of Siebold's most trusted students. Written evidence suggests that she did not leave home until later. Nevertheless, there is little doubt that Ine and her mother had a deep and continuing association with Keisaku. Their families eventually became related through the marriage of Keisaku's nephew Mise Shūzō (1839-1877) to Ine's daughter Tada.[241] Even if the legend is an elaboration, it is clear that Ine studied medicine and obstetrics with Keisaku between the years of 1854 and 1861, and that two of those years were spent in Unomachi.

Keisaku was born into a farming family, but his talents led him to travel to Nagasaki as a young man to study Western medicine with Mima Junzō (1795-1825). He entered Siebold's Narutakijuku along with his teacher in 1823. During the Siebold Affair, Keisaku came under scrutiny for his activities with Siebold, particularly for his surveying of mountains during their journey to Edo. After his trial, he was exiled from Nagasaki and Edo, and he returned to his homeland to practice medicine and open a private school in 1830, settling in Unomachi in 1833 with the support of Uwajima Domain. Keisaku was reputedly a skilled surgeon. By 1845, his contribution to Western medicine in the domain was recognised by *taitō*, the permission to wear a sword.[242]

According to Ine's résumé, however, she began her medical training first with Ishii Sōken in 1845 at the age of eighteen, specializing in obstetrics.[243] If indeed, this was her first experience of medical study, it was a late age to be beginning her studies. Typically, medical apprentices lived and worked with their teachers for a period of seven to ten years. Their work began with simple errands, followed by the study of Chinese classics or the Dutch language and mixing medicines. Only then did students progress to accompanying their teacher on visits, and the study of medical textbooks.[244] Some historians have suggested that Ine probably lived as an apprentice in Sōken's house, studying obstetrics in the time remaining after she had helped with the housework.[245]

Sōken was the son of a village doctor from the province of Mimasaka. He had travelled to Nagasaki in 1823 to study with Siebold and become one of his closest disciples. He wrote a number of articles in Dutch for his teacher and, along with Ninomiya Keisaku, accompanied him on his visit to Edo in 1826. Eventually, he was recognised by Katsuyama domain and was employed as a salaried domain doctor. He moved to Edo in 1853, when he was given an appointment as an official *bakufu* doctor.[246]

Ine lived in Okayama for several years until her studies were brought to an abrupt halt by a violent incident. While alone with her on a boat, Sōken raped her and made her pregnant. The incident is described in some detail in Takako's narrative.[247] Ine returned to Nagasaki in 1851, shortly after giving birth. In Nagasaki, she brought up her baby girl with the help of her mother. The name she gave her daughter was Tada, meaning "free". Takako (as she later became) explained that it was a way for her mother to come to terms with her fate: that heaven had granted her "for free".[248] The rape was a personal tragedy, but not even this was enough to put a halt to Ine's determination to become a doctor. There is some evidence that Sōken later wished to adopt, or somehow be involved in the upbringing of his daughter, but Ine refused him. This gives an indication of the strength of her convictions.[249]

After returning to Nagasaki, Ine undertook further studies in obstetrics for a period of three years with a doctor by the name of Abe Roan. He had trained in Western medicine with Aoki Shūsuke (1803-1863) and appears to have had some involvement in smallpox vaccination.[250] His teacher Shūsuke had studied with Tsuboi Shindō (1795-1848) and Udagawa Genshin (1769-1834), two of the most highly regarded scholars of *rangaku* (Dutch learning) at the time.

It was not long, however, before once again Ine drew upon the support of the Siebold network, and in 1854, she left Tada in the care of her mother and travelled to Shikoku to study further with Ninomiya Keisaku. There, she studied alongside Keisaku's nephew, Mise Shūzō. Under the enthusiastic patronage of the domain lord Date Munenari (1813-1889), Uwajima Domain had been experiencing something of a boom in Western learning, and it was a lively environment in which to pursue the study of Western knowledge. Munenari was so interested in Western learning that he had harboured the famous *rangaku* scholar and fugitive Takano Chōei from 1848-1849 following his escape from prison.[251] Munenari also employed prominent military expert Murata Zōroku (later known as Ōmura Masujirō). He, along with Keisaku, was one of Ine's travelling companions in 1854.[252] Ine remained in Unomachi until 1856, when Keisaku suffered a stroke and returned to Nagasaki for treatment, taking Ine and Shūzō with him.

### Siebold's Return

In 1859, the same year that the Dutch station of Dejima was abandoned in favour of a consulate at Edo, and Nagasaki, Yokohama, and Hakodate were opened as treaty ports, Siebold was pardoned and allowed to return to Japan, bringing his son Alexander, from his German marriage, with him. His return to Nagasaki in August of 1859 opened up new doors for Ine, who by this time was in her early thirties.

It was decided that Shūzō, who by then spoke and wrote Dutch fluently, would become Siebold's personal assistant, translator, and student, in addition to teaching his son Alexander Japanese.[253] During this period, Siebold, Ine, and Shūzō exchanged a number of letters (generally written in Dutch) that provide an important insight not only into their personal interactions, but into Ine's medical activities.[254]

Of the Dutch letters, Shūzō's are the most numerous, numbering around thirty. Ine appears to have been close to Shūzō, even before she arranged for him to marry her daughter. He wrote several of Ine's letters on her behalf, and was privy to some of the more personal aspects of her relationship with her father. Most of them are short communications concerning patients, the exchange of items, and other domestic matters. Ine's letters reveal her involvement in helping with Siebold's domestic affairs, including managing his maids, making mosquito nets, and sending food. Some of the letters reveal a number of difficulties between them, particularly over a certain maid employed to serve him.[255] She appears to have struggled to communicate in Dutch, and after an especially bad argument, Ine blamed her poor language skills for their failure to communicate:

I know well that such a misunderstanding occurred because I cannot yet speak Dutch, and that your words for me and my words for you were not very comprehensible, although I attended to you as well as I can. Taking such thoughts in my heart, I was prepared to travel to Kokura in Buzen, where my Master lives,[256] to learn the Dutch language. But I cannot because my mother and Keisaku have forbidden it. So I shall learn from Shūzō at home. I am sincerely grateful for the greeting you sent through Keisaku, but I have decided in my heart that I should not stay in your house so long as I cannot speak a little Dutch. I hope that you will not be offended.[257]

It is worth noting that Ine was advised to learn Dutch with Shūzō, twelve years her junior, and supposedly less experienced than herself. Her skills were obviously inferior, and we must suspect that her training had been less vigorous. However, it should also be said that not all *rangaku* scholars learned to speak Dutch, and Shūzō's linguistic talents were by all accounts exceptional.

After this unhappy beginning, Ine and her father appear to have come to an agreement about the way their relationship should proceed, and Ine decided that she would not live with her father any longer. She asked him instead to help her with her studies and medical practice.[258]

In many of the other letters, there was a recurring theme in which Ine repeatedly requested that her father come to help her with the more difficult medical cases. In addition to the help he gave her, Ine was also able to use the strength of his reputation to attract patients of her own, and to broaden her own medical experiences. For example, a letter written by Shūzō and dated November 25, 1860, described how Ine had been examining a patient with a growth on the tongue who had requested her father's help.[259]

Other letters indicate that Ine was not only seeing patients herself, but prescribing and mixing drugs as well. Two separate notes written by Shūzō demonstrate this:

Oinesan says many thanks for your efforts yesterday, and requests very respectfully that you might be so kind as to get the opodeltoch[260] and other items quickly. She would now like in addition some extract of hyoscine, senna, and a medical set of scales, if they are available.

... I examined with Oinesan today the sinus of a doctor from Chikuzen ...[261]

I helped Oinesan to prepare the medicines because if she had done it alone they would not be ready for three or four days. So I cannot come to you now. I will come early in the morning. Ine sends her greetings and thanks you very much.[262]

Thus, from the letters above it is clear that Ine worked closely with Shūzō and was involved in a variety of cases. She saw patients and prescribed and prepared medicines. There are no examples of obstetric cases in the letters to Siebold, despite her having trained in obstetrics with Ishii Sōken.

It is likely that Siebold's presence in Nagasaki also fostered Ine's relationships with other European doctors. Further evidence of Ine's activities in Nagasaki comes from the memoirs of Pompe van Meerdervoort (1829-1908), a doctor who came to serve the Dutch community in Nagasaki and who contributed much to Japanese medical education. Ine counted Pompe among her teachers in her résumé. It is likely that she received an introduction from her father, since she began working with him shortly after Siebold's arrival in Japan. While he was unimpressed with Japanese obstetrics in general, Pompe does appear to have regarded Ine's abilities highly. In a memorandum about the dissection of a criminal published in the *Journal of the North China Branch of the Royal Asiatic Society of Great Britain and Ireland* in 1860, he wrote under the entry for November 1, 1859:

This time there were more than sixty spectators, and what is most remarkable *one Japanese Lady* was present! She is an accoucheuse, who has studied the medical science, and she earnestly requested me to permit her to witness the dissection, which I allowed, and I must say that she neglected nothing. She always was very attentive and asked me several questions which proved her to be very intelligent; she assisted also in the operations.[263]

Although on this occasion Pompe described Ine as an accoucheuse, he later wrote about her in his memoirs in most laudatory terms, describing her as a physician-obstetrician:

When mentioning this complete lack of scientific knowledge of obstetrics, I forgot to mention that there is one very fortunate exception. At Nagasaki, there lives a woman physician-obstetrician, the natural daughter of one of the earlier physicians in Japan; this woman, after her father's departure, was truly worshipped by some of his students who protected her and taught her medicine and obstetrics, in which she really made good progress. This woman had an unlimited enthusiasm for this work, and she asked me to be allowed to attend the medical exercises on the corpse as taught by me to the Japanese students. She showed at those occasions that she certainly was one of the most experienced Japanese anatomists. She also often attended the clinical classes in the hospital in the women's ward, and she was often called upon for consultation by her colleagues. Twice I saw her serving as an obstetrician for European women, and she really was most satisfactory. In one of her rooms I noticed pictures of famous physicians and medical men.[264]

These are the only available concrete examples of Ine's training. It is not clear whether she was able to participate in the lessons to the same degree as the male students, but the fact that she assisted in the operations suggests that she was permitted to take an active role. Furthermore, she was clearly working in the women's ward at the Nagasaki Yōjōsho, the Western-style hospital planned and opened by Pompe with the assistance of the shogunate in 1861. According to Ine's résumé, she also learned from other European doctors in Nagasaki during this period, including Pompe's successors Antonius Bauduin (1822-1885), and C.G. van Mansvelt (1837-1916).[265]

**Uwajima Domain 1861-1868**
During the 1860s, Ine's increasing profile and her connections with the community of *rangaku* scholars in Uwajima allowed her to obtain the patronage of the *daimyo* of Uwajima, Date Munenari. As mentioned previously, Munenari had a strong interest in *rangaku*. She appears to have gone there shortly after Siebold departed for Edo to advise the *bakufu* on foreign matters, taking Alexander and Shūzō with him in 1861. Ine spent the 1860s going back and forth between Nagasaki and Uwajima. Her gender did not prohibit her

from travelling, nor from making use of scholarly networks in the same way as her male *rangaku* colleagues did. In many cases, her travelling companions were male scholars of Western learning (she does not seem to have travelled unaccompanied).

In Edo, Shūzō's linguistic prowess and his close relationship to Siebold aroused the suspicion of anti-foreign elements in the government, and he was arrested on the grounds of impersonating a samurai in the tenth month of that year.[266] Despite the enthusiasm of some daimyo for Western learning, the possession of Western knowledge could still arouse hostility in these politically volatile times. Around this time, Ine wrote a letter in Japanese which provides evidence of the extent to which she had been taken under the *daimyo*'s wing. It is dated the twenty-seventh of the fifth month, and from the content, can be dated to 1862.[267]

> ... I had been intending to write to you before now, but since I came here I have been ceaselessly bombarded by patients day and night without a moment's respite, so I have been unintentionally silent. ... As you know, my daughter Taka has been working ... at the castle since the autumn of last year ...[268] I too, have been called to the castle for audiences with the retired Daimyo,[269] his wife, and his son and his wife as well. All of them were most kind, especially the retired Daimyo who summoned me many times and spoke to me most kindly. Among other things, he has made efforts to intervene in Edo and is worried about obtaining [Shūzō's] pardon as soon as possible. I am overwhelmed with gratitude for everything ...[270]

Thus, Ine had not only established a flourishing medical practice in Uwajima, but gained the favour of the *daimyo* for both herself and her daughter. The letter reveals, moreover, the efforts made by Date Munenari on behalf of Shūzō. When Shūzō was eventually released from prison in 1865, he was made a retainer first of Ōzu Domain, then of Uwajima Domain. He and Takako were married the following year under the auspices of the Uwajima *karō* (chief retainer), another indication of Ine's rise in social status.[271]

Ine was even honored with an official stipend from Date Munenari. Miyoshi cites material from domain records dated the twenty-second of the third month 1864 that Ine had come to Uwajima and presented gifts to Munenari and his son, the reigning *daimyo*. Furthermore, the entry reads: "Itoku the daughter of Siebold recently came to Uwajima. On this day, for her medical activity she received a rice stipend for two, and was told that she should also be ready to serve in the women's quarters in the castle."[272] Although the salary was modest, it was comparable to the salaries given to men of commoner status.[273] Domain records also show that two male students of medicine came to study with Ine for a short period in 1865.[274] In the eighth month of 1867, Ine attended the *daimyo*'s wife Yoshiko in childbirth, along with two male doctors.[275]

In 1866, the British doctor William Willis described Ine as the "Chief Physician of the Uwajima family" when he accompanied Sir Harry Parkes on a visit to Uwajima in September of that year. He noted that she was a "clever woman with some ideas of European medical knowledge", and commented on the ease with which she and her children conducted themselves: "... her children [sic], nieces and nephews of our interpreter, are most handsome and seem to be upper class retainers. At all events they moved freely about and seemed a part of the family."[276]

There is further evidence in the Uwajima Domain documents uncovered by Miyoshi that Ine lived for some time with a samurai retainer by the name of Ōno Masasaburō (?-1880).[277] This relationship is interesting not only in terms of Ine's personal life, but also because Masasaburō was a samurai and a scholar of Western learning, who specialised in the English language. It shows the extent to which Ine was steeped in *rangaku* culture: through her training, her medical activities, and through her personal life as well. She appears to have been comfortable moving in these scholarly samurai circles, where she was accepted and supported in her medical activities.

### Tokyo 1870-1877

After her sojourn in Uwajima and the death of her mother in Nagasaki in 1869, Ine made a series of moves from Nagasaki to Osaka, and finally to Tokyo. In these activities, she was supported again by the network of doctors who helped to shape her life. Her move to Tokyo, however, introduced her to an expanded group of contacts, whose enthusiastic patronage led eventually to her prestigious appointment at the Imperial Court.

At the time of her move to Tokyo, Ine's teacher of medicine in Nagasaki was Antonius Bauduin. Bauduin had recently returned to Japan after undertaking studies in obstetric surgery in London from 1867-1868. He then pioneered the technique of ovariotomy in Japan.[278] It is likely that Ine's move was prompted by Bauduin's appointment at the Tōkō (later Tokyo University Medical School) in 1870.[279]

Through her connections with Bauduin and Shūzō, Ine became reacquainted with a doctor called Ishii Kendō (1840-1882), who was none other than the son of Ine's former teacher, Ishii Sōken, and hence Takako's half-brother.[280] For Ine and her daughter, it was the beginning of a fresh relationship with the Ishii family. Kendō and Shūzō both obtained prestigious Tokyo appointments in the early 1870s: Kendō first to the Tōkō and then the Bureau of Medicine (*Imukyoku*), and Shūzō as a medical advisor on prison reform to the government.

Kendō had been educated by prominent Western learning scholars, including Mitsukuri Genpo, and Matsuki Kōan in Edo, and Ogata Kōan in Osaka from 1858-1860. Prior to entering Kōan's school, he had spent about six months in Nagasaki, where he probably met Ine and Takako.[281] His warm relationship with the women and Shūzō alike is recorded in his Tokyo diary of 1874.[282]

Kendō was a close friend of many other doctors and proponents of Western learning, including Nagayo Sensai and Fukuzawa Yukichi, famous educator, and advisor to the government. With the support of Fukuzawa, Ine's name was put forward to the Imperial Household in 1873.[283] The birth which she attended was that of the Emperor's concubine, Hamuro Mitsuko. It took place on September 18, 1873, in a house belonging to the Imperial Household Ministry. The child was a boy, but sadly, he was stillborn, and Mitsuko died four days later.[284] For her "remarkable" efforts, Ine received a hundred yen.[285] For other work, Ine received more modest payments. When she attended Kendō's wife Ai in childbirth in November 1874, she received *kamigata* tea worth one *ryō,* and some bonito flakes.[286]

It is known that Fukuzawa apprenticed his sister-in-law Imaizumi Tō to Ine in order for her to study obstetrics, but this arrangement was only short-lived.[287]

In addition to the support she received from Kendō, Ine was also occasionally in contact with her half-brothers Alexander and Heinrich. Alexander had remained in Japan after his father left and was employed at the British legation. Heinrich had arrived in Japan in 1869 and was employed as an interpreter for the Austro-Hungarian legation. In a letter Heinrich wrote to Alexander in 1877, he complained that he had written several times to Ine, but had never obtained a reply. Nevertheless, she did write to him to inform him of Shūzō's death that year.[288] Ine's granddaughter Tane recalled that when she was about seven or eight years old (around 1895), her family moved with Ine into a Western-style house that Heinrich had built in Azabu.[289]

The heyday of Ine's Tokyo career was brought to an end by Shūzō's sudden illness and death in Osaka in 1877. He and Takako had returned to Osaka the previous year, where he was working as a doctor at Osaka Hospital. More tragedy was to follow. Takako, newly widowed, became pregnant to an acquaintance she did not care for, and gave birth to a boy in 1879. Ine adopted the boy as her heir and named him Shūzō, an action which speaks for itself. Takako later married Yamawaki Taisuke, another doctor, and gave birth to three more children, only to be widowed again in 1886.[290]

In the midst of this family drama, Ine returned to Nagasaki for a time, and applied for her midwifery licence there in 1884. It is unclear how long she continued her midwifery practice after returning to Tokyo in 1889. She may have retired around 1895, when she moved in to Heinrich's house with Takako and the grandchildren, for her granddaughter Tane reported that Ine had looked after them while Takako went out to study the *koto*.[291]

**Conclusion**

The examination of Ine's life story in the context of the social networks in which she participated adds to the growing body of evidence that certain women were able to participate in activities beyond the private sphere in Edo-period Japan. Anne Walthall has demonstrated, for example, in her book on Matsuo Taseko, how one woman defied convention to participate in the politics of the Meiji Restoration. She argues convincingly that there are rewards in viewing her life not simply as an episode in women's history, but in terms of her impact on the male sphere.[292] Indeed, as Patessio has noted, those women who did attempt to enter the public sphere in the late Edo period often moved in social worlds that were entirely male.[293] This is particularly noticeable in the case of Ine.

Walthall has suggested, further, that the turmoil of late nineteenth-century Japan provided special opportunities for some women to blur the roles between public and private, to take advantage of "marginality."[294] Ine took advantage not only of the turbulent social world of the *bakumatsu* period, and the lack of medical regulation within it, but also of the exceptionality of her birth. Much of what she achieved was due to the fame of her father Siebold. He provided for her not only a comfortable inheritance that allowed her to remain unmarried throughout her life, but also a tight network of his many students and admirers who shared their knowledge with her and welcomed her into their male world, even in her father's absence. Indeed, as Pompe noted, some of Siebold's students "truly worshipped" her.[295] For Ine, as well as for those who assisted her, her female gender was of far less consequence than her genealogy.

This article has attempted to show that Ine was above all, a *rangakusha*, a practitioner of Western learning like the men with whom shared her working life. She freely associated with these low-ranking samurai and medical men, and frequented important centers of Western learning in Nagasaki, Okayama, Uwajima, and Tokyo. She worked not only with Siebold's own students, but also with followers of Pompe, Ogata Kōan, and Mitsukuri Genpo, some of the most important figures in Western learning at the time. Fukuzawa Yukichi's support in Edo was instrumental in her invitation to serve the Imperial Palace, however the fact that she had already worked for Date Munenari, the *daimyo* of Uwajima, must also have counted in her favour. Ine's decision to obtain a midwifery licence rather than a medical one came at the end of a remarkable career in the early modern period. Her failure to obtain a licence must be interpreted within the broader context of the position of Western Learning in Japan's medical modernisation.

## CHAPTER FIVE

# MIXED MESSAGES: INTERRACIAL COUPLES AND BIRACIAL CHILDREN FROM THE NAGASAKI FOREIGN SETTLEMENT PERIOD TO WORD WAR II

LANE EARNS

## Historical Background

Nagasaki's long history of interracial relationships between Western men and Japanese women dates to the port town's founding in 1571, when Nagasaki became the Japanese entrepôt for Portuguese trade in Chinese silk (out of Macao) for Japanese silver, and the center of, and safe haven for, Christianity. The Portuguese were followed soon thereafter by the Spanish, Dutch, and English—the latter two based primarily in nearby Hirado.

A mixture of relatively unregulated short-term and long-term interracial relationships between European traders and local Japanese women continued until the maritime prohibition (*sakoku*) edicts of the Tokugawa *bakufu* in the 1630s attempted to control foreign trade and eliminate the Christian influence in Japan. In 1636, the Japanese "wives" of the Portuguese and the offspring fathered by the Portuguese were deported to Macao and ordered not to attempt to return to Japan on the penalty of death. Three years later, a similar directive was applied to the "wives" and children of the Dutch and English, who were deported to Batavia.

Starting in 1641, the only Westerners allowed to remain in Japan were a small contingent of Dutch traders and officials, who were ordered to move from Hirado to the artificial island of Dejima in Nagasaki Harbor. Japanese authorities did not allow the Dutch to bring their wives (or any European women for that matter) with them to Dejima.[296] The only female contact the Dutch were allowed at Dejima involved Japanese prostitutes from the neighboring brothel quarters at Maruyama and Yoriai in Nagasaki. These women were usually natives of the desperately **85** poor rural areas of Shimabara and Amakusa, just northeast of Nagasaki, who came to work in the city's so-called "tea houses."

Throughout the seventeenth and eighteenth centuries, the biracial children produced by these interracial relationships on Dejima usually lived with the family of the Japanese mother, sometimes with the financial support of the Dutch father. When the father returned home to Europe, any children had to remain behind in Japan, although the father was allowed to continue financial support of the child/children from afar.

By the nineteenth century, however, some Japanese women and their children began to live openly with their Dutch partners on Dejima or even off-site in the city. In 1801, Hendrik Doeff, the Dutch Director of Trade at Dejima, fathered a daughter (Omon, died 1810) with a Japanese woman (Sono) from a local teahouse. As had long been the custom, Omon lived with her mother. Doeff also had a second relationship with a woman named Uryuno from a neighboring Maruyama teahouse that resulted in the 1807 birth of a son, Michitomi Yokichi, and in this case, father, mother, and son lived on Dejima. But when Doeff left Japan for the Netherlands in late 1817, his son, by law, had to remain behind. Yokichi died seven years later of leukemia and was buried in a Buddhist cemetery on a hill behind a temple in town.[297]

The German physician Philipp Franz von Siebold, who worked for the Dutch in Nagasaki from 1823 to 1830, began living with a sixteen-year-old woman named Kusumoto Taki (1807-1865) from a local teahouse soon after his arrival in Nagasaki. Together, they had a daughter, Ine, born on Dejima in 1827. The family lived in a residence in the Narutaki district of the city. When Siebold returned to Europe, he asked one of his Japanese medical students, Ninomiya, to help look after his daughter Ine with money that he provided.

Kusumoto Taki married a Japanese man after Siebold left town, and, Ine, at the age of nineteen, went on to study medicine in another province in Japan under the guidance of Ninomiya. When Siebold returned to Nagasaki in 1859, Ine moved back to town and continued her medical studies under him. With his assistance and her great efforts, Ine became Japan's first female obstetrician (see Ellen Nakamura's chapter in this volume for more on this woman). Kusumoto Ine passed away in 1903 at the age of seventy-six.[298]

### The Opening Decade of the Foreign Settlement

As the decade of the 1860s opened, many had high expectations of Nagasaki because of its long experience with Westerners, its excellent harbor, its proximity to Shanghai and the China coast trade, and its ample supply of coal. A U.S. naval chaplain predicted Nagasaki was "destined from its convenient position to become very populous—another New York and also influential, instantly there will be a rush and indeed it has already begun,"[299] and a U.S. commercial agent speculated Nagasaki would become the "Honolulu of Japan."[300] And, indeed, for a decade, before the opening of Hyōgo (Kobe) and Osaka, Nagasaki competed with Yokohama as the most active trading port in Japan.

As outlined above, by the time Westerners began arriving for the opening of the foreign settlement in the fall of 1858, a tradition of Japanese women living with Dutch men at Dejima and nearby in the city had already been established. Because the foreign settlement was not ready for its scheduled occupation in July 1859, the first Westerners took up temporary residence at Dejima and in the neighboring district of Hirobaba, where they witnessed firsthand Dutchmen in living arrangements with Japanese women.

While missionaries and consular officials made their presence known in Nagasaki, most of the Westerners who arrived in Nagasaki in the opening decade were rowdy sailors and merchants— adventurers in their twenties, who made arrangements through local tea houses for Japanese female companionship. The majority of these interracial relationships were relatively short-term trysts, but there is also evidence of longer-term liaisons, extended common-law arrangements, and occasionally decades-long marriage commitments.

Because many of the Japanese women in these relationships came from desperately poor circumstances, often having been contracted by their parents into prostitution for economic survival, one can imagine a motivating factor for entering into a relationship with a Western merchant-sailor might have been the perceived opportunity to escape poverty, attain some sort of financial security, and garner improved social status. As with some of their male partners, some Japanese women also seem to have taken the opportunity for companionship, love, and occasionally even the development of a stable family life. For a few of the Western men in this opening decade of the foreign settlement, a relationship with a Japanese woman could also provide help with the fledgling businesses they opened in the hopes of stability and profit.

What these interracial couples sought as they entered these relationships, what they eventually achieved in these partnerships, and what hopes they held for their children, not only shaped their own lives, but also shaped the avenue of opportunities available to second- and third-generation biracial children raised in Nagasaki, in cities across Japan and East Asia, and around the world. How people reacted to these issues not only varied between families but among family members. In searching for definitive patterns and themes involving biracial offspring, one would be hard-pressed to tie a neat bow around the package of their experiences, but for most of them, the shifting context of Japan's relationship with the outside world is reflected in the choices they made.

While some of the biracial children born in the early years of the foreign settlement were raised in their father's household, it was more common that their upbringing took place in the confines of the mother's family. It was usually easier for these children to move seamlessly among the Japanese mother's support group (which usually lived in the area) than it was among the support group available to a Western father (usually visitors or short-term residents in Nagasaki).

In 1883, the Surgeon-General of the U.S. Navy published a report stating in part that:

> Since 1860 a large number of Eurasian children has been born [in Japan] every year, and they apparently thrive through infancy and early childhood and are then lost sight of, so that it is an unusual thing to recognize one of these children apparently more than twelve years of age. Many doubtless die, but many more, I think, are so thoroughly Japanese that the paternal portion of their inheritance is not readily recognized. The Japanese characteristics, color, hair, and features, are much more strongly impressed on these children than any element of foreign race. ... The Japanese women who live with Europeans and manage their households are, to all outward appearances, like other Japanese, and their children are brought up as Japanese children, in most instances speaking only the Japanese language, so that in later life all traces of foreign origin are lost and they become an integral part of the mixed race from many sources, which we call Japanese.[301]

Western consular courts in Japan sometimes afforded themselves the luxury of ignoring "all traces of foreign origin" if the Western father of a biracial child chose not to support his offspring. The jury could simply assert there was no foreign blood in the child, and the father would be absolved of any financial obligations to mother and child.

This report sets the stage for a look at one of the most interesting interracial relationships between a Westerner and a Japanese in Nagasaki during the raucous opening decade of the foreign settlement in Nagasaki, a relationship between a Japanese prostitute named Takashino from a local tea house and an American sailor-turned-merchant named George Lake.

George Lake became one of most controversial Westerners ever to set foot in Nagasaki. He registered his arrival at the U.S. Consulate in Nagasaki in September 1860, just days shy of his twenty-first birthday. Soon thereafter, he established Lake & Company, a butcher, compradore, and general trading business, and, by the fall of 1862, he had been joined in Nagasaki by his seventeen-year-old brother, Edward.[302]

Even before George Lake came to Japan, he had had an affair with a neighbor that resulted in a daughter, Georgiana, being born in his hometown of Topsfield, Massachusetts in 1858. But George had absconded to China on a whaling vessel prior to the birth, abandoning the pregnant mother.[303]

Lake developed an early and lengthy criminal record in Nagasaki in spite of the fact that he was the marshal at the American consulate. He eventually fled the country in 1869 over a trade dispute and returned to his Massachusetts home to avoid arrest. While there, in 1870, Lake married a woman from the neighboring town of Middleton named Lucy Wilkins. The following year, Wilkins gave birth to a daughter. Despite this, Lake soon thereafter decided to return to Nagasaki, without his wife and daughter, in hopes of clearing up the legal mess that he had left behind.

One resident of Nagasaki especially irate over the news of Lake's marriage in America was a woman named Takashino, who went by the professional name of Toka or Tako. In July 1871, she brought a paternity and child-support suit against Lake in the U.S. Consulate at Nagasaki, in which she claimed that she had been his mistress and housekeeper for eleven years (the latter position continuing even during his two-year stay in the United States) and that he had fathered her seven-year-old son. Takashino also said in her petition that upon Lake's return to Nagasaki he had beaten her, and that he had been brought up on assault charges at the British Consulate for also beating an Englishman that Lake had accused of sleeping with her while he was away. George Lake admitted that he had obtained

Takashino from a Nagasaki house of prostitution, and that she had lived with him from early 1861 to 1869, but he denied being the child's father.[304]

Takashino also argued that it was only with her assistance over the years that Lake was able to transform his struggling butchery business into a successful provisions company. She said that she stayed by his side as the business grew and believed his promises over the years that he would adequately provide for her and their child. It appeared to her that Lake had changed his mind about supporting them and recognizing her child as his son after marrying the American woman in Massachusetts, and after listening to what Takashino said were false rumors of her infidelity while he was away.[305]

According to the first of Takashino's two petitions:

> Lake told me that he intended ... to send for his wife ... and that he [would] separate from [me because my] living with him [would make] his wife disagreeable on her arrival to this port. ... I complied with such [a proposal] ... because the woman's feelings are of the same, generally, [anywhere] in the world. ... If I gave the child to any man as an adopted son—this child was born seven years ago—I would not be troubled myself so much as I am now. ... I cannot conceive that Mr. G. W. Lake, who thought at first the child as his own one, and took great care in rearing him up by having a wet nurse, etc., tells me now many difficulties, saying that the child is not his own. ... I thought often it would be better for me that I lost my life, but I did not [do] so, having thoughts of the child, and I am now in great distress. ... Mr. G. W. Lake told me once that if he married with [his] country woman he shall marry me off to some Japanese, but I believe that I cannot immediately marry unto any man, for not only [am I accompanied by] a child, but I [am] already twenty-eight years old, instead of being seventeen or eighteen years old.[306]

In the second of Takashino's petitions, she stated that she continued to raise their child with great love:

> Because I believe him to be my true one since his

birth; but Mr. G. W. Lake expressed [to] me his pretext that the above child was made through my [lewd] intercourse with [a] Japanese in [the] town of Nagasaki, instead of his true child, while he was no doubt present when the birth of the child took place. ... Under these circumstances, I have been overwhelmed with a deep sorrow, [and I] went [to] the sea-side one or two times for the purpose [of committing] ... suicide by drowning, but this was prevented [by] the grief of my young child ... [being] left alone [by] me. ... Although I am, of course, a foolish woman, and should not be good for Mr. G. W. Lake, yet I was engaged [to] him [for about] eleven years. ... If he persists upon such a pretext, how [can we] keep our livelihood, [especially since I am too old and will be unable] ... to marry with anybody.[307]

In the trial at the U.S. Consulate in Nagasaki, a jury of four American assessors from the foreign settlement deliberated on the matter, declared the child to be pure Japanese, and found Lake not guilty of the charges. The trial, in spite of its legal outcome, would prove to be the last straw for Japanese government officials in town, as they had decided in advance to enforce Japan's treaty rights and order him deported for his previous offenses. U.S. Consul Willie Mangum supported the decision and gave Lake three months to leave the country. This thus set the stage for the end of Lake's tumultuous decade-long stay in the city. As we shall discover, although Takashino was clearly wronged, she would turn out to be the luckiest of George Lake's many female partners.

When George Lake left Nagasaki in October 1871, his brother Edward stayed on to conduct business at Lake & Co. under a power of attorney. George returned to Massachusetts and resumed living with his wife Lucy; not long thereafter, they had a second child. Soon thereafter, however, he divorced her on grounds of adultery. He later claimed that the suit was decided in his favor because he denied fathering either of Lucy's two children.[308] This action legally set him free to pursue his latest love interest—his sixteen-year-old illegitimate daughter, Georgiana, who he had abandoned in 1858.

Lake's pattern of avoiding responsibility for the children he fathered unfortunately got worse before it got better. By 1874, he had sired four children by three women and not admitted his paternity in any of the cases. Instead, he blamed each of the women for their adulterous behavior and shirked all responsibility.

When Georgiana became pregnant with George's child in 1875,

she came to work for him as a housekeeper/ bookkeeper at his New York City business office. In 1876, she gave birth to a baby girl— fathered by her father. The couple made headlines in New York in 1878 when George had another child by Georgiana, but it was not until 1883 that George was arraigned on charges of cruelty to his children and abandonment. His four children and his wife were by then in an alms-house.[309] Soon thereafter, Lake was convicted of incest, but the verdict was appealed on a procedural error. It took until March 1886 for a new trial to end in a conviction on the charge of incest and for Lake to be sentenced to nine and one-half years of hard labor. According to newspaper accounts of the day, during the commotion surrounding the case, Georgiana's mother died, Georgiana went insane, and four of his five children from the unfortunate affair were institutionalized.[310]

After his release from prison, Lake, now an ex-convict unlikely to find work in New York, decided to return to Nagasaki in January 1893, in an effort to regain control of the family business. The U.S. Consul in Nagasaki was far from pleased to see him, because not only was his original deportation order still in effect, but Lake's criminal record had grown even longer since he left Japan.

Lake's by-now notorious past—his scandalous affair, abandonment, and trial twenty years earlier with the unfortunate Takashino in Nagasaki, not to mention the list of crimes and tragic outcomes in the United States—became the talk of the town in 1893 when he returned to Nagasaki to reclaim his business. Through legal maneuvers and stubbornness, he managed to remain in the city until January 1894, when he was again arrested for violating the deportation order, his business closed, and his property confiscated by the U.S. Consulate. A comedy of errors then ensued, in which Lake was deported on three separate occasions to Shanghai, returning to Nagasaki each time. When he showed up in Nagasaki a fourth time in July 1894, he was deported again—this time to Korea, where he decided to pursue business opportunities until late August 1898, when his life ended suddenly and violently: he was apparently murdered in Inchon, Korea.[311]

It is not difficult to make a correspondence between Lake's (mis)adventures and one of the most celebrated cultural examples of Japanese-Western relationships in Nagasaki during the foreign period—the famed *Madame Butterfly*. In 1886, the French seaman Louis Viaud (pen name Pierre Loti) participated in a month-long relationship with a seventeen-year-old Nagasaki girl that became the basis for his novel *Madame Chrysanthème*, just as the young American sailor and budding merchant George Lake had settled in town twenty-five years earlier and begun his own nine-year live-in relationship with another seventeen-year-old Nagasaki resident.

It is likely that Jennie Correll, the Methodist missionary who lived in Nagasaki in the 1890s and sister of John Luther Long, the author of *Madame Butterfly* (1898), was aware of both Viaud's *Madame Chrysanthème* (1887) and the account of George Lake's affair, which was the talk of the town upon his failed attempt in 1893 and 1894 to reclaim his business and property in Nagasaki. Nor does one have to strain much to see the Viaud and Lake affairs in both the book and in *Madama Butterfly*, the immensely popular Puccini opera set in Nagasaki that debuted in 1904, even while acknowledging other additional influences. Takashino's lament in her trial testimony— "If I gave the child to any man as an adopted son ... I would not be **troubled** myself so much as I am now"—provides a tantalizing bit of conjecture as a herald for Cio Cio San's operatic son, Trouble.

As George Lake's sordid story was unfolding in the first period of this study—the so-called "raucous" period of the early foreign settlement in the 1860s—other Westerners in Nagasaki pursued their professional ventures in the city and interacted with Japanese women in a manner that was not quite so destructive. For example, two Western consuls from this period, the American Consul John Walsh[312] and the Portuguese Consul Jose Loureiro,[313] began long-term relationships with Japanese women. While neither married their Japanese companions while in Nagasaki—Japanese law prohibited legal unions until March 1873, by which time they had left town— these common-law relationships did produce biracial children who were raised as members of their families.

The uniqueness of these relationships was probably due to the fact that Walsh and Loureiro were both merchant-consuls who maintained separate businesses as their primary vocation and performed consular duties on the side, as opposed to consular officials whose full responsibilities commanded their attention as representatives of their countries.

### The Quieter Life of a Supply Station: 1870-1894

In the decades after the opening of the foreign settlement, after the first generation of restless young adventurers, Nagasaki itself began to change, losing some of its importance as a trading port in the years following the opening of Osaka and Kobe in 1868, and with this, the influx of rowdy young men. From 1870 to the beginning of the Sino-Japanese War in 1894, Nagasaki became little more than sleepy supply station that provided coal to visiting ships, and sundries, curios and alcohol to visiting sailors and tourists. From this time, however, we find a shift in the patterns of relationships between Japanese women, with evidence of relatively stable, longer-term unions between them, and more Japanese women and their biracial children living together in households with their Western husbands/fathers. The closing in 1888 of the Nagasaki branch of the Eurasian Children's Trust Society of Japan[314] signaled the fact that fewer biracial children had to rely on the charity of the Western community in the foreign settlement to support their well-being.

Among the interracial couples who lived together in Nagasaki and built successful long-term relationships in this period were the Jewish merchant Haskell Goldenberg and Kita Ide, who remained together for a dozen years in Nagasaki; the American ship captain Samuel Lord and Satsue Yoshitake, who were together for a similar time in Nagasaki and Shanghai; the British-born Russian merchant George Denbigh and Teshi Moritaka, who lived together for over three decades in places like Nagasaki, Vladivostok, Sakhalin and Hakodate; and the American-born Japanese physician Mary Gault and Motonosuke Suganuma (the only recorded biracial couple in Nagasaki in which the woman was a Westerner and the man Japanese) who resided in Nagasaki as husband and wife for twenty-nine years.[315]

Two other financially successful merchants in Nagasaki had long-term relationships with local Japanese women—more than one of them in fact—in this period. An American ship captain, John Breen, had relationships with two women, Shie Tomonaga and Yoka Miyahara, and fathered children with both of them over the course of at least seventeen years in Nagasaki. Likewise, the American merchant R.H. Powers had relationships with two Nagasaki area women—Funaki Sato and Naka Iida—that resulted in children over multiple decades.

As mentioned earlier, some Western merchants, consular officials and military personnel in town had more practical reasons for entering into relationships with local Japanese women. Quite often, these Westerners sought help with establishing and developing their businesses and/or with caring for their residences, and themselves, in return for Japanese "housekeepers" acquiring the Westerners' estates upon their deaths.

Among this group were the African American bartender J.J. Johnson, who fathered a child by Naka Morita, who raised the child at her nearby residence just outside the foreign settlement. Another American bartender, William Thomas, employed a live-in housekeeper who also helped him tend to his tavern.[316] The American consular official and compradore Frank Nevells had a resident housekeeper named Oshige Honda from 1888. Their relationship was such that when he passed away in 1925, his funeral service was held at Kosaiji Temple, he was interred at Honda's Buddhist cemetery lot at Tanohira, just above the former foreign settlement, and Oshige Honda inherited all of his possessions.[317]

## A Decade of Resurgence, Subsequent Decline and the Rise of Militarism: 1895-1941

As the nineteenth century neared its end and the foreign settlement period began to wind down, sleepy Nagasaki briefly re-awoke and there was a dramatic spike in commercial activity from 1895 to 1905, fueled by wars and military operations in China, Korea, Russia and the Philippines. This activity led not only to more military personnel seeking "rest and relaxation," but it also resulted in a corresponding spike in the number of sailors and soldiers passing through and looking to take their discharge in Nagasaki, often setting up small businesses (usually bars and/or cheap hotels) with the assistance of female Japanese companions.

Because of Nagasaki's deep and naturally-protected harbor, its quality coal supplies, its proximity to other East Asian port cities, its ship repair facilities, its long tradition of Western intercourse, its natural beauty and its neighboring resort spas, Nagasaki was a popular port-of-call for ships: warships, transports, passenger ships and mail ships. Some of the soldiers and sailors who came to town from 1895 to 1905 chose to take their discharge in Nagasaki seeking either business opportunities or the chance to live out their years in beauty and comfort. Members of both groups sometimes looked for Japanese women to help them realize their dreams and ambitions.

James Schon took his discharge from the U.S. Navy, for example, and became a merchant in Nagasaki in 1896. In September 1910, Schon (51) married a young woman from Nagasaki named Hisame Shimoda (20), who over the course of the next decade gave birth to four children.[318] Also from the U.S. Navy was James Hatter, who after retiring to Nagasaki opened a tavern. Later, Hatter and his wife ran the Seamen's Home[319] in town, where he eventually died after a long illness. James Oliver retired from the U.S. Army, and with the help of his Japanese wife, Saku Yamaguchi, operated a small hotel in town until his death.[320] The Dutch-born British citizen Ary Van Ess came to Nagasaki after retiring from years of service with the British government in China. In Nagasaki, he married Kizue Kotani, and they lived together for a decade before his death.

Also coming to Nagasaki in this period was Nicholas Russel, the Russian-born American physician, newspaper publisher and populist who fathered two sons by his two housekeepers while living in Nagasaki. He later died in China, surrounded by the second housekeeper and his children in 1930.

This spike of activity in Nagasaki was short-lived, however, for by 1905, the war-fueled trade had once again declined as the military threats in China temporarily subsided and the Japanese war with Russia ended. Once again, Nagasaki settled into a routine that seemed to replicate the sleepier days of the 1870s and 1880s, a lull that continued through World War I, until it was roused again by the rising tide of militarism in the 1920s and 1930s.

As domestic and global events in the 1920s and 1930s led to increasing tensions, however, the rise of militarism also began to change social acceptance of interracial relationships and biracial children in both Japan and the West. It became increasingly difficult, and even dangerous at times, to be different, and the multicultural characteristics and skills once lauded, suddenly became suspect, as people became suspicious of possible traitors in their midst.

David Hatter (a half-Japanese and half-American with a biracial wife) and Edward Zillig (who had a Japanese wife) were put in internment camps in Japan; John (Ian) Denbigh, the biracial grandson of the Russian merchant George Denbigh, was placed in a camp by the Japanese in Shanghai; and Jack Golden, the half-German and half-Japanese son of the Nagasaki merchant Haskell Goldenberg who was living in the American Midwest, burned records of his past so he would not be interned with thousands of other Japanese, Japanese Americans and Germans. Nagasaki may have had a long tradition of international relations between various racial, ethnic and national groups of people, but when militarism and warfare reared their ugly heads, it was safer to hide one's differences and accentuate one's similarities.

**The Legacy of Interracial Couples: Biracial Children between Japan and the West**

Through the arc of this study, from the opening of the foreign settlement to the outbreak of World War II, the legacy of interracial relationships between Japanese women and Western men is most evident through their children, born between two cultures and left to negotiate their racial identities in different ways. Numerous factors helped determine the course these children took as they moved into adulthood, but the primary determinant related to how they were raised—whether their parents wanted them to be predominantly Western or Japanese, or whether they sought some combination of the two. Sometimes this choice varied among children in the same family. Factors such as their given names, their education, their primary language, their marital partners, and, finally, their geographical destinations—did they remain in Nagasaki or leave to seek different opportunities?—all helped influence their life courses.

Some interracial couples chose to raise their children in the Western style of the fathers. These included, for example, the German merchants Oscar Hartmann and Carl Lehmann. Sada, the Japanese mother of Taru and Sadakichi (1867-1944) Hartmann, and the wife of the German merchant Oscar Hartmann, died months after the birth of Sadakichi and was buried in a Japanese cemetery in town. The father sent the boys away to Germany to be raised by his brother there. Sadakichi Hartmann later moved to the United States, where he became a flamboyant critic, poet and actor.[321] Oscar Hartmannn's business partner, the German merchant Carl Lehmann, came to Nagasaki in 1862 and soon afterward developed a relationship with a Japanese woman (Kija Otoki). The couple had a daughter (born 1864) named Louise Charlotte Otoki Lehmann. On a trip to Germany in 1867, Carl Lehmann had his daughter christened. Both Oscar Hartmann and Carl Lehmann sent their children to Germany, both left Nagasaki for Kobe for business reasons, and both eventually died in Germany. Their children, likewise, lived their lives in the West.

Another Westerner in Nagasaki, the Irish-born American merchant John Breen, who was mentioned earlier, lived in a large house at Minamiyamate with two different Japanese women between 1870 and his death in 1886. In the first relationship with Shie Tomonaga, he had two children, Henry (born 1870) and Catherine [Kate] (born 1872) and with the second woman, Yoka Miyahara, he had a daughter, Margaret [Mary] (born 1882). Upon Breen's death, Miyahara successfully petitioned the U.S. Consulate for the right to claim his estate on her behalf and that of the children. Not only did the three children have Western names, but when Miyahara died in 1913, she was buried in her husband's grave, and her Christian name "Elisabeth Breen" was added to his tombstone.[322]

All the Breen children were educated in Nagasaki. Margaret married a Westerner in Nagasaki in 1904 and left town. Henry later moved to Kobe to work. The Breen house was sold at auction, according to Henry's instructions, to a Japanese merchant in 1920. The house still stands in Nagasaki today. Henry Breen died in Kobe in 1929 and was buried in a Western cemetery there. His descendants live in the United States.

Another American, ship's pilot Samuel Lord, had four children with Satsue Yoshitake: Annie (born 1881), Edward (born 1883), Minnie (born 1884) and Mary Lord (born in the late 1880s), all born in Nagasaki. Samuel and Satsue officially married in Nagasaki in 1889[323] and returned with the family to Shanghai shortly thereafter. Samuel Lord died in 1891. In the Shanghai foreign settlement, Satsue Lord remarried, again to a Westerner, as did all of her children. The Lord family provides clearly one of the most obvious examples of biracial children who were raised to be part of a Western tradition and not a Japanese (or Chinese, for that matter) tradition.

Another family that maintained its strong Western traditions, even among its biracial children, was the family of the British-born Russian George Denbigh and Teshi Moritaka (a native of Nagasaki). The Denbighs had five children—Alfred (1879), Alexander [Ted] (1873), George Washington [Wash] (1885), Lisa [Kin] (1886) and John [Vanya] (1888)—most of whom were born in Sakhalin but raised in Nagasaki. All five married Westerners and three died abroad (two in Canada and one in Hawai'i). Teshi, George, and Lisa are buried in Nagasaki's Sakamoto International Cemetery,[324] while other family members are buried in Western cemeteries in Yokohama, Hakodate, and Victoria, Canada. All members spoke varying degrees of Japanese, English, and Russian. A grandson, John (Ian) Denbigh, was placed by the Japanese government in an internment camp in Shanghai, where he met his future wife.[325] Denbigh descendants are currently scattered across Japan, Canada, and the United States.

For other couples, the context of their births presaged a predominantly Japanese upbringing. For example, John Powers, the son of the American merchant R.H. Powers and Funaki Sato, was born in 1870 and raised in Nagasaki. John became an employee in his father's firm and married a local Japanese woman. The couple had a son who later worked for years at the Nagasaki Prefectural Library. Though John died at the young age of thirty-seven, his descendants still live in Nagasaki as Japanese citizens. R.H. Powers and his son were buried together in a Western cemetery in Nagasaki under a tombstone provided by John Powers' mother.[326]

In 1891, R.H. Powers also had a daughter, Masa Powers, with Naka Iida, one of his female employees from the neighboring town of Kikitsu. Like her half-brother, Masa was born and raised in

Nagasaki. Masa Powers attended Kwassui Jo Gakkō, the Methodist mission school for girls in town. She then spent a brief period abroad, earning her baccalaureate degree in the United States at Wesleyan University in Ohio in 1916.[327] Upon graduation, she returned to teach English at Kwassui. Masa later married a Japanese man, Fukuzō Nakayama, and they moved to Osaka. Both became politicians. In 1960, Masa Nakayama became the first woman to hold a cabinet position in Japan when she was appointed Welfare Minister.

For some biracial children, cultural influences from both their Japanese and Western parents informed their lives and their choices as they moved into adulthood. For example, the only daughter of the U.S. Consul John Walsh and Rin Yamaguchi, Ai Yamaguchi (born 1864), was given a Japanese first name and her mother's maiden name. She lived with both parents in the foreign settlements of Nagasaki and Kobe. While Ai married a Japanese man, some of the family descendants married Westerners and others Japanese. Her daughter studied art in Tokyo with a biracial friend from Nagasaki. One of her uncles, Robert Walsh, married a Japanese woman in Kobe. Descendants of the Walsh and Yamaguchi families are spread across Japan, the United States and Europe, and some continue to communicate with each other on a regular basis.

Another American born and raised in Nagasaki was John F. Johnson, the son of the African American bartender J.J. Johnson and his Japanese housekeeper Naka Morita. He was probably born in the early 1870s, although he was not registered at the U.S. Consulate until 1883. The elder Johnson passed away in 1888, and was buried in a Western cemetery in town. The younger Jefferson obtained the mortgage to his father's property in 1890. He tried his hand at operating the hotel, but the venture was unsuccessful, and in November 1895 he transferred the lot to the Board of Directors of the Seamen's Home.[328]

Whereas J.J. Johnson had managed to carve out a relatively successful living for himself as a hotel and tavern proprietor for more than a quarter century, his half-African American, half-Japanese son found the going more difficult. Within two years of selling the family tavern/hotel, he was gone from his hometown. Where he went after leaving Nagasaki is unknown, as is the fate of his Japanese mother.

Tracing the offspring of the Russian-born Jewish merchant Haskell Goldenberg captures the diversity of experiences of biracial children in the foreign settlement. With Kita Ide, Goldenberg fathered Lena [Rie] (born 1888), Arthur (born 1889) and Jacob

Goldenberg (born 1891).[329] The couple legalized their relationship through a marriage ceremony in Nagasaki in 1894 after the birth of their children. Lena, the eldest, was sent to a mission boarding school in Shanghai, where she converted to Catholicism. Arthur and Jacob, although raised in the Jewish tradition by their mother at home, both attended Kaisei, a French Catholic mission school for boys in Nagasaki. After the death of her husband Haskell, Kita Ide married a Japanese man named Tadakimi Yoshiki around 1900. The couple had one son, Tadamasa.[330]

Arthur Goldenberg left Nagasaki in 1904, looking for a better life in Europe. After a few years in Berlin, he moved on to Massachusetts upon an invitation from a cousin. There, he changed his name to Golden and worked as a sign painter for five years. Arthur then moved to the Midwest and made arrangements for his brother to join him. Jacob, who changed his name to Jack Golden, became a university student. With their mother's financial support, they returned to Nagasaki one final time in 1913 to see their sister Lena marry a Japanese Christian named Manabu Sakurai.[331] The couple had four children between 1915 and 1920.

After their return to the United States, Arthur and Jack both married—Jack in 1914 to a woman from Milwaukee and Arthur in 1916 to a woman from Chicago. Both couples had three children. By 1917, Jack was a dentist in Michigan and Arthur was an industrial painting contractor in Chicago.

Lena and her family relocated to Manchuria because of her husband's work, but they moved to Tokyo in 1933, where they were joined by her mother, step-father and step-brother. The outbreak of World War II caused considerable difficulties, especially for Arthur and Jack who were living in the United States at the time. Both their passports listed their German father and Japanese mother. Given the fraught politics of the moment, Jack Golden burned all traces of his background on December 7, 1941.[332] Lena had fewer difficulties, because she was married to a Japanese and her language skills were native.

All of the Goldenberg children safely navigated the war and lived without any difficulty in the post-war world. They met once in Hawai'i in 1955 on a reunion trip. Both Lena and Tadamasa had children who maintained ties with the United States. And, in 1974, three of Arthur and Jack's children came to visit Nagasaki, the place of their parent's birth.[333]

As mentioned earlier, the ex-seaman James Hatter married a Japanese woman who helped him first with his tavern business and then with managing the Seamen's Home. The couple had one son, David, who worked for the U.S. Consulate in Nagasaki for a few years and then left for Kobe. There, he married a biracial woman, Mary Anna Kizue Kotani, whom he had known from his Nagasaki days. Mary Anna was the daughter of the British merchant Ary Van Ess and Kizue Kotani.[334] David Hatter was placed in an internment camp in Kobe by Japanese military officials. After the war, he worked for the U.S. Occupation forces in Osaka and then as a businessman in Tokyo.

Another example of children embracing a combination of Japanese and Western cultures within a single family were the offspring of the German merchant Carl Scriba (originally Sciba) and his Japanese wife Miwa Naitō. The couple married in 1899 and had five children: Johana, Karl, Adolph, Hugo and Elsa.[335] The eldest daughter, Johana, died in 1902 and was buried in the Western cemetery in Nagasaki. Both her father, who died in 1912, and her brother Hugo, who passed away in 1964, are buried next to her.

In 1925, Karl Scriba (born 1905), a graduate of Tozan, the Reformed Church mission school for boys in Nagasaki, went to California to study engineering.[336] There, he met and married a woman from Wisconsin. They went back to Japan for his work but immigrated to the United States after his retirement. For his part, Adolph Scriba was adopted into a Japanese family. He later married a Japanese woman and had a son.

One of the most colorful and cosmopolitan individuals ever to make Nagasaki his home was a Russian-born populist who gained and lost his American citizenship on at least three occasions. Born Nikolai Sudzilovskii in Mogilev, Russia, in December 1850, the man known as Nicholas Russel was a champion of individual liberty and freedom. He fought government oppression wherever he found it—and he found it everywhere. A disillusioned dreamer who never abandoned his college idealism, he confronted governments in Russia, Bulgaria, Romania, the United States, Hawai'i, China, Japan and the Philippines, all the while working as a physician, pharmacist, coffee plantation owner, scholar, politician and newspaper publisher.

In Japan, Russel had one son, who he called Dick (born 1907), by Tomo Takagi, a Japanese housekeeper from Shimabara. A second son, who he called Harry (born 1909), was born to a second housekeeper, Natsuno Ohara of Amakusa.[337] Both boys spoke English to their father, who did not use any Japanese. Another child, Flora, was born to Ohara in 1919, but there is some confusion as to whether Russel was the father or not. Ohara and the three children went with Russel to Tianjin, China in 1920. There, Russel died in 1930 in relative poverty and obscurity, a pensioner of the Russian government who earned his stipend based upon his lifelong contributions to socialist causes. Russel also had two daughters by his first Russian wife (whom he later divorced) and fathered his two illegitimate Japanese sons while married to his second Russian wife in Nagasaki.

Few couples contributed a larger number of biracial offspring to the cultural melting-pot of Nagasaki than the Italian Carlo Urso and his Japanese wife, Take Urso,[338] who gave birth to sixteen children in Nagasaki between 1889 and 1909. Of these, eight died in infancy and are buried in Western cemeteries there. Among her surviving children, Caterina married a Japanese man named Nakahara. She died in 1950 and is buried next to her parents (Carlo died at the family residence in 1918 and Take passed away in 1939) in Sakamoto International Cemetery in Nagasaki. Four of Take's other children (Angela, Eugenio, Maria and Camillo) lived into their seventies, and were also buried there between 1976 and 1980. The family has numerous descendants who continue to make Japan their home.

## Conclusion

With its unique history of international exchange and interaction, Nagasaki provided a relatively prosperous opportunity for interracial relationships both to occur and to succeed, and, as we have seen, some families stayed and thrived in its (mostly) accepting environment. Of course, exactly how the interracial partners treated each other and what expectations that they had for themselves and their children unfolded somewhat differently for each family. Given the economic trajectory of much of the period in question, when Nagasaki experienced brief stretches of intense trade activity, followed by years of economic stagnation, parents and especially children, often had to search beyond Nagasaki's famous harbor for opportunities to succeed. With the rise of militarism and the onset of World War II, biracial children were forced to downplay their differences from those around them and do their best to accentuate the commonalities that they shared with the general population.

## CHAPTER SIX

# JAPANESE INTERNATIONAL MARRIAGES (*KOKUSAI KEKKON*): A LONGUE DURÉE HISTORY, FROM EARLY MODERN JAPAN TO IMPERIAL JAPAN

ITSUKO KAMOTO (TR. NADIA KANAGAWA)

## Introduction

The term *kokusai kekkon* (international marriage) is a concept that originated in modern Japan. I have previously proposed two socio-historical conditions for such an international marriage to exist.[339] First, the marriage must be socially recognized, both within and outside of Japan, as part of a legitimate marriage system. Second, the marriage must be between one person who, prior to the marriage, has nationality of the modern nation-state of Japan, and another person who has nationality of a different modern nation-state.

Recently, there has been an increase in research related to *yosomono* (literally, "strangers" or "outsiders") in the Edo period, when the modern Japanese nation-state had yet to be established.[340] I am, however, uneasy with historians who use the modern term *konketsuji* ("mixed blood child") uncritically in writing about the early modern period. "Mixed blood children," like the term "international marriage," became commonly used around the beginning of the twentieth century.[341] This was also the time when the term "outsiders" was established, along with a national consensus on who the "us" was that could be distinguished from the outsider "them."

The early twentieth century was also the period when the ideas associated with Social Darwinism circulated on a global scale.[342] The English term "intermarriage" exists for marriages that transgress against social boundaries by bringing together those who, even if they hold the same nationality, are determined to be "strangers."

Each era has its own way of distinguishing strangers or outsiders, whether as aliens, foreigners, foreign nationals, or those from a territory beyond. In the case of Japan, "outsiders" in international marriages were those who did not have nationality in the modern nation-state of Japan. In particular, during the era of Japanese colonization, marriages between "people in the inner territory" and "people from the outer territory"—even if both held Japanese nationality were differentiated from marriages between two inner territory people. Just as the English term "intermarriage" applied to marriages between white and black people of the same nationality, so it was for marriages between people of the inner and outer territories of the Empire of Japan.

Broadly speaking, the history of international marriages can not only be tracked vis-à-vis the treatment of "others," but also vis-à-vis society's treatment of women who become a part of these relationships and the children born from such marriages. In this chapter, I will focus on how the "outsider" was defined in Japanese society as the foundation of a socio-historical analysis of international marriages and similar relationships from the Edo period through the Japanese colonial period. In particular, I will focus on how the notion of "us Japanese people" ("*tainai teki nihonjin*" as found in "family registers" or *koseki*: *ko* means household unit and *seki* means enrollment or membership) was developed in contradistinction to the notion of nationality (*kokuseki*, wherein the *koku* means state or nation), which could include those who were "Japanese *de jure* (*taigaiteki nihonjin*)" under colonial rule. Japanese colonization developed a system of treating "minority peoples" of the empire—such as Han Chinese or Korean people, island peoples such as the Taiwanese, or the Ainu—as "Japanese *de jure* (Japanese in legal sense)" who belonged neither to Japan's interior territory nor to the Yamato people (*Yamato minzoku*).

### International Marriage and Intermarriage

On March 14, 1873, the year after the Jinshin *Koseki* (Family Registration), the Grand Council of State issued Edict 103. Also known as the Regulations on Japanese-Foreigner Marriage, this was the first Japanese law to regulate international marriage, although the term "international marriage" was not used. Approximately 10 years later, Yoshio Takahashi would translate the English term intermarriage as *zakkon* (literally "miscellaneous" or "mixed marriage") in his *Nihon jinshū kairyoron* (*Thesis on Improvement of the Japanese Race*). Takahashi argued that in order to improve the Japanese race, Japanese men should establish mixed marriages with White women from advanced civilizations and produce mixed-race descendants.

Clara Whitney, a 14-year-old American girl who had come to Japan, offers an opinion on this kind of intermarriage that could be said to be representative of white American society at the time. Clara's diary from the day describes her feelings on meeting an English woman who was married to a Japanese man.

### On Friday, December 17, 1875

The lady must have been anxious for a husband. If she could not find one among the brave, handsome, and gay of her country or mine, there might have been some excuse, but I did not ask the circumstances under which the member of two nations, so different in every way, married, but hastened to change the subject, for it disgusted me that a member of the Anglo-Saxon race should contrive such intimate relations with a Mongolian. Still this is not as bad as the *American*, yes *American* (I blush to write it) girl, blue-eyed, goldhaired, who mated with a Chinaman. Yes, pigtail, almond eye and all complete. Disgraceful. It is painful to dwell upon, so I dismiss the subject.[343]

The Western notion of intermarriage focused on "Whiteness" being mixed with something else. For a young American like Clara, it was a question of what would be mixed with the White (race), Anglo-Saxon (ethnicity), and Protestant (religion). If each of these social categories matched in a marriage between an American person and English person whose only difference was nationality, Clara likely would not have found it so "disgraceful." But in this case, even continuing to talk about marriage to a "Yellow," Mongolian, Buddhist (or Shinto) Japanese person was repugnant to her. At this time, Clara could hardly have dreamed that she would one day marry Umetarō Kaji, the child of Kaishū Katsu and his mistress.

In some states in America, anti-miscegenation laws had been enacted and intermarriage was defined as a "marriage of persons deriving from those different in-groups and out-groups other than the family that are culturally conceived as relevant to the choice of a spouse."[344] In American intermarriage, even people of the same nationality were not accepted as having a legitimate marriage if they were of a different race. Thus the social boundaries in American intermarriage were different from those in Japanese international marriage.

Japan's legal framework, as embodied in Edict 103, permitted marriages with foreigners holding other nationalities regardless of race, ethnicity, and religion. Moreover, the Meiji government had only just begun the process of nation building and did not yet have either the first socio-historical condition of international marriage (the Civil Code), nor the second (the Constitution and Nationality Act), and the determination of one's status as a Japanese person was regulated through the marriage system. The enactment of the Constitution and Nationality Act would not come until a quarter of a century later; thus Edict 103 was in effect until the revision of the unequal treaties were signed with Western nations following the opening of Japan. What made this possible? The answer lies in the operation of social mechanisms that I will refer to as "the household (*ie no hako*, i.e., container of household)" and "the ship (*fune no hako*, i.e., container of ship)."

**Closing the Country: The Formation of the Framework of "the Household"**

The *Nippo Jisho* (Portuguese: *Vocabulario da Lingoa de Iapam com a declaração em Portugues*, English: *Japanese-Portuguese Dictionary*) was published in the first year of the Edo period (1603). Though it had entries for marriage and mixed residence, it did not have entries for "mixed child" (*ainoko*), "mixed blood" (*konketsu*) or "international marriage" (*kokusai kekkon*). What it did have were entries for "seed" (*tane*) and "seed child" (read *xuji* in Chinese, according to the entry, as *tane* in Japanese), with a further explanation of the phrase "*tane ga kawaru*" that referred to a situation "when two or more children have the same mother but different fathers." In this case, "seed" represents bloodline and lineage. In a society that values lineage, a family with children who had different fathers will be faced with the important question of whose "seed" each child came from. As most of the "foreigners" who came to Japan were men, it is likely that their "seed" was discernible at a glance. Because there were women who had relationships and children with foreign men but later remarried local men, it is apparent that, at least until the early Edo period in the areas of Nagasaki and Hirado, there was no aversion to women who had relations with foreign men.[345]

Policy makers did not prohibit marriages between Japanese people and "outsiders" until the regulations that closed off Japan gained momentum; Gary Leupp, both in this volume and elsewhere, has described the government approach at that time as generally laissez-faire.[346] From a different vantage point, Yasunori Arano has divided long-term intimate relationships between European men and Japanese women in the Edo period into the following four types:

1) marriage, 2) service as a concubine, 3) female kabuki entertainers, and 4) prostitution. However, exactly what constituted marriage in the early modern period varied by time, region, and status, and applying the modern state's notion of marriage to this period is not meaningful. From the perspective of the Western men, many relationships with Japanese women were no more than "interracial intimacy" as Leupp has termed it.[347]

Although there were no "modern" marriages, there were children who were born of intimate relationships with "outsiders." It was in 1636, when the closing of the country began, that the children who are described as "seeds" in Nishikawa Joken's *Jagatara bumi* and their parents were forcibly sent away to Macao.[348] Three years later, eleven people, including Oharu of Jakarta (Jagatara Oharu), the well-known mixed-race Japanese woman, drifted from there to Jakarta. However, the policy of expelling these children and their parents was replaced by policies legislating how such children should be raised during the period of Japan's isolation.

From a socio-historical perspective, the closed-country policies brought a number of important changes to these intimate relationships. First, under the closed-country policies, both the men and women in these relationships and the children born of them were expelled. Second, the *bakufu* limited the movements of foreign men, and while they permitted relationships with prostitutes (*yūjo*), they were not permitted to have ordinary Japanese women or prostitutes as "wives." Third, the *bakufu* shifted to a policy that emphasized how "seeds" (i.e., mixed children) should be raised in 1715. Children born to prostitutes were to be raised by their mothers as Japanese. This was because there were policies prohibiting Japanese people from traveling across the seas during the period of Japan's isolation. Thus, it was impossible to take these mixed race children abroad, regardless of the wishes of their foreign fathers. Fourth, policies in the period of isolation were marked by fear of Christianity, which led to the systematization of the religious affiliation registry (*shūmonchō*) that would become the basis for the framework that took the "household" unit as foundational to the organization of society. Finally, with the eventual loosening of the closed country policies, there was a need for the government to develop some means of certifying to the external world that someone was Japanese.

In the Kan'ei era (particularly during the 1630s), the Tokugawa bakufu issued a series of so-called Closed Country Edicts one after another. In the Nagasaki area, people were required to step on images of Jesus and Mary to test whether or not they were Christian (a process known as *fumi-e*, literally "stepping on images"). At the same time, religious affiliation registries were created with the goal of eliminating Christianity.

As the fear of Christianity, which was the original reason for creating the registries, faded, the temple parishioner system (*danka seido*), in which wives who belonged to one temple would join the temple of their husbands, was created. Letters of temple transfer are generally believed to have been the model for transfers of legal domicile in later times. However, Akira Hayami, a leading scholar of historical population studies and an expert on Tokugawa era economic history, has criticized the idea that there is a close relationship between these religious affiliation registries and the later Meiji government's establishment of the Jinshin family registries.[349] He argues that there were some domains that did not produce religious affiliation registries and that there was regional variation in their production, such that these registries could not have been used to manage the people of an "entire nation."

There are many unresolved debates within the field of historical population studies as to when exactly the household system was established. Nevertheless, I would like to argue that the establishment of the apparatus that I call the "household" framework (*ie no hako*) was initiated with the production of the religious affiliation registries during the period of Japan's isolation. In other words, "Japanese" could not be "Christian" during this period and by the regular certification of "Japanese" people as members of Buddhist temple parishes, this system of religious affiliation identification also served as a mechanism for defining who belonged to a properly constituted "household" in Japan. This household framework would later constitute the boundaries of who constituted the "people of Japan" in the form of the so-called Jinshin *koseki* (family registries) of the Meiji period. With the end of the period of Japan's isolation, the original purpose of the religious affiliation registries disappeared as the practice of Christianity was permitted again. These registries thus came to act as censuses.

During the period of Japan's isolation, government policies that affected relationships between Japanese and "outsiders" primarily focused on the assignment of prostitutes to serve "outsiders." Prostitutes held licenses similar to work permits (*kansatsu*), and were dispatched to designated "outsiders."[350] Since it was clear who had been designated which prostitute, it was even possible to specify the paternity of any children. The only women who could frequent Dejima, where the Dutch trading post was located, and the Chinese Residences also in Nagasaki, were prostitutes. However, there was no societal recognition that these prostitutes might become the official wives of foreign men.

One example of a child born in such circumstances is "O-Ine of Holland" (for more on Ine, see Ellen Nakamura's chapter in this volume), born to Philipp Franz von Siebold and a prostitute of the Maruyama district named Taki. An order from the Nagasaki Magistrate dispatched to Maruyama and Yoriai-machi in 1715 stated: "children of Chinese and Dutch should not be given coarse upbringings," or in other words, children born of relationships between foreign men and prostitutes would be raised as Japanese by their mothers. In 1829, as a result of the so-called "Siebold incident," Ine's father was permanently expelled from Japan, and was unable to bring his beloved daughter home with him when he left. Overseas travel was forbidden during the period of isolation, and no Japanese person could cross the seas.

As the Meiji government sought to establish a modern nation, it created the Jinshin family registries. These registries were the systematized, modern form of the "household framework" that would govern who was *de facto* Japanese and would control an "entire nation" regardless of class. But as the new modern nation state developed and the old "closed country" order disintegrated, a new category of Japanese people who could not be recognized domestically through the household framework emerged.

**The "Opening" of the Country: The Creation of the "Ship" Framework**
Just as the construction of large-scale ships that were capable of sailing across the seas was prohibited during the period of Japan's isolation, boarding a ship and traveling overseas was similarly strictly forbidden. Where once only the flags of the various Japanese domains flew on ships traveling the coastal waters of Japan, the opening of Japan saw the arrival of vessels flying the flags of a variety of countries, and in 1854 it became necessary to establish a symbol for all Japanese ships. A sun on a white background was chosen.[351] In 1863 it was further declared that in the interest of national security: "For warships, a sun on a white background will be the national symbol." In this way, the *hinomaru* (the red sun on a white background) went from being a Japanese shipping symbol to functioning as a national flag. The "ship" framework for distinguishing between insiders and outsiders was also directly connected to another critical part of nation building, namely, the question of how far Japanese territory extended. In English, the word "nationality," which can signify the legal rights of belonging

to a particular nation, ship registration, and/or ethnicity is used in its international sense, while "citizenship" is as a term within the domestic realm as a marker of belonging. Establishing the use of the *hinomaru* to represent ships registered to Japan can thus be said to closely linked to the opening of the country after centuries of isolation and to a new era when the crossing of the seas by ship engendered new possibilities and delimitations on relationships between insiders and outsiders.

Under the overseas travel prohibition of the Edo period there was no need for passports, but with the dissolution of the closed country policies, the ban on overseas travel was lifted. According to Tsunekichi Yoshida, the reasons for lifting the ban began with requests from Westerners who had employed Japanese servants and wanted these servants to continue to serve them as they traveled to other ports in Japan. This then expanded to permits for travel to foreign ports and little by little the entire ban on overseas travel fell apart.[352] The first passports were given to Namigorō Sumidagawa's foreigner-employed troupe of acrobats.[353] The passports served as an international form of identification that certified that one was a Japanese person while overseas. The idea of Japanese people in the passports, which was authorized or issued by Japanese central government, emerged together with the new "ship" framework. The passport represented the notion that the modern nation state of Japan would provide nationality to all Japanese persons. This was a development in sharp contrast to the Edo-period status system where one's status as a samurai, merchant, etc., played a critical role in one's place in each domain. In this new era, a Japanese person traveling internationally had to have a status that was not bound by the old status system. It would be this recognition as a "Japanese" in the international sphere that would come to have meaning in new marriages to "outsiders."

Therefore, by the early Meiji period, these two frameworks of the "household" and the "ship" were already influencing the possibility of "international marriages," well before Japanese society had legally systematized either family registries or nationality law.

### The Napoleonic Code and Edict 103

After the opening of Japan, in 1862 the consulates of various foreign governments were notified that children of foreign fathers would henceforth be considered "foreign persons" in contrast to previous policies.[354] However, this proclamation was met with resistance from many countries and likely had little effect internationally. More significant for mixed roots children were the revisions to the family registry system and how it treated the broader category of "illegitimate children" (*shiseiji*, literally "private children"), such as those born to prostitutes. The Illegitimate Children Act was announced only two months before Edict 103 (the Regulations on Japanese-Foreigner Marriage), and stated that children born to mothers who were not an official wife or concubine would be added to their mother's registry.[355] Ultimately, this would also apply to those children born to foreign men and Japanese women (particularly prostitutes) who were not part of an official marriage. In 1872, as the Jinshin family registries were launched, the Maria Luz Incident led to the Emancipation Decree for Prostitutes.[356] The emancipation of prostitutes was an important event in opening a path towards becoming an official wife for Japanese women who had relationships with foreign men.

It was in this period that the British consulate made two inquiries related to international marriages. It was a result of these inquiries that the Grand Council of State Edict 103 was issued on March 14, 1873. How was it possible to enact this law on international marriages without a Constitution, a Civil Code, or a Nationality Act? The answer lies in the fact that the law relied on an imitation of the recently translated Napoleonic Code.

In the Napoleonic Code, established at the beginning of the 1800s, the principle was that married couples shared same nationality. The law prioritized the paternal bloodline, and thus wives switched to their husbands' nationality upon marriage and children inherited the nationality of their fathers. However, Edict 103 added a new section on adopted foreign son-in-laws that was not in the Napoleonic code. This part of the law only applied to foreign men who took part in Japanese *engumi* customs such as the adoption of a son-in-law, or, in a case where the adoptive parents-in-law had died, becoming an "incoming husband (*nyūfu*)" who took his wife's name and joined her family. In such a relationship, the adopted foreign son-in-law would be included in the "household" framework of his Japanese wife. Because he was then considered to have received "the status of being Japanese (*nihonjin taruno bungen*)," he would at the same time be included in the Japanese "ship" framework.

Two examples of this kind of adoption of Japaneseness include the well-known writer Lafcadio Hearn, who had an Irish father and Greek mother, becoming Yakumo Koizumi and the Australian-born professional storyteller (*rakugoka*) Henry James Black[357] (also known as Kairakutei Black I and Black Ishii). In Black's case, he entered Japaneseness by pledging loyalty to the Emperor in a written oath, and despite his known homosexuality, his marriage into his wife's family was permitted.[358] As in Hearn's case, these foreign husbands were afforded their wives' nationality and their children would inherit their mothers' nationality—an extremely unusual version of the legal principle.

Even though it took the Napoleonic Code as a model, Japanese law was not necessarily based on the principle of prioritizing the patriline. Instead, it was based on a principle of "*bungen* (social status or standing)" that prioritized the framework of the "*ie* (household)."[359] By moving from one household to another and thereby gaining the position of daughter- or son-in-law, it was possible also to provide "outsiders" with the status of being Japanese. In contrast to the ideas of nationality as deriving from *jus soli* (right of the soil) and *jus sanguinis* (right of the blood), we might call this the right of "*bungen*"; the status shift that occur when becoming a bride or an adopted son-in-law, which are shifts between *koseki*, "family registries" as inseparable from the simultaneous shifts between *kokuseki*, "nationalities" that constitute acquisition of the status of being Japanese.

The reason that the Meiji government could enact Edict 103 before there was a Constitution, a Civil Code, a Nationality Law, or a Naturalization Law, was that the "household" and "ship" frameworks already existed. However, the "ship" framework that certified people as Japanese on an international stage and the "household" framework that certified people as Japanese within the domestic Japanese sphere increasingly were interlocked. Therefore, one could both transfer or lose Japaneseness through movement between "household" or "ship" frameworks.

The reality of international marriage was what taught the Meiji government that it would be necessary to separate these two apparatuses and systematize them into *koseki* (family registry) law and *kokuseki* (nationality) law. In order to achieve parity with other civilized nations, the laws regulating transfer in and out of "households" would have to reflect a monogamous marriage system. The Brinkley trial would test exactly this point – whether the international marriages recognized by the Meiji government were up to the standards of civilized nations. The King Kiku Kingdon case would go even further, and force the Meiji government to deal with the question of how to determine the nationality of an "illegitimate" child born before the parents took part in a modern marriage. Thus the necessity of differentiating between family registry laws and nationality law became imperative for the new Meiji government.

In the first case, Francis Brinkley brought suit against the British Attorney General in 1890. The focus of the trial was on whether or not a marriage recognized under Japanese law was a Christian (i.e., monogamous) marriage or not. Brinkley's marriage to Yasu Tanaka was authorized under Edict 103.[360] However, as the Meiji government had not yet enacted a civil code at the time of his suit, the only answer they could give was that notification of the transfer and record of household registration was what determined the presence or absence of a legal marriage. Fortunately, "concubines" had been removed from the law eight years prior to this suit. In 1889, the year before the suit was brought, the Meiji Constitution (the Constitution of the Empire of Japan) had been promulgated. Thus, the British court made the following statement: "We all know that Japan has long taken its place among civilised nations, whose forms and laws and ceremonies are not to be treated as on the same footing with those of the Baralong tribe of South Africa."[361] Here, the British court acknowledged Japan as a civilized nation and Japanese marriages as legitimate, even though they were not Christian. The key point of contention was whether marriages recognized in Japan were monogamous (i.e., equivalent to Christian marriages) or not. The Brinkley trial revealed that prior marriages recognized under Edict 103 might have been considered invalid by foreign states. In other words, it revealed that women who had forfeited "the status of being Japanese" might have been left stateless.

Another legal case that illustrates the status of mixed roots Japanese of that time is that of King Kiku Kingdon. A document titled "The matter of reinstating nationality to King Kiku, child of N.P. Kingdon, a British resident of Yokohama, and Utagawa Mura of Japan[362]" includes exchanges between the Ministry of Justice, Ministry of Foreign Affairs, and Ministry of Home Affairs, as well as various offices on the British side. The Meiji government studied this case, which dealt with a situation in which a child was born in a foreign settlement protected by unequal treaties at the end of Edo period, and only after his birth did his parents became part of an "international marriage," and posed the question of which society this child should be recognized as belonging to.

First, let us look at the letters sent to the Kanagawa Prefectural Governor and Minister of Foreign Affairs by the British Ambassador and Consul. A letter was sent to the Kanagawa Prefectural Governor from British Consul Enslis on September 20, 1889, which notes the litigant: "A British subject, Mr. N. P. Kingdon having applied to have his son King Kiku Kingdon requested as being under British protection." The letter goes on, "I propose allowing him to do so as in view of his having in 1884 contracted a marriage with Utagawa

Mura, the mother of King Kiku Kingdon."

King's British father, Nicholas Philip Kingdon, was influential among people living in the foreign settlement and played a leading role in organizing opposition to the revision of the unequal treaties in 1890. In response to the father's request that his son be taken under "British protection," the British consul wrote that by marrying Kingdon, King's Japanese mother could be admitted to "British protection" and he intended to give his approval to the request, but he wanted to check if there was any objection from the Japanese side.[363]

Utagawa Mura was born in 1847, the sister of the *ukiyoe* master Utagawa Kunitsuru II, and gave birth to King before she was 20 years old. King was born in the foreigner settlement in 1866, at the end of the Edo period. In the late Edo period, the foreigners living in the settlements established in newly opened ports like Yokohama and Kobe were protected by the extraterritoriality agreements in the unequal treaties. King's parents received permission from the Meiji government to marry on April 28, 1884, just over 10 years after the 1873 proclamation of Edict 103. King would have been 18 years old at the time of their marriage. The beginning of the council for the revision of the treaties was in 1882, two years before the Kingdons submitted their "Petition to Marry a Foreigner," and they likely wanted to confirm the status of mother and son after the revision of the treaties.

King's father submitted applications not only to the British Consul in Yokohama, but also to the Japanese Ministry of Foreign Affairs. This we know from a letter dated October 1, 1889 sent by the British ambassador, Hugh Fraser, to the Japanese minister of Foreign Affairs, Shigenobu Ōkuma:

> I have received from Her Majesty's Principal Secretary of State Foreign Affairs copies of a correspondence which has passed between the Foreign Office in London and Mr. N.P. Kingdon a British Merchant residing in Yokohama relative to the nationality of Mr. Kingdon's son Mr. King Kiku Kingdon.
>
> It appears that the latter was born in Yokohama in 1866, his mother being a Japanese subject who was not at the time of his birth married to his father. Subsequently, however, his mother was married to Mr. Kingdon in accordance with the required formalities the

marriage being registered in the British Consulate at Yokohama. Mrs. Kingdon thus became a British subject, but the son Mr. King Kiku Kingdon having been born out of wedlock, could not by this marriage acquire the nationality of his parents.

Under these circumstances, Mr. King Kiku Kingdon applied to the Kencho Authorities in Yokohama on the subject of his nationality, and was informed by them that in consequence of his mother being no longer registered as a Japanese subject he could not be registered as such himself but was simply in the position of an alien, and that he could only become a Japanese subject by adoption.

I am accordingly instructed by Lord Salisbury to enquire officially from Your Excellency whether the Japanese Government claim Mr. King Kiku Kingdon as a Japanese subject. [...][364]

Clearly, British Consul Enslis' plan and the views of British Ambassador Fraser differed. King had been born to a mother who was not officially married. Fraser gives the opinion—directly opposite to that of Enslis—that due to the circumstances of the marriage, it was not possible for King to acquire the nationality of his parents. We can also see that in their response to British Consul Enslis's query, the Kanagawa Prefectural Office had replied that with the official marriage of his parents, King was no longer Japanese. Fraser goes on to say that Foreign Minister Salisbury also would like to confirm with the Japanese government whether or not King was Japanese.

On the Japanese side, the Ministry of Foreign Affairs and Ministry of Home Affairs clashed, and the Ministry of Justice had to intervene. The Ministry of Foreign Affairs argued that the "illegitimate child" of a foreign father and Japanese mother should be entered into the household of the Japanese mother. However, they stressed that had the parents been officially married, their child would be legitimate and also that the mother would have transferred to her foreign husband's nationality and lost the status of being Japanese due to her "international marriage." So as to the official marriage of his parents, the illegitimate child would become legitimate and acquire his father's nationality. Here, we can see how the "household" framework comes to be nested within the "ship" framework.

On the other hand, the opinion of the Ministry of Home Affairs was that moving from being an "illegitimate" to a "legitimate" child was a change of status, and thus nothing more than a movement within the "household" framework. Because a change of nationality was a change in the "ship" framework (i.e., recognition of status on an international stage), they argued that this should be thought of as a different issue. In other words, the Ministry of Home Affairs suggested that a distinction between nationality (*kokuseki*) and household registration (*koseki*) was necessary.

At this point, the Ministry of Foreign Affairs argument had been formed by Shūzō Aoki, Vice-Minister at this time and later Minister of Foreign Affairs. Aoki, himself part of an international marriage with a German woman, saw through the logic of the British side's distinction between "British protection" and "British nationality." The details must be omitted, but it was Aoki who grasped how far Japanese laws were from those of the so-called civilized nations. Fraser asked Aoki only two questions, but Aoki felt it necessary to answer on five different counts and accordingly wrote to the minister of justice, requesting a response on the points below.

First, "What is the law of the Japanese Empire on these subjects and where is it to be found?" This was one of Fraser's questions, and it struck a nerve. At a time in which there was no Civil Code, the only answer that could be given was that the notification of transfer of the household registration was a legal marriage. The second question was regarding the laws on legitimate and illegitimate children. The Ministry of Justice response was that concubines had no legal status.[365] Undoubtedly the British side would have been surprised at this reply. Third, was it possible, even if a child was "illegitimate" at the time of birth, for him or her to become legitimate if the parents subsequently married (if not, was this possible in any other circumstances)? The reply to this query was a blatant dodge, stating only that children born to concubines recorded in the household register and children born to those who were not registered but whose fathers later recognized them were both referred to with the term "miscellaneous children" (*shoshi*). The fourth question was about where one could look for the laws regulating these issues, as no Civil Code had been established. The response was that a compilation of all the declarations of the Grand Council of State existed. Finally, in the case that an "illegitimate child" was born to a mother who was Japanese at the time of the child's birth and that the parents of the child married after the child was born, what were the Japanese state's thoughts on the circumstances in which an "illegitimate child" could retain the status of being a subject of Japan? The Minister of Justice's response was that if Kingdon's father had been French, then under French law the imperial government would naturally reach the same decision regarding King Kiku Kingdon, even if he was a legitimate child. In short, the Meiji government would also conclude that he was a Japanese subject. There was a postscript to this reply, noting that all this might change as there was "a draft of the Civil Code currently being compiled," that had not been promulgated after all.

The Meiji government re-registered King into his mother's side family registration because he had been revealed to be without registration and stateless. Then, her relatives made a request to transfer registration to Great Britain. After her "international marriage" was recognized by the Meiji government, King's mother lost not only the status of being Japanese but also had her name removed from her family register. It is not clear whether Utagawa Mura became a British citizen or not. We do not know this because the so-called Directives of the Three Ministries issued on April 5, 1890, approximately two months after the Brinkley trial, do not contain even a single reference to the Brinkley case, which centered on the question of whether Japanese women who lost their legal status as a Japanese person by marrying a foreigner might be left stateless.

The 1890 Directives of the Three Ministries were issued by the Minister of Home Affairs, Aritomo Yamagata; the Minister of Justice, Akiyoshi Yamada; and the afore-mentioned Minister of Foreign Affairs, Shūzō Aoki. The problem of "illegitimate children" between Japanese people and foreigners had previously been addressed in the 1873 so-called Illegitimate Children Act. The children would, without exception, be entered into the mother's registry. If the "illegitimate child" had been acknowledged by the foreign father as being his, or, if the father and mother had gotten married through proper procedures and the child was to be considered legitimate and allowed to gain foreign nationality, documentation of the consent of the mother and maternal relatives, as well as that of the child if they were of age, would have to be submitted through the appropriate Japanese office and receive authorization from the Japanese government. Based on this legal premise, the Kingdons had already applied for King's nationality to the Japanese Foreign Ministry. They had also submitted their request to the Meiji government to register him as a British person. Having received it, the Meiji government granted the request to transfer registration, and issued a directive stating that the transfer of King's registration from the Empire of Japan to the British Empire had been authorized.

However, the British government then made the decision that "Mr. King Kiku Kingdon is not a British subject in the eye of the law of England." The reason given was that he was an illegitimate child born before his parents entered into an official marriage. Since the British side would not grant British nationality, the Japanese responded by saying: "We rescind the directive of last year regarding the registration transfer of this person and admit him into the registries of this state." Thus ended the matter of reinstating Japanese nationality to King Kiku, which had lasted approximately six years from the time of his parents' marriage.

It was this legal case that highlighted the complexities involved in international marriage that prompted the Ministry of Justice to establish a Civil Code and Nationality Law in addition to the household registration laws. In other words, although the new government could see how transferring persons between "households" could work as a system domestically, when it came to transferring persons across the sea through various "ship" frameworks, there was a need for new laws that would permit transfers of nationality.

The Civil Code of the Empire of Japan was eventually enacted in 1898, and legal guideposts regarding private matters such as the principle that "divorce is governed by the law of the husband's state" were established. These legal precedents were in effect until they were revised nearly a century later in 1989. In 1899, the Nationality Act was proclaimed, and in the same year the Treaty of Amity and Commerce with the British was concluded (incidentally, it was Shūzō Aoki who signed the treaty for Japan). Japan, victorious in the two foreign wars that bracketed the beginning of the 20th century—the Russo-Japanese and Sino-Japanese wars—and successful in revising the unequal treaties, began to take pride in having joined the club of civilized nations. But how would they handle marriages to "outsiders" in the various colonial territories they had acquired?

**Inclusion and Exclusion: The Expansion of the Colonies and Intermarriage between Japanese and Koreans**

During the interwar years, determining whether a ship belonged to an ally or enemy depended on the nationality of a ship's registration. As Japan continued the process of nation building and colonized the Korean peninsula, Taiwan, and southern portions of Sakhalin islands, the territory included under the Japanese "ship" framework expanded and an era in which Japan governed a variety of different ethnicities began. The various peoples of the areas now subsumed in the Japanese "ship" framework had to be recognized as Japanese on the international stage. As Eiji Oguma has noted, household registries were used to exclude people, while nationality was used to include them[366]. Thus, in governing the various ethnicities that fell within Japan's expanded zone, the "ship" framework was used to include new members, while the "household" framework was simultaneously used to exclude them. The principle that made this differentiation in usage possible closely resembled the rules of Edict 103 (the Regulations on Japanese-Foreigner Marriage).

The terminology of intermarriage reveals that real distinctions were made between "inner-territory" Japan and the "outer-territory" colonies. Marriages between inner-territory Japanese people and outer-territory people of the Korean peninsula were called *naisen kekkon* (Japanese-Korean marriage), and those to Taiwanese people were called *naitai kyōkon*[367] (Japanese-Taiwanese marriage). Here, I will limit my examination to Japanese-Korean marriages.

According to Yong-dal Kim, who has examined changes in the legal system alongside statistics on Japanese-Korean marriages, 90% of these marriages took place in Japan, with fewer than 10% taking place on the Korean peninsula.[368] The basic principles of Edict 103 were adopted for transfers of household registries between inner and outer territories. The major difference was that Edict 103 had not conceived of a situation in which a Japanese man would be adopted as the son-in-law of his foreign wife's family (i.e., that a Japanese man would forfeit "the status of being Japanese"). Rules for intermarriages, however, enabled both Japanese men and Korean men to become adopted sons-in-law or adopted husbands.

Meanwhile, on the Korean peninsula, adoption of non-relatives was not normally permitted. Thus, it would have seemed impossible for a Korean man to enter the "household" of an inner-territory Japanese woman as an adopted son-in-law or incoming husband, or for a Japanese man to enter the "household" of a Korean woman as an adopted son-in-law or incoming husband. Even if it was possible to imagine a situation in which a Japanese man was adopted as a son-in-law in a Korean woman's family (i.e., a marriage in which a man from the colonizer class became the adopted husband in a colonized status household), such a marriage would be particularly unlikely to actually occur. In fact, there are only three instances of such marriages. By contrast, there are many cases of marriages in Japan in which Korean men entered the "households" of inner-territory Japanese women as adopted sons-in-law or adopted husbands. What explains this difference?

The notion of a household registry was originally imported from China in the classical age. However, the modern household registration of the Meiji period and afterwards was based on rules unique to Japan. The rules for China, Taiwan, and the Korean peninsula's families and relations were different from domestic Japanese rules, which prioritized the "household," and therefore the outer territories of the colony could not compile household registries by the same rules as the inner territories. The household registries created were referred to as "outer territory household registries" (*gaichi seki*) or "ethnic registries" (*minzoku seki*), implying that the Japanese government viewed those in newly-acquired Japanese territories as a part of Japan, but also understood that part of Japan to be constituted of members of a different "ethnic" grouping.

It was in the Meiji period that Japanese women came to take the lineage name (*uji*) of the "household" into which they had married. But in Korea, Taiwan, and China, one's name was not part of the household. Instead, in those territories, one's surname (*sei*), which preserved the paternal bloodline, was prioritized. In a truly patrilineal system, a woman would not take her husband's surname. Of course, their children would have the father's surname. In Japan, if there were three generations living together, everyone in the house would take the lineage name (*uji*) of that household. In contrast, on the Korean peninsula, a man's mother had a different surname than he did and his wife would also have a different surname, so there might be people with three different surnames living together in the same house. Furthermore, on the Korean peninsula there was, in principle, no adoption of non-relatives (i.e., those of different surnames). It was possible to adopt those of the same surname—nephews, for example, if a younger brother had several sons. Sharing a surname and birthplace registration (*honkan*) meant being of the same clan, and the principle of surname and registration exogamy (*dōsei dōhon fukon*) lasted until quite recently in Korea.

The genealogies in the Jinshin household registries defined who was considered "Japanese" within the domestic realm and these functioned as inner-territory household registries. The colonies (or outer territories) did not have the same household framework rules as the inner territory. Instead, the outer territory or ethnic registries were governed by the customs of the each outer territory. Thus while the new framework of the Japanese "ship" had expanded, non-Japanese peoples (*iminzoku*) would be governed through the construction of households with different rules for household registries. At the same time, in order to recognize Japanese-Korean marriages and Japanese-Taiwanese marriages as legitimate, it became necessary to adjust and unify some laws. Accordingly, in 1918, the Common Law (*Kyōtsū hō*) was established. Southern Karafuto had been deemed part of the inner territories, and thus the areas in which variant laws existed were: the inner territories, Korea, Taiwan, Guandong, and the South Pacific Mandate. Article 3 of the Common Law stated that a person entering a household (*ie*) in one area would have to leave their former household (*ie*) from another area. At the same time that these people were being included as subjects of the Empire of Japan on the international stage, they were being domestically excluded through the discriminatory use of the framework of the "household." Just as Great Britain had differentiated between British nationals and people under British protection, the Meiji government may have seen colonial subjects as "internationally Japanese," i.e., under Japanese protection, but they were not treated as equal to other subjects domestically. That said, it was still possible to become a "*de facto* Japanese national" if one entered an inner-territory "household" as a son- or daughter-in-law.

If they had been seriously considering the promotion of Japanese-Korean marriages, then the infamous policy that forced Koreans to take Japanese names (*sōshi kaimei*) would likely have been implemented at the same time as the Common Law. However, the name change policy was implemented over twenty years later, in 1941. Furthermore, if the policy was just focused on taking Japanese-style surnames and personal names, they could have called it "changing names and changing surnames" (*kaisei kaimei*). So why was the policy termed *sōshi kaimei* (literally "creating a lineage (*uji*), changing surname")? The answer is that the Japanese-style households depended on the creation of a lineage (*uji*). The only legitimate way to take a Japanese-style lineage name without "creating a family name and changing surname" was to enter an inner-territory household through a Japanese-Korean marriage. In governing the colonies, the Japanese government was concerned that Japanese-Korean marriages would lead to an inability to distinguish between inner-territory people and those who were originally Korean.[369]

Including people as "internationally Japanese" while excluding them from being "domestically Japanese" was a way of separating and marking Japanese-Korean and Japanese-Taiwanese marriages as culturally and societally undesirable intermarriages. In the outer territories the Japanese government pretended to be respectful of old customs while actually systematizing the separation between inner and outer territory household registries.[370]

## Intermarriage as a Strategy for Survival

From around 1938, as the Sino-Japanese war gained momentum, the number of Japanese-Korean marriages in the inner territories in which Korean men became incoming husbands or adopted sons-in-law to Japanese women increased rapidly. The reason that there were particularly large numbers of incoming husbands likely lies in the advantages these marriages held for Korean men (rather than the existence of numerous Japanese women whose parents wanted to adopt a son-in-law). However, entering an inner-territory household registry meant that these men, like all inner-territory men, ran the risk of being conscripted. As with the "creating a lineage, changing surname" policy, the legal system for conscription of colonial subjects was not established until near the end of colonial rule, but the Empire of Japan did use a sort of draft system to exploit the labor of colonial peoples. Many Korean men were drafted and forcibly transported to the coalmines of Hokkaido, Kyushu, and the Sakhalin islands, and made to work for low wages or no pay. Shūko Takeshita describes two instances of "marriage to Japanese women as a means of survival." One man, who was forced to work in poor conditions in a coalmine, said that he thought: "If I marry a Japanese woman not only will I survive, but also I will be trusted." According to another man, "I managed to marry a Japanese woman who worked at the barracks, and then I received the same wages as a Japanese person."[371] The odds are high that men were becoming incoming husbands or adopted sons-in-law either as a means of survival or to receive the same wages as a Japanese person.

Whether in the inner or outer territories, it was necessary for women to rely on men for survival. There were cases of Japanese-Korean marriage in which it was only after the marriage took place that it became known that the husband was not Japanese, but there are also many cases in which women became estranged from their parents because they knowingly married Korean men. Just after the San Francisco Peace Treaty was signed in 1951, inner-territory women who married Korean men forfeited their inner territory household registries and were placed under the Japanese governmental category of Korean (Chōsen) registries in Japan. There were also Japanese wives who only discovered when they "returned" to Korea with Korean men that theirs was only a common-law marriage.[372] Some of them were stateless whilst living in South Korea.

There are also cases in which boys from the Korean peninsula were adopted as a way of pro-actively making up for the scarcity of labor in the inner territories. According to the *Osaka Asahi* of March 26, 1935, families from a fishing village outside of Hagi City in Yamaguchi Prefecture who were without sons were going to Korea "where many people received children, returned home, and raised them as adoptees, naturally leading to many Japanese-Korean marriages."[373] These young Korean men who were raised from a young age to be fishermen were completely assimilated into the customs of their Japanese villages, and the article concluded that they were "uniting in a lovely Japanese-Korean harmony." On the Korean peninsula, eldest sons were prioritized, but second and third sons were sometimes given up for adoption.

In these ways, the people of the inner territory strategically adopted Korean sons or sons-in-law and men from the Korean peninsula made use of marriage rules that would be inconceivable in colonial Korea as strategies for survival.

**Conclusion**
While the "household" remains the primary framework for demonstrating one's belonging and status as a Japanese, modern Japan still has one kind of intermarriage in which there is a barrier to the transfer of persons from one household to another; namely marriage to a member of the Japanese imperial family, which has no family registry (*koseki*). Women of the imperial family join a family registry for the first time if they marry a Japanese subject and take his surname. The current Crown Prince's younger sister, Sayako Kuroda, is one example. Even if a Japanese royal like Kuroda bore a son, regardless of whether the son was born in or outside of Japan, he would have no claim to the throne. In the current imperial family, only Prince Akishino has a son. The daughters of the imperial family will eventually marry out, and only the immediate family of Prince Akishino's son, Prince Hisahito, will continue to exist as the imperial family. In the present law of the imperial family, only male members have the right of ascending to the throne, and there is no provision for adopting sons-in-law. In a similar vein, even after losing the war and the creation of the postwar Constitution that prescribed equality of men and women, children born to Japanese women in international marriages did not automatically receive Japanese nationality, but only the nationality of their fathers.

Even now, though it is said that the system allows for choice, almost all Japanese women choose to take their husband's name when they marry and they are not bothered in the least that their children inherit the name of their husband's household. Even after the adoption of the postwar Constitution that emphasizes gender equality, it is as if the Meiji Civil Code regulations on the legal incompetence of wives were still in effect. Under the postwar Nationality law, Japanese woman does not lose the status of being Japanese when she marries a foreign national. But up until the mid-1980s, the Japanese government might have considered Japanese women who had married foreign men as legal incompetent. It is as a result of this viewpoint that they did not allow these women's children to inherit Japanese nationality.

As a condition for the ratification of Convention on the Elimination of All Forms of Discrimination against Women, adopted in 1979 by the UN General Assembly, the Japanese government was required to revise domestic laws to treat all genders equally. One of these was the "Partial Revisions of the Laws Regarding Nationality and Household Registration." In 1986, the system in which children of international marriages had until the age of 22 to choose between the nationality of their mother and father was established. The so-called Equal Employment Opportunity Law was also created around this time. However, it was not until 1989 that Meiji era legal precedents that regulated laws on private relationships, such as the principle that divorce would be governed by the laws of the husband's state, were revised. In spite of the postwar Constitution and the ratification of the Convention on the Elimination of all Forms of Discrimination against Women, gender equality in the imperial family has yet to change.

Recently, there has been an increase in examples of the failure of an international marriage leading to a Japanese woman returning to Japan (usually from her husband's country) with her children but without the consent of the husband. The Japanese government has for a long time avoided joining the Hague Convention on the Civil Aspects of International Child Abduction (Hague Convention), but in 2014 Japan finally became a signatory country. When the Hague Convention was created at the 1980 Hague Conference on Private International Law, the Japanese Nationality Act stated that the children of Japanese women in international marriages would hold the nationality of their fathers, and it was thought inconceivable that a wife might kidnap her children.

A product of the modern nation state, international marriages force us to constantly face the problem of how to deal with "outsiders," and the question of which society children of international marriages should be seen as belonging to. After the creation of the Napoleonic Code, the principle that married couples should share nationality was adopted throughout Europe. But with World War I, which made allies or enemies of the various European states, transfers of nationality and transfers of status by marriage were differentiated, and the tide turned in favor of nationality laws based on the principle of individual nationality. Still, children born of international marriages fell under a dark shadow during the world wars. If their father's country and mother's country became enemies, these children had to confront the difficult question of whether they could become a soldier for their father's country and kill the people of their mother's country. In 1923, after the end of World War I, a proposal titled *Paneuropa* was put forth by Richard Nikolaus Coudenhove-Kalergi, whose father Heinrich had traveled to Japan as an Austrian diplomat, and whose mother's original name was Mitsuko Aoyama. This would later become the foundation of both the European Economic Community (ECC) and the less-economically-focused European Communities (EC). This man of mixed roots with a Japanese mother envisioned a world less governed by national borders, but issues for children torn between nations at war or parents in conflict continue to this day.

## CHAPTER SEVEN

## BLOOD TALKS: EUGENIC MODERNITY AND THE CREATION OF THE NEW JAPANESE[374]

JENNIFER ROBERTSON

"Blood talks" (*chi wa mono o iu*).[375] So Shigenori Ikeda began his eugenic manifesto for Japan, published in the January 1927 issue of his journal, *Yūsei Undō* (Eugenic Exercise/Movement).[376] Blood continues to "talk" in Japan today, and is a loquacious interlocutor on the subjects of sexual attraction, kinship, mentalité, national identity, and cultural uniqueness. Blood-type, moreover, is the basis for a very popular "sanguine horoscopy," in addition to other systems of fortune-telling and personality analysis based on East Asian cosmology. Ikeda's invocation of the narrative agency of blood reflects its widespread, contemporary use as a metaphor for "shared heredity" or "shared ancestry," and even for the essential material imagined to constitute *the* Japanese race. In Japan and elsewhere in the industrializing world at the turn of the nineteenth century, race was conceptualized both as a mix of discrete biological and cultural characteristics, and as the specific group or human type that possessed and manifested those characteristics. Blood remains an organizing metaphor for profoundly significant, fundamental, and enduring assumptions about Japaneseness and otherness both within and outside of Japan. Eugenics, which I shall summarize for the moment as "instrumental and selective procreation," provided a framework in *fin-de-siècle* Japan within which blood became a cipher for specifically modern ideas of "disciplinary bio-power."[377]

Obviously, I am not the first scholar to point out the connection between blood and nationality in Japan; the theorists and ideologues about whom I write long precede me, and several of my contemporaries have addressed related subjects employing different methodologies, theories, and interpretations.[378] The link between blood and nationality is certainly not unique to Japan but it is inflected in ways that distinguish the Japanese phenomenon from others. My most general objective is to layer into a coherent and demystifying narrative the cacophonous popular debates and welter of folk and scientific assumptions specifically about "Japanese"—and the Japaneseness of—blood and bodies. My specific and original scholarship addresses two large themes that bleed into each other, so to speak: the application of eugenic principles and propositions in fusing kinship and biology, and the normalization through popular eugenics of "ethnic national endogamy" as a dominant and modern cultural ideal.[379]

I must emphasize at the outset that "the popular" and "the scientific" did not inhabit opposite ends of a continuum of credibility. In *fin-de-siècle* Japan, eugenics constituted a synergism of theory, ideology, and practice that blurred and even fused any hypothetical boundary between the street and the laboratory. This blurring and fusion were symptomatic of "eugenic modernity," by which I mean the application of scientific concepts and methods as the primary means to constitute both the nation and its constituent subjects.[380] As my cited references attest—references that are at once factual and artifactual—established scientists used the mass media to foster an appreciation of race betterment through customized procreation, and impresarios organized traveling hygiene exhibitions and eugenic beauty contests (the judges for which included some of the same scientists). Through eugenics, science was popularized, and the public was prevailed upon to cultivate a modern attitude of scientific curiosity.[381]

The new scientific order in Japan was introduced under the aegis of nationalism and empire-building. Beginning with the colonization of Okinawa in 1874 followed by that of Taiwan in 1895, Korea in 1910, Micronesia in 1919, Manchuria in 1931, North China by 1937, and much of Southeast Asia by 1942, the state consolidated through military force a vast Asian-Pacific domain, the so-called Greater East Asia Co-Prosperity Sphere (*daitōa kyōeiken*), a rubric coined in August 1940. Although empire-building forms the backdrop of this chapter, my focus is on colonizing practices pursued and implemented *within* Japan among the Japanese people, who constituted a proving ground for such practices throughout Asia and the Pacific. If East Asian prosperity was the euphemistic metaphor for Japanese dominance abroad, "family" was the operable image at home. The concept of a family-state (*kazoku kokka*) system was invented by late nineteenth-century ideologues to create a familiar and modern community—the nation—where one had not existed before. Some ideologues stretched out the family metaphor and likened nationality to membership in an exceptional "bloodline" (*kettō*).[382]

## Bones, Flesh, Seeds, and Blood

According to cultural historian Tomomi Nishida, it was during the seventeenth through nineteenth centuries that "blood" (*chi*, *ketsu*), equated in earlier periods with death and ritual pollution, gradually acquired a positive metaphorical meaning of "life force" and lineage. It also became the main criterion of nationality, which, ever since the promulgation of the first constitution in 1890, continues to be based on the principle of *jus sanguinus*.[383] Before the seventeenth century, the dominant symbolism of blood was negative, located as it was in the ritually polluted female body; menstruation and parturition were classified in Shinto and Buddhism as "dirty" and especially dangerous to males.[384] In addition to banishing females from certain "sacred" sites and spaces, males could avoid "blood poisoning" by undertaking Shinto purification rituals.[385]

Nishida surmises that the terms *ketsuen* (blood relationship), *kettō* (blood line), and *ketsuzoku* (blood relatives), indicative of an affirmative meaning of blood, were coined around the mid-nineteenth century when they began to appear in a wide range of literary sources. The Japanese dictionaries compiled by Jesuits in the late 16th and early 17th centuries did not define blood in terms of heredity or lineage.[386] Before blood acquired its new, positive meaning, heredity was denoted by the term *kotsuniku*, or bone–flesh, where "bone" (*kotsu*) referred to paternity, and "flesh" (*niku*) to maternity.[387] Another term in use since at least the tenth century to identify paternity specifically was *tane* (seed). From the late-nineteenth century onward, the Japanese-style term *hitodane* (lit. person [*hito*] seed [*t(d)ane*]) was used to denote heredity in the sense of "germ plasm," as then understood. Thus, the phrase *tane ga kawaru* (seed changes) refers to children with the same mother and a different father.[388]

Nishida notes that in Japan, unlike in China, "blood relations" (qua heredity) were not privileged over other types of social intimacy, such as adoption, which continues to be widely practiced in Japan.[389] Important to realize in this connection is the fact that adoptions were and are arranged for pragmatic reasons, most commonly to secure a male to occupy the *situs* of household (*ie*) successor. They were not undertaken for personal or emotional needs, objectives that can be realized without actual co-residence and even through *post mortem* adoptions and ghost marriages.[390] An increasingly positive interpretation of "blood" was accompanied by the normalization of patrilineality as the dominant rule of household succession. Moreover, within the framework of the Meiji constitution, "blood" was the basis of and for a person's civic and legal provenance and attendant rights. Until its codification, patrilineality was especially characteristic of pre-modern samurai, or warrior, households in particular, which comprised less than eight percent of the population of roughly twenty-seven million persons during the Tokugawa (or Edo) period (1603-1867), and specifically the 1720s.[391] Although bonafide membership in the samurai class was determined by the paternal "seed," intra-class adoption was also widely practiced.[392] The Meiji Civil Code sanctioned both the patriarchal household as the smallest legal unit of society and father-to-son succession as the most general, normative pattern of household continuity—a pattern referred to as "samuraization." Today, by contrast, under the auspices of the postwar constitution individuals are legal entities in their own right and succession a subjective arrangement. Although equal inheritance is mandated in the postwar constitution, the majority of Japanese continue the earlier practice of male primogeniture. Furthermore, as in the pre-modern period, sons need not be the biological offspring of fathers; rather, the terms "father" and "son" denote gender roles and social (including adoptive) statuses and not necessarily a biological relationship (although they may *connote* one).

Despite the normalization of patrilineality as an extension of the Meiji state's authority, eugenicists were unanimous in stressing the importance of reckoning kinship bilineally in order to build what they believed to be a scientific foundation on which launch their collective project of bettering the Japanese race and creating a foundational generation of New Japanese. They also critiqued sharply the deleterious consequences of patriarchy and patrilineal ideology on the health and hygiene of girls and women. For example, writing in January 1945, Tōgō Minoru, a eugenicist, bureaucrat, and colonial administrator, echoed his predecessors in declaring that the physical and mental health of females had been woefully neglected under the feudal, androcentric, and xenophobic regime of the Tokugawa shogunate.[393] Although early feminists supported many aspects of the eugenics movement, such as birth control and modern, scientific approaches to pregnancy and childbirth, the eugenicists' critique of patriarchy and patrilineal ideology was not motivated by overtly feminist concerns.[394] Shigenori Ikeda, for example, who had doctorates in eugenics and women's history from Jena University in Germany, addressed the difference between the women's and eugenics movements in a 1929 article:

Many people believe that the objectives of eugenics are contrary to those of the women's movement; namely, that eugenics calls not for women's liberation but for women's fulltime role as birthmothers and childraisers. Actually, the eugenics movement wishes to encourage all of the above—liberation, birthing, and childraising. Of course, a female's primary role is to give birth, a fact that should not reduce but greatly elevate her social status. Those who think otherwise have a poor understanding of eugenics.[395]

The creation of the Eugenic Marriage Popularization Society (Yūseikekkon Fūkyūkai) on November 11, 1935 provided an institutional dimension to Ikeda's notion of a gynocentric eugenics.[396] The Society, the majority of whose members were female, was established under the auspices of the Japan Association of Race Hygiene (Nippon Minzoku Eisei Kyōkai), founded by Hisomu Nagai in 1930. Nagai was a professor of physiology at Tokyo University who played a central role in the drafting and passage of the National Eugenics Law of 1940.[397] He was preceded by a decade by Ikeda, a journalist *cum* eugenicist who also devoted much energy toward popularizing eugenics among girls and women. Ikeda differed in important ways from Nagai with respect to the social applications of eugenics. His Japan Eugenic Exercise/Movement Association (Nippon Yūsei Undō Kyōkai), founded in 1926, was the first such organization to actively recruit girls and women into its various programs, some of which I introduce subsequently.

The (non-feminist) gynocentric, maternalist bent of these early eugenics associations was reflected in the postwar Eugenic Protection Law of 1948, which, in addition to preventing "the birth of eugenically inferior offspring," aimed to "protect maternal health and life." The 1948 law was replaced twenty years ago with the Maternal Protection Law of 1996, from which references to "eugenically inferior offspring" were omitted and a singular emphasis placed on the protection of motherhood and maternal health.[398] The historical debates about blood and recent legal developments concerning maternity help us to understand why in Japan (unlike in Germany, Israel, and the United States), "eugenics" is neither an avoided nor negatively charged term.[399]

## Mixed Blood Versus Pure Blood

The concept of "pure blood" as a criterion of authentic Japaneseness began circulating in public discourse by the 1880s in many venues and media. "Purity" referred metaphorically to a body—including the national body—free from symbolic pollution and disease-bearing pathogens as well as to genealogical orthodoxy. As a newly dominant concept, "pure bloodedness" also effectively tightened what historically had been a loose sense of consanguinity. Although intellectual and ideological rivals, the founders of eugenics associations were nevertheless alike in seeking to improve *the* Japanese race by making bloodline synonymous with household succession.[400] Their emphasis on the necessary bilineality of a national genealogy consisting of "pure bloods" was not represented in the Meiji Civil Code, which instead privileged male primogeniture and Japanese paternity, or the "male seed," as the sole criterion of nationality and citizenship. This criterion was retained in the postwar Civil Code until 1985, when the nationality law was changed as a result of legal pressure brought by feminists to have the "blood" of Japanese females recognized as an independent and authentic agent of Japanese nationality and citizenship.

In contrast, bilineal kinship continues to supersede all other modes of reckoning the familial, legal, social, and political status of *burakumin* ("outcastes") and spirit-animal possessors, that is, persons or households thought to control, or to be controlled by, supernatural animals.[401] In the Tokugawa period, their symbolic pollution and marginality was imagined to be "infectious," and later, with the conflation in eugenic discourse of blood and heredity, inherited and inheritable. In these cases, the new "affirmative" meaning of blood as life force and lineage did not replace the earlier, "negative" meaning of blood as a polluting substance, but rather congealed as both a coeval and a mutually constitutive system of belief. These tenacious popular beliefs, including the dangers of "female blood," represent another or an alternate world of local practices revolving around the negative valences of blood.

By the same token, the blood-type fads today represent both a continuation and a distortion of nineteenth-century scientific ideas about bodies and blood that were embraced by leading intellectuals and introduced to the public at the turn of the century through a centralized education system and burgeoning mass media. (Although many of these ideas are no longer perceived as "scientific" they nevertheless persist in various guises.) The specific field of science that took up the "positive" meaning of blood as its subject was eugenics and race science, and it fueled a discourse that permeated all aspects of everyday life in Japan by 1900. The public sphere shaped by the discourse of eugenics and race science was premised on a future-oriented vision of a racially improved nation-state, one peopled by taller, heavier, healthier, and fertile men and women whose anthropometrically ideal bodies would serve as the caryatids of the expanding Japanese empire.

At this juncture it is necessary to backtrack in order to review the beginnings of the imperial New Japan. The defeat of the xenophobic shogunate and the restoration of the emperor Meiji in 1868 within a German-style parliamentary system ushered in unprecedented social reforms based on a policy of selective and controlled Westernization. Among these reforms was the creation of a nation informed by the utopian ideology of the family-state system, noted earlier. People who had had primarily identified themselves and who were identified by region, domain (*han*), locality, and fixed social and domestic status, had to imagine themselves first and foremost as "Japanese." These layers of identity were contained by the new, umbrella-like category of *kokumin*, or "citizen," in the sense of subject of the imperial nation-state, itself imagined as having an organic, corporeal form (*kokutai*). Eugenicists and nationalists believed that New Japan (*shin Nippon*) could "compete successfully with the West in international affairs" and pursue an imperialist agenda of expansion and colonization only if it were peopled with New Japanese. Just how New Japanese could and should be created was the subject of a heated and divisive debate among the ideologues of blood that has shaped the discourse of eugenics to this day.

Eugenics, coined by Francis Galton in 1883, was translated into Japanese as the romanized *yuzenikkusu* and as the neologisms *yūseigaku* (science of superior birth) and *jinshukaizengaku* (science of race betterment). These terms were used synonymously with two terms coined a little earlier: "race betterment" (*minzoku/jinshu kairyō*) and "race hygiene" (*minzoku/jinshu eisei*).[402] *Minzoku* and *jinshu*, the two Japanese words for "race" in both the social and phenotypical senses, for the most part were used interchangeably, although *jinshu* remains the more clinical, social-scientific term (cf. *Rasse*) and *minzoku* the more popular and populist term (cf. *Volk*).[403] When prefixed with names, such as Nippon and Yamato, *minzoku* signified the conflation of phenotype, geography, culture, spirit, history, and nationhood. All of these semantic and semiotic inventions were part of the ideological agenda of the Meiji state and were incorporated into the postwar constitution of 1947, which retained the definition of nationality and citizenship as a matter of blood, or *jus sanguinus* (as opposed to *jus solis*).

Eugenics, in the sense of instrumental and selective procreation, was hardly a new concept in *fin-de-siècle* Japan. Historically and mytho-historically, as well as across classes and statuses of people, the maintenance of genealogical integrity was a key strategy of household succession. Integrity in this historical context was understood as continuity; that is, the successful augmentation or replacement of household members from one generation to the next through strategically arranged marriages and adoptions.[404] Eugenics, in contrast, was equated with broad societal and nationalist goals, such as the propagation of New Japanese and the rationalization of marriage, with respect to both partner choice and the betrothal ceremony. Introduced under the auspices of eugenics was a new national premium on "pure blood" and "wholesome" (*kenzen*) heredity as a necessary condition of race betterment and modern nation-building. Heredity (*iden*) was understood in a general sense as whatever one received from one's parents and ancestors, making them morally as well as medically culpable should their offspring and ascendants be less than wholesome. Japanese race scientists thus also worked to reform marriage and sexual practices more generally because it was through sex, regulated by the institution of marriage—as well as licensed prostitution—that either positive or negative eugenic precepts, or both, were most effectively implemented.[405]

Positive eugenics, promoted by Shigenori Ikeda, refers to the improvement of circumstances of sexual reproduction and thus incorporates advances in sanitation, nutrition, and physical education into strategies to shape the reproductive choices and decisions of individuals and families. The effects of biology (genetics) and environment are conflated. In this connection, "eugenic" was often used in the early twentieth-century Japanese literature as both an adjective meaning, and a euphemism for, "hygienic" and "scientific." Negative eugenics, enthusiastically advocated by Hisomu Nagai, involves the prevention of sexual reproduction, through induced abortion or sterilization, among people deemed unfit. "Unfit" was an ambiguous term that included alcoholics, "lepers," the mentally ill, the criminal, the physically disabled, and the sexually alternative among other categories of people. Some traditional or premodern categories of stigmatized alterity, such as the *burakumin*, were recast in scientific terms and deemed uneugenic, while others, such as horoscopic identity, were dismantled as "superstitions and folk beliefs" (*meishin*) of no eugenic consequence, although they could impede the implementation of scientific practices.[406]

Eugenics provided an avenue for the application of science to social problems, including public health, education, and hygiene. The fields of eugenics and public health shared much jargon and many assumptions, attitudes, and aims, not only in Japan, but in other countries as well.[407] What Martin Pernick notes about early twentieth-century America pertains equally well to Japan, namely, that "eugenic methods often were modeled on the infection control techniques of public health": "infections were caused by germs; inheritance was governed by germ plasm. In both cases, 'germs' meant microscopic seeds. Both types of germs enabled disease to propagate and grow, to spread contamination from the bodies of the diseased to the healthy" through the medium of blood, a metaphor for heredity and a vehicle for infection.[408] Like their international counterparts, Japanese eugenicists tended to collapse biology and culture, and, consequently, held either explicitly or implicitly Lamarckian views on race formation and racial temperament. Thus, even those who were environmentally inclined, also assumed that complex phenomena, such as the "uniquely Japanese *ie* (household) system," were "carried in the 'blood,' if only as 'instincts' or 'temperamental proclivities'".[409] The melding of biology and culture, nature and culture, is also evident in the interchangeability of *jinshu* (race) and *minzoku* (ethnic nation), and in the prescriptions for race betterment. Through networks of modern institutions and industries, such as the army, schools, hygiene exhibitions, immigration training programs, the press, fashion, advertising, popular genealogies, and so forth, the Japanese people were encouraged to think in totally new and different ways about their bodies. They were to think of their bodies as plastic, in the sense of capable of being molded, and as adaptable, pliable, and transformable through new hygienic regimens of nutrition and physical exercise.

For males, these regimens were part of their military training beginning in 1873, when a modern conscription army was established, replacing the hereditary warrior (samurai) class that epitomized the Tokugawa period. Females, exempt from military service, were exposed to these regimens at the many private sector schools and academies that competed to enroll girls and women whose education was more or less neglected by the Meiji government, a least initially. Clothing also fell under the eugenic gaze. Whereas boys and men were encouraged to wear crewcuts and Western-style outfits to symbolize the modernity of New Japan, girls and women were to represent through costume and hairstyle a nostalgically re-imagined traditional Japanese culture, although they were urged to loosen the normally tightly cinched *obi*, or sashes, of their kimono, and to simplify the traditional chignon to facilitate the regular cleaning and combing of their hair. All Japanese were advised by public health agents to learn how to walk properly, to use chairs whenever possible, and to avoid kneeling for long lengths of time, which was thought to cause bowed legs and pigeon-toedness.[410] The desirable corporeal results and aesthetic effects of these new hygienic practices were perceived as transmittable by blood through "eugenic marriages" (yūsei kekkon), as elaborated below.

In Japan, the discourse of eugenics clustered around two essentially incommensurable positions concerning blood: the "pure-blood," or junketsu, position, and the "mixed-blood," or konketsu, position. The proponents of each position acknowledged the "mixed-blooded," or multiethnic, ancient history of Japan, an idea developed in the late-nineteenth century by the German physician and genealogist, Erwin von Baelz, who had spent thirty years in Japan (1876-1906) studying the racial origins of the Japanese people. Baelz, applying the then dominant teleological evolutionist paradigm, proposed that the so-called Yamato stem-race, associated with the Imperial Household and its allegedly unbroken lineage stretching back over 2,500 years, had, by the sixth-century, conquered and subjugated the different racial groups co-existing on the islands. These groups, he maintained, were assimilated selectively and slowly, so that by the nineteenth century, "Yamato blood" was a refined and superior substance.[411] Japanese pundits favoring the pure-blood position were keen on preserving the eugenic integrity of the pristine Yamato stem-race; those promoting the mixed-blood position, enumerated the eugenic benefits of hybrid vigor through the mixing of Japanese and non-Japanese blood.[412]

The "mixed-blood" position was first articulated in an 1884 essay, A Treatise on the Betterment of the Japanese Race (Nippon jinshu kairyōron), penned by the Keio University-educated journalist Yoshio Takahashi. Invoking a Social Darwinist scenario, Takahashi argued that Japan was undergoing a transition from a "semi-civilized" to a "civilized" status represented, in his view, by northern European countries and their taller, heavier, and stronger populations. This "civilized" status could be expedited through the marriage of Japanese males and Anglo females, or, as he phrased it, the "mixed-marriage of Yellows and Whites" (kōhaku zakkon).[413] Mixed-blood marriages, Takahashi hypothesized, would create a taller, heavier, and stronger, in short "a physically superior Japanese race, thereby making it possible for the Japanese to compete successfully with Europeans and Americans in international affairs."[414]

The "pure-blood" position was advocated by Hiroyuki Katō, a veteran politician, imperial advisor, and chancellor of Tokyo University. Katō's scathing critique of the mixed-marriage plan was published in 1886 in both an academic journal, *Tōyō Gakugei* [Oriental Arts and Sciences] and the *Tokyo Nichinichi Shinbun*, a leading daily newspaper. To summarize, Katō first of all objected to the notion that the Japanese were less civilized than Europeans.[415] Second, he argued that interbreeding "Yellows" and "Whites" would create a completely new hybrid category of person whose political and social "status" would be unclear and perplexing. Miscegenation, Katō concluded, would result in race *transformation* and not race betterment, and would, over the course of several generations, seriously dilute the pure blood—or racial and cultural essence—of the Japanese. He declared emphatically that whereas mixed-blood marriages between Yellows and Whites would insure the "complete defeat" (*zenpai*) of Japan by Westerners, pure-bloodedness would insure for eternity Japan's distinctive racial history, culture, and social system.[416]

Although the pure-blood position emerged fairly quickly as the dominant one, the pros and cons of both positions were hotly debated in the eugenics literature through 1945, and continue today in other guises. For example, in an article published in the May 1911 issue of *Jinsei-Der Mensch* (Human Life), the first eugenics journal published in Japan, zoologist Jirō Oka'asa scoffed at the proposal of "white–yellow marriages," dismissing it as one example of the "maniacal fascination with the West" (*seiyō shinsui*) that defined the early Meiji period.[417] Over twenty-five years later, in 1939, political theorist Susumu Ijichi published an article in *Kaizō* (Reconstruction), a popular, generally liberal, literary periodical, advocating the intermarriage of Japanese males and "carefully selected" Manchurian females. He referred to his proposal as a "racial blood transfusion" (*minzoku yūketsu*) and argued that "mixing superior Japanese blood with inferior Manchurian blood would stimulate the development and civilization of inferior peoples by producing hybrid offspring who would mature as natural political leaders."[418] Ijichi's ideas in turn were rebuffed by Minoru Tōgō, noted earlier, whose ideas about blood circulated widely during the 1920s through1940s. Tōgō reiterated Katō's objections to mixed-blooded offspring, arguing that they constituted a "new race" (*shinminzoku*); miscegenation by definition could only fail to produce the cultural objective of colonial assimilation, namely Japanization (*nipponka*). Mixed marriages between Japanese and non- Japanese Asians, he asserted, would effectively corrupt and "dissolve the soul (*tamashii*) of the pure Japanese race and national body" and thwart the imperial expansion of the Japanese people.[419]

I realized, in the course of my research on blood ideologies, that the central tenet of the "pure-blood" position was anchored in a centuries-old construction of radical otherness transposed in a new vocabulary. Although he used mathematical charts and invoked modern science, Hiroyuki Katō's argument for preserving blood purity was strikingly similar to the persistent "one-drop" folk theory regulating marriages between symbolically pure and polluted Japanese. Briefly, according to this theory, *burakumin* and spirit-animal possessors are labeled "black stock" (*kurosuji*) and their opposites are labeled "white stock" (*shirosuji*). The term *suji*, or "stock" or "line," is very close to the nineteenth-century meaning of blood as an inheritable biological *and* cultural substance, but its affective range is much broader and the transmission process analogous to infection and contamination. Miscegenation among black and white "stockholders" would turn both a "white stock" person and that person's entire household "black".[420] Katō seemed to define the nation in terms of *shirosuji*, a "white stock" lineage that could be irrevocably sullied—or turned "black"—by the mixing Japanese and non-Japanese blood.

## Blood Marriages

The central focus in the Japanese eugenics movement concentrated on the physiques and overall health of girls and women. Japanese eugenicists argued that the physical development of Japanese girls and women had been neglected for centuries, resulting in their physiological inferiority. The need to grow the population in order to generate the human capital with which to fund nation- and empire-building motivated agents of the Japanese state and private sectors alike to focus their undivided attention on improving the bodies of females, who were, after all, the biological reproducers of the nation.[421] This part of the nationalist and imperialist enterprise was supported by some of the leading Japanese feminists, whose agenda of popularizing methods of birth control and promoting maternal health was incorporated into the discourse of eugenics, as I noted earlier.[422] In this connection, note that the early twentieth-century (1940) *and* postwar (1948 and 1996) eugenics legislation and laws alike have been understood as measures to protect the reproductive health of mothers. "Maternal protection" (*bosei hogo*), in fact, is one of the many euphemisms for eugenic practices today.

Generally speaking, the pronatalist state encouraged the improvement of the conditions surrounding female reproductivity instead of advocating sterilization as a way to reduce the reproduction of the unfit. The Welfare Ministry (Kōseishō), established in 1938, inaugurated a "propagate and multiply movement" (*umeyo fuyaseyo undō*), which included the staging of healthy-baby contests throughout the country. Especially fertile mothers were eulogized in the mass media as comprising a "fertile womb battalion" (*kodakara butai*). The Ministry also organized awards ceremonies, many of which were staged at department stores, where such mothers, babies in tow, were presented with certificates honoring their reproductive success.[423] Already in 1930, Education Ministry (Monbushō) together with the *Tokyo* and *Osaka Asahi Shinbun* (newspaper) companies, had inaugurated an annual nationwide contest to identify the top ten—of 260,000 contestants— "most healthy, eugenically fit children in Japan" (*Nippon ichi no kenkō yūryōji*). Contestants were selected from elementary schools throughout Japan and underwent further screening at the prefectural level before the finalists were selected by a central committee. In addition to a female and male winner, four pairs of runners up were selected along with five pairs of semi-finalists. Photographs of the scantily clad winners were published in the daily press along with charts detailing their physical measurements, medical histories, educational backgrounds, and maternal and paternal genealogies

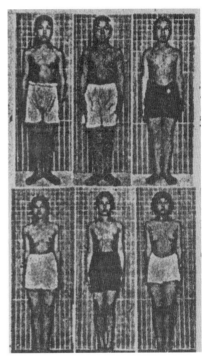

Figure 7.1 The most eugenically fit children in Japan. Photograph by author of *Nippon'ichi yūryōji* (The Most Eugenically Superior Children in Japan)

(see Figure 7.1).[424] Eugenicists referred to this contest as a new (*shin*) *nenjūgyōji*, a term for the "annual events" comprising the agricultural calendar. In doing so, they sought to naturalize and traditionalize the incorporation into everyday life of eugenic practices as central both to the persistence of historical cultural practices and to the corporeal development of Japanese children.[425]

Worries about the anthropometric status of women and children were equaled by and linked to worries among a majority of eugenicists about the "high rate" of consanguineous marriages in Japan. One of the most prevalent topics in the four eugenics journals that I have scrutinized—*Jinsei-Der Mensch*, *Yūsei Undō*

(Eugenic Exercise/Movement), Yūsei (Superior Birth), and Yūseigaku (Eugenics)—was the "detrimental consequences" of "marriages among blood relatives," or ketsuzoku kekkon.[426] Much was made of how consanguineous marriages, mostly between first cousins, amounted five to six percent of all registered marriages.[427] It is not always clear from the Japanese literature what standard in relation to which this percentage constituted a "high rate." The statistics provided by Ethel Elderton, a Galton Research Scholar writing in 1911 and much cited by her Japanese colleagues, may offer a useful cross-cultural comparison. Elderton concluded that the percentage of first-cousin marriages "among all classes in England" was around three percent, although she found a "very high percentage" of cousin marriages, seven to eleven percent, in cases of deaf-mutism and albinoism.[428]

Using population and registered-marriage statistics compiled by the Japanese government between 1933 and 1943, I calculated that five percent would amount to an annual average of somewhere between 24,000 and 33,000 registered marriages.[429] The actual percentage of consanguineous marriages is actually much higher since many—in some cases over a third or more—marriages were not registered. Unfortunately, the number of unregistered, common-law marriages, or naien, for this period are not available, much less information as to what percentage of them were among "blood relatives."[430] Some villages, such as Narata and Yūshima in the Minamikoma district of Yamanashi Prefecture, were known as "blood-marriage hamlets" (ketsuzoku kekkon buraku) because the vast majority of inhabitants had married their first cousins, half cousins, second cousins (hatoko), uncles, or nieces. These two villages were the subjects of a survey initiated in September 1943 by the Welfare Ministry, the results of which were published in 1949.[431] Yōko Imaizumi, a demographer employed by the same Ministry, notes that the proportion of consanguineous marriages in Japan averaged 16 percent in the 1920s.[432] Curiously, the American anthropologist John Embree elected not to explore the phenomenon of the "frequent cousin marriages" that he encountered while conducting pioneering fieldwork in rural Kyushu during the late 1930s. He did, however, note that "missionaries" of the eugenic marriage campaign were active in the area, and that the practice of consanguineous marriage was "being discouraged by more educated people on the questionable theory that it is biologically harmful."[433]

The countrywide practice of consanguineous marriage reflected the premium placed on what I call the "strategic endogamy" practiced during the 250 years of relative isolation maintained by the Tokugawa shogunate. By "strategic endogamy" I am referring to the transaction of marriages exclusively among and within certain categories of people defined by social status and geographical location; in Japan, "blood marriages" were not limited to elites. Familiarity was another desirable criterion, as it was popularly assumed that marriages between blood relatives were more stable and diplomatic in that they were free from disruptive anxieties about unknown or hidden factors.

Eugenicists in Japan and elsewhere argued among themselves over the negative and positive benefits of inbreeding among blood relatives. A minority in Japan pointed to Galton's thesis of "hereditary genius" and other seemingly positive examples of consanguinity, including the ancient Athenians.[434] Applying quasi-Mendelian logic, they argued that in order for inbreeding to be risk-free, the blood of each party must be absolutely pure.[435] The catch, of course, was that pure-bloodedness, while good to think, was never completely ascertainable. The majority of Japanese eugenicists believed that the transmission and manifestation of diseases and defects were expedited and multiplied through inbreeding. They echoed and cited their foreign counterparts, such as Ethel Elderton, in linking a host of disorders and diseases to the hereditary transmission of faulty germ-plasm (iden)—the word gene was not coined until 1909. In Elderton's words:

> The real danger of cousin marriage lies not in the existence of patent defects in the stock. Nor can we recommend cousin marriage because the stock has certain patent valuable characteristics. Behind the obviously advantageous quality may exist the rare but latent defect. The danger of cousin marriage lies in the probability that the germ-plasm of each individual contains numerous latent defects, each of which is rare in the community at large, and each of which is of small danger to the individual or the offspring unless the mating is with another individual whose germ-plasm contains one or more of the same latent characters.[436]

These "latent defects" included sterility, mental illness, alcoholism, feeblemindedness, physical deformities, disabilities, dementia, deaf-mutism, myopia and blindness, "deviant" sexuality, and proneness to tuberculosis, syphilis and criminal behavior. Obviously, not all of these conditions are inherited, and those that are may be hidden in "normal-looking" carriers.

The vocabulary and vectors of eugenics were also used to pathologize and contemporize historical constructions of radical otherness, as in the case of *burakumin* and spirit-animal possessors. Their stigmatized status was eugenically respun as the consequence of defective germ-plasm. Curiously, of the several articles I read by eugenicists dismantling superstitions surrounding marriage practices, not one made an argument *against* the systematic discrimination of *burakumin* in all arenas of Japanese society. Moreover, eugenic discourse was instrumental in creating a caste-like category of "stigmatized other." Not only were those Japanese who exhibited a newly identified hereditary defect ostracized, but their households were also marked as eugenically unfit. Whereas historically, symbolically impure groups were allowed to marry and reproduce among themselves, persons and groups classified as eugenically unfit, such as persons with Hansen's disease (leprosy), were quarantined, exiled, and prevented from marrying (unless sterilized) and reproducing.[437] Eugenicists such as Eitarō Taguchi expressed alarm that although "genetically defective" and "feebleminded" individuals constituted only two percent of the population, they reproduced at two to three times the rate of "normal and ordinary" (*futsū*) individuals. Taguchi even invoked Gresham's Law in arguing for the passage of the 1940 National Eugenics Law.[438]

The imperial state and its agencies chose early on to pursue a eugenics-dictated agenda that called for the eradication of the apparently widespread practice in Japan of consanguineous marriage. Beginning in 1883, numerous "hygiene exhibitions" (*eisei tenrankai*) were staged countrywide, sponsored first by a Buddhist temple, the Honganji in the Tsukiji district of Tokyo, and subsequently by the Japanese Red Cross and, after 1938, by the Welfare Ministry. By the late 1920s, the theme and content of many of these exhibitions were based on public opinion polls; the relationship between heredity and marriage practices proved to be one of the most popular themes.[439] The sensationalistic and sometimes grotesque exhibits—such as a realistic wax model of a man's face riddled with syphilitic lesions—along with numerous articles in the popular press, drummed home warnings about the deleterious effects of both unregulated sex and inbreeding. Schoolchildren, along with the general public, were encouraged to attend the lectures that accompanied the exhibitions. Presented by doctors and university professors, these "blood talks" greatly simplified eugenics for the lay public, who apparently attended by the thousands. The speakers harshly censured superstitions and folk customs related to marriage, such as matchmaking based on horoscopy, the sexegenary cycle, and the five elements (wood, fire, water, earth, metal). But their sometimes facile presentations of genetic diseases helped to spawn new superstitions based on popularized science, such as the attribution to consanguinity of a host of non-genetic conditions such as leprosy, tuberculosis, and symbolic pollution and marginality.[440]

## Eugenic Marriages

The tenacious persistence of "blood marriages" despite private and state efforts to condemn their transaction provoked intensified efforts to eliminate that tradition. One of the first lines of offense was the "eugenic-marriage counseling centers" (Yūsei Kekkon Sōdansho) that were first opened in Tokyo and regional cities in 1927. The earliest centers were sponsored and staffed by Ikeda's Japan Eugenic Exercise/Movement Association. A year earlier, Ikeda had founded the Legs Society (Ashi no kai) as a means of popularizing eugenic principles. Like the earlier German Wandervogel and Czech Sokol movements that inspired Ikeda, the Legs Society sponsored, through its Tokyo and regional branches, collective hygienic regimens, nutrition lessons, group hiking, and wholesome folk-dancing in the countryside as ways to improve the bodies and minds of young Japanese so that they could "properly oversee the nation's global expansion."[441]

Ikeda regarded the ostracism and sterilization of the unfit a crude and simplistic approach to the project of race betterment. Citing the evolutionary categories proposed by Lewis Henry Morgan in *Systems of Consanguinity and Affinity* (1871), Ikeda argued that monogamous marriage practices, together with the systematization of physical education, was the golden key to improving the Japanese race and modernizing Japan.[442] Article after article in his journal, *Yūsei Undō*, emphasized that "monogamy was the foundation of eugenics" and that a eugenically sound marriage insured the development of a prosperous, physically fit, and moral society.[443] Ikeda and his colleagues followed Francis Galton in emphasizing the dialectical relationship between eugenics and marriage:

> Eugenic belief extends the function of philanthropy to future generations, it renders its actions more pervading than hitherto, by dealing with families and societies in their entirety, and it enforces the importance of the marriage covenant by directing serious attention to the probable quality of the future offspring ... [and] brings the tie of kinship into prominence.[444]

Dismissing as bunk the folk belief that the familiarity shared by married blood relatives insured household diplomacy and stability, Ikeda lectured throughout Japan on the need to shift the basis of and for desirable familiarity between females and males from close kinship *per se* to the modern alternative of equal co-education and shared hobbies. In his lectures and essays, Ikeda repeated the slogan of his association, "superior seeds, superior fields, superior cultivation" (*yoi tane, yoi hatake, yoi teire*) which, he explained, was a metaphor for "superior genes (or germ plasm), superior society, superior education" (*yoi iden, yoi shakai, yoi kyōiku*).[445] Civic and educational institutions, not consanguineous households, were promoted by him as ideal sites for revising the terms of interpersonal familiarity and ultimately insuring marital success among persons unrelated by blood. Ikeda argued that a desirable intimacy among strangers could be facilitated through educational programs and leisure activities, such as those offered by the Legs Society, that replaced pervasive folk beliefs about "shared blood" as a key criterion of and for affinity and harmony.[446]

A number of the eugenic marriage counseling centers, including Ikeda's, were opened in department stores—such as Shirokiya in the elegant Nihonbashi section of Tokyo—in order to make information about social and race hygiene, and associated behaviors and practices, easily available to consumers. Women especially were targeted, for "female citizenship" was defined not in terms of legal rights but in terms of procreation and consumption.[447] Modern scientific—specifically hygienic and eugenic—knowledge was dispensed as a commodity. Because consumption was inextricably associated with the body and its cosmetic, nutritional, and sartorial enhancement, the link between women's consumer citizenship and eugenics was naturalized by the state and commercial sector alike.

The staff of the eugenic-marriage counseling centers also provided matchmaking services, introducing potential spouses to each other based on the autobiographical health certificates they had completed and filed at the centers. According to the health profile (*shinshin kensahyō*) of a eugenic couple appearing in *Shashin Shuhō* (Photograph Weekly) in April 1942, by which time the centers were well established throughout Japan, the ideal woman was 154 cm tall, weighed 51 kg, had a chest size of 80 cm and was 21 years old or younger.[448]

The ideal man was 165 cm tall, weighed 58 kg, had a chest size of 84 cm and was 25 years old or younger. Both were free from disease and had "normal" genealogies. As the quintessential eugenic couple, they were committed to observing the "ten rules of marriage," which were: choose a lifetime partner; choose a partner healthy in body and mind; exchange health certificates; choose someone without bad genes; avoid marriage with blood relatives; marry as soon as possible; discard superstitions and quaint customs; obey your parents; have a simple and economical wedding; and, reproduce for the sake of the nation. The health profile was accompanied by photographs of the couple and their health certificates, scenes of a simplified, eugenic marriage ceremony, and a cartoon of the desired outcome of eugenic marriage counseling; namely, a family of eight children (see Figure 7.2).[449]

Figure 7.2 A eugenic couple and their health certificates. Photograph by author of *Korekara no kekkon wa kono yō ni* (1942)

Below the photograph of the ideal bride was the following declaration:

> Only people can accomplish the construction of Greater East Asia. Superior (*yūnō*) people are greatly needed for our future. There is one condition that must be fulfilled in order to increase the number of superior

people and that is the promotion and encouragement of marriage. For every Japanese child born, seven children are born in China, five in India, and three in the Soviet Union. However important it is to increase the population, the birth of physically weak and mentally impaired children will harm the national body (*kokutai*). Therefore, let us be sure to think carefully about marriage and to transact a wholesome union in order to bring forth superior offspring. Then, in ten or twenty years, the strong children who will lead East Asia will have increased in number to the point where by Shōwa 35 [1970], the population of the main islands (*naichi*) of Japan will have topped 100 million. Is that not a wonderful scenario to contemplate?[450]

Center staff also attempted to discourage marriages between Japanese women and Korean men who had been recruited from the peninsula as laborers following its annexation by Japan in 1910. In the ethnocentric words of one survey report, filed in 1942, "the Korean [male] laborers brought to Japan, where they have established permanent residency, are of the lower classes and therefore of an inferior constitution. ... By fathering children with Japanese women, these men could lower the caliber of the Yamato *minzoku*."[451]

Not only were women the primary audience for eugenic marriage counseling, they were also encouraged early on to undertake meticulous hygienic and eugenic surveillance work in their official gender role of good wife, wise mother. Married women were recruited by eugenicists to undertake the ethnographic surveys of their marital and natal households necessary to establish genealogical, or blood, orthodoxies within families as a foundational step toward race betterment. In 1887, the hygiene section of the Home Ministry established the Greater Japan Women's Hygiene Association (Dai Nippon Fujin Eiseikai) in Tokyo under whose auspices married women in particular were organized as blood-marriage whistleblowers. An Osaka branch was established three years later.[452] Encouraged to regard themselves as amateur ethnographers, the women were instructed to collect as much information as possible on the life histories of living and deceased relatives. The households and relatives of prospective marriage partners and their extended families were to be similarly scrutinized in order to prevent inbreeding.

By the early 1930s, detailed "eugenic marriage" questionnaires were printed in or inserted into popular magazines for public consumption, and the accompanying instructions underscored the slippery nature of questionnaires in general. The amateur ethnographers were reminded that because there was often a huge difference between what people say they do and what they actually do, they could not take anything at face value and were obliged to maintain a healthy skepticism.[453] By and large, the questionnaires were designed to foster a modern, anti-traditional attitude of scientific- mindedness.

An exemplary eugenic-marriage questionnaire was published in 1933 in the *Fujin Kōron* (*Women's Review*), a leading, mainstream women's magazine. The insert was titled, "A marriage survey that amateurs can undertake" (*shirōto de dekiru kekkon chōsa*). There were nine categories of investigation: personal history; disposition and character; personal conduct; health status; hobbies, tastes, and habits; religious beliefs; political orientation; lifestyle; and financial status. According to the author of the survey, "since females make a career of homemaking, it is not necessary to survey their social relationships [outside of the home]."[454] Thus, whereas males were asked about their "future worldly aspirations," females were assumed not to have any. Instead, women were questioned as to whether they had any "problems with the concept of wifehood." The types of wifehood listed to prompt their responses were: good wife, wise mother-type; harlot-type; faithful companion-type; household-type; working wife-type; and, wants-to-be-a-nun-type.[455] Eugenicists may have been gynocentric in select respects but they were not feminists as this questionnaire makes clear, for their aim was not about empowering the agency of females as we understand that concept today, but rather to rationalize and justify the modern, patriarchal institution of marriage and the unequal sexual division of reproductive labor.

Clearly, the successful completion of these eugenic-household questionnaires was ultimately contingent upon the literacy and diligence of the surveyor; namely, an urban, middle-class educated woman with enough free time to devote to the task. If necessary, however, detective agencies could be commissioned to assist. In fact, one historian of science, Yutaka Fujino, claims that the first detective agencies (*kōshinjo*) were founded in Osaka in 1892 to conduct background checks on potential marriage partners, a service that remains in high use today.[456] Eugenicist Shigenori Ikeda, writing in 1928, noted that rapid urbanization and the social confusion it occasioned, called for new strategies of matchmaking, including the use of detective agencies to carry out background and character checks—"it's a welcome sign that they are increasing in number."

However, he continued:

> detective agencies do not and cannot locate and
> provide eugenically fit marriage candidates; rather, they
> only investigate particular individuals already identified
> as potential spouses. Thus, systematically organized
> eugenic matchmaking and marriage counseling offices
> are a necessary social institution.[457] Ideally, according
> to Ikeda, these offices would administer confidential
> census-like surveys in order to create a database of
> eugenically fit women and men available for marriage.

> The surveys will consist of five categories of information
> provided by clients: (1) the client's name, age,
> occupation, height, chest diameter, weight, general
> health, educational history, talents, hobbies, siblings,
> income, and photograph; (2) the client's description
> of an ideal spouse, including age, occupation, health,
> social status (mibun), income, and so forth; (3) the
> client's parents: father's name, age, occupation, health,
> siblings, hobbies; mother's name, age, occupation,
> health, siblings, economic history, hobbies; and the
> present circumstances of both; (4) the same details
> for the client's paternal and maternal grandparents,
> including the cause of death if deceased; and (5) a
> list of the names of the client's primary [i.e. blood]
> relatives. The office staff will solicit further information
> from the client and others on the client's bloodline
> (kettō), [his or her] household's character (iegara),
> and [his or her family's] genetic (iden) makeup. These
> surveys will be kept confidential; actual names will be
> substituted with pseudonyms when providing spouse-
> seekers with copies of the documents to peruse. The
> actual names will be released to both parties only when
> an arranged marriage meeting is formalized.[458]

Ikeda was convinced that these marriage surveys would not only insure the eugenic fitness of spouses [459]but also help avoid class differences that could disrupt and even destroy a marriage. Moreover, he explained, the surveys would be augmented by information from a eugenic couple's children. Ultimately, the goal was to create a database of individuals and their entire households—and ultimately "all Japanese households"—which would enable eugenicists to conduct in-depth surveys of any given family's genealogy (*kakei*). Because, Ikeda declared, the government did not yet have an institutional framework for administering a comprehensive eugenic marriage counseling office—the Welfare Ministry was established in 1938—the Japan Eugenic Exercise/ Movement Association was prepared to undertake this service (Ikeda 1928: 61). Ikeda's association took the lead in 1928 by declaring December 21 "blood-purity day" (*junketsu dē*) and sponsoring free blood tests at the Tokyo Hygiene Laboratory. Two thousand persons, mostly women (wives and daughters), were tested by early afternoon, and a second day of free tests was offered on December 26 to accommodate the crowds, whose presence was construed by Ikeda as evidence of the popular acceptance of eugenic precepts.[460]

Ikeda's eugenic marriage counseling activities, which included the "mixers" sponsored by the Legs Society, "blood-purity" testing clinics, the eugenic-marriage questionnaires, and the public hygiene exhibitions among other things, illustrate the extent to which scientific culture was popularized and popular culture "scientized" by social engineers keen on modifying and modernizing the behavior of the Japanese people. Additionally, articles and advice columns on eugenic themes appeared frequently in national daily newspapers and popular magazines. Eugenicists contributed regularly to the media, and the eugenics journals *Jinsei-Der Mensch*, *Yūsei*, *Yūsei Undō*, and *Yūseigaku* all included columns and articles devoted to summarizing the coverage of eugenics themes in the daily press.[461]

### Eugenic Marriages as National Strategy

In addition to concerns, real and imagined, about the negative consequences of inbreeding among blood relatives, it occurred to me that the state—that is, the repertoire of agencies and institutions that reinforces and reproduces dominant ideologies and normalizes everyday practices—had another investment in the eradication of consanguineous marriages.[462] What eugenics offered was a motive and rationale for the imperial state to more closely engineer and orchestrate the sexual, gendered, marital, and reproductive practices of its subjects. Nation-states have always maintained a vested interest in the sexual and social reproduction of the population, and New Japan was no different in this regard. In fact, in some respects, the imperial state was following a powerful precedent set by the Tokugawa shogunate, which had brokered and controlled all marriages and adoptions among the vassal daimyo as one means of insuring their subordination.

The imperial state differed from this precedent in two major ways. First, the patrilineal orthodoxy undergirding the Tokugawa regime extended to the prevailing ethno-embryology, which is best described as male monogenesis, or the notion that the female body serves as a vessel to contain the active life-producing agent supplied by the male alone. With the popularization of eugenics came an explanation of sexual reproduction that emphasized the critical and equal contributions of females and males to heredity. The imperial state thus recognized the importance taking both maternity and paternity into account in promoting the creation of New Japanese despite the persistence of patrilineality as the singular criterion of nationality and citizenship.

The second major difference between the Tokugawa regime and the imperial state was the global scope of the underlying ideological agenda of New Japan, which was informed by the utopian ideology of the family-state system that characterized Japanese nationalism. By promoting eugenic marriages, the imperial state and its agents aimed to redefine historical and traditional boundaries of endogamy (dōzoku kekkon) and exogamy (zokugai kekkon). The state sought to replace one type of kin group endogamy with another system that I shall call "eugenic endogamy," which basically amounted to the introduction of "universal exogamy" among theoretically pure-blooded Japanese. Eugenic endogamy in short, was at the foundation of the family-state system, or state familism. In seeking to instill in its subjects an awareness of the New Japan and their Japanese nationality, the state aimed to dissolve the boundaries that engendered local affinities—boundaries that were intricately shaped by historical and traditional endogamous practices based on kin group, pedigree, class, region, and "superstitions and folk beliefs."

An article published in 1889, in the journal of the Great Japan Association for the Betterment of Public Customs and Morals (Dainippon Fūzoku Kairyōkai), is one of the earliest calls for the practice of universal exogamy in Japan. In it, the author drew attention to the allegedly higher percentage of deformities and mortality among the offspring of couples related by blood.[463] Citing and agreeing with Hiroyuki Katō's opposition to "mixed marriages," the author recommended what they termed both shūshi kōkan, or "exchange of seeds," and man'en kekkon, or "marriage between widely dispersed individuals":

> marriages partners should be selected not from the
> narrow parameters of blood relatives within a village or

circumscribed regions, but from all over Japan. A man from Satsuma [in the south] should marry a woman from the north; a woman from Shikoku [in the south] should marry a man from Niigata [in the north].[464]

Forty years later, Shigenori Ikeda reiterated the pressing need for a new geography of marriage in his arguments for the establishment of eugenic matchmaking centers, which would have the effect of "greatly expanding the circle (han'i) of eligible spouses."[465]

From a perspective *inside* Japan, universal exogamy was advocated; from a vantage point *outside* of Japan, eugenic or national endogamy was promoted—that is, the principle that Japanese should marry other pure-blooded Japanese comprising the imaginary national family based on eugenic criteria that replaced traditional endogamous practices. Limited exceptions were also made for politically strategic purposes, such as arranged marriages between members of the Japanese aristocracy and their Korean, Manchurian, and Mongolian counterparts. Arguments in favor of so-called "mixed-blood marriages" and "hybrid vigor" continued as part of the public discourse of eugenics, and have remained a foil for assertions today about the cultural and racial uniqueness of *the* Japanese.

### Epilogue

I have reviewed the Japanese ideologies of blood that came into prominence in the twinned contexts of nation-building and imperialism. The Japanese people themselves were the proving ground of colonialist schemes in Asia and the Pacific for the reason that they needed to be claimed and remolded as a national community and recruited into the imperial enterprise as a supporting cast. The popularization of eugenics, race hygiene, and eugenic endogamy as elements of quotidian life was a (bio) powerfully effective method of national mobilization. In Japan, ideologies of blood vacillated between the two incommensurable theoretical positions of pure-bloodedness and mix-bloodedness. Scrutinized from another perspective, we can see that these positions themselves were premised on competing notions of either the vigor or the vulnerability of *the* Japanese as agents of cultural encounter and transformation.

These positions were also refracted in the condemnation of consanguineous marriages and the promotion of universal exogamy within Japan among pure-blooded Japanese. The tension between these positions persists today in many popular forums.[466] Manichaean arguments are waged in the mass media about whether or not the Japanese were imperialist aggressors, anti-colonial liberators of Asia, or victims of Western imperialism— tautological and essentially moot arguments that, since 1945, have worked to erode memories and records alike of tangible historical events. Scientists have been no less willfully amnesiac: Ei Matsunaga, a geneticist writing in 1968 on birth control policy in Japan, made the preposterous and fallacious claim that "no eugenic movement has ever existed in this country."[467] Similarly, postwar demographers and biologists writing on consanguineous marriages in Japan somehow overlook or ignore the active role of the state and eugenics associations in fostering a negative image of inbreeding and instead attribute the decline in such marriages to an agentless "loss of traditional values".[468] Moreover, the journal *Minzoku Eisei* (Race Hygiene), launched in 1931, continues to be published, despite the disturbingly fascist allusions of the title

It is clear that eugenic formulations—"blood talks"—about Japanese nationality remain suspended in a *continuous present* where they shape and support political social, cultural, and aesthetic perceptions of ethnic and racial identity.[469] Only by recognizing and researching historical patterns of social engineering and nation-building, and only by remaining alert to their contemporization and to the continuous presence of their past, can we begin to frame a critical discourse of first- and second-wave eugenics both relevant to Japan and possessing comparative potential.

## CHAPTER EIGHT

# CULTURAL BROKERAGE AND INTERETHNIC MARRIAGE IN COLONIAL TAIWAN: JAPANESE SUBALTERNS AND THEIR ABORIGINE WIVES, 1895-1930[470]

PAUL D. BARCLAY

### Introduction

Scholars have long recognized the importance of interethnic marriage to European commercial expansion into the Americas, Africa, and Asia. George Brooks Jr. has chronicled the evolution of French-Senegalese marriages in eighteenth-century West Africa under the rubric of "Signareship" to demonstrate how ambitious Wolof and Lebou women "provided [European merchants] access to African commercial networks ... and proved indispensable as interpreters of African languages and cultures."[471] Theda Perdue has analyzed a similar pattern of opportunistic intermarriage between British merchants and daughters of Choctaw, Cherokee, Chickasaw, and Creek chiefs in eighteenth-century North America.[472] For late nineteenth- century northern Sumatra, Ann Stoler writes of "an extensive system of concubinage" on the plantations of the Deli region, where Dutch tobacco companies encouraged European liaisons with Javanese women to initiate subalterns into the local languages and customs of a booming frontier economy.[473]

In all these cases and others the necessity of linguistic facility for the conduct of commerce in commercial hinterlands is assumed, and the benefits of interethnic marriage toward attaining this end are taken as self-evident. Moving forward from these truisms, scholars have gone on to sketch the historical dynamics of these unions in terms of their local meanings and wider political ramifications. Interethnic marriages are said to have provided benefits for both local societies and European immigrants for a time. However, as power relationships shifted between Europeans and non-Europeans—that is, as trading peripheries became colonial spaces—interethnic unions lost their symbiotic character, either disappearing from the historical record or becoming occasions for violent altercation, heated debate, and general instability.

Two compelling explanatory frameworks have been proposed to account for these patterns. The first focuses on conditions in Europe's peripheries and points to the erosion of an early modern "middle ground." In this model, frontier conditions of mutual need produce a modicum of respect for local "customs of the country." On the "middle ground," foreigners constitute a small minority, whose power consists solely of supplying desirable imported trade goods and occasional political contacts. Host communities sanction these marriages, bringing them within the ambit of time-honored norms and safeguards. When immigration, state building, or trade dependency bring about outsider dominance, however, locals lose control over the terms of interethnic unions, and European males act wantonly, provoking resentment and vengeance.[474]

The other explanatory framework is decidedly more "metro-centric" and emphasizes European anxieties about racial mixture. In this model, changing European conceptions of race, respectability, and national identity open up a rift between subaltern males who marry into local societies and European elites who attempt to stop the practice of interethnic marriage. In part these European racial anxieties are driven by fears that hybrid loyalties or progeny will undermine a solidarity that must be maintained against threats of rebellion from the majority local population.[475] At the same time, intellectual currents within Europe, partly fueled by the fruits of maritime expansion, dispose colonials toward a racialist, biological view of human variety, creating the conceptual ground for casting interethnic marriages as unnatural, as "miscegenation".[476]

The literature on interethnic unions in the context of European expansion has thus provided scholars with an opportunity to relate material conditions, cultural predispositions, gender relations, and intellectual currents as they affect and are transformed by a major watershed in global history: the movement from an early modern world of empires and local societies, in which fluidity, porous boundaries, and interethnic mixing were the norm, to a modern world of putatively homogenous and distinct nations, created and preserved through practices of physical and symbolic boundary maintenance. In this literature, the search for a prehistory of Western racism is never far from the surface.[477]

As a non-Western example that straddles the early-modern and modern periods, the case of interethnic marriage in Taiwan under Japanese colonial rule takes on special significance. Resembling the Senegalese, Five Civilized Nations, and Sumatran examples cited above, interethnic marriages in Taiwan served a number of political and commercial functions in the early modern era. When Han Chinese immigration began to overwhelm Aborigine communities in the eighteenth century, however, instances of abuse became prominent. Conforming to the larger pattern, Han-Aborigine unions eventually earned the opprobrium of Qing elites who feared the destabilizing consequences of Chinese settler marriages into Aborigine families and polities. This cycle would repeat itself under Japanese colonial rule but with an interesting twist. Marriage between Japanese colonists and Aborigine women did not fade from the scene as an early modern marchland became a colonized territory—nor did these unions provoke official horror over the security ramifications and image problems associated with mixed progeny and men "gone native." Instead, the government-general embraced interethnic marriage as a solution to the problem of "Aborigine administration" in Taiwan's rugged mountain interior, where armed resistance to Japanese rule simmered well into the 1910s.

From 1908 through 1914, political alliances cemented with interethnic marriages paved the way for Japan's conquest of the northern Aborigine territory. The participants themselves, Japanese males and Atayal women, however, ended up divorced, abandoned, dead, or disgraced as a result of the "political-marriage" policy. I will argue that political marriages were a Japanese response to the Qing legacy of ethnic segregation policies in Taiwan's foothills and mountain ranges. Thus, the case of Aborigine-outsider intermarriage in Taiwan provides an occasion to analyze the role of interethnic unions in territorial expansion in both early modern and modern settings.

From the late Ming period on, when Chinese immigration to Taiwan reached significant proportions, interpreters known in Mandarin as *tongshi* conducted commerce and diplomacy and collected taxes among the Aborigine population. In the late Qing period, the role of *tongshi* was frequently performed by bicultural couples, Sinophone husbands and their Aborigine wives. In this milieu, a gender division of labor emerged in which the task of treating with lowlanders was relegated to women. This gender division of labor established the ground for the first wave of Japanese-Aborigine marriages in Taiwan, producing a number of *tongshi* who functioned much like their late Qing counterparts. The quasi-official status and uncertain loyalties of these interpreters, however, drew a chorus of steady criticism from Japanese policy-makers. But instead of banning interethnic marriage, the source of *tongshi* power, the Japanese state attempted to supercede marriages brokered by local headmen and Japanese freebooters with government-brokered marriages. The antecedents and consequences of the political-marriage policy illustrate how the conscious manipulation of Japanese and Atayal gender norms and family structures worked for and against the construction of empire in Taiwan's uplands.

As was the case in many arenas of Western colonial expansion, interethnic marriages between Japanese and Aborigines provoked official consternation. Western concerns with monogamous marriage and racial purity were much less pressing, however, for Meiji (1868–1912) and Taishō (1912–1926) Japanese, although these issues burned hotly in metropolitan Japanese discourse on modernity. Rather, the evidence suggests that everyday Japanese attitudes toward marriage and sexual propriety, based on notions of male prerogative and the maintenance of the stem family, were often consonant with late Qing-period Atayal practices of marrying out daughters and sisters for the benefit of the village or tribe. Atayal strictures about monogamous marriage and expectations that in-marrying males would act as political allies were more likely to cause frictions related to interethnic marriage than race or class anxieties generated in the metropoles of Taipei or Tokyo. To understand the dynamics and importance of interethnic marriages on expanding colonial frontiers, we need to enlarge the compass of our research and consider factors beyond Western notions—be they subaltern or elite—of race, class, and gender before we can build global models. The following chapter is an attempt to make a start on this project.

### "Acquiring Intimate Knowledge of the Barbarians and Their Language": Interpreters As Merchants, Local Bullies, and Subofficials

Over the centuries of Qing rule (1683–1895) in Taiwan, *tongshi* endured numerous historical vicissitudes to survive as primary conduits of trade and diplomacy across the shifting geographic, cultural, and political divide separating Aborigines from Han Chinese. This so-called savage border (*bankai/fanjie*) evolved from a porous, vaguely defined frontier to a meticulously demarcated, state-maintained boundary line over the course of the Qing period (see Figure 8.1). The English word "interpreter" is a good approximation for *tongshi*, since linguistic prowess was central to the role. At the same time, *tongshi* participated in commerce and rural administration, tasks which separated them from mere translators. Moreover, *tongshi* were primarily associated with oral interpreting, which lowered

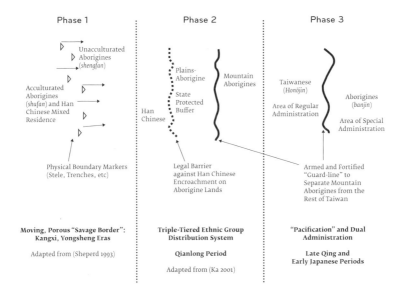

Phase 1 | Phase 2 | Phase 3

Unacculturated Aborigines (shengfan)

Acculturated Aborigines (shufan) and Han Chinese Mixed Residence

Physical Boundary Markers (Stele, Trenches, etc.)

Plains-Aborigine

State Protected Buffer

Han Chinese

Mountain Aborigines

Legal Barrier against Han Chinese Encroachment on Aborigine Lands

Taiwanese (Honōjin)

Area of Regular Administration

Aborigines (banjin)

Area of Special Administration

Armed and Fortified "Guard-line" to Separate Mountain Aborigines from the Rest of Taiwan

**Moving, Porous "Savage Border":
Kangxi, Yongsheng Eras**

Adapted from (Sheperd 1993)

**Triple-Tiered Ethnic Group
Distribution System**

**Qianlong Period**

Adapted from (Ka 2001)

**"Pacification" and Dual
Administration**

**Late Qing and
Early Japanese Periods**

Figure 8.1 Schematic diagram of the Han-Aborigine frontier. Phase 1 represents an early period of makeshift boundaries and mixed residence patterns (adapted from Shepherd, 1993). Phase 2 brings a clearer separation of Han Chinese from Plains Aborigines as a result of the Qing strategy to use the Aborigines to defend against the Mountain Aborigines and restrain the Han (adapted from Ka, 2001). Phase 3 marks the disappearance of the Plains Aborigines as a major force in border affairs after the 1875 campaign to "Open the Mountains, Pacify the Aborigines" (*Kaishan fufan*).

their official status and salaries vis-à-vis the more text-oriented "translators" (*tsūyaku*) of the Japanese period. For comparative analysis, *tongshi* can be best characterized as cultural brokers, described by Daniel Richter "as simultaneous members of two or more interacting networks (kin groups, political factions, communities or other formal or informal coalitions), [who] provide nodes of communication ... with respect to a community's relations with the outside world."[478] The niche filled by *tongshi* reflected the topography, ethnic composition, and political economy of Qing- and early Japanese- period Taiwan.

In the earliest records of Aborigine-outsider interaction, the themes of trade dependency, intermarriage, and official suspicion punctuate descriptions of *tongshi* in Taiwan. Chen Di's 1603 *Account of the Eastern Barbarians* (*Dongfan ji*) explains that Fujianese traders brought "agates, porcelain, cloth, salt, and brass" to Taiwan to trade for deer horns, hides, and meat. Chen lamented that Aborigines had "developed some desires" leading "rascals [to] cheat them with junk."[479] Two decades later, Commander Cornelis Reyersen observed Taiwan Aborigines exporting diverse animal products for "coarse porcelain and some unbleached linen." These exports were brokered by the "Chinese living there, who ... married local women."[480] A February 1624 VOC (Dutch East India Company) record suggests that trade dependency gave Chinese immigrants near Fort Zeelandia leverage disproportionate to their numbers: "In almost every house [in Soulang] ... one, two, three, nay sometimes even five or six Chinese are lodged, whom [the Aborigines] keep very much under control. ... Likewise they themselves are bullied by the Chinese for not giving them food or not working hard enough. *The Chinese immediately threaten to deprive them of salt, which means they are dependent on them.*"[481] (see Figure 8.2).

In 1697, travelogue writer Yu Yonghe described *tongshi* as quasi officials who took advantage of Aborigine trade dependence and the early Qing's weak state capacity in Taiwan. Yu's account became a template for subsequent records:[482]

> In each administrative district a wealthy person is made responsible for the village revenues. These men are called "village tax-farmers" [*sheshang*]. The village tax-farmer in turn appoints interpreters (*tongshi*) and foremen (*huozhang*) who are sent to live in the villages, and who record and check up on ... the barbarians (*fan*). ... But these [interpreters and foremen] take advantage of the simple-mindedness of the barbarians and never tire of fleecing them. ... Moreover, they take the barbarian women (*fanfu*) as their wives and concubines (*qiqie*).[483]

To the consternation of literati such as Yu, the lands beyond Qing-administered territory were havens for fugitives from justice. Renegade *tongshi* and the so-called village bullies (*shegun*) operated in close cahoots, according to Yu's damning account:

> With the passage of time [village bullies] acquire an intimate knowledge of the barbarians and their language. ... The affairs of the villages are left to the machinations [of the bullies]. ... [The bullies] take advantage of the simplicity of the barbarians. ... [E]ven if there are some who appeal to justice, the judge cannot get at the facts of the case because of the language barrier, and he still has to ask the interpreter

## Taiwan Political Map

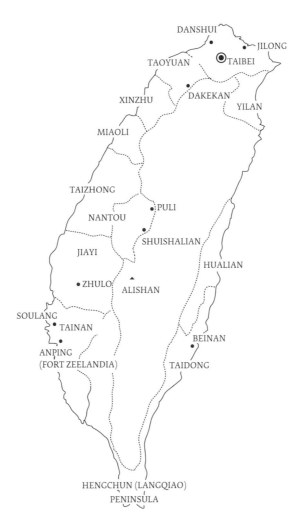

Figure 8.2 Locations of major villages and cities mentioned in this chapter. Prefectural and district boundaries are for October 1909 through September 1920 (adapted from Chen, 1993, 105).v

........................................................................................

to explain. The interpreter turns right into wrong and wrong into right, and it is the barbarian instead who gets a scolding. ... Therefore the barbarian dreads the village bully even more, and serves him like God

**159**

Himself.[484]

Although local bullies and assorted ne'er-do-wells exerted considerable pressure on Aborigine villages in the southwestern "core region" of former Dutch- (1624–1661) and Zheng-period (1661–1683) settlement, *tongshi* did not terrorize the whole island. Interpreters operating near the major Aborigine settlements of Alishan, Shuishalian, and Hengchun (see Figure 8.2) had little actual contact with more-remote tribes known as *shengfan*, or "raw barbarians."[485] *Tongshi* were linked to Taiwan's deep interior via relay trade with more-acculturated *shufan* (cooked barbarians).[486] Huang Shujing, a contemporary observer, described the relay trade in Paiwan country circa 1722: "In every village the raw barbarians carry on trade in beads, cloth, salt, and iron with the *shufan*; while the latter emerge to trade with the interpreters."[487] *Tongshi* "tax collection" in early eighteenth-century Alishan has the appearance of exchange, rather than extraction, betraying the government's lack of authority in the highlands: "The interpreter has built another hut ... for distributing [goods] to braves from these villages, stocking tobacco, cloth, sugar and salt to supply the needs of the local barbarians. [Here also the latter] sell their deer meat, skins, sinews and such, in order to pay their taxes. ... Altogether, trade and tax-paying can be carried on for ten months."[488]

The above descriptions of *tongshi* activity from the seventeenth and early eighteenth centuries confirm that the character of cultural brokerage and the power of *tongshi* to oppress Aborigines were indeed variable across space and over time. The standard periodization scheme for Taiwan's past—the Dutch, Zheng, Qing, Japanese, and Kuomintang (KMT) (1946–2000) eras—posits the entire island as the subject of history and cannot accommodate the geographic variation so characteristic of cultural brokerage along the moving "savage border." World-systems theory, in contrast, does not use the nation-state as its organizing principle. Instead, its spatial units of analysis are derived from fluctuations in relative power relations, concentrations of capital, and technological capabilities. Such a framework, as Richter has argued, is useful for longitudinal and comparative studies of cultural brokerage.[489]

The world system, as defined by Thomas Hall, is an "intersocietal system that has a self-contained division of labor with some degree of internal coherence. ... It is a key unit of analysis within which all other social structures and processes should be analyzed."[490] For our analysis, the area of Taiwan that encompasses a coherent political economy, in conjunction with the external economies to which this area is linked, constitutes a world system. Hall's definition of a frontier as "a region or zone where two or more distinct cultures, societies, ethnic groups, or modes of production come into contact" will be used to describe Taiwan's so-called savage border.[491] Hall defines three ideal types of frontier based on relative *degrees of incorporation* into a world system, which will be used as analytical tools to make general claims about the emergence, vicissitudes, and disappearance of cultural brokerage in Taiwan. They are the "contact periphery," that is, a frontier with little or no sustained connection to a core after initial contact; the "marginal periphery," which participates in an intersocietal division of labor while retaining a separate corporate existence; and the "dependent periphery," whose economy requires sustained involvement in (unequal) exchange relations with the core. Through trade dependency and/or political conquest, dependent peripheries are *incorporated* into the world system to which they had once been external or marginal.[492] The Han-dominated side of the frontier is herein considered the "core" because it contains the linkages to other cores beyond Taiwan's shores (Fuzhou, Beijing, Tokyo, Nagasaki, or London). Moreover, Aborigine societies have historically been incorporated into Han- or Japanese-centered political economies, while movement in the other direction has been infrequently observed.

By definition, contact peripheries exist astride but beyond intersocietal divisions of labor. A cultural broker may conduct profitable trade with peoples on a contact periphery but will exert little political influence. In a dependent periphery, acculturation will proceed to such an extent that cultural brokers are no longer necessary. The middle position (the marginal periphery), presents the best opportunities for cultural brokers to proliferate and exert influence. Here, societies on either side of the frontier, core and periphery, remain distinct, yet are economically interdependent, providing the niche for brokerage to emerge as a valued and necessary service. When power relations or concentrations of capital are asymmetrical, the core expands and incorporates marginal peripheries, pushing the terrain of cultural brokerage into new marginal peripheries farther afield. If core expansion is unchecked by topography, resistance, or a third party, cultural brokers will disappear altogether.

## Territorializing Ethnicity in Qing Taiwan
In the decades following Taiwan's Kangxi era (1683–1722), Han settlement expanded to the foothills of Taiwan's island-length central mountain spine. A combination of Aborigine initiative (acquisition of language and business acumen), Qing policy

(Aborigine schools, suppression of Han *tongshi*), and Han Chinese ambition (expansion of acreage under cultivation) transformed marginal peripheries into dependent ones throughout the lowlands, seemingly dooming Taiwan's Han *tongshi* to extinction.[493] In the aftermath of major rebellions in 1731 and 1737, however, Qing grand strategy intervened. From the 1740s on, the court brought a near halt to the expansion of Han settlement, giving the *tongshi* a second lease on life.

During the Qianlong era (1736–1795), the court formulated Taiwan policy with two contradictory objectives in mind: promote agricultural development and maintain frontier stability.[494] The Qing balanced the goals of increased acreage under the plow and reduced incidents of frontier violence by physically separating "Han Chinese," *shufan*, and *shengfan* into ethnically demarcated zones of residence. Under the "three-tiered ethnic-group settlement system" (*sancengzhi zuqun fenbu jiagou*), so called by Ka Chih-ming, the Plains Aborigines, formerly known as *shufan* (cooked barbarians), acted as armed buffers against Han encroachment beyond the limits of Qing administration. At the same time, they protected the rice-producing regions from raids and attacks by mountaineers, whose violence against plainsmen stemmed from a mixture of self-defense, revenge, and culturally sanctioned head taking. This three tiered system was cheaper than garrisoning the savage border with Qing troops from the mainland, and it was preferable to letting Han immigrants continue to stir up trouble by stealing land, poaching resources, and hatching plots in the foothills.[495]

From the 1740s on, the government stepped up protection of Plains Aborigines' rights as landlords and reduced their tax burdens.[496] Over the subsequent decades, Qing officials clarified the boundaries between "raw barbarian" (*shengfan*) territory in the mountains and arable acreage in the foothills. The newly surveyed foothill land was then reserved for "cooked barbarians" (*shufan*). In the 1780s, *shufan* military colonies were built on the new reserve land to solidify the triple-tiered system.[497]

In the Kangxi and Yongzheng (1723–1735) eras, the savage border was a moving frontier characterized by settlements of interspersed Aborigine and Han villages on either side. The Qianlong savage border, in contrast, starkly separated Plains Aborigine military colonies and reservations from the *shengfan* lands beyond the pale. In the triple-tiered system, *tongshi* became brokers between Taiwan's mountains and plains. *Tongshi*, both Han and *shufan*, paid government bribes to *shengfan* in return for access to water rights to irrigate newly expanded agricultural territory. *Tongshi* also

# Taiwan Aborigine Ethnic Groups

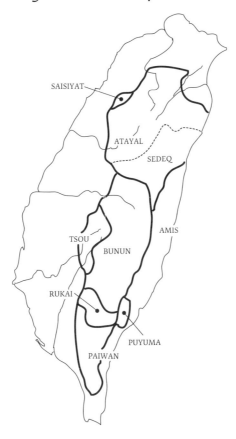

Figure 8.3  Major ethnic divisions of Taiwan Aborigines as recognized by the government-general during the Meiji and Taishō periods, with approximate contemporary boundaries (Nihon Jun'eki Taiwan Genjūmin Kenkyūkai, 2001, 8).

continued to farm taxes for *shufan* villages distant from centers of government and Han settlement. Other *tongshi* engaged in private trade. As in earlier times, interpreters were frequently blamed for fomenting revolts, oppressing Aborigines, and illegally opening up new land for cultivation.[498]

As early as 1722, officials expressed the fear that frontier intermarriages were reducing the number of eligible brides for Aborigine males, thereby decimating the Aborigine population. Imperial scholar E Ertai warned that Han marriages into Aborigine society would discourage Han agrarian productivity and social stability. Other observers complained the Han were marrying

Plains Aborigine women to gain influence and accrue property in matrilineal societies beyond the reach of government supervision. In 1737 the Qing finally banned interethnic marriages. Since such unions produced the *tongshi* necessary for keeping tabs on the population beyond the passes, however, they were secretly tolerated by local officials. Examples of men who violated the prohibition to become prominent in the annals of rural administration and reclamation included Wu Sha, who married into Sandiao Village near Taipei in the late eighteenth century, and Huang Qiying, who married into a Saisiyat Village in Nanzhuang during the 1810s[499] (see Figures 8.3, 8.4, and 8.5).

## Gender Division of Labor and Cultural Brokerage

The wives of enterprising Han settlers and officials such as Wu and Huang likely emerged as an important class of female interpreters during the implementation of the triple-tiered system in the mid- to late eighteenth century. The militarization of the savage border undoubtedly reduced the opportunities for Aborigine males to descend the mountains peacefully for commerce.[500] In addition, the forced-segregation policies would have impeded the diffusion of Minnan and Hakka into the interior. Biculturals continued to thrive on an island whose political segregation could not forestall its economic integration.

In the 1850s, Taiwan began to export significant amounts of tea and camphor to Western buyers, yoking the island's economy more tightly to the Euro-American core area of the nineteenth-century world system. The high return on products grown in elevated, cooler climates shifted Taiwan's economic center of gravity away from the southwestern plains northward and inland. During the treaty-port period (1860–95), the foothills and valleys of northern Taiwan, once contact peripheries at best, fast became marginal peripheries of the global economy.[501] The new mania for the "riches of the interior" moved Qing literati, who once portrayed the uplands as miasmic, cruel, and treacherous, to reevaluate the interior as a verdant source of wealth.[502]

Western visitors to Taiwan in the treaty-port era observed that Aborigine women were central to cultural brokerage in the marginal periphery. In 1857 future British consul Robert Swinhoe wrote: "I had the pleasure of seeing a few [Aborigine] women, who were married to Chinese at ... [Hengchun]. ... [A] Chinaman named Bancheang, of large landed property, traded with the Kalees [Paiwan] of the hills. ... He was constantly at variance with the Chinese authorities who had outlawed him, but could not

# Northern Taiwan Under Japanese Colonial Rule

Figure 8.4 Division of the northern tribes of Taiwan under Japanese rule (adapted from Deng, 2001, 191; Asai and Ogawa, 1935; Kusaka, 1936).

touch him, as he was so well defended by his numerous Chinese dependants, and the large body of Aborigines at his beck. This man was wedded to a Kalee..."[503]

A few years later, William Pickering, a well-known interpreter in his own right, described the chief of one village as a "T'ong-su" (*tongshi*), the "headman of the tribe, responsible to the Chinese government." Pickering wrote that the "women had some knowledge of the Celestial tongue, from being employed as go-betweens in their bartering with the Chinese. ... This old woman [our interpreter], named Pu-li-sang, was no novice to the ways of civilization, as she had, years ago, been married to a Chinese, and also had lived from some time with the [shengfan] Bangas. ..."[504] On the eve of the Japanese invasion in 1874, American naturalist Joseph Steere confirmed the role of Aborigine women as mediators in commerce between mountain and plain: "The Kale-whan [Paiwan], in times of scarcity, frequently sell their daughters to the Chinese and Pepo-whans [Peipoban/Pingpufan], who take them as supplementary wives and make them useful as interpreters in thus bartering with the savages. While we were among the Kale-whan the chief offered to sell us three girls of the tribe at twenty dollars each."[505]

Japanese infantryman Takeshi Iriye, observing conditions just after the cession in 1895, attributed such practices to increased cross-border trade:

> In *shufan* territory, *shengfan* give their daughters away and force them to marry. This is a recent occurrence; it did not happen in former times. ... All these types of marriages are related directly to *shufan* trade. ... A meeting of the minds is reached between man and woman, and the marriage is arranged. Before any immorality is committed, the chief's permission is sought and the marriage carried through. When a *shufan* takes a *shengfan* concubine, the new bride is given Chinese clothing, and so on. ... For the return trip home, they are given a water buffalo, two jars of liquor, and black and red cloth.[506]

As Iriye explains, the need for access to trade goods was tempered by the desire to preserve distance from Qing surveillance and Han exploitation:

> Again, a female *shufan* may marry a *shengfan* man. This is always a result of a young girl being lured away into the mountains and then becoming accustomed to *shengfan* ways—once she learns the language, she can act as an interpreter when the *shengfan* come to trade with the *shufan*. So, when the *shengfan* spy a girl they are attracted to, they wait for an opportune moment to lure her away. ... The parents of the girl are angry at the request for marriage, but they do not have any way

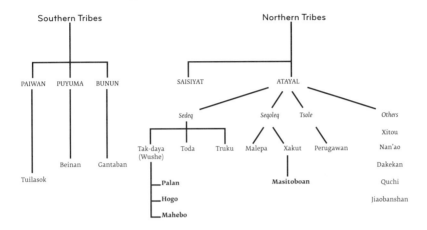

Figure 8.5 Divisions and subdivisions of Taiwan Mountain Aborigines as they were understood during the period of Japanese rule. There is no standard orthography for these names in Chinese, Japanese, or English. I have followed the spellings in Deng, 2001 where possible and have used pinyin renderings of Chinese place names/ethnonyms where necessary. This chart is not exhaustive.

to take the girl back from the savage *shengfan*, and then again, they stand to make large profits from the *shengfan* trade. The *shengfan* bring gifts of monkey, opossum, and mountain animals. When the girl has become accustomed enough to her new life, she is permitted to return to her hometown. She is greeted with great warmth and happiness, but her parents and siblings are not allowed into the "savage territory" (*banchi*), only she can go there and move about freely; she is singular for not being tattooed and for wearing Chinese clothing.[507]

Two features of Aborigine out-marrying practices described above should be underscored. First, whether the bride was *shengfan* or *shufan*, intermediaries were used and public exchanges of gifts took place, indicating that a degree of social recognition was being conferred upon these marriages. Ushinosuke Mori, who did extensive fieldwork throughout Atayal country from 1900 through the early 1920s, asserted that bride price—in the form of red cloth skirts (up to one hundred in extreme cases), cattle, pigs, guns, daggers, farming implements, and even farmland—was customary at Atayal weddings.[508] Second, *shengfan* parties to these unions were careful to assure that marriage alliances did not result in *too much* familiarity between lowlanders and highlanders. A number of episodes from the early Japanese period indicate that paramount chiefs and other enterprising headmen enriched themselves and accrued political power by interposing themselves between villages farther inland and delegates of foreign powers, thereby monopolizing outflows of mountain products and inflows of imported prestige goods. Thus, although Steere's observation that desperate families sold off daughters to outsiders for cash may have held in certain localities, there is much evidence to suggest that out-marrying was part of a complex political strategy to maintain power in a decentralized political world in which the distribution of gifts and the monopolization of access to goods was a key to maintaining leadership status.[509]

In response to the booming export economy in resources extracted from the interior, governor Liu Mingchuan established the Fukenju (Bureau of Reclamation and Pacification) in 1886 to regulate relations between the Mountain Aborigines and Taiwan's Han population.[510] By then the association of indigenous women with cultural brokerage had been cemented. The Fukenju charter specified that "*banba* [Aborigine women] should ... greet and feast *banjin* [Aborigines] who come down from the mountains." The Japanese gloss to this passage added: "these are taken mainly from *banpu* [Aborigine women] married to *shinajin* [Chinese men]."[511]

### Interpreters under Japanese Colonial Rule
When Japanese troops arrived in Aborigine strongholds in summer 1895 to announce the regime change to their new subjects, they hired *tongshi* to conduct them through the mountain passes. The first such mission, under garrison commander Watanabe, met seven Aborigines at a clearing in front of Caoling Mountain on August 29. The discussions took place within a couple miles of Dakekan, former headquarters of Liu Mingchuan's Fukenju. The soldiers distributed gifts of liquor, tobacco, silver coins, and tinned mackerel to secure an agreement to meet again. The elder female Aborigine, named Yūkaimā, wore a simple blanket, sported tattoos, and went barefoot. The younger female Aborigine was around eighteen, wore manufactured Chinese clothing, and "could pass for Japanese but for her braided hair."[512] Named Fuwanhō, the younger woman appeared to be the Aborigine village's delegate in

dealings with Chinese.

On September 8, future Taipei governor Bunzō Hashiguchi led an expedition to Caoling to follow up on Watanabe's initial overtures. The Japanese party, with one official translator in tow, distributed daggers, red woolen cloth, hairpins, calicoes, tinned meat, tobacco, and alcohol to twenty-two Dakekan-area residents at the rendezvous point. Five of them were persuaded with promises of additional blankets to return to Taipei to meet government officials. A well-circulated photograph of these five appeared in various Japanese periodicals. One of the five, an Aborigine woman named Washiiga, hailed from Jiaobanshan. Unlike the other four, her hair was bound and she wore some "old Chinese clothing." Washiiga understood the "Formosan language somewhat" because she had married a Chinese man at the age of sixteen.[513] With Washiiga's assistance, Hashiguchi recorded the Aborigines' names, domiciles, and ages in his all-important register.[514]

A week later, Hashiguchi ordered subprefect Shuichirō Kawano to lead Japan's first official embassy to Yilan's Aborigine territory. Kawano's mission set off with only a Japanese *tsūyakukan* or *tsūyakusei* (official translator), for fear that a Chinese *tongshi* would cause trouble. Eventually Kawano located four *tongshi* of former Qing employ and their *banpu* wives at Yilan's old Fukenju locations. Kawano described the women as "pure Aborigines with facial tattoos."[515] The men were *kabanjin/huafanren*, or "transformed barbarians."[516] Kawano deputized the women as *tsūben* (another word for "interpreter") because the male "transformed barbarians" were likely to be rebuffed or worse by Xitou tribesmen. The women then went inland and convinced a Xitou chief to meet Japanese officials on neutral ground. On November 16, Kawano's party distributed a Japanese flag, gifts, drink, and food to the assembled villagers. The Xitou contingent firmly refused Kawano's entreaties to visit the walled city of Yilan for further parleys and also resisted Japanese requests to travel farther inland. The Xitou emissaries did offer to distribute the remaining gifts to other tribes and act as intermediaries between the Japanese and the other inland villages.[517] Awai, one of the *tsūben* hired by Kawano, appears in an ethnographic note published just after the Yilan mission as an informant on language, village names, and local songs. She was thirty years old and married to *shufan* Chen Xilai for eight years. Although she wore some Chinese clothes, she retained distinctive tattoos and spoke the local Aborigine dialect effortlessly.[518]

The government-general initiated diplomacy in southern Taiwan's Aborigine country much later than it did in the north.

Because Paiwan and Puyuma country were close to centers of organized Han armed resistance, conditions were quite turbulent into late 1895 and early 1896. By summer 1896, thanks to the timely aid of a bicultural Han-Aborigine *tongshi* couple, the government-general was able to establish a presence on the Hengchun peninsula and in Taidong District (see Figure 8.2). The Beinan interpreter variously referred to by Japanese as "Dada," "Xi Lu Niu," and "Tata Rara" played a pivotal role in this enterprise. Tata was born in 1864 to a paramount chief named Ansheng. During the Charles LeGendre and Tsugumichi Saigō expeditions of 1872 through 1874,[519] Ansheng collaborated closely with Americans and Japanese.[520] Tata married a Chinese man named Zhang, who appears in documents as both an interpreter and prosperous merchant—one source calls him Yichun, the other Xinzhang.[521] Tata spoke Minnan as well as the Beinan, Paiwanese, and Amis languages. She earned a salary of six yuan per month as a Qing *tongshi*.[522]

When future prefect Nagatsuna Sagara arrived in Taidong in February 1896, Tuilasok (Chorōsoku) chief Pan Wenjie, a powerful Hengchun headman who also collaborated with Westerners during the late Qing period, arranged a meeting for the village heads to pledge their cooperation with Japanese officials. Sagara soon learned that demobilized Qing troops were pressing locals for rations; Ansheng and Pan sought Japanese intervention. In May, Pan, Japanese translator Yūsuke Nakamura, interpreter-merchant Zhang Yichun/Xinzhang, and *tongshi* Tata Rara organized a militia of three hundred Aborigines in Beinan to expel the Qing remnants. Tata's work as the liaison among Beinan chiefs, Pan, and Nakamura earned her a commendation from the government-general in 1901, which came with forty yen.[523]

As Japanese officials drew on the expertise and networks of Qing-period *tongshi* to establish a presence, however faint, among the highlanders, they began to replicate Qing discourse on *tongshi* perfidy. The following description of the frustratingly complex process of mediation in Taiwan's interior is typical of the period:

> An interpreter (*tongshi*) is a Chinese who is good at Aborigine languages and is conversant with conditions among them.[524] Each hamlet or group of hamlets has an interpreter (a hamlet is similar to our *buraku*). The "local man" (*sheding/shatei*) works under the interpreter, procuring whatever is needed for each side to facilitate communication, diplomacy, and so on. Each hamlet without fail has a *sheding*. These local

men and interpreters are not always to be found in the hamlets, though. They have their own households with affairs to attend to, and they hire themselves out to people. Moreover, these interpreters can apply for government service. Officials screen them, and ... they become responsible for relaying directives and taking care of all manner of things related to the Aborigines. ... One imagines that their income is not small. ... The interpreters and local men assume an arrogant and insulting manner towards the Aborigines, who in turn treat the interpreters very humbly.[525]

A minimum of two interpreters, but usually three, brokered Japanese-Aborigine communication in the early years of colonial rule. Japanese men known as official translators interpreted for government officials to the Chinese interpreters. These Chinese interpreters stood between the official translators and the intermediaries known simply as "local men" (*sheding*) or "Aborigine women" (*banpu*). Despite their low official status, these *sheding* and *banpu* were indispensable for sojourns in the Aborigine territories. When Fukenju chief Otosaku Saitō's Japanese official translator, Kunitei Shōjiro, was incapacitated with malaria during an early circuit of Alishan's environs, Saitō's mission continued to function. Saitō would not proceed, however, without local men.[526] An official from the interpreter's bureau in Miaoli underscored the point: four different languages were spoken behind the mountains abutting Miaoli City. It was simply impossible to conduct business there without local interpreters.[527]

## Japanese Discontent with the *Tongshi* System
In Taiwan under Japanese rule, the messages conveyed by officials to Aborigines were simple at first: the victors had come to announce the defeat of the Qing and demand recognition from local chiefs. Moreover, in the first months of Japanese rule, the Japanese came to the savage border bearing gifts—textiles, foodstuffs, tobacco, and alcohol—with few strings attached. These ceremonial presentations were well understood by Japanese emissaries and Aborigine headmen as the substance of relations that centered on the distribution of gifts, the formal recognition of government authority, and the initiation of commercial relations.[528] Under such circumstances, the limited ability of each side to understand the nuances and subtleties of the other's verbal proclamations appears to have sufficed. As the government-general settled in for the long haul, it began to directly adjudicate conflicts between Han and

Aborigines and to take an active interest in the profitability of the camphor industry. Deepened involvement in the affairs of Atayal country in turn placed greater demands on Japan's interpreters.

On March 31, 1896, the Japanese chartered the Bukonsho (Office of Pacification and Reclamation) to establish friendly relations with Aborigines, develop the camphor industry, and canvass the *banchi* for information on the unknown mountain tribes (Inō 1918/1995, 1:13–20). Article 9 of the Bukonsho charter indicates official dissatisfaction with the ad hoc system of cultural brokerage inherited from the Qing:

> The most urgent matter for Aborigine pacification
> is obtaining adequate or appropriate (*tekitō*)
> interpreters. ... History has shown that interpreters
> often take advantage of mutual unintelligibility, and
> as middlemen deceive both sides for their own great
> profit. There are examples of Aborigine sensibilities
> being wounded. Therefore, it is very important to
> consider the interpreters' character and the Aborigines'
> feelings toward them before employing one. Aborigine
> languages are not exceedingly difficult to learn, so if
> Bukonsho officials will make efforts to learn them, it will
> benefit and open new avenues for us all.[529]

Despite these optimistic pronouncements, it turned out that Aborigine languages were not easy for Japanese officials to learn, so the government-general made due with the *tongshi*, *sheding*, and *banpu* who dwelled among the passes to the mountain country. Otosaku Saitō, posted to Jiayi District in 1896 to head the Bukonsho, wrote that the village of Dongpushe was "under the control" of a *tongshi* named Du Tingdong. Saitō described Du's associates (*sheding*) as sullen and crafty Chinese men who dressed in Aborigine clothing. Provisions could be had for fair prices in direct negotiations with Aborigines, wrote Saitō, but once the *sheding* intervened, prices rose and commerce became difficult.[530] Zhang Shichang, Saitō's own interpreter, learned his craft in the Fukenju under the Qing regime, where he began service around 1887. He headed a somewhat prosperous house and managed the trade between three Chinese villages and two Aborigine settlements. Saitō wrote that Zhang took hefty profits as a provisioner on the Jiayi Bukonsho expedition to Tsou country.[531]

An early editorial in the *Taiwan shinpō* (*Taiwan News*) excoriated *tongshi* for exploiting the Hualian-area Aborigines and paying them mere pittances for their laboriously produced hemp blankets.[532] Until Aborigine languages were understood, a Bukonsho official wrote in 1898, Japan was doomed to rely on local intermediaries who cheated Aborigines at trade after plying them with booze. These seedy men also trafficked in contraband rifles, threatening Japan's security.[533] But despite these complaints, there was little that the Japanese could do to decrease their reliance on *banpu*, *sheding*, and *tongshi* because official translators were prohibitively expensive and of little use beyond the walled cities where standard dialects of Chinese were understood.

In Taidong, district chief Nagatsuna Sagara reinstated the Qing-era interpreters as village officials, thereby resurrecting a system of indirect rule. Government-general inspectors made the usual complaints about interpreter greed and untrustworthiness. Nonetheless, they recommended that *tongshi* be deputized and paid stipends as local officials on the "devil-you-know" theory.[534] A number of Japanese-language training institutes were established among Aborigines in Paiwan country beginning in 1896, the first under the aegis of Pan Wenjie, Sagara's partner in Hengchun. These southern schools graduated a core of reliable Aborigine intermediaries at a relatively early date.[535] In northern Aborigine territory, however, things took a much different turn. Among the Atayal and Sedeq peoples (see Figure 8.5), a cooperative strongman of Pan's stature was not to be found. Instead, the Japanese dealt with a host of aspirants for the role of middleman, involving the government in the complex politics of marriage alliance across the so- called savage border.

### Marriage, Concubinage, and Brokerage in the North

Puli subprefect Tetsusaburō Hiyama was the first prominent Japanese official to marry into an Aborigine polity. In early 1896, Hiyama wed the daughter of a paramount Wushe (Musha) chief named Bihau Sabo.[536] To seal the alliance with Bihau, Hiyama slaughtered two oxen and numerous pigs in addition to distributing jars of liquor and blankets at the wedding feast. Ignorant of the local languages and oblivious to Wushe's historical enmity with Toda, another cluster of villages to the east of Wushe, Hiyama admitted several non-Wushe guests to enjoy the largesse. After the celebration, Wushe warriors ambushed the returning Toda men and took their wedding gifts away, upset that Hiyama would treat visitors from afar with the same generosity shown to the tribe that provided his bride. Hiyama later distributed an ox and a jar of liquor to neighboring Toda, Perugawan, and Truku to display his impartiality, which only brought Bihau back to fire off his matchlock at Hiyama's gate for assuming the paramount chief's prerogative of distributing gifts among the subsidiary tribes.[537]

Hiyama's most notorious associate, Katsusaburō Kondō (b. 1873), would spend the rest of his life in Taiwan, achieving fluency in Taiwanese and at least one dialect of Atayal. Under Hiyama's patronage, Kondō was granted a permit to "trade in Aborigine products" in Puli on May 19, 1896.[538] Contemporary references to Kondō label him as *tongshi*, *shokutaku* (commissioner), or *buppin kōkanjin* (Aborigine trader).[539] As a first step to becoming a celebrated "Aborigine hand" (*bantsū*), Kondō wed Iwan Robau, the daughter of a Palan village headman named Chitsukku, sometime in 1896.[540]

In January 1897, Kondō and Iwan joined the ill-fated Yasuichirō Fukahori expedition as interpreters (see Figures 8.6 and 8.7). Fukahori's fourteen-man crew was subsequently ambushed and murdered while surveying routes to link Taizhong to Hualian.[541] Before the expedition entered the high mountains beyond Puli, however, Kondō succumbed to malaria and was spared a gruesome death. Iwan accompanied the mission as an auxiliary interpreter, working with Kondō's replacement, a *shufan* named Pan Laolong, also a merchant specializing in the "Aborigine trade".[542] Pan and Iwan survived because they abandoned the mission before it came to grief, rightfully fearing danger as the troupe traveled beyond areas previously secured through parleys with local chiefs. Aborigine-language *tongshi* such as Pan and Iwan were of limited or no utility beyond narrowly circumscribed territories, much to the chagrin of the Japanese. The search for Fukahori's remains was greatly impeded and finally called off for want of willing local trackers in Toda and Truku. In retaliation for the Fukahori debacle, the government-general cut off traffic in guns, ammunition, salt, and matches to the Puli trading posts, Wushe's main supplier, for a period of eight years.[543]

ウバロンワュ妻の郎三勝藤近
（女長のクッッチ目頭社ソラーバ）

Figure 8.6 Iwan Robau, daughter of a Palan headman and interpreter on the Fukahori expedition of 1897 (Ide, 1937, 278).

On August 20, 1897, Kondō left his wife, Iwan, and headed north to Truku-Toda country, since Japan's punitive embargo had forced Kondō's trading post near Puli to close down. He brought two of his employees, Yoshitsugu Nagakura and Shūkichi Itō, in addition to securing the services of Itō's wife, a Toda native named Tappas Kuras.[544] After a grueling, rain-soaked march, Kondō secured the patronage of a trade-minded Toda headman named Bassau Bōran, a former customer at Kondō's Puli establishment. As Bassau's trading partner, houseguest, and adopted son, Kondō literally "went native" in the course of his twenty-month stay, earning the sobriquet "Seiban Kondō" (Kondō the Barbarian).[545] While Kondō and Itō bartered their way around Toda-Truku territory, unions between Japanese men and Aborigine females became commonplace in Taiwan. As in Qing times, officials worried about the deleterious effects of these pairings on political stability in the colony. In 1899 Sanjiaoyong district officer Yoshimasa Satomi complained to Taipei governor Yoshio Murakami that Japanese-*banpu* unions were causing undue friction with local males. Satomi suggested that Japanese civilians be forced to apply for permits before taking *banpu* as wives. Murakami then proposed a system of punishments for Japanese men who abandoned *banpu* mates. In addition, Murakami recommended state support for the abandoned women, whose local marriage prospects had been ruined by public association with foreigners. Murakami's questionnaire, circulated to magistrates and police posted in Aborigine territory, illuminates official concerns with intercultural marriage along the savage border:

深堀大尉近藤と亡人三郎
（深藤近蕃生と緯名された人）

Figure 8.7 Katsusaburō Kondō is here pictured with the widow of Yasuichirō Fukahori, who was killed in early 1897 while surveying a railway line across Atayal country (Ide, 1937, 278).

- To what extent are there contracts or gifts of cash or merchandise on the occasion of a wedding (*kashu no sai*)?
- The name and occupation of the person who married a *banpu* (*banpu o metorishi mono*).
- Is it possible for one who has been a secondary wife/concubine of a Japanese to remarry an Aborigine (*naichijin no shō/mekake to naritaru mono wa futatabi banjin ni kasuru*)?
- In the case of abandonment, how is the *banpu* managing? How do the Aborigines feel about the

situation?

- Was the union with a Japanese (*naichijin ni kasuru*) entered into as a lifelong commitment, or was it rushed into avariciously for the short term?[546]

The operative verbs in the Satomi-Murakami correspondence are *metoru*, *kasuru*, *kekkon o yaku*, *kekkon suru*, and *kongi o musubu*. All these terms can be translated as "to marry" or at least "to enter into a household." Accordingly, Japanese men are described as "married to Aborigine women." The noun "wife" (*tsuma/sai*), however, is not used by Satomi or Murakami. One passage specifically uses the character *mekake/shō/qie*, which has two different possible Japanese readings. Read as *mekake*, it referred to a woman kept for a man's pleasure, whose children had no legal standing as members of the household. A *mekake* might be understood as a "mistress" in Western parlance. On the other hand, the character could also be read as *shō*, or "secondary wife/ concubine".[547] Japan's 1871 Civil Code (*Shinritsu-kōryō*), an amalgam of Ming, Qing, and older Japanese codes, considered *shō*, like wives, to be "second-degree" relatives of their husbands. A *shō*'s sons, to be sure, had less claim than a principal wife's sons to inheritance. Nonetheless, there was enough legal equality between wives and concubines to cause Arinori Mori, a famous Japanese critic, to consider the distinctions made by the 1871 Civil Code meaningless.[548] The husband-*shō* relationship received further sanction in the 1872 Household Registration Law (*Koseki hō*), which stipulated that *shō* be listed next to wives in the household register. The Illegitimate Child Law (*Shiseiji hō*) of 1873 declared that children of *shō* were "legitimate" by making their fathers responsible for support.[549]

Legal prescriptions allowing more than one female partner for husbands were abhorrent to a vocal contingent of Meiji-period social engineers, modernizers, and moralists. How, they asked, could Japan call itself a civilized nation when its civil code tolerated "secondary wives/concubines" and considered their progeny legitimate?[550] This debate was partially resolved on the side of "civilization" in 1880, when the government drafted a new civil code abolishing "the *shō*'s legal status as spouse."[551] The practice of keeping *mekake*, however, remained widespread among Japanese lawmakers and men of means long after. Movements to stamp out concubinage persisted into the Taishō and Shōwa (1926–1989) periods.[552] Thus, the men who took Aborigine wives in Taiwan, as well as their superiors, subscribed to a variety of notions of what sorts of arrangements were "normal" and might justify the terms "marriage" and "wife."

Some fourteen years after *shō* had been banished from Japanese civil law, the editors of *Fūzoku gahō* (*Folkways Illustrated*) supplied the *furigana* reading "*shō*" (secondary wife) for the character *qie* in reference to Tetsusaburō Hiyama's Atayal bride.[553] That same year, a Tokyo newspaper referred to the same couple as "man and wife" (*fūfu*) in its florid description of their mutual attraction and emotional entanglement.[554] In 1929 the intrepid and generally reliable author Seinosuke Fujisaki referred to Katsusaburō Kondō as Iwan Robau's "common-law husband" (*nai'en no otto*). Kawata Ide, perhaps Japan's most encyclopedic chronicler of the colonial experiment in Taiwan, referred to Iwan as Kondō's "wife" (*tsuma*).[555] The *Taiwan nichinichi shinpō* called Ōita Prefecture native Eijirō Watanabe's Aborigine spouse a "wife" as well.[556] Remarkably, Watanabe's household registry (*koseki*) lists her as *tsuma* under the name "Mei-hai." Mei-hai's parents, Watan Naui (father) and Chugas Neehan (mother), were also entered into Watanabe's Ōita Prefecture *koseki*.[557]

Prior to December 1898, former Sino-Japanese War translator Jiku Sho Min married the daughter of an heirless Atayal headman to become successor to a chieftainship in Quchi. Taking the name Watan Karaho, Jiku styled himself a local king. His marriage is specifically referred to as "entering his wife's house" (*irimuko*) in two issues of *Taiwan kyōkai kaihō* (Bulletin of the Friends of Taiwan).[558] This usage seems apt, as men such as Hiyama, Kondō, Itō, Jiku, and Watanabe played the role of *mukoyōshi* in their new Taiwanese families. In Japan, *mukoyōshi* entered the households of wives as both bridegrooms and adopted sons. This arrangement solved the problem of succession for lineages lacking male heirs while increasing prospects of second and third sons in a society in which primogeniture was the norm.[559] By the lights of Meiji Japanese practice, then, many of the more remarkable intercultural unions between Japanese males and Aborigine females are plausibly called "marriages" and the spouses called "husband" and "wife."

The Taiwan government-general, however, did not publicly acknowledge Japanese-Aborigine marriages. The government-general's vital statistics reports for the years 1905 through 1934 record not a single "Aborigine wife-Japanese husband" marriage. In contrast, these reports assiduously tallied thousands of mixed *shufan-shengfan* and Han-Aborigine marriages.[560] Moreover, not all "Aborigine hands" were as scrupulous as Watanabe in confirming their families' legal status by entering them into the *koseki*. The 1917 version of Kondō's *koseki* contains no entries for Iwan Robau, a glaring omission, considering the very public nature of the marriage and the loyal service rendered to the government by Iwan.[561]

In stark contrast to Eijirō Watanabe, many Japanese males treated their Aborigine mates as *mekake* or worse. These men crossed a line that cost hundreds of Japanese dearly. In December 1900, the governor of Taipei accused camphor men of "recklessly defiling Aborigine women," thereby provoking incidents of head taking.[562] A 1901 editorial in *Taiwan minpō* (*Taiwan People's Daily*) blamed illicit interethnic relations for causing a rout of Japanese forces in Xincheng, Taidong Province, in 1900.[563] Even Jiku Sho Min, the great "Watan Karaho" himself, appeared to be little more than a "local bully" to the Quchi men who sacked his office and destroyed his possessions for perceived abuses of power. Government-general Samata Sakuma (1906–1915) later blamed two major uprisings on resentment caused by illicit Japanese male-Aborigine female relations, and preached restraint to his underlings.[564]

Meiji-period Japanese ethnographic reports, in addition to journalistic accounts, were uniform in asserting that Atayal severely punished adulterers and were monogamous by custom. So although late Qing and early Japanese evidence shows that out-marrying, accompanied by ample bride price and public ceremony, complied with long-standing Atayal practices, casual liaisons between Japanese adventurers and Atayal women could provoke violent retribution (as could cases of adultery within Atayal society). Kyōta Inuzuka contrasts traditional Atayal regard for premarital chastity, monogamy, companionate marriage, and gender equality with prewar Japanese traditions of male dominance and gender inequality in marriage. Inuzuka hypothesizes that diametrically opposed male attitudes toward women collided in northern Taiwan under colonial rule.[565] Anthropologist Scott Simon's observations, based on fieldwork, recent Taiwanese anthropology, and Japanese ethnological reports, call attention to Atayal valorization of chastity and monogamy as well. Simon's research, however, emphasizes the patriarchal character of Atayal gender norms. Arranged marriages and anti-divorce and anti-adultery prohibitions functioned, in his view, to subordinate Atayal women to the dictates of family and village leaders.[566] Historical evidence indicates that at least some young Atayal women were cast out of their local societies to live for life as "barbarians" among the lowlanders as intermediaries. This being the case, the thesis of "clashing gender systems" requires modification. In certain instances, Japanese and Atayal patriarchy were symbiotic, provided that each party to the alliance had common interests. When these interests clashed, however, what affective or institutional tie remained to bind an out-married daughter to the cause of her natal community?

On December 16, 1902, the Puli Subprefect dispatched a *"banpu* named Iwan" to sound out the Wushe tribes about an upcoming Japanese punitive expedition to the north. Japanese officials commonly sent northern Aborigine women to the mountain villages as emissaries during the first decade of colonial rule.[567] Iwan's case is particularly interesting for illustrating how Atayal out-marrying practices could backfire on the men who sent their daughters and sisters to the plains. The description of Iwan's route and domicile indicates that she was none other than Katsusaburō Kondō's wife, Iwan Robau.[568] In Palan, Iwan learned that Wushe sought a truce with Japan in order to resume trade in salt and to "be treated like the *shufan* tribes." Besides, they were engaged in a cycle of revenge feuding with Toda and needed arms and ammunition.[569] Of course, the price of resuming the salt trade was the forfeiture of firearms and pledges to cease head taking. Under such conditions, Wushe was vulnerable to neighbors who either had yet to surrender or had already thrown their lot in with the Japanese as guard-line soldiers. For these reasons, it would seem, Wushe and Japan failed to come to terms in the ensuing months.

The direct evidence linking Iwan Robau to this disaster is spotty, though plausible. Local historians Aui Heppaha and Pixo Walis claim that Iwan and several other women arranged this meeting at the behest of the Japanese.[570] We will probably never find evidence much firmer than these dim recollections, both undoubtedly affected by years of exposure to the "Wushe incident testimonial" industry. The whole purpose of using brokers such as Iwan seems to be their semi- and nonofficial status, which exempted much of their activity from the normally rigorous Japanese practice of colonial record keeping. At the least, the infamous October 5, 1903, incident illustrates the devastating effects that Japanese officials could wreak through a combination of trade embargoes and adroit manipulation of local rivalries. The capacity to punish recalcitrant villages, however, was not the same as governing them directly in accordance with Japan's ideals of colonial administration. Consonant with the trends of the times, these ideals included the economic rationalization of the uplands and the tutelage of the Aborigines, projects that would require much more prolonged and intimate contact with the northern tribes.

## Breaking the Gordian Knot: The "Political- Marriage Policy" in Atayal Country

Following the Russo-Japanese War (1904-1905), which had diverted energy from Japan's ambitions in Taiwan, Governor-general Samata Sakuma's administration (1906-1915) executed a "get-tough" policy toward the Atayal villages who had refused to surrender their rifles and sovereignty during the previous decade of colonial rule. Although Wushe had formally submitted in 1906, many of the tribes farther upland and inland still remained armed and defiant. Sakuma pledged to break the resistance of the northern tribes once and for all by extending the heavily armed "guard line" to the heart of Atayal country to encompass Xakut, Truku, and Toda.[571]

Sakuma's right-hand man on Aborigine policy, Police Bureau chief Rinpei Ōtsu, inspected the forward posts of the guard line in spring 1907. His report proposed to remedy the alarming interpreter situation with a "political-marriage" policy. Ōtsu implied that operators such as Katsusaburō Kondō, Eijirō Watanabe, Iwan Robau, or Tata Rara, although linguistically competent, were too scarce and unreliable to carry out Japan's new positive policy in the highlands. The government-general's efforts to train Japanese beat cops and rural officials in Austronesian languages had failed miserably. To break through this impasse, Ōtsu called for a more bureaucratic form of interethnic marriage to bring the central government closer to the villages hitherto ruled from a distance:

> I have sensed an extreme paucity of Aborigine translators at every installation on my tour. This being the case, it is not difficult to imagine that many, many more translators will be necessary as we bring the Aborigines within the fold of government. I need not mention that success in managing the Aborigines hinges upon the ability of our translators. ... The quickest route to cultivating translators would be to give occasional financial assistance to the appropriate men and have them officially marry *banpu*. While it is recognized that such marriages cause trouble (Aborigines ... will say that such marriages are unfair and benefit only the villages or lineages of the *banpu*'s new husband; again, if the Japanese husband is rotated to another post and abandons his wife, it will offend Aborigine sentiment), our present lack of translators is troubling. Because marriage to a *banpu* will raise living expenses, occasional moneys should be provided for the low-ranking men who can ill afford it.[572]

It is significant that Ōtsu called for the cultivation of *tsūyaku* (translators) instead of *tongshi* in his long disquisition on the failings of the government-general's Aborigine policy. As we have seen, *tsūyaku* in colonized Taiwan were attached to high-ranking

Japanese officials. *Tsūyaku*, native Japanese who spoke at least one standard dialect of Chinese, operated at physical and linguistic removes—bridged by *tongshi*—from the myriad upland villages and hamlets of Aborigine Taiwan. *Tongshi*, often in conjunction with *banpu* and *sheding*, aided or displaced *tsūyaku* in government dealings with uplanders as a rule. Ōtsu's radical plan to fuse the roles of *tsūyaku*, *tongshi*, and *sheding* into the person of a single Japanese police officer represented yet another attempt to make the savage border's cultural brokers, creatures of the Qing triple-tier ethnic settlement system, obsolete. Ōtsu's call to streamline Japanese-Aborigine relations proved to be a very tall order indeed.

In the final analysis, the rapidity of state-led, forced political integration in upland Taiwan under the Sakuma plan impeded language acquisition by Japanese officials just as the new positive policy increased demands on their linguistic capacities. We should recall that "translation" and "interpretation" require different levels of competence on the part of cultural brokers, depending on their structural position in a world system and the balance of power obtaining on each side of a border or frontier. In contact peripheries, transactions can be brokered in the absence of interpreters. Many such examples are documented in P. J. Hamilton Grierson's 1903 *Silent Trade: A Contribution to the Early History of Human Intercourse*. In the "silent trade," nonverbal symbols, markers, barriers, and gestures are employed to facilitate exchange and preserve distance between groups who are economically interdependent but politically at war.[573] In other contact-periphery settings, which lie on the edge of marginal peripheries, Yasuhide Kawashima and Jonathan Spence have shown that minimal levels of linguistic competence can serve quite well for transactions of brief duration and limited range.[574] Business conducted in treaty ports and at trading posts are good examples of this phenomenon.

Examples of true biculturalism are the province of the marginal periphery. European interpreters among Amerindians, in certain periods and places, displayed fluency in the highly figurative, stylized, and nuanced speech acts that were expected at tribal councils in the northeast. These interpreters spent long years of residence among Native Americans. By the same token, Native Americans became skilled at European languages and played their part in the complex political economy in the interstices of competing empires. A significant number of these interpreters had married across ethnic lines or were the progeny of bicultural marriages.[575] Johannes Fabian's insights into the dynamics of language acquisition in colonial frontiers explain why marginal peripheries, like the one partially frozen by the Qing triple-tiered ethnic settlement policy, are conducive to the emergence of biculturalism. Fabian writes: "Practical language learning needs time. ... Above all, practical language learning demands humility, a willingness to risk shame and ridicule for mistakes and lapses in competence. It hardly needs pointing out that all this fits neither the typical scientist conducting research nor the typical explorer commanding a caravan, both of whom, in different but related ways, need to be in control of situations at all times."[576]

According to Fabian's logic, the degree of intimacy and the length of time required for immersion-style language acquisition—the only effective method for languages unknown in the colonial metropole—were beyond the reach of colonial agents on a rapidly moving frontier. For one, most officials were promoted, reassigned, or decommissioned before they could master a local tongue. But even when colonial officials stayed put, their metaphysical and practical relationship to native speakers involved the distancing mechanisms of hierarchy, abstraction, and armed conflict. Under such conditions, fluency is nearly impossible to obtain, especially at an institution-wide level.

In marginal peripheries, however, especially those where intermarriage is common, many of the mitigating forces described by Fabian are muted. As Richard White so eloquently argues in *The Middle Ground: Indians, Empires, and Republics in the Great Lakes Region, 1650-1815* (1991), symbiosis and mutual interdependence, even where power relations are asymmetrical, produce flexible attitudes and a willingness to be taught. Add to this the familiarity and suspension of the colonizers' "stiff upper lip" that attends cohabitation and family life, and the possibilities for language acquisition through immersion are increased. These marginal peripheral or "middle ground" conditions describe the circumstances surrounding the marriages of Kondō, Jiku, Watanabe, and Hiyama into Atayal polities in the late 1890s. In sharp contrast, the government-general's Aborigine-language institutes for guard-line soldiers were mired in surroundings resembling those that Fabian rightly considers inimical to empathy and language acquisition. Stationed on the front lines of an offensive war against the native speakers of the target language, Japanese soldiers were reduced to studying vocabulary lists on their own, for lack of conversation partners. Consequently, these institutes failed miserably, prompting Ōtsu's formulation of the political-marriage policy.[577]

In August 1908, Ōtsu circumvented his linguistically incompetent guard-line officers by commissioning Katsusaburō Kondō to secure Wushe allies for a military operation against the "hostile" Toda and Truku tribes in his path. Kondō balked at the mission but reconsidered when Ōtsu offered him a land grant of thirty hectares outside Puli in return. In October Kondō found ready allies in Hogo (headman Aui Nukan) and Mahebo (headman Mona Ludao), two Wushe tribes that considered Truku and Toda enemies.[578] According to Kondō, Mona and Aui demanded that he and his younger brother Gisaburō take wives in Wushe to seal the bargain. Kondō paid the price of one pig to Palan's chief to ratify his "divorce" from Iwan to pave the way for his second marriage.[579]

In January 1909, the brothers Kondō were married to Obin Nukan and Diwas Ludao, in a government-sponsored feast that saw the slaughter of six oxen and the distribution of twenty oil cans of distilled spirits. Soon after the formalization of the alliance, Katsusaburō Kondō led some 654 Wushe warriors in the general attack on Toda and Truku in late February, which was successfully concluded by March 1909.[580] The official report states that Wushe had blamed Toda for recent attacks on the guard line. Japanese officials were skeptical but thought it expedient to use Wushe's manpower to gain a strategic foothold in difficult terrain, so a government force of 580 fighting men with about 660 coolies (probably Kondō's 654 Wushe warriors) prepared to attack Toda.[581] These early 1909 maneuvers secured commanding heights for Japanese cannon and mortars as well as strategic passes for communication, which allowed the government-general to effectively cut the northern Atayal country in two.[582]

As an oldest son and a future *koshu* (household head), Kondō expected to secure his Japanese family's future by obtaining a large, government-registered farm near Puli for the care of his aged father, per Rinpei Ōtsu's promise in August of 1908. Indeed, Kondō's father, who had immigrated to Taiwan by this time, passed away in March 1909, leaving Kondō legally responsible for the care of his mother, younger brothers, younger sisters, and a number of nieces. Kondō spent the years 1909 though 1916 pressing claims for the promised acreage while continuing to accept government commissions as a guide and an interpreter. As the years wore on, Ōtsu returned to Japan; other officials familiar with Kondō's case left Nantou Prefecture; and finally Wushe district police inspector Shōsaburō Kondō (no relation) deeded the land to his own relative, preempting Katsusaburō's claim. This perceived slight angered Katsusaburō's younger brother Gisaburō to the boiling point. Gisaburō immediately tendered his resignation in Taipei but was instead transferred out of Wushe to a new post in Hualian District.[583]

Sixteen-year-old Gisaburō Kondō had come to Taiwan in 1901.

Gisaburō worked his way up through the ranks to become a sergeant in the Aborigine-territory police by 1916, thanks to his facility with the Sedeq dialects spoken near Wushe. Ishimatsu Igarashi, a Japanese official of long experience in Wushe, recalled Gisaburō as a companionable husband to Diwas Ludao and figure of local respect. Igarashi claimed that Diwas's devotion to Gisaburō allowed the Japanese to squelch an uprising by Xakut and Salamao in 1913. Overhearing the plan from her brother Mona Ludao, Diwas alerted Gisaburō, who in turn sounded the alarm and averted disaster for the Japanese.[584] Such timely intelligence is all that Rinpei Ōtsu could have hoped for when he called for "political marriages" back in 1907.

From Mona Ludao's perspective, though, the alliance with Japan created a number of intractable problems. By the Mahebo headman's logic, the surrender of weapons and the marriage alliance with Gisaburō Kondō should have spelled preferential treatment for the allied Wushe villages. According to Katsusaburō Kondō, however, the government-general was stingy with their rations of ammunition and gun loans to Wushe headmen, their putative allies, while they were relatively generous to Wushe's rivals. Because Mona had engineered the alliance, he was held responsible for the shortage of ammunition and guns. According to Katsusaburō Kondō, Mona became an object of scorn and abuse among his own men. Adding to Mona's problems, Gisaburō Kondō disappeared from sight sometime in 1916, leaving Diwas Ludao bereft. Diwas eventually was remarried to a local man but was never compensated in the form of death benefits, nor was she given a sinecure, as was commonly done with high-born Aborigine wives of Japanese men in Sedeq country.[585] Katsusaburō Kondō recalled that Diwas had not been entered into Gisaburō's household register, making it impossible to file a claim on her behalf.[586] Katsusaburō Kondō himself complained that his Wushe men had donated twenty thousand man hours of labor to building the guard line in early 1909, while their fields lay unattended.[587] He argued that long-term resentment at the government's ingratitude, which could have been allayed with a few kegs of sake and an official "thank you" or a few more guns and bullets for Mona Ludao and his allies, ultimately led many locals to sympathize with and participate in the Wushe rebellion of 1930.[588]

From 1909 to 1914, Samata Sakuma's "Five-Year Plan to Subdue the Northern Tribes" (*goka nen keikaku riban jigyō*) brought most of Atayal country under direct colonial rule. The Banmu honsho (Bureau of Aboriginal Affairs), the temporary organ established to administer Sakuma's five-year plan, was disbanded in July 1915 and victory was declared in the north.[589] Thereafter, the northern Aborigine country was governed by Japanese police officers who possessed the power of life and death over their colonial subjects. Police boxes were erected among the villages in upland Taiwan as the state's most prominent institution. The Aborigine police were charged with peace keeping, judicial, educational, and medical functions, becoming the eyes, ears, hands, and feet of the Taiwan government-general in the lands under "special administration."

The dissolution of the Banmu honsho in 1915 is of paramount significance for our story. Katsusaburō Kondō's inability to secure his land contract or a public "thank you" for Wushe in addition to the government-general's discontinuation of support for Mona Ludao stemmed from a single cause: after 1915 the bicultural brokers, intermediaries, *banpu*, and *tongshi* of the savage border were expendable. The space of indeterminate sovereignty between the plains and the highlands, instantiated and given durability in the Qianlong period under the "triple-tier ethnic-group settlement" system, had been reduced to an administrative boundary between Han Taiwanese and *banjin*. Henceforth, Japanese "Aborigine hands" would reside among the tribes and villages that they governed, take direct orders from their superiors, and rule over their in-laws through the blunt threat of punishment through force or economic embargo.

Two particularly well-known Japanese-Aborigine marriages, both initiated to advance the guard line in Atayal country, survived the dissolution of the Banmu honsho in 1915. One ended in 1925 with the sacking of Jihei Shimoyama after a drunken altercation with his superior officer; the other ended in 1930 with the murder of Aisuke Sazuka during the Wushe uprising. As ex-guard-line men turned "mountain policemen," Shimoyama and Sazuka functioned something like salaried *tongshi*, with all the contradictions that this oxymoron entailed. To wit, their careers illustrate why conditions in a dependent periphery were less than propitious for would-be cultural brokers.

Shizuoka native Jihei Shimoyama arrived in Taiwan in 1907 as a young army veteran. During Sakuma's five-year campaign, the Malepa dispatch station was overrun and its staff wiped out. To reestablish control, the Nantou district head of Aborigine Affairs sent Shimoyama to run things, after ordering him to marry Pixo Doleh, the daughter of Malepa's headman. According to Pixo's niece, Malepa assented to the marriage out of economic desperation in order to obtain needed patron interpreters age and rifles.[590] According to their son Hajime, Pixo became proficient at Japanese conversation. Shimoyama, on the other hand, could not speak Atayal. Pixo bore him two sons and two daughters. Shimoyama's other betrothed, Shizuoka native Nakako Katsumata, arrived in Wushe after he and Pixo had started their Malepa family. Katsumata also began to bear Shimoyama's children. For a time, Shimoyama shuttled between Wushe and Malepa. No longer able to afford two households, he finally moved his Japanese family to Malepa. Pixo, the daughter and sister of local headmen in a fiercely monogamous society, was humiliated to be treated publicly as a *mekake*.[591]

Jihei Shimoyama's bigamy, an open display of contempt for Atayal "customs of the country," came to the attention of Neng'gao district commander (*gunshu*) Nagakichi Akinaga in 1925. Akinaga broached the delicate issue in front of assembled Malepa men. Shimoyama explained that Pixo Doleh's relatives had consented to this arrangement. Besides, an angered Shimoyama replied, he had been assured that he could break off the political marriage to Pixo after three years' time, even if there were children. Akinaga took umbrage at being contradicted publicly by a subaltern and threw Shimoyama down on a table. Shimoyama was dismissed for insubordination the next day, demonstrating clearly that the government-general believed it could handle affairs in Malepa without his intercession with the locals. Although his abrupt departure left Pixo bitter, Shimoyama secured a job for her at a Wushe infirmary at a salary of forty yen per month before he left. Shimoyama's son Hajime recalled that his mother was never entered into Shimoyama's *koseki* as a "wife" but merely as a "coresident *banjin*".[592]

At the tail end of Sakuma's five-year campaign, in 1914, Aisuke Sazuka married Yawai Taimu, daughter of a Masitobaon headman. Sazuka was born the same year as Shimoyama, in 1886, in Nagano Prefecture. Soon after mustering out of the army's Hokkaidō 7th Division in 1908, Sazuka married his aunt's daughter. Sazuka, however, could not abide impoverished country life in Japan's "snow country." One January morning in 1909, Sazuka fled to Taiwan via Tokyo with money stolen from his father.[593] Sazuka's wife is remembered as one who spoke unusually graceful Japanese and worked harder than other Atayal women to assimilate.[594] When Sazuka returned to Nagano in 1915 on a two- day leave from government duty in Tokyo, he divorced his Japanese wife and turned over the family headship to his younger brother. So unlike the Kondō's or Shimoyama, Sazuka cut his ties to Japan for a future in Taiwan. In many ways, then, the Sazuka-Yawai political marriage should have been a model for the Rinpei Ōtsu plan of 1907. Instead, it confirmed Ōtsu's worst fears: although the efforts of Sazuka and

Yawai facilitated surveillance and cooperation in Masitoboan, they hurt Japan's cause in Sedeq country.

The poverty and ambition that made Sazuka a willing Aborigine hand had its dark side. He was a notorious embezzler who regularly skimmed Aborigine wages for public-works projects.[595] Nonetheless, he was considered preferable to a man such as Shimoyama, whom he replaced in Malepa after the 1925 incident. Sazuka was finally promoted to chief of the Wushe branch station on March 31, 1930.[596] Whether he was "kicked upstairs" to preempt the emergence of another local power base or genuinely promoted for recognition of his efficacy, the reassignment to Wushe turned out to be a death sentence for Sazuka. Because of their roots in Masitoboan, Yawai and Sazuka were viewed as enemies by local Wushe men, who included Mahebo headman, Mona Ludao. Heavily reliant on his wife's networks for local knowledge, which provided little useful intelligence in the new setting, Sazuka downplayed information that he received about Sedeq men stockpiling supplies for a prolonged war against the Japanese. When Mona's coalition of disaffected headmen and warriors struck on October 27, the Japanese were completely blindsided and Sazuka was among the first to perish. Yawai survived by jettisoning her kimono and fleeing to Puli dressed as an Aborigine woman. In recognition of her service, Yawai, like Pixo Doleh, received financial support from the government-general after Sazuka's death.[597]

## Conclusions

The annals of colonial conquest in Taiwan from 1895 through 1930 illustrate Ann Stoler's contention that divisions between colonizer and colonized are drawn and redrawn during the process of colony building, creating communities of interest and lines of separation which may little resemble the identities that existed *status quo ante*.[598] In Taiwan, Qing-period headman Pan Wenjie and interpreter Pu Jing, both of Aborigine ancestry and lacking knowledge of the Japanese language, were hired by the government-general as salaried officials for contributing to the colonial enterprise with great zeal. On the other hand, the government-general kept native-born Japanese adventurers such as Katsusaburō Kondō at arm's length. Atayal women Iwan Robau and Pixo Doleh were recognized by the state with sinecures of steady employment after their Japanese husbands abandoned them, but neither was entered into a Japanese family register as a full-fledged wife. Assertions of iron-clad racial exclusionary practices among Japanese colonists notwithstanding, Eijirō Watanabe entered the names of his Atayal wife and her parents into his household registry for all to see.

At the other extreme, Diwas Ludao was not only excluded from Gisaburō Kondō's registry; the government-general itself refused to contribute to her livelihood after his disappearance.

In Western examples drawn from French colonial Indochina, Dutch-governed Indonesia, German colonial Africa, and United States–governed North America, scholars of colonial ideology have shown that nineteenth-century Euro-American notions of racial purity and superiority existed in a dialectical relationship with nefarious legal distinctions and physical barriers that separated whites from Others in colonial situations. In colonized Taiwan, ethnic boundary drawing was central to Qing policy in the eighteenth century. The Japanese, as intrepid students and practitioners of modern colonialism, etched their own lines on Taiwan by writing the administrative boundary line between "Taiwanese" and "Aborigine" over the old triple-tiered ethnic settlement system of Qing times. Fears of racial contamination or colonial hybrids, however, never dominated colonial discourse on the Japanese–Taiwan Aborigine marriages that facilitated this project. The modern "bourgeois family" as it was constructed in Meiji Japan, much to the horror of Japanese reformers, was based neither on monogamy nor on the concept of pure bloodlines. Rather, the maintenance of the stem family, the *ie* that was enshrined in the 1898 Civil Code, was Japan's modern alternative to the monogamous, nuclear family of the West. Within the *ie* structure, adoption and concubinage were not only permissible but were laudable when they contributed to the survival of the *ie*.

"Tensions of empire" were certainly felt along the axis of interethnic marriage in colonized Taiwan under Japanese rule. Japanese Aborigine hands, heirs to the role of *tongshi*, often became dutiful *mukoyōshi* in their adopted new families in upland Taiwan. The role of *mukoyōshi* in this context, however, meant showing partiality to one's own relatives at the expense of other imperial subjects—rival neighboring tribes—a contradiction that the Japanese were never able to resolve. Again, when Japanese men treated their Aborigine mates as *mekake* (mistresses) instead of *tsuma* or *shō* (wives), they angered their superiors and offended their in-laws, with often dire consequences for themselves, their families, and the state. To be sure, Japanese of the Meiji and Taishō periods harbored notions of ethnic and even racial superiority vis-à-vis other Asians and Taiwan Aborigines. At the level of practice, however, in situations in which intermarriage could further personal and political agendas for both Atayal and Japanese parties involved, the preservation of racial purity did not emerge as a central feature of discourse or contention.

## CHAPTER NINE

## KEY MOMENTS IN JAPANESE AMERICA'S MIXED-RACE HISTORY, 1868-1945

DUNCAN RYŪKEN WILLIAMS

The narrative of an increasingly multiracial Japanese America has become a prominent point of discussion both among scholars and within that community as this ethnic group becomes the first Asian American subgroup that will become majority multiracial in the next several years. But perhaps less recognized is the significant role that multiracial Japanese Americans have played throughout that community's history.

Rather than simply viewing Japanese America as originally "pure" and increasingly "hybrid," this chapter argues that "mixed-ness" has been a significant feature of this community from its earliest beginnings and throughout the course of its development. This was particularly the case in the early Japanese community in Hawai'i and the non-West Coast (Midwest, South, East Coast) Japanese American communities. This paper examines three key moments in early Japanese American history (1868–1945) to highlight the place of mixed-race persons in this community: 1) Issei Pioneers as a Part of Multiracial Families, 2) Anti-Miscegenation Laws and the Inclusion/Exclusion of the Multiracial Japanese Americans in American Society, and 3) the World War II Incarceration of Hapa Japanese Americans and their Participation in the U.S. Military.

### The First Japanese Americans: Issei Pioneers as a Part of Multiracial Families

Unlike the many Japanese who sojourned in the Americas as laborers, students, or businessmen for relatively short periods in the late nineteenth century, the first Japanese Americans—the first Japanese who put down roots and permanently settled as migrants in Hawai'i, 189

California, and Oregon—were all involved in multiracial families. Most histories of Japanese America have completely missed this reality.

Hawai'i was the starting point for Japanese migration eastward across the Pacific, primarily because American sugar plantation owners on the islands developed an urgent need for cheap labor as sugar replaced whaling as the islands' primary industry. The American plantation owners viewed the Japanese as a good option to fill this labor shortage because they had not been colonized by any European power. The Hawaiian monarch, King Kalakaua, saw them as a "racially cognate" group that could eventually rejuvenate Hawai'i's decimated native population through intermarriage.[599] The recruitment of Japanese in the late nineteenth and early twentieth century brought about the largest wave of labor migration to the Hawaiian Islands, roughly 150,000 migrants.[600]

The mass migration of the Japanese began in earnest in 1868 when the first group of 153 laborers emigrated to Hawai'i aboard the 800-ton British ship *Scioto*.[601] The group left Japan for the purpose of working on Hawai'i's sugar plantations without official sanction from the shogunate. The trip from Yokohama Bay to Honolulu was a month-long journey across rough Pacific Ocean waters. The group was later dubbed the "Gannenmono" because they were people (*mono*) who had left in the first year (*gannen*) of the newly established Meiji government in 1868, which secured power a few months after their departure. In Hawai'i, the twelve-hour workdays on the sugar plantation, the wretched housing conditions, the language barriers with the plantation overseers, and the mistreatment of the laborers proved too much for many in the group to endure. The Japanese government sent a special envoy, Kagenori Ueno, to investigate these labor conditions. Ueno and his visit nearly led to an early end of Japanese migration to Hawai'i and the Americas.

However, the Hawaiian Kingdom swiftly put in place new policies that would better laborers' work conditions, and allowed any *Gannenmono* who wanted to get out of their three-year contracts to do so. Forty of the original 153 went back to Japan immediately and another thirteen left after their contracts ended. And about ninety of the original group requested and were given official permission to settle in Hawai'i with a Japanese-government passport.[602] This group of Japanese, a number of whom remained in Hawai'i permanently, represented the beginnings of a major migration and settlement of Japanese in Hawai'i and the Americas.

Among the small handful of those who settled permanently in Hawai'i were men like Matsugorō Kuwata, Tokujirō Satō, and

Toyokichi Fukumura, all of whom married and had children with local Hawaiian women.[603] The children of the unions between *Gannenmono* Japanese men and native Hawaiian women were hapa Japanese Hawaiians who represented the first Japanese born in the new land.

One of the *Gannenmono* fathers was Toyokichi Fukumura, a samurai who left Japan with this first group of Japanese migrants because he fought on the side of the shogunate, and with the restoration of the Emperor was fearful of persecution by imperial forces. Toyokichi married a Hawaiian woman, Kahā Lu'ukia (also spelled Lukia Kaha) and had two children: Solomon and Mary. Other *Gannenmono* who married native Hawaiian women were Matsugorō Kuwada (a tailor on Maui), who married Meleana Auwekoolani, and Tokujirō Satō (in Pahao on Big Island), who married Kalala Lamekona.[604] Thus the first *permanent* Japanese American population in the Hawaiian islands was almost entirely multiracial.

In Hawai'i—still a sovereign nation at this time prior to U.S. annexation—multiracial encounters and unions were common in a way quite different from North America. Indeed, Toyokichi Fukumura's hapa Japanese son, Solomon, married another mixed-race individual, the Hawaiian-German woman Mine Haines, and had six children with her. King Kalakaua set the tone, with his belief that racial intermarriage would be the key to revitalizing the Hawaiian population. Indeed, in 1881 the King went as far as to propose to the Japanese Emperor that a union take place between his six-year-old niece, Princess Kaiulani, and the young Japanese prince Sadamaro Yamashina.[605] And though the royal union did not come to pass, Japanese-Hawaiian relations improved because of such gestures.[606] At the same time, among *Gannenmono* descendants, was Charles William Fukumura (born 1907), a Japanese-Hawaiian-German American, later known as Charles Kenn after the family changed their last name in 1916. Celebrating his various ethnic and cultural heritages, Kenn appreciated his Japanese samurai heritage, his European family name, and his native Hawaiian heritage—he became a well-known expert on ancient Hawaiian culture and the secret art of lua, a Hawaiian martial art.[607]

Hawai'i became an intermediary zone between white America and Japan where multiple frameworks of race and ethnicity, held by native Hawaiians, by Japanese and other Asia Pacific migrants, and by Euro American migrants, encountered each other. Certain sectors of the Japanese American population valorized the mixing and encountering of peoples and culture in Hawai'i. Several decades after the first hapa Japanese Hawaiian children were born, a

Japanese American woman in Kona, Hawai'i, referring to a funeral banquet that consisted of traditional Japanese foods along with Hawaiian-style fruit salad, bread, and doughnuts, commented: "Everything here is hapa—food, talk and all."[608]

Such intermixing in Hawai'i certainly increased when the Japanese government sanctioned migration of laborers to Hawai'i to work on the sugar plantations. This wave of migration brought roughly 30,000 Japanese, the so-called *kanyaku imin* (contract migrants), to Hawai'i before the system was replaced by immigration not organized by the government. Accompanying the first official group of 943 Japanese contract laborers aboard the steamship, *City of Tokio*, in 1885 was Robert Walker Irwin, the Kingdom of Hawai'i's Minister to Japan, appointed to that post by King Kalakaua during the King's visit to Japan in 1881. Irwin had arrived in Japan in 1866 to head the Yokohama office of the Pacific Mail Steam Company, and prior to the King's visit served as the Consul-General of Hawai'i in Japan. Irwin ended up being central to the negotiation of the treaty between the Japan and Hawai'i, signed a year after the *City of Tokio*'s arrival, that permitted the mass migration of Japanese, including his own Japanese wife (Takechi Iki). The Japanese Foreign Minister Kaoru Inoue, who had worked with Irwin before his government position as the head of a major trading company, arranged their marriage in 1882, which constituted the first legal marriage between an American and a Japanese citizen.[609] Their six children, including their oldest daughter Bella (who later founded the Irwin Gakuen School in Tokyo), are among the earliest hapa Japanese Americans.[610]

Another key multiracial Japanese American in Hawai'i central to this massive labor migration from Japan to Hawaii was Fred (Kinzaburō) Makino, born in Yokohama in 1877, the third son of a Japanese woman, Kin Makino, and a British silk merchant, Joseph Higgenbotham.[611] He established the Makino Drug Store in Honolulu in 1901—one of the first Japanese-owned stores in the city—two years after immigrating there. His involvement in Honolulu's Japanese community extended beyond his small business, as he served as a lawyer for many Japanese who faced problems ranging from immigration to marital legal issues. His skills eventually led him to represent the Japanese community, especially in the labor issues that plagued the majority of the Japanese migrants, who worked on the sugar plantations where racially discriminatory work conditions provoked numerous labor strikes. The Higher Wage Association elected Makino president during the 1909 Oahu plantation strike, and his role in the labor movement led the Hawai'i Territorial Government to jail Makino for four months. Other multiracial families involved in the strikes included the parents of Bessie Yoneko Ibrao Fooks, who remembers her Japanese Buddhist mother always cooking for the strikers at the Buddhist temple, despite the fact that her father was a Catholic Filipino and that "prejudice was prominent and their relationship was ostracized."[612]

Though mixed race, Makino's stature in the Japanese community only increased when in 1912 he founded one of the most influential and long-lasting ethnic newspapers, the *Hawaii Hochi*. Through the newspaper, Makino expressed community sentiment around labor issues (including the largest labor strike in 1919), immigration issues (including the forced mass weddings of Buddhist and Shinto picture brides in Christian ceremonies), citizenship issues (fighting for U.S. citizenship rights for Japanese who served in World War I), and the Japanese language school cases (that resulted in a 1927 U.S. Supreme Court victory for the schools, which were targeted by the Territorial government, bent on an English-only education policy). Makino's biography provides clear evidence that the early Japanese American community in Hawai'i generally viewed multiraciality in a positive light, and that mixed-race individuals could be advocates for and representatives of Japanese America.

The initial migration of Japanese further east to the mainland U.S. was also marked by the presence of multiracial families. The first Japanese family to settle in California was that of John Henry Schnell, a Prussian national who arrived in Japan prior to the Meiji Restoration under the auspices of the Dutch (the only Western nation with whom Japan had diplomatic relations at the time) to deal in arms, including heavy artillery and Gatling guns, for the Shogunate-allied forces. While John's elder brother, Edward Schnell, consulted with the Shogun and served as a translator for the Prussian consulate, John himself came under the direct employ of Lord Matsudaira of the Aizu Domain and was given status as a samurai. Lord Matsudaira had given Schnell permission to marry a Japanese woman from the samurai class, Oyo. He then proposed to Lord Matsudaira that his then-pregnant wife and a group from the Aizu-Wakamatsu region (present-day Fukushima Prefecture) emigrate to California and establish a colony. In April 1869, with Lord Matsudaira's consent and funding, Schnell commissioned the steam-powered clipper ship the SS *China,* to carry his wife, their first child Frances, their nursemaid, Okei, and twenty farmers and craftsmen to the U.S.

This group, the first Japanese to settle in North America, established the Wakamatsu Colony in Placerville, California, also known as the Wakamatsu Tea and Silk Farm Colony, in 1869.[613] The arrival of this group from Japan in San Francisco on May 20, 1869 caught the attention of the *San Francisco Alta Daily News*, which noted that the colonists brought the means for their agricultural productivity with them, including "50,000 three-year old *kuwa* (mulberry) trees," used for the cultivation of silk worms, as well as six million tea seeds.[614] They came with the hope to establish a new agricultural community in the Americas that highlighted Japanese practices.

Unfortunately the colony was a failure, and after two years Schnell returned to Japan with his wife and two daughters, but in this experiment we see that the first Japanese community to develop in the continental U.S. was a multiracial one. This included the birth of the first Nisei American (second-generation person of Japanese ancestry) in 1870 with Schnell family's second daughter, Mary, born in California. The multiraciality of the earliest communities can further be seen with one of the Wakamatsu colonists, twenty-year-old carpenter "Kuni" Kuninosuke Masumizu (1849-1915), who married Carrie Wilson, the daughter of a Blackfoot Indian woman and a former African American slave, in Colma, California in 1877. Masumizu was the only one of Schnell's group to settle permanently in the U.S. and raise a family. The couple had three children and their descendants, the present-day Elebeck Family, were "discovered" when a local newspaper ran a story on the one-hundred-year anniversary of the Wakamatsu Colony.[615]

The first Japanese to settle in Oregon were also members of a multiracial family. Miyo Iwakoshi arrived in 1880 with her Australian-Scottish husband, Andrew McKinnon, and her brother Riki, and their adopted five-year-old Japanese daughter, Tama Jewel Nitobe.[616] The couple had met in Japan, where McKinnon, at the invitation of the Japanese government, had been teaching the Japanese new animal husbandry techniques for raising cattle and dairy farming in Hokkaido, as a part of a government campaign to learn from Western expertise that ultimately brought 10,000 so-called *oyatoi gaikokujin* (hired foreign specialists) to the island nation. The Iwakoshi-McKinnon couple was among the many interracial couples that resulted from this effort to modernize Japan.[617]

The couple set up a sawmill in East Multnomah County, outside of Portland, that McKinnon, eventually named after his wife. The settlement was called "Orient," and this small township of Orient still exists outside of Gresham, Oregon.

These examples of multiracial families in Hawai'i, California, and Oregon demonstrate that multiraciality is not only a recent phenomenon in the Japanese American community, but rather, it was present and significant from the very beginning of the Japanese American experience. The notion that hapa Japanese are a recent addition to the Japanese American community may be traced to the so-called picture bride period, during which the Japanese American community became predominantly monoracial in Hawai'i and on the West Coast of the U.S., but even during that period, in regions such as the Midwest, the South, Alaska, and the East Coast, multiracial Japanese American families continued to be a noticeable feature of the community (see Greg Robinson's chapter in this edited volume for more on these cases). Indeed, as the Japanese American community grew in the last decade of the nineteenth century and the first two decades of the twentieth century, the problem of "miscegenation" or racial intermixing would become a major element in the dynamic of inclusion and exclusion for the Japanese in American society.

### Anti-Miscegenation Laws and the Inclusion/Exclusion of the Multiracial Japanese Americans in American Society

In the years following World War I, the growth of the Japanese American community was driven primarily by the birth of children in United States. The second generation, called "Nisei" in contrast to the "Issei" sojourners and immigrants from Japan, was afforded United States citizenship by virtue of their birth on American soil. With a high mortality rate for infants and women in childbirth (in Seattle in the early 1900s, the mortality rate for childbirth deaths averaged twenty-six per 1000), the Japanese population, limited also by a number of new anti-Japanese immigration laws, grew at a slow but steady pace.

Despite this, the white public's image of the Japanese was one of a people who reproduced at an alarming rate. This image was due to misinformation spread by people like Miller Freeman, the prominent Seattle publisher of the Pacific Fisherman, who gave speeches (with titles like, "This is a White Man's Country") to audiences of hundreds in 1919, falsely claiming that Japanese women bore five times more children than white women.[618] The growing Japanese population also concerned the U.S. government. In May 1918, army intelligence officer Major H. C. Merriam issued a report titled, "The Increase of Japanese Population in the Hawaiian Islands and What It Means." It attributed the Japanese population increase to the so-called "picture brides," stating "These Japanese women are prolific."[619] Government and media interest in a growing "yellow peril" represented by the fecundity of Japanese women certainly helped to shape popular opinion.

In the early decades of the twentieth century, the addition of Japanese women, particularly the picture brides, to the initial Japanese population of male laborers, made for a much more robust community. The presence of women allowed for family formation, a process that tended to reduce out-marriage, given that most Japanese male migrants preferred to marry Japanese women. With very few women in the initial sojourning community of laborers, as an increasing number of Japanese men began to contemplate a longer-term commitment to living in the U.S., the desire to marry meant either returning to Japan temporarily to find a wife or, with increasing frequency, hiring marriage arrangers to find someone appropriate (often from the same village or region in Japan) with whom they might begin a courting process, including exchanging photos.

This led to so-called "photo marriages" (*shashin kekkon*) which were registered in Japan in the local family registry, and after the six-month waiting period required by the Japanese government for a wife to have been married, a "picture bride" was allowed to board a ship to the Americas.[620] Between 1908 and 1924, over 21,000 young women (14,000 from mainland Japan and 7,000 from Okinawa), usually from ages 16 to 20, arrived in the Americas from Japan as new wives to husbands who were often a decade older.[621] Many women were dismayed upon arrival in the Americas to find that their new husbands had sent misleading information about themselves, such as photos of themselves taken when they were much younger or false information about their immigration status.

Prior to the arrangements that made Japanese women more available, Japanese male migrants often looked to women of other races, including Mexican and Filipina Americans, as well as white American women. Probably the best-known example of the pre-picture bride period, was a marriage between the Japanese writer Yone Noguchi and the Irish American educator and journalist Leonie Gilmore (see Greg Robinson's chapter in this volume for a more detailed treatment of this family). Their son, Isamu (1904–1988), who self-identified as a "hybrid" Japanese American, would in later years become an internationally celebrated sculptor, architect, and furniture designer, with works that included public art like the Rockefeller Center Skating Rink Atlas motif and his sculpture in the Yale University Beinecke Library courtyard, with the Noguchi Museum in New York City now dedicated to showcasing his works.[622]

As noted earlier, King Kalakaua and the Kingdom of Hawai'i initially promoted the concept of inviting the Japanese as a "cognate race" to repopulate the decimated native Hawaiian population through intermarriage. Even as an American territory, Hawai'i continued to permit and, at times, celebrate racial mixture. And in South America, a Japanophile Peruvian president changed a law prohibiting interracial unions to welcome the Japanese in the early 1900s. Further, Brazil also permitted such marriages, enough so that potential Japanese emigrants in the 1920s would see, in books like *Burajiru no Jisseikatsu* [*The Real Life of Brazil*] by Hisaichi Kōdo, "a photo of young Brazilian women with the caption, 'What a group of lovely senhoras! The beauties of Sao Paulo state hope for marriage with young Japanese.'"[623]

However, North America, especially in the Western states, was a different story. In stark contrast, many states expressed fear of Asian immigration and integration into the American mainstream by passing a series of laws to prevent racial mixing with white America. As early as 1880 the California Civil Code explicitly forbade the issuance of marriage licenses to couples consisting of a white person and a "negro, Mulatto, or Mongolian." In 1910, for example, two Los Angelenos—George Masaki, a Japanese gardener, and Juliette S. Schwann—traveled to Goldfield, Nevada to get married because they could not marry in California due to the state's anti-miscegenation laws. While the County Clerk in Nevada duly issued them their marriage license and a Judge Stevens performed the first "Asiatic marriage in Goldfield," a hostile crowd gathered outside the courthouse. Fearing violence from a public ready to lynch the couple, the sheriff's department had the marriage immediately revoked, rushed the couple rushed to the train station, and told them never to return to Goldfield.[624]

In the four decades that followed, virtually every Western state except Colorado and Washington passed similar anti-miscegenation laws that had roots in the southern U.S. tradition of prohibiting marriage and integration between Whites and Blacks, but this time adding Asians (otherwise known in that period as "Orientals" or "Mongolians") as a primary target of the laws. In 1910, 28 states had anti-miscegenation laws that prohibited white-black marriages, with six Southern states enshrining this prohibition as a provision of their state constitution.[625] During the early twentieth century, Asians were added to this fundamental ban on intermarriage into white America (these laws did not prohibit interracial unions between non-white racial groups), albeit with varying terminology and definitions; Arizona, California, Mississippi, and Utah used the term "Mongolian," while Nevada and Oregon used the term "Chinese," and Montana both "Chinese" and "Japanese."[626]

The heightened regulation of "Oriental" miscegenation with

white America seemed to go hand in hand with growing public anti-Japanese sentiment. In Idaho, the state statute included a ban on white-"Mongolian" marriages, a term which seemed to refer only to the Chinese. This law was amended in 1922 with the explicit addition of "Japanese" to the list of persons illegal for white Americans to marry.[627] By 1922, even the federal government became involved after the passage of the congressional Cable Act, which eliminated American citizenship from women who married aliens but maintained it on those marrying aliens "ineligible" for citizenship (most often a code word for Asians, given that this new law allowed continued citizenship for American women marrying European immigrants or aliens eligible for citizenship).[628]

These laws directly impacted mixed-race couples such as Gunjirō Aoki and Gladys Emery Aoki, who left California to marry in Washington in 1909, or Fusatarō Nakaya and Edith W. Morton, who went as far as Mexico to sanctify their marriage in l921.

With newspaper articles in the San Francisco area blaring headlines such as "Cleric's Daughter Will Marry Samurai" or "Throw Bricks at Japanese Suitor, Corte Madera Men to Treat Miss Emery's Fiancée to Tar and Feathers," the Aoki couple enduring legal and social barriers to their union (in 1909, California legislators had passed the Polsley Bill, adding Japanese to the list of people prohibited from marrying Whites and it was not until 1933 that Mrs. Helen Gladys Aoki regained her citizenship stripped from her due to the Cable Act).[629]

Though they met in the Midwest, Nakaya and Morton ended up in California, despite its anti-miscegenation laws, where Dr. Fusataro Nakaya became a prominent community leader and worked at the Japanese Hospital in Los Angeles. Edith Morton, who lost her American citizenship due to the Cable Act, also managed to regain her citizenship through a legal effort.[630]

One of the most publicized cases around white-Asian intermarriage was that of Emma Fong Kuno (née Emma Howse), who in 1897 married a Chinese man (Walter Fong, a Stanford graduate and Christian pastor) in Colorado because of California's anti-miscegenation laws. After his death, she married a Japanese man, Yoshisaburō Kuno (a graduate of UC Berkeley and in 1901 the first instructor of Japanese studies at the University of California).[631] Not only had a white woman married an Asian man, but she also did so twice and proudly and publically detailed her relationships in a 1922 serialized piece in the San Francisco Bulletin: "My Oriental Husbands: The Story of a San Francisco Girl, Who Married a Chinese Graduate of Stanford University, and a Year After His Death Became the Wife of His Lifelong Friend, a Japanese Instructor of the University of California."[632]

The Emma Fong Kuno case suggests that despite the increasing number of discriminatory pieces of legislation barring white-Asian marriages, couples found ways to circumvent these state laws and legalize their unions. Less sensational but also in the news was the case of the daughter of a Christian Archdeacon who had fallen in love with her family's Japanese "houseboy." Fiercely opposed by her father, the young woman's mother supported their union, supposedly telling her husband, "Aren't you a Christian? In God's eyes, the Japanese, Americans, English, and all other people are the same."[633] A newspaper article in a San Francisco paper was highly critical of this white-Japanese marriage, especially because the bride was the daughter of such a prominent family. Other Christians of the time, such as the Rev. N. L. Ward of Canada, thought of this type of union as the "acid test" of tolerance: "Would you like your sister to marry a Chinaman or a Japanese? ... Surely, God does not expect that you should call anybody and everybody a brother-in-law!"[634] The Archdeacon divorced his wife over the marriage, and she ended up living with her daughter, her Japanese son-in-law, and her five mixed-race grandchildren who were born thereafter. Apparently, the Christian pastor never forgave his daughter for breaking this social taboo, but towards the end of his life decided to include one of the grandsons in his will.

The tension between the Christian teaching of equality in the eyes of God, invoked by the archdeacon's wife and the notion of an Anglo-Protestant America that needed to be protected was also evident in the case of a Japanese steward residing in lower Manhattan waterfront district—a certain K. Moto according to legal records—and his marriage to Winifred Corman in New York in 1899. The historian Mary Lui chronicled the legal case against Moto that came about after city officials found out that Winifred was only 14 years old (and not 17 as she had told the Rev. O. R. Boulton of the Five Points Mission, who had married them). The Japanese Issei was charged with abduction as defined by Section 282 of penal code (though eventually those charges were dropped) and the marriage dissolved. The court reserved a particularly strong reprimand against the Christian minister for officiating a marriage between "a heathen and a Christian."[635]

In contrast, Christianity was invoked to justify the interracial union that produced Aiko Tokimasa Reinecke. Her Japanese father was a convert to the Methodist Church and served as a minister in it. In the 1920s, the father and white mother permitted the daughter to marry a white man and his son to marry a white woman.[636] Here, the rhetoric of the equality of all peoples in the eyes of God was invoked to counter the rhetoric of God's creation of a hierarchy of beings that was promoted by people like the Washington State attorney Joseph Cheney who was a fierce advocate of anti-Japanese legislation. His argument in the 1920 *Wapato Independent* newspaper was based on a fear of racial mixture: "White and yellow skins will not blend into a veril [sic] nation. ... God, the almighty Creator put the yellow races in Asia, Red in Americas, the white in Europe." The slogan of the day, according to Cheney was, "THE JAP MUST GO. Make your choice. Are you white or are you yellow?" He followed this up with a December 1920 letter to sympathetic white Americans, including Christian clergy:

> Do not let the cheap yellow cur or renegade white man bought by yellow and tainted money obscure the real issue. As long as this universe exists, the offspring of a white man and a Japan (sic), or a white woman and a Jap, the half-breed will never be a man. It will be a mongrel insult, neither white nor yellow, neither man nor beast. As long as there is an ounce of pride or self respect in your veins you will not have your children intermarrying with the Jap.[637]

Some Japanese parents also exhibited concern at interracial unions. An advocate of intermarriage, the Superintendent of the Hawai'i's Department of Public Instruction, Vaughan MacCaughey, noted in 1919 that, "In general, Japanese marry only Japanese; they show remarkable racial allegiance, more so, as a race, than any other in Hawaii. A few Japanese men have married Hawaiian, part-Hawaiian, and Portuguese women; only one has married an American woman."[638] An Issei father in the 1920s declared, "My son is not going to marry a Haole, a Chinese or a member of any other race. He is the only son in the family and it is expected that he should take our family name. Can a 'happa' take the name Tokunaga and be the head of the Tokunaga family? 'Happa' is not worthy of such an honorable position in a Japanese family."[639] Another Issei parent in the 1920s in Hawai'i suggested, "I am well convinced that marriage with members of other races always ends in divorce. See, Mr. A, a dentist, Mr. B., a doctor, returned from the mainland with Haole wives. How long do you think they lived together? Every one of them had separated after a year or two. You can't expect to be happy with a Haole woman or a Portuguese woman because our culture, our modes of living, our philosophy are not the same as theirs."[640] This type of interethnic tension has been chronicled by historian Eichiro Azuma, who documented the saga of a Filipino boycott of Japanese businesses in Stockton, California that had its roots in an intermarriage between a Nisei woman and a Filipino laborer. He also notes the fear among Japanese Americans of Filipino males vis-à-vis Nisei women in Japanese ethnic newspapers in the Delta region of California. The newspapers claimed that male Filipino laborers were "seducing" young Nisei women because so few Filipina women lived in the region. Azuma suggested that, "Japanese immigrants worried about intermarriage because it signified Filipino 'contamination' of their 'pure' bloodline," which he attributed to the racism of imperial Japan as it expanded its empire in Asia.[641] In Brazil, although 20% of all marriages in the 1920s involved a non-Brazilian partner, the Japanese were less likely to intermarry (which sometime provoked attacks of ethnocentrism) than other ethnic groups. According to Steward Lone, although the number of Japanese marrying Brazilians went up in the 1930s, there were those who thought such marriage to be negative, with one Issei quoted as saying, "To marry with another race is ethnosuicide for we Japanese."[642]

In other words, resistance to interracial unions came from racial ideologies founded on notions of blood purity that were present in both Euro-American and Japanese perspectives. Such resistance, however, did not eliminate multiracial unions and the multiracial and multiethnic individuals born of them. In most cases in this era, the father was Japanese and the mother non–Japanese, which is in stark contrast with postwar interracial unions where the dominant pattern was of a Euro-American or African-American man and a Japanese woman.

But in one early mixed family—the Kojima family—we can see both patterns in two generations of the family. Born Kenji Edward Gordes, Kenji was a hapa Japanese American with a half-Japanese and half-French man, Henri Gordes, as his father and a Japanese woman, Harue, as his mother. Kenji's parents divorced after having four children, and the mother took three of those children to America, including Kenji, where she met and married a Japanese miner named Kojima, from whom Kenji took the family name he used until his death. We know about Kenji Edward Gordes Kojima because he was memorialized after dying in one of the worst mining accidents in the history of the American West: the August 1923 collapse of the Kemmerer Coal Company's Mine Number 1 in Frontier, Wyoming.[643] Here we can see how the patterns of interracial individuals were complex even in this early period.

But by this period in the 1920s, the anti-Japanese movement had become even more aggressive, further discouraging intermarriage especially between Japanese and white America. For example, the Asiatic Exclusion League in California developed a six-point rationale for barring the further immigration of Japanese, including the clause "It should be against public policy to permit our women to intermarry with Asiatics." As one spokesman put it, "an eternal law of nature has decreed that the White cannot assimilate the blood of another without corrupting the very springs of civilization."[644] The secretary of the Canadian Oriental Exclusion Association, Harry Langley, went as far as to say that he would "murder" his children rather then "see them fall prey to Orientals for husbands."[645]

In his testimony at the 1920 federal Congressional hearings on immigration and naturalization, Miller Freeman, president of the Anti-Japanese League of Seattle, focused on the fact that he believed the Japanese to be non-assimilable—that "it is not possible for the two races to mix." In an interview with the *Seattle Star* newspaper, he cited the cultural evolution theories of Herbert Spencer and suggested that intermarriage of human races would have negative consequences much as the interbreeding of animals would. In another part of the federal hearing, Congressman John Miller of Seattle claimed that white blood was the weakest in the world, meaning that racial intermarriage between Japanese and white Americans would result in the diluting of the white race. Giving an analogy in reference to white and Native American mixes, he explained, "In other words, the half-breed Indian partakes more of the Indian than the white man."[646]

The fear of white blood and white civilization becoming overwhelmed by "Oriental" or "Asiatic" blood was stoked by the rise in the study of eugenics and so-called race sciences. Madison Grant and Lothrop Stoddard, two of the most prominent proponents of this movement, hierarchized race and emphasized not only the value in preserving the purity of a race, but also linked this to marriage laws and immigration policies. Madison Grant, with his book *The Passing of the Great Race* (1916) and articles in popular journals and magazines like the *North American Review*, brought new racial theories to the emerging eugenics field, wherein he advocated the sterilization of the "unfit," including "worthless race types" along with criminals, the diseased, and mentally unstable people.[647] When it came to miscegenation, as Patricia Roy noted, Grant argued that when "'two distinct species are located side by side' either one or the other drives the other away or they amalgamate to form 'race bastards' (where the 'lower race,' predominates)."[648]

Grant's disciple Stoddard developed these theories and more explicitly linked them to national identity and legal measures to prevent Asian immigration. As historian Jennifer Snow observed, Stoddard "ranked Asian immigration above war, revolution, or economic competition in dangers to white domination,"[649] and as historian Roger Daniels noted, within four years of the publication of Stoddard's best-selling book, *Rising Tide of Color* (1920), it went through fourteen editions, just at the same time as the restrictive Immigration Acts of 1921 and 1924 passed.[650] In *Rising Tide of Color*, Stoddard claimed:

"Colored migration is a *universal* peril, menacing every part of the white world ... The whole white race is exposed, immediately or ultimately, to the possibility of social sterilization and final replacement or absorption by the teeming colored races. ... There's no immediate danger of the world being swamped by black blood. But there is a very immediate danger that the white stocks may be swamped by Asiatic blood. ... Unless [the white] man erects and maintains artificial barriers [he will] *finally perish*. ... White civilization is today coterminous with the white race. ..."[651]

The notion that race and civilization are conterminous meant that the earlier fears expressed by Christians bemoaning the arrival and integration of Asian "heathens" as a threat to Christianity. This further split the Christian community, with a majority opposing equal treatment of Asian and European immigration on the basis of so-called heathenism, racial hierarchy, and fear of miscegenation. For some, like those who belonged to the study groups on race relations in the United Church in Canada, Stoddard's work was required reading.[652] On the other hand, a minority, especially those who engaged in prior missionary work in Asia, believed the immigration of Asians created a great opportunity for Christian conversion and an affirmation of the idea of equality of humans under God.

But even these more open-minded Christians generally opposed, for public purposes at least, racial mixing of Asian immigrants with white Americans. Sidney Lewis Gulick, a liberal Christian who was normally known to be sympathetic toward the Japanese and who worked against anti-Japanese discriminatory legislation, initially opposed "free intermarriage of the races" and "unlimited immigration." Yet in his 1914 book, *The American Japanese Problem*, he allowed that "half breed" Japanese were not mentally ill nor morally deficient and even seemed to shift his views to favor the interbreeding of various races in Hawai'i in his 1937 book, *Mixing the Races in Hawaii*.[653] In Canada, Henry F. Angus of the University of British Columbia, who was a champion of the rights of Japanese Canadians, feared intermarriage and argued that it "would be deplorable at the present time, as our social atmosphere is not yet favorable to it."[654] Though very likely an undercount, Canadian statistics, which show only eight white-Asian interracial marriages recorded in the early twentieth century (six Chinese men married white women and two Japanese men married white women) seem to bear this out this sentiment.[655]

The former Christian missionary, Robert Speer, was also generally sympathetic to Asians, argued that "Amalgamation had always happened in the past, is happening now, and will happen in the future. No existing race was a pure race including the 'White.'" But as Jennifer Snow noted, Speer "opposed intermarriage on a practical basis" and worried that "children of intermarriage were often abandoned by their white fathers and in many nations mixed-race children were also rejected by mother's society. His vision was that God created a diversity of races and each should stay apart.[656] The idea of equal but separate was seemingly the farthest mainstream Christians in North America, however liberal, felt they could go.

At this time, the Japanese also began to adopt certain forms of racial and eugenics theories from the West, as noted above, Issei immigrants also held some qualms about race mixing on practical grounds, but some Buddhist leaders expressed admiration of hybridity. In an essay for the popular Buddhist magazine *Dōbō*, Bishop Imamura commented on Hawai'i and mixed-race peoples, writing, "The hybrids will control the future world. ... Children of mixed blood will necessarily develop and prosper."[657] This was in sharp contrast to the increasingly common view in mainstream white America and Canada of "race degeneration" through interracial unions. Canadian journalist J.S. Cowper, in his series, "The Rising Tide of Asiatics" in 1921, claimed that mixed-race children, whom he termed "hybrids" between Japanese and Whites, had the negative characteristics or "vices" of both parents.[658]

These mixed-race individuals found themselves facing such negative stereotyping when it came to marriages of their own. David Yoo has noted the case of Mary Kunimoto, the daughter of a Japanese American physician and an Irish American woman born in Denver, Colorado. Just two days before her wedding in 1929, her white fiancé skipped town, claiming that his change of mind came about "because he did not want to marry one who was 'A Daughter of Two Worlds.'" Mary, upset and humiliated by the incident even while wedding gifts were still arriving, was "found dead inside of her father's car with a revolver at her side."[659]

By this period, the term "amalgamation" gained currency in both popular and legal discussions of immigrant assimilation via race mixture. This was particularly evident in U.S. Supreme Court cases concerned with citizenship. The best known of these were the 1922 cases *United States v. Ozawa* and *United States v. Thind*, in which a Japanese and a South Asian, respectively, challenged the discriminatory laws that afforded first-generation European immigrants citizenship, but not immigrants from Asia. Ozawa's petition for American citizenship was denied even though he was an English-speaking UC Berkeley graduate and professed Christian, seen by some as conforming to an Anglo-Protestant normativity in regards citizenship.[660] Since 1790, the right of naturalization was restricted to aliens who were "free white persons," though this was amended in 1870 to include "aliens of African nativity and persons of African descent." Cases to include Asians as eligible for naturalization (at times curiously argued on the basis that Asians were "White" or "Caucasian") failed. In an important "racial prerequisite" precedent, the 1878 *In re Ah Yup* case, Judge Sawyer declared: "I am of the opinion that a native of China, of the Mongolian race, is not a white person."[661] Until the 1922 Ozawa case settled the matter, some legal scholars like John Wigmore, in 1894 in the *American Law Review*, argued that while the Chinese should not be considered "white persons," the Japanese had as good a claim to the color "White" as "southern Europeans and the Semitic peoples," or were at least not "Mongolian" and should be eligible to naturalized as Americans.[662] Some 1,368 Chinese and 420 Japanese naturalized American citizens had apparently slipped through the legal cracks according to the 1910 Census, but after the Ozawa Supreme Court case, Japanese were grouped into the category of persons "ineligible to citizenship."

The move towards racial purity and exclusion meant not only that virtually no Japanese could naturalize, but that mixed-race Japanese (some of whom were at least partially White) also found themselves unable to lay claim to American national belonging. These laws impacted many who had naturalized as U.S. citizens in 1898 when all residents of Hawai'i automatically earned American citizenship upon the transfer of sovereignty when the Hawaiian Islands became an American territory, including Jō Makino, the older brother of Fred Makino (the half-Japanese, half-Scottish founder of the *Hawaii Hochi* newspaper mentioned above). Makino was stripped of his citizenship in New York when authorities learned of his half-Japanese heritage; he took his case to a New York state court, but lost.[663] Similarly, William Knight, despite having served in the U.S. Navy for over twenty-five years and receiving a medal in the battle of Manila Bay, found himself in front of Judge Thomas Chatfield of the U.S. District Court (Eastern District of New York) in 1909, who denied his application to naturalize as an American citizen, stating that despite a white father, because his mother was half-Japanese and half-Chinese, he was "literally a half-breed ... the application must be denied."[664]

Another mixed-race Japanese who took his case for U.S. citizenship to court was Albert Henry Young, who, as a half-Japanese, half-German, was denied his U.S. naturalization by federal District Court Judge Cushman of Washington State on August 15, l912. Judge Cushman opined:

> In the abstraction of higher mathematics, it may be plausibly said that the half of infinity is equal to the whole of infinity; but in the case of such a concrete thing as the person of a human being it cannot be said that one who is half white and half brown or yellow is a white person, as commonly understood.[665]

These legal determinations prior to the better-known 1922 *United States v. Ozawa* case made it clear that those with even partial Japanese heritage were not going to be included in the national citizenry.[666]

The exclusion of the "Oriental" and "half-breeds" through immigration policies and citizenship laws had real consequences. The designation of Japanese immigrants as "ineligible for citizenship" by extension made it impossible for them to earn the right to vote or to purchase and own land, after a series of "anti-alien land laws" and other laws based on citizenship were passed in California and other Western states. These anti-Japanese and anti-hapa Japanese sentiments of exclusion would manifest in their worst form during World War II with the incarceration of nearly 120,000 Japanese and Japanese Americans by the U.S. government.

# World War II Incarceration of Hapa Japanese Americans and their Participation in the U.S. Military

*I am determined that if they have one drop of Japanese blood in them, they must go to camp.*

*—Colonel Karl Bendetsen (1942)*

White Americans often invoked the "one drop rule" to define multiracial black Americans as "Black." Many believed that "one drop" of Japanese blood was enough to take from white-Japanese individuals not only the right to become an American, such that like other Isseis, hapa Issei immigrants would have to wait until the 1950s to have a claim on citizenship, though their American-born children had citizenship rights.

But even with American-born children, the exclusionary nature of white America towards Asians and mixed-race Asians was extended, or even heightened, during World War II. The quotation above shows how the "one drop" rule, defining the non-White "other," was used by Colonel Karl Bendetsen, one of the key architects of the U.S. government's policy of rounding up and incarcerating nearly 120,000 persons of Japanese ancestry, purportedly for the sake of national security, after the February 1942 issuance of Executive Order 9066 by President Roosevelt, which defined a military zone in the western U.S. from which all persons of Japanese ancestry were to be removed.

Despite being at war with Germany and Italy as well as Japan, the U.S. government's wholesale targeting of all Japanese Americans (even those with only a single "drop" of blood), while selectively targeting small numbers of German American and Italian American individuals with particular ties to Nazi and Fascist organizations, demonstrated the racial bias in the policies of the U.S. government.

These policies led to the indiscriminate targeting of Japanese Americans, including mixed-race Japanese Americans, who lived in zones of the western United States that had been designated vulnerable to potential "fifth column" activity. This was despite the fact that Pearl Harbor in Honolulu had been attacked and the equally large population of Japanese Americans in Hawai'i was not subjected to mass incarceration. As a result of these policies, West Coast Japanese Americans lost their homes, businesses, property, and communities when they were relocated to high-security camps run by the Department of Justice or to one of the ten camps run by the War Relocation Authority (WRA).

Mixed-race Japanese were not exempted from this situation. Indeed, confusion reigned within interracial families about what exactly to do. Stories like that told by the Rev. Daisuke Kitagawa were common. Kitagawa met a woman at a sanatorium in the White River Valley region of Washington State on the day before the first train was to leave for camp (around May 10-12, 1942). He recalled:

> I happened to meet at the hospital a young Nisei woman, married to a Filipino, who had just had a baby. Neither she nor her husband knew for sure whether she and their children were entitled to stay where they were or, if they had to be evacuated, whether her husband was entitled to accompany them to camp. The evacuation order was quite clear on that point: anyone of Japanese blood, of whatever degree, must be evacuated. Whether this resulted in a temporary separation of that man from his wife and children or whether he accompanied his family to the camp, I can no longer remember. Most likely the young mother and her children caught one of the three trains while her husband remained behind, hoping that in the not-too-distant future arrangements could be made for their reunion.[667]

In time, the government issued a policy that they would make an exception to the "one drop rule" by exempting those with less than fifty percent Japanese blood from the relocation policy, though such exceptions were rarely put into practice.[668] Indeed, more common would situations such as one observed by the Quaker sympathizer to the Japanese American, Rev. Herbert Nicholson, who witnessed an older white woman, her adult mixed-race children, and their children crying on one of the "evacuation" buses leaving Covina, California. Apparently, the older woman was a Russian mother who had had the adult children years ago with a Japanese man, who had since passed away. She had remarried a Russian and had raised the children from the first marriage without telling them that they were half-Japanese. These half-Japanese, half-Russian sisters had never met their Japanese father and it was only when one of them had applied for a defense industry job, that after government investigation, discovered her heritage and got the whole extended family ensnared in the mass incarceration. Rev. Nicholson was able to persuade a Colonel Severance, who was in charge of the mass "evacuation" in the San Gabriel area, to make efforts to release them after six weeks.[669]

Among the very rare exceptions made to the policy of West Coast exclusion for those with Japanese heritage were two naturalized World War I veterans: Inomata Kinji (aka Kenji Inomata) and Nisuke Mitsumori. The two received special permits directly from U.S. Attorney for the Southern District, William Fleet Palmer, permitting them to remain in Los Angeles and Pasadena respectively. In the case of Inomata Kinji, the war veteran was able to avoid incarceration along with his Alabama-born "Creole" (wartime documents refer to her as a "Negress") wife Genevieve Beckham-Kingi and seven hapa Japanese-American children.[670] However, lengthy service in U.S. military alone seems not to have been sufficient for an exemption. A Nisei veteran in the U.S. Marine Corps with thirty years of service, Frank Fukuoka, who had three sons in the U.S. Navy at the time of Pearl Harbor, was forcibly removed to the Santa Anita detention center. And U.S. Army Captain Robert S. Kinoshita, his white wife Evelyn, and hapa Japanese American son, Robert, were all detained initially at the Portland Assembly Center in Oregon and later in the WRA Minidoka camp in Idaho, despite his years of service in the Medical Corps reserves after earning his M.D. from the University of Nebraska in 1934 (he would later serve in the famed 442nd Regimental Combat Team receiving two Silver Stars and three Pearl Hearts).[671]

The U.S. government also forcibly removed to the WRA camp in Minidoka over 120 Alaskans, among whom were quite a large number of children or grandchildren of Eskimo women and Japanese men.[672] Alaskan government officials, concerned less about the Japanese and more about the native Alaskan women and the mixed-race children, wrote to General Simon Buckner, head of Alaska Defense Command, in April 1942, inquiring if it might not be better for entire families to relocate to Idaho: "Would children be allowed to accompany parents or older relatives on a voluntary basis to prevent hardship? Undoubtedly, numerous native women married to Japanese would be left behind without material support."[673] Alaska Governor Gruening also appealed to General John L. De Witt at the Western Defense Command in San Francisco in regards to the case of Henry Hope, a seventeen-year-old Japanese-Eskimo boy (born to a Japanese father, but adopted by Lucie and Sammy Hope, an Athabaskan Indian and an Eskimo). Naske notes that, "The governor regretfully reported that his request had been denied and that 'no exceptions can be made.'"[674]

By early 1942, the government had removed families like

those of Amelia Kito, a woman of Tlingit-Japanese descent with three children, from their homes. Kito was taken from her home in Petersburg, Alaska to Minidoka, while her Japanese American husband, Saburo "Sam" Kito, Sr., was taken to a high-security camp run by the U.S. Army in Lordsburg, New Mexico, where he recalled "wearing clothes with 'POW' on the back" before being transferred to a Department of Justice-run camp at Santa Fe and eventually to a road construction labor camp in Kooskia, Idaho.[675]

Hundreds, perhaps over a thousand, mixed-marriage families like the Kito family had lived in the affected West Coast areas as of October 1, 1943.[676] This situation tore families apart. Among the Japanese-Eskimo families, for instance, the head of the household— the 66-year old Yahei Shioda (originally from Kumamoto Prefecture), had been removed from Alaska to the high-security U.S. Army-run Camp Lordsburg (New Mexico). He had left behind his native Alaskan wife, children, and even one young grandchild, not knowing where they had ended up. Several months after his incarceration, he suddenly passed away. A Buddhist priest, Daishō Tana, recalled that the deceased had carried a photo of his mixed-race grandchild, and out of respect for the deceased's affections, had that photo placed on Mr. Shioda's chest when he was buried. He also brought together over thirty Buddhist priests behind barbed wire to perform Mr. Shioda's funeral with a volunteer to serve in the place of the mixed-race children and grandchild to offer incense to honor the deceased.[677]

Often the non-Japanese parent in the multiracial family had to decide whether to enter camp with the rest of the family. These persons without Japanese ancestry who voluntarily entered the World War II camps for the sake of their families included Mary Kimura (a Portuguese woman who had married into a Japanese American family, that ended up in the Topaz WRA camp)[678] and Estelle Peck Ishigo (a Euro American woman who lost her job at the Hollywood Arts Center after Pearl Harbor because of her Japanese family name, and who became renowned in the post-war period for her candid sketches of camp life). Shizu Hayakawa, a neighbor to Mrs. Kimura, recalled that after the FBI took away her neighbor's Japanese American husband, she was in a difficult situation:

> [Mary] had three children, and in those days they were called *happa* [half and half] and were looked down upon. The Japanese called them *keto keto* [hairy foreigner] and they had a very hard time. ... but since this lady was white, she could take a night job ... Mrs.

Kimura, my Caucasian friend, had one daughter, who was just about ready to graduate from high school. The mother thought that perhaps they would not have to go to camp, since she at least was Caucasian. But her daughters had Japanese boyfriends and preferred to go into the camps. I persuaded the mother to prepare to go with her children. On the very day we were to leave, the father was released by the authorities and came home. I was very thankful and relieved, because even though I had advised the mother to go with the girls to camp, down in my heart I was afraid they would be ridiculed and called bad names. Later we were all to meet again at Tanforan [Assembly Center].[679]

In contrast, for some families, the non-Japanese parent remained out of camp to help protect the family's home or farm. For example, Ginger Matsuyama Masuoka's German American mother remained on their family farm in Sonoma, California, while Ginger and her seven other mixed-race siblings were sent to Tanforan Assembly Center and then onto Topaz; meanwhile, the government eventually transferred her Japanese American father to Denver, Colorado (in the so-called "free zone") to help train the Denver police force in Japanese martial arts (which he had done previously as the martial arts instructor to the San Francisco Police Department).[680] Several of the Masuoka children were released from camp.

Other cases of release from camp involved young mixed-race children. One of the most prominent families in this situation was the Yoneda family. Karl Yoneda (a Japanese Issei and well-known Communist activist who took on the name Karl from his hero Marx) and his equally radical labor activist wife, Elaine Black Yoneda, and their young son all went into the WRA camp. Before the war, the San Francisco-based couple had married in 1936 at the non-sectarian, social activist Church of the People in Seattle (due to California's anti-miscegenation laws) and their mixed-race son, Thomas Culbert Yoneda, was born in 1939. The Catholic nun, who ran the hospital in San Francisco where Thomas had been born, commented to one of the doctors, "Had it been known that it was a 'half-breed' birth, admittance would have been refused. Don't ever bring such a patient here again."[681] Despite this and other incidents such as white neighbors successfully circulating a petition to bar the mixed-race family from their apartment complex or even the Communist Party's ban on Japanese nationals in the U.S. from being party members, Karl Yoneda was one of roughly 800 Japanese

Americans who volunteered for an advance party to help build the WRA Manzanar camp. The father thought that his white wife and mixed-race son would be allowed to remain in Los Angeles, where they had moved to in early 1942, but on April 4, 1942, U.S. government announced that those who were already at Manzanar would be subject to the mass "evacuation." Elaine Yoneda decided to join her husband in Manzanar, but was told by officials that as a white woman, she was not required nor encouraged to enter camp and that her son "Tommy" would be "put into a 'Children's Village' to be 'manned' by nuns." She refused to give up her son to an orphanage and insisted on accompanying her son to camp. Because of Tommy's asthmatic condition, the father Karl was furious upon seeing his wife and son arrive at the terribly dusty desert camp, shouting "Are you bringing our child to be killed?" not knowing that the compulsory mass incarceration had begun. A dust storm blew the first night and it would be the first of many asthma attacks and hospital visits for this mixed-race child.[682]

It was only after the military decided that Karl Yoneda's leftist leanings that critiqued Japanese militarism and strong bilingual skills could be used by U.S. military intelligence for propaganda development against the Japanese in the Pacific theater, that he was released to serve in the Burma-India-China theater as a linguist for the American cause. His wife and son were also permitted to leave Manzanar for San Francisco, but only under the condition that the mother report on a monthly basis "to military authorities on the child's whereabouts."[683]

Another woman, Chizuko Doi and her three mixed-race children were also released, but not before she was separated from her Hispanic husband, Andy Campos, and forced to take her children, including her three-week old infant, into the Fresno Assembly Center in California's Central Valley. She recalled, "Baby formula was in scarce supply and the barracks did not have refrigeration or cooking facilities."[684] These types of family separation were particularly difficult for families with very young multiracial children.

And yet another family was torn into three, but at least the children were old enough to be students in college. The Japanese father, Takeshi Okazaki (an importer living in Los Angeles) was interned at the high-security Department of Justice-run Santa Fe camp, while Barbara, his 44-year old Austrian wife, remained free in Los Angeles, and his two college-age mixed-race children (Takeshi and Florence) were behind barbed wire at the WRA-run Manzanar camp.[685]

The U.S. government had conflicting views about the incarceration of non-Japanese spouses in these camps. Paul Spickard (see his chapter in this volume) details how these multiracial family situations were viewed from the U.S. government's perspective, starting with memos such as the "Mixed Marriage Leave Clearances" drafted by Major Herman P. Goebel, Jr. in July 1942, and another Western Defense Command memo from November 1942 that proposed allowing mixed-race families to leave camp to return to their homes in exclusion zones, as long as the father was White and the children were minors. These children could leave camp, but not return to the exclusion zone if the father had Japanese ancestry or if the non-Japanese parent was not White.[686] The rationale was that forcing such families to live in a WRA camp "would expose them to infectious Japanese thought."[687] James Ong has further noted that authorities were somewhat inconsistent with the early release of mixed Japanese American families, with freedom "generally granted on the basis of racial 'whiteness' rather than nationality." For example, Ong has highlighted how the WRA camps Jerome and Rohwer, despite both being located in Arkansas, had very different records with regard to mixed Japanese and Latino/Hispanic families.[688]

While mixed-race Japanese American families on the West Coast faced mandatory incarceration, it was not as if multiracial families in the so-called "free zones" were completely free from government harassment. Indeed, in 1942, the FBI raided the farm and home of Torata Akagi and his Euro American wife, Beatrice, near Sheldon, Texas. Thomas Walls reported on the raid:

> While one [FBI] man herded the family and hired
> help into the living room, four others searched the
> house—the term 'ransacked' would be more accurate,
> since the contents of drawers and closets were strewn
> around. In one corner of the house stood a small
> wooden Buddhist altar called a *butsudan* ... During
> the search one of the men strode towards the corner,
> and, in obvious contempt, swept the *butsudan* from
> its pedestal, smashing it on the floor. Later one of the
> official intruders sneeringly asked Beatrice, the only
> non-Japanese in the family and the wife of Torata
> Akagi, whether she wasn't now sorry she had married a
> 'Jap.' 'No, of course not' was her icy reply. Powerless to
> defend themselves, the Akagis sat stoically throughout
> the ordeal. But when one of the federal agents asked

how much money was in the house, two of the younger Akagi girls ran into their rooms and retrieved a bowl of pennies they had been saving. In a symbolic act of defiance, the two young girls sat on the living-room floor and counted their pennies one by one, slowly, meticulously, and quite loudly. The FBI's search of the Akagi homestead turned up a long-forgotten crystal radio set receiver made by the two Akagi boys when they were younger. In spite of its crude construction and dubious danger, it was confiscated. Beatrice's Kodak box camera was also taken.[689]

For this family, the FBI took away the mixed-race children's grandfather, Fukutarō, for internment, though three months later, after Beatrice and her sympathetic white neighbors vigorously campaigned for his release, he was returned to the family when a parole hearing found no evidence of any anti-American activity.

Perhaps the most egregious example of racial bias in the U.S. government's internal security policies was the policy of relocating young Japanese American children who had been living in West Coast orphanages and incarcerating them behind barbed wire at the Manzanar WRA camp. Many of these children were mixed-race, third-generation (Sansei) orphans under the age of seven without any family, including some as young as two, exposing the gross absurdity of the U.S. government's claim that anyone with even a drop of Japanese blood represented a threat to national security. Among the children of the Manzanar Children's Village, roughly one in five were of mixed-race background, very possibly abandoned due to social pressures from both the Japanese and non-Japanese sides of their families.[690] James Ong notes that of those children of mixed ancestry, the non-Japanese part of their heritage included Mexican, Indian, Filipino, Italian, Irish, French, and Native American backgrounds.[691]

The three tar-paper barracks at Manzanar that were dubbed the "Children's Village," housed over sixty children drawn primarily from Shonien and the Maryknoll Catholic Home (both orphanages in Los Angeles) and the Salvation Army Home (in San Francisco). Others, such as Dennis Tojo Bambauer, were pulled out of the Children's Home Society in Los Angeles (filled primarily with white orphans), and sent to Shonien (the Japanese children's orphanage) before being shipped off to Manzanar.[692] Still others, such as Ronald Kawamoto, were mixed-race children born after the incarceration process had begun. Kawamoto was born to a Japanese American father and a Mexican American mother (Teresa Rose Kawamoto), separated from his parents at Santa Anita, and brought to the Manzanar Children's Village.[693]

The mixed-race children in this orphanage, already experiencing the loss of their parents, faced a second form of isolation when they were rejected by their fellow orphans because of their mixed heritage. Dennis Tojo Bambauer, recalled, "because I was half Caucasian, I think the kids picked on me."[694] That he shared a name with Japan's infamous Prime Minister naturally contributed to his difficulties. Non-mixed-race children confirmed this; former orphan Takatow Matsuno recalled, "*Hapas* were picked on more [because they] looked different."[695] Elsewhere, though, there were signs of a more accepting monoracial Japanese American opinion on hapas. A young Hatsune Helen Kitaji, noted in her dairy during her time in the Salinas Assembly Center: "There are certainly interesting people in a place like this. There is a lovely girl by the name of Alice Hirabayashi who is very Caucasian-looking. Her mother is Italian and her father is Japanese. There is another lovely young woman whose father is Chinese and mother Japanese. Of course, that is not unusual."[696]

Despite the complex racial dynamics of the period, many Japanese Americans, including hapa Japanese Americans, volunteered to serve in the U.S. military. Perhaps most well-known was the segregated Japanese American 100th Battalion/442nd Regimental Combat Team that served in the European theater, the 100th even earning the moniker the "Purple Heart Battalion" for their valor and high casualties in battle.

Hapa Japanese American Virgil (Nishimura) Westdale served with the 442nd after being removed from his position as a flight instructor in the Air Corps after Pearl Harbor. Born to Sunao Nishimura and Edith Loy and spending his childhood in the Midwest, phenotypically he could pass as Caucasian and had little cultural connection to the Japanese side of his heritage. It thus came as a big surprise to him in May 1942 that after he had earned his private plot license from the Civilian Aeronautics Administration (CAA) and volunteered for the War Training Service (WTS) hoping he could fly in the Air Corp rather than being drafted into the Army or Navy, he was abruptly told he could no longer serve in the program. He recalled, "It didn't even matter that I had an excellent reputation at the flight school. My government was treating me as untrustworthy. Suddenly, I was a second-class citizen. Overwhelming degradation flooded over me. I felt the moral anguish of being half Caucasian and half Japanese."[697] Another individual who was fired from his job at the McClellan Air Field in Sacramento, California due to his half-Japanese heritage was Inomata S. Kingi, Jr. described above as one of the few exempted from EO9066's evacuation orders. The young Inomata Kinji had been training alongside other young pilots to fly for the Army Air Force, when he was dismissed despite passing a FBI background check regarding his loyalty.[698]

In Virgil Nishimura's case, in October 1942, he legally changed his family name to Westdale from Nishimura. He recalled:

> When we attempted to directly translate Nishimura from Japanese to English, however, we ran into problems. *Nishi* means *west*, and *mura* means *village*, but *Westvillage* didn't sound like a name. Finally, someone suggested *Westdale*, which we liked. ... First, I met with a lawyer. Then, for about two weeks, an announcement ran in the local paper that my name would be changed in court on such and such a day. When I appeared in court, the judge asked me to state the spelling of my name and my nationality. Then he asked why I wished to change my name, and I explained that it was hard for people to spell and pronounce. I didn't admit that prejudice was a key factor in changing my name.[699]

By the summer of 1943, Westdale became an instructor for the War Training Service, training other young pilots in instrument flying, but suddenly, he received a notice from the War Department transferring him. He was abruptly told he was no longer an Air Corp flight instructor and now an Army private. He recalled, "I could see no reason for this demotion to army private, where I would make $21 a month (13 cents an hour!) as compared to the $9 per hour I had been earning as an instructor. I felt the deadly sting of my government's distrust of me, which was a blow to my pride. I felt as if I were being punished for being half-Japanese."[700]

Westdale had been placed with the 442nd Regimental Combat Team for basic training at Camp Shelby, Mississippi and found that First Sergeant Wakamatsu of Company F was just as confused as he was about why this somewhat Caucasian-looking man was joining the segregated Japanese American unit. He was only consoled by the fact that another hapa Japanese American had arrived to the unit at the same time, recalling, "With [Cliff Hana]'s light reddish hair and freckles, he, too, appeared to be Caucasian. Wakamatsu took one look at Cliff and me and thought we had reported to the wrong outfit. ... I stood a full head taller than most of the others. I felt as if I were in the Foreign Legion. ... Cliff Hana, in the same proverbial boat as I, was a consolation to me."[701]

He served in this most highly-decorated unit of World War II, as a part of the 522nd Field Artillery Battalion, as it saved the Texas "Lost Battalion" in France, broke through the Gothic Line, and liberated the Nazi death camp of Dachau.[702] Especially ironic to Westdale was liberating one of the sub-camps of Dachau on April 29, 1945. He recalled that the "Dachau prisoners took one look at our almond-shaped, black eyes and yellow skin and stepped back in fear. They thought they'd been freed from the Germans only to fall into the hands of the Japanese! ... It took some work to convince them that we were American soldiers. When they finally understood, they dropped to their knees and laughed and cried for joy."[703] Here was a hapa Japanese American who had experienced the discrimination by "looking like the enemy," with many families of his fellow combat team behind barbed wire in the U.S. involved in the liberation of another persecuted group, in this case, of Jews and political prisoners from behind barbed wire in Germany.

Westdale, along with Cliff Hana mentioned above, were among the small number of hapa Japanese Americans born and raised in regions outside of the Pacific Coast, such a Robert Chino, who joined the segregated unit in the European theater. As Greg Robinson describes in his chapter in this volume, Chino had been raised with his brother in Chicago by his Japanese father, Haruka "Frank" Chino, and a white American woman from St. Louis, Mercelia Hicks. Originally a critic of the war and a draft resister who spent eighteen months in a Minnesota prison, he eventually joined the 442nd Regimental Combat Team as a supply sergeant in Italy and France and was wounded on three occasions.

These hapa individuals were also joined by a contingent of mixed-race/mixed-roots Japanese Americans from Hawai'i. They included William Kato, Robert Kapuniai Jr., Jesse Oba (all half-Japanese, half-Hawaiian), Alvin Planas (half-Japanese, half-Filipino), William Goo (half-Japanese, half-Chinese), and Ed Nishihara (half-Japanese, half-Portuguese) who volunteered for or were drafted into the 100th Battalion and 442nd Regimental Combat Team.[704] The historian Masayo Duus notes that as many as 20 mixed-race soldiers from Hawai'i were a part of the 100th Battalion, including the battalion band leader, Sergeant James Kaholokula (father was Hawaiian and mother Japanese) and his half-brother, Eddie (who pretended he was part Japanese so that he could continue to be with his half-brother with whom he had been together since their enlistment in the National Guard). According to Masayo Duus, "some had Hawaiian surnames like Kaleialoha or Kelaloha, and some Japanese surnames. There were also soldiers with Japanese-Portuguese, Japanese-Chinese, or Japanese-Filipino parents. Issei who succeeded financially often took mistresses, as was common for well-to-do businessmen in Japan, so a number of the soldiers had been born out of wedlock."[705]

Among those in the 100th Battalion was a young father, Corporal Hideo Uchida from Company B, who was wounded in action during the first days of combat in Italy. Shrapnel had hit him in the chest just an inch away from his heart and he was put on a hospital ship back to the U.S. in February 1944. His white wife, Helen, was extremely worried because he had hovered between life and death from the injury. But, the authorities refused to allow her and their 14-month-old mixed-race child, Greydon, to visit their father who was in an army hospital in northern California. They told her that she could visit her husband, but that her half-Japanese American son, Greydon, would be violating the ban on persons of Japanese ancestry in the Western Defense Command zone. This family would not be fully reunited until later that year when the war veteran Uchida was moved to another hospital in Honolulu.[706]

While mixed-race children like Greydon were impacted by notions of segregation and exclusion, others like Benjamin (Benny) Franklin Ogata, a young 442nd hapa Japanese American soldier, paid the ultimate price for embracing both his American and Japanese heritage. Born in 1925 to Harry Ogata (the Japanese American owner of the Ogata Art Studio in Dallas) and Antoinette Hildeman (a native of the Dutch West Indies) in Texas, he had volunteered for the Navy right after the bombing of Pearl Harbor. Eventually, Benny joined the all-Japanese American unit at Camp Shelby in Mississippi, where other Japanese Americans called him "Tex." With the 442nd, 2nd Battalion, he died in action in Italy, south of Leghorn in the course of taking Hill 140 during the predawn darkness of July 6, 1944 while the Allied forces were pushing the Germans towards Pisa.[707] Not only did hapa Japanese Americans serve in the 442nd, they also died to uphold the notion that all Americans, regardless of their racial makeup, were equal under the law.

Another Texan hapa Japanese American served on the other side of the world. Frank "Foo" Fujita was the only Japanese American combat soldier taken prisoner by the Japanese. Fujita was born in Lawton, Oklahoma in 1921 as the second son to Tsuneji "Frank, Sr." Fujita (a Japanese traveling salesman who had emigrated from Nagasaki to the U.S. in 1914) and Ida Pearl Elliott (an Oklahoman of English-Scottish, German, and Catawba American Indian descent).[708] Although his older brother, Herbert, also served in the U.S. military with the 442nd Regimental Combat Team during the campaign in France, it was Frank Fujita, Jr. who became something of a celebrity in his hometown in Texas (where the family had moved to in 1937) as part of the so-called "Lost Battalion" that had disappeared in Java (Netherland East Indies).

Frank had enlisted just after high school in the Texas National Guard: Headquarters and Headquarters Battery, 1st Battalion, 131st Field Artillery Regiment, 61st Field Artillery Brigade, 36th Division. The unit was mobilized in November 1940 and by the time the unit was assigned to the Pacific theater in anticipation of clashes with the Japanese in January 1941, Fujita was making $54 a month as a sergeant.[709]

While most of the Texas National Guard's 36th Division (or the "T Patch" Division) was mobilized to Europe (well-known for their efforts at Salerno, Anzio, and Rapido River in the Italy campaign), Fujita's 2nd Battalion was sent to Java (present-day Indonesia) to assist the Dutch in its defense against a possible Japanese move in that region. It was while en route on the Pacific Ocean that his unit heard that Japan had attacked Pearl Harbor. Fujita recalled, "One day someone asked on the information program if 'there was a Jap on board this ship?' I wrote a short reply to this and gave it to the MC of the program and he read it on the next day's program. It read: 'I do not know if there is a Jap on board or not, but there is an American army sergeant who happens to be half-Japanese—I know, for I am that person, Sgt. Frank Fujita.' I never heard more of this, but was very apprehensive for awhile."[710]

The Dutch, who commanded the Allied troops in the region, capitulated quickly, and though Fujita wanted to fight from the mountains, he and the small contingent of Americans on Java had to surrender on March 8, 1942. Just prior to becoming a POW of the Japanese, Fujita couldn't sleep because he "had heard that the Japanese considered anyone with Japanese blood, regardless of where their citizenship was, as also a citizen of Japan. If this were indeed the case and they found I was—in their eyes—a Japanese fighting against the Japanese, their reaction against me could be quite gruesome."[711] During the initial assembly at the POW camp at Jaarmarkt, his friends in E Battery "pleaded with me to change my name to a Spanish or Filipino name, for they were certain that when the Japs found out about my Japanese ancestry I would be summarily shot. ... However, I felt that if I changed my name and I should die for any reason during the war then, if my death were reported at all, it would be reported under my assumed name and my parents would never know what happened to me."[712]

Eventually, he would be transported to Japan to the Fukuoka POW camp, which held roughly 1,200 British, Dutch, and American POWS, and forced to work as a slave laborer at the Nagasaki shipyard. It was here, on June 1, 1943, that his half-Japanese identity was discovered and he was brutally beaten by the Japanese guards, especially after he would not renounce the United States.[713] But because of his heritage, he was permitted to make radio announcements about what had happened to his unit (bringing some sense of relief to the people of Texas) and in December 1943, he was moved to Tokyo to work at a secret Japanese radio propaganda project housed at the Bunka Gakuin Kanda. It was not just that his Japanese language ability was very limited, but Fujita adamantly refused to cooperate with the Japanese authorities in these broadcasts. Indeed, Fujita's resistance was used as a point in the prosecution's case in the so-called Tokyo Rose trial and in other investigations of Americans who did collaborate with the Japanese propaganda unit, and Fujita was called upon to testify.[714] Another hapa Japanese American who worked directly against Japanese propaganda efforts, Clarke H. Kawakami, is described in Greg Robinson's chapter in this volume, as a Japan specialist in the U.S. Office of War Information's Psychological Warfare Section, working in the India-Burma theater.

On the same day as the surrender of his unit in Java, Fujita's younger sister, Naomi, was featured in the local newspaper. The March 8, 1942 issue of *The Abilene Reporter News* carried a story about her dismissal from her job at the local Woolworth's. In a piece sympathetic to the hapa Japanese American high school senior, the article reads in part:

> Naomi has a brother with the presumably hardpressed American Forces in Java, and another in training at Sheppard Field. But she isn't working at the five-and-ten any longer because their father is a Japanese, making them children of a mixed marriage. Naomi used to stand there [at Woolworth's] and sell jewelry, cards, phonograph records and assorted other merchandise. ... Because of repeated complaints heard by [Woolworth's manager] Davis, however, [she was asked to move to] the stock room. Manager Davis, expressing regret, said he proposed a transfer to spare both Naomi and the store criticism from persons he

described as "Fanatics." "The story was going around that we had a Jap girl working in the store," he said, "and I even heard of people inquiring if I myself was a Nazi Agent." ... Naomi refused the stockroom job. 'That would be hiding,' she said. She added that Davis had been completely fair and that she regards him as her friend. The store manager, reporting "the girls in the store are for Miss Fujita 100 percent," said her work was above reproach. ... At least two other Woolworth girls are of German blood, but Manager Davis said that there have been no complaints regarding them. Naomi Fujita is a pretty, dark eyed girl of 18. She enrolled in Abilene High School last fall as a senior.[715]

Facing discrimination for their half-American and half-Japanese heritage—the brother at the hands of Japanese POW camp guards and the sister from racially biased "fanatics" in Texas—they struggled with these challenges until the end of the war. Ultimately, Fujita was liberated from the Omori POW camp by U.S. Naval forces on August 29, 1945. In his "exit interview," he went to see a colonel who was doing the debriefing, who asked him, "'Are you the half-Japanese sergeant that was captured with that bunch of Texans down in Java?' I said, 'Yes Sir.' He then asked me if the Japs had been rough on me for being part Japanese, and when I told him that they had, he said, 'By damn I'm glad to meet you! I've heard how they treated you at this camp. Always stand tall and don't ever be ashamed of your heritage.'"[716]

In the Pacific theater, Fujita was the only Japanese American to directly assigned to serve as a soldier in a combat battalion. But several thousand Japanese Americans served as linguists in the MIS (Military Intelligence Service) in the Pacific, providing services as translators of captured documents, interrogators of Japanese POWs, creators of propaganda encouraging surrender, or as intermediaries between civilians and the U.S. military especially during the Okinawa campaign. A subset of the Nisei MIS linguists were embedded with front-line troops (often with guards so that they would not be killed by friendly fire) in numerous campaigns across the Pacific. Of these, the Nisei assigned to the 5307th Composite Unit Provisional under the command of Brig. General Frank Merrill, better known as "Merrill's Marauders," conducted some of the most dangerous missions in the Pacific theatre. This covert unit operated deep behind enemy lines on what were called "Dangerous and Hazardous Missions." The 15 Nisei volunteers of this unit used their combat and linguistic skills to help disrupt

Japanese advances.

The leader of the Japanese Americans attached to the Merrill's Marauders was a hapa Japanese American, Captain William Alfred Laffin. He had been born in 1902 in Yokohama, the son of a naturalized American (born Canadian) Thomas Laffin and Miyo Ishii Laffin. When the war broke out, his father, who had been operating a business in Yokohama, was promptly interned by the Japanese authorities, but the family's two sons (William and Thomas Jr.) were fortunate enough to board the last exchange ship in June 1942. Their mixed-race sister was unable to leave Japan on the exchange ship, and, after being apprehended by the Japanese authorities, died in a Japanese internment camp in 1944. William, who had been working for Ford Motor Company in Yokohama, returned to the headquarters in Michigan to find that he had been terminated. Facing rejection in both Japan and the U.S., he discovered that the U.S. Army was looking for qualified bilingual linguists to serve in the Army Military Intelligence Service. After receiving a commission as a captain—he graduated from the Japanese Language School at Camp Savage, Minnesota—Laffin was assigned to lead the Nisei attached to the Merrill's Marauders, which was tasked with attacking the Japanese in northern Burma. Laffin's last mission with the unit was to seize the critical all-weather Myitkyina airfield from the Japanese. The unit succeeded, but Captain Laffin never lived to receive honors from the U.S. military for his service as he was killed in action by a Japanese Zero plane on May 17, 1944 while flying over Myitkyina in a L-1 to examine the Japanese defenses. [717]

Hapa Japanese Americans in the U.S. military thus served with family members left worried in Hawai'i or the U.S., some incarcerated behind barbed wire in camps run by the War Relocation Authority or the Department of Justice, and some in internment camps run by the Japanese for enemy aliens in Japan. It was especially during the context of war that racial and national difference came under extreme scrutiny as mixed-race and mixed-roots Japanese Americans found themselves in between various national ideologies of race.

### Conclusion: Hapa Effects on the Postwar

This chapter highlighted how hapa Japanese Americans have been integral to the key moments in early Japanese American history: the migration and settlement of Issei pioneers in both Hawai'i and the continental U.S., the development of the community in the birth and growth of the Nisei generation, involvement in challenges to racially-biased laws around citizenship and marriage, and the World War II experiences of both incarceration and military service. Many of the themes in the prewar period of inclusion and exclusion, of assimilation and resistance to assimilation, of name and phenotype changes, of abandonment and belonging, all continue into the postwar period.

Just as the first Japanese Americans were multiracial, following World War II, a second major wave of Japanese migration to the U.S. was spearheaded by multiracial families, in the persons of the Japanese war brides and their mixed-race children who came to the U.S. to join their GI husbands in the 1950s.

Discrimination against Japanese Americans continued following the war. A notable example was the government's differential handling of European and Asian "war brides." When Congress passed the War Brides Act in December 1945 and the GI Fiancées Act in June 1946, it eased previous restrictions on emigration from Europe—in the three years immediately following, over 113,000 brides and 4,500 children emigrated from Europe—but these laws did not apply to Asian war brides and their children, whose entry to the U.S. was still restricted by the anti-Asian immigration laws passed in the 1920s. [718] It was not until August 1950, a full five years after its initial passage, that the War Bride Act was amended to cover all brides regardless of race, allowing the immigration to the U.S. of the Japanese wives and children of American servicemen. [719]

In the years following, with the changing attitudes about race in the U.S., and with the elimination of anti-miscegenation laws, there has been a rise in out-marriage rates among subsequent generations of Japanese Americans, and the hapa population has naturally continued to increase as a percentage of the Japanese American community. I hope that this chapter's survey of multiraciality in prewar Japanese America, will encourage further research on the historical arcs of the hapa Japanese American experience, rather than focus simply on presentist concerns, as these stories are critical to getting a fuller understanding of both Asian American history and global mixed race studies.

## CHAPTER TEN

# THE EARLY HISTORY OF MIXED-RACE JAPANESE AMERICANS

### GREG ROBINSON

Japanese Americans in the twenty-first century represent an increasingly exogamous group. Recent statistics reveal rates of intermarriage around 50% among individuals of Japanese ancestry in the United States, leading to a significant birth rate of hapa (mixed-race) children of these marriages.[720] The coming of age of this new multiracial generation has led various writers to speculate on the reshaping—even the disappearance—of the traditional ethnic group.[721] Strangely, however, the past history of mixed-race Japanese Americans has remained largely obscured in such discussions. In fact, hapa individuals ranked among the earliest and most visible Nikkei public figures, and it is worth investigating their lives and contributions in order to properly understand the larger history of Nikkei in America.

Scholars of Japanese Americans, as well as popular commentators, have tended to assume that until recently mixed unions and their offspring were a rare and marginal phenomenon.[722] The are some rational grounds for such a belief: while the idea of intermarriage between Whites and ethnic Japanese did not trigger the level of panic among elite white Americans—in the South and elsewhere—as black-white sexual relations during the first half of the twentieth century, there was palpable opposition to sex and reproduction (as well as to the social leveling that interracial unions implied).[723] In some cases, race-baiting West Coast journalists and politicians brandished the threat of intermarriage to justify racist exclusion.[724] Most notably, during the 1920s, West Coast farmers and businessmen angry over economic competition from Issei (Japanese immigrants) trumpeted the menace of intermarriage in lobbying for immigration restriction.[725] Even Franklin

D. Roosevelt, a liberal easterner who campaigned for better relations between Japan and the United States, expressed agreement with West Coast Whites that legal bars to entry of Japanese, as well as discriminatory laws to prevent Japanese aliens from naturalizing or owning property, were reasonable and justified because they preserved white "racial purity" against intermarriage and the menace of mixed-race children. "Anyone who has travelled in the Far East, " FDR wrote in 1925, "knows that the mingling of Asiatic blood with European or American blood produces, in nine cases out of ten, the most unfortunate results."[726] Throughout the first half of the century, every state in the West Coast and Mountain region (apart from New Mexico and Washington), plus a handful of others enacted laws forbidding Asians to marry whites. In the Territory of Hawai'i, where white-Japanese unions were not formally barred, they likewise remained stigmatized.

Still, despite the various (and varying) legal and social obstacles to white-Asian marriages in the West, they occurred in signficant numbers. The incomplete War Relocation Authority (WRA)[727] roster of approximately 109,000 Japanese Americans from the Pacific Coast and Alaska "relocated" during World War II lists 192 Nikkei of mixed white and Japanese ancestry, plus another 183 whose ancestry was listed as "Japanese and other" (a category that included those with African American, Hispanic, Chinese and Filipino ancestry, as well as a group of inmates from Alaska who were partly Inuit).

At the same time, such unions were quite common in the cosmopolitan urban areas of the Northeast and Midwest, where ethnic Japanese communities were sufficiently small and unobtrusive not to trigger the same level of hostility as on the West Coast. According to one Nikkei community survey in New York taken during the mid-1930s, at least one-third of its members—and possibly as many as half—had non-Japanese partners.[728] Not only did Eastern states not bar white-Asian intermarriage, but Issei there had extra incentive to find non-Japanese spouses. Unlike on the West Coast and Hawai'i, few Issei brought wives or families with them, while the greater distance from Japan made contracting "picture bride" marriages or returning home to find a Japanese bride less practical. Many of these Issei were educated young male professionals who were well integrated into mainstream society, with the result that they more easily met white women (frequently from working-class or white ethnic backgrounds) with whom they had children.

In any case, a review of the contributions of the mixed-race Japanese Americans who came of age in the first half of the twentieth century reveals a panoply of often exceptional individuals, who left their mark in fields as diverse as literature, visual and performance arts, sports, science, business, and political activism. While a discussion of their overall contributions, or their reception within ethnic Japanese communities, is beyond the scope of this essay, a set of capsule biographies might serve as a useful indication that, even at that early date, the presence of mixed-race Nikkei in American society was already significant and visible.

## Literature

Any discussion of creativity among ethnic Japanese starts with Sadakichi Hartmann, the uncrowned "King of Bohemia." Karl Sadakichi Hartmann (1867-1944) born in Dejima, Japan of a German father and a Japanese mother, and raised in Germany, arrrived in the United States in 1882 and settled in Philadelphia. He soon became attached to the poet Walt Whitman, and visited him in nearby Camden, New Jersey. After the poet's death, Hartmann produced a slim volume, *Conversations with Walt Whitman* (1895) about their relationship. Meanwhile, Hartmann toured Europe, met contemporary writers and artists, and undertook a career as an international journalist and art critic for such journals as the *Weekly Review* and the *Boston Transcript*. He founded his own short-lived journal, *The Art Critic*, in 1893. His *History of American Art* (1901) became a standard textbook for Art History classes. Hartmann was notable for discovering talented but unknown young artists. In addition to reviewing painting and sculpture, Hartmann was a pioneering essayist on photography and modern dance. He also worked as a painter, but never found success as an artist.[729]

Hartmann also distinguished himself as a poet and playwright. In 1893, he produced a symbolist religious drama, *Christ: A Dramatic Poem in Three Acts*, the publication of which led to Hartmann's spending a week in prison for blasphemy. He continued to write religious dramas, including *Buddha*, *Confucius*, *Mohammed*, and *Moses*, as well as a privately printed novel, *The Last Thirty Days of Christ* (1920). He also worked as a performer. The most notable (or notorious) of his productions was a 1902 vaudeville act, "A Trip to Japan in Sixteen Minutes," styled as a "perfume concert." In this performance, with the help of a large electric fan to blow different perfumes to the audience, Hartmann attempted to evoke sensual impressions in his listeners through sense-memory triggered by smell. The show was not a success, to say the least, and closed after a single performance.[730]

Despite his renown as a critic and playwright, Hartmann's

health and fortunes declined in later years. Debilitated by tuberculosis and alcoholism, he moved to Los Angeles in the 1920s in hopes of working as a scenarist for the movie industry, but was unable to find steady employment. Instead he lived with and served as companion to the famed actor John Barrymore. Hartmann continued to write poetry (some of which was published in the Nisei press) and worked on an essay collection, *Esthetic Verities* (which was completed and deposited with the Library Company of Philadelphia, but which remained unpublished in the author's lifetime).

Another early hapa writer was Kathleen Tamagawa [Eldridge] (1893-1979). In her 1932 memoir *Holy Prayers in a Horse's Ear*, she distinguished herself by her painful account of her biracial identity, which made her, in her own words, a "freak of nature."[731] Born in 1893 to a Japanese father and an Irish-American mother, Tamagawa spent her early years in Chicago. Throughout her childhood she was regarded by friends and neighbors as Japanese and treated as an exotic—a living "China doll." Feeling marginalized by such reactions, Tamagawa welcomed the family's decision to move to Japan in 1906, since she assumed she could now be with others of her kind. Once in Japan, however, Tamagawa felt even more foreign. Unable to identify or communicate with the Japanese, she wrote of feeling herself without any "race, nationality, or home." Although she ultimately found a place for herself in Yokohama's multicultural foreign settlement, Tamagawa deliberately chose to marry an American diplomat, Frank Eldridge, because she perceived him to be "ordinary." Once back with her husband in the United States, she assimilated rapidly into mainstream white American culture.

At the end of the 1920s, while working at Columbia University and taking creative writing courses, she was inspired to write a memoir. It first took shape as a set of articles that were published in *Asia* magazine in 1930, and were then expanded into a book-length manuscript. In her memoir, Tamagawa treats her racial and cultural difference as incidental and mythical, rejecting all reference to it as an absurdity. The most revealing aspect of Tamagawa's reaction to her hapa identity comes in the book's conclusion. She relates being told by the Japanese government that, because her birth was not formally registered, she does not exist for official purposes. Tamagawa presents that statement as the apex of the absurdity engendered by her mixed identity, which she then renounces:

I do not approve of Eurasian marriages. I do not approve of inter-national marriages ... because there are so few among the many in Europe, in Asia or America who have the wit and ability or the moral and spiritual stamina and determination, or the keen, blind, deaf and dumb intellect that will allow them to drive their psychological horse in triumph to its goal. Why venture on such a marriage, a marriage which must include chasms of misunderstanding? But all this may be my conventional mindedness, that is, of course, if I, who do not exist, can have a mind.[732]

Although after completing her memoir, Tamagawa started a second book, she soon gave it up, and moved to Washington D.C., where she worked as an assistant to her husband, Frank Eldridge (Eldridge worked in the U.S. Commerce Department during the 1930s, then after World War II became one of the early staff officers for the Central Intelligence Agency). Apart from lecturing on Japan at George Washington University during World War II, Tamagawa spent the rest of her life outside the public eye as a housewife and civic worker.

Another early hapa Nisei author who moved at different times between Japan and the United States was Clarke H. Kawakami (1909-1985), a man who made his mark in many different fields. He was born Clarke Hiroshi Kawakami in Momence, Illinois. His mother, Midred Clarke, was a white American from a local family. His father, Kiyoshi Karl Kawakami [K.K. Kawakami] (1875-1949), was a well-known journalist who became the author of several widely read books, including *American-Japanese Relations: An Inside View of Japan's Policies and Purposes* (1912); *Asia at the Door* (1914); and *The Real Japanese Question* (1921). The young Clarke and his sister Yuri moved with the family to San Francisco in 1913 (a younger sister, Marcia, was born that year), and in 1922 the family established itself in Washington, D.C., where Clarke attended Central High School [today known as Cardozo High School]. He then went on to attend Harvard University, where he studied government and international relations, and starred on the tennis team, of which he was named captain. Hoping to enter a career as a diplomat, he applied to the State Department upon graduating from Harvard in 1930, but despite his stellar record he was turned down. It is not clear how much the refusal was based on racism and how much American officials were wary of the influence of his father, who had become a supporter of and propagandist for Tokyo's foreign policy.[733]

In the end, Clarke Kawakami was awarded a fellowship from

the Ecole Libre des Sciences Politiques for a year of graduate study in France. After his fellowship period ended, he moved to Geneva. With help from his father's connections, he was hired as an interpretor by the Japanese delegation at the World Disarmament Conference at the League of Nations (in the months before Japan withdrew from the League). While in Europe, Clarke met and married Helen Machilda, a German woman who worked at the Japanese legation as a secretary. For a time, Clarke and Helen moved to Washington, D.C. There Clarke served as a press attaché for Yōsuke Matsuoka (according to legend, despite the young Kawakami's poor Japanese, Matsuoka preferred Clarke because of his striking good looks). In summer 1933, Kawakami moved to Japan with Matsuoka, where he was hired as a reporter for the Japanese news agency Shinbun Rengo (later known as Dōmei); since he could not write in Japanese, he wrote all his articles in English. Helen joined him in Japan, and worked as a secretary for Kokusai Steam Company. During this period, Clarke also joined a Harvard classmate in touring occupied Manchuria. Following his trip, he collaborated on production of a bilingual propaganda volume about the Japanese puppet state of Manchukuo.[734]

In late 1935, Clarke met Chieko [Susuga] Takehisa, a famous stage and screen actress, at a Christmas party. The two soon fell in love, and Clarke asked Helen for a divorce. Helen was not pleased, but finally agreed in exchange for Clarke assisting her to get U.S. citizenship as his spouse. As a result, the divorce took several years to be officialized. In 1939, Clarke moved to London as European correspondent, and then in June 1940 he returned to Washington, D.C. While in Washington he lived at his parents' house and filed a series of English-language articles on American foreign policy to Dōmei. He had great difficulty securing a visa for his wife because of the Japanense exclusion laws. Finally, he persuaded Secretary of State Cordell Hull to order the State Department to issue her a one-year student visa.[735] One year later, in April 1941, Chieko came to Washington, and the two were wed in August.

Pearl Harbor led to drastic changes in Clarke Kawakami's life. His father K.K. Kawakami was briefly interned as a potentially dangerous alien. Once the war began, Chieko decided to go back to Japan, and left on the first exchange ship, despite Clarke's opposition. Clarke's job with Dōmei was suspended by the outbreak of war. Clarke formally resigned from his post, and publicly condemned Japan's attack as shameful and double-dealing. In a letter he wrote to his Washington newspaper colleagues explaining his position—and which was then publicly released by the U.S. State Department—Kawakami described the attack as "The blackest and most shameful page in Japanese History" and expressed his intention to enlist in the U.S. Army so that he could help "Crush forever the type of militarist rule which drugs and drags peaceful people in to war, wherever it exists."[736] He tried to volunteer for the Army (from which he had obtained a deferment before the war) but was declined permission. Clarke wrote many articles on Japan and sent them to journals such as the *Saturday Evening Post*, *New York Times*, and *Washington Star*, without success. After several months he was able to secure a position as correspondent with the *Washington Post*. The series of articles he produced on Japan during mid-1942 reveal a clear understanding of Japanese society.[737]

In spring 1943, Kawakami enlisted in the U.S. Army Military Intelligence Service (MIS) program, and was sent to Camp Savage camp in Minnesota to be trained as Japanese specialist. His fluency in Japanese was much greater than that of the average Nisei. In spring 1944, Clarke was attached to the Office of War Information's Psychological Warfare Section and was sent to the India/Burma front. Two prominent leftist Nisei, Koji Ariyoshi and Karl Yoneda, were also in his group. Clarke drafted propaganda flyers that were translated into Japanese by Yoneda, and worked with State Department diplomat John Emmerson on reports of interrogations of Japanese POWs.[738] In early 1945, he was sent to China. Once the war was over, he returned to Japan and was reunited with Chieko. The couple would have three children in in the following years. During the U.S. Occupation of Japan, Kawakami was attached to General MacArthur's staff at GHQ, initially as a soldier, then after his discharge as a civilian War Department employee. At first he was employed translating articles from the Japanese press. He later worked with the G-2 Historical section to produce a history of MacArthur's wartime campaigns. Kawakami was assigned as chief American editor of a history of Japanese military operations.[739]

Kawakami and his family returned to the United States in 1950, following the death of his father. Back in Washington, D.C. Kawakami served as research assistant to Commodore Richard Bates of the Naval War College on a history of the Battle of Leyte Gulf. Kawakami wrote articles for *The Reporter*, notably one on anti-Americanism in Japan. Meanwhile, he helped translate and edit a book by two Imperial Navy officers, *Midway: The Battle That Doomed Japan* (1955). In 1955, Kawakami was hired as a staffer by the new United States Information Agency, and was named Associate Editor of the USIA's journal, *Problems of Communism*. He remained with the USIA until his retirement in 1976. He died nine years later.

A mixed-race author prominent in some unusual fields was

Milton K. Ozaki (1913-1989). Born in Racine, Wisconsin, Ozaki was the son of Frank Ozaki, Issei owner of a local restaurant, and a white woman, Augusta Rathbum. Milton, who lost a leg in early childhood, developed a love of reading and writing. He edited his high school newspaper, and worked briefly for the *Racine Times*. In 1933, Ozaki entered Ripon College, a small liberal arts college, where he majored in English, but spent a good deal of his time playing bridge. In the years after college, he opened a pair of beauty shops in Chicago, but later claimed to have earned his living largely by playing bridge for money.[740]

Exempted from military service during World War II due to his handicap, Ozaki remained in Chicago. Inspired by the writings of pulp author James M. Cain, he determined to write mystery stories himself. In 1946, Ozaki's first mystery, *The Cuckoo Clock*, was published by Ziff-Davis. The dust jacket noted that the author was a "newspaper man, artist, writer and ... well-known Chicago tax accountant." The plot revolved around three characters: the narrator, Bendy Brinks, a graduate student at "North University"; Professor Caldwell; and Detective Phelan of the Chicago Police. Ozaki soon produced two more novels, *A Fiend in Need* (Ziff-Davis, 1947) and *The Dummy Murder Case* (Graphic, 1951), using the same characters. Meanwhile, beginning with *The Black Dark Murders* (Quinn, 1949), Ozaki produced a series of books under the pen name Robert O. Saber (a pun on Ozaki's name, as "zaki" is Japanese for "saber") featuring such detectives as Carl Good and Max Keene. In *The Case of the Deadly Kiss* (Fawcett, 1957), Ozaki created a novelty in the character of Japanese American detective, Lieutenant Ken Koda, a policeman in suburban Stillwell, Illinois. After 1960, as the hardboiled detective industry declined, Ozaki returned to his former focus on bridge and wrote widely on the subject, including a humorous guide, *Bridge for Absolute Beginners* (1965). He also became a stamp broker and published a magazine, *Philatelic Investor*. During this time, he moved to Arizona, where he spent the rest of his life.[741]

Born the same year as Ozaki, but with a very different career, was a writer and poet with the magnificent name Ambrose Amadeus Uchiyamada (1913-2002), known to family and friends as "Ambie". He was one of four surviving children of Thomas Morikiyo Uchiyamada, a university-trained engineer from Japan who obtained further schooling in the United States, and his Irish-born wife Mary. Following a tragic accident, Mary Uchiyamada developed cancer and died young, while her husband, worn out by sorrow and alcoholism, was confined at a state farm, and likewise died some years later. Even before their mother's death, Ambie and his younger sister, who had been raised in their mother's Catholic faith, were sent to live at the Maryknoll Home. At the Maryknoll School, Uchiyamada distinguished himself as a writer and actor. He left the orphanage as a teenager, and supported himself through high school by work as a houseboy and domestic for white families. During these years he also rode the rails throughout the Western states, accumulating material for a (never published) book on the lives of tramps and hoboes.[742]

With help from sympathetic Maryknoll brothers, Uchiyamada won a scholarship to Marquette University, where he majored in journalism and earned awards for oratory and poetry. After leaving Marquette in 1935, he returned to California. In the following years he published numerous works in the West Coast Nisei press and literary magazines. His selection in the 1935 journal *Leaves*, edited by Yasuo Sasaki, was a greenroom dialogue between two musicians on the relative importance of talent and fearless initiative. His contribution to the 1936 journal *Gyo-Sho*, edited by Eddie Shimano, was a wistful poem, "Ah, Love—Do You Remember?" It concluded:

> Ah love, I have found ...
> That the world is only a bubble
> And the night's cloak merely a shadow
> And the stars—(ah, fool!)—the stars were never diamonds...
> Ah, if you can, forgive your long-ago lover
> For those blind eyes that could not see ...
> For the rash promises he could not keep.

Uchiyamada made a strong impression on his colleagues. Mary Oyama [Mittwer] later recalled him as a "dashing Irish-Japanese poet-thespian-vagabond" who gallantly kissed her hand. Larry Tajiri, English editor of the *Nichi Bei Shimbun* and an arbiter of taste, referred to Uchiyamada's poetry as a highlight of Nisei writing.[743]

Uchiyamada's later life is somewhat more hazy. Sometime before World War II, he moved to New York, where he worked as an editorial assistant at *TIME* magazine and as assistant editor at *Architectural Forum*. Following the outbreak of World War II, his sisters and younger brother were confined by the U.S. government. He was conscripted into the U.S. Army, but protested being drafted because of his family's treatment. To avoid prison, he ultimately agreed to join the U.S. Army Medical Corps, and was stationed in Chicago. There he met and married Hilda Castle [Kastelowitz], a University of Chicago physicist working on neutron cross-sections for the Manhattan Project. Ambie was ultimately sent for service in

England and Germany before being discharged in mid-1945. In the postwar years, he enrolled at the New School, where he received a bachelor's in literature, and then pursued graduate work in literature at Boston University and New York University. In addition to several years of working together with his wife at the General Dynamics Corporation on submarine control systems, Uchiyamada worked for a time as professor of English literature, first at what is now Alfred State College and then at Penn State Altoona. He does not appear to have published either scholarly articles or creative literature. The couple lived their retirement years in Maine.

One other versatile author was Mitsu Yamamoto (1920-2006), who mixed classic literature with popular writing. Yamamoto was born Mitsie Ethel Yamamoto in Ohio and grew up in Philadelphia, the daughter of a Japanese immigrant father, Sannosuke Yamamoto, and a Swedish mother, Hilda Nelson Bernharina. Mitsu enrolled in 1939 at the University of Pennsylvania. After the start of World War II, her father Sannosuke was engaged teaching Japanese language to U.S. Marine recruits, and was subsequently hired as an "informant" by Penn's linguistics department. He collaborated on a Japanese dictionary for the military, which was also commercially published in 1944 as *Japanese for Military and Civilian Use*. Perhaps as a result of her father's defense work, and what she later termed her "white-bread appearance," Mitsu Yamamoto was permitted to enroll in the graduate school after receiving her BA, despite the Penn trustees' unpublicized policy decision to exclude Japanese American students. There she took classes in English literature. In 1945, after leaving Penn, she was maried to George Anderson. Meanwhile, she enrolled as a student in Dropsie College, a Philadephia-based center for Jewish and Hebrew Studies, as "Mitsie Y. Anderson." She likewise studied at Columbia University during the 1950s.[744]

It is not known precisely when Yamamoto began writing. However, in 1956, a one-act play of hers won a prize in the Fourth Collegiate Playwriting Contest, sponsored by the Samuel French Co. (It may have been "Pride Goeth," which she copyrighted under the names "Mitsu Yamamoto" and "Mitsie Y. Anderson" in 1962).[745] In November 1957, her short story "The Good News," about two women who meet when they are roommates in a hospital, appeared in *The New Yorker*. It was the first of a set of stories that she published in national magazines in the following years. For example, her story "In Any Language" appeared in *Redbook* in 1962, and a trio of pieces were featured in *The PTA Magazine*. She also contributed a mystery story in 1973 to the magazine *Alfred Hitchcock Presents*.

Perhaps most notably, her stories "Miss Kemper Comes Home in the Dark" and "Karen Stixx and her Jigsaw Puzzle" appeared in *The Saturday Evening Post* in 1972-73. The first of these concerned a woman attacked by a mugger on the street, and the curious consequences that resulted from her defending herself. It was later included in the anthology volume *Best Detective Stories of the Year, 1973*. The second was a Faust story of sorts, in which a mysterious stranger offers an unhappily married man a new life in exchange for a service. Meanwhile, she published a nonfiction book for children, *Bridges to Fear: A Collection of Strange but True Stories* (1977).[746] Yamamoto also produced various book reviews for *Library Journal*. One pithy statement (and perhaps revealing of her own identity) came in her review of the pioneering Asian American literary anthology *Aieeee!*:

> [These writers] pronounce themselves a unique American minority, Asian Americans —not Asians, not Americans, not an uneasy combination of both. Overlong and overwrought prefaces repeat this valid identification while tossing around words like 'yellow goons,' 'racist henchmen,' and 'manhood.' Apart from this consciousness-raising, what? Mainly fiction and drama, with a rich, varied content not often matched by a like expression.[747]

In addition to her own writings, Yamamoto became a prolific children's book author, adapting classic novels such as Jack London's *The Call of the Wild*, Robert Louis Stevenson's *Dr. Jekyll and Mister Hyde*, and Charles Dickens's *Great Expectations*, plus the Bible, into abridged editions. She died in New York City.

## Arts

In the history of mixed-race Japanese Americans in the visual arts, the figure of sculptor-designer-architect Isamu Noguchi (1904-1988) dominates. Born of a liaison between the Japanese poet Yonejirō (Yone) Noguchi and Léonie Gilmour, the white woman he hired as his secretary, Isamu Noguchi was abandoned by his father when he was only two. He grew up between Japan and America, never really accepted—he later referred to himself as a "waif." After studying in Paris, where he worked with the sculptor Constantin Brancusi, Noguchi settled in New York. There he established himself as a modernist sculptor, while making his living doing portrait busts of rich Manhattanites. During the 1930s, Noguchi worked on various projects, flirted with leftist politics, settled for a time in Mexico

City (where he had an affair with Frida Kahlo). He gained additional fame when his stainless steel frieze was picked for installation in Rockefeller Center.

Following the Japanese attack on Pearl Harbor, Noguchi threw himself into defending Nisei civil rights and supporting the war effort. In partnership with journalist Larry Tajiri, and a group of progressive writers, Noguchi formed an antifascist group, the Nisei Writers and Artists Mobilization for Democracy, which produced reports on Nisei in California agriculture and on employment and housing conditions, and sought assistance from government allies. (Noguchi wrote directly to President Franklin D. Roosevelt, asking him vainly to preserve the basic rights of Americans of Japanese ancestry.)[748]

On February 19, 1942, President Roosevelt signed Executive Order 9066. The order, which authorized the Secretary of War to designate certain areas as military zones from which persons could be excluded, led to the mass exclusion and ultimately confinement of Japanese Americans from the West Coast. Once the order was announced, Noguchi travelled to Washington, D.C. for consultations. There he was recruited by John Collier, director of the Bureau of Indian Affairs (BIA), to work at the new camp being set up for confined Japanese Americans at Poston, Arizona. Although as an East Coast resident he was not subject to Executive Order 9066, Noguchi volunteered to be placed in the camp. He deemed it a worthy sacrifice for democracy. Noguchi arrived at Poston in mid-1942. However, he had trouble working in the primitive conditions of camp life. Worse, despite his romantic notions of uplifting the Japanese Americans, his "people," Noguchi's mixed race identity, as well as his ties to the WRA administration, made him a figure of suspicion among inmates. In November 1942, he left Poston, having stayed only six months, and swiftly returned to the East Coast, where he remained for the rest of the war. He resumed making sculptures and designed sets and costumes for Martha Graham ballets, including the notable *Appalachian Spring* (1945). Noguchi found small ways to assist Japanese Americans, but did not seek to integrate into Japanese communities.

After the end of World War II, Noguchi became an internationally known and much-travelled artist and designer. The three-sided glass coffee table he designed for Herman Miller in 1947 soon became a classic of modern furniture. In 1948, Noguchi visited Japan, where he immersed himself in creating pottery as well as sculpture. In 1951, he premiered his designs for *akari* (Japanese paper light sculptures), which became one of his signature works. He remained in Japan for several years. In the early 1950s, he married actress Yoshiko Shirley Yamaguchi (a.k.a. Li Xianglan or Ri Kōran to Japanese fans). Beginning in the 1960s, he collaborated with stone carver Masatoshi Izumi on the island of Shikoku, Japan, where he ultimately established a studio. In addition to producing sculptures that were featured in collections around the world, Noguchi created a large number of playgrounds, parks, and gardens, including the famed UNESCO garden in Paris and Bayfront Park in Miami. In 1987, Noguchi received the National Medal of Arts from President Ronald Reagan. In 1985, he designed and opened his own museum, the Isamu Noguchi Garden Museum, in New York City.

If Isamu Noguchi achieved worldwide renown as a Japanese American visual artist, his half-sister Ailes Gilmour (1912-1993) remains more obscure, despite her achievements as an early modern dancer. Born in Yokohama, Japan, she was the daughter of Isamu Noguchi's mother Léonie Gilmour and an unidentified Japanese father—her mother never revealed her father's identity, though later evidence suggests he was a university student in Tokyo. Ailes spent her early years with her mother in Chigasaki, Japan. In 1920, Léonie returned to live with her daughter in the United States, settling in San Francisco and then in New York. Ailes attended the Ethical Culture School, and later was sent to the Cherry Lawn School in Connecticut, where she attended as a scholarship student. During her time there, she became editor of the school literary magazine, *The Cherry Pit*. In 1929, following her graduation from high school, Ailes went to New York to study at the Neighborhood Playhouse. There she met modern dance pioneer Martha Graham. Invited to join Graham's company, Ailes danced with her company for four years during the 1930s—they performed an experimental work, "Choric Patterns," at the newly-opened Radio City Music Hall in 1932. She also danced in "How Long Brethren?" a dance drama based on "Negro Songs of Protest," with choreography and direction by Helen Tamiris, and a musical score by Genevieve Pitot. In 1938, she performed at Mecca Temple (later called City Center).

She was most closely associated with choreographer Bill Matons. In 1937, Ailes and Matons performed in dance recitals held at the Brooklyn Museum and The New School, under the auspices of the Dance Theater project of the Works Progress Administration, a Depression-era government jobs agency. She also performed with him in *Adelante*, a WPA-sponsored Broadway musical in 1939. In September 1939, she appeared on stage as one of the "Calypso Dancers" in a show by Matons. Following World War II, Ailes retired from the stage. In 1948, she married art historian Herbert

Spinden. The couple had a son, Jody Spinden. She died in Santa Fe, New Mexico, in 1993.

During this time there were two other hapa women dancers who became Broadway stars. The first was Marion Saki, about whom not much is known. She claimed to have been born Hatsuko Sakakibara, the daughter of New York art dealer Gitsuo Sakakibara (himself a mixed-race Japanese). As a teenager, she studied for two years with the legendary ballerina Anna Pavlova at the Hippodrome Free Ballet School, but then decided to go into vaudeville and musical theater. Her first large role was in *The Sweetheart Shop*. She appeared in *Everything* (1919), a mammoth musical spectacle by R. H. Burnside, with music by John Philip Sousa and Irving Berlin, among others. After appearing in George M. Cohan's *Little Nellie Kelly* (1923), she appeared in several shows including *The O'Brien Girl, Hit the Deck,* and *Plain Jane* in 1924, and *Some Day* in 1925. Her first starring role was in *Sweetheart Time* (1925).[749] When she starred opposite Billy Taylor in London with *Happy Go Lucky* (1926), their dance was recorded on film by British Pathé. Upon her return to the United States, she performed in Vaudeville and played the famous Palace Theater with the team of Snow and Columbus. After appearing in a supporting role in the short-lived *Polly* (1929), starring Fred Allen, she switched to study singing. She recorded the song "Morning and Evening Comes my Love for You" (1932), and sang soprano opposite Charles Hackett in a production of Franz Lehár's operetta *The Land of Smiles* (1933). Although the production was not a success, she received a glowing review from the *New York Times*, whose critic noted that she had led the audience to applaud because she "brought a light touch and a lively spirit into far too solemn a [group] performance."[750] After it closed, Saki sang on the radio for a season, after which she disappeared from sight.

The other performer, a more versatile dancer and celebrated figure, was Sono Osato. Born in Omaha, Nebraska in 1919, she was one of three children of Shōji Osato, a Japanese immigrant who ran a photo studio, and Frances Fitzpatrick, an Irish/ French-Canadian mother. Frances left to make a career in Hollywood, returned to Omaha, then in 1927 took her children to Europe. It was while on a trip to Monte Carlo that the young Sono saw her first performance of the Ballets Russes. In 1929, the family returned to the United States and settled in Chicago, where Osato started to study ballet with Adolph Bolm and Berenice Holmes. In 1934, after Holmes secured an audition for her, she was accepted into the Ballets Russes de Monte Carlo, directed by Vassilli de Basil. She toured Europe and the United States with the company for the next six years, leaving her family behind. She mostly performed in the ensemble, with occasional brief solos.[751] In 1941, she left the company, tired of appearing in the chorus, with few solo roles and no credit (or extra money) for those she acccepted. She soon joined Ballet Theatre [today called American Ballet Theatre] as a lead dancer. She stayed two years with the company. Among her most memorable performances with Ballet Theater were in two works by Antony Tudor—*Pillar of Fire* and *Romeo and Juliet* (1943); in the latter she played Rosaline, a role developed specifically for her.[752]

Osato's life was turned around by the Japanese attack on Pearl Harbor and the outbreak of war in December 1941. Osato's father was arrested and interned for ten months as a dangerous alien by the U.S. government. For a time, Sono danced under her mother's maiden name, Fitzpatrick, to defuse anti-Japanese hysteria. Further, she was barred from joining her colleagues on a transcontinental tour to the Pacific Coast during 1942, because of the restrictions against all people of Japanese ancestry imposed by the Western Defense Command.

In mid-1943, Osato left the company. By that time, she had fallen in love with and married Victor Elmaleh, a young architect and real estate developer. She intended to start a family. However, both her love of performing and the couple's parlous financial situation led her to resume her career. Nora Kaye, the Ballet theatre's lead dancer, told Osato to write to Agnes de Mille, who was choreographing a Broadway show, *One Touch of Venus* (1943). She was soon hired (once more under her own name), and the comic solo that de Mille eventually created for Osato won her *Billboard* magazine's Donaldson Award and launched her as a theatrical star. After 9 months in *Venus*, she was hired to create the nonsinging dance role of Ivy (a.k.a. Miss Turnstiles) in the Leonard Bernstein musical *On The Town* (1944), which featured choreography by Jerome Robbins. She remained with the show for a year. In 1945, she signed to play the lead in an upcoming American adaptation of the French stage hit, *Undine*, by Jean Giraudoux, but withdrew during rehearsals.

In 1947, Osato went to Hollywood. In the end, however, she appeared only in a single film, *The Kissing Bandit* (1948), with Frank Sinatra and Kathryn Grayson.[753] However, she faced limited choice of roles, due to her racial background, as well as the threat of blacklisting for her political activities. She returned to New York and had two children in the following years. Osato continued to work sporadically, then retired from performing, and later worked as an installation artist. In 2005, she created the Sono Osato Scholarship Program in Graduate Studies at Career Transition For

Dancers, which funded retraining for retired dancers entering second careers. Her memoir, *Distant Dances* (1980) won critical praise for its candid account of her career.

One hapa artist/creator who developed a pair of careers—and identities—was Earle Goodenow, also known as Kyōhei Inukai. Born in Chicago in 1913, he was one of three sons of Kyōhei Inukai, a Japanese immigrant artist who became a popular society portraitist (and fencing champion) in New York, and Lucienne Goodenow [later Lucene Taliaferro], a sculptor of portraits in ivory. The two had met when they were fellow students at the Art Institute of Chicago, and married in early 1910. (When they became engaged, Goodenow's parents objected until they learned that Inukai was of noble ancestry and was a convert to Christianity!)[754] A few years later the Inukais split up—Kyōhei had a child by another woman. Earle and his brothers Girard and Julian stayed with their mother and took her family name. Earle grew up in Battle Creek, Michigan and Chicago; like his parents, he attended the Art Institute of Chicago. During the 1930s, he moved to New York City, where he attended the National Academy of Design and the Art Students League. He meanwhile worked in advertising, while also painting. The artist held his first one-man show at the California Arts Club in 1934. The next year, he contributed to a show at the Louis Comfort Tiffany Foundation in New York. In the following years, his work was displayed in shows at Pittsburgh's Carnegie Institute and the Corcoran Gallery in Washington D.C. In 1943, he exhibited in a show of American artists at the Brandt Gallery in New York. *New York Times* critic Howard Devree described his work as "attractive" but "sober-hued."[755] The next year, Devree reviewed his show at the Ferargil Gallery:

> The Flemish masters, one feels, have been among his mentors, and a curious folk-art strain is also evident. But Goodenow has been working out an individual style in these portraits and figure pieces and the soundness and earnestness of the work is impressive.[756]

Meanwhile, around the time that his daughter, Ariane, was born, he began illustrating children's books. Goodenow's painstakingly illustrated edition of *The Arabian Nights* (1946)—a book briefly withdrawn from sale over charges of anti-Semitism in the text—proved his most popular work. He soon went on to write and illustrate a series of popular children's books on animals, starting with *Cow Concert* (1951) and continuing on with an alliteratively titled series that incuded *The Lazy Llama* (1954), *The Bashful Bear* (1956), and *The Careless Kangaroo* (1959). It is an open question whether his mixed background affected his stories, many of which involve individuals dealing with being different. For instance, his book *The Peevish Penguin* (1955) tells the story of a penguin who is disturbed that he cannot fly, and tries to think up alternate plans. *The Last Camel* (1968) tells the story of a maladjusted dromedary. Among his most creative and whimsical stories was *The Owl Who Hated the Dark* (1969).

Meanwhile, following his father's death in 1954, Earle Goodenow took over the name Kyōhei Inukai for his painting and sculpture (since he did not use a "junior," the use of the name has prompted continuing confusion with his painter father).[757] Under this new name, he participated in shows in the White House Rotating Exhibition, the U.S. Embassy in Tel Aviv, and the USIA Print Exhibition at the 1970 Osaka World's Fair in Japan. In 1967, he had a show at the Goodenow Gallery (presumably family-run) in New York. In 1970, he had a solo painting and sculpture show at the Spectrum Gallery on Manhattan's Soho district. Ten years later he put on a second solo show at the Suzuki Gallery. In 1981, he shared a show with his brother Girard "Gig" Goodenow (1912-1984), himself a well-known book illustrator and artist of animal prints.[758] Inukai was known for his use of bright colors. In Les Krantz's book *American Artists: An Illustrated Survey of Leading Contemporary Artists*, he is described as "an abstract pattern painter" who "worked in a variety of styles from expressionism to constructivism and hard-edged geometric abstraction."[759]

Inukai also became known for his abstract sculptures, especially in aluminum and steel. Inukai's work is included in such collections as those of the Albright-Knox Museum, Buffalo; the Portland Museum of Fine Art, Oregon; the Rose Art Museum, Waltham, Massachusetts; and the Wichita University Museum of Fine Art. His sculptures can be found in such places as Knoxville, Tennessee; the Monmouth Mall in Eatontown, NJ; and Riverside Mall in Chicago.

### Activism
One of the aspects of early hapa life (like that of Japanese Americans more broadly) that has been lost through time is the varied history of social and political activism that individual Nikkei as well as organized groups have engaged in. In many cases, mixed-race individuals, whether because of their education or superior connections—or sometimes their wish to fit in with other Japanese

Americans—have been in the forefront.

One of the earliest and most notable activists was the Issei journalist and organizer Fred Makino (1877-1953). Born Kinzaburō Makino in Yokohama, Japan, he was the third son of Joseph Higgenbotham, a merchant/trader from Manchester, England, and Kin Makino, a native of Kanagawa Prefecture. He suffered the loss of his father in September 1881, when he was just 4 years old. Like Kathleen Tamagawa a generation later, Makino came of age in Yokahama's multiracial foreign settlement. In his teens, he was hired as a clerk by his older brother Eijirō, who ran an import/export business. However, in 1898 the young Kinzaburō was involved in a well-publicized incident while frequenting prostitutes in the red-light district of Yoshiwara. His brother Eijirō then determined that he should leave Japan and travel to Hawai'i, where the family's eldest brother, Jō, was living.

Makino arrived in Hawai'i in 1899. After working for his brother for a time, he moved to Honolulu, opened a drug store and set up a "law office" there as well (while Makino was not licensed to practice law, in the absence of other Japanese attorneys he was called on to serve as a consultant and advocate for immigrant laborers). In 1909, following the outbreak of a mass strike by workers on Hawai'i's sugar plantations, Makino was elected president of the Higher Wage Association, which served as negotiating body with the Hawaii Sugar Planters Association. Despite opposition from Hawai'i's political and economic elite (as well as two of the territory's three Japanese-language newspapers) he continued his efforts, until the strike ended with a raise for the workers in late 1909. However, Makino then faced reprisals from the planters. In 1910 he and a dozen other strike supporters were arrested on trumped-up charges of conspiring to hinder plantation operations. Makino was convicted and sent to prison, where he spent three months. Upon his release, he determined that Hawai'i needed a Japanese-language paper that would support workers and lobby for progressive reform. As a result, in 1912 he organized a team of workers, and founded a new daily newspaper, the *Hawaii Hochi*. Although Makino had no previous experience with journalism, and the newspaper struggled financially (Makino was forced to fund its operations by drawing from his drugstore), under Makino's editorship it established itself as the voice of the immigrant workers against Hawai'i's plantation elite.

Probably Makino's most notable achievement was his defense of Hawai'i's Japanese language schools. In the years following the end of World War I, xenophobic white elites targeted the territory's

Japanese schools as subversive and anti-American. Legislators enacted a series of discriminatory statutes with the intent of shutting them down. In mid-1922, Makino funded a suit challenging the regulations as discriminatory and unconstitutional. Makino's action was controversial even among Japanese Americans—it was bitterly opposed by Christian minister Takie Okumura and by *Nippu Jiji* editor Yasutarō Soga. Even the Consul General of Japan was opposed. With the aid of a crusading attorney, Joseph Lightfoot, Makino launched an appeal to the U.S. Supreme Court. In 1927, the U.S. Supreme Court agreed in *Farrington v. Tokushige* that special rules and regulations against Japanese language schools were unconstitutional, and allowed Japanese language schools to continue.

Makino continued to edit the *Hochi* for the quarter century that followed (he assigned George Wright to edit the paper's English-language section, inaugurated in 1925). Following the Pearl Harbor attack in December 1941, he was detained for questioning by military authorities, but was not interned, and his newspaper (renamed *Hawaii Herald* for the duration of the conflict) was allowed to reopen. In the postwar era, he was a strong supporter of the alliance of Nisei veterans and unions in the Democratic Party that would come to dominate Hawaiian politics.

A longtime activist on the opposite side of the country, one who combined letter-writing with organizing, was Yone U. Stafford (1902-1981). Yone Ko (or Yone-Ko) Ushikubo was born in New York. Her father, Daijirō, was a wealthy Japanese importer and art dealer for the Yamanaka Company who settled on the Upper West Side of Manhattan with his wife, Louisa, the daughter of German immigrants to the United States. Yone was their only child. In 1918, Yone was sent by her parents to Japan, and lived there for two years, attending the Sacred Heart Academy, before returning to the United States. Sometime in the early 1930s, Yone married another New Yorker, Bradley Stafford, and moved with him to Springfield, Massachusetts.

Yone was long attracted to social reform. In the 1930s she joined the Socialist Party and became involved in the Women's International League for Peace and Freedom (WILPF). Both Staffords also were active in the local branch of the America First Committee, the isolationist group that opposed all intervention in Europe's wars.

Although as an easterner, Yone was exempt from Executive Order 9066 during World War II, she reacted strongly and immediately to what she termed the "atrocity." First, she sought to influence public opinion against the action by writing protest letters to newspapers. The *Springfield Republican* refused to publish any of her letters, though she ran a letter in the *Springfield Union*. Meanwhile, she wrote letters to the Wisconsin-based weekly *The Progressive* (under the name Mrs. Bradley Stafford), in hopes of persuading its editors and readers to pay more attention to the treatment of Japanese Americans. Yone's challenge to official policy led to surveillance by the FBI; it also brought great strain to her marriage, especially when the president of Bradley Stafford's company threatened to discharge him if Yone continued writing letters. When she threatened to leave her husband rather than stop, the couple compromised and Yone agred to sign her letters to newspapers under the pseudonym "America."

Less controversially, Yone worked with the WILPF and the Fellowship of Reconciliation (FOR) during 1942 to collect a 250-pound shipment of clothing and blankets, which were sent to the Heart Mountain camp. She agreed to help sponsor resettlers, and when two young Nisei women were authorized to leave camp and settle in Springfield, Yone labored to provide them assistance. She was outraged when the discriminatory treatment the two resettlers experienced from townspeople led them to leave. In 1945, after the government finally allowed confined Japanese Americans to return to the West Coast, the WRA announced that the camps would be closed at the end of the year. Yone was furious over the WRA's abandonment. Since the United States was busy educating Germans and Japanese in the ways of democracy, she snapped, perhaps they could "spare a few gauleiters for our Department of the Interior and the War Relocation Authority?"

During the postwar years, in the shadow of the atomic bombing of Japan, Yone returned to her primary interest in pacifism. She began a column in the *Los Angeles Tribune*, an African American newspaper, entitled "I Go Crying Peace, Peace;" the column ran off-and-on for the next few years. She also published letters in *Christian Century* and other journals. In the 1960s, she was on the national committee of the War Resisters League. Her political activism remained tied up with her prewar isolationism and her feelings about Japan, as well as her continued outrage over the treatment of Japanese Americans. These feelings appeared in a 1973 letter she wrote to the conservative *Chicago Tribune* to complain (with some exaggeration) that she was sick of hearing about President Nixon and Watergate, when Nixon's was a minor crime compared to those of other presidents. "We have been conditioned to so much worse under former presidents, beginning with F.D.R., who gave away 50 destroyers without a 'By Your Leave,' imprisoned and improverished citizens because of their race, and dropped atomic bombs on people already beaten." In her last years, she supported lobbying for redress.

Franklin Chino (1911-1962) and Robert Chino (1919-1987), hapa brothers who grew up (like Sono Osato) in the tiny Japanese community of prewar Chicago, provide two very different models of political activism.[760] The brothers were the sons of Haruka "Frank" Chino, the youngest son of a samurai-class family from Odawara who settled in St. Louis in 1904 and married a local white woman, Mercelia Hicks[761], before moving to the Windy city.

Franklin Kiyoshi Chino (who used Franklin H. or Frank, Jr.) attended Walter Scott and Hyde Park High Schools, and grew interested in legal work. Following a period of self-study, he enrolled at John Marshall Law School and was admitted to the bar in December 1937. Soon thereafter, he opened up a law office, Chino, Iversen, and Shultz, and also signed on as an attaché with the Japanese consulate in Chicago. Meanwhile, he sought to promote the status of Nisei as Americans. In 1937, he became president of the Japanese Young People's Association, a club for local Nisei. He organized the building of a community center, ran social events, and formed a Nisei Boy Scout troop (with his friend and fellow attorney Minoru Yasui as scoutmaster). In early 1940 he proposed a nationwide contest to select a "Nisei of the year"—a forerunner of the later JACL "Nisei of the biennium" award. His goal was to celebrate the achievements and point up the Americanism of "second generations." Chino wrote to First Lady Eleanor Roosevelt to ask her advice on the plan. He described the psychological malaise of the Nisei, who were American citizens, yet not fully accepted:

> On the one hand it is charged that we do not "assimilate" and on the other, social barriers are erected against us to rebuff our attempts to take a real place in the American scheme of things. The result has been that many of us have a definite inferiority complex and persecution mania, all of which is bad not only for the individual but also for Society as a whole.

With the endorsement of Mrs. Roosevelt, who praised the project as inspirational and a "splendid idea," Chino founded the Sansho Yamagata award (named for a local Issei businessman). It sparked widespread nationwide interest and nominations among Japanese Americans. The award was given twice, to JACL President Walter Tsukamoto in 1940 and to Mike Masaoka in 1941, before it died with the coming of war.

Meanwhile, he spoke out against United States intervention in World War II. In a letter published in the Black newspaper *Chicago Defender* under the name "F Chino", he recounted incidents in which free speech had been crushed in Japan, France, and Germany. He concluded that Americans should "mind our own business," for once war came, he argued, "we can say good-bye to the Bill of Rights and the last remaining vestige of democracy on the globe."[762]

Once war came, it must be said, Franklin Chino withdrew from public activities, apart from assisting the Chicago Commission for Civil Defense. Meanhile, under the guidance of his wife Marie, an Italian-American, he became a devout Catholic. He spent a good deal of time in church activities, such as directing his parish's Holy Name Society and joining the Knights of Columbus. He did not involve himself deeply in Japanese American community activities, although he did sign JACL legal briefs in civil rights cases and joined political education programs with the Chicago JACL. In 1948, he drew derision from Nisei intellectuals for his public statements in the *Chicago Shimpo* newspaper urging Nisei to support the Republican Party, on the grounds that the Roosevelt Administration had been responsible for Executive Order 9066, while the Republicans had passed evacuation claims legislation. In 1950, he wrote a letter to the *Pacific Citizen* advising Nisei not to form separate political organizations, but to participate in elections through interracial groups. He is commemorated by Franklin Chino Park in Hoffman Estates, the suburban Chicago community he helped create."

Although Franklin Chino publicly warned of restrictions on civil liberties in case of war, it was his brother, Robert, who was most directly touched by official action. A strapping youth and star athlete at Hyde Park High School, Robert also wrote poetry and stories. As a teenager, he ran away from home and rode the rails as a hobo, then returned and founded a Chicago chapter of the American Lincoln Brigade (the name given to the American volunteer battalions in the Spanish Civil War). He married a fellow activist, Marilyn Fillis, the daughter of a distinguished local doctor and medical school professor.

Like his brother Franklin, Robert opposed U.S. intervention in the war in Europe during 1940-41, and he became active with the pacifist group War Resisters League (WRL). After Pearl Harbor, Robert was assigned a new draft classification of 3-A (deferred due to dependents). Unlike other Nisei, his classification was not 4-C (enemy alien). Even though he was barred from conscription, he returned the draft card he was sent to his Draft Board, and assisted the WRL in draft counseling. As a Nisei, Chino faced additional burdens due to his actions, because they could be read as support for the Japanese enemy.

On February 17, 1942, after Robert Chino escorted a fellow resister, David Nyvall, to the police station, he was arrested for draft evasion and charged with failing to keep his draft card on his person. Lawyer Francis Heisler, a World War I veteran who defended conscientious objectors, took his case—Franklin Chino was inexplicably absent during the entire affair—and entered a plea of not guilty. (Chino could not meet the $5,000 bond required, but Georgia Lloyd, a millionaire with radical sympathies, provided funds for his release.) Once out on bail, Robert threw himself into organizing with the Fellowship of Reconciliation (FOR), a pacifist and social justice group. When a young African American FOR staffer, James Farmer, put together a proposal for a civil rights protest group inspired by Mahatma Gandhi's nonviolent approach, Chino was among the half-dozen activists who attended the organizing meeting, and Farmer adopted his suggestion that the new group be called Congress of Racial Equality (CORE). As part of CORE's "race relations team," Chino then participated when CORE launched its first restaurant "sit-in," at Jack Spratt's Coffeehouse in Chicago on May 15, 1942, to protest denial of service to blacks.

On May 26, Francis Heisler appeared before Judge William Holly and informed him that Chino wished to plead *nolo contedere*, in essence leaving his sentence to the judge—Chino presumably believed that the judge would less hostile than a jury. He admitted that he had returned his draft card, but now insisted that he had done so in protest against the board's discriminatory treatment of him. His case was continued while the probation board examined his record. On June 25, Judge Holly sentenced him to three years in prison for failing to carry a draft card. Robert Chino spent the next eighteen months in prison in Minnesota. In order to secure his release, he then agreed to join the Army, and enrolled in the celebrated all-Nisei 442nd Regimental Combat Team. He served as supply sergeant with the unit in Italy and France, and was wounded on three occasions.

Robert Chino remained in France and Italy in the decades after the war. He left the Army in 1948 and settled in Nice with his new wife Claude. They soon had twin sons, Denis and Bruce, but the marriage did not work out. He left the family after a few years and remarried. He and his third wife, Gisele, had a son, Philippe, in 1954. In the decades that followed, Chino occupied various jobs and moved several times. For a time, he specialized in electronics. He kept up his military connections, and in 1954 he was named adjutant of the French division of the American Legion. A devotee of fly fishing, Robert wrote articles for fishing magazines and published a translation of French pediatrician Jean-Paul Pequegnot's book, *French Fishing Flies* (1987). In 1987, while living in the South of France, Robert fell ill. His family was able to arrange a military plane to fly him to Walter Reed Hospital, where he died in December 1987. His lonely episode of draft resistance and protest over the treatment of racial minorities remained forgotten.

A very different path to activism was taken by Toshi-Aline Ohta Seeger (1922-2013), who collaborated with her longtime husband, Pete Seeger, in his musical career and support for progressive causes. Born in Munich, Germany, in 1922, she was the daughter of Takashi Ueda Ohta, the son of a prominent Japanese family, and a white American mother, Virginia Harper Berry; as a baby, she was brought to the United States at the age of six months, not long before the Oriental Exclusion Act barred further entry.[763] Takashi Ohta had first come to the United States in 1915, accepting banishment from Japan in place of his father, a supporter of Sun Yat-sen who had fallen afoul of the Japanese government for his revolutionary political activities. He presented a fictionalized version of his unusual story in a cowritten 1929 book, *The Golden Wind*.[764] After a stay in Pennsylvania, where Toshi's brother Allan was born, the family settled in New York's Greenwich Village. There Takashi worked as a painter and supported himself by various jobs, including being caretaker at the nearby Henry Street Settlement House and set designer at the Provincetown Playhouse. Some years later, the family moved for a time to the Woodstock artists' colony in upstate New York, where Takashi became set designer and scenic painter at the Woodstock Playhouse. In the depths of the Great Depression, the Ohtas lived off what they could grow and sell. The young Toshi attended The Little Red School House in New York City and graduated from the High School of Music and Art in 1940. In 1939, she met the folk singer and activist Pete Seeger at a square dance, and agreed to help him put together a book of labor songs. Soon, the two started dating. Meanwhile—in what would prove a rare case of her activism within ethnic Japanese communities—Toshi joined the Japanese American Committee for Democracy during 1942. She was elected to the group's Executive Board, and served as a program committee volunteer. (According to JACD members, it was Toshi who attracted folksingers Leadbelly and Woody Guthrie to perform at JACD dances.)[765] In June 1942, she hosted a tea party for Nisei girls to encourage them to become active in the war effort.[766]

In 1943, Toshi married Pete Seeger, who was then in the Army.

In 1949, the two moved to Beacon, New York, where they built their own cabin (at first without electricity or running water) and raised three children. Though Toshi was primarily involved in caring for home and children in the early postwar years, she joined her husband in various political activities, including campaigning for Henry Wallace's 1948 presidential candidacy on the Progressive Party ticket, and attendance at political protests. Toshi also became increasingly active as a supporter of Pete Seeger's career as a folk music performer and freelance activist, first as a member of the renowned singing group the Weavers, later as a soloist. Her contribution as booking agent, publicist, and secretary made his career possible. She ultimately branched out to serve as booking agent for other music groups as well.

Meanwhile, she embarked on a career as a filmmaker and musicologist/ethnologist. During the late 1950s, Pete Seeger was blacklisted for his Communist Party membership and left-wing associations, and for some years was largely unemployable. During this time, the pair took a trip around the world and visited musicians on several continents. Although untrained in cinematography and filmmaking, Toshi co-produced, directed, shot, and edited films of the visit. After returning, she continued to travel around the United States, recording musicians. For example, her 1966 film, *Afro-American Work Songs in a Texas Prison*, depicts music made by inmates. In 1965, when her husband was no longer banned from television by blacklisting, she produced his Public Television show, *Rainbow Quest*. In later years, Toshi continued her eforts. In 2007, at age 85, she served as executive producer of an Emmy award-winning documentary on her husband, *Pete Seeger: The Power of Song*.

In addition to supporting her husband directly, Toshi worked in various ways to meld music with political activism. She served as chief organizer in the early years of the Newport Folk Festival, and helped discover bluesman Mississippi John Hurt. Meanwhile, she attended civil rights demonstrations in the South and marched with Dr. Martin Luther King from Selma to Montgomery in 1965. Her support for singer and activist Bernice Johnson Reagon, herself a leader of the Albany, Georgia civil rights campaign, led Reagon to name her daughter, singer Toshi Reagon, in Seeger's honor. In later years, Toshi Seeger was honored by being appointed to the New York State Arts Council.

Beginning in the 1970s, Toshi Seeger became best known for her work with the Hudson River Sloop Clearwater organization, a nonprofit organization that the Seegers founded in 1969, using a replica of an old sailing ship as a vehicle for advancing the goal of cleaning the polluted Hudson River. She organized the annual Clearwaters Great Hudson River Revival, ran the events (such as dropping the stone in the "stone soup" symbolizing community cooperation) and recruited performers for benefit concerts.

## Conclusion

The portraits sketched in this essay can only hint at the galaxy of different activities in which hapa Issei and Nisei have proven noteworthy. The historian could as easily point to other areas of life where early mixed-race Japanese Americans made visible contributions, such as sports (Arthur Matsu, Eddie Townshend), cinema (Lotus Long [Pearl Suetomi]), music (George Hirose), science (William T. Thomson), business (Arthur Hirose, Eben Takamine), or health care (Jokichi Takamine III, George Omura, Marilyn Takahashi Fordney, Augusta Nakahama Oguri). In the same vein, there were mixed-race Japanese on the international stage who visited the United States or influenced American life (Henry Mittwer, Ian Mutsu, Kokou Yamata, Count Richard Coudenhove-Kalergi).

It would also be interesting to study the careers of the hapa who, like Robert Chino, served in the 442nd Regimental Combat Team during World War II—including Virgil Westdale of Indiana, or the Hawai'i-born William Kato and Willie Goo (a Japanese-Hawaiian and Japanese-Chinese hapa, respectively). Sono Osato's younger brother Timothy Osato not only served in the 442nd, but became a career military officer following the war, as well as professor of Military History at West Point and elsewhere, and later served in both the Korean and the Vietnam Wars. Such an inquiry would further demonstrate the variety and depth of Nikkei life, even before today's proudly multicultural era.

## CHAPTER ELEVEN

# "I AM 'MIXED' AND IDENTIFY WITH ALL THE CULTURES EQUALLY": JAPANESE-ABORIGINAL AUSTRALIAN AND OTHER MIXED-HERITAGE PEOPLE IN BROOME, NORTH WESTERN AUSTRALIA

### YURIKO YAMANOUCHI

Broome is a town located 2,200 kilometres north of Perth, Western Australia. From the 1880s to the 1960s Broome had an influx of Asian migrants, including Japanese, for its pearl shell industry. Despite the migration restrictions of the White Australia Policy, the internment of Japanese during World War II, and their deportation after that, some Japanese people stayed and intermarried with the local indigenous people. This paper explores one of their descendants' statements: "I am 'mixed' and identify with all the cultures equally." I argue that his claim of "mixed" identity could be interpreted, not simply as an aspect of generic notions of ethnic/racial identity formation, but as a product of the legacy of the polyethnic pearl shell industry in Australia. "Mixed" identities are particular to the local histories and it is through understanding these local matrices that we might expand the study of "mixed-race" peoples and ethnic/racial systems.

The phrase I focus on here comes from a conversation I had with a man of Japanese, Chinese, Scottish and Australian Aboriginal heritage who was born and brought up in Broome, and who will be called "Jason" in this paper. When I asked his identity he said, "mixed," and then added: "I identify with all the cultures [I inherit] equally." Many of Broome's residents have Asian—including Japanese—and Aboriginal Australian heritage, shaped by Broome's pearl shelling history. They often claim "mixed" identity as well as each individual ethnic and racial heritage. For example, one person of Japanese, Filipino, and Aboriginal Australian descent called his family "Ja-Fili-Gene." At the same time, they usually classify themselves according to the groups their Asian ancestors have been associated with (in this person's case, Japanese).

The question here is: what made them identify in this way? In contemporary Australia, which advocates multiculturalism, Broome is sometimes said to have been "multicultural" since before World War II.[767] Jason's hybrid identity seems to conform to this multiculturalism. However, historians argue that although the pre-war population of Broome was multi-ethnic, there was a fine hierarchy between these ethnic groups, which is different from what current advocates of multiculturalism would advocate and assume.[768] Understanding why people like Jason assert their identity as mixed requires careful unravelling of their historical, social and political background.

Although academic interest in the topic of "mixed race" can be traced to the nineteenth century, the field of interdisciplinary mixed-race research has developed from the 1990s, mainly in North America and Britain.[769] Many of these scholars identify as mixed race and emphasize the category of race as social construction. How a mixed ethnic or racial background affects a person's identity has often been the focus of these studies. Some scholars argue the possibility that mixed-race people are members of simultaneous plural groups, which challenges the notion of the "race" category itself.[770] However, this standpoint has limitations. Ropp points out that trying to transcend racial thinking by using the term "mixed race," which itself includes the word "race," leads to the re-inscription of the concept race.[771] After all, "mixed race" is only significant where there are racial categories. By drawing on the example of the Caribbean, Ropp argues that neither "being biologically mixed" nor having the category of "mixed race" necessarily weakens the social significance of "race." In these countries, social stratification based on white supremacy is still strong, even though being biologically mixed is common, and a category designating some people as being mixed, exists. He asserts that a "more effective way of developing a critical race theory through the multiracial subject is the engagement of social formations (political, economic, and cultural) as they are constructed along racial lines."[772]

Empirical research indicates that mixed-race people report their racial identities inconsistently, and that this identity shifts and changes through their life course.[773] Along with the effects of ethnic/racial stratification, the mixed-race individual's identity is affected and influenced by many factors. Csizmadia and others note, "Friendship groups, school environment, region, and family dynamics intersect with race in myriad ways to produce a racialized sense of self"[774]

The arrangements of these factors are locally and historically specific. As Ropp mentioned in the case of the Caribbean, the categories that designate mixed race do not necessarily challenge social stratification based on ethnic/racial thinking.[775] For example, in Latin America, integration through racial mixing—so-called "racial democracy"—has often been proffered as an ideal, but Arocena observes that this ideology of racial mixing prevents the full recognition of social disadvantage and discrimination experienced by those of Indigenous American and African descent.[776] Their struggle has been against this "racial democracy" which glosses over inequality. The "pan-ethnic/racial" identity has a similar problem. In Hawai'i, where mixed ethnicity/race relationships are viewed in a more positive light than in other parts of the United States, the salience of a pan-ethnic/racial (or "local") identity has been noted since the 1960s.[777] This "local" category designates the descendants of Indigenous Hawaiians and Asian immigrants who shared subjugation by the dominant white planter and merchant oligarchy before World War II. Okamura argues that due to the external social and economic forces of change, "local" identity has developed, and the term "local" come to be considered as those who appreciate the quality and style of life in Hawai'i. However, even though these Indigenous Hawaiians and Asian immigrants have a history of mixing with each other, the usage and the emphasis of this term "local" is criticized as glossing over the fact that the Asian immigrants were settlers who exploited indigenous land and resources.[778] As these cases indicate, the "mixed" or "pan-ethnic/racial" category does not necessarily transcend ethnic/racial categories. The social significance of these categories is different between societies.

These points support Ropp's argument. Rather than pointing out how "race" could be mixed, unravelling how the racial system is created to give meaning and justification to practices of social inequality is more effective to challenge the overall system of race itself. The category of race may be socially constructed, but it is real in everyday social practices. An important point here is that social, political, economic, and cultural formations constructed along racial lines are locally and historically specific, and people develop their regional and historical identities in response to these formations. The fact that the majority of mixed-race studies are produced in the North American and British contexts limits the understanding of how various factors work to form social stratification along ethnic/racial lines. This chapter provides an example of Japanese-Aboriginal Australian (and other Asian) mixed people in Broome to expand the horizon of the academic literature.

Categories that designate people as "mixed race" or which straddle more than one ethnic/racial group are not rare throughout the world. How these categories operate in their own specific ethnic/racial system and how these operations are similar or different between each other have not been explored as often. In Broome, being Japanese-Indigenous Australian mixed is not unusual. However, the social meanings of "being mixed" are not the same as in Latin America or Hawai'i. As Christian points out, hybrid identity is locally and historically specific.[779]

In the rest of this chapter, I first describe the history of Japanese migration to Broome and the multi-ethnic situation from which Jason's "mixed" identity originates. Then, I move to the social and political change surrounding Broome after World War II, which became the backdrop for Jason's assertion of "mixed" identity. As Bauman has observed, identity is argued because it is not taken for granted.[780] Finally, I discuss some episodes that have affected the "mixed" identity of Japanese descendants in Broome. If a "mixed identity" is constructed and asserted against a specific historical and social background, it is not immune to change, even if the "mixed" identity is never extinguished. These findings are based on field research conducted in Broome for two weeks in 2009, one month in 2010, and one week in 2012.

## Japanese Descendants in Northern Australia

It goes without saying that race has been a powerful structural force in Australia. With Federation in 1901, the well-known White Australia Policy was embodied in the *Immigration Restriction Act 1901*, barring non-white people from migrating to Australia. Although the White Australia Policy was gradually dismantled after World War II, it was not officially abolished until 1973. Australia has long been viewed as a "white country," though the introduction of official multiculturalism in the 1970s has helped change that image.

The northern part of Australia, however, had a different trajectory from the south. It was believed by those in the white power structure that the tropical climate did not suit Europeans. Instead, Asian and Pacific Islander workers, including Japanese, were recruited for its industries. Their migrations into northern Australia continued even under the White Australia Policy. Northern Australian society before World War II was multi-ethnic, although the relationships between these ethnic groups were not necessarily harmonious. Recently the history of this "mixed society" has become subject of research.[781] The "mixed" identity that is based on this history has also been expressed in music and performance arts during the last couple of decades.[782] The pearl shelling industry, responsible for attracting numerous different populations to northern Australia, declined in the 1960s, which stopped the flow of the workers. Although this recent historical research and artwork explains the roots and asserts the existence of "mixed identity," it does not explain why it is expressed now, more than four decades after the 1960s.

From the 1870s to the 1960s, Japanese workers flowed into northern Australia for industries such as pearl shell and sugar cane.[783] They quickly became sought-after workers in these industries. Although the 1901 White Australia Policy restricted their migration and most of the sugar cane workers went back, the pearl shelling industry—the second largest industry in northern Australia at that time—was exempted. As a result, Japanese pearl shelling workers continued flowing in. In 1919, there were about 600 Japanese on Thursday Island in the Torres Strait and 1,200 in Broome, the two main centers of the pearl shell industry.[784] Pearl shell was, at that time, a popular material for the button industry in Europe. For Japanese migratory workers, work in Australia was a significant opportunity: In 1926 the per-worker remittances from Australian workers to their Japanese families was the second largest next to those from the United States back to Japan.[785]

During World War II almost all Japanese in Australia were interned and then deported after the war. The post-war reintroduction of Japanese migratory workers started in 1953 and continued until 1969, around when the pearl shell industry practically ceased.[786] Throughout these periods, Japanese people (migratory workers and others) stayed, intermarried, and created families with the local people, who had diverse ethnic and racial backgrounds such as Indigenous Australian (Aboriginal Australians and Torres Strait Islanders), Malay, Filipino, and Chinese.

At the time of my research in 2010, there were about ten Japanese surnames in the Broome phone directory. Some families have a history there since before World War II, though most came after the war. There are also some Japanese descendants who, for various reasons, do not use or have Japanese surnames. The experiences of those with Japanese heritage vary greatly according to their generation and their relationship with their Japanese ancestors. They neither concentrate in ethnic enclaves nor regularly meet with each other. The term "Japanese community" is used actively at some events, for example the annual town festival, *Shinju Matsuri*.[787] The prime movers of the festival and of the public face of the

Japanese community are from two families of ex-pearl shell divers. Some Japanese descendants, however, do not join these community activities.

### "The Polyethnic North"

What these Japanese descendants have in common are their historical roots. Their Japanese ancestors came to Australia with other Asians to work in the pearl shell industry or to do business in the Japanese community created by the pearl shell industry. Starting in the late nineteenth century, the pearl shell industry attracted the largest number of non-Europeans to northern Australia. These "non-Europeans" included Japanese, Chinese, 'Malays', which, in this context, referred to those from Singapore, Malaya the Indonesian archipelago, including Koepang (Timor), Ambon, and other islands. Their presence shocked the "White Australia" advocates from southern Australia. Ganter calls the northern part of Australia before World War II, the "polyethnic north." Polyethnicity refers to "the close proximity of peoples from different ethnic background, and the frequent family formation across ethnic boundaries."[788] Members of these ethnic groups, as well as Aboriginal Australians and Torres Strait Islanders, married each other, and their mixed descendants also married each other. "In the third generation a child in such a mixed family may have four grandparents speaking four different languages."[789] There were also cohabitations and casual relationships between Asian men and Indigenous Australian or part-Indigenous Australian women.[790] Since most Asians in Broome were indentured labourers, there was a severe shortage of Asian women. For example in 1901, there were 303 Japanese men and 63 Japanese women in Broome. European women were, in most cases, inaccessible as partners.

The increasing number of Asian-Aboriginal Australian people—so-called "mixed bloods"—became a government concern. Their presence disturbed the colonial authority's expectation that Australian Aborigines would die out, bowing to the force of evolution. The bureaucracies sought to distinguish these "mixed blood" people from Aboriginal people of "full descent." In Western Australia, the Aborigines Act 1905 prohibited non-Aboriginal men and Aboriginal women from cohabitation, and the Chief Protectors of Aborigines had the power to permit or forbid the marriages of Aboriginal women and non-Aboriginal men, permission that was rarely granted. Some Asian men were deported for living with Aboriginal women in violation of the 1905 law. Mixed-descent children were often taken from their parents or mothers and put into institutions run by missionaries and nuns. Nonetheless, the "mixed-blood" population continued to increase. In Broome in 1954, the number of "mixed-bloods" was 347 out of the total population of 1,261, constituting a significant proportion of the town population.[791]

Relationships between Asians and Indigenous Australians were ambiguous. While they shared subjugation to the colonial government and white master pearlers, Asian migrants were also settlers. Sometimes these two groups had positive interactions. For instance, Aboriginal people preferred to work with Asians, including Japanese, rather than Europeans because they were not as "flashy" as Whites. Some Aboriginal people on the northern coastline developed informal and mutually beneficial trade relationships with Asian crews of pearl luggers.[792] On the other hand, an ethnic/racial hierarchy existed. Ganter writes, "northern polyethnicity was underwritten by finely graded rules of etiquette that dictated where one lived, which school one attended, with whom one socialized, and even where one sat in the picture theater."[793] Japanese stayed in the Japanese quarters and spent most of their time there. In the Sun Picture Theatre in Broome, white people sat in the best seats in the middle, Japanese sat behind them, and the "Blacks" (i.e., the Aboriginal people) at the back.

Interethnic relationships in the polyethnic north were complicated and differed from place to place, and time to time. For example, in 1932 some Japanese seamen were killed by Aboriginal people in Caledon Bay, Northern Territory. Ogawa, who collected the life stories of Japanese ex-pearl shell divers, including recollections of incidents like the above, writes that Aboriginal people were sometimes considered by the Japanese to be cannibalistic barbarians.[794] Although some assert good relations, these were also shaped by the hierarchies in the polyethnic north, including that of varying Asian groups.[795] As the example of the Sun Picture Theatre indicates, Japanese ranked next to the Whites in the hierarchy of the polyethnic society, due to the fact that they almost monopolized the divers' jobs in the pearl shelling industry. Koepangers, Ambonese, and other South-East Asians, who were classified as "Malays," had less power and prestige. They often were under the command of Japanese divers on pearl-shelling ships and were ill-treated, although there were quite a few Malay divers as well. Chinese had more prestige than Malays. Although these differences do not necessarily mean that they were on bad terms all the time, ethnic conflicts and riots happened. For example, in Broome in 1907, 1914, and 1920, street fighting between Japanese, Koepangers, and Ambonese, caused several deaths.[796]

In examining the history of race and ethnicity in Broome, we need to keep in mind from which vantage point these histories are written. For example, what, from one perspective, is taken to be "Aboriginal women's sexual exploitation by Asian men," might alternatively be viewed as a "good idea" for exchange practices between Aboriginal people and Asians.[797] For example, Dalton wrote in the 1960s that a Japanese who married an Aboriginal woman was expelled from the Japanese community, whereas Nakano, dealing with the same era and people, reports a case where a marriage between a Japanese diver and an Aboriginal woman was celebrated.[798] I have heard descriptions from local Asian, Aboriginal, and mixed people of more amicable relationships than those reported in historical records. Even with the possibility of biased historical records, why amicable relationships are only being claimed, or/and listened to, now should be considered in the current social and political context.

**After the Polyethnic North: Broome Changes**
Asian, Aboriginal, and mixed heritage people like Jason share the historical background of the pearl shell industry. To understand their identity, however, we need to see local history past World War II. Ganter maintains that the "polyethnic north" went into decline with the outbreak of World War II, when almost all Japanese in Australia were interned.[799] Only nine of the Japanese who were forcefully removed from Broome during internment and deportation returned to Broome. The effect of war was huge on the pearl shell industry. In 1953, Western Australia again permitted Japanese indentured labourers into the area, but the industry never fully recovered. The town once called the "queen of the southern sea" shrunk. With the decline of industry, significant change occurred to the ethnic composition of the local population. In 1955, 106 Japanese were working in Broome. In the late 1970s it was about 20. The cultured pearl industry, which started in the 1950s as a Japanese-Australian joint project near Broome, became successful and provided some employment, but not as much as the pearl shell industry had.[800] Many Japanese thus left Broome. Most of those who stayed had families or long-term relationships with local people.[801] Nakano suggests that during this period of time, Japanese attitudes towards Aboriginal people changed.[802] When Masataro Okumura, a pearl shell diver who came to Broome in 1953, started to live with an Aboriginal woman named Mary in the mid-1950s, some celebrated. But some Japanese people also gossiped, "how low Okumura fell to get together with a black woman!" By the mid-1960s, more Japanese people "got together" with Aboriginal or mixed-blood

Aboriginal women. One Japanese ex-pearl shell diver in Broome told me that when he got together with an Aboriginal woman in the 1970s, "everyone celebrated." Ganter writes that the Japanese descendants in northern Australia are now well integrated in the Aboriginal community.[803]

Historical factors such as the history of mingling ethnic groups in Broome, the relatively recent decline of the pearl shell industry, and the fluctuating number of indentured labourers have influenced Jason's identification. Broome's recent changes also play a part. Since the 1970-1980s, Broome has become a popular tourist spot. The town population has increased drastically as people have moved to Broome for the new industry. Dalton reports that the town population was 1,261 in 1954, mainly consisting of Asian, Aboriginal, and mixed people.[804] It was 1,272 in 1971;[805] 4,869 in 1981;[806] 7,932 in 1991;[807] 17,811 in 2001;[808] and 14,997 in 2011.[809] The Asian, Aboriginal, and mixed population became a minority. One person who has known Broome for more than twenty years wryly said that Broome is now a "white town." Together with the white sand beach, its "multicultural" history has become a tourist attraction. Plaques and statues commemorating Broome's multiethnic past have been built. The central part of the town was rebuilt and named "Jonny Chi Lane," after a successful Chinese businessman before World War II. However, although some reconstruction of old buildings and houses is evaluated favourably by Broome residents, these signs and symbols do not seem to be connected with the Asian, Aboriginal, and mixed peoples' sense of history and identity. Some said that "Jonny Chi Lane" before World War II was in a different place. Others noted that new people (often perceived as "White") do not understand the history of Broome.[810]

This kind of feeling was exposed when the documentary film *The Cove* was released in Broome in August 2009. We can gain insight into the nature of ethnic relations in Broome, by examining the reaction of the townspeople to the movie. The film, whose depiction of Japanese dolphin hunting in Taiji, Japan, raised an outcry amongst environmentalists and others. In Broome, this led the Broome City Council to nearly suspend Broome's sister-city relationship with Taiji, in Wakayama Prefecture, Japan. Broome and Taiji had become sister cities in 1981, as many of Broome's pearl shell divers originally came from Wakayama and from Taiji, in particular. In Broome, more than half of the gravestones in the Japanese cemetery are for people from Wakayama, including Taiji.[811] After World War II, many Japanese workers also came from Taiji.[812] Taiji was also a well-known whaling town, where whales and dolphins were hunted.

The Cove, a film about the annual dolphin hunt in Taiji, created an international sensation, and within two weeks after the release of the film, some people submitted a petition to suspend Broome's connection with Taiji at the monthly Broome City Council meeting. The petition was accepted immediately at the city council meeting. This decision was protested by the "old Broome residents," especially Asian, Aboriginal, and mixed people, as well as some Whites whose families had been in Broome since the pearl shelling era. They requested a special meeting with the City Council to rescind the decision. They argued that the decision was made without consulting them, and that the historical relationship between Taiji and Broome should be given greater respect.

After the special meeting, the Broome City Council rescinded their decision.[813] Kaino suggests that the fact that other Asian-Aboriginal Australian groups joined Japanese descendants in protest shows the continuous ties between Japanese and Aboriginal Australian communities.[814] For them all, the tie with Taiji was not just a tie with a Japanese town, but symbolized the polyethnic history of Broome. I agree with Kaino about this point. However, I would argue that the reason Japanese and other Asian and Aboriginal group members worked together is not simply that they have ties and identification with the pearl shelling history, but that they sensed a threat to their identity. One Asian group member said that he joined the protest because it was important for Asians to get together, since their numbers had diminished. The protest was joined by some people of Japanese descent who usually do not join Japanese community activities.

Jason's claim of identity as "mixed" was made against this backdrop. He maintained that the people in Broome had known about dolphin hunting in Taiji for ages. It was only the "new Whites" (the newcomers to Broome) who did not know. Against these newcomers he asserts his mixed identity as someone who has roots in Broome's pearl shelling history. His identification as "mixed" is also a response against contemporary Aboriginal regulation. Since the early 1980s, categories of Aboriginal people are limited to those (1) of Aboriginal descent, (2) self-identifying as Aboriginal, and/or (3) accepted as Aboriginal by the Aboriginal community.[815] Jason, who is of Aboriginal descent, would be classified as "Aboriginal" since he identifies as "Aboriginal." In practice, government policies are based on the "black or white" binary and do not give room to Aboriginal people to identify concurrently with other ethnic groups. The recent changes in Broome, contemporary Aboriginal regulations, and the protest against dolphin hunting in Taiji, are considered foreign concepts, brought by "white" outsiders ignorant of local history. Against this, Jason claims that he is "mixed," with roots in the polyethnic past of Broome. This assertion is not the same as accommodating "multiculturalism" espoused by Australian policy-makers.

What about Jason's claim that he identifies with all his inherited cultures equally? I wrote of the ethnic and racial mix at the time of the polyethnic north. The inter-ethnic/racial tensions have loosened since the 1950s. In many ways, Asians, Aboriginals, and their mixed descendants have come together through their mutual attachment to the town of Broome. As reported by Nakano, at his friend's funeral in 1979, Okumura asserts: "we created this town."[816] He says:

> We made the company (pearl shelling) big, not the Whites. It is not them who made this town big. It's all "us" who did it. We dived under the cold water and worked. It was so cold, so cold that we had to drink. Kaino [his late friend] worked hard too. For a white person's funeral, not so many people would attend.[817]

Nakano indicates that the funeral was well attended by Japanese and Aboriginal people. Further, he suggests that what Okumura meant "us" were those "colored" (Asian, Aboriginal Australian and "mixed") people who lived and worked in the pearl shelling industry. This indicates that these people who worked in the pearl shelling industry share a sense of "creating Broome." Jason's claim of identity can thus be interpreted not within a flat and neutral ethnic/racial heritage, but within the legacy of the polyethnic pearl shell industry that shaped the region.

### After *The Cove*

In June 2011, seven delegates including the Broome Shire President, a Japanese former pearl shell diver, his daughter, and two grandchildren visited Taiji. They re-confirmed the ties between the two sister cities. Taiji renamed its main civic street "Broome Street." The student exchange between Broome and Taiji, which was suspended in 2009, restarted in 2010. The crisis started by the showing of *The Cove* in Broome ultimately strengthened the sister city ties between the two towns. For the Japanese descendants who have relatives in and around Taiji, this move created the opportunity for strengthening their transnational familial ties.

A liquefied natural gas plant project to be constructed at James

Price Point, 52 kilometers north of Broome, caused huge controversy and protest in Broome. Some Japanese descendants of Broome joined the protest together with environmentalists, who tend to be considered newly arrived outsiders by the old Broome residents. This cooperation indicates the possibility of ties between the two groups, which can lead to a common identification, although in 2013 the project was delayed indefinitely. Even though one of the project joint-owners was Japan Australia LNG Pty. Ltd (Mitsui and Mitsubishi), it did not lead Japanese or Japanese descendants in Broome to support it.[818]

In August 2012, the traditional Japanese summer ancestral festival, the Obon Festival, was conducted at the Japanese cemetery in Broome, organized by some Japanese descendants, their family members, and a Japanese migrant artist. They invited a Japanese Buddhist priest from Sydney. The ceremony attracted not only Asians, Aboriginals, and their mixed descendants, but a large number of Broome's residents, as well as some delegates from Taiji. Some Japanese descendants seemed shocked by the size of the crowd. On the other hand, some Japanese descendants seemed comfortable to include non-Asians, Aboriginals, and their mixed descendants, even those who were newer residents of Broome. After the ceremony there was a dinner at one Japanese descendant's place, where I chatted with a white woman. She told me that she came to work in Broome just a couple of months ago. She was invited by one Japanese descendant woman who was working together with her.

These events indicate that there have been, are, and will be continuous changes in the social, political, and economic situation of the mixed people of Broome, which creates, strengthens, but can also weaken, their connections with different people. But how these forces affect identity is not simple. As the presence of the white woman at Obon festival dinner suggests, social events that would strengthen the old Broome "mixed identity" of Japanese descendants also includes the possibility of new ties and connections. Although mixed identity originates from the strong connection with pearl shelling history, there might develop a new "mixed identity," which can include those who came to the town after the pearl shelling era.

## Conclusion
This article analyzes the "mixed" identity of Broome, Western Australia and reveals its historical roots and the social and political context in which it is claimed. This mixed identity has become

significant against the social changes in Broome since the 1960s, as well as with respect to contemporary Aboriginal regulations. This identity is shared not only by Japanese, but also other Asian, Aboriginal, and their mixed descendants whose Asian ancestors came to Broome for the pearl shelling industry. The pan-ethnic "local" identity in Hawai'i and the "mixed" identity in Latin America obscured the recognition of the disadvantages experienced by Indigenous people. As Trask pointed out, Asian immigrants in Hawai'i were settlers and so, too, can Asian immigrants in Broome be viewed as settlers.[819] However, Indigenous Australians have not vocally criticized Asian migrants or their descendants as settlers. This might be a matter of time, but then again, the conditions shaping the populations in Hawai'i and Broome differ. Unlike Hawai'i, where Asian migrants' descendants—including Japanese—are dominant in society, Japanese or other Asian descendants do not dominate Broome. Most of the Asian migrants were long-time indentured laborers who could not bring their families to Australia. Now most of their descendants in Broome have Aboriginal ancestors as well. They are now a minority, their town and their place within it have been changed by external factors. These factors might not give much motivation for Broome's Aboriginal people to criticize Asian migrants and their descendants, although this topic needs further exploration. The meaning of being "mixed" differs from place to place. Further research on this difference, and also on how various factors make people connect and conflict would facilitate our understanding of ethnic/racial systems.

## CHAPTER TWELVE

# INJUSTICE COMPOUNDED: AMERASIANS AND NON-JAPANESE AMERICANS IN WORLD WAR II CONCENTRATION CAMPS[820]

PAUL R. SPICKARD

During World War II the United States put Japanese Americans in prison camps in remote, desolate parts of the Western states. The politics and the human cost of this event—the imprisonment of a people, on the sole ground of shared ancestry with one of America's enemies—have been richly documented by other authors.[821] It is less well known that a number of non-Japanese Americans, mainly wives and husbands of Japanese men and women, and hundreds of children of mixed parentage, also were sent to those camps. Their story is one of bureaucratic bungling, twisted racism, and petty cruelty suffered by people who had, even by the federal government's standards of the time, no business being in prison.

The war began on December 7, 1941, when Japanese warplanes bombed the American Navy at Pearl Harbor. By March 1942, members of Congress, the Roosevelt administration, and the Army's Western Defense Command (WDC) knew that they wanted to incarcerate most Japanese Americans. But they were not quite sure what to do with those Issei and Nisei (first and second generation Japanese Americans) who had married non-Japanese people. The Japanese American population at large was imprisoned for a variety of reasons. There were rumors, unfounded but persistent, that Japanese Americans were engaging in espionage and sabotage for the Japanese government. As Japanese forces marched unimpeded across the globe, West Coast Whites grew increasingly fearful of the Japanese in their midst. This fear was based on an unreasoning racism that equated American citizens and resident aliens (who were denied citizenship on racial grounds) with Japanese subjects—and accused them of sinister intent—simply on the basis of shared ancestry. Fear turned to hysteria and finally to a massive public clamor for their

## WEST COAST JAPANESE AMERICAN IN-MARRIAGE, OUT-MARRIAGE, AND MIXED RACIAL STATUS BY GENERATION AND REGION, 1942

| STATE OR REGION | SINGLE PURE JAPANESE | SINGLE MIXED ANCESTRY | MARRIED TO JAPANESE | MARRIED TO NON-JAPANESE | TOTAL |
|---|---|---|---|---|---|
| **Issei** | | | | | |
| Washington | 501 | 2 | 4,132 | 77 | 4,712 |
| Oregon | 175 | 1 | 1,175 | 12 | 1,363 |
| California | 4,807 | 10 | 26,107 | 717 | 31,641 |
| Hawaii | 28 | 0 | 104 | 1 | 133 |
| Other US | 34 | 0 | 115 | 9 | 158 |
| TOTAL | 5,545 | 13 | 31,633 | 816 | 38,007 |
| **Nisei** | | | | | |
| Washington | 6,455 | 30 | 1,216 | 6 | 7,747 |
| Oregon | 1,725 | 15 | 320 | 16 | 2,076 |
| California | 47,063 | 200 | 11,735 | 301 | 59,299 |
| Hawaii | 691 | 3 | 221 | 2 | 917 |
| Other US | 174 | 15 | 26 | 8 | 223 |
| TOTAL | 56,979 | 274 | 13,533 | 376 | 71,162 |

Figure 12.1 Source: War Relocation Authority, Census Form 26, Japanese American Evacuation and Resettlement Study Archives, Bancroft Library, University of California, Berkeley [henceforth, JERS]. I am grateful to Richard McIntosh for doing the computer work on this project, which involved a complete tabulation of over 100,000 WRA census forms. A small number of Japanese Americans from outside the West Coast were imprisoned by the WRA during World War II. Numbers for non-West Coast Japanese Americans should be treated with extreme caution, for those inmates did not represent anything like a cross-section of the Japanese American populations of their home areas.

ouster. This fear factor was the main cause of imprisonment. Greed was also evident. Some non-Japanese saw an opportunity to take over thriving farms and businesses for a fraction of their value if the Japanese Americans were ordered out. Then, too, there were the machinations of professional race-baiters and the endorsement of the Roosevelt administration. Finally an element of empire building by certain WDC officers existed. Together, these various factors led to the incarceration of one hundred nine thousand West Coast Japanese in the spring of 1942. The WDC rounded up West Coast Japanese Americans and held most of them in temporary assembly centers—hastily converted fairgrounds and racetracks, for the most part—administered by the WDC's civilian arm, the Wartime Civil Control Administration (WCCA). Gradually, through the summer and fall of 1942, the WDC turned their prisoners over to the War Relocation Authority (WRA), as that civilian agency built more permanent prison camps.

Among those imprisoned were at least fourteen hundred intermarried Japanese Americans, a few of their non-Japanese spouses, and at least seven hundred people of mixed racial ancestry (see Figure 12.1).[822] The Army seems to have had some doubts about the wisdom of putting such people into prison camps. The Japanese American population at large was imprisoned chiefly on the ground of suspected disloyalty. (Political fictions such as "protective custody" need not detain us here.) The WDC very early expressed a desire to take some of the intermarried families out of the prison camps and return them to their homes. This was partly because the WDC thought intermarried Japanese Americans were likely to be loyal Americans. But, more importantly, it was because they did want Amerasian children who had grown up among Caucasians to be tainted by contact with Japanese people. In July 1942, the WDC developed an elaborate set of criteria by which certain categories of people might be granted clearance to return to those portions of California, Oregon, Washington, and Arizona from which Japanese Americans had been excluded. Those individuals who seemed least likely to present a threat to American security would be allowed to return home. Certain others would be permitted to leave the camps, but they would have to stay away from the West Coast. Others had to remain in prison. The criteria for choosing these groups had little to do with individual loyalties. Rather the groups were chosen by racial and gender attributes.[823]

Maj. Herman P. Goebel, Jr., set forth the initial criteria for "Mixed Marriage Leave Clearances," as they were called, in a memo circulated on July 12, 1942. Intermarried couples might leave the camps, but only if they had minor children. The reasoning behind this decision was indicated in another WDC memo (this one from November 13, 1942): "The mixed marriage non-exclusion policy is predicated upon the desirability of providing the issue thereof [i.e., Amerasian children] with an opportunity for rearing in a non-Japanese environment. ... If the parties to mixed marriages have successfully discharged their obligation [sic] with respect to the rearing of their children in a non-Japanese environment, it seems reasonable to reward them with the privilege [sic] of remaining within the excluded area [i.e., western California, Oregon, and Washington, and southern Arizona]. ... To send them to a War Relocation Project [i.e., prison camp] at this time would not only expose them to *infectious Japanese thought*, but would also compel them to live in an environment from which they sought to escape."[824]

The objective, insofar as it was clearly thought out, was to take children of mixed ancestry who had grown up among Caucasians or other non-Japanese people out of prison and deposit them back in their presumably healthy, prewar, non-Japanese environments. There was a not-so-subtle sexism that went with the racism in this selection system. The WDC assumed that males would dominate the culture and loyalties of their households. Thus, mixed children who had white fathers and Japanese mothers would return to the West Coast, because their Caucasian fathers presumably had created American environments for their families. By contrast, mixed children who had white mothers and Japanese fathers could leave the camps, but they could not go home. Because their fathers had made them, presumably, more than half Japanese, they did not qualify for a complete return to normal life. Yet, on the off chance that Caucasian mothers had had some salutary effects on their offspring, such children were offered a limited kind of freedom. They could leave camp, but not return to the jurisdiction of the Western Defense Command. It is interesting to note that the WDC saw this environment business, not in terms of conflicting *national* loyalties and cultures (that is, American versus Japanese), but rather in terms of *racial* loyalties and cultures. Whenever they spoke of the kind of environment they wanted for these children, they labeled it "Caucasian" not "American" or "Western," or even "wholesome." Though such an appellation would confound an anthropologist, presumably it meant something to the WDC's planners. In either case, whether the offending Japanese parent were the mother or the father, the entire family was allowed to leave prison together.[825]

An intermarried couple who did not have children, or one whose children had reached majority, had to stay in prison; that is, the Japanese spouse had to stay. Theoretically, the non-Japanese spouse could go whenever he or she pleased, since it was only the Japanese partner who represented a threat to national security. But any non-Japanese who had stuck with his or her partner through the rigors of imprisonment was hardly likely to abandon the family at this point. The only intermarried Japanese Americans who lacked minor children, yet were permitted to leave camp, were a few women whose husbands were serving in the armed forces. Like Japanese women with Amerasian children, they were allowed to go back to the West Coast, apparently in reward for their husbands' service. The WDC also allowed adults of mixed ancestry to leave prison if they wanted to, but only if they had "fifty per cent, or less, Japanese blood," and could demonstrate that their prewar environment had been "Caucasian."[826]

There were some matters that Goebel's July memo did not settle. Goebel and other WDC officers assumed that all the non-Japanese spouses would be Caucasians. In fact, some were Filipinos, others Chinese, others Koreans or Blacks or Chicanos or European nationals. It took the WDC some time to decide what to do with Japanese Americans who were married to such people. At first they treated non-white spouses with somewhat greater disdain than Caucasians; Japanese women whose husbands were Filipinos, Chinese, or British subjects of Indian extraction were allowed to leave camp, but they were banned from the Coast. Apparently the WDC felt that dark-skinned men were not as skilled as Whites at resisting the infection of Japanese thought.[827] By January 1943 this particular sort of discrimination had been altered: now the requirement was not color but citizenship. If the husband of an intermarried family was either a "United States citizen or citizen of friendly nation" such as Britain, China, or the Philippines, then the couple might return to the West Coast, provided they could meet the other requirements.[828]

The WDC's mixed marriage policy soon came under fire from at least two directions. Dillon Myer, head of the War Relocation Authority (WRA), the civilian agency charged with maintaining the Japanese American prison camps, wrote a letter in January 1943 to John McCloy, Assistant Secretary of War. Myer asked McCloy to review and broaden the categories of people to be allowed back into the WDC's jurisdiction. He wanted the WDC to grant full freedom to any loyal Japanese American woman who was married to a non-Japanese, whether or not her husband was a United States citizen, and whether or not she had children. Myer also wanted freedom for all loyal Amerasians whether their non-Japanese gene pool satisfied the WDC's fifty per cent standard or not. Myer also tried to wrest some power from the military by suggesting that security checks on those leaving camp be made by the civilian FBI, not by Army Intelligence as in the past. McCloy did not act immediately, but in February he passed on Myer's recommendations to Lt. Gen. John DeWitt, commander of the WDC. Eleanor Roosevelt also put pressure on the WDC. In May she contacted Secretary of War Henry Stimson, stating in strong terms her feeling that Theresa Takeyashi should be allowed to rejoin her family in Seattle because she was an Amerasian and a loyal American, even though she did not meet the WDC's re-entry requirements. Stimson passed Roosevelt's letter on to DeWitt and his aide, Col. Karl Bendetsen.[829]

DeWitt was quick to respond to these pressures. He saw correctly that Myer and Roosevelt were questioning the very basis of his unit's policy. They asked the Army to give permits to people based on their loyalty to America. DeWitt, in letters to McCloy in February and June, and Bendetsen, in a May phone conversation, held out for the WDC's narrower criteria. As DeWitt wrote McCloy in February, "If the present mixed-marriage policy is modified in the theory that loyalty can be determined and Japanese wives who are allegedly loyal be permitted to return to the evacuated areas, there would be no real justification for not allowing any such Japanese to return. The proposal to extend the policy to include childless families is highly objectionable because it would pave the way for large numbers of Japanese women to return to the evacuated areas, and has no relation to the original objective of protecting mixed-blood children and adults from a Japanese environment."830

The various actors in this drama had different motives for the positions they took. Roosevelt made her petition on behalf of an individual woman for the humanitarian purpose of reuniting a family and did not address the policy implications of her request. Myer acted out of a desire to undercut the racial basis of the incarceration of Japanese Americans. It was Myer's goal, from the day he took over the WRA, to get the Japanese Americans out of prison camps and back into their normal roles as contributing members of society. If he could change the crucial factor in determining mixed marriage leave permits from the existence of children of mixed ancestry to the loyalties of the candidates for release, then he stood a good chance of converting the entire evacuation to a loyalty issue. He was confident that he could establish the loyalty of the vast majority of his Japanese American prisoners. If they were loyal, and if disloyalty were the sole reason for their imprisonment, then they would have to be released. DeWitt's motives for resisting any policy change were partly bureaucratic ("the mixed-marriage policy has gone forward satisfactorily since its inception"; that which works should not be disturbed) and partly racist (Myer's changes "would lead to the presence of many hundreds of Japanese on the coast.").831

DeWitt won in the short run. The mixed marriage leave clearance policy was not changed. But over time Myer won his goal. By administering a loyalty test to all the inmates in the spring of 1943, and then segregating those who flunked, he gradually convinced most Americans that their Japanese fellow countrymen probably were not actively disloyal. Myer arranged to have large numbers of Japanese Americans, mainly young Nisei, let out of the camps to go to work and school in the East and Midwest. By January 1945, thanks to a favorable Supreme Court ruling, all Japanese Americans deemed "loyal" by the WRA were allowed to go back to the West Coast, over the feeble protests of the WDC. But even the Army was softening its stand. Throughout 1943 DeWitt and his successor, Delos Emmons, showed an increasing willingness to grant individual exemptions to their formerly rigid mixed marriage policy. They made it clear that they did not want large numbers of Japanese Americans in their area, but a few might be okay. They seem to have recognized that public opposition to Japanese Americans on the West Coast was declining. By December 1943, the soldiers felt confident enough about popular opinion to make public for the first time the fact that they had been letting some intermarried Japanese Americans reside on the West Coast all along.[832]

The procedure by which an individual from a mixed family got clearance to leave a WCCA or WRA prison camp was fairly simple. If that person fell within one of the WDC's approved categories he or she could fill out an application that included questions about his or her background, job history, family relationships, connections with Japan, and employment prospects. The person would then be checked against the files of Army Intelligence or the FBI. If that check showed no criminal or subversive history, the individual then was required to present evidence that he or she had a job offer on the outside or else sufficient savings "to prevent their becoming public charges." Finally, the WDC had to ask the sheriff or chief of police of the place to which the prisoner wanted to go, to see if it were okay for him or her to go there. If the local law enforcers said it was okay with them—and frequently they expressed reservations—then the inmate got a travel permit, a photo identification card; and an order to report monthly to the Army near where he or she intended to live. This procedure was the same for Amerasians and intermarried Japanese as it was initially for others who applied for leave permits. Over time, however, the procedures were made less stringent.[833]

Just how many Japanese Americans got out of the prison camps under the WDC's mixed marriage policy in 1942 and early 1943 is unclear. Neither the WDC nor the WRA kept the kind of records that would show such information. The WRA kept track of how many people left their prison camps permanently each month, but did not indicate how many of those were intermarried Japanese or people of mixed parentage, nor how many went back to the West Coast versus how many went east. Altogether, the WRA released less than 900 inmates between July and December 1942, and less than 1,000 more in the first two months of 1943. Thereafter, the WRA encouraged large numbers of Japanese Americans to resettle in the eastern part of the United States.[834] The WDC kept a rough tally of the intermarried Japanese Americans and Amerasians they allowed to return to the West Coast, but those numbers offer no help in trying to determine how many people from mixed families went to other parts of the country. In February 1943 only 113 intermarried families and 15 single adults of mixed ancestry were living in the Western Defense Command. In April the total number of intermarried Japanese Americans and Amerasians was 520. In June, the total was 554; 90 Japanese women who were married to non-Japanese men; 44 Amerasians married to non-Japanese; 90 single adults of mixed parentage; 323 mixed children; and 7 full-blooded Japanese children living with white foster parents. The numbers had increased only slightly when the WDC took its last count in September 1943.[835] The upshot of all this was simply that several hundred intermarried Japanese Americans and Amerasians were allowed to leave the WCCA and WRA prison camps in 1942 and early 1943, in an effort spearheaded by the WDC to keep certain categories of children untainted by contact with other Japanese.

What of the thirteen hundred intermarried Japanese and three hundred people of mixed ancestry who remained in WRA custody? The effects of life in the prison camps were not very different for the intermarried than they were for other Japanese Americans. Japanese Americans lost hundreds of millions of dollars in property that had to be abandoned or sold at fire-sale prices. They suffered the anger and frustration, the fear and hopelessness of being sent to prison camps without cause and without recourse. Once-strong Japanese families lost cohesion as fathers found their authority and their breadwinning capacity usurped by the government. Issei community leaders lost their positions to members of the second generation. Lives were interrupted, careers sidetracked, goals abandoned. Intermarried Japanese Americans suffered all these privations in much the same degree as their homogamous friends and neighbors.

But there were some differences for the intermarried. One crucial difference had to do with family unity. The evacuation put great strains on ordinary Japanese American families, but at least most of the families were able to stay together in the first months of the war—albeit behind barbed wire. By contrast, most intermarried families were broken apart by the evacuation. There was a large number of Japanese American women in camp who were married to non-Japanese men. Almost none of the husbands joined their wives in prison, though the WRA would have allowed them to do so. Nearly all the non-Japanese husbands elected to stay at their prewar homes and jobs while their wives and children went off to prison. Mike Torrez (pseud.) stayed in the Los Angeles area while his wife

Yuriyo (pseud.), seven months pregnant, was taken to Manzanar. The Army did not show much concern for the welfare of another pregnant Nisei woman, Ethel Taylor. The WDC refused to allow her to stay with her husband Larry in Sacramento, though she, too, was seven months pregnant. Herman Goebel responded to her plea by saying that "this office declines to extend the mixed marriage policy to cover pregnant women. Until the child is born, Mrs. Taylor is not eligible for residence in the evacuated area." Goebel showed hard-hearted consistency when he decreed that Grace Record had to leave her white husband Vernon at Mare Island naval station in Vallejo, California. The Records ordinarily would have been allowed to stay together, because Vernon was a ship's cook in the Navy, but Goebel disapproved of their common law marriage. Toshi Griner had to endure separation from her husband because his job in the Merchant Marine did not qualify as service in the armed forces for purpose of her leave clearance. Tamiko Johnson (pseud.) and her daughter Mary (pseud.) also stared out from behind the fence at Tule Lake while Eric Johnson (pseud.) minded the family store in Quilcene, Washington. Liwa Chew had to leave her husband Joe and son Samuel behind in Oakland when she went off to prison. Mary Asaba Ventura fought in court to be allowed to keep her family together, but her petition was denied and she went off to camp anyway. Riyoko Patell had no better luck with her attempts to avoid imprisonment. She was a Japanese woman who fifteen years earlier had married a man from India and taken British citizenship. The Patells were harassed so badly by the Japanese government that in 1939 they fled to America. They intended to travel on to Europe and then India, but World War II began and they had to stay in California. There Mrs. Patell got caught up in the Japanese American evacuation, She and her husband appealed to people at all levels of government, but to no avail.[836]

It was a rare non-Japanese husband who was willing to join his wife and children behind barbed wire. Doubtless both husbands and wives thought it better to have even one of them free, earning a living and keeping up a semblance of their former existence, than to have both incarcerated. One husband who did end up in a WRA camp was W. J. Farrell. He and his Japanese wife were visiting the United States from their home in South America in the fall of 1941. They planned to return home in early December, but found themselves stuck here when all sailings were cancelled in the aftermath of Pearl Harbor. Soon they were both bundled off to the WRA center at Rohwer, Arkansas. Some intermarried couples fled the West Coast before the Army could evacuate them, but such people had an extremely difficult time. John Hayes, a draftsman, and his Nisei wife left the coast and went to Denver to avoid her imprisonment. There, friendless, jobless, running out of money and hope, Hayes suffered a "nervous and physical breakdown" in a skid-row hotel. In desperation he wrote to the WRA for help, but Dillon Myer had no help to offer.[837]

Many Japanese men also had to leave their non-Japanese wives when they were taken to prison camp. Sonny Ujimasa (pseud.), Kazuo Ota (pseud.), Karl Yoneda, and Fred Uchida (pseud.) all left wives on the outside, though Yoneda and his wife Elaine were later reunited in camp. Sey Sugi was separated from his wife Bernice and two-year-old daughter by the evacuation. He had to petition the WDC to have them join him in camp. Ella and Yoshitaro Amaco were separated when the Army took him off and left her at home in Los Angeles. Once interned, Yoshitaro refused to leave camp because the WDC would not let him return to the coast, and Ella refused to join her husband in prison. Fred Korematsu, an Oakland nurseryman, was engaged to a Caucasian woman when the evacuation orders were published. Desperate to remain near the woman he loved, he went into hiding. He changed his name and tried to alter his features through plastic surgery in the hope of passing as non-Japanese. He was caught, arrested, convicted, and sent off to camp anyway.[838]

Perhaps the greatest sufferers in such cases were children who had to endure separation from one or both parents. Little Lamarr Torrez (pseud.) was born in a concentration camp and not allowed to see his father for many months. Grace Record's baby Eunice was only a few months old when they were torn away from husband and father Vincent. Mary Beth Wong (pseud.), John Thomas (pseud.), Ramon Ramirez (pseud.), Donald and James Halog, and Penney Alindungen likewise all were small children when they were forced to leave their fathers and go to prison with their Japanese American mothers. Some Amerasian children had to do without parents entirely in the prison camps. Before the evacuation, the Los Angeles Japanese Children's Home was taking care of nineteen orphans of mixed parentage and eighty-two youngsters of pure Japanese descent. The relatively large number of mixed children in the Home's population is to be explained by the reluctance of Los Angeles Japanese families to take in children of mixed parentage, while they were quite willing to provide homes for most pure Japanese orphans. The entire orphan population of the Japanese Children's Home was taken to the Manzanar prison camp in 1942, where they were installed in a "Children's Village." One of these orphans was Richard Honda, aged six. He had spent the previous five years as a foster child of Sam Spandrio near Oxnard. Apparently he was viewed as a threat to national security. When the Army came to take Richard away, the Spandrios protested, but the Army denied their petition because there was "no policy applicable" to Richard's case. Another, unnamed Amerasian child—a two-year-old girl—was luckier: the WDC said she could stay with her foster family.[839]

Some of the intermarried families that had been broken up by the evacuation managed to get back together in late 1942 and 1943, when the WDC decided to let a few of them out of the prison camps. Some of these were lucky enough to be allowed to return to their West Coast homes. But many were able to reunite only somewhere away from the war zone, usually in Chicago or elsewhere in the Midwest. Many more families remained separated because they did not fit any of the WDC's leave clearance categories.[840]

A number of the intermarried families managed to stay together throughout their imprisonment. For the most part, these were families of Japanese American men and non-Japanese women, such as Jim and Daisy Miyata and their four teenage children; Ikaru and Ida Homa and their daughter Yuriko; Sakuji and Rose Matsumara; Kotarō and Josephine Uyeda; and Fukuzō and Nellie Ogawa. Couples comprising Japanese husbands and non-Japanese wives were more likely to enter the camps together, while couples with the reverse combination usually split up. Apparently, this was because men were usually the breadwinners. If the family wage-earner was interned then the whole family went with him, but if he was not, then he remained at work while the rest of the family was imprisoned. Though the families of Japanese men and non-Japanese women benefitted from being able to stay together, they suffered greater economic losses than the families that split up. A non-Japanese spouse on the outside could keep the family home and business going, an option that was not available to families stuck together behind barbed wire.[841]

A number of adult Amerasians also suffered imprisonment. Some had only remote Japanese ancestry, but they were sent to concentration camps anyway. John, Richard and Karl Watanabe (pseud.) were Los Angeles teenagers who had to grow up fast when the government took them away from their parents and interned them at Manzanar. Emily Simmons (pseud.) was a woman of mixed Japanese and Hawaiian descent who made the mistake of teaching school in Bakersfield rather than back home in Hawai'i. James Oastler, Francina Van Pelt, and Marion Swanson (pseud.) were all elderly half-Japanese who got caught in the evacuation. Harry Haleala (pseud.) was a sawmill worker from Aberdeen, Washington, who may have been part-Japanese but who was raised by a Hawaiian couple. Though he knew no Japanese and never had anything to do with Japanese people, he was interned. The nine brothers and sisters of the Hayward family had one Japanese grandparent, of whose existence they were unaware until the Army came to take them away. The Roberts (pseud.) family comprised over twenty children of a Portuguese-Japanese couple, some of them married to Japanese Americans, others to Whites. All were incarcerated. Julius Down's nearest Japanese ancestor was a grandparent, but he, his white wife Eunice, and their daughter Juliette all went to prison for his Japanese ancestry. Perhaps the most prominent person of mixed parentage to languish behind barbed wire was Isamu Noguchi, the noted sculptor and son of Japanese writer Yone Noguchi.[842]

Most people of mixed parentage and intermarried families were not welcomed to the camps by their fellow inmates. A University of California report on life in the Tule Lake camp found that Japanese partners to mixed marriages were routinely harassed by other Japanese Americans. Japanese Americans had wanted little contact with such people before evacuation, and they were not pleased to be stuck with them in such close quarters now. They had a sense that they might be affected adversely by contact with the intermarried. The report told of one Nisei woman who roomed at Tule Lake with two Issei women: "As soon as her roommates found out that she was married to a Chinese they became very unpleasant and began to pick on her on every occasion." To escape their harassment she moved in with an aunt and uncle, but had little better luck there. The uncle beat her and both complained that "their daughters would not have much of a chance to marry if she were living with them." Thrown out of their apartment, she finally got a short term pass to leave camp to go to work, went AWOL to see her husband in Seattle, was arrested, and ended up in jail. Rose Hayashi (pseud.) had several friends of mixed parentage in camp. An outcast herself because of her reputation as a wanton woman, she sought out the company of other unwanted people. "I began to associate with some of the half-Japanese kids who were living near me," she said, "because they hated the camp too. The other Japanese thought that they were inferior and they did not get along with them." One of Hayashi's particular friends was a Nisei girl who had dated a Filipino boy before the war. "I felt sorry for her. ... She was very lonely too as the other Japanese would not talk to her." Hayashi's attitude toward intermarriage was rather different from that of most of her peers. She had dated a white boy before the war. After she had been imprisoned she said that "it occurred to me then that I should have married [him] and I could have escaped this camp life.

It was too late to do anything then."[843]

Accorded an even frostier welcome were those non-Japanese who found themselves interned. Some, like Elaine Yoneda, Hazel Araki, and Bernice Sugi, fought the bureaucracy to be allowed to go to camp because they wanted to share their husbands' fate. Others went for the sake of the children. Maria Kageyama (pseud.) had long been separated from her Japanese American husband, but she volunteered for internment because her daughters had to go and she did not want them to go alone. Estelle Ishigo went at least partly because she and her semi-employed actor husband Arthur had been having a very tough time supporting themselves on the outside. One white woman named Laverne had been married to her Nisei husband Yukio for six years, but had never had much to do with other Japanese Americans. Inside Tule Lake she felt herself the· object of curiosity and some hostility from her fellow inmates. Estelle Ishigo wrote diaries and manuscripts to pass the time at Manzanar. She contended stridently that there was no difference between people of different races and that she felt as Japanese of any of her neighbors, but it is clear from her writings that they did not feel a similar kinship for her. Elaine Yoneda felt another kind of hostility in camp. She was bothered, not by Japanese fellow inmates, but by a WRA officer named Ned Campbell, who made it clear that he did not approve of her marriage to a Nisei.[844]

Not all of the non-Japanese inmates were relatives of Japanese Americans. In a few bizarre and tragic cases, people of other ethnic groups got caught up in the evacuation and were unable to find a way out. Peter Ogata (pseud.) was one such person. In 1942, the Army took 145 Japanese Alaskans from their homes and put them in the prison camp at Puyallup, Washington. About 50 of those were the children of Japanese fishermen or cannery workers and Indian or Eskimo women, among them Ogata's two half brothers. Peter Ogata was born at Taku Harbor in 1915. His Indian mother had become pregnant by an Indian man. To salvage her respectability she married Hajime Ogata (pseud.) while Peter was still in her womb. She and Hajime had two boys of their own before Hajime deserted the family. The boys were brought up by missionaries among other Indians. They had never been to a city, much less around Japanese Americans, before the government took them to camp. Peter, tall, powerfully built, and dark-skinned, was a full-blooded Tlingit Indian, as were his wife and infant son. But the government took them anyway because they had a Japanese last name. At the same time they left free full-blooded Japanese Alaskans who had taken Indian names. Peter complained that, "When we got to camp all the Japanese people gawked at us." The Ogata family were treated as curiosities by their fellow inmates and were very lonely in camp. But things got worse when they managed to get a leave clearance to settle in Chicago. Unemployed and unused to city life, they grew depressed and bitter, longing for their woodland home. When Peter was interviewed by Charles Kikuchi in 1944 he was bitter against the bungling government bureaucracy for forcing his family into such a degraded state, against the Japanese Americans who had mistreated him in camp, and against his stepfather—both for deserting the family and for giving him the name that had caused him so much trouble. He vowed, "Someday I'm going to slit his neck open if I ever find him, by golly." Ogata was not the only non-Japanese who suffered imprisonment through a quirk of government bungling. Richard Lora (pseud.) was a Chinese boy who played on the basketball team at Belmont High in Los Angeles. For reasons that remain unclear, the government decided he was a threat to national security and sent him to Manzanar, leaving his parents at home.[845]

The wartime experience of intermarried Japanese Americans and their mixed offspring were, in sum, rather different from those of other Japanese Americans. Like other Japanese Americans, most of them suffered imprisonment on account of their Japanese ancestry, but some were let out of the prison camps rather quickly because the government did not want children of mixed ancestry who had been raised among Caucasians to be tainted by contact with Japanese. Others languished in prison. There, in addition to the indignities heaped upon the other inmates, they had to endure separation from their families and harassment from other prisoners. Like other prisoners, many were eager to get out of camp when the WRA made that option available in 1943. But many feared the hostility of their fellow Americans and elected to remain behind barbed wire.[846]

# CHAPTER THIRTEEN

## FRATERNIZATION REVISITED: POST-WAR LEGACIES OF JAPANESE-DUTCH UNIONS

EVELINE BUCHHEIM

On the battlefields of World War II, fraternization—intimacy between occupying military and the occupied population—was generally considered a transgression in multiple senses. In the Dutch East Indies (colonial Indonesia) under Japanese occupation, intimate relations between Japanese military and local women from all ethnic backgrounds were a common phenomenon. These unions were not viewed favorably by either the Dutch or the Japanese. Therefore, for a long time these narratives have remained outside public discourse. If not for the children born out of these unions, these contested relationships would receive little attention today. In this chapter, I will examine the relations between Japanese men and Dutch women and show how the assessment of fraternization relationships can shed light on the "tensions of Empire" that continue to haunt us until this day.[847] I will argue that the abhorrence people experienced with offspring from fraternizing relations was not primarily about fear of miscegenation, since interracial unions had been part and parcel of the colonial experience. As Damon Salesa aptly summarizes: "... racial crossings were not intrinsically troublesome to colonialism ... [they were seen as] strategies *of* colonialism not challenges *to* it."[848] What was considered problematic in these unions seems more closely linked to the tensions on different axes of the intersections of race, class, and gender and a wide range of adjacent categories in a changing colonial context.[849] The changing power relations in the colonial arena and the changing power relations in families and households were the causes of trouble. These changing power relations need to be closely analyzed when we want to understand what meaning is attributed to the mixed backgrounds of Japanese-Dutch descendants.[850] My research is based on life stories of Dutch and mixed-descent Dutch (*Indisch*) women who fraternized with the Japanese enemy, and the children that resulted from these unions. The data have been collected from two different sources: personal interviews with children of Japanese fathers and a few of their mothers, and material from social reports in the archives of *Stichting Pelita* at the Hague.[851] These reports were part of the procedure to appeal for compensation for war damage incurred during or after World War II.[852]


## Historical Background

The early decades of the twentieth century marked a period of great change in colonial landscapes. Japan's drive for expansion became more and more obvious, eventually resulting in Japan's invasion of Manchuria and China in the 1930s. To support their imperialist aims, the Japanese Imperial Army needed increasing amounts of oil, amongst other resources. They targeted the Dutch East Indies, a strategically important region because of its abundant raw materials. Two Japanese economic missions visited the Dutch East Indies in 1940 to convince the government to grant the Japanese government larger oil supplies. Once the negotiations ran aground, war seemed inevitable. Nonetheless, the Allied forces were taken by surprise when the Japanese Imperial Navy attacked the American Pacific Fleet in Pearl Harbor on December 7, 1941. The Dutch government was the first country to declare war on Japan the day after the assault. Within a month, the Japanese armed forces advanced on the Dutch East Indies, starting their invasion on Kalimantan, Sulawesi, and the Moluccas. The battle for the colonial center of power, Java, started in early February and soon after, on March 9th, the Dutch Commander-in-chief, Lieutenant General Hein ter Poorten, surrendered. And although in some places, like Sumatra, guerilla warfare continued for some time, from that moment on Dutch colonial possessions in the Indonesian archipelago were under Japanese military command. The swift Japanese conquest provided a huge blow to the alleged European superiority of the Dutch colonizers in the Indies. It would profoundly change the existing power balances and the defensibility of Dutch colonial rule. The presumed magic of colonialism had broken and the genie was out of the bottle, even though the long-term consequences of this could not immediately be fully grasped.

Since the Japanese military legitimized their acquisitions on the basis of replacing the Western imperialistic order, one of their first priorities after occupying the Indies was to ban all Dutch influence from society. One of the ways they attempted this was to intern a large part of the Dutch population as POWs or civilian internees. As a result, almost all families were separated and most of the women stayed behind without men, who had traditionally earned the family income. The women who remained outside the internment camps had no other choice then to come up with alternative means to support themselves. The Japanese officials thought that people of Dutch and local mixed descent, called *Indisch*, would sympathize with the Japanese ideal of a Greater East Asia Co-Prosperity Sphere. Therefore, many women and elder men of *Indisch* descent were not interned and remained outside the camps. Being able to move around more freely than those women interned, it was mainly Dutch women with a mixed *Indisch* background that could establish personal contacts with the enemy. However, the Japanese were mistaken in their assumption that the *Indisch* people would identify with the Japanese cause. In the first half of the 20th century, the mixed blood *Indisch* who belonged to the juridical group of Europeans, associated themselves with the Dutch colonial elite who had been ousted by the Japanese. Many of them stressed their Dutch identity and underplayed the Eurasian one. Another reason for the Japanese military not wanting to intern inhabitants of mixed descent was more practical: the enormous logistic operation of interment had its limits. It was simply an impossible task to accommodate the whole European population, which, in 1942, consisted of more than 300,000 people.

## The Status of *Indisch* in Colonial Indonesia

From their outset, colonial encounters led to racial mixing, and over time different terms have been used to describe the phenomenon. In the Dutch East Indies the term used for people of mixed European Indigenous background was *Indisch*, an expression that has many levels of meaning because it was used for different categories of people: for the mixed bloods of European and indigenous descent, for Europeans born in the Indies without indigenous roots, and for Europeans born outside the Indies who considered the Indies their homeland.[853] In *Being Dutch in the Indies* this has been summarized as: "So, broadly speaking, we can say that Indisch refers either to a power relationship or to racial mixture."[854] In this chapter, when referring to *Indisch*, I am talking about people of mixed ancestry.

Like in other colonies, in the history of the Dutch East Indies the position of people of mixed ancestry has been complicated and contested for cultural and socio-economic reasons. The white colonial community and the mixed *Indisch* population simultaneously despised and needed one other, and the dividing lines between the different groups were more porous than clear-cut distinctions suggest.[855] The social construction of "racial purity" turned out to be extremely powerful in widening the yawning gap between purely White and *Indisch*, and from this many ambiguities in daily colonial life arose. And although "Whiteness" without doubt constituted an important marker, the differences in everyday life were not so much primarily based on color but on unstable and fluid intersections of color, gender, social class, education and culture.

Although the colonial government divided the population in three different groups, "Natives" (these days rather replaced by the less pejorative term "Indigenous"), Europeans, and Foreign Orientals, the legal status of members of these categories was not fixed. Switching to another category was possible through a juridical process of equation or marriage. Through "equation" some members of the "Indigenous" category could apply to become a member of the "European" category on the condition that they were both Christian and fluent in written and spoken Dutch. Change of category through marriage was clearly gendered: the legal status of the husband was always leading; a woman belonging to the "Indigenous" category could become "European" when marrying a man from this category. If a Dutch woman decided to marry an Indigenous man—something that happened rarely—she would not be considered European anymore and pass over to the Indigenous category.[856]

The juridical status did not account for the nationality of the inhabitants. Being "Dutch" could either refer to the possession of a Dutch nationality (as was the case for the Dutch members of the "European" category) or refer to being a Dutch subject (as was the case for most members of the legal category "Natives"). Both within the "Native" and the "European" category we find Eurasians, those *Indisch* who are the concern of this chapter. Their belonging to one category or another mainly depended on the official recognition by a European father. The legal, social, economic, and cultural positions of different members of the *Indisch* population were extremely diverse, and those who were part of the upper strata of colonial society definitely considered themselves Dutch. From 1899 onwards, when the *Japannerwet* (Law on the Japanese), was passed, the Japanese inhabitants of the colony were also included in the European category. With this law, which resulted from a trade agreement, every Japanese inhabitant of the Dutch East Indies who possessed a Japanese passport was considered a member of the juridical category of Europeans.[857] This included the Japanese prostitutes who lived and worked in the Indies, which shows how commercial agreements were more important than the moral, cultural standards of what constituted European superiority.[858] The different laws for different categories of inhabitants of the colony suggest an ideology of clear-cut divisions between category of persons, but daily colonial practice was much more complicated. Everyday practices turned out to be very arbitrary and fluid. Following the Japanese occupation, new tensions arose.

### Researching Dutch-Japanese Fraternization

Before we delve deeper into how fraternizing relations were narrated by the women who engaged in these relationships and by their children, we need to address a few methodological issues. Researching fraternization is a challenging endeavor: it is very difficult to get access to sources of primary actors. I did not find primary contemporary sources like diaries or letters in which people describe their personal experience with these wartime unions. Although Japanese soldiers were keen journal keepers, journals from members of the military who served in Indonesia are hardly available.[859] In Dutch diaries and in interviews recorded in the collection of the Foundation for Oral History on Indonesia, one can find occasional comments on relationships that Dutch or *Indisch* women had with Japanese men.[860] But in almost all cases these comments are given *about* fraternizing women and not *by* them, and, as is to be expected, the judgments are often disapproving. The writers and interviewees often allude to the mixed descent and the low moral standards of *Indisch* women.[861] The subtext is that real Dutch women would never betray the nation like *Indisch* women did. Fraternizing was used as further evidence that *Indisch* women could not be trusted, despite their claims to be loyal Dutch citizens. According to many Dutch inhabitants of the Dutch East Indies fraternization was another proof of *Indisch* disloyalty.

Interviewing the primary actors—those men and women whose fraternization resulted in children—turned out to be difficult. After the Japanese defeat most of the men returned to Japan and most of the *Indisch* women decided to gloss over their wartime experience. Especially after their post-war return to the Netherlands, the wartime liaisons were relegated to oblivion. For this research, it is problematic that those who engaged in these unions have been motivated to keep the relationships secret. I interviewed some of the mothers, but they were the minority that had finally decided to speak out. Their stories therefore represent a biased sample— those who choose to tell their story are most likely those who are not ashamed of what they did—and we see that these stories are of women who did not see Japanese men as enemies and who stress the consensual nature of their relationship. Although their experiences were a welcome addition to the negative stories in the interviews in the oral history archive, more diverse testimonies were needed to be able to draw a complete picture.

The stories of the fathers turned out to be even more difficult to access. Not only because of language difficulties, talking about fraternization during a war is never comfortable with soldiers who returned home defeated. Upon their return to Japan, Japanese World War II veterans did not speak of their wartime lovers or the children they had fathered. I spoke at length with two Japanese men who were in Java during the occupation, but did not engage in any relationships with Dutch women. One was a liaison officer at the time. In 1945 he worked in the harbor of Jakarta, Tandjong Priok, and witnessed some of the Dutch women leaving for Japan to follow their lovers.[862] The other man is a veteran. He worked at the Radio Signal Unit for the Imperial Army in Java. Since 1995 he has been very active in doing research and helping to find the fathers and families of the Japanese-Indisch descendants.[863]

My primary material therefore consists of interviews with children born out of these unions. And although the importance of their testimonies is evident, they can only partly judge the relationship between their parents, as they can only consider it from their personal perspective. The interviews with mothers or children are, unfortunately, subject to a selection bias: those mothers and children who wanted to be interviewed represent a "coalition of the willing." Only those who want to tell their stories will be included, and their experiences quite probably were rather different from the experiences of those who do not wish to tell their story.

Eventually I managed to find another source in which relationships between Japanese men and Dutch women were mentioned. The Stichting Pelita archives in the Hague keeps the social reports that were part of the procedure to appeal for compensation as a result of war damage during or after World War II.[864] Of course one has to bear in mind that this data is also biased; these reports have been produced with the very specific goal of telling the life stories of the interviewees in such a way that it becomes evident that they are eligible for compensation. These reports revealed different and additional information: we can find allusions to children who after the war were left behind in Indonesia by their mothers and who not only never came to know their father, but neither their mother. They were either adopted by families or put in orphanages, and some of them repeatedly stated that it was difficult for them to understand the reasons why their mothers engaged with Japanese men. Was it out of coercion, necessity, or love? For almost all Japanese-Indisch descendants, the background of their parents' relationship is very important in making sense of their origin. In some cases, they were able to learn the identity of their biological mother at some point, but then again this often led to feelings of betrayal or of not being acknowledged. This was particularly so in those cases where somebody they had always known as a distant relative or acquaintance turned out to be their biological mother.

In the Stichting Pelita archives, stories of children can be found who recalled their mothers' experiences with Japanese men primarily in the context of rape and force. The bias inherent in an archive of compensation claims stands in contrast to, and acts as complementary data to, the bias found in stories told by those who want to tell their story. The Stichting Pelita sources also revealed another category of stories, namely of half-Japanese children born in internment camps from mothers who were either said to have been raped by a Japanese man inside the camp or of mothers who were already pregnant when they moved to the camp. These stories can also be found in the collection of the Foundation for Oral History on Indonesia, explanations differ from those in the Stichting Pelita archives. In the oral history collection, the women in the camps who gave birth to a half-Japanese child were often considered prostitutes. In the Stichting Pelita reports, these women were more often presented as victims of sexual aggression.

The fraternizing relationships took place in a changing social and political context and this remains one of the challenges in evaluating them. The relations were measured and evaluated differently at different times (during or after the war), and in different locations (in colonial Indonesia or in the Netherlands). The decision to start a relationship with a Japanese man could meet with antagonism of family and friends during the occupation, but such antagonism was often unexpressed because of the possible advantages in having positive relationships with the occupiers. As long as the war lasted and the outcome remained unclear, Japanese-Indisch unions were mainly judged on the basis of how useful they could be for the Dutch community. As soon as the Japanese army was defeated, a moral evaluation returned to the foreground again.

### Japanese-Dutch Intimate Relations
Let us now turn to fraternizing relations between Japanese men and Dutch women in more detail. On the basis of two of the interviews

I conducted with mothers, I here present two short vignettes. They are only two examples of the very diverse and multifarious histories behind fraternization:

Soon after the war started Luisa's father died and a very difficult period started for her mother and sisters who now had to earn the family income. Recalling how she first met Takashi, the Japanese man who would become the father of her eldest daughter, Luisa's look softened. "We both were single and felt sympathy for each other from the start. I saw him at the military rest and relaxation centre for Japanese military in Surabaya. I had found a job as a cashier there. He used to be a schoolteacher in Japan and now he worked at a storehouse in Surabaya. At work all intimate contact with the Japanese soldiers was strictly forbidden, therefore we only met outside. Since I had worked at a Japanese company before the war, I was used to working for Japanese people and I did not feel any animosity. I was simply in love and did not think about the future and did not discuss that with Takashi either. At our last meeting Takashi gave me a picture of his mother and brother. I was still very much in love with him but I did not think of following him to Japan, we split up without making promises or plans." Glancing at her daughter Luisa says, "I have always been so happy with her, she is my souvenir from that period.[865]

Anna was still a child of only 14 years old when the war started. "My two elder sisters were both engaged in relations with Japanese men. The eldest dated a pilot and she even went to Japan after the war for a few years. But life in Japan proved too difficult for her. Afterwards her sister came back and got engaged to a Dutch man, I raised her half-Japanese child. Because of my sisters' contacts Japanese men visited us now and then at our house. I first met my Japanese partner, who was ten years my senior, when I was very young. Our intimate relationship began when I started working in a restaurant. I was around 16 years then. I was puzzled and in retrospect I did not know what was happening to me. The first time was a pure case of rape. And even though I hated him our contact continued, especially once I got pregnant. You get used to each other and I really have to say that he took good care of me, especially when I was pregnant. When the war was over and shortly before he left he even provided me with money and goods for the baby. He also apologized for what he had done to me. Only in hindsight I realized that this was a very immature love, I was so young, what did I know about intimacy? Afterwards I often have asked myself why I had not offered resistance at the time. One of the reasons was the material advantages this relationship offered in the very difficult wartime.[866]

Although very different, these two short vignettes reveal one basic and maybe general condition that encouraged fraternizing relations. A lot of *Indisch* women lived outside the Japanese internment camps, and with fathers and husbands gone, they had to provide the income for their families. They were forced to find jobs outside of the conventional opportunities and jobs that they might have filled prior to the occupation. It was under these circumstances that they came in contact with other men, including Japanese soldiers. It has to be stressed that only a few of these women, like Luisa in the first vignette, had always been open about their wartime relationship. Of course not only relations with Japanese men occurred. During the war period Dutch women also had relationships with Chinese and Indonesian men, and right after the end of the war unions with British Indian soldiers from the British army.[867] However, these unions were much less contested, primarily because of the different statuses involved. For the moral assessment it made a huge difference whether your lover was considered an enemy, a non-enemy, or even a liberator.[868]

Because of the taboo surrounding them, fraternizing relations with Japanese soldiers were kept discrete both during and after the liaisons. Under the Japanese occupation, the majority of relations took place outside the public domain, because neither Japanese officials nor the Dutch community favored these unions. Soon after the war it became clear that as a result of the Japanese occupation in the Dutch East Indies, the existing gender and race balances had been severely challenged. The global phenomenon of (mostly only temporary) change in gender roles was due to war related necessities, leading to women entering the labor force or military service.[869] In the Indies, the temporary change was mainly the result of the gender-segregated internment of the European population, which had led to a forced separation of couples and families. If we look more closely at fraternizing women we see that they were judged by their contemporaries as having transgressed several moral colonial boundaries: firstly they had challenged the unwritten rule that only white men were allowed to choose non-white women as their companions, the opposite was highly condemned; secondly, they had neglected to maintain the ideal of European superiority; thirdly, they had betrayed both "their" men and the nation. Since under the Japanese occupation most European men were absent and out of sight, they had not been able to protect women against the Japanese invaders. The resentment that many men felt after the war was played off against fraternizing women on a personal and national level.

Changes in the assumed social balances turned out to be more radical for the colonial order. The demand for more political influence that Indonesian nationalists already had started in the 1920s had become a full fight for independence. Only two days after the Japanese surrender, Indonesian leaders Soekarno and Hatta declared Indonesian independence. The Dutch government tried to fight this for a few years, but to no avail. In December 1949, they finally had to hand over power to Indonesians. The years between 1945 and 1949 saw a fierce colonial war instead of the long-awaited peace after the Japanese occupation. As a result of this new fight, the ranks in the European community closed and women who had fraternized with the Japanese in the Indies were not publicly punished as harshly as women in the Netherlands who had fraternized with German soldiers.[870]

The small group of women who decided to follow their lovers to Japan right after the war, made the wartime unions visible in official Dutch bureaucratic papers for the first time.[871] These files form a bureaucratic trail from which we now can clearly read the disdain of civil servants. In these archives we can see that these liaisons were not only rejected by Dutch officials, they were considered a serious affront against the moral order and against the nation. The dominant social position of Dutch men had been contested and severely weakened during the Japanese occupation and now they felt it was their time to restore this dominance and to chastise the women who had underscored their humiliation. This was deemed especially necessary because the Japanese defeat had not brought the long awaited peace and a restoration of the colonial order.

### Legacies of Japanese-Dutch Unions

Post-war Indonesia saw fundamental social and political change.

After the Japanese occupation and the subsequent fierce fighting between the Dutch colonials and the Indonesian nationalists, many of the Dutch inhabitants of the Dutch East Indies returned to the Netherlands. Their numbers included people of mixed descent who had never before set foot on Dutch soil. The Dutch East Indies was their birthplace and the land where they felt they belonged; now they were leaving that home for a new and unknown country. Many of the mothers who decided to keep their half-Japanese children also returned to the Netherlands at some point. Within the *Indisch* community in the Netherlands, the Japanese occupation was considered a very dark period responsible for the complete loss of the colony. Therefore most members of the *Indisch* community felt, and continue to feel, strong resentment against anything Japanese. This was one of the reasons that *Indisch* women in the Netherlands glossed over their wartime unions and that even many children were unaware of their Japanese fathers for a long time.

The background of most Japanese-Indisch children was kept secret, even for the children themselves, because they were considered illegitimate in a national and moral sense.[872] As a result these children often had to put together the information of their background on the basis of hearsay. Fairly common in memories of half-Japanese children is the idea of a general and all-encompassing feeling of exclusion and non-belonging and a feeling of vicarious shame for what many *Indisch* inhabitants had experienced under Japanese occupation. The negative attitude of the *Indisch* community in the Netherlands towards anything Japanese was and remains an important problematic factor for children of Japanese fathers.

Nonetheless, after decades of prolonged silence in both national and family narratives, some of the children born out of these unions succeeded in getting their parents' war experiences into the public discourse both in Japan and in the Netherlands. In the late 1980s, they first started talking in public about this part of their mothers' war experience in colonial Indonesia and soon thereafter they went on a search for their fathers. The nickname "children of the enemy" is now used with pride and the Japanese-Indisch descendants have organized themselves in support groups whose main goal was to find their Japanese fathers. Their stories can make the trans-generational effects of the war very clear. Even though Japanese-Indisch descendants do not have many memories of the Japanese occupation, their existence up to the present day is strongly influenced by the conflict.

One of the recurring themes in interviews with mothers and children is that some of the fraternizing relationships originated from genuine love relations. In that respect the stories of Japanese-Dutch unions can shed a more nuanced light on the slanted image of all Japanese men as sexually aggressive, brutal villains. Despite the unbalanced power relationships created by the Japanese occupation, many of these relationships developed in a fashion similar to the development of relationships in other contexts, with the power relationship being secondary to the development of real affection. If we take into account memoirs from Japanese soldiers, we can see that a lot of Japanese soldiers were conscripted and that they had to leave behind their families, friends, and work to embark on a journey to an unknown land. It was only natural that when far away from home they tried to look for affection and a homely environment.

## Conclusion

In this chapter, I argued that the reason that children born out of, mostly illegitimate, unions between Japanese men and Dutch women under Japanese occupation met so much resistance was not primarily their mixed background. By putting emphasis on the context and historicizing the phenomenon under which they came into being I showed how judgments of Japanese-Dutch children were influenced by discourses blurred by a range of discrepancies, uncertainties, and myths.

Like the fraternizing unions that at the time took place outside the public eye, the true background of the children of these unions remained hidden for decades. Even today it remains difficult to sketch a clear picture of these unions, because the limited range of (contemporary) sources. However, the data that are available clearly show how changing gender, race, and class discourses shaped the boundaries of approval and disapproval of fraternizing relations between Japanese men and Indisch women. In a previous publication, I analyzed ways in which these discourses affected the descendants of these relationships.[873] In postcolonial Netherlands the children born out of these unions, during their lives, have found themselves at the intersection of competing identities with Dutch, Japanese and Indisch components. Discourses about Japanese-Dutch fraternization took place and were silenced on several levels (in the private sphere, in the Indisch community, and in Dutch society at large) and at different times (during and after the war). Since a lot of these discourses were fragmented, it remains difficult to make a coherent analysis of this phenomenon. Trying to take into account all the influencing factors is a challenging project. I have focused on differences and tensions along the axes of race, class, and gender. These factors cannot be judged in isolation, but their effect has to be analyzed in connection to each other.

Fraternizing women trespassed colonial mores in engaging with the Japanese enemy. Because they did not adhere to what was considered proper female behavior, they embodied one of the tensions of empire. Whether they did so from their own will or under pressure remains difficult to assess in hindsight, but their actions made clear how white prestige had been undermined under the Japanese occupation. Most of them chose to remain silent about their wartime relations. Their wartime unions were seen as a clear sign of their alleged low morals and a lack of loyalty to the Dutch colonial cause. In a way, this was what many Dutch expected of *Indisch* women who, because of their "mixed racial origin," were despised.

In trying to disentangle the different aspects that played a role in the assessment of these fraternizing relations, we find that a range of factors influenced the judgments. They include, first, the contested nature of *Indisch* identity in the colonial and post-colonial context of the Dutch East Indies and later in the Netherlands. Secondly, the humiliation that especially Dutch men had felt first by being overrun by the despised Japanese army and then as a result of losing their colonial power altogether. These factors relate to changing geopolitical power relations and to changing power relations in families.

## CHAPTER FOURTEEN

## "ENEMIES IN MINIATURE": THE MIXED-RACE CHILDREN FROM THE ALLIED OCCUPATION OF JAPAN[933]

WALTER HAMILTON

Following the capitulation of Imperial Japan in 1945, and as the American-led military Occupation got underway, newspapers, radio broadcasts, posters, and leaflets urged the population to remain calm. In particular, Japanese women, these voices of authority proclaimed, should "maintain dignity."[934] Many feared the worst. A member of the local assembly in Kanagawa Prefecture (a major base for Occupation troops) predicted that "by this time next year we can imagine the thousands of girls selling themselves in places like Yokohama Park, holding celluloid, doll-like children in their arms."[935] In the general election of April 1946, a female candidate campaigned on the slogan "We don't want any blue-eyed babies in Japan."[936]

Anticipating trouble, an American missionary approached Col. Crawford Sams, chief of the Public Health and Welfare Section of SCAP in Tokyo, seeking his permission to establish a special home for unwanted mixed-race children.[937] Sams refused. "The worst thing that can be done is to call a child a GI baby or stigmatize him in any way ... There've been Eurasians in Japan for many years. They've all been absorbed very well by the population."[938] What the colonel conveniently overlooked was that most Eurasians in pre-war Japan were, or could be presumed to be, the children of white engineers, doctors, and other professionals—and were not likely to be equated with the offspring of white or black servicemen. As one Japanese commentator put it, the mixed-race citizens of former days were "romantic ... elegant ... fragrant," whereas, metaphorically speaking, the *konketsuji* of the Occupation gave off a dirty smell.[939]

Because Japanese women were ineligible to enter the United States, the American military initially refused GIs permission to marry Japanese women, rendering the children "illegitimate" and subject to a policy that required them to stay in Japan.[940] It was the perfect catch-22, in which racial exclusion (through the Immigration Act of 1924) justified mandatory racial inclusion (the "absorbed very well" dictate of SCAP). This situation evoked little public comment because of strict press censorship in force during the first four years of the Occupation.[941] The topics most often targeted by American military censors were sexual fraternization and miscegenation.[942] Prejudice and fear rushed in to fill the information vacuum.

Japanese men resented how easily females seemed to pass into the post-war milieu, from which they felt excluded. The former enemy was beating them again—this time in manners, dress, spending power, and sex appeal. It was bad enough that women fraternized shamelessly, but their sexual congress with foreigners also threatened the nation's racial integrity. The writer Jun Takami approvingly recorded the observation of a friend: "Regarding these ugly Japanese women, it's not ignorance, but something in their blood. Whatever you say, Japanese are originally a cross-bred race, and the cross-breed seeks out contact with foreigners."[943] Bitterness welled up. Japanese women, it was said, "soaked in the swimming pools of Americanism" or were "sunk into the mud" of Occupation-swamped Japan.[944] One commentator jokingly suggested that they seemed to acquire plumper, shapelier bodies from inter-racial contact: "Is this the result of blood exchange with 'tall men in small cars'?"[945]

In the eyes of society, konketsuji were the end product of a transformative process that began simply by showing a preference for something non-Japanese. The most obvious agents of this betrayal were the flamboyant panpan streetwalkers, or "women of the wall," as they were sometimes called.[946] The mother of a konketsuji, writing in a popular magazine at the end of the Occupation, protested against the silent malediction attaching to all women in her situation:

> People in society treat mothers of konketsuji the same as panpan. But most mothers of konketsuji I know are good-natured, and were inexperienced in the ways of the world. People never try to understand the misery of girls who produced babies, dreaming of official marriage in the future, while being abandoned by their families and despised by society.[947]

Right-wing commentators implicated the panpan in Japan's loss of sovereignty and the poisoning of the nation's moral traditions.[948] They were "weeds and toxic grass ... taking advantage of the authority of Occupation soldiers who reign over the citizenry."[949] Left-wing commentators, though more inclined to see the women as victims, linked them to the unwanted foreign military presence. Socialist opponents of conservative Prime Minister Shigeru Yoshida mockingly referred to his *"panpan"* government.[950]

In the absence of an official response to the situation, private charitable organizations stepped into the breach. An order of Roman Catholic nuns, the Franciscan Missionaries of Mary, established Our Lady of Lourdes Baby Home (*Seibo Aiji-en*) in Yokohama in 1947. By June the following year they were looking after 130 *konketsuji*.[951] Around the same time, Miki Sawada, a granddaughter of the founder of the Mitsubishi *zaibatsu*, began receiving children at the Elizabeth Saunders Home at Ōiso, also in Kanagawa Prefecture.

Among Sawada's first intake was the son of an Australian soldier. The mother had been working as a dancer when they met; the man disappeared after she became pregnant. She persevered for a year trying to raise the baby by herself before making the journey to Ōiso.[952] Sawada did not just wait for mothers to surrender their children—she actively encouraged them to. In 1952, a war widow wrote to her from Osaka explaining how she had been persuaded by a friend to spend an afternoon with a "young and handsome" Australian. She saw him off at the station, without learning his name, only to discover later that she was pregnant. Her parents stuck by her, making it possible for her to take care of the child; but now the boy was approaching school age, she wondered what to do:

> I am working now ... and my mother is looking after the boy ... I want to tell about that time, about the child who was produced in three hours. I really wish my child could see his father. Looking at his eyes and at his skin colour, and when people admire his beautiful face, I always think about his Australian father ...

Sawada traveled to Osaka and urged her to give him up: "She and her mother talked it over. Even though they knew it was for the best, emotion prevented them from releasing the child ... I went home empty-handed."[953]

Not everyone appreciated the work of the Elizabeth Saunders Home. Hostile graffiti were carved in the gate soon after it opened, and a prominent American missionary in Japan, the Reverend

Charles Iglehart, accused Sawada of engaging in "an experiment in genetic development."[954] It took a well-publicized visit by Emperor Hirohito to put the enterprise beyond reproach. The Home's operating expenses were covered by public welfare subsidies and private donations. The U.S.-based Christian Children's Fund was an important conduit of money and adoption requests. In March 1952, Sawada was caring for 118 konketsuji. Nearly one in three was Black, about twice the proportion of African-American troops taking part in the Occupation.[955]

Adoptions proceeded slowly at first, as was the case for other institutions.[956] These became easier to arrange after the United States relaxed its immigration rules for foreign orphans in 1953, and then removed all quotas four years later. Although Sawada sometimes expressed doubts about sending the children to adoptive families abroad, celebrity friends—including the performer Josephine Baker and writer-philanthropist Pearl Buck—were invited to take children.[957] Of the 500-600 konketsuji given shelter at the Home by 1960, around two-thirds eventually went overseas for adoption.[958]

Miki Sawada was a big personality and a major influence on Japanese understanding of the konketsuji issue. She retailed anecdotes suggesting an epidemic of abandonment: bodies dumped in rivers and drains.[959] In promoting her cause, she fostered a distinction between victimized women of the early Occupation (returnees from China, girls without families, and destitute war widows) who took up with foreign soldiers out of desperation and foolish younger women of the later period who fancied they could make themselves "American" by going with a GI.[960]

Sawada regarded the konketsuji as a race apart, with a limited future in Japan.[961] Although her Christian concept of cleansing Original Sin was not part of mainstream Japanese culture, the emphasis she put on parentage certainly was:

> The only way by which the terrible stigma on these unfortunate children who must shoulder the fearful guilt of their parents can be washed off is not by training them to become merely clever, but by training them to become men of worth—gentlemanlike and ladylike. I was thus brought up, and so my desire is to train them in the same manner.[962]

Notwithstanding Sawada's insistence on the "guilt" of the

parents, according to information obtained from the Elizabeth Saunders Home and other institutions, two-thirds of the mothers had been through some form of marriage ceremony and surrendered their children because of financial hardship, family opposition, or desertion by the fathers. Only 10 percent could be identified as prostitutes.[963]

Sawada insisted that public hostility towards the *konketsuji* was based on moral disapproval, not color prejudice.[964] Yet her own contributions to race and class folklore embraced both morality and heredity: black girls were "more highly sexed" than white girls;[965] "many" world criminals were of mixed race;[966] backward children were good at painting because "the worse the brain, the more they use beautiful colors"; and, quoting an anonymous policeman, "the prostitute produces prostitute blood down two generations."[967] While others attributed low IQ test scores among children at the Home to the effects of institutionalization, Sawada blamed the parents: "retarded" *panpan* and "illiterate" soldiers, she called them.[968]

A strongly built woman, Sawada was not loath to give an unruly child a hard slap across the face, followed by a perfumed hug. Potential runaways could find themselves tied up to a post by the ankle.[969] Some children felt she played favorites and feared, more than anything else, not gaining her affection.[970] During a speaking tour of the United States, she exploited well-established notions of mixed-blood misery to boost her fund-raising campaign for the building of special schools inside the home.[971] Though it was always her intention to keep her charges separated from Japanese society, she justified her stance with exaggerated claims about local public schools spurning the children.[972] Friend and biographer Elizabeth Hemphill muddies the waters when she refers to critics who misguidedly "believed in the melting pot mythology."[973] Disagreements went deeper than that. One of Sawada's early backers, the Episcopal Church in America, suspended funding in 1953 in opposition to her isolation policy, accusing her of being autocratic and unprofessional.[974] An Australian missionary with first-hand experience of her methods labeled her "an unprincipled schemer."[975] It is undeniable, however, that she got things done, while others dithered, and innocent lives would have been lost without her efforts.[976]

In April 1952, a week before the Peace Treaty came into effect, the president of the YWCA in Japan, Tamaki Uemura, addressed an open letter to the wife of General Matthew Ridgway (who had replaced General Douglas MacArthur as Supreme Commander for the Allied Powers) on the exploitation of Japanese women by American servicemen:

> These girls are quickly seduced and eventually become prostitutes ... [They] have reportedly mothered 200,000 illegitimate children,[977] and deserted many of them during the past six and one-half years. These mothers were of low education, but I doubt if the fathers deserve the name of gentlemen or were very faithful to Anglo-Saxon morality.[978]

The well-connected Uemura was among the first Japanese allowed to visit the United States after the war, and her letter received wide publicity. She lent credence to fears of a massive *konketsuji* legacy and, by portraying all the mothers as "fallen women," framed the issue solely in terms of moral collapse following the war defeat.[979]

Provoked into action, the Welfare Ministry now made the first serious attempt to discover exactly how many *konketsuji* there really were.[980] Officials distributed a questionnaire to registered obstetricians and midwives and were shocked to come up with a tally of just 5,013.[981] A field survey to determine how many of the children remained in Japan identified 3,490 living with mothers or guardians, plus another 482 in institutional care.[982] Although, by this time, following the relaxation of U.S. immigration restrictions, more than two thousand mixed-race children had left Japan with their parents, and a small number had been adopted abroad, to most informed observers the official estimate still seemed too low.[983] They recognized that many mothers, especially those determined to keep their children, would try to avoid the prying eyes of officialdom. A more credible estimate of ten thousand *konketsuji*, including those who had already departed the country, was put forward.[984] It was also assumed many times this number had died from natural causes, neglect, infanticide, or abortion.[985]

To come up with a policy response, the Japanese government formed the "Mixed-Blood Children's Welfare Committee." Its twenty members included the social critics Kiyoshi Kanzaki and Sōichi Ōya, Miki Sawada, and specialists in psychology, sociology, paediatrics, education, child physiology, and eugenics. The convenor was Yoshio Koya, the head of the National Institute of Public Hygiene (*Kōshū Eisei*), whose eugenic views on *konketsuji* had been influential during the war.[986]

Koya insisted on looking beyond "sentimental" concerns about child protection to the consequences of race mixing per se. Eurasians and other mixed-race minorities, he warned, always formed a "foreign stratum" in society, prone to exploitation by "communists or nationalists." This made the sociological dimension of the problem even more serious than the biological one, though he anticipated some "disharmony of genes" in the konketsuji population. Either way, the problem should not to be taken lightly, since "the stamp" (kokuin) of the fathers would last for generations: "It will not be easy to get rid of black peoples' characteristic shape of nose, lips, and curly hair."[987] Paradoxically, he also celebrated the power of the blood of a defeated race to "take revenge on the armed conqueror" by eventually obliterating his genetic footprint.[988] Koya was just as equivocal about whether the konketsuji should be segregated into special schools, since "the final objective should be harmony with Japanese forever."[989]

The key point—whether to integrate the children into society or separate them with a view to their final adoption abroad—was never resolved. Although the Education Ministry wanted all konketsuji who were registered as Japanese to attend ordinary public schools, both the Elizabeth Saunders Home and another facility, Keimei Gakuen in Hakone, were allowed to establish special schools,[990] and the Welfare Ministry began subsidizing inter-country adoptions in 1960.[991]

In keeping with standard practice for all Japanese children taken into care, the konketsuji placed in institutions were physically and psychological assessed.[992] They aroused more-than-usual curiosity because, until then, scientists had not had the opportunity to study such "hybrids" in significant numbers.[993] The testing regimes represented a significant invasion of the subjects' lives. Teeth casts were made twice a year for a study of "human variability and evolution." Other researchers, looking for signs of deviation from the Japanese norm, took X-rays and body measurements, tested emotional and sensory responses, analyzed artistic expression and patterns of play, and undertook post-mortem examinations.[994]

Some media reports distorted the research findings. A skin color analysis of black konketsuji was said to have found them to be "strongly black," when the actual study described them as falling "between Japanese and Negroes" in pigmentation. To another finding, that mixed-race children were "more emotional and strong-willed" than other Japanese children, a reporter appended the conclusion: "This may lead to anti-social behaviour."[995] The same newspaper used the expression "mentally impaired" (seishin *hakujaku*) to describe *konketsuji* (mainly children in the Elizabeth Saunders Home) who fell below "normal" in their IQ test scores—a phrase that does not seem to have been used by the researchers.[996] It became commonly accepted that "many" mixed-bloods were "sort of idiotic."[997]

It was not merely a case, however, of misreporting. Researchers contributed to the public's misunderstanding by careless handling of data and ambiguous or unscientific commentary.[998] The chief fault lay in attempting to categorize the *konketsuji* through test results obtained exclusively from those living in institutions. The well-known tendency of institutionalized children to lag behind in psychological and social development was insufficiently acknowledged. Differences between "pure Japanese" and mixed-bloods in early age groups were emphasized, even though other data suggested that, by the age of four or five, *konketsuji* were statistically indistinguishable from other institutionalized Japanese children. Given the sampling methods used, the search for an answer to the question of whether the mixed-bloods' IQ and sociability test scores were determined by nature or nurture yielded no defensible results. Ultimately most serious researchers were inclined to give greater weight to the unusual social and environmental factors involved (which included children being permanently harmed by failed abortion attempts and early post-natal neglect), but their conclusions came too late and too timidly.[999] A leading newspaper quoted one medical academic as saying "the inundation of future *konketsuji* could be more significant for Japan's racial history than the atomic bomb." Professor Fumio Kida was adamant that Japanese did not want the children and expressed satisfaction that a liberalized abortion law would help contain their number.[1000]

Belated and equivocal official responses to the *konketsuji* issue reflected contradictions bedevilling early post-war Japanese society more generally. The writings of Sōichi Ōya, a well-known commentator and member of the government's expert panel, illustrate how competing impulses clouded the public debate. Ōya could be broad-minded: "It is pointless appealing to the 'purity of racial blood' just like the Nazis. ...There is no 'Japanese race,' only a 'Japanese ethnic group.' If Anglo-Saxons or Negroes have been added recently, what's the problem?" He could also be bigoted. An article published under his name referred to black *konketsuji* as "miniature King Kongs" and confined the employment prospects of mixed-race children to sport and entertainment: "We should not expect a lot to become academics or succeed in endeavours requiring brain power."[1001]

Kiyoshi Kanzaki was equally ambivalent. He wanted society to overcome racial discrimination and give the children a happy life, outside institutions: "That way Japan can truly be a great and tolerant world citizen." But Kanzaki always saw the issue through the filter of his disdain for the American military and their camp followers, who give birth to *konketsuji* "like methane gas." Teachers with mixed-bloods in their classes, as he saw it, faced a conflict between promoting humanitarian values and fostering a spirit of national independence—as if, by treating all children the same, they risked sending an unwholesome message.[1002]

The issue became more vexed as the Occupation gave way to an on-going American military presence. In December 1953, the welfare scholar and Socialist Diet-member Katsuo Takenaka described a nation gripped by fear:

> People see their homeland turning into something like a colony and sense a *panpan*-like change appearing among female Japanese nationals. Blood purity is becoming cloudy... gentle and strong Japanese women are giving birth to black and white children. I wonder if we are not witnessing the pollution of Japan's heritage and race, leading to their eventual ruin.[1003]

One image more than any other dramatized the national anxiety about lost cultural and political sovereignty: the black Japanese. People did not know whether to laugh or cry over anecdotes about black mixed-bloods trying to scrub the color from their bodies and mothers secretly swapping them for other children at bathhouses. It was widely assumed that sexual encounters involving black soldiers were violent, perverted, or strictly commercial, and that black offspring alienated the affections of their unfortunate mothers.

Every mixed-race child learned to expect taunts of *ainoko* (half-caste, mongrel) or *harō no ko* (child of "hello"), but the mixed-black child also heard cries of *kurombo* (nigger) or *dojin* (earth person, aborigine) in the street or playground. Media commentators based predictions of the children's future behavior on skin color: those who were white would become bossy due to feelings of superiority; those who were black would become destructive because of society's hostility or, some even suggested, their "savage" ancestry.[1004] A preoccupation with externals blinded observers to the inner life of the children: the anguish at witnessing a mother's mistreatment; the guilt at being the cause of a family dispute; or, for those sent abroad for adoption, the sadness of giving up friends and familiar surroundings. The son of a black *konketsuji* has expressed this well: "My mother loved Japan, but Japan did not love my mother."[1005] They were never—as typically imagined and depicted[1006]—intrinsically separate from society. Regarding themselves as Japanese, they were constantly forgetting and being reminded of their other perceived identity. "Only when I saw my reflection in a mirror or in a train window at night," said one young woman, "I knew I was different."[1007]

Following the Education Ministry's decision to integrate all *konketsuji* registered as Japanese within the regular schooling system, it became doubly important that the names of children without natural fathers supporting them be entered into a *koseki* (household register).[1008] Many *konketsuji* were unregistered; in the eyes of the law, they were stateless. Only when a *koseki* registration was completed (leaving the column for the father's name blank) did a child obtain Japanese nationality. Mothers who still hoped for their partners to return held back from declaring their child officially illegitimate, since *koseki* records at the time were semi-public documents that could damage a person's prospects when entering senior high school, applying for a job, or seeking a marriage partner.

A way around the dilemma was to register the child as the son or daughter of a married family member (another reason that official counts understated *konketsuji* numbers). Recognizing that some mothers lacked the necessary family support, the mixed-race author Imao Hirano publicized his willingness to become a nominal "father" to anyone in need. By 1965, he had reportedly lent his name to sixteen children.[1009]

As the 1953 school year got underway, some voices in the mainstream press sought to calm public fears. The *Mainichi* newspaper wrote wistfully about *konketsuji* turning up with "blue eyes and black faces shining."[1010] The *Yomiuri* described them "already running around the playground hand-in-hand with other good children."[1011] Many doubted, however, whether the children's innocence could cure society of its disdain; the *konketsuji* were too easily drawn into the nation's struggle to throw off feelings of shame and bitterness.[1012] The *Tokyo Nichi-Nichi*, for instance, chose this moment to serialize a lurid account of the corrupting effects of the Occupation.[1013] Yokosuka was so far gone, it said, mixed-blood children were "not even an issue" there.[1014] The "issue" would not be allowed to rest.

302  The following year, when Our Lady of Lourdes Baby Home

applied to build a new Boys' Town for thirty-nine *konketsuji* (mainly the offspring of African-American fathers) in Yamato City, near the U.S. Navy air base at Atsugi, the local primary school refused to accept them, forcing the institution to purchase a bus and take them to and from Yokohama for their schooling, a two-hour round trip. Three years later, the school agreed to admit a few of the children, on a trial basis, until parents complained that they were a disruptive influence. Another three years passed. The Boys' Town applied again, and the school board offered to make a special class for the *konketsuji* (as a school typically would for handicapped children). Only after the teachers insisted on spreading the children among their regular classes was the barrier finally breached—in 1960. A female teacher recorded the following episode in her class diary:

> When I was tidying up a shelf, a child called me, "*Sensei*" [Teacher or Miss] in a fawn-like voice. I pretended to pay no attention. Then the child called me in a low voice, "*Okā-san, Okā-san*" [Mother, Mother]. I wondered if this was because the child had heard the word "*Okā-san*" in conversation with classmates and wanted to experience using it once.[1015]

The novelist Yaeko Nogami addressed an open letter to Pearl Buck in May 1952:

> We cannot imagine without shivering the possible friction or hostility these black children will cause in primary schools and the bad influence this will have on them. However, in your country [the United States] where there are more than ten million splendid black citizens—among them, world-class singers, boxers, and academics—black children such as these would not be unusual. Surely they would blend naturally, like a flock of small black birds under cover of night.[1016]

Nogami's appeal reduced the issue to one common denominator: the children's physical differences. She did not recognize the true complexity of their lives as Japanese, which can be gleaned from various first-hand sources: interviews, memoirs, and contemporary surveys.[1017] These reveal that most mothers of *konketsuji* (Black or White) were not engaged in formal prostitution;[1018] many black mixed-bloods were lovingly raised by their mothers or other family members;[1019] women frequently described their black partners as kinder, more attractive, and more generous than white soldiers;[1020] Japanese neighborhood children mixed with *konketsuji* of all complexions;[1021] and, while black infants suffered a higher rate of abandonment, their fathers were no less likely than white soldiers to acknowledge them.[1022]

Not all Japanese wanted to ship the black *konketsuji* off to the United States. Some thought Japan's own racial humiliation in the war provided an incentive to combat prejudice against the children.[1023] The novelist Taiko Hirabayashi commented: "We don't need to copy the heartlessness of their fathers. Raising these mixed-blood children is a task for the Japanese."[1024] Others argued that black *konketsuji* would be better off remaining in Japan because Americans were greater racists.[1025] (The same was said of Australians, in respect of white *konketsuji*.) The critic Fumiko Matsuda felt it was not a question of tolerance, but duty, to look after every child born in Japan to a Japanese mother: "We need to have the attitude not to make any unhappy Japanese."[1026]

Such opinions often reflected a desire for a more mature national life, free of "feudal" attitudes, and capable of withstanding international scrutiny.[1027] They could also serve, however, to celebrate a one-dimensional, Japanese ethnic identity. "Let them gorge on *natto* [fermented soybeans] or *misoshiru* [soybean-paste soup]," wrote the war veteran and editor Keiichi Aoki.

> Let them play *takoage* [kite flying] or *hanetsuki* [Japanese badminton]. Let them get together and go to *kamishibai* [card picture-shows] or candy shops. All we have to do is raise them as members of the same racial family. This … will show that Japanese are a superb race capable of governing a first-class, law-abiding nation.[1028]

With his checklist of peculiarly Japanese food and amusements, Aoki clearly was not appealing to the values of diversity and universality.

Formal studies into the best way of handling the mixed-race children continued for years. Changes of approach over time were reflected in an annual series of "*konketsuji* guides" issued by the Education Ministry, which brought together case histories contributed by teachers, research papers, and essays.

Once the children began attending school, the influence of a generally sympathetic teaching profession took effect.[1029] Non-discrimination became the watchword, and narratives that emphasized *konketsuji* differences or treated them as a separate minority were discouraged. Inferior IQ test scores were put down to institutionalization and social maladjustment was attributed to "personality" rather than breeding. Emphasis shifted away from guiding the children and towards guiding society to a more enlightened view.[1030]

Within a few years, the professional approach swung back again. *Konketsuji* were said to require "scientific" guidance, because fault-lines of apprehensiveness and "mental instability" could lie beneath the surface of even seemingly well-adjusted individuals.[1031] A developmental psychologist at Hiroshima University, Mitsuya Yamauchi, applying theories pioneered by the American social psychologist Kurt Lewin, found that the mixed-race children exhibited typical minority-group behaviour.[1032] This was due to the discrimination they experienced, resulting from their different physical appearance, dysfunctional families, low socio-economic status, and social isolation. They were noticeably "clingy" towards their teachers, he said, because they were using them to "restore their privileges" when excluded from the majority group. Yamauchi believed *konketsuji* needed to be provided an objective understanding of why they were members of a minority, instead of trying to ignore the fact.[1033]

Researchers attempting statistical analysis of *konketsuji* under care recognized that their sample groups were becoming increasingly unrepresentative.[1034] By 1958, the winnowing effect of adoption had pushed up the proportion of black children in care to 30 percent, and boys outnumbered girls two to one.[1035] Other research on children living in the community (in Kure and Yokohama) showed a strong correlation between IQ test scores and the level of family support, offering scientific evidence—if any were needed—that capable mothers could raise smart *konketsuji*.[1036]

On many basic points, however, the experts disagreed. Some said better dress standards and grooming would make *konketsuji* less prone to playground bullying; others insisted that personality traits, not untidy clothes or poverty, made them unpopular. Some believed those raised in bilingual households suffered a disadvantage; others played down the significance of having to adjust between Japanese and Western cultural norms. Fundamental was the divide between those teachers, welfare workers, and psychologists who remained convinced *konketsuji* could be understood only on a case-by-case basis—focusing exclusively on individual circumstances—and other professionals who believed the children's proper adjustment within society depended on their attaining an understanding of why they met discrimination and being able to identify with others in the same minority.[1037]

In October 1952, in response to "inflammatory" press coverage, American expatriate business, church, and veterans' groups formed the "American Joint Committee for Assisting Japanese-American Orphans."[1038] The U.S. Embassy lent support and the American Chamber of Commerce in Tokyo provided the committee with office space.[1039] It began slowly, gathering information, counseling mothers, and distributing a small amount of financial aid. It took a direct hand in arranging only nineteen adoptions prior to April 1954—a tiny proportion of the several hundred placements with American families by then.[1040] (By December 1952, the 2,585 children of more than 11,000 interracial marriages had also received passports to travel to the United States.)[1041] In a separate initiative, one hundred American servicemen were given free passage back to Japan to take responsibility for their offspring,[1042] while American military units also donated substantial sums to orphanages.[1043]

Although *yōshi engumi* (adoption of an heir) was familiar to Japanese as a means of securing the family line, in the absence of a natural son, there was no tradition of philanthropic adoption (which is also a comparatively modern phenomenon in the West).[1044] The cultural aversion to adopting a child of obscure parentage found expression in the proverb *"Doko no uma no hone ka wakaranai"* ("One does not know from which horse the bone has come").[1045] As one scholar has noted, "a vein of unsentimental pragmatism" ran through the practice.[1046] In the social confusion following Japan's surrender, numerous secret or informal arrangements were made between unwed mothers and childless couples, and the doctoring of *koseki* records was not uncommon.[1047] But institutions found it almost impossible to place *konketsuji* with an unrelated Japanese family. Some welfare workers actively discouraged local placements because prejudice against the children was so severe any Japanese offering to take one might be assumed to have a dubious motive. A newspaper reported in May 1952 on what it said was "the only blue-eyed boy being raised by a Japanese foster-parent in Tokyo."[1048]

The majority of early adoptions to foreigners were arranged directly between individuals or between adoptive parents and an institution. Three hundred children were placed with American military families stationed in Japan by April 1954.[1049] Many other adoptions were completed by proxy—using legal agents acting on behalf of overseas clients. Unfortunately, these proxy adoptions resulted in a disturbingly high proportion of unsuitable placements. An early investigation found:

> Instances have occurred of abuse of children, breakdown of adoptive homes, adoption of children by persons who were unstable or mentally ill or who had serious physical illness, and placements of upset or emotionally disturbed children with persons unprepared or unable to help them.[1050]

Specific expertise in inter-country adoption was not brought to bear until International Social Service (ISS) joined the work of the American Joint Committee.[1051]

The Geneva-based ISS had taken on work begun in the 1920s by the YWCA assisting migrants, refugees, and displaced persons. After World War II, ISS led the first professional effort to resolve the problem of "lost" children fathered by foreign servicemen. It also helped formulate reforms to better regulate inter-country adoption.[1052] The organization's Far East representative, Florence Boester, travelled to Tokyo in April 1955 and put in place a team of social workers paid for by the U.S. State Department.[1053]

Boester found it hard to break down existing practices that gave "perfunctory" consideration to whether adoptive parents and children were well matched.[1054] Because demand outstripped supply, any delay in matching a child to suitable adoptive parents abroad could result in the natural mother, or the institution, accepting another offer. ISS found it expedient to place children with American military families living in Japan: the couples were close at hand and inclined to be flexible in the selection of children; and the natural mothers were happier knowing who would be raising their child (this ran counter to the usual practice of discouraging contact between adoptive and natural parents). ISS America, as a result, became anxious that insufficient Japanese children would be available for its clients in the United States.[1055]

In March 1956, ISS had 143 "orphans" under investigation or being processed for adoption.[1056] Boester set out to increase this enrolment by soliciting referrals from prefectural child welfare departments and urging institutions to make use of ISS before the U.S. Refugee Relief Act expired at the end of the year. She met limited success. She found welfare officers preferred dealing directly with American families because they could obtain a "personal benefit," and institutions relied on adoptions to bring in much-needed donations.[1057] Miki Sawada spurned Boester's overture.[1058]

Nevertheless, well over two thousand children went to the United States for adoption by June 1958, the overwhelming majority *konketsuji*.[1059] By now ISS was handling a significant share of new cases. As the exodus gathered pace, Florence Boester noted an improvement in the tone of Japanese press and public responses to the issue.[1060]

It was around this time that ISS became aware of a fresh challenge. The Occupation of Japan had not been an exclusively American affair. Troops from Australia, Britain, India, and New Zealand, comprising the British Commonwealth Occupation Force (BCOF), also took part. BCOF was based in the bombed-out port city of Kure, Hiroshima Prefecture, and its area of operations extended over nine prefectures. Force strength peaked at thirty-seven thousand in February 1947.[1061] The largest contingent of troops came from Australia; BCOF's commanding officer was an Australian; and the Australian military presence lasted much longer than the other participants' (until 1956).

Unlike the Americans, BCOF enforced a policy of non-fraternization right through the Occupation. BCOF also refused to permit any marriage between a serviceman and a Japanese woman to be registered, whereas the Americans relaxed the restriction for some GIs (between 1947 and 1952, eleven thousand U.S. military and civilian personnel in Japan registered marriages to Japanese).[1062]

During the early years of the Occupation, a BCOF serviceman taking up with a woman, and asking permission to marry, could expect to be placed under arrest and shipped home. Some men stowed away on ships and planes to get back to their de facto wives and children, only to face deportation and, in some cases, lengthy prison sentences.[1063] In the later years, there was a tendency to turn a blind eye when BCOF chaplains blessed couples in Christian marriage services, but even these unions could not be registered––a situation one senior officer publicly condemned as "morally horrible."[1064] As men were rotated back to Australia, at the end of their tours of duty, they were forced either to leave their families behind or quit the service and seek local employment, which was extremely difficult to find. Those that did stay were stranded—because they could not take their Japanese wives to Australia (until the policy was changed in 1952).

In February 1956, an Army sergeant went public with the claim that 200-300 *konketsuji* were living in Kure in miserable circumstances, and that some mothers were being forced into prostitution to survive. The Australian government moved swiftly to discredit and silence the soldier, who was "severely reprimanded" and charged with stealing Army stationery (which he had used to launch a relief fund for the mothers and children).[1065] No serious investigation of his claims was undertaken.

Already by now the Immigration Department had received applications from several civilians and servicemen in Japan and Korea wanting to adopt mixed-race children and take them to Australia. Their entry, however, would have been contrary to the "White Australia" policy that, among other things, excluded persons of mixed race unable to prove they were at least three-quarters European. The Commonwealth Immigration Advisory Committee responded to this "very awkward"[1066] situation by making it a condition that a foster parent seeking to bring in a mixed-race child would first need to have spent six to nine months taking care of the child in situ. It was tantamount to a prohibition.[1067] As to whether an adoption order granted under Japanese law would be recognized by an Australian court, this was left—conveniently for the authorities—up in the air.[1068]

It took another two years for the Immigration Minister, Alexander Downer Sr., to make the policy public: "The illegitimate children of servicemen in Japan are not generally eligible for admission to Australia."[1069] Downer went on to tell parliament: "A bid for the children is a bid for the mothers and, by the time the whole operation were carried out, quite a small colony of Japanese migrants would be coming to this country." He would have none of that.[1070]

Kure was a city with a proud naval tradition; it is where the mighty battleship *Yamato* had been built and based. Kure's location on the Inland Sea, and unusual topography (many small neighborhoods separated by steep hills), fostered a somewhat insular outlook among its residents. It was a long way from teeming Tokyo or Yokohama. Even one fair-haired child wandering downtown was likely to be noticed in a place of Kure's size and character.

"People in Japan, when they see something unusual enter society, strongly reject it," says Mayumi Kosugi, the daughter of a BCOF serviceman. "Many mixed-blood children like us were bullied."[1071] Early one morning, while heading to school, Mayumi came under attack in the street from a stranger, who threw stones at her.

Another of the Kure Kids,[1072] Karumi Inoue recalls:

I'd be walking down the street by myself, and men—I'm
not talking about young kids, teenagers, but much
older—would start charging. I'd turn around because
I could hear their footsteps. Bang! Across the back
of my head, they'd hit me They'd see me, I guess, as
having to do with the dropping of the atomic bombs ...
Other times, they'd walk past and go "Phut." Spit at you.
People never stopped and thought—never once.[1073]

Joji Tsutsumi realized—though only after he became an adult—
why people had targeted him. Joji was born in June 1950 but lost his
Australian father in the Korean War six months later:

The children's faces were the faces of those who,
not so long ago, were dropping bombs. The faces,
by themselves, provoked animosity. For those who
had been educated to hate, I guess it was natural to
feel hatred when they saw miniatures of their enemy
hanging around ... I understand this now. But at the
time I wondered why I was singled out for bullying.[1074]

Teruko Morimoto met her future husband, a Scottish-born
Australian Warrant Officer in 1948, and later shared a rented
house with him in the Kure hills. Unable to formally marry (until
1953), Teruko lived in constant fear of her partner being sent home
without her, and took the necessary precautions.

Kure's [mixed race] kids had a dreadful time. They were
treated as "children of prostitutes" and looked down
upon. Returned soldiers were especially hostile, saying,
"We left kids like that in places we conquered." They
emphasized how it was a disgrace for Japan. I made
up my mind and determined not to have a child in
those circumstances.[1075]

The British Commonwealth Forces Korea (successor to BCOF)
lowered the Australian flag in Kure for the last time in November
1956. The brief ceremony moved one local newspaper to publish this
bitter eulogy:

It began in 1946, with Occupation soldiers in broad-brimmed hats, like cowboys. ... Then, in the absence of a peace treaty, the city became known as a "town of violence," and was taken up in parliament. ... And during the Korean War, Kure "R & R Center" provided ten thousand supplemental UN troops [i.e. Japanese workers], comfort women, and training (or was it an export campaign) for international war brides.[1076]

The Peace Treaty had done little to sweeten relations between the over-staying foreign guests and their impatient hosts. As soon as the lid was lifted on public criticism of the Occupation, the media gave full vent to coverage of crimes by soldiers. "Lawless" Kure leapt to national attention, bringing a parliamentary delegation from Tokyo to investigate.[1077] Public meetings were called to discuss the moral hazard posed to children by the city's active sex industry; lecturers condemned the "colonial atmosphere" of "cabarets and beer halls, with women's sexy voices, jazz, U.S. soldiers' [sic] red faces and quarrels."[1078]

Journalist Kiyoshi Kanzaki used the image of the wrecked naval shipyards being turned into scrap metal as an unflattering metaphor: "It seems Kure citizens have not only made the dead flesh of the past war their prey but they also try to suck a profit by driving a vulture's beak against the flank of the current war, or BCOF." As for the Occupation soldiers, they had had

a shortage of objects to conquer. It's said there were many devastating discharge activities with women regardless of who they were—whether panpan or vagabonds—and wherever it took their fancy—in tunnels or under bridges. How on earth have foreign soldiers, supposedly from civilized nations, transformed defeated Kure into the "town of beasts"![1079]

Women associating with "beasts" could hardly be otherwise themselves. Press stories, in reporting prostitute numbers, routinely lumped together onrii (short for "only one," a woman with one boyfriend) with panpan.[1080] The official barriers to marriage and emigration that dictated how inter-racial couples had been forced to live were only occasionally, if ever, acknowledged. Similarly, there was, at best, an ambivalent attitude to the war brides' normative influence. The comparison to "an export campaign," in the editorial quoted above, carried the implication of a low, commercial purpose.

International Social Service first became aware of the situation in Kure in 1957 from an American missionary, Pastor Milton Lundeen, who was concerned about the plight of destitute mothers and children. Kure (population two hundred thousand) was a hard place for anyone to live: 40 percent of households were receiving official livelihood assistance and the unemployment rate was among the highest in the country.[1081] The Augustana Lutheran Mission provided funds for ISS to send a social worker from Tokyo who collaborated with city officials in identifying the number, backgrounds, and circumstances of mixed-race children and determining how many were available for adoption. A copy of his report was sent to the Australian Council of Churches, which agreed to fund the adoptions of eight Kure Kids to American families and pay for a full-time ISS social worker to reside in Kure. The Australian Government was asked to help—but, at this stage, refused.[1082]

The ISS Kure Project represents the best-documented longitudinal study of a group of *konketsuji* living in the Japanese community. It was a unique undertaking that ran from 1959 until 1977, providing professional counseling and disbursing direct assistance, school scholarships, and living expenses to 130 clients. About half its budget of almost ¥70 million (approximately ¥700 million at today's values) came from Australian and Japanese charitable donations and half from the Australian government, which finally agreed to start contributing funds in 1964 (while not relaxing its stand against adoptions).[1083] The project's enduring value for a clearer understanding of the *konketsuji* issue is that it preserves an encounter, lasting several decades, with identifiable people in a defined social setting. Claims repeated in many accounts of the Occupation and its aftermath—that all *konketsuji* were corralled into institutions or sent abroad, or denied an education and confined to menial jobs, or could never marry and lived only miserable lives— are contradicted by the Kure Project.[1084]

. . .

**Mari's Story**[1085]
Names signify our connection to family and announce us to the world. Whether through adoption or marriage, at a whim, or from a desire to take control of their lives, a number of the children of the Occupation have put on and taken off names, like changing clothes according to the seasons.

She started out as Mary when she was a baby. But her grandfather, fearing the foreign name might cause problems, changed it to the Japanese-sounding Mari. This remains her everyday name, but above the door of her restaurant in Hiroshima, written in cursive style, she is also "Mary" again: more befitting the condiments, cure-alls, and other imported bits and pieces she sells at her shop. The strongly-built woman, in a heavily-starched chef's tunic, stands behind the counter preparing the speciality dish of the region, *okonomiyaki*: cabbage, flour, egg, seafood (or whatever you like), mixed and fried on a hotplate, topped with tangy sauce and powdered seaweed—a dish admitting of no identity problem.

Mari Ishikuni's story really begins three generations ago, in the early Meiji era, when her great-grandfather migrated to Hawai'i. It is where the key person in Mari's life—her grandmother—was born.

> My family circumstances were a bit unusual and my upbringing was different from normal Japanese. When I was small, my grandmother cooked Italian food; she was always making minestrone. I was scolded if I dropped rubbish, for example, and when I sat in a chair I was told to keep my knees together. I keep a photograph of my grandmother on the wall, just over there, where I can always see it.

At the age of seventeen, displaying the family's trademark independence of spirit, Mari's grandmother ran away from Hawai'i to avoid an arranged marriage and returned to Japan. She met a man, had two children by him, divorced, and then took up with Mari's grandfather, a sign-painter. The couple tried their luck in 1930s Manchuria, where they prospered, only to lose everything by the end of the war, including several houses they had bought in Hiroshima.

By the time they returned to the devastated city, a year after the war's end, it was too late for the couple to start over again. It was now the turn of their two daughters to strive for a better life. Mari's mother succumbed to the confusion and exhilaration of the post-war freedoms.

> My mother was nineteen when she had me [in December 1948]. I knew my father's name once, but I've forgotten it now. [Laughs.] Maybe this sounds odd,

but I didn't think about it as much as people might
expect. I wasn't curious. I thought: "That one [my
father] perhaps has his own life." I didn't dwell on it.

She learned nothing about her father—mainly because Akiko,
her mother, left home when her daughter was still an infant. Later
she took off for Australia, apparently with another man. "The
reason she went to Australia, according to my grandfather, was to
rebel against her parents. It seems she wanted to be an opera singer.
But my grandfather got angry, because you can't make a living that
way." Akiko disowned her daughter, telling acquaintances about
the "stranger" who had left a *konketsuji* with her parents back in
Hiroshima.

Mari's grandfather adopted her by entering her name in his
*koseki*. A fourth person was living in the house, Mari's aunt, who
worked as an interpreter at Iwakuni city hall. Mary/Mari had been
named for this aunt's favourite teacher at college, an American,
who kept sending them regular parcels of powered milk and
clothing even after she returned to the United States. Money was
short, but the home atmosphere was warm and relaxed. In this
family no shame attached to foreign blood.

If the family did not like the fact I was half-Australian,
I wouldn't have been comfortable at home. But it
wasn't like that. Whether it was that, or because my
grandparents made a special effort to ensure I wouldn't
be lonely, it seemed a natural thing my mother wasn't
present. I didn't try to find out about her or wish for
her. I didn't think so much about it when I was small. I
didn't feel sad, although I faintly remember when I saw
someone with parents I cried [tears well up in her eyes
and her voice thickens]. But I think I was fulfilled.

Life became more difficult, however, once Mari started school.

Because I was bullied going to and from school, my
grandmother escorted me every day. An old woman
who used to live in my neighborhood once told me
about an episode her husband witnessed one day when
my grandmother couldn't pick me up. He saw me in
the street, surrounded by other children, being bullied.

He watched from a distance to see whether he needed to intervene. He heard me yelling, "We are the same human beings, so what's the difference?" And because I continued to be taunted with "*gaijin, gaijin*," I yelled back, "Why don't you become a *gaijin*?" I heard that story, though I don't remember the episode myself.

During her childhood, Mari had long blonde hair that reached down to her waist, and she was proud to show it off.

Every day my grandmother would iron a ribbon and tie my hair with it. One day, a primary school teacher, who often gave me a hard time, yanked my hair and said, "Cut this off." My grandmother demanded to know why, but no reason was given. Just, "Cut it!" There was no alternative; otherwise I'd be bullied. School was bad, but the reaction to me from adults in the street was sometimes worse. They would turn back and look at me. Throw stones. A lot of things happened. However, my friends in the neighborhood protected me, because they knew me well.

The family first learned about International Social Service following a visit to Iwakuni by the social worker Yone Itō. "She came to the [Iwakuni city] office asking whether there were any *hafu* [half or mixed-blood] children in the area. My aunt said there was one at her house. That's how the relationship with ISS began."

A case report was prepared on Mari: "She is a cheerful girl who loves music and going to the movies. At first sight she looks gaudy. She helps out a lot with the housework."[1086] It also mentioned that Mari wanted to go to Australia. Since the age of eleven, after her grandmother was crippled by a stroke, the girl had been bearing the main burden of cooking and cleaning at the family home.

The Vietnam War was just getting started. My auntie was very busy; she hardly came home. I was a "housewife." I had to do chores such as carrying my grandmother on my back and bathing her. I did everything. Maybe it was useful for me; I didn't have time to dwell on negative things. I used all of my being just to live.

Though the hard work took a toll on her health, she never thought of quitting school. She liked study and regretted not being able to find time for her books at home.

> In the first year of junior high school, I was really absent-minded. My teacher asked me, "What are you thinking about?" And I said, "I'm thinking what I should cook for tonight," wondering what would please my grandmother. Every day was like that. I wasn't able to play like other children.

According to ISS, she wrote letters to her mother in Australia but never received a reply. Then, out of the blue, when Mari was seventeen, Akiko suddenly appeared at the front door.

> Simply because the house was the same one she had left, she came there. She said something to the effect that she had divorced and was running a gift-shop by herself [in Melbourne]. Her trip was mainly for business. It seemed that she lived a rich life: her outfit was gorgeous; she said she drove a BMW. That was the first time I ever saw her. When they heard all her talk, my grandfather, grandmother, and auntie got angry, saying, "Why didn't you do anything for your daughter?" They were furious. She simply turned her face away and went back [to Australia]. [Laughs.] So, my impression was, she was that sort of person.

Mari was more self-assured by now than she had been as a small child. Back in primary school, her tactic for combating prejudice had been to keep a low profile: "I never uttered a word in class. I tried to be invisible." The tactic did not help, however, once she started junior high and new children saw her for the first time; the bullying began all over again. She came to realize—as did many of the Kure Kids—that unless she fought back, she would not be able to survive.

> I became stronger, little by little. Now, as you can see, I speak my mind. I run a restaurant, I deal with customers. My friends from childhood say I have become a different kind of person. They say, "You are not the Mari-*chan* of past days." This might be because

I found my own way of surviving, my defense.

Most of my friends in junior high were Koreans. It was easier for me to be with *gaikokujin* [foreigners], because they were bullied too. They were called *"Chōsen-jin"* [people from Chōsen, the old name for Korea, sometimes used pejoratively]. I had many of these sorts of colleagues.

A scholarship provided through ISS enabled Mari to enter senior high school. The bullying stopped; she became a class leader. School friends, aware of her situation at home, occasionally sent gifts of food. "I studied desperately. My teachers, because they saw what I could do, looked after me. I put a lot of energy into that." ISS records confirm she was "a bright girl, studying hard every day, and liked by many friends." She joined the English club at school and acquired a penfriend in Sydney. The ISS scholarship did not cover Mari's living expenses, so she needed to undertake part-time work. "I did sewing: other students' sewing class homework. [Laughs.] Something like, five hundred yen per skirt. I also washed dishes at a department store restaurant."

Riding on a bus one day, she encountered her old nemesis: the primary school teacher who had ordered her hair to be cut. He displayed condescending surprise on learning that she had been able to enter senior high. "He knew we didn't have money. That's the sort of person he was." Many years later, the same man walked into her restaurant in Hiroshima. Sitting opposite her at the counter, taking his meal, he quietly apologized: "I'm sorry." But he did not come again.

Mari married in her early twenties and had two children, a boy and a girl. Watching them grow up, she felt a strong desire to show them to her mother. Having had no contact for twenty years, she hardly knew where to start looking, until a relative in Hawai'i sent a newspaper article about war brides that mentioned Akiko, who was still living in Melbourne. Through a friend, whose aunt had married an Australian, Mari made inquiries—shrugging off the embarrassment of having to reveal her unhappy secret to a stranger.

The children were almost teenagers when Mari and her family set off to see Akiko. The reunion left her feeling dissatisfied:

I have two younger brothers in Australia, but my mother

never let me have contact with them. I don't know, but it may be we have different fathers. While we were there she would introduce us to people as her "Japanese relatives." [Laughs.] So it seems she doesn't want to talk about me! No. She was that sort of person. That one *is* that sort of person. [Laughs.] There's no point asking her how she got me. She's cold, my mother. [Laughs.] These days, my daughter sometimes says, "Do you want to give her a call?" I say, "No." Maybe I'm cold too! [Laughs.]

When Mari's son was in his twenties, he went to Australia to stay with his grandmother for several months. It seemed they did not get on well, but he liked the place, and so Mari has kept in touch with her mother—despite everything.

I understood by her silence that she didn't want to talk about the past. So I thought, "Even if I blame her, nothing will come of it." I often thought about these things and finally decided, since a time may come when my two children will want to go to Australia, if I quarrel with my mother, and as a result she and my children don't get along, that would be bad. So I thought I should stop blaming her. I told my mother that, regardless of all else, she was the person who brought me into the world. I appreciated her for that. Of course, it was not just my mother; she had a partner. That's why I was born and was able to get married and have children. And there's another thing: my customers often tell me my way of thinking is not Japanese. [Laughs.] I don't know whether it's my DNA or my upbringing, but I appreciate these things. So I don't blame anyone.

· · ·

To head up the Kure Project, ISS appointed a twenty-nine-year-old, Tokyo-born graduate of Japan Women's University and the Kent School of Social Work at the University of Louisville in Kentucky. Yone Itō initially identified eighty-eight *konketsuji* living in and around the city, including fifty-two with Australian fathers.[1087] As Christmas 1959 approached, she sent word to the families to come to town, and bring *furoshiki* [carrying cloths] with them, to collect food parcels. They hauled away chunks of cheese and tins of powered milk sent from Australia.[1088] Had the donors been present, they would have noticed the processed cheddar being carved up later and sold to buy food more palatable to Japanese tastes. They would have realized, too, that children turning up at school in Western style hand-me-downs might actually be worse off.[1089]

The majority of the children, Itō reported, were at a critical stage of their psychological development, between the ages of nine and twelve:

> Encountering social prejudice, they feel they are the greatest victims in the world and make themselves out to be heroes of anguish and emotional instability. For those ones with a strong inferiority complex, proper support and careful guidance are necessary. Forty-five percent of children are in a situation where they cannot even live with their natural mothers. Frustration and social pressure often lead them in an evil direction.[1090]

To succeed in her work, the social worker needed to win the confidence of the mothers. While the children, in her report, come across as troublesome, the mothers seem almost heroic; Itō admired them for speaking fondly of their former soldier-partners and imparting a generally positive image of them to their offspring. An element of self-justification in their nostalgia did not make it less real, as far as she was concerned.[1091] She overturned the view, favored within ISS, of "pathological" mothers versus "innocent" children.

Most families, Itō found, were suffering "mental stress" (*seishinteki kunō*).[1092] A bar girl over the age of thirty (no longer a "flower," as the social worker put it) entered a downward spiral, chasing meaner jobs at lower pay. Mothers of *konketsuji* met swift rejection if they sought serious employment, and one in four had shifted address over the past year.[1093] Society treated them coldly because people remembered how women associating with foreign soldiers had lived comparatively luxurious lives while others were doing it tough. Their subsequent descent into poverty seemed a just retribution. The antipathy was so strong she doubted whether she could obtain any cooperation outside official circles.[1094] A "Mixed-Blood Children Rescue Advisory Committee," made up of local government officials and prominent citizens, helped shore up her position.[1095]

Mayumi Kosugi's mother was so mentally scarred by the

trauma of childbirth, the child's grandmother and aunt had to take responsibility for raising her. "When reporters asked me about my father," recalls Mayumi, "I had nothing to say: no name, no place of birth, no explanation. I felt sick being asked such questions."[1096] Participating in the Kure Project eased her anxiety. "Where I lived, I was the only mixed-blood. Going to ISS for the first time, I found lots of children like me. Being there made me feel emotionally calmer."

Once it became obvious the adoption route to Australia was blocked (indeed the great majority of Kure families declined this option), Itō decided the children would have to succeed or fail as "Japanese."[1097] The immediate challenge was education: compulsory and free up to junior high, selective and expensive thereafter. Three years of senior high school was considered the minimum requirement for obtaining skilled work in Japan: a standard then being met by two out of three children in the wider population.[1098] Of the Kure Kids graduating from junior high in 1962, however, just one in four would remain at school.[1099] As the Japanese economy expanded, school retention rates would keep rising. There was no time to waste.

Itō put increased emphasis on group activities to build confidence and social skills among the children—and keep them off the streets.[1100] She arranged club meetings, excursions, English language classes, and music and typing lessons. Volunteers from the Maritime Self-Defense Force ran sporting events, conducted brass band practice, and helped out at summer camps. Group activities were arranged for the mothers, too, to break down their social isolation and foster home-making skills. Itō adhered to a simple philosophy of "learning ways of better living by doing."[1101]

ISS penetrated almost every aspect of the mothers' and children's lives: education, medical care, counseling, entertainment, job-hunting, matchmaking, and the provision of living expenses (down to the supply of underwear and toiletries). Itō was on call, night and day, to deal with problems as they arose: a mother wanting money for urgent medical treatment, a boy caught stealing and in police custody, or a girl missing from her school dormitory. By 1964, she had two, sometimes three, full-time assistants running programs and providing guidance to more than one hundred children and their families. That year, six out of the nine Kure Kids completing junior high would go on to senior school: a retention rate equal to the national average.

The ISS policy was to avoid, if at all possible, placing children in institutional care. Even those without mothers living at home, and barely under the control of elderly relatives or acquaintances, were considered better off remaining in the community. Inevitably, a small number turned delinquent: skipping class, getting into gang fights, and dabbling in petty crime. Physically conspicuous, they readily caught the eye of the police.

Around the age of ten, Joji Tsutsumi, a tall, stocky boy, underwent a sudden personality change. Previously gentle and obliging, he became moody and destructive. His mother had disappeared, and he was growing up with little or no adult supervision. He spent more time wandering the streets than attending school. "Even if I went to school, it was no use learning. There was nothing to look forward to: no plan to go higher, no possibility of dropping lower." Joji gave the ISS social workers a torrid time. The day he tossed an explosive into the office stove, he and Yone Itō came to blows. The boy was headed for the reformatory; but ISS managed to trace his mother, and Joji's life began moving in a better direction.[1102]

As the Kure Kids got older, there was more need for one-to-one counseling. Itō commented at the time: "The children often get mad about [being ostracized] and ask their mothers why they were born. Their mothers cannot handle this problem and it usually falls to me to explain to them marriages which the mothers felt were binding but the fathers did not."[1103] The youngsters would drop by the ISS office after school to release their frustration and anger: in this "oasis of their mind," as she put it, they could relax and talk freely.[1104]

Her "psychiatric method" was to refrain from giving direct advice and let them arrive at their own solutions.[1105] She tried to be patient and objective, withholding her emotions, seeking to establish a "professional-technical human relationship," as distinct from "private or friendly" contact.[1106]

The most common criticism noted in case reports was that a child "lacked guts" or was "weak-willed." The Kure Project fostered group identity partly as a substitute for parental recognition. Since only a small number of children could expect to trace missing fathers, the aim was to toughen them to accept the situation. A caseworker became the custodian of a child's personal story: keeper of the records and agent for "over there" (Australia, the United States, etc.). ISS exercised discretion when deciding how much to tell clients, even as adults. There was, for instance, the case of a married man who contacted the Kure office after being out of touch for many years, begging to be given the name of his "Australian father." He had never been told that his father—whose name and address in Auckland, New Zealand, remained on file—was not the same man who fathered his two "sisters." Consistent with other cases like it, ISS preserved the secret.[1107] Some of the Kure Kids came to resent the power exercised by ISS, and Itō in particular. Others, however, remained dependent on the organization as a place to belong, a source of strength, and a touchstone of their identity.

Approaching adulthood, the next big hurdle for Japan's *konketsuji* was employment. Prestigious firms such as banks, major manufacturers, and trading houses would tactfully decline to hire people whose antecedents were murky. The mixed-race children were pushed towards small and medium-sized firms paying lower wages and offering less job security.[1108] The same was generally true for the Kure Kids. After graduating from university, Mayumi Kosugi found work as a hotel receptionist. "After a month or two my boss called me over and said: 'You're a *konketsuji*, and your appearance is different from ordinary Japanese. You're not suitable for the reception desk; it's better you work in the back office.' I was furious. I told him it was unfair. I was fully aware I might be sacked, but I felt I needed to claim my rights." Supported by her female colleagues, she protested loudly until her boss relented.

One sector of the labor market that lay wide open was the world of entertainment. So many exotic new faces began appearing in modeling and acting roles, commentators spoke of a "*konketsuji būmu.*" The long-legged, dark beauty Bibari (Beverly) Maeda led the way with an enormously popular poster campaign for Shiseido cosmetics. Seizing the opportunity, Itō arranged for several of her girls to sing on a television variety show and encouraged talent scouts from Osaka to cast an eye over the children. She escorted one good-looking teenager to Tokyo to enrol in an actors' workshop. After featuring in a popular hair tonic commercial, he was offered the lead role in a prestigious television production, but suffered a breakdown and dropped out of sight.[1109]

Sport was another field in which *konketsuji* were expected to excel. Several times during the 1950s and 1960s, Australian swimming stars were invited to Kure. The mixed-race children were organized to join them in the pool, both as an encouragement to their athleticism and a public relations exercise. It turned out the strongest athletes among them were better suited to track and field: Kiyotaka Kawasaki went on to represent Japan in the discus, setting a national record that has never been broken.

Itō's use of Maritime Self-Defense Force volunteers to serve as role models and help with group activities encouraged several boys to take up careers in the Japanese military. A case report on one individual noted: "The reason [he] wants to go into the Navy is because there is no bias against mixed-bloods. His mother lost her job several times because she had a mixed-blood child."[1110]

After employment came marriage: a daunting prospect for most *konketsuji*. "When I came of age, some people said, 'Because of the [fair] color of your hair, you won't be able to marry,'" recalls Junko Fukuhara, the pretty daughter of an Australian Army officer. "It seemed my friends had a lot of offers of *omiai* [a meeting with a suitor], but I had none. So I felt a little bit lonely."[1111] Better-off families took great care to protect their pedigrees. Private investigators were skilled at digging up even the most obscure personal details of a prospective bride or groom, and an absent foreign father was hardly obscure.

Contrary to expectations, few *konketsuji* married other mixed-bloods (there was one case in Kure). Mayumi Kosugi became fond of a boy she met through ISS. "He told me, 'I will absolutely never marry a woman from ISS; you can imagine what the child would look like! It would have a face totally "over there" [foreign].'" Some chose partners from other ethnic groups—a Filipina wife, for example—especially if they, themselves, could not "pass" in Japanese society. The fabled beauty of mixed-race girls, on the other hand, exerted a definite appeal. A businessman from Hiroshima once turned up at the ISS office and asked Itō to introduce his son to one of the Kure Kids. A marriage resulted.[1112]

The first to marry was a nineteen-year-old nurse who had met her husband at the company where they worked. The wedding, in the spring of 1968, was a milestone event to which local and international media were invited. The couple settled down in the city and raised a family. One thing led to another, and the woman felt sufficiently encouraged to start a search for her natural father. Almost thirty-seven years after her birth, father and daughter were finally reunited in Sydney.

By 1977, out of the eighty-four Kure Kids registered as having Australian or "British" fathers, a total of thirty-six (twenty-one females and fifteen males) were married. This proportion, though well below the national average, was higher than had been generally predicted.[1113] The stigma of their birth and marginalized social position hampered male *konketsuji*, in particular, in the search for a marriage partner.[1114] Being the mixed-blood child of a foreign soldier was not, however, in and of itself an insurmountable barrier to a socially advantageous marriage. A notable example involved an Australian ex-soldier, Jimmy Beard, who stayed on in Japan after the Occupation and saw both his daughters into celebrity marriages. The elder girl, a model, entered the Ishibashi family (of

Bridgestone Tires fame) and her younger sibling, an actress, became the sister-in-law of a future prime minister, Yukio Hatoyama.[1115]

By the time the Kure Project was wound up, one in five of the Kure Kids was living abroad: in the United States, Australia, Brazil, Taiwan, or Papua New Guinea. Half of those who remained in Japan resided close to where they were born. A few had died or lost contact with ISS. Some researchers have suggested, based on anecdotal evidence, that *konketsuji* experienced a higher-than-average rate of suicide.[1116] Among the Kure Kids, one or two individuals are known to have taken their own lives. In addition, however, a significant number of others have continued to bear psychological scars from their childhood experiences.[1117]

The Kure Project's finest achievement was providing access to a level of education unattainable by most other *konketsuji*: fourteen university graduates (including two with master's degrees), two college graduates, and twenty-four senior high school graduates.[1118] Mayumi Kosugi: "If I were not able to go to high school, if I were not able to go to university ... there is a possibility my life could have gone in the wrong direction. I can imagine the negative result. Without help, there may have been no choice. Because I was given a scholarship, I can lead a life nobody can point at with a finger of derision."

In 1967, a sixteen-year-old black *konketsuji* was arrested in Chiba Prefecture for the rape and murder of three women. The case caused a sensation. The boy told police he never knew his father and his mother died when he was small. Unhappy at school, he began stealing and drifted around the country: "Young women always laughed at me as they passed by. I started to hate women."[1119] The words the boy reportedly screamed as he confessed his crimes—"I hate my hair and skin"—pricked the nation's conscience.[1120]

Public interest in the *konketsuji* during the 1960s wavered between voyeurism and sympathy. The popularity of mixed-race hostesses hired by the glitzy bars of Tokyo's Akasaka and Ginza districts could produce this kind of reportage:

Growing up insulted as "*ainoko*," now the center of a boom, with their mixed blood as a sales point, they have advanced into the neon-lit streets in search of the greedy life. People say the feature of *konketsuji* hostesses is that they express their instincts in a foreigner's way, while their way of thinking is Japanese. Hearing them talk, it's hard to believe they are

Japanese.[1121]

The *konketsuji* hostess was considered a captive of history like her parents: "Beneath her cheerful tone was the sound of loneliness, the shade of war."

As the Vietnam War escalated, and thousands of free-spending American servicemen rotated through Japan on leave, a familiar pattern seemed to be repeating itself. A television documentary on the life of an eighteen-year-old *konketsuji* left novelist Mitsuharu Inoue "grief-stricken." The young woman was the child of a BCOF soldier—she kept a photograph of her father but had no memory of him. Raised by her grandparents, while her mother went out to work, she had turned delinquent in her early teens: "Since everybody hated me, I felt I needn't care what happened to me. I could be a good girl, yet I'd still be bullied. People would say, 'the child of a *panpan*.'"[1122] She now worked as a hostess in a bar in Yokosuka. "The way things are going," commented Inoue, "she will give birth to the child of an American soldier returning from Vietnam. And her child will murmur the same words as her."[1123]

Not every portrayal looked backwards or promoted negative stereotypes. A respected weekly magazine ran a feature on mixed-blood success stories. The captions accompanying the wholesome photographs included, "maintaining positive attitude towards society," "lives peacefully as a housewife," and "wishes to be a poet."[1124] The *konketsuji*-rights advocate Imao Hirano insisted that "sad and soapy dramas" of mixed-race misery were out of date: "They have been patient, honing their skills and cultivating an independent spirit. Meeting these 'new people' I am very much encouraged."[1125]

In the 1957 Oscar-winning film *Sayonara*, Marlon Brando plays an American airman who falls in love with a Japanese entertainer. At the climax of the film, Brando's character pleads with his girlfriend to marry him. "But what would happen to our children?" she asks. "What would they be?" To which he replies: "They'd be half Japanese, half American; they'd be half yellow and half white; they'd be half you; they'd be half me. That's all they're going to be."[1126] Hollywood's rather gauche answer to the centuries-old doubt about race mixing was at least a beginning.

At some point in the lives of every parent of a mixed-race child, whether living in Japan or the United States or Australia, the question would arise, "Why am I different?" The child might be told he or she was lucky to be half-Japanese or half-Australian, and that other children should be envious. Or the answer might be,

"You are not 'half,' but 'double.'" Yone Itō consoled one anxious child by telling her, "You have the blood of two races running in you; so you have more potential than others."[1127]

More recent studies of mixed-race Japanese-Americans living in Japan and the United States lean towards the view that marginality is not the straitjacket it was once considered to be. Some individuals, questioned about their self-image, strenuously objected to the suggestion they needed to choose between their different heritages.[1128] They could manage several personal and social identities, bonding and interacting with different groups, without ill effects. Though other individuals gravitated strongly to a single identity, whether Japanese or American, both groups possessed the ability to manage the distinction between how they perceived themselves and how society perceived them.[1129] Even Japanese-oriented konketsuji, with comparatively low self-esteem and high sensitivity about society's tendency to deny their identity, evidently felt secure in their personal cultural preference: they valued Japanese culture above any other.[1130]

While it was usually easier for white konketsuji to "pass" as Japanese, the desire to "pass" was by no means limited to those with the necessary physical attributes. Even individuals conspicuously not "pure" Japanese might insist that they were, and disassociate themselves from their other ethnic heritage. Such individuals avoided contact with foreign nationals and even expressed negative views about mixed-race people.[1131] A mainstream Japanese identity—taken on, for instance, to protect the "good name" of a spouse's family—required a lifetime's vigilance. Several of the Kure Kids contacted by the author declined to be interviewed because they were concerned it might upset workplace or family relationships.

Accounts of the konketsuji experience that put emphasis on unresolved identity and discrimination tend to overlook a wider pattern of marginality in Japanese society. Classical definitions of race are inadequate to explain the fluidity or rigidity of Japanese uchi-soto (inside-outside) relationships. Not even one drop of foreign blood may be required for someone experiencing marginality to regard him or herself as an "incomplete" Japanese and seek an explanation in some hidden foreign connection or imagined previous life as a foreigner.[1132] A real link to the outside world—a grandmother's past sojourn in Hawai'i; a spouse's sister's American husband; a cousin successfully settled abroad—often turns up in the life stories of the better-adjusted Kure Kids, like a talisman validating their difference. It is not the *fact* of difference that counts the most, in the end, but the *explanation* one can supply for it.[1133]

Down the centuries, the concept of race served not only to codify but also entrench human differences—because differences could attract as well as repel. The mixed-race child subverted power structures, defied class barriers, and altered nations from within. Colonizers and occupying powers planted this assumption wherever they planted their flags. The *konketsuji* of the post-war Occupation of Japan seemed perfectly matched to the stereotype of mixed-race misery fixed in the minds of Americans, Australians, and Japanese.[1134] Many observers assumed the children were rejected because of what made them noticeable, their physical differences, whereas society's attitude was shaped mainly by the perceived low socio-economic status of the mothers and bitterness over Japan's war defeat. Politicians and journalists portrayed them as unwanted waifs, even though the great majority were raised by relatives and acculturated as Japanese. Academics claimed they could not obtain a proper education, marry, or find a decent job. And yet, as the Kure Project demonstrates, with guidance and financial assistance positive outcomes were possible. Many could and did lead productive lives.

## CHAPTER FIFTEEN

# FROM KYOTO TO NEW ENGLAND: A MULTIRACIAL MAN'S JOURNEY IN THE POST-WAR PERIOD[1135]

LILY ANNE Y. WELTY TAMAI

*"I was constantly dreaming about the U.S. I thought some day I was going to get there, even though I had no clue how I was getting there. I just never stopped dreaming."*[1136]

### Introduction

This chapter examines the experience of what it was like to be *hafu*, or mixed-race, during the post-war period in Japan. Born in 1950 to a Japanese mother and an American father, Kaoru Morioka, who later adopted the name Karl Lippincott, experienced tremendous hardship because of his mixed racial background and persevered by finding strategies to cope and to improve his situation. Kaoru Morioka's life details a rich micro-history that illuminates post-war Kansai and his experience of immigrating to the U.S. and coming of age on the East Coast during his teens.

Being mixed race in Japan was not always a source of pride, a source of envy, or seen as *kakkoii* (cool or chic). It was not always associated with a cosmopolitan and international lifestyle, with overseas trips, bilingual skills, and international schools. It did not always mean perceived privilege, cross-cultural access, a complicated family life, and international marriage. Neither did it mean that one automatically became a model or worked in the entertainment industry as a *tarento* (celebrity talent). These more positive and international images of mixed-race Japanese came to be in vogue during the 1970s and 1980s in Japan and persist to this day.[1137] In the decades immediately following World War II, possessing a mixed-race appearance meant something entirely different. For many *hafu* in 1950s Japan, possessing a mixed-race appearance was riddled with assumptions. People often assumed that their fathers were in the American military and that their mothers were morally loose women, which carried a negative stigma, especially if their fathers were absent and they were raised in Japan with their mothers, other relatives, or with an adoptive family. Whether the assumptions about their parents were true or not, the stigma of their visible racial mixedness affected mixed-race individuals by creating shame and guilt for cultural crimes they had never committed.

Their physical features alone could immediately reveal to a stranger their parents' sexual choices—something private and intimate—for which the children had no responsibility. Mixed-race children carried around the proof of their parents' intimate relations in their genes and on their faces. For many of them, their inability to speak English suggested that their English-speaking parent was absent from the household, perhaps because their parents' relationship did not last. All of these things could be assumed—whether they were true or not—if the children looked racially mixed and spoke Japanese and limited English.

Kaoru recalled, "I was one of the three mixed children in the area school district. Not being able to speak English meant I was *konketsuji* or *hafu*. There was no way to hide being a *hafu*. I had very little confidence, no pride, and felt that I had no future prospect in Japan."[1138] Not living with their fathers meant that they did not learn English at home: another strike. In Kaoru's case, his physical features might have allowed him to pass as a Westerner. But because of his lack of English ability, he was immediately pegged as mixed race.

People in Kyoto often mistook Kaoru for a *gaijin* (foreigner). When they tried to practice speaking English and realized their mistake because he could not speak English back to them, they would say, "*gaijin no marudashi!*" (impostor) or call him *ainoko* and then run off leaving Kaoru feeling let down. Their words were harsh: *yappari ainoko wa eigo dekinai de sho. ainoko wa yappari ainoko* ("I knew it. Those love children can't speak English. A love child is nothing but a love child").[1139]

Kaoru was constantly being flung between two extremes, one where people initially praised him for being a *gaijin*, and the next moment when they realized that he couldn't speak English, and therefore dismissed him and called him a love child.

If I were able to speak English, it could have helped me gain so much self-respect and confidence. I could have at least tried to pass as an American kid or a *gaijin*, instead of being a *nise no gaijin* (a fake). Not being able to speak English was a dead give away about my being *hafu*.[1140]

The treatment Kaoru received at the hands of his peers reflected the anxieties of Japan at the time. At the end of World War II, Japan was occupied by another country for the first time in its history as a nation. Citizens watched as thousands of U.S. military servicemen descended upon a defeated Japan in August of 1945 for what would be an undefined period of occupation. We know now that the U.S. military maintained its presence on mainland Japan until the end of the Occupation in 1952, and on Okinawa until 1972. During the Occupation, nearly one million Americans served in some capacity. As the military emerged into cities and neighborhoods across Japan, intimate relationships between the American servicemen and Japanese and Okinawan women flourished. Dating an American meant fraternizing with the former enemy. Some of these relationships formed initially from the short-lived Recreation and Amusement Association, the government-regulated sex industry and later from the private-sector sex industry.[1141] But the vast majority of couples paired up, began dating, and sometimes married, outside the context of brothels. As a result of these new relationships, there was a surge in the birthrate of mixed-race children during this period.

The historical record has missed the nuanced stories of mixed-race people who grew up in post-war Japan. It has dealt with the war brides, the servicemen, and the children born between them as separate groups in isolation of one another. Some accounts mention their children as a by-product of these wartime relationships. The few studies that have looked at the mixed-race children have focused mostly on the hardships and racial pathology they faced as mixed-race individuals.[1142]

Through the lens of Kaoru, this chapter examines the lives of the children of those interracial relationships, rather than focusing on the war brides and the G.I.s who served in Japan. Those post-war children are currently reaching retirement age, and many are now grandparents. By the 1950s, there were an estimated 10,000 mixed-race children, some of whom were raised by one or both parents while others were placed in orphanages or in the care of adoptive families.[1143] The debates and discussions in the Japanese media surrounding what to do with the mixed-race children were dubbed the *konketsuji mondai* or "the mixed-blood problem." Mixed-race people were labeled a range of names including, GI babies, Occupation babies, and war babies in English; *konketsuji* (mixed-blood), *ainoko* (love child or child of mixture), and the offensive term, *panpan no ko* (prostitute's child) in Japanese.[1144] None of these were labels of their own choosing.

## Mixed-race Scholarship

Much of the scholarly research and writing that focused on mixed-race Japanese began in earnest in the late 1970s and 1980s.[1145] The scholarship on mixed-race people tended to focus on younger people under the age of thirty years old.[1146] In popular culture, the stories and media articles that existed about mixed-race people were often sensationalized accounts describing them as examples of unwanted children born out of the war and out of wedlock, their lives laden with tragedy.[1147] Some children were sent to orphanages that sprang up across Japan during the 1950s and their caretakers described the children's tough beginnings and lamented over their futures.[1148] These stories are true for some but not all mixed-race individuals. Another motif was the story of mixed-race people who were famous and "made it big" in Japan's entertainment industry.[1149] Although cinematic, these stories are extreme examples of tragedy and success detailing what happened to the baby boomer generation of mixed-race individuals. The lives of mixed-race American-Japanese are complex, and most of their life experiences were neither monolithic nor as extreme as the two stereotypical stories described above.[1150]

As a historian, I set out to find out what happened to these individuals in the last seventy years since the end of World War II because few firsthand records on this period existed.[1151] These mixed-race individuals were often stereotyped as illegitimate, with lives full of difficulty. Certainly, many people faced tremendous challenges, but those challenges were met with strategies to cope and to survive. In addition, their mixed heritage suggested that their parents' relationship was haphazard, hasty, or even financially profitable. Although some women may have been sex workers, not all were. Although some military fathers were absent in the lives of their mixed-race children, not all were. There were unplanned pregnancies, and there were planned pregnancies. This chapter seeks to separate the image of the red light district from the mixed-race individuals whose images and identities grew up in the shadow of these stereotypes.[1152]

## Oral History as a Methodology

When we use oral history as a methodology, we can reveal untold histories. Oral history is not a new method, but rather one that has been renewed in recent times to recount individual narratives. As stated by historian Peter Thompson, "In fact, oral history is as old as history itself. It was the *first* kind of history."[1153] Using a traditional method to obtain non-traditional narratives gives us a look into the extraordinary lives of ordinary people. Often, ordinary people do not leave a tidy paper trail in the archives for researchers to easily follow. They may leave few written records. Their voices are not immortalized in policy, books, and papers. Thus, oral histories like this are valuable and provide insight into the lives of mixed-race individuals.

In addition, archives are usually silent regarding the emotions and perceptions of individual life experiences. Oral histories provide a level of depth, detail, and nuance that may not be included in secondary sources like newspaper articles. Moreover, oral histories serve as primary sources that shed light on life histories that privilege the individuals to tell their versions of their life events and their life history. Giving mixed-race individuals the chance to tell their stories helps to set the record straight, even seventy years after the end of World War II.

## Growing up in Kansai

Kaoru Morioka was born in 1950 to a Japanese mother and an American father in post-war Kyoto. While growing up in the 1950s and 1960s, he received harsh treatment because of his mixed-race background. People called him *ainoko* and *konketsuji*.[1154] His mother was called *pan pan* (or woman of the night) and assumed by others to have been a loose woman.[1155] He grew up as a native Japanese speaker, and did not learn English until he formally studied it in high school and worked diligently to perfect it as an adult.

He attended public schools: primary school at Rokuhara Shōgakkō in Higashiyama-ku, junior high school at Yasaka Chūgakkō, and high school at Horikawa Kōtō Gakkō, not far from Kiyomizu-dera, arguably one of Japan's most famous temples (see Figure 15.1). Kaoru attended evening classes to complete his courses while working part-time at a bookstore delivering books and magazines. He grew up with his mother and his Japanese stepfather, and did not know his biological father, an American GI from Tennessee who served in Japan following World War II. His parents had a relationship but never married. According to his mother, after his father was shipped off to serve in Korea, they

Figure 15.1 Kaoru with his mother, Setsuko, on the first day of elementary school at Rokuhara Shōgakkō, located in Higashiyama-ku, circa 1957 Kyoto, Japan. Used with permission by Karl Lippincott.

never made contact again.

Kaoru's mother, Setsuko, came from a proud family that traced its ancestry to a samurai lineage. According to Kaoru, she was a very strong-willed and often *ganko* (stubborn) Japanese woman. As a twenty-five year old single mother of a mixed-race child in the 1950s, she endured social stigma and judgment from society.

When she was in town with Kaoru, people made the connection and looked at her with contempt. Hecklers called her a *panpan* even though she was not a prostitute and had never worked in such a capacity. Kaoru recalled,

> When I was in about second grade, I remember my mother and I were walking down the street talking, all of a sudden out of nowhere, this young boy started calling her *panpan*. I remember my mother picking up a tiny piece of stone and hurling it at him, to get him away from us. She was yelling, but I don't remember what she was saying to that boy. I also remember my mother was very, very upset. I had never seen her like that before.[1156]

Even the simple act of being with her mixed-race son in public caused people to make assumptions and prejudge her. Setsuko and Kaoru could never just be mother and son or shake the association of *panpan* and *ainoko* because Japanese society at the time automatically deemed them as such. Setsuko made the choice to be a mother and raise her son rather than give up her child for adoption. This choice had severe consequences. She was ostracized from her family and shunned by her brothers. Kaoru remembers, "I have no recollection of being with my uncles. I had no contact with my cousins or any other relatives. We were in complete isolation from the rest of the family."[1157] By the time Kaoru was in junior high school, Setsuko had married a Japanese man who was a supportive stepfather.

Kaoru's upbringing was a humble one. For most of his childhood in Kyoto, he grew up with a single mother (see Figure 15.2). Thrift, austerity, and food rationing were commonplace in post-war Japan. Kaoru and his mother did not have the luxury of acquiring American goods from the PX because they were not associated with the military or connected to the bases. Kaoru recalled, "We were poor, even by Japanese standards. I was at the bottom of the caste system, because I was poor. I was not living on the army bases. I ate Japanese food. I was Japanese. I went to a Japanese school."[1158] Even after she remarried, they remained extremely poor because her husband, Mr. Yamada, did not have a steady job and his income fluctuated. He often gambled on races making their family's finances even less stable. For mixed-race individuals like Kaoru, the difficulty they faced at this time stemmed from their racial status, socioeconomics, and limited membership within Japanese society.

Coping strategies were necessary for survival. Mixed-race

Figure 15.2 Kaoru, his mother Setsuko, Baya-san, and the family dog. Baya-san was not related, but a very kind Obasan to Kaoru. She sometimes served as his babysitter. This picture was most likely taken when Setsuko's partner left to return to the U.S. Kyoto, Japan, circa 1957. Used with permission by Karl Lippincott.

children were cast as outsiders because their physical features reminded others of the defeat Japan suffered during the war. Kaoru endured *ijime* or bullying from his peers, sometimes on a daily basis. As soon as he left the house, he was taunted and jeered at. The constant reminders of his racial difference became burdensome and nearly unbearable. However, he found ways to cope by building model airplanes and studying English. He mostly built American airplanes and tanks with American insignias on them. He recollected, "This gave me some sort of comfort and made me feel a bit closer to my father and the United States."[1159] This pastime continued into adulthood, and even today he displays his model airplanes in his basement at home. The relentless *ijime* also fueled Kaoru's desire to study English:

> I studied conversational English and thought some day I will be able to speak it fluently enough to gain respect. I listened to The Beatles' records and learned their songs and tried to pronounce the English words in the lyrics correctly. I watched many American movies including Western movies starring John Wayne, who was my hero. I pretended I understood English, even though I had to read the [Japanese] subtitles.[1160]

For an adolescent like Kaoru caught in the reality of post-war racism, it is easy to understand his reasoning for making model airplanes and furiously studying English. He was unable to solve the greater issues of post-war multiraciality, poverty, and bullying. The logic behind his motivation and pastimes helped Kaoru to deal with the illogic of racism.

Things were difficult, but they improved as time went on. Part of this was because Kaoru was fearless and resourceful. The other part was that as a teenager he was able to have some control over the choices in his life (see Figure 15.3). And he had a solid support group of school and church friends to help him. An American missionary friend of his gave him the name Karl because it was very similar to his name, Kaoru. "When we first met him in Kyoto, he called me Karl instead of Kaoru, and it stuck."[1161]

> Without having a very good support group, while growing up in Japan, I really don't know how I would have ever survived. My mother and my stepfather, Mr. Yamada, were really there for me. They kept me stable, even though we were poor. My schoolteachers, my friends, and pastors from my church: they were all taking part in trying to keep me together so I could stay focused with my life, whether they knew it or not. They were a very important part of my life in Japan.[1162]

Figure 15.3 Kaoru sitting on a motorcycle belonging to a friend whose family owned a udon-ya (noodle shop). The motorcycle was used to deliver soba and oyako donburi (chicken and rice bowls). Kyoto, Japan, 1965. Used with permission by Karl Lippincott.

Although he had a supportive environment, Kaoru's desire to come to the U.S. never subsided. "I was constantly dreaming about the U.S. I thought, some day I was going to get there, even though I had no clue how I was getting there. I just never stopped dreaming."[1163] His yearning put him into situations where he would gain the leverage to do so.

After completing the tenth grade, the Pearl Buck Foundation sponsored Kaoru to travel to the U.S. as an exchange student (see Figures 15.4, 15.5, 15.6). This occurred because in addition to having a solid support group, Kaoru's life intersected with various influential people in Japan. One figure who served as a supporter and a catalyst for Kaoru's eventual journey to the U.S. was the author, Imao Hirano. Born in 1900 to a Japanese mother and a French-American father, Hirano grew up in Japan when being mixed race was not commonplace. He came of age during a time when a mixed background did not have the stigma of the military

Figure 15.4 Class photo, Yasaka Junior High School, circa 1964 Kyoto, Japan. Used with permission by Karl Lippincott.

and war. By the time Kaoru's generation of mixed-race children was born, Hirano was already in his fifties. The public debates of the *konketsuji mondai* and questions about what to do with the children swirled around in the media. To address the issue, Hirano authored several books of semi-autobiographical juvenile literature using a mixed-race character named Remi.[1164] He chose the name Remi because that was his own nickname while growing up. During the 1960s, Hirano became an activist for mixed-race individuals by publishing articles and organizing grassroots group discussions called *Remi no kai*, where mixed-race youth could come together for camaraderie and dialogue.[1165] Kaoru attended a *Remi no kai* meeting in Kyoto after reading one of Hirano's articles, "I Will Be Your Father: Raising the War's Innocent Mixed Blood Children," which spoke to Kaoru deeply.[1166] His reaction to it garnered an unexpected result that changed the course of his life.

Figure 15.5 An article about Kaoru receiving the Pearl Buck Foundation Scholarship. Title, "Mixed Bloods Who Achieve," *Kyoto Shinbun*, November 14, 1966.

In 1967, when I was about 15, I read an article written by Mr. Imao Hirano in the monthly magazine, *Bungei Shunju*.[1167] The article was about me, and others like me. He described how Japanese people treated us. The article really left me with a lasting impression; I was compelled to write to him and thank him and let him know just how happy I was to have found someone like him. He himself was a mix blood.

He wrote me back and told me he was coming to Kyoto in the near future. When he came to Kyoto, he invited me to come and see him. We had a very interesting and meaningful conversation. It was like talking to a psychologist. Suddenly, there was this person who really and literally understood what I was going through living in Japan.

When Miss Pearl S. Buck read about him, she contacted him and told Mr. Hirano that she was going to pay a visit to him, on her way back from Korea. When they met, Mr. Hirano mentioned me to her. In turn, Miss Buck wanted to see me. The arrangement was made to meet with her in her next trip back from Korea. I met her with Mr. Harris, the President of the Pearl S. Buck Foundation, along with a Japanese judge who was there to translate for us.

I did my best to answer their questions with my limited English. I expressed to them just how much I wanted come to the States. At the end of our meeting, I was told by Mr. Harris to come see them later at the Miyako Hotel in Kyoto.

That night at the Miyako Hotel lounge, I was told they were interested in bringing me back to the States. They offered me a full scholarship to study in the States. That truly was a life changing moment. I will never forget that moment as long as I live.[1168]

E-2   EVENING TRIBUNE   ②   San Diego, Wednesday, June 28,

AUTHOR AND FRIENDS—Author Pearl Buck attends American Legion Auxiliary convention yesterday to receive cash gift from auxiliary for Pearl Buck Foundation, Inc. With her are Karl Morrioka and Paul Iiyama, Amerasians whom the foundation has helped. She's 75.

Figure 15.6  An article about Kaoru receiving the Pearl Buck Foundation Scholarship with Pearl Buck. Title, "Author and Friends," *San Diego Evening Tribune*, June 28, 1967.

Kaoru came to the U.S. as a scholarship student funded by the Pearl Buck Foundation. Founded in 1949 by Pearl Buck, as the Welcome House Adoption Agency, the Pearl Buck Foundation initially served as an adoption agency for mixed-race and monoracial children in places like Korea, Taiwan, and Vietnam. In 1964, the name was changed to the Pearl Buck Foundation. [1169] In Japan and Okinawa, the Pearl Buck Foundation was not an adoption agency but rather provided scholarships, financial support and job training for mixed-race individuals. [1170]

## Journey to New England

*"I wanted to be an ordinary person and blend in with everyone else, just like 'an average Joe.'"*[1171]

Kaoru traveled to the U.S. via Hawai'i. He flew into Honolulu and stayed for a one-week layover with Pearl Buck and other students. Looking out of the hotel window with the view of Diamond Head, he recalled, "The reality hits you, that we were in the U.S. We were saying, 'Look how beautiful it is. We are in the U.S.' This was in June 3, 1967. It was so exciting. Finally my dream came true."[1172] Initially, Kaoru came to the McCall School in Philadelphia to study basic English to prepare to enter the local schools. One year later, he attended the Friends Select School, which was run by Quakers. By the fall of 1969, Kaoru's English improved enough that he enrolled at Pennridge High School in Perkasie, Pennsylvania, near the office of the Pearl Buck Foundation. His first host family, the Robinsons, worked at the Pearl Buck Foundation. After a brief stay there, Kaoru moved in with another host family, the Lippincotts, who were Pearl Buck's adopted daughter Jean and her son-in-law Joe. He completed high school in the U.S. in 1970 on the Pearl Buck Foundation Scholarship.

> The image I had of the USA was that I was finally going to be free of prejudices, once I arrived in the States. It was the country where my biological father lived before he came to Japan. I thought everyone was going to accept me as one of them with open arms. I no longer had to be ashamed of being a mixed blood, because I thought the majority of Americans were a mixture of races. I also thought that I no longer had to worry about being spotted and finger pointed any more in public. My problems were over now, or so I thought.[1173]

Kaoru's life in the U.S. was not without difficulty. He faced challenges adjusting and the process of acculturation was nowhere near instantaneous. Pennsylvania, at that time, was not without its own biases. During the 1970s and 1980s, the racial make up of Perkasie, Pennsylvania was nearly ninety-eight percent White. Kaoru physically blended in with his peers and the community, but once he opened his mouth to speak, things did not match up. Since English was Kaoru's second language, others immediately picked up on his foreignness when he spoke. Although he was integrated with the community in Pennsylvania, due to his language ability and Japanese background at times he was perceived as an outsider. He faced questions about race and his mixed background no matter where he was.

Figure 15.7 Kaoru and Joy on their wedding day, July 22, 1972 at the St. James Episcopal Church in Keene, New Hampshire. Used with permission by Karl Lippincott.

For Kaoru, the reality of America was quite different from his initial impression.

> I thought to myself, 'I have finally come to the States.' I thought now everything was going to be all right, but I was not free from prejudices in America, either. It was easy for me to be picked out as an alien because English was not my first language. In high school I remember I was ridiculed because some of my test scores were low. I had difficulties with reading assignments and was not able to participate in class. When the teacher would pick me and I wouldn't be able to give a good answer, it was really embarrassing.[1174]

After graduating from high school in 1970, Kaoru went to Windham College in Putney, Vermont. In 1971, while at a local club, Kaoru noticed a woman named Joy and asked her to dance with him. They married a year later in 1972, and have been married ever since (see Figure 15.7). After getting married, the couple moved to Keene, New Hampshire, for Kaoru's job and Joy worked at the local hospital as a registered nurse. Their last name Morioka was printed on her hospital badge. Patients had a hard time pronouncing the Japanese last name and asked a lot of questions about it like, "What kind of name is Morioka? What nationality is that?"[1175] Both Kaoru and Joy figured that the name would give their children problems when they went to school in the future. So, instead of continuing to use his last name, Morioka, and to bypass the constant stream of inquiries, the couple asked Kaoru's former host family, Joe and Jean Lippincott, for permission to use their name legally. The Lippincotts agreed. Once they made the change, Kaoru and Joy received fewer questions about their name because Lippincott was easier for Americans to pronounce like the other European surnames in their New England community.

Living in the U.S. and being away from Japan was bittersweet for Kaoru and his mother. He had a once-in-a-lifetime opportunity to travel abroad to the U.S. to study on a scholarship. They had divided up their small family for Kaoru's future.

> My mother was very supportive, excited, and was also very proud. In her own view, Japan was not kind to her. She sacrificed great deal in raising me. It was her vindication to see me sponsored by the Pearl Buck Foundation to come to the States. She knew I needed to leave Japan. She witnessed what I went through as a child growing up in Japan. She also realized I may not be back for a long time to see her again.[1176]

In fact, Kaoru went back to Japan only three times after his departure as a teenager. He and Joy were busy raising their own family and working to put their children through college. During the 1970s and 1980s, international air travel to Japan cost a small fortune. As an adult, he was not able to be present for the day-to-day care of his aging parents. His mother and stepfather were involved in their church and could depend on the congregation's members as they got older and needed assistance.

During a visit to Japan in 2000, Kaoru saw his mother for the last time. She had been struggling with bladder cancer and in 2001 she passed away. Kaoru was not able to attend her funeral, or visit her grave. Due to the excessive cost of a gravesite in Japan, Kaoru's parents did not have the ability to purchase a private cemetery plot. Instead, they are memorialized with other members of their church on a community gravestone.

People like Kaoru faced adversity but leveraged their situation. In particular, this generation of mixed-race people received harsh treatment from society because the memory of World War II was so fresh. They were the physical reminders of a complex atomic war.

> I have been referred to as 'Jap or 'Nipponese,' numerous times. I just was not expecting that from Americans and it really hurt. I thought I was one of them, even though I did not have my citizenship. I thought I qualified to be one of them because my father was an American citizen. I had an identity crisis. Am I Japanese or American? Am I Asian or Caucasian?[1177]

The embarrassment and discrimination Kaoru faced echoed the treatment he had received in Japan. This was very disconcerting to him because the image of the U.S. he had in Japan was very different from the actual place to which he arrived. These experiences motivated Kaoru to perfect his English fluency. Despite having a late start in learning English, he mastered the language to near perfection by his late twenties.


## Conclusion

Biology is not destiny. The historical record does very little in the way of describing the life stories of mixed-race people. For mixed-race Japanese born in the post-World War II generation, their lives and experiences were not only negative; but there were also examples of life histories characterized by survival and success. When using oral history as a methodology, we can get at a different set of information that describes their lives in personal detail. We can see how the lives of mixed-race Japanese born at the end of World War II intersected with significant historical events during this period. People who were born immediately after World War II often went under the radar, while their stories were recounted as tragic ones, or they were thought to be in the entertainment business. Certainly people like that existed; however, most were ordinary individuals who were largely unknown.

The history books on the U.S. Occupation of Japan have left people like Kaoru invisible, or told their stories in a way that reflects problems and generalizes their experiences. In the media of the period, their stories are told as tragic, hopeless, and dire. Yet, when we gather the details we find that despite the predictions of racial pathology most multiracial people were not destined for failure. In fact, many of the racial biases and issues originated from others who had predetermined notions of race that fueled the anxieties of the *konketsuji mondai*. Mixed individuals like Kaoru were questioned about their identity, but that did not warrant the label of an identity crisis. Rather, others had a crisis with their identity. Oral history provides a method to see that there is not a problem with the bullied, but instead, perhaps a problem with the bully.

Kaoru's oral history renders him visible in the historical record and provides a window into what his life was like in post-war Japan from *his* point of view. Some mixed-race people left Japan while others never did. Having his voice provides the reader with an understanding of his experience coming from Kansai and ending up in New England. We gain a better understanding not only of the post-war mixed-race experience, but also influential individuals like Imao Hirano and Pearl Buck from the standpoint of Kaoru.

Kaoru went from one extreme to the other, from a primarily Japanese population speaking Japanese in Kansai, to complete immersion in a white English speaking population in New England.[1178] His assumptions about what it meant to be mixed race, his image of America, and his position as a son, husband, father and grandfather help us understand the subtleties of race relations and mixed-race studies in the post-war period. Certainly, Kaoru's life experience is extraordinary because his life intersected with influential individuals like Hirano and Buck during in the 1960s. However, the racism, nativism, poverty, periods of loneliness and triumph he endured were widespread.

## Epilogue

Karl Lippincott currently resides in New Hampshire with his wife Joy, where they recently celebrated their forty-third wedding anniversary together. They are the proud parents of four children, Kristen, Andrew, Alex, and Trevor, all of whom are college graduates. Karl and Joy recently became grandparents to a beautiful baby girl named Paisley.

## CHAPTER SIXTEEN

# CHERRY BLOSSOM DREAMS: RACIAL ELIGIBILITY RULES, HAPAS AND JAPANESE AMERICAN BEAUTY PAGEANTS

### REBECCA CHIYOKO KING-O'RIAIN

*As I peek out from behind the curtain of the Cherry Blossom Queen Pageant stage, I can feel the noise and excitement levels rising. The queen pageant candidates giggle nervously behind me and one slips her hand into mine asking me in a whisper, "How do I look? Do I look okay?" I produce a compact mirror for her to check her "Japanese up hair do," which is thickly padded with cotton and heavily adorned with bells and birds to complement her kimono. She wets her finger and draws it carefully over the front of her hair and then her eyebrows to mat them down so they won't stick out and will look smooth and sleek. 'There!' we both say in unison and we are ready to begin the beauty pageant to see who will represent the Japanese American community as the Cherry Blossom Queen (excerpt from field notes San Francisco, 1996).*[1179]

### Introduction

Japanese American beauty pageants are prime sites of collective identification, cultural production and representation. They are interesting case studies of popular culture as they produce both symbolic racial representations of collective identities (the racialized beauty queen) and representative collective cultural meanings (what it means to be Japanese American culturally) through the symbols of the queens. But not everyone can be a queen and there are racial eligibility rules that determine who can and cannot be deemed an authentic representative of the Japanese American community. This chapter explores the intersection of culture and race in Japanese American beauty pageants by focusing on the process of racial and cultural production where beauty queens are symbols on which race/culture is inscribed as text, but also sites of and agents in the active production of race/culture. Analysis of this process reveals that notions of culture are produced that serve to naturalize race in the pageants, which can be seen in debates about the community and authenticity.

### Eurasians are the Poster Children of Globalization

They are the "mixed-race chic"[1180] of the East. The explosion of mixed-race models and interest in multiraciality and beauty has been analyzed in Japan primarily as a consequence of global capitalism, postcolonial racialization and patriarchy.[1181] Matthews argues that the appeal, allure and persuasions of Eurasian/mixed race are as much an effect of its commodified production as a cosmopolitan figure with automatic racial, cultural and national border crossing attributes, as its capacity and potential to claim for itself a local space of visibility.[1182]

Mixed-race or hapa models in Japan then are racialized and sexualized as more desirable and attractive than their monoracial counterparts in part because they are often represented as half White. But are they always in every situation considered in this way?

In this chapter, I examine mixed race representation and turn it on its head to argue that in fact, in the context of Japanese American beauty pageants (a non-white hegemonic context), mixed-race Japanese American women may NOT be deemed more attractive, chic or good representatives of the Japanese American community. As Eric Liu writes, "The blurring of race labels is neither the dawn of colorblindness nor the dusk of racism."[1183] Instead, the presence of mixed-race beauty queens within Japanese American communities may be seen as a harbinger of cultural dilution.

But what is the relationship between cultural dilution and racial mixing? To be a Japanese American beauty queen one must be racially (enforced by racial eligibility rules which require "at least 50% Japanese ancestry") Japanese and ALSO culturally Japanese American (speak the Japanese language, be familiar with cultural values such as *gaman* (perseverance) and possibly cultural arts (such as *ikebana* flower arranging and *taiko* drumming). Pageant organizers and participants were clear that if one is racially Japanese, then one naturally has the corresponding culture. Japanese American beauty pageants in this way could be seen as an example of the Production of Culture perspective.[1184]

Within Asian American Studies, Chin, Feng, and Lee argue that the term "cultural production" is understood as:

not simply an epiphenomenal manifestation of a pre-existing culture, but rather the product of hybrid cultural trajectories....culture is not an essence but a process of production and reception, an active social relation. Created by individuals with vested interests, cultural production is always historically situated, reflecting such social relations as crafted through the dialogic and syncretic processes of production and receptions.... Hence, the question 'who is producing what for whom and why?' is critical to understanding complexity of cultural production.[1185]

Asian American cultural production in this sense has an activist tendency to challenge racist stereotypes,[1186] but it can also serve as the bridge between relations of cultural production (with mainstream but also with other racial/ethnic minority groups, globalization, etc.) and the nuances of lived experiences.[1187]

In terms of race theory, the rejection of biological determinism and the focus on the social construction of race[1188] has meant that some racialization theorists have tended to throw the body out with the biology. Some race theorists have moved away from analyzing embodied practices of racial and cultural production to focus on organizational and institutional understandings of race and racial meaning making.[1189] However, racial/ethnic beauty pageants are different to other forms of cultural production precisely because the product being produced and the surface on which meanings are created and attached is a real racialized human body.[1190]

The racial element (primarily enforced through racial eligibility rules) in the selection of Japanese American beauty queens makes them different types of cultural objects (as living symbols of racial/cultural communities) and they concomitantly have different types of cultural production processes. Firstly, the Japanese American beauty pageants studied here do not operate within a pageant industry. There is no television coverage, no agents, no paid consultants, and they do not represent a pyramidal pageant scheme, i.e., if one wins they do not go on to the regional Miss Japanese America pageant, etc.[1191] These pageants take place within a context where the culture being produced is not an object or thing (such as art work or music) but embodied—the queen herself is produced with cultural meaning but is not just an object but a person and social agent. Finally, the beauty pageants and queens are not commodified and sold, per se, within a market to benefit producers but seen primarily as an ambassadress—both agent and symbol of—ethnic/racial and cultural capital which is seen to be naturally authentic.

In the Japanese American case, antiquated versions and notions of culture are racialized and gendered in particular ways by the pageant organizers, the queens, and the judges so as to attempt to tie together, maintain, and hold onto what they deem to be authentic Japanese American culture. Linked to the homeland (Japan) through social and gift relations (the giving/receiving of *omiyage* souvenirs), common past historical experiences (World War II internment) and art forms (dance, music, flower arranging), dress (*kimono*), and cultural values (*gaman*, filial piety, and some would argue versions of retro femininity), the pageants work on the beauty queens to reinforce relationships between culture and race which essentialize and fix Japanese American culture to racial identities.

Japanese American beauty pageants are cultural productions that are also consumed (although not in a strictly economic form of consumption) as a way of creating and shaping social networks along ethnic and racial lines. The Japanese American pageants as cultural forms tend not to just be appropriated by other groups, but also by Japanese Americans themselves to bring together individual and communal level anxieties about the increasing role of mixed-race participants in the pageants and communities. But the pageants have always reflected the current issues of local Japanese American communities.

**The Changing Nature of Japanese American Beauty Pageants (1935-2010)**

The Nisei Week Queen Pageant was first held in 1935 in Los Angeles. Japanese Americans at the time faced increasing racial discrimination and were forbidden from participating in many mainstream popular cultural realms including mainstream pageants like Miss America or Miss California. The pageant's connection to cultural festivals served to highlight the local context of the pageants.[1192] However, the audiences for different parts of the festival differed. Nisei Week in Los Angeles was founded to focus on the *Nisei* Japanese Americans, who were born in the U.S., and were U.S. citizens. On the eve of World War II, the festival and pageant served the dual purposes of uniting the Japanese American community in Los Angeles and Southern California and to celebrate their American born and succeeding generations. To the *hakujin* (white mainstream) community, it was an attempt to prove the ability of Japanese Americans to assimilate and become truly American.

By the 1970s and 1980s, Japanese American pageants shifted to focus on cultural nationalism and declare that, "Japanese American is Beautiful Too." The Asian American Power Movement following from the success of the Black Power Movement in the 1970s, embraced the "Black is Beautiful" ideal as a way to accept and reaffirm the natural beauty of minority women. The Japanese American community was not immune to this and Japanese American beauty pageants, while fairly traditional in terms of feminism, did incorporate some elements of culturally nationalist discourse on the resistance of white feminist hegemonic norms of beauty. Unlike the earlier era, the proponents of the pageants in the 1970s argued that Japanese American women could be beautiful in their own right. While transgressive perhaps in a racial challenge to white norms of beauty, the pageants maintained strong notions of Japanese American femininity.[1193] Japanese American pageants shifted from being a model of assimilation to a platform to claim pride in Japanese American racial and cultural identity.

By the 1990s and 2000s, the pageants were focused on "Preserving Japanese American Culture." During this period, the issue of the dilution of the Japanese American community, primarily though interracial marriage, was at the forefront of the minds of local Japanese American community members in San Francisco, Los Angeles, Seattle, and Honolulu where my research was conducted. The N2K or Nikkei 2000 "Ties that Bind" conference in San Francisco was centered on the question "Will there be a Japanese American community in the future?" As community newspapers and organizations shut down and demographic dispersion took its toll, community leaders worried about the future of the Japanese American community. With an aging population and low immigration, they focused clearly on intermarriage as a challenge, which brought to the fore debates about who was Japanese American and what that meant for cultural definitions of Japanese Americaness if the majority of the community (in places like San Francisco) became racially mixed rather than monoracial.

The argument followed that if a person was only half Japanese racially, they were also only half Japanese culturally and were therefore losing culture and blending into the mainstream—racial dilution was causing cultural dilution and, in turn, community dilution. The pageants became a vehicle to preserve Japanese American culture with a focus on maintaining authentic Japanese American culture and the quest for authenticity came to re-inscribe certain notions of culture as true. One example of this was the continued use of racial eligibility rules, which were often justified based on the argument that if racial rules were eliminated, anyone could be the queen and that this, in the end, would dilute the meaning of the queen for the community. In general, organizers of the pageants argued that it would be better to do away with the pageant all together rather than open it up with no racial eligibility limitations. For people outside of the Japanese American community, the queen represented Japanese American culture as a commodity to be consumed as an exotic experience connected to the festival. The queen functioned as a public relations stunt to bring non-Japanese people into Japantown to eat and experience a little bit of Japanese American culture, but it certainly was not intended to invite them to *be* the queen.

## Methods

This chapter analyzes the cultural production of racial, ethnic, and cultural meanings embodied in the selection of Japanese American beauty queens in four cities: Los Angeles (1935-present), San Francisco (1968-present), Seattle (1960-present), and Honolulu (1950-present). Sixteen months of participant-observation fieldwork was conducted in the mid 1990s, again in early 2000 and 2011, by the author as a member of the San Francisco Cherry Blossom Queen Pageant Committee. This included all visitations—to local shops to open new businesses, volunteer and public relations activities, as well as all training sessions and official visitations to the other cities. Sixty in-depth interviews were conducted with past and current court members, organizers, judges, and sponsors through purposive sampling. Gaining access to the pageant as a committee member came from volunteering to help out at the first press conference and then being put to work assisting the candidates and court. This allowed me to gain a backstage perspective and observe closed rehearsals and confidential instructions given to the candidates and queens before traveling and watching how the pageant organizers, chaperones and judges shaped behavior, deportment, and discourse. Being behind the scenes for an extended period of time allowed me to see how culture affects social action, but also the ways in which culture itself changed over time and was collectively produced.

## Producing Culture, Community, and the Beauty Queen as Symbol

The pageants are a public, collective Japanese American conversation about what it means culturally *and* racially to be Japanese American across the four cities studied, but there were particularly lively debates in Los Angeles and Honolulu in the 1990s. The Japanese Americaness of the queen was deemed important. A Nisei Week Queen pageant organizer from the early 1990s explained why the queen is of such cultural importance:

> The queen is really a real feeling about being Japanese, being Japanese American, I'd say. And it is the love of what our community represents and of the culture we have and this is something that we have really tried to instill, not just sending someone out because she is pretty but because she is intelligent and, as you have seen, because of the queens, who they are, being very articulate and they do these things that are very Japanese. It is more to preserve our culture and to have a representative to make it a positive thing to be a Japanese American.

Within the latter era of Japanese American beauty pageants, the multiculturalist (but particularly the multiracial) narrative threatened the authenticity of Japanese American racial and cultural claims. Some used debates about racial eligibility rules to express their worries that the community will be diluted and blended away through racial (and assumed cultural) hybridity into indistinct American culture—thus losing their unique racial and cultural identity.

Culture in the Japanese American pageants was used as a foil to thwart feminist critiques of the pageants. Pageant advocates argue that the pageants importantly function to "preserve culture," are focused teaching about and maintaining culture, and are *not* about beauty and therefore do not objectify women like mainstream pageants do. The focus on culture is a rationale for the continuation of the patriarchal practice of annually crowning a woman as queen to represent the community.

Culture was also used in part to determine authenticity, in conjunction with race and social networks. Claims to authenticity were based on criteria such as: *racial capital* (looking Japanese American enough to serve as the symbol of the local community), *cultural capital* (having competency in, for example, the Japanese language, Japanese arts, or Japanese ways of being) and *social capital* (Japanese American social networks and community ties that legitimate the queen as part of the Japanese American community). In fact the queen candidates reproduced this connection between notions of culture and race when they took on the task of learning more about Japanese American culture in order to be, embody, and enact a better queen as a symbol of the community. This is because, as Inglis claims:

> Body techniques learned from the group tend to be experienced an enacted by the individual unconsciously rather than consciously, he or she generally feeling that the specific ways bodies move are just 'natural'. But of course these ways are not just 'natural' because they have been created by the culture of the group to which the person belongs... each social group has a distinctive lifestyle. ... Another way of saying this is that the social group instills its cultural values not just into the minds of each of its members, but into their bodies too.[1194]

This natural racialized cultural body is made manifest and drawn into consciousness in the pageants because the queen candidates are shown, trained and practice how to "be" Japanese American in bodily terms through the pageant. They put tremendous effort into learning to walk in *kimono*, bow, and carry themselves in a Japanese American way. Training sessions in preparation for the pageant emphasized moving in ladylike ways but also moving in racialized Japanese ways – walking with toes pointed in, gliding or shuffling and not striding, which was seen as a western way of walking in kimono. The queens wear symbols such as the *kimono*, but also work to become symbols themselves. Interestingly, the women were trained to walk in a more western way (striding, with pivot turns and using their arms more freely) during the evening gown section of the pageant where the focus was questions and answers, but not during the opening preview section of the pageant where they were dressed in kimonos where the emphasis was on "walking Japanese" and flirting with the audience through moving the neck and head and small movements with the sleeves of the kimonos.

Culture was also inscribed on the bodies of the queen candidates through the emphasis on racial appearance and racial eligibility rules. Even with a focus on the commonality of Japanese culture across local Japanese American communities, racial meanings mattered highly in the context of the pageants studied here. In Los Angeles in the 1980s, a heated debate was sparked within the community by the selection of a mixed-race queen. The main argument was that mixed-race queens did not represent the community *because* they were mixed.[1195]

In Hawai'i, the Japanese American community continued to insist on maintaining a rule that Cherry Blossom Queen contestants must be "100% racially Japanese" until 1998. Even in 2008, after many mixed-race women had been named Cherry Blossom Queen, there was still a sense of nostalgia for when the queen was racially pure in Hawai'i and a continuing pride in being the last to change the racial eligibility rules to 50%.

Racial eligibility rules defining who was eligible to run in the pageant and hence who could represent the local Japanese American community are not just specific to Japanese American pageants, but in fact, exist in many ethnic pageants more generally (e.g., Miss Chinatown must be at least 25% Chinese, the Narcissus Queen in Hawai'i must be "nearly 50% Chinese," and Miss Asian American must be of 25% Asian ancestry). In the contemporary era, these racial rules usually exist NOT in mainstream pageants but primarily in racial/ethnic pageants concerned with maintaining and celebrating authentic ethnic culture and legitimating who can represent them. Most mainstream pageants have very strict rules around marriage and motherhood (which are not allowed) but few around race or ancestry, which might be deemed illegal.

But how do these racial rules play out in cultural practice? In the pageants studied here, many people were trying to impose racial definitions on candidates for Cherry Blossom Queen in San Francisco in asking, "Are you Japanese?" Mixed candidates responded to these racial challenges with cultural symbols such as using Japanese names, the Japanese language, or Japanese cultural arts to demonstrate their legitimacy as Japanese American community members and therefore authentic representatives as queen. They deployed certain cultural repertoires that they thought would be authenticated as truly Japanese American in order to improve their chances of winning.[1196]

There was an ever-present process of racial assignation in the pageants for example, when one is seen as "not White" by the mainstream, but not Japanese American by Japanese Americans in bodily/beauty terms in the pageants.

> Such racial projects highlight the importance of 'culture' in terms of the intangible but very real markers of language, dress, demeanor, and cultural capital that in addition to phenotype, make race so pervasive in everyday life.[1197]

In fact, in the Japanese American pageants that I observed, there was a downplaying of competition because they were not beauty pageants, per se, but cultural pageants. The implication was that by moving away from physical beauty as a criterion for judging, that somehow looks didn't matter.

But appearances clearly mattered in the pageants. The exterior presentation of self was constantly enacted in a bodily manner and was an important way to relay information visually to others – in order to be effective, the cultural strategies of the candidates had to take on an embodied form. Craig illustrates this when she argues that race is an embodied identity—one is a member of a cultural group in part because of one's body.[1198] She writes,

> Since race is constructed as an embodiment identity, challenges to racist hierarchies are often expressed as contests over the representation of racialized bodies … images of beauty practices can serve as a focal point for viewing the complex project of racial articulation.[1199]

Bodies in the context of the pageants were seen as natural and racialized. Certain parts/characteristics of the body (skin color, hair color, nape of the neck, etc.) were emphasized as part and parcel of the authenticating process in the pageants. The judges, who were mainly Japanese American community insiders, read and reinforced bodily cues, including racialized cues, to select the candidates who were the "nice girls."[1200]

Japanese American beauty pageants, while for the most part not televised, were similar to a television production in two respects. They were highly controlled by the producers/organizers, and they were also often loosely linked to the commodification of Japanese American culture through the selling of Japanese culture to outsiders by, for example, encouraging them to come into Japantown during the pageant/festival to shop, wearing a sash with a company logo embossed on it as advertisement, and so on. However, the sponsors were not commercial entities but tended to be local Japanese American churches (Buddhist and Christian), the Nikkei Lions Club (or VFW), or local Japanese American community groups. There were a few local Japanese American owned businesses (e.g., Benihana restaurant) who sponsored queen candidates in San Francisco, but they were only involved with the pageant for the month before the pageant and the sash with the sponsor's name was discarded after the pageant took place and once the queen candidates had earned their titles (such as Cherry Blossom Queen,

Princess, Miss Tomodachi).

## Authenticity

In the Japanese American beauty pageants, racial and gender appearance were worked at and worked on in order to make the claim to authenticity and the right to speak and represent the community as the queen ambassadress. Culture was used to justify racial rules and assignation but the pageant itself was also justified as a way for the Japanese American community to define itself in cultural terms.

For example, although not an official requirement, speaking Japanese was often seen by the judges as an advantage to the queen in her selection and duties (visiting Japan, dealing with Japanese businessmen, etc.). One former Cherry Blossom Queen pageant judge in San Francisco from the 1990s told me:

> I heard a story that one of the Japanese dance teachers was a judge. She asked someone if they spoke Japanese. They said, "No." Then she said, "We have nothing else to say to each other." I don't know how much of that is fact and how much myth. We get candidates who say, "I don't speak Japanese," and are really apologetic.

Language was a cultural tool used to make cultural claims to authenticity within the pageant. Others used their Japanese middle or last names to emphasize their Japaneseness in hopes that it would help them win. One Nisei Week Queen in Los Angeles in the early 1980s recounted:

> Queens who change or use Japanese names must see an advantage to doing that. They think, "Right. I am going to manipulate these factors and get every single one on my side that I can. I can't change my hair color or my eyes, but I can change my name." One girl, she changed her name. The story was that her father was Japanese but he changed his name because he married into a Chinese family and was going into the family business. Some people said they made that up ... they are Chinese and they want to run in the pageant. Other people said, "it makes sense to me." Other people said, "Who cares? If she wants that badly, let

her run."

Cultural authenticity in the pageant was decided by a shifting group of judges who brought to the stage different notions of what type of culture they were looking for. In the name of preserving culture and being a positive role model for Japanese American women, certain notions of ethnic Japaneseness (competent in the Japanese language, connected to the local Japanese American community, etc.) and certain notions of gender (articulate, well spoken, intelligent, but also pretty) were selected and reproduced by the judges, audience, and organizers each year in the pageant. When there was disagreement between the judges and audience about who should win, dissent was known almost immediately through the process of booing the titleholders.

In order to control for this, the pageant committee organizers conduct subtle orientations or training of the judges each year to shape the criteria (both formal and informal) that are used to select a winner. The scorecard is carefully explained to the judging panel before the pageant begins and concepts such as poise and confidence are explained, often in cultural terms. In 2000, when I sat in on the judging panel, the chairman of the pageant explained poise in strictly cultural terms, saying, "we wanted a queen who would represent us well, who is calm, classy, carries herself well, and isn't too outspoken." This closely mirrored a Japanese American cultural preference for silence over verbosity, and conformity over uniqueness part of a philosophy that the "protruding nail gets hammered down." There was no need to articulate this to the local Japanese American youth community worker or the Japanese dance teacher on the judging panel, who both began nodding in agreement almost from the moment he spoke. Only the non-Japanese American judge asked for clarification as to how to determine poise on the scorecard.

What was interesting was how *culture* was invoked in the pageants in order to claim and authenticate *racial* identities. One Cherry Blossom Queen from Honolulu in the 1990s explains,

> The queen appears in **kimono** a number of times in public. I think when you hear the public ask for the queen, a lot of people want you to be in **kimono**. It is the whole flavor of the Japanese American community. You can look very awkward in **kimono** if you don't walk correctly, if you don't handle yourself nicely. I think they are just worried. The person who donates the **kimono** –

that is a very large gift. He would just cringe if he saw people crossing their legs in it or waving their arms around, wiping their mouths on their sleeve. I think a lot of it is just the traditional look.

The correctness of the *kimono* matters because to violate a cultural norm and appear rude in it would make the committee and by association the local Japanese American community look bad. Not knowing culturally appropriate behavior is naturalized as "something we should just know" in the *kimono* segment. There was also intense social gendered and cultural control of the queens, which was often rationalized as "think what the community will think." The women's behavior as representative of the community was tightly controlled and there were strict rules about not drinking in *kimono*, appearing in revealing clothing, not getting pregnant etc.

Gender was also used in the context of the pageants as a rationale for maintaining culture, but also at the same time maintaining control over Japanese American women's bodies via the queen selection and pageant. The queen candidates were closely controlled by a chairperson, usually a man, who dictated and defined (through the training of the judges) appropriate femininity and womanhood that the queen was intended to represent. There were conflicts between the queens and the chaperones who tried to enforce rules around appropriate femininity (no smoking in *kimono*, no drinking with the tiara and sash on, etc.). Within this effort to control the behavior and appearance of the queens, it was difficult for the chaperones to regulate something that was supposed to be natural. In this instance, beauty culture was:

> a resource used by collectivities and individuals to claim worth, yet it is an unstable good, whose association with women and with sex, and its dependence upon ever-changing systems of representation, put its bearer at constant risk of seeing the value of her inherent beauty or beauty work evaporate. If beauty is ever capital, it is a somewhat stigmatized capital. It must appear unearned if it is to be authentic, as opposed to purchased, beauty.[1201]

## Naturalizing Culture

Race then was seen as natural and authentic beauty in the pageants, but it also was a social force and clearly played a role in naturalizing culture. If one was monoracially Japanese, it was assumed that by definition one had more culture. If one was mixed race, there was an assumption that one would have less Japanese American cultural knowledge or understanding. Race allowed some to make claims about culture and in doing so naturalized culture as something one has instead of something one does. Mixed-race beauty queens were under particular strain because without full racial credentials, their culture was suspect. This was in part because "Performers without this full [racial] pedigree ... have to do special authenticity work to gain acceptance."[1202]

Ironically, many of the mixed-race contestants had mothers from Japan (generationally quite close to Japan) and spoke Japanese and many monoracial candidates were often third, fourth or fifth-generation Japanese Americans with no Japanese language and little familiarity with Japanese American culture.[1203] One monoracial former Nisei Week Queen from the 1980s in Los Angeles explains,

> We have had some girls who are half Japanese and half various other things. Some of them have been more trained to the Japanese culture, more exposed to the Japanese culture than some of the girls who are biologically all Japanese American. Tami, she was bilingual but half Caucasian. Are they more Japanese than me because they speak Japanese or are they less because both my parents are Japanese American? I think her mom is from Japan. The current queen (1996) is only half Japanese but she does *taiko* (Japanese drumming) and works in Little Tokyo. She is definitely a part of the Japanese American community. I think she is an ideal representative, she knows the community. She is a part of the community.

Even though the queen in 1996 was half Japanese in terms of ancestry (race), she was a deserving queen in the eyes of this former queen because she participates in Japanese culture (*taiko*) and is connected to the ethnic enclave/network community in Little Tokyo in Los Angeles. Cultural practice and social capital help her to overcome racial deficiency. In both Los Angeles and San Francisco, efforts to impose strict racial and biological thinking were fairly unsuccessful because others argued for community inclusion based on culture rather than race. On a group level, many mixed queens appealed to the idea of community over the idea of race. When they successfully made the argument that they were a part of the community despite their mixed racial make-up, they exploded the racial basis of membership. They in fact, went a step farther to argue that they were trying to save the community by participating in it, and in the process taking the existing meaning of community, and changing the basis of it by removing race as the sole criterion. They argued that they were the "face of the future" in the community and they were ultimately successful because they used family connections (my mother is Japanese American, how can they say I am not?), culture (I know *odori* - Japanese cultural dance), and language (I speak Japanese) to legitimate their claims to represent the community. In fact, their ethnic claims posed problems for some monoracial candidates whose Japanese cultural practices were quite minimal—they had race, but no culture. However, even those candidates with impeccable racial credentials were under pressure to prove themselves ethnically because the assumed link between race and culture had been broken. This apparent struggle between ethnicity-based community and race-based community seems to be particularly obvious in Los Angeles and San Francisco where the community is on the demographic cusp of becoming a predominantly mixed community.

Likewise, if one of the queens was not behaving in a way that was considered Japanese American, if that queen couldn't back it up with the cultural characteristics attributed to Japanese Americaness, they were not considered to be authentically Japanese American. One monoracial *Sansei* (third generation) San Francisco Cherry Blossom Princess from the mid 1990s explained:

I think some of the candidates do Japanese talents because they can't speak Japanese. They think, let's stick something in there that is something to do with Japanese or they will say I don't have any aspects of Japanese culture in my whole presentation. I think that has something to do with it. The candidates that are half Japanese––the only differences are visual in some cases. Someone who is full Japanese ancestry, whose culture is American, I think they kind of have to strive to prove that too, but maybe they don't have to prove it as much as someone who doesn't look Japanese American.

The work that the half Japanese American has to do to unhitch race from cultural practices (Japanese talents) is more of a burden because they don't look Japanese. They then deploy these cultural presentations as a ploy or tactic to convince the judges of their Japaneseness.

One mixed-race contestant from San Francisco in the mid 1990s describes how she dyed her hair darker and did her eye make up to make her eyes look "more Japanese." When I asked why she did this, she replied that she felt that she needed her face to "look more Japanese" in order to do well in the pageant.

### The Visiting Queen and Claims to Authenticity Through Japanese American Culture

Culture was also used in the pageants as a tool to increase social capital through the queen's visitations to other Japanese American communities. These visits were taken as confirmation of the queen's authenticity but also allowed the four local Japanese American communities to gain support from each other in the face of continued minoritization in the U.S. In the pageants, physical attractiveness mattered and significant time was spent on physical appearance issues, but culture was deemed more important by the pageant organizers, chaperones, and judges[1204] than beauty or racial appearance, because the queen's main role was as a symbolic link to the other Japanese American communities. By collectively saying, "This is our queen," and by clarifying who she is, the pageants produced definitions of culture designed to reassure the Japanese American community both locally and afar that this is who 'we' are. Potts et al. found that the production and consumption of creative products (like computer games) are often constituted by social networks.[1205] Pageants, like the creative culture Potts describes, are also produced and constituted by social networks defined by racial and cultural criteria. The key aspects of the courtesy visitations by the queen as a representative and ambassadress were: 1) to strengthen ties between the local Japanese American communities in the four cities, 2) to reinforce notions of authentic and common culture and the power of the queen to claim authenticity, and 3) to legitimize the local pageant's claim to the right to produce and select the queen each year.

The visit the queen makes between the cities actually builds the social ties between the cities. While the pageant winners making the visits are different each year, the pageant organizers in the cities remain fairly consistent and the same people organize and facilitate the visits between the cities each year. In fact, the obligations incurred by past visits motivate reciprocating visits with each other. During field work, I observed much emphasis on the gifts that would be given to the visiting courts (chosen by the organizers, not the queen and court) and being sure to raise enough money to host (i.e., pay for the dinners and event fees for the visitors), because, in the past, their local queen and court had been similarly hosted when visiting the other cities.

This on-going social network was dense and strong friendships developed between the organizers, so, for example, the chief organizer of the visit in Hawai'i was the best man at the wedding of the second-in-command in San Francisco. Both were Japanese American men in their late 20s and early 30s at the time and both had served as judges for the other's pageant. The visits were about much more than the queen and the cities becoming sister organizations and pageants to each other. In fieldwork, the chaperones often used a family metaphor, arguing that the cities were sisters, as were the pageant organizers and queens. At social events, the queen and her court often formed 'court circles' protected by chaperones, to thwart unwanted social attention by drunk older men at receptions and the like. The cross-pageant relationships were often described as analogous to ancestral family ties that were to be cultivated and respected. This was done primarily through the use of Japanese American culture to reinforce notions of authenticity surrounding the pageants. There were in-depth discussions throughout watching each other's pageants (often the visitations were timed to have the visiting royalty make an appearance at the local Japanese American pageant) and about the level of authentic Japanese American culture in each pageant.

While doing fieldwork in Hawai'i, I was told by the San Francisco queen and court that I must note in my field notes that the Hawai'i pageants, while in *kimono*, did not wear the traditional *zori* (wooden flip flops) that they do in San Francisco. Rather than note that the *zori* are expensive and difficult to walk in, they queen and her princesses felt that the absence of the *zori* made the Hawai'i *kimono* segment less authentic than the San Francisco one. The Hawai'i court countered with the fact that they don't just receive training in walking, make up and *kimono*, but instead also take classes on Japanese arts and culture such as *taiko* drumming, *ikebana* (flower arranging), and Japanese singing. These contests of localized ethnic authenticity ran consistently throughout the pageants. They argued that the costuming was more real or authentic to Japanese culture or that the cultural training was more in depth and therefore authentic. The reference, however, was not to contemporary Japanese American culture, but to an antiquated notion of Japanese culture. Ironically, this linked culture to appearance in strong ways and the wearing of the *kimono*, while present in all the pageants and discussed as something a "true Japanese woman would wear," in fact was increasingly infrequent in contemporary Japanese culture. In contemporary Japan, the *kimono* is not worn very often (only for weddings and similarly formal occasions) and Japanese women also have to learn how to wear it and walk in it, as few own one to wear in the first place. Most Japanese women rent a *kimono* for their wedding or special occasion. However, when pageant participants were dressed (and they were literally dressed by elderly Japanese women who spoke little English and found it difficult to communicate with the queen, but who were experts in tying the *obi* (sash) in *kimono*) they talked about feeling like they were "putting on the layers" of Japanese history and felt like "real Japanese women." They didn't complain about the heavy, tight layers of material wrapped around them, but instead discussed how great it felt. The beauty and culture in wearing the *kimono*, while meant to appear effortless and culturally authentic in the pageant, in fact, was highly produced, learned, and put on (literally) by others and enacted in an antiquated notion of culture by the queens thus naturalizing culture on the body.

In addition, by reinforcing notions of authentic culture in the pageants, queens on the visitations also used other pageants to authenticate their own pageant's cultural productions and practices. Again, when the San Francisco Queen traveled to Hawai'i for their pageant, they were struck by how quiet, slow and traditional the *kimono* segment of the Hawai'i pageant was and they noted the fact that it was narrated in both Japanese and English. They argued that because San Francisco also had a similar *kimono* segment, that it was proof that in fact their own pageant was authentic. They argued that "If they do it and we do it", it must be authentic Japanese American culture. There were also contemporary examples of this as when the San Francisco court were given gifts of t-shirts which had 12 different types of Spam *musubi* (Spam rice balls) printed on them. The San Francisco court immediately recognized the food as Japanese American and the humor in the portrayal of the different ways to prepare it as an inside cultural joke. This move of reinforcing and even poking fun at oneself and one's culture allowed them to recuperate Japanese American culture through food even in a time of increasing anxiety about the loss of culture.

However, as a collective symbol, the queen sometimes found it difficult to represent many different cultural versions of Japanese Americaness. One Cherry Blossom Queen from Honolulu in the late 1990s said:

No matter what you do, someone is always unhappy. The Japanese businessmen will complain, or the young people will complain, or the sponsors. When we get candidates, we always tell them "remember, this is a volunteer organization; no two years are ever the same." If you look at how the queens are chosen and who the judges are, I think you begin to see a pattern. When you have celebrity judges or people who are involved in movies or TV, you usually get a more glamorous looking queen. When you get judges who are more of a local personality you are going to get someone who has been involved in the community. It is natural that their personal biases are going to become involved.

Finally, the pageants also used the presence of the visiting queens to local pageants as a way to legitimize the local pageants' right to produce the queen using racial and cultural criteria. The use of racial eligibility rules was often compared from city to city; Hawai'i had a 100% rule until the late 1990s and the others had 50% rules, with the rule being most loosely enforced in Seattle. This can be seen again through social networks, as the judges in the local pageants often were either past queens or organizers from other cities who knew who they should choose, and which criteria they should use almost without being told – including racial and cultural criteria which were often tacitly implied. For example, in the 1990s in San Francisco, one of the candidates clearly ran in the pageant to create career opportunities for herself in the local media (she was an aspiring reporter) and not to "further the cause of the local Japanese American community" or "spread interest in Japanese American culture." One of the judges who came from the Seattle pageant organizing committee commented afterwards that he didn't give her high marks, because he felt that culturally it wasn't very "Japanese American of her" to be promoting herself and not the community—his interpretation, perhaps, of a longstanding Japanese American ideal of the importance of the group over the individual. Ironically, in the pageant, one had to be unique and individual enough to stand out from the rest of the candidates, while also manifesting the narrative of putting community first in order to win and be the queen.

The symbolic role of the queen in representing community in international ties was clarified in this way by one former 1980s Nisei Week Queen upon her trip to Brazil to the Miss Nikkei International Pageant:

I would think there is a sense of trying to feel connected amongst the communities. The queens are just a visible link. We are the link. Everywhere I went, people are looking for "do you know so and so and are you related to X?" We are each a Japanese community, but we are all Japanese American. Even going to Brazil, we are all very different. I did feel that. More in Brazil than anywhere else. We were so different. There were the Portuguese-speaking girls; there were girls from Argentina and Mexico. The North American girls, Canada and all over the U.S. When you don't speak each other's languages you have to resort to bad Japanese and you don't speak any. You are third and fourth generation. That is what you have in common. There is something you have in common – Japanese culture. All of a sudden you felt it!

Anxieties about cultural loss have been recuperated through the pageants. By connecting with others and in trying to preserve the cultural traditions (however antiquated), the pageants have served as a focal point for Japanese American cultural production through bodily not linguistic recognition of Japanese culture.

## Conclusion

Japanese American pageant organizers and queens practice and enact their own conception of race as lived cultural experiences and in doing so produce both racial and cultural meanings. The Japanese American beauty queen is a site where social actors authenticate and naturalize race to make race look like a natural cultural attribute rather than a production.

The pageants also highlight the cultural strategies used to make claims to authenticity (using language, names, and Japanese talents) that are then judged by others within the pageants. Culture is also a basis of social capital, linking Japanese American communities in various locations together through recognition of cultural similarities. Cultural similarity serves as a basis for ethnic networks and the "ties that bind" Japanese American diasporic communities in California, Hawai'i, and further afield in Japan and Brazil. The ambassadress queen is chosen as a representative of the local Japanese American community in order to solidify ethnic ties, and to celebrate, perpetuate, and produce cultural meanings. Ultimately, the cultural production of the pageants naturalizes notions of culture (as something one has naturally) and links them inextricably to race. Many mixed-race queens deploy cultural repertoires in racial strategies in order to convince audiences of their authenticity. Finally, culture serves as a source of strategic action when it is mobilized to connect the queen to other Japanese American communities. The body, race, and culture are inextricably linked through social interaction, which serves, in this instance, to naturalize culture through an assumed connection with race and appearance.

## CHAPTER SEVENTEEN

# PLEASE CHOOSE ONE: ETHNIC IDENTITY CHOICES FOR BIRACIAL INDIVIDUALS[1206]

## CHRISTINE C. IIJIMA HALL

During the late 1970s, 30 half black and half Japanese individuals were extensively interviewed on their experiences of and attitudes about being racially mixed. This exploratory research project was initiated to uncover the ethnic identity choices made by these individuals, the factors affecting their choices, and life experiences/ attitudes of these mixed individuals. In the past, most research had been conducted on mixed children in psychiatric hospitals or clinics.[1207] Consequently, research on this population yielded data that indicated maladjustment. Very few published works could be found, at the time of the present study, on a nonclinical sample of biracial individuals. Therefore, I endeavored to interview a nonclinical sample of individuals with black fathers and Japanese mothers.

Park coined the phrase "marginal man" to represent a person who lives in two cultural worlds.[1208] Stonequist, Park's student, popularized the term but took a different perspective on the marginal person.[1209] Stonequist viewed the position as a negative one, with the marginal person being one who is poised in psychological uncertainty between two or more social worlds; reflecting in his soul the discords and harmonies, repulsions and attractions of these worlds, one of which is often "dominant: over the other; within which membership is implicitly based on birth or ancestry (race or nationality); and where exclusion removes the individual from a system of group relations.[1210]

Stonequist's view of marginality was challenged by other sociologists and psychologists.[1211] The most prominent complaint was that Stonequist made no distinctions among marginal person, marginal status, and marginal personality.[1212] A marginal person is biologically or culturally from two or more races or cultures. Marginal status exists when an individual occupies a position somewhere between cultures but does not wholly belong to any. This person is tied to groups culturally, socially, and/ or psychologically. The individual has a marginal personality when he or she has trouble dealing with the marginal status position, is torn between cultures, and develops psychological problems. With these distinctions, Goldberg made the important determination that the mere fact of being a marginal person does not lead to a marginal personality.[1213] In fact, there was growing belief that marginal people may be multicultural, with the ability to identify with more than one culture and acquire a wide range of competencies and sensitivities.[1214]

> The fate which condemns him [the marginal person] to live, the same time, in two worlds is the same which compels him to assume, in relation to the world in which he lives, the role of a cosmopolitan and a stranger. Inevitably he becomes, relative to his cultural milieu, the individual with a wider horizon, the keener intelligence, the more detached and rational viewpoint. The marginal person is always relatively the more civilized human being.[1215]

One group of individuals living in the United States who must live in two worlds is people of color who are living in white America. This group has at least three identity choices: to identify with their ethnic group, to identify with the white group, or to meld the two into a third (sometimes "hyphenated") identity, such as Japanese American (or Japanese-American).

Americans of mixed racial/ ethnic heritage must also live in two worlds. Mixed individuals who have minority and majority (ethnic and white) heritages have similar choices to those mentioned above. The choices are multiplied when the individual is a dual-minority combination (e.g., Black-Japanese). Ethnic identity for all racially mixed groups is exacerbated by the fact that they are racially mixed in a nonmixed society. They are a numerical minority, have few role models, and are usually not totally accepted by either ethnic group with which they share heritage.

The present study looked at a group of "marginal people" gathered from a nonclinical population to investigate ethnic identity choices, factors that influenced these choices, and attitudes and experiences regarding their bicultural and biracial existence.

## Method: Respondents and Questionnaire

A total of 30 (15 women and 15 men) black-Japanese respondents were recruited through word of mouth and newspaper articles in the *Los Angeles Times* and the *Rafu Shimpo* (the primary Japanese American newspaper in the Los Angeles area) describing the proposed research.

Respondents, ages 18-32, were from the greater Los Angeles area. The requirement that they be over the age of 18 was included in an attempt to eliminate adolescent "identity crisis" as a factor in their responses.[1216] Additionally, only individuals with black fathers and Japanese mothers were interviewed. (If other combinations had been included, the number of participants would have had to increase exponentially due the cell sizes needed to obtain statistical power.)

Respondents were interviewed using a researcher-designed questionnaire (The Hall Ethnic Identity Questionnaire) that consists of a self-administered section and an interviewer-administered section. The self-administered section contains established measures of self esteem with some adaption for the Black-Japanese sample population.[1217] In Dien and Vinacke's Ideal Self measure of self-esteem, a list of adjectives are presented to respondents, who rate themselves on a 6-point Likert-type scale (strongly agree to strongly disagree).[1218] Two adjectives added to the scale for this research study were *Black* and *Japanese*. The 10-question Rosenberg Self-Esteem Measure was used without adaptation.

The interviewer-administered section was of my own design; it solicited information on the areas described below.

*Ethnic identity choice.* For this study, *ethnic identity* was operationally defined as the category chosen by the respondent on a multiple-choice question commonly used for affirmative action purposes at many institutions. It is a questionnaire that instructs a person, "Please choose one" of the ethnic categories. Then listed are the usual federal delineations of ethnicities (Black, Hispanic, Asian, American Indian/Alaskan Native, White, and so on). An option of "Other: Please specify" was also included.

*Demographics.* Respondents were asked questions on their sex, age, and generation of mother (immigrant to the United States, first generation born in the United States, and so on).

*Ethnic composition of neighborhoods and friends.* Respondents were asked to give ethnic breakdowns of their past and present neighborhoods and friends.

*Subjective measure of cultural knowledge.* Respondents were asked how much they knew about the Black and Japanese cultures (answering items using a scale of 1to 6).

*Objective measure of cultural knowledge.* This section was composed of questions adapted from the Chitling Test and comparable Japanese culture questions.[1219] Sample questions were "How do you say rice in Japanese?" and "What is a blood?" This section is now endearingly titled the Sukiyaki-Chitling Test.

*Racial resemblance to a particular ethnic group.* Respondents were asked to self-assess their resemblance to various ethnic groups (Japanese, Black, Filipino, Polynesian, White) on a 4-point scale ranging from "very much" to "not at all."

*Involvement in political movements.* Respondents were asked questions about their participation in Asian, black, and other movements.

*Acceptance of and by particular ethnic groups.* The Bogardus Social Distance Scale was adapted for this measure.[1220] Bogardus discusses individuals' acceptance of particular groups as being a criterion for identification or inclusion with the group. For this particular research, acceptance by particular groups may have been additionally important for ethnic identity choice.

*Ethnic identity decision process.* Respondents were asked whether they had experienced periods when they had to decide to be Black, Japanese, or any ethnic identification.

## Results and Discussion

Of the 30 Black-Japanese interviewed in this study, 18 (60%) chose the category "Black" on the "Please choose one" question, 10 chose the "Other" category (7 of whom specifically identified themselves as Black-Japanese), 1 identified as Japanese, and 1 chose not to place himself into a racial or ethnic category. The 10 people who chose "Other" commented that they did not wish to be categorized simply as Black or Japanese, which would deny one of their cultures. They found that checking "Other" on a list that instructed "Please choose one" was a viable choice. Statements such as the following illustrate the frustrations and discovery: "It made me so mad to have to choose one." "It took me a long time before I realized that there was a place to check 'Other.'"

The one person who identified as Japanese did so because she had lived in Japan most of her life. The respondent who did not wish to categorize himself from a checklist was not much different from the rest of the respondents in his reaction to the interview and the questions. He simply did not believe in racial categorization.

In order to perform statistical analyses on the ethnic identity (dependent) variable, the ethnic choices were divided into two categories, Black (n=18) and Other Than Black (n=12). Dichotomizing this dependent variable was necessary to conduct the primary statistical analyses for the study—regression with the aforementioned factors hypothesized to influence ethnic identity as the independent variables (demographics, ethnic composition of neighborhoods, and so on).

**Ethnic Identity Choice Regression**

To determine the relative influence of each of the variables on ethnic identity, a regression was computed (see Figure 17.1). The ethnic identity choice regression, with Black as the dependent variable, yielded four significant variables accounting for 56% of the variance ($F = 8.3$, $p < .01$). It showed that those Black-Japanese who were young, had knowledge of the black culture, had predominantly black friends, and perceived non-acceptance by Japanese American peers tended to identify as Black. When these variables were regressed on the Other than Black dependent variable, the regression showed that those Black-Japanese with the opposite attributes—who were older, had less knowledge of black culture, reported fewer black friends, and were accepted by Japanese Americans—had a greater likelihood or choosing a category other than Black. Because these "Other" respondents did not possess the attributes needed to predict black identity, their category choice should not be seen as a fallback choice. If this were a fallback choice, it most likely would have influenced self-esteem. As reported earlier, this was not the case. There was no significant correlation between ethnic identity choice and self-esteem. Thus the choice of a category other than Black was not seen as choosing a "marginal" or "outcast" category, but as choosing a viable racial category that respondents felt comfortable with and proud to report.

## ETHNIC IDENTITY CHOICE REGRESSED ON BLACK IDENTITY

| ANALYSIS OF VARIANCE | DF | SS | MS | F | $R^2$ | ADJUSTED $R^2$ |
|---|---|---|---|---|---|---|
| Regression | 4 | 4.05 | 1.01 | 8.03* | .56 | .49 |
| Residual | 25 | 3.15 | .13 | | | |

| VARIABLES | BETA | STANDARD ERROR | $R^2$ |
|---|---|---|---|
| Age | -.29 | .02 | .06 |
| Percentage of times the respondent reported having Black friends | .42 | .002 | .24 |
| Subjective knowledge of Black culture | .38 | .19 | .14 |
| Perceived acceptance by Japanese American peers | -.36 | .12 | .12 |

*$P < .01$

Figure 17.1

*Demographics.* The mean age of respondents was 24 years. Age was correlated, although not significantly, with ethnic choice ($r$=-.29). (However, age made a significant contribution to ethnic identity choice in the regression analysis.) It appears that younger respondents had a greater tendency to identify as Black than did other respondents. Cheek has reported similar findings with his Black respondents.[1221] His explanation for this age difference is that with youth comes race militancy and a stronger race ideology. This militancy stage is also discussed by Cross as a necessary stage in the process of "Nigrescence."[1222] Kitano and Piskacek/Golub also theorize a stage where a minority individual may choose to reject one culture.[1223] The young Black-Japanese interviewed in this study may, therefore, have been experiencing this stage of strong identification with and/ or rejection of one culture.

Another explanation can be found in Goodman's book on race awareness.[1224] Goodman observes that young children see race as a unidimensional trait; it may be that the younger Black-Japanese individuals in this study view race as an "either/or" category. The older Black-Japanese may have reached a point in their lives where they can conceive of race as being multidimensional, and thus are able to identify as both Black and Japanese. These respondents concluded that a biracial category was a viable alternative; they actualized that a multiracial and multicultural existence was possible. This awareness may occur through maturation, experience, and self-evaluation.[1225] For example, one respondent reflected, "When I was younger, I thought I had to choose between the Blacks or the Japanese. Now I realize that can be both and who cares what other people think I should be."

No sex differences in ethnic identity choice were indicated in the analysis. Contrary to past research, females in this study did not differ from males in their ethnic identity choice.[1226] Same-sex identification was not substantiated. An interesting possible explanation for this lack of sex difference is that sex roles may be less important than race/ ethnic roles for minority males and females.

A total of 24 of the respondents' mothers were first-generation immigrants from Japan (Issei); 6 were second-generation Japanese Americans (Nisei). It was surprising that no generational effects developed, given that past research has shown generation to be a salient factor in ethnic identity among minorities in the United States.[1227] Perhaps this lack of influence was due to the respondents' belief that they were a new people or new race.[1228] Generation of mother would have no significant influence on their ethnic identification if they considered themselves the first generation of Black-Japanese.

*Ethnicity of Neighbors and Friends.* Respondents reported that, averaged over their lifetimes, approximately 46% of their neighbors had been White, 31% had been Black, and 14.5% had been Japanese. Percentage of times they reported having white, black, and Japanese friends were 42%, 67%, and 26.4%, respectively. There was a greater tendency toward black identification when the respondent s reported a predominance of black neighbors ($r = .39$, $p < .05$) and friends ($r = .49$, $p < .01$). These results are in accordance with past research findings.[1229] It should be noted, however, that strong correlation does not explain the direction or timing of the choice. That is, a person could have a predominance of black friends and thus chose a black identity or he or she could have had a black identity and thus chose to have more black friends.

*Knowledge of Culture and Language.* Ethnic identification choice and the objective and subjective measures of culture were significantly correlated ($r = .48$, $p < .01$). The more a respondent knew about Black culture, the more likely he or she was to choose a Black identity. Though not significant, strong correlations similarly indicated that the more knowledge a respondent had about Japanese culture, the more he or she tended to choose a category other than Black. Again, correlations do not give information about causality. Knowledge of culture may also have been the consequence of ethnic identity choice. If an individual identifies with a particular group, he or she is more likely to practice the customs and rituals of that group more often than an individual who does not identify with the group. Conversely, knowledge of culture could be the antecedent in this case, since many of the respondents reported practicing black and Japanese customs at home (before the social influence of friends could come into play). As they grew older, they may have realized that these customs were group specific and may therefore have sought others who would maintain and accept these customs. This process may have led to an identification with a specific group.

There were 16 respondents who felt they could speak Japanese well, somewhat, or a little, and 19 who felt they could speak black English well, somewhat or a little. There was no significant correlation between language proficiency and ethnic identity choice. This was surprising, given that language proficiency has been shown to be a powerful influence in ethnic identity.[1230] In fact, of all the cultural knowledge measures, it had the lowest correlation with ethnic identity.

The lack of influence of Japanese language proficiency may have been due to the Black-Japanese respondents' referent group for Japanese identity. That is, the respondents tended to see Japanese Americans, close to their ages, as their Japanese peers. Since most Japanese Americans around the age of 24 tend not to speak Japanese very well, it was not surprising that the Black-Japanese respondents' criteria for Japaneseness did not include language proficiency.[1231]

The lack of influence of black English proficiency is, however, confusing, because many respondents commented that being able to participate in street talk was necessary for relating to the black experience. The ability to speak black English may be important for interaction with Blacks but may not necessarily be a criterion for Blackness or black identity. For example, many black leaders (e.g., Martin Luther King, Jr., Jesse Jackson, Ralph Bunche) do not speak black English in their public addresses and yet still have strong black identities.

*Political involvement.* The only significant variable in this area was that of involvement in other ethnic movements ($r = .38$, $p < .05$). This variable seemed to predict that those involved in other ethnic movements (e.g., United Farm Workers and MECHA) tended to put themselves in a category other than Black more often than those not so involved. This could mean that those who chose this category saw themselves as more multicultural and were able to become involved with other ethnic movements besides those of their black or Japanese heritage.

The lack of influence of participation in black and Asian movements was surprising, however. Perhaps involvement was viewed as a forced choice—as having to choose Asian over Black or Black over Asian. In the 1970s, Blacks and Asians were pitted against one another. Involvement with human rights and other ethnic issues was more diverse and cut across racial lines.

*Perceived Acceptance By and Of Various Groups.* Perceived acceptance by black peers and lack of acceptance by Japanese American peers showed moderate but nonsignificant correlations with ethnic identity ($r = .32$ and $-.23$, respectively). However, lack of acceptance by Japanese Americans did emerge as a significant predictor in the ethnic identity choice regression that will be discussed later.

The perceived acceptance by groups may have been an antecedent or a consequence of ethnic identity choice. The perceived acceptance by Blacks as an antecedent to black identity is logical. That is, if one is accepted by a particular group (of which one is at least partially a member), the probability of one's identifying with that group increases, because membership is readily accessible. This may have occurred in this study, as comments similar to the following were made repeatedly: "They accepted me while others didn't" and "Blacks have accepted me for a long time." As a consequence of ethnic identity, perceived acceptance by Blacks could have been high because the respondents had already identified with the group.

The perceived lack of acceptance by Japanese American peers was not unexpected. Much has been written about the lack of acceptance among Japanese of other groups, especially Blacks, and this was supported by comments made by many respondents.[1232] Since many of the Black-Japanese were aware of this lack of acceptance by Japanese Americans, they may have decided to identify with their other ethnic group, Blacks. As some respondents stated, "They [Japanese] did not accept me, but the Blacks did."

The results of acceptance of various groups by the respondents was also interesting. Both acceptance of Blacks and acceptance of Japanese correlated with black identity, although the acceptance of Blacks was significant (r = .46, p < .01) while acceptance of Japanese was not (r =.34; n.s.). Here again the direction of influence is unknown. Respondents may have accepted Blacks and therefore choose to identify with them. Conversely, they could have chosen to identify with the Blacks and then began to accept them. Logic seems to predict the former explanation of acceptance and then identity, while cognitive dissonance theory could suggest the latter.[1233]

*Racial Resemblance.* The self-reported racial resemblance to different groups varied among the Black-Japanese interviewed (see Figure 17.2). Most, however, felt they looked more Black than they did any other race. Only one respondent, however, in my opinion, looked completely Black; he made the same judgment about himself. There was only one respondent who looked all Japanese (to me), but that respondent did not report that she resembled Japanese to a great extent. Most respondents did not believe they resembled Japanese very much. The other races they did feel they resembled were Polynesian, Filipino, and Malaysian.

Most reported they felt that Black-Japanese are very attractive people; *exotic* was the word many used for personal descriptions. Skin color varied from dark brown to very light; hair texture ranged from very coarse to fine and from curly to straight. The most

## PERCEIVED RACIAL RESEMBLANCE (IN PERCENTAGES)

| RACE | VERY | SOMEWHAT | A LITTLE | NOT AT ALL | N |
|------|------|----------|----------|------------|---|
| Black | 57 | 37 | 6 | 0 | 30 |
| Japanese | 0 | 23 | 54 | 23 | 30 |
| Latino | 10 | 24 | 35 | 31 | 29 |
| Polynesian | 34 | 23 | 37 | 6 | 30 |
| Filipino | 28 | 24 | 20 | 28 | 29 |
| Malaysian | 17 | 21 | 38 | 24 | 29 |

Figure 17.2

prominent Japanese feature to emerge was usually the eyes; but, again, this varied from very Japanese looking (one respondent said that his eyes were more Japanese than most full Japanese he knew) to slightly Japanese.

Some respondents were asked if they could recognize another Black-Japanese, and most said yes. Thus it seems that just as most Blacks can recognize another Black (even those who are fair-skinned enough to look White), so it seems many Black-Japanese have the ability to determine whether another person is Black-Japanese. It is difficult to explain to a "nonmember" what the salient characteristics are in determining another member, but it appears that many mixed individuals experience the same phenomenon. It seems that Whites concentrate primarily on skin color, while people of color (who vary tremendously in skin color and ancestry) attend to other features, such as eyes, hair, nose, body build, and stature.

None of the racial resemblance variables emerged as significant in correlations with ethnic identity choice. This was surprising, given that Cooley and Clark/Clark found that an individual's physical image has much to do with the manner in which society (and the individual) reacts to him or her.[1234] It was believed that the more one resembled a particular ethnic group, the more likely one would be to identify with that ethnic group. This lack of correlation could perhaps have been due to the lack of variability in the self-ratings of racial resemblance. That is, almost everyone in this sample felt she or he looked very Black, and few felt they looked Japanese. With little variance, it is difficult to obtain significant correlations.

Resemblance to Blacks and Japanese did not emerge in the ethnic identity decision regression. This was unexpected, since, as one respondent said, "I looked Black, lived with Blacks, and was accepted as Black; there was no decision to make." Two other respondents made similar comments.

The only variable that did produce a strong, but nonsignificant, correlation to the ethnic identity decision process was that of resemblance to Polynesians. The respondents who felt they resembled Polynesians were more likely to experience ethnic identity decision processes than those who did not resemble Polynesians. This may be because resembling Polynesians represents perhaps the epitome of Black-Japanese "physical marginality." That is, Polynesian characteristics seem to be a combination of black and Japanese features. Thus, if individuals look Polynesian, they are perhaps able to have a larger choice in their ethnic identification because they are physically able to enter many groups.

*Self-esteem.* There was no significant correlation between self-esteem scores and the ethnic identities chosen by the respondents. It seems that regardless of whether the respondents chose Black or other than black identities, their self-esteem was unaffected. This shows that the choice of a category other than Black can be called neither "marginal" nor "maladjusted."

### Ethnic Identity Decision Process
The majority (n = 18, 60%) of respondents experienced a period in their lives when they had to decide on an ethnic identity. Of these 18 respondents, 10 identified as Black and 8 identified as other than Black. The identity decision process reportedly began around the age of 14 or 15 and lasted approximately three to four years. Experiencing this process seemed to have no influence on whether the respondents chose the Black or other than Black category. Thus it seems that the process was a normal one, experienced by many but not correlated with the respondent's ethnic identity choice.

It was interesting that there was no significant correlation between experiencing an ethnic identity decision process and ethnic identity choice. It could be that respondents actually experienced decision processes without being unaware that those processes had occurred. Erikson believes that all individuals (multicultural or otherwise) must experience a decision process for adequate adjustment.[1235] Indecision may result in a marginal personality. That the respondents seemed to be adjusted (as shown by self-esteem scores) suggests that all must have encountered conscious or unconscious ethnic identity decision processes. For example, many respondents who lived with Blacks, looked Black, and were accepted as Black said that they had not experienced a decision process. However, they may have made a decision (unconsciously) to be Black. That is, there are Blacks who live in black communities, look Black, and so on, who decide not to identify as Black.[1236]

### Interrelationships between Black and Japanese Cultures
A multiple-choice, forced-choice question is designed to measure dominance of one variable over another. Thus the ethnic identity question of "Please choose one" was used to assess which racial identity was dominant over the other. To assess choice in a more liberal manner, the adjectives *Black* and *Japanese* were included in the Likert-type Ideal Self Measure. The respondents rated their

"Blackness" and "Japaneseness" on a scale of 1 to 6; 28 (93%) of the respondents rated themselves as high on Blackness and 26 (87%) rated themselves high on Japaneseness (see Figure 17.3). The correlation between the respondents' Blackness and Japaneseness was also very strong (.74). This can be seen as a measure of multiculturality using an analogy to Bern's theory of androgyny.[1237] Bern found that when people were forced to choose between identifying as masculine or feminine, they usually chose the sex-appropriate category (i.e., men chose masculine and women chose feminine). When asked how feminine they were, however, separately from how masculine they were, data showed that many people were both feminine and masculine simultaneously. In a similar manner, when having to make a forced choice between Black and other categories, the majority of respondents in this study chose Black. However, when asked about their Blackness and Japaneseness on two separate continua, 26 reported that they were high on both; they were biracial and bicultural—their version of androgyny.

### DEGREES OF BLACKNESS AND JAPANESENESS

|  | STRONGLY AGREE | MODERATELY AGREE | SLIGHTLY AGREE | SLIGHTLY DISAGREE | MODERATELY DISAGREE | STRONGLY DISAGREE |
|---|---|---|---|---|---|---|
| Black | 10 | 13 | 5 | 1 | 0 | 1 |
| Japanese | 8 | 8 | 10 | 2 | 1 | 1 |

Figure 17.3

Since many believe that society forces one to make a specific racial choice, the majority of racially mixed people probably choose one race over another. When allowed, however, to express the many facets of themselves, the respondents in this study tended to identify highly with both of their racial and cultural backgrounds.

### Experiences and Attitudes of Black-Japanese
When asked about the negative and positive points of being racially mixed, the respondents made positive comments twice as often as they made negative comments. Their negative experiences occurred primarily during the early years of the respondents' lives. Some negative experiences were still sometimes encountered, but most respondents commented that being mixed was more difficult for them when they were children. Problems consisted of people

calling the respondent derogatory names, not being understood or not having anyone to relate to, being the focus of jealousy from others, having conflict between cultures, and developing self-hatred.

As Stonequist hypothesized, some of the respondents reported that one of the negative points of being biracial is not being totally accepted by either group.[1238] This difficulty was reported by 9 of the respondents; 3 others said they were not totally accepted by Blacks, and 3 reported a lack of acceptance by Asians. Thus a total of 15 (50%) of the respondents reported a marginal status position.

The choice of identifying with both cultures was positive for some in the respect that it helped the individuals realize they did not have to try to fit into a single racial mold. The negative aspect of this, however, was that with so few Black-Japanese, they become a minority within a minority. Role models, reinforcement agents, and support groups were scarce for this group and alternate "others" had to be sought by individuals in this group

Other problems stemmed from the dating situation. In fact, racial identity decision processes seemed to begin around dating age—15 years old. Two respondents could not decide whom to date. Six other respondents reported that dating Blacks was difficult because many potential dates did not accept the respondents as all Black and refused to date them.

Again, positive comments far outnumbered the negative. The most frequently mentioned positive comments concerned the benefits of being from two cultures and heritages and obtaining the best qualities of both, and the ability to accept, empathize with, and understand people of other cultures and races. The next most popular responses were that being biracial made one novel, and gave one the "best physical features of both races." Many commented that Black-Japanese were very beautiful people. Having good parents and a strong family unit was also mentioned by many. Several respondents said that being multiracial and multicultural had made them strong people with diverse and positive perspectives on life.

This Black-Japanese group could be seen as at risk for developing marginal personalities. As Garmezy (1978) has shown, however, these "at-risk survivors" emerge stronger than the average individual.[1239] Thus, in spite of (or because of) all the detours and adjustments, the Black-Japanese in this study were well adjusted in their heterogenous heritage. In fact, most found their biracialism and biculturalism to be assets, as reflected in the following comments: "I feel like a richer, more diverse person"; "I've got the best of both worlds"; "It makes me more sensitive and understanding to other minorities." These Black-Japanese are, indeed, the "cosmopolitan people" discussed by Park (1937) and the "multicultural people" considered by Ramirez et al. (1977).[1240]

## CHAPTER EIGHTEEN

# THE NEW NIKKEI: TOWARDS A MODERN MEANING OF "JAPANESE AMERICAN"

CYNTHIA NAKASHIMA

### Introduction

According to demographic projections, there is a good chance that 2016 will go down in Nikkei history as the year that the Japanese American community became "majority mixed": in other words, of the United States citizens who identify themselves as "Japanese", more than 50% will also identify with one or more *other* ethnic and/or racialized groups. For a people who have historically associated "pure-bloodedness" with "Japaneseness" this shift will undoubtedly be a meaningful one. [1241]

Interestingly, thousands of miles away in the Nikkei homeland of Japan, a different but overlapping moment of transition is occurring in terms of a population decline that, if patterns remain unchanged, will result in almost 50% of the nation's citizens over 65 years of age by 2060. A typical response by an industrialized nation to this sort of population projection would be to increase immigration—if for no other reason but to maintain a youthful work force. But again, associations of "purity" with definitions of "Japanese" have led the country to maintain some of the strictest immigration and naturalization policies in the world, even while it is a leading force in the global exchange of goods and ideas.

The Japanese and their diaspora are in major flux. Regardless of the possible reasons for these patterns, what will be the response? In Canada, Japanese Canadians have the "highest proportion of out-group pairings" of any "visible minority group": 75% in 2006. [1242] In Peru and Brazil, two other countries with sizable Japanese populations, out-marriage rates and the proportion of Japanese who are "mixed" are similarly high. [1243] Narrow definitions of who and what looks/sounds/acts Japanese are becoming more and more meaningless every day. Can the Nikkei challenge themselves to complicate their category(ies)? Can they accept themselves as a "New Nikkei"?[1244]

In this chapter I will explore the path thus far towards complicating one iteration of the category "Nikkei"—that of the Japanese American. In the final hours of a majority "pure" ethnic community, let us reflect on the evolution of a cultural identity.

## The Discourse on Mixedness in the Japanese American Community

### Part I: A Major Ethnic Disaster

Appendix to Executive Order 9066
(by Ronald Tanaka, 1980)

the people who put out that book
i guess they won a lot of awards.
it was a very photogenic period
of California history, especially
if you were a white photographer
with compassion for helpless people.

but the book would have been better,
i think, or more complete, if they
had put in my picture and yours, with
our hakujin wives, our long hair and
the little signs that say, "what? me
speak japanese?" and "self-determination
for everyone but us." and then maybe
on the very last page, a picture of
our kids. they don't even look like
Japanese.[1245]

Ronald Tanaka (1944-2007) was a poet with a Ph.D. in British literature. He lived and taught English in California. And he was born behind barbed wire, in the War Relocation Authority's Poston, Arizona facility. The above poem is a powerful, pain-filled expression of his anger towards the incarceration of Japanese Americans during World War II and the affects of that incarceration on the people and the community. It is also an example of a belief in the genetic and cultural "purity" of the Japanese and the value in maintaining that purity.

Prior to the 1967 *Loving v. Virginia* case, which struck down anti-miscegenation laws as unconstitutional, the incidence of interracial marriage and social acceptance of mixed race couples and families were low. After the Supreme Court's ruling, Japanese Americans— by this time into their third generation—joined other Americans in this early version of "marriage equality" and the resulting "biracial baby boom". By 1980, when Tanaka's poem was published, he was by no means the first or only person to worry about what some were calling the Japanese American "genocide" through out-marriage.

In February 1977, UCLA sociologist Harry Kitano spoke at a Japanese American Citizens League (JACL) awards dinner with the announcement that by the year 2000 there would be "no pure Japanese American in our group." This caused an intense debate in the organization's newspaper, the *Pacific Citizen*, spurred by an article on March 25, l977, entitled "A Major Ethnic Disaster" by a Jon Inouye:

> While we are economically and scholastically a successful minority, in order to maintain this success we must confront a major ethnic disaster, and this is intermarriage. ... If we as Japanese Americans view racial "assimilation" (extinction) as something good, then I stop my "sermon" here. But if we desire a continuance of a cultural, ethnic tradition carried to us by our Issei forebears, then we cannot do anything but confront the interracial marriage problem.[1246]

Inouye finishes his article with this incendiary thought:

> What is the greatest threat to our race here in the U.S.? Is it the FBI? White Racism? Is it the media? The intermarriage problem is by far the worse [sic] threat to our existence than a hundred million Manzanars, Tule Lakes, or Pearl Harbors.[1247]

The *Pacific Citizen* experienced a flurry of angry letters to the editor following the Inouye article, many of them from Nisei who spoke on behalf of their grown children's marriages and their half-Japanese grandchildren. In an effort to resolve the controversy, the paper's April 18th issue featured an article by well-known columnist Bill Hosokawa entitled "The Intermarriage Question", where he called out Inouye on his "language that smacks of Nazi rhetoric," and questioned "the judgment of the editor in publishing insulting and patently racist material in the newspaper of an organization dedicated to human rights and racial equality." He noted:

> Inouye's column is insulting to the hundreds of JACL members not of the "pure Japanese blood" so precious to him, members who were attracted by the organization's human ideals rather than racial pride. It is insulting to thousands of Japanese Americans married to spouses who are not "pure-blooded Japanese," and to other Japanese Americans who have accepted non-Japanese sons-in-law and daughters-in-law as beloved members of the family circle.[1248]

Finally, Hosokawa concludes his rebuttal with a reference to World War II, which is frequently used in Japanese America as a reference point for civil rights issues:

> Just how repugnant the column is can be demonstrated by imagining an essay written from the opposite view by a Caucasian urging other Caucasians not to marry Japanese because the white heritage is superior and must not be diluted by the infusion of other than pure Caucasian blood. If that had happened today—as it happened frequently during World War II—*Pacific Citizen* would be deluged by bitter and angry protests. And rightfully so.[1249]

### Eligibility "Rules"

While it rarely got as heated as it did in the months following Kitano's assertion in 1977, debates about the changing nature of the Japanese American community were revisited every couple of years throughout the next decade, often centering around authenticity and eligibility rules for Japanese American beauty pageants and sports teams (also see King-O'Riain's chapter in this volume). While these rules and the motivations for having them still exist today, the discourse around them reached a high point during the 1980's, as young people born in the early days of the "biracial baby boom" began to enter community institutions and compete for community resources.[1250]

## R.I.P. Midori Tanaka, Pageant Queen

While beauty pageants are problematic in many ways, they are interesting as sites for the articulation of an "ideal" female type. As sociologist Rebecca Chiyoko King-O'Riain has demonstrated in her exhaustive study of Japanese American beauty pageants, they can also be an opportunity to imagine and contest ideas about authenticity and representativeness of an entire ethnicity.[1251] In the Japanese American community there is a tradition of beauty pageants associated with important festivals that dates back to the 1930's; even today there are four regional Japanese American beauty pageants held annually in the Japanese American communities in Honolulu, Los Angeles, San Francisco and Seattle.

Prior to 1974, there was an occasional mixed-race or mixed-ethnic (e.g., Japanese/Chinese) contestant in the various pageants, but, as King-O'Riain observes, "It wasn't until 1974 that the Nisei Week Queen was mixed. Elsa Akemi Cuthbert started a trend, which caused outrage, and for many she marked the beginning of the debate over the mixed-race queens."[1252] As more and more mixed women began to participate in—and sometimes win—the various Japanese American beauty pageants, the arguments against them took many forms and attempted many angles. For example, one argument was that a woman with only one Japanese parent wouldn't be as culturally Japanese as a woman whose entire family had Japanese ancestry. This assertion didn't last long as, in fact, many of the mixed race contestants had mothers from Japan and were therefore bilingual and very familiar with "real" Japanese culture, whereas the "full-blooded" contestants tended to be Sansei (third generation) and much more "Americanized."

Another argument was that a mixed person often didn't "look" Japanese on paper (i.e. he or she would have a non-Japanese surname), which made it difficult for others to recognize that she was, in fact, Japanese. Historian Lon Kurashige, whose work has looked specifically at the Los Angeles Japanese American community and its festivals, describes how George Yoshinaga, who has been a regular columnist in community newspapers since the 1950's, has written many times over the years about this "problem". For example:

> It's getting so that "pure bred" Japanese American candidates are things of the past. Two years ago we had (Elsa) Cuthbert as the Nisei Week Queen. Up in San Francisco a girl by the name of Anna Przybyiski

won the Miss Cherry Blossom crown. In fact, there were five entries in the San Francisco contest with non-Japanese names. ... will we have another queen named simply "Midori Tanaka" in our lifetime?[1253]

But contestants could generally respond easily to the name problem by deploying their Japanese name/middle name/mother's maiden name. Which left what, at the end of the day, seemed to be the most persistent problem with electing a mixed queen—racial phenotype (e.g., "she doesn't look Japanese"). Linden Nishinaga wrote to the editor of the *Rafu Shimpo* (Los Angeles' largest Japanese/English paper) in August 1982:

> Of the nine candidates, four on the basis of surnames and Eurasian looks, were half Japanese and half Caucasian. ... This disproportionate selection and seeming infatuation with the Eurasian look not only runs counter to what I consider pride in our Japanese ancestry but also to the very idea of the Nisei Week Queen tradition itself ... in order to appreciate the particular Japanese beauty one must look through a different set of glasses and discover the many other special qualities, features and mannerisms one normally wouldn't be looking for in our often superficial commercialized Hollywood glamour-model environment ... why then should we stop with the half Caucasian? Why not half-Black women? Or why not wholes of other races, e.g., blondes?[1254]

Both King-O'Riain and Kurashige describe a hierarchy in the pageants where the ideal queen would be "100% Japanese", the next "best" would be a mixed Asian (e.g., Japanese/Chinese), the third would be a mixed Japanese/White and the last choice would be a mixed Japanese/Black.[1255]

It is important to recognize that within the beauty queen debates there were many people who disagreed with the opinion that mixed women should not represent the Japanese American community. Dwight Chuman, editor of the *Rafu Shimpo* at the time, responded to Nishinaga's letter and the ensuing debate by questioning the ethics of the pageant as a whole: "Now, not-so-subtle overtones of racism are emerging ... Why not ban 'Eurasian' girls from entering 'our' pageants ... I find this kind of talk ironic and tragic. ... The importance placed on these pageants is inappropriate." Similarly, JACL member and civil rights activist Ray Okamura, wrote to the *Pacific Citizen* that he did "not much care for beauty contests", but that a "Nikkeijin is anyone of Japanese ancestry, regardless of percentage." And finally, from mixed-race people themselves, as expressed in this powerful letter to the editor from the 1980 Nisei Week Queen, Hedy Ann Posey:

> I think it's about time that one of the subjects of this controversy voiced her side as well. First of all, I may only be 50 percent Japanese, but I'm as proud of that 50 percent as I would be if I were 100 percent ... What is the definition of a Japanese American anyway? I know a lot of full-blooded Japanese who know a lot less about their heritage than some of my Eurasian friends. I grew up in a Japanese neighborhood of Los Angeles, with Japanese food, culture and language in my home and attended Japanese school for 11 years ... still some prejudiced Nisei and Sansei think that I am not "Japanese" enough to represent them. ... It breaks my heart to think that the very people that I have been so proud to represent aren't proud that I'm representing them.[1256]

## Gatekeeping on the J-League

The other major Japanese American community institutions that regularly make eligibility decisions on who is and is not Japanese are the various community sports leagues. Japanese American baseball and basketball leagues began in the 1920s in response to discrimination and segregation that kept Issei, and particularly, Nisei from playing in mainstream leagues. These teams were sponsored by Japanese American businesses and institutions, and community members would volunteer their involvement. After World War II and the Civil Rights Movement, Japanese American sports continued to be popular as a community activity that would bring families together on the courts and fields, as well as at fundraisers and celebrations.

In addition to the community aspect of it, Japanese American sports—basketball in particular (the J-Leagues)—were meant to give Japanese American boys and girls the opportunity to play with and against people of a similar physical size and stature to themselves. As the community has became more and more geographically dispersed and increasingly diverse in everything including "size and stature", the J-League teams have continued in their popularity, and are often the only community activity that young Japanese Americans regularly engage in. But *which* young Japanese Americans are invited to and are *allowed* to play has been a point of contention.

In her dissertation, *Hoops, History and Crossing Over: Boundary Making and Community Building in Japanese American Youth Basketball Leagues*, sociologist Christine Chin finds that much "gatekeeping" goes on in the J-Leagues, and that birth certificates, names and physical appearance are all utilized by the leagues as determinants of a potential player's Japanese ancestry. She also finds that if a player's authenticity is in question, the "burden of proof" (i.e., proving one's Japaneseness) is on the player him or herself. Apparently, those questions can continue even once a player is "safely" on a team:

> Given that players have to "look Asian," mixed race players were scrutinized the most, particularly in highly competitive settings such as tournaments ... Rachel, a 12th grade player, recounted to me ... "We had two Black girls on our old team and they're like a quarter Japanese but we got so many complaints, especially during tournaments ... Sometimes parents (from opposing teams) were really rude to them. They are Asian, but they don't look full Asian so (parents) would just give them dirty looks ... I feel like if you don't look full Asian or like somewhat Asian, you don't feel as welcomed."[1257]

While it varies depending on the league, and much of it is unofficial, eligibility rules still exist, governing the percentage of Japanese ancestry a player must have to qualify, as well as the number of non-Japanese players allowed on each team. There is much disagreement within the Japanese American community and even within the J-League community about the rules and if they are practical and/or ethical. But many others continue to be protective of these boundaries. For example, the 2015 "Discover Nikkei" website asks:

> Japanese American Basketball Leagues have been a part of the Japanese-American (JA) community for

generations. ... It is not as clear cut as it was for the Nisei and (for the most part) the Sansei. As a result of intermarriage with other ethnicities, many self-identified Japanese-Americans are now of mixed heritage. ... If J-Leagues were formed to give Japanese-Americans a chance to play but many Yonsei and Gosei are of mixed heritage, what criteria should be used to decide who is allowed to play?[1258]

## Part II: Negotiating Inclusion

Although the gatekeeping impulse still exists, by the early l990s, overtly questioning the inclusion of mixed Japanese Americans in the community had become much less acceptable. In 1993, Professor Harry Kitano, either trying to relive the excitement of 1977 or simply making a revision to his earlier Year 2000 claim, announced that the Japanese American community "will be no more in 2050 in the face of the rising rate of intermarriage." But this time, instead of weeks and weeks of follow-up articles and letters to the editor, the only major response was that another venerable Japanese American professor: Lane Hirabayashi (who is, himself, a mixed race Sansei) responded immediately with his own essay entitled, "Is the JA community disappearing? Or is the choice up to us?" Hirabayashi quipped:

> While I always appreciate data on the current rates of Asian American intermarriage, as a person of Japanese and Norwegian ancestry, I had a serious objection to UCLA Prof. Harry Kitano's assertion ... Dr. Kitano seems to assume that the survival of Japanese American culture and community revolves around the purity of Japanese "blood" down through the generations ... contrary to this view, most contemporary social scientists agree that culture is learned. In turn, learning has to do with exposure within the family context as well as in institutions where the values, norms and typical practices of a given group are enacted, whether this be a school, church, club, interest group, or even a "slo pitch league."[1259]

How did intermarriage and mixed race—or the "hapa controversy" as Lon Kurashige calls it—lose its status as most volatile subject in such a short period of time?[1260] Had the community simply resigned itself to the "dilution" by then? Did every Japanese American family

393

have so much intermarriage and so many little hapas running around by the 1990s that to debate it seemed irrelevant? Perhaps, yes, to some degree, but I think that there was also a shift in the community where Japanese Americans began to consider the possibility that a person might not have to be "100% Japanese" to be Japanese American. This shift was the result of the determined efforts of a small group of mixed-race Japanese Americans, who pioneered the dialogue around identity and inclusion for mixed-race people in the Japanese American community (see Figure 18.1).

Figure 18.1 Pacific Citizen, vol. 106, no. 18, Friday, May 6, 1988, page 4.

### Bill Smith, Japanese American

Between 1980 and l986, four doctoral dissertations were published on the subject of mixed-race Japanese Americans, all by mixed race people with Japanese immigrant mothers. It started with Christine Iijima Hall and her 1980 dissertation, *The Ethnic Identity of Racially Mixed People: A Study of Black-Japanese*, and was followed by the work of George Kitahara Kich (1982), Michael Thornton (1983) and Stephen Murphy-Shigematsu (1986). This established a group of "experts" who could, would, and did speak to the community on behalf of intermarriage and mixed-race concerns. Other notable mixed race voices in these early discussions were professor of Asian American Studies Lane Hirabayashi, playwright and poet Velina Hasu Houston, attorney/activist Philip Tajitsu Nash, and writer Chiori Santiago, each of whom approached the subject from different angles. Together and separately they moved the discourse with the Japanese American community forward in a thoughtful and productive way.

Perhaps the most tangible indicator of a turning point in this discussion was the 1985 "Holiday Issue" of the *Pacific Citizen*, which was devoted to the subject of "Interracial Families". This enormous (over 100-page) special issue featured articles by Hall, Hirabayashi, Houston, Kich, Murphy-Shigematsu and many other mixed and interracially married Japanese Americans. Most of them approached the subject in a clear and factual way: the outmarriage rate of Japanese Americans is between 60-70%, interracial marriages are not destined to fail, mixed-race children are not doomed to identity crises, mixed families can hold on to their Japanese American cultural ties, the support and inclusion of mixed families and people by the Japanese American community is important to their happiness and well-being. In many ways it was a guidebook for the Japanese American community for how to think and talk about the reality of a mixed race future. In their piece "Interracial? Wakarimasen", Kich, Mary Ann Leff, Grace Wakamatsu Fleming and Murphy-Shigematsu wrote:

> Ethnicity is important to all of us. Preserving a passing way of life, something of ourselves, is important. Interracial families are a vivid reminder of our rapidly changing world and challenge us to answer a basic question: "What is Japanese American?" Is the answer based on a mythical purity of race? Does it require a Japanese name or looks? Can someone whose name is Bill Smith, who has green eyes and brown hair, be Japanese American? ... Let's hope that someday a Bill Smith, with brown hair and green eyes, who has been called "Jap" and blamed for Pearl Harbor and who cares deeply about his Japanese heritage, can say with ease and prideful assurance, "I am Japanese American."[1261]

## A Multiracial Movement

On a separate but overlapping front, I-Pride, the first organization for interracial families and people, was founded in Berkeley, California in 1979 with George Kitahara Kich as its first president. Over the next two decades there was a pervasive trend in similar grass-roots organizations in communities and on university campuses across the country. The Amerasian League was formed in Southern California in the early half of the 1980's to consider the issues of specifically mixed-race Asians in the U.S. and abroad, followed by the Multiracial Asians International Network (or MAIN) in the San Francisco Bay Area in 1989. Most other organizations were pan-mixed race.

It is interesting to note that many of the people who were at the forefront of what is now called "The Multiracial Movement" of the 1990's were the very same mixed-race Japanese Americans who first asserted their identities within the Japanese American community. The idea that these people were actively identifying around their "mixedness" as well as their "Japaneseness" was surprising to many within the Japanese American community, who expected them to repress their mixedness in favor of a monoracial identity (i.e., to try to "pass" as Japanese). I believe that this phenomenon was actually a critical piece of the great progress that was made during the period in terms of expanding notions of the category "Japanese American." These people weren't "pretending" to be Japanese by trying to cover up their other ethnicities or their true identities; they were asserting themselves as mixed-race Japanese Americans and demanding that it be included in the definition.

Within the context of the growing "Multiracial Movement", the next generation of mixed-race Japanese American activists took form and took the discussion to the next level. In l992, three undergraduate students at UC Berkeley—Greg Mayeda, Steve Ropp, and Eric Tate—took a course in Japanese American history taught by Jere Takahashi, where they found themselves in the company of many other mixed-race students as well as many "full-blooded" Japanese and Asian Americans. At one point in the semester, Takahashi invited two graduate students to present their findings on the topics of mixed-race Asian Americans and Asian American interracial dating and marriage. One young sociologist who focused on interracial relationships presented the argument that Asian American intermarriage represented an effort to "move up" the social and economic hierarchy, and that increasing interracial marriage would ultimately cause the dissolution of Asian American communities because mixed-race people do not identify as Asian as strongly as non-mixed people.

Not surprisingly, the mixed-race students in the class responded very negatively to this sociologist's assertions. They stated that her theory was based on assumptions that were baseless, incorrect, and offensive to themselves and to their parents. Most importantly, they told her that she should not and could not speak for mixed-race people about how they do or do not identify.

After this pivotal day in class, Mayeda, Tate, and Ropp formed a group called the Hapa Issues Forum—a name modeled after a public policy and advocacy institute called the Latino Issues Forum—with the stated purpose of representing mixed-race Japanese Americans in dialogue with the Japanese American community (see Figure 18.2). In an interview with Tony Yuen for his master's thesis on the subject, co-founder Eric Tate stated:

> We did know that there were specific things that we wanted to achieve ... if we had a mission at that point, it was to open up and educate the Japanese American community, to make it more ... accepting of Japanese Americans of mixed race. And so if we did this ... we could actually ... change it so it's better and more accepting and ... make for a stronger community overall.[1262]

### The Changing Face of Japanese America

FIRST ANNUAL CONFERENCE

# What Does The Future Hold For Japanese Americans?

Explore The Following Issues:

• Over 60% of Japanese Americans marry outside of their community.
• By the 21st century, the typical Japanese American will be a Hapa.
• What does this evolution mean for the future of the community?
• Learn how Hapas will effect the Japanese American community.
• Interrracial Marriage, Community Cohesiveness, Ethnic Identity

**WHEN:** SATURDAY, MARCH 12, 1994 (9AM-4PM)

**WHERE:** 10 EVANS HALL, U.C. BERKELEY

**ADMISSION:** FREE!

**FOR MORE INFO CALL:** (510) 466-0682 OR (510) 339-1153

Hapa (hāp'a) From the Hawaiian term *hapa haole* (half-white foreigner). Also describes a person of partial Japanese ancestry.

Figure 18.2

Hapa Issues Forum began right away to network with Japanese American community institutions. They produced fliers that they distributed at street fairs and festivals and many other kinds of community events. The wording on the fliers was strong and provocative:

> To remain a viable community, Japanese Americans must accept the reality of the changing dynamics and use it to their advantage. If those in positions of leadership and authority fail in their responsibility of resolving the contemporary issues facing the Japanese American community, many segments of the community will become dissatisfied, despondent, and ultimately cease to participate (or) identify with the community as we know it today. Without the meaningful participation of Hapas and reconciliation of Hapa issues, the Japanese American community will find itself moving toward extinction. This will mean the loss of a rich heritage, and, in the end, the only thing the world will know about Japanese Americans is from studies by sociologists who will write, "There once lived a people who ..."

Within a year of its start as a student group on the UC Berkeley campus, Hapa Issues Forum (HIF) became a non-profit community organization with a steady stream of invitations to speak at meetings and conferences of Japanese American organizations, to serve on panels and focus groups, and to write articles for community newspapers. Co-founder Greg Mayeda explained that as a history major writing his senior thesis on the Black Panthers, he was inspired by the story of young people, many of whom were college students, who became agents of social change. At their first annual conference called "Hapas: The Changing Face of Japanese America", HIF committed itself to "broadening the understanding of Japanese Americans to include people of partial Asian ancestry" and to "ensure that Hapas are never put in the position where they must 'prove' they are Japanese or where they must surrender part of their ethnic identity as a condition of full participation in the Japanese American community." The activism of HIF opened the door for a much greater representation of mixed-race people in Japanese American institutions, which has gone a long way in proving that mixed people are committed to the community and do, in fact, identify as Japanese Americans. Ultimately, HIF was instrumental not only at the Japanese American community level but at the national policy level, as they went on to testify in front of the Office of Management and Budget (OMB) regarding models for revising the United States Census to accommodate mixed-race people. They also consulted on the subject with the JACL, which then became the first national civil rights organization to explicitly support a multiple check format—the model that was eventually adopted by the OMB.

As Rebecca King-O'Riain found in her study, "the increased participation of mixed-race Japanese Americans in traditional Japanese American institutions has motivated a private and public discussion of *who* is Japanese American and how this relates to changing meanings of race, ethnicity, community and gender." These changes were evident at the "Ties that Bind" conference in Los Angeles in 1998 and the "Nikkei 2000" conference in 2000, two large-scale gatherings where the stated goal was to address the demographic changes in the community.[1263] According to the published conclusions of the Nikkei 2000 conference, "... over 600 students, professionals, community organizers, artists, politicians and individuals from across the United States, Canada, Peru, Brazil and Japan gathered ... to brainstorm ideas and [create] action plans." When participants were asked to describe their vision of the future:

> the idea of an all-inclusive, dynamic community topped the list. From the start, conferees concluded that traditional ideas of a "Japanese American" community were quickly becoming obsolete; the "Nikkei" community has become increasingly multi-racial and reflective of the gender identity issues that are a part of American society.

As for mixed people, there was a snowball affect to these shifts: the more of them there were in the community, participating in Japanese American activities and institutions, the more they felt welcome and represented; this, in turn, made them more likely to increase and deepen their participation.

## Part III: Imagining a "New Nikkei"

### Alternatives to Assimilation

The Japanese American community has thus moved from a very exclusive and narrowly defined community to a relatively inclusive ethnic group in an impressively short time. And rather than it being a resignation that the community has "assimilated" into the American mainstream, this inclusiveness seems to be an inspiration and a motivation to re-invent what it means to be "Japanese American". But the question is—in what form?

One idea that's been discussed is "pan-Asianism," whereby things Japanese American would shift from being ethnic-specific to becoming "Asian American" in general. This argument has mostly been discussed in relation to institutions such as Japanese American churches or the aforementioned "J-Leagues",[1264] but some individuals, like sociologist Larry Shinagawa, have proposed pan-ethnicity as an ethnic identity strategy. In a *New York Times* article from 2004, Shinagawa is paraphrased as having said that, "most Japanese-Americans face only two directions—assimilating into 'whiteness' or adopting a 'pan-Asian' identity."[1265]

While this idea has some merit, it does not seem likely that it will be the dominant direction for Japanese Americans. As some have pointed out, a pan-ethnic Asian American identity runs the risk of reducing the Japanese American community to only its experiences as a racialized minority in the United States. While this is an enormous piece of the Japanese American story, its provincial scope misses too many of the connections that Japanese Americans have with the past, present and future of Nikkei, all over the world. As Greg Kimura, the current CEO and President of the Japanese American National Museum (JANM) in Los Angeles, found in his recent research on young Japanese Americans in Southern California: "Increasingly for Gen Y and millennials, the shift is happening that our American-ness is already assumed and we're trying to figure out our Japanese heritage and what does that mean. How do we integrate that into our personal identity?"[1266]

This desire to connect with a Japanese heritage seems to be a trend for young Nikkei not only in the United States, but globally. The Nikkei Youth Network, a nonprofit organization started by a Chilean-Japanese from Costa Rica and a third generation Japanese Brazilian (and funded by the Nippon Foundation) is built around the Japanese concept of "kizuna" which they define as having "strong bonds and emotional ties". They begin with the premise that "Nikkei all share a common root", and with the goal of creating "an international network ... to share knowledge and work together."[1267] This network is ostensibly a community in cyberspace where time zones and language differences (they currently operate in English, but are planning to be multilingual) are irrelevant to the shared interests of communication of information, inspiration and ideas, as well as crowdsourcing for tangibles such as involvement (i.e. volunteer labor) and funding.

So, perhaps in this era of technology, globalization and transnational identities, a more productive direction for the future of Japanese America is a re-articulation of ethnicity that is flexible and dynamic, and that acknowledges and seeks out connections both within and outside of the United States. When Greg Kimura (who is, himself, a mixed race Yonsei from Alaska) took over as CEO/President of JANM in 2012, he immediately set out to expand all of these dimensions and others, in relation to the thirty-year old institution. For example, recent exhibits and events have built or strengthened connections with a pan-Asian American perspective and cultural aesthetic; with people interested in issues of social justice and civil rights; with the very diverse population who are attracted to the culture of Japan (from tattoos to Hello Kitty!); and with the mixed race/ethnic people and families within the Japanese American community. As an article on the V3 Digital Media Conference's website (now held annually at JANM) said, "This isn't your father's Japanese American National Museum."[1268]

While Kimura initially experienced community push-back on his bold new vision, it was, in fact, what he was hired to do to: museum membership and attendance was dwindling, and they were operating at a net loss with a growing deficit. Gordon Yamate, the current chair of the JANM's board of trustees acknowledged that "When we hired Greg we were looking for someone to undertake the huge challenge of broadening the audience of this museum, someone who would be transformative."[1269] The transformation has been a success—JANM is again profitable and growing.


**Summary**

In summary, much of the dialogue that has taken place in the Japanese American community around the growth of intermarriage and mixed people reflects two outdated beliefs: 1) that until recent patterns of intermarriage, Japanese were genetically and culturally "pure" and 2) that interracial marriage is an inevitable path towards "assimilation" into a white/European American mainstream. The reality is, there has never been a time or a place where genetics and behavior have remained stagnant, including (or especially) in the here and now, where transnational lifestyles and the "worlding" of contemporary culture make it difficult to pinpoint a meaningful mainstream. Japanese Americans were never "pure" ... and they aren't disappearing into Whiteness.

But, the Japanese and their diaspora are in major flux. What will be the response? Can the Nikkei challenge themselves to complicate their categories? Rather than continuing to move forward as a series of reactions to changing conditions, there seems to be a growing effort within and outside of the United States to "treat the present as an historical moment"[1270] and proactively construct a community, culture and identity that is a combination of old and new, of domestic and international, of real and "imagined" aspects and structures that will shift and adjust with the times. This expansive, inclusive version of Japaneseness is much less concerned with percentages and generations and authenticity. It is not worried about "proving" how Japanese or American (or Brazilian or Canadian) one is. This New Nikkei looks, sounds, and acts differently than anything that we have known before.

# NOTES

## INTRODUCTION

1. National Institute of Population and Social Security Research 2012 report.

2. See http://www.japantimes.co.jp/news/2016/03/05/national/one-29-babies-2014-least-one-foreign-parent/#.VwB4vUvXfot and http://www.e-stat.go.jp/SG1/estat/eStatTopPortal.do

3. Hoeffel, Rastogi, Kim, and Shahid 2012, pp. 1-5, 15 for all information from the U.S. Census Bureau on the 2010 Asian American and Japanese American population. The Census terminology is "Asian in combination" and "Asian alone." For the "Black and Asian" combination data, see Jones and Bullock, 2012, 9.

4. Jones and Bullock, 2012, 20. The Japanese American case also contrasts with Americans who identify as White (only 3.2% report being multiracial) and Black (only 7.4% report being multiracial). Only Native Hawaiian/Other Pacific Islander (56%) and American Indian/Native Alaskans (44%) had a higher percentage of multiracial individuals as a percentage of the overall community compared to Japanese Americans.

5. See http://www.nytimes.com/2015/05/30/world/asia/biracial-beauty-queen-strives-for-change-in-mono-ethnic-japan.html?emc=eta1&_r=0

CHAPTER ONE

6. Abbreviations used throughout this chapter are: KT *Kokushi taikei*. 60 vols. Tokyo: Yoshikawa Kōbunkan, 1964-1967; NKBT *Nihon koten bungaku taikei*. 100 vols. Tokyo: Iwanami Shoten, 1958-1966; and SNKBT *Shin Nihon koten bungaku taikei*. 100 vols. Tokyo: Iwanami Shoten, 1989-2005. The primary sources used in this chapter include the following texts: *Nihon sandai jitsuroku*. KT 4; *Nihon shoki*. NKBT, vols. 67–68; *Nihon kōki*. KT 3; *Ruijū sandai kyaku*. KT 25; *Ryō no shūge*. KT 23; *Shoku Nihongi*. SNKBT, vols. 12–16.

7. For the official English translation of the statement, see: http://www.kunaicho.go.jp/e-okotoba/01/press/kaiken-h13e.html; and for the original Japanese, see: http://www.kunaicho.go.jp/okotoba/01/kaiken/kaiken-h13e.html, both accessed February 25, 2015. I follow Joan Piggott's use of "tennō" for the premodern Japanese ruler in place of the common translation, "emperor." See Piggott, 1997, 8.

8. Description of the Emperor's role from Article 1 of the Constitution of Japan. For an official English translation, see http://www.kunaicho.go.jp/e-about/seido/seido01.html#H2-01, accessed February 25, 2015.

9. The family that Kammu claimed as maternal relatives was the Kudara no Konikishi, whose title is discussed below. For the edict in which he makes the claim, see the *Shoku Nihongi*, Enryaku 9th year, 2nd month, 27th day. For more on Kammu's relationship with his mother's family and the Kudara no Konikishi, see Tanaka, 1997, pp. 72-103.

10. The text is known as the *Shinsen shōjiroku* (815), or "Newly Compiled Record of Names and Titles." For the authoritative version of this text, see Saeki, 1981.

11. For examples of such arguments in English, see Kiley, 1969, 177, and Ooms, 2009, 103. The sources make it clear that for most of his life, Kammu was not expected to come to the throne. It was only with the fall of Crown Prince Osabe and his mother—accused of treason and exiled—that the possibility of Kammu ascending to the throne was raised. Many scholars have argued that having a mother from a relatively unimportant family said to be descended from Paekche immigrants was a significant disadvantage for Kammu (then Prince Yamabe). While he was made Crown Prince and eventually took the throne as Kammu Tennō, his relationship with his maternal family remained an important theme throughout his reign. Exactly how this relationship shaped his mindset and policies, including those

related to integrating and configuring people from outside the realm, is extremely difficult to determine.

12. The early state on the Japanese archipelago was known as Yamato or Wa (倭), and in this I will use Yamato, rather than the anachronistic "Japan." The written name of the realm was changed to 日本 (now read "Nihon" or "Nippon" but also read "Yamato" in early sources) at the beginning of the eighth century. The 702 CE envoy to the Sui court marked the shift in Chinese sources, indicating that this new names for the realm had been acknowledged as the official name of the realm by the Chinese court. See Kōnoshi, 2005, pp. 10-18.

13. For a concise summary of his three stages, see Tanaka, 1997, pp. 281-285.

14. A nearly complete version of the Yōrō code has been reconstructed from the *Ryō no gige* and *Ryō no shūge*, and consists of 30 administrative sections and 12 penal sections. The Taihō Code is not extant, but sections of it have been reconstructed from the *Koki* commentary of the *Ryō no shūge*.

15. For the most famous articulation of the ancient East Asian world, see Nishijima, 1983, pp. 397-467.

16. See Yoshie, Ijuin, and Piggott, 2013, 379 and Enomoto, 2010, pp. 6-12. In fact, Enomoto has argued that there is almost no evidence that the 681 Asuka Kiyomihara administrative code was directly influenced by Tang institutions. He cites the work of a number of scholars who have traced the antecedents of various early Japanese institutions to the Western Wei, Northern and Southern Dynasties, and Korean states of Paekche and Silla.

17. Tanaka, 1997, 202. See also Batten, 2003, 29.

18. The phrase carries the implication of approaching the realm of one's own volition, submitting to the *tennō*, and being transformed into a subject of the *tennō*. The term *kika* and *kikajin* are also used in the present day to refer to naturalized aliens, but this should not be confused with its usage in this earlier period.

19. Article 70 of the Yōrō Codes "Laws on Official Documentation" (*Kūshikiryō*). The translations for the titles of each section of the codes follow those in Yoshie, Ijuin, and Piggott, 2013. The authoritative edition of the *ritsuryō* codes is Inoue, 1976.

20. Article 16 of the Yōrō Codes "Laws on Residence Units" (*Koryō*).

21. Article 15 of the Yōrō Codes "Laws on Taxes" (*Buyakuryō*).

22. The translation of *koseki* as "residence unit registries" follows Yoshie, Ijuin, and Piggott, 2013 and Tanaka, 1997, 199.

23. During his lifetime, the prince appears in the records as Prince Kamitsumiya or Prince Umayado. For more on the differences between the historical figure and later legends, see Como, 2008, pp. 4-5.

24. *Nihon shoki*, Suiko 23rd year, 11th month, 15th day. NKBT 68: pp. 200-201. Aston, trans., 1896, 146.

25. *Nihon shoki*, Suiko 29th year, 2nd month. NKBT 68: pp. 205-206. Aston, trans., 1896, pp. 148-149.

26. The *ritsuryō* codes do acknowledge the possibility of people leaving the state by being captured or taken prisoner in wars. See the Yōrō Codes, Laws on Residence Units, article 26, for an example of a law that acknowledges this possibility.

27. Tanaka, 1997, pp. 177-203.

28. *Nihon shoki*, Keitai 24th year, 9th month. NKBT 68: pp. 43-44. Aston, trans., 1896, II: pp. 22-23. The character read *kara* here is an ambiguous character that is often used to refer to states on the Korean peninsula or to the states of the Korean peninsula collectively. What it might signify in this compound, however, is not certain.

29. The only other time that these characters appear in the *Nihon shoki* is in the discussion of an individual named Soga no Karako Sukune who appears several times in Yūryaku's reign. While the *Nihon shoki* account describes Soga no Karako as being involved in various maneuvers on the Korean peninsula, there are no notes similar to that which appears above and "Karako" seems to have been considered merely part of the name.

30. *Nihon shoki*, Kinmei, 2nd year, 7th month. NKBT 68: pp. 72-77. Aston, trans., 1896, II: pp. 45-47.

31. See below for a discussion of the *kabane* system of ranked noble titles granted by rulers. Nasol was the sixth of sixteen Paekche court ranks. For the structure and dating of Paekche bureaucracy, see Best, 2006, pp. 41-51.

32. *Nihon shoki*, Kinmei 2nd year, 7th month. NKBT 68: pp. 72-77. Aston, trans., 1896, II: pp. 45-47.

33. *Nihon shoki*, Kinmei 5th year, 2nd month and Kinmei Tennō, 5th year, 3rd month. NKBT 68: pp. 78-89. Aston, trans., 1896, II: pp.

49-55. For a full list of officials with mixed names and discussion of their significance in relations between the Japanese archipelago and Korean peninsula, see Lee, 2014. pp. 124-127.

34. Tanaka, 1997, pp. 202-203.

35. *Shoku Nihongi*, Enryaku 8th year, 10th month, 17th day. SNKBT 16: pp. 444-447.

36. The rulers were: Shōmu, Kōken, Junnin, Shōtoku, Kōnin and Kammu (Kōken-Shōtoku took the throne twice). The two dynasties were the Tenji-line and the Tenmu-line. The *Shoku Nihongi* entry cited above does mention that he was a particular favorite of Shomu Tennō, but given that he served under Shōmu quite early in his career it can hardly explain his continuous rise through the ranks in later reigns.

37. In 684, Tenmu had added four new titles for a total of eight, and re-arranged the ranking of the titles to reward those who had supported him in the civil war that put him on the throne. The eight titles were: *mahito, ason, sukune, imki, michinoshi, omi, muraji,* and *inagi*. For details, see Miller, 1974, pp. 1-17 and Piggott, 1997, 314. Robert Borgen's article on the Haji family also offers an excellent case study of the significance of *kabane* in the Nara and Heian periods.

38. A literal translation of the first title would be something like: "Paekche royal family."

39. The characters for Koma are the same as that in the Koma no Konikishi family mentioned above. Although the two names are the same, the Koma no Konikishi and Koma no Ason had no connection other than the name. For details, see Tanaka, 1997, pp. 53-57.

40. One possible explanation for this combination of names is that several members of Fukushin's family were appointed as envoys to foreign states but not while they were the Sena no Konikishi. It was only once they received the name Koma no Ason that they served as foreign envoys. Fumio Tanaka argues that the Japanese court knew that the *konikishi* title would not be accepted by other states and therefore took the precaution of changing the name to something less likely to offend. If true, this could suggest that the Japanese ruler's performance of *ritsuryō* universality was primarily for a domestic audience. Tanaka, 1997, pp. 61-62.

41. *Shoku nihongi*, Enryaku 8th year, 10th month, 17th day. SNKBT 16: pp. 444-447.

42. Park, 1996, 107.

43. Kōken Tennō was the only woman ever designated heir to the throne. Earlier female sovereigns have often been understood as "place-holders" who occupied the throne until a younger male heir was prepared to rule. As an unmarried female sovereign without children in a court increasingly invested in the patriarchal paradigm of the state embedded in Tang texts, Kōken faced a variety of real and potential challenges to the legitimacy of her rule. For further details, see Piggott, 2003, 47-74.

44. *Shoku Nihongi*, Tenpyō-hōji 1st year, 4th month, 4th day. SNKBT 14: 184.

45. *Nihon Kōki*, Enryaku 18th year, 12th month, 29th day, as cited in Sugasawa, 2001, pp. 209-220.

46. Tanaka, 1997, pp. 132-139.

47. Tōru Ōtsu and Jun'ichi Enomoto have argued pursuasively that because the supplementary legislation and protocols were included as two of the four types of law in the classic *ritsuryō* system, they should be understood as a continuation of the *ritsuryō* process into the Heian period. Collections of supplementary legislation and protocols include the *Kōnin kyakushiki* (820), *Jōgan kyaku* (869) and *shiki* (871) and *Engi kyaku* (907) and *shiki* (967). See Enomoto, 2010, 5.

48. The date of the *Ruiju sandai kyaku* is unclear, although it is thought to have been compiled in the eleventh century. It contains *kyaku* issued from 702 CE to 907 CE.

49. *Ruiju sandai kyaku*, Jōwa 9th year, 8th month, 15th day, Edict of the Council of State. For an excellent French translation with annotations, see Herail, 2011, pp. 568-570.

50. Ishii, 2003, 61.

51. *Sandai jitsuroku*, Jōgan 14th year, 1st month, 20th day.

## CHAPTER TWO

52. These Europeans were overwhelmingly male. Some European women settled in Batavia and elsewhere with their husbands but for the most part western men in Southeast and East Asia had relations with local women.

53. Massarrella, 1990, 234. The Dutch East India Company (VOC) controlled part of Taiwan from 1633 to 1662.

54. Hapa, a Hawaiian word meaning "half," is actually an English loanword. It's the precise equivalent of the Japanese loanword *hafu*, which is also derived from the English word "half" and used to refer to a part-Japanese—usually half-White or sometimes half-Black. Although there are perfectly good words for "half" in the pre-contact Hawaiian language as well as in Japanese, these terms of alien origin have been applied to "mixed-race" people to draw special attention to their exoticism, their (at least "half") foreignness. In eighteenth century Hawai'i, hapa usually connoted a half-Hawaiian, half-white (*haole*). But as the Polynesian population plummeted and the Asian population swelled, the term *hapa-haole* came to refer, more typically, to a part-white, part-Asian person. (Growing up in Hawai'i in the 1970s, I had hapa friends who were part-White, part-Chinese or Filipino or Vietnamese, but most self-defined hapa I knew were part-Japanese.) On the West Coast of the U.S., hapa has come to describe any part-White (European), part-Asian. On my campus in Massachusetts, the newly-formed Hapa Club includes half-European, half-Indian, or half-Pakistani students. And there are hapa who are part-Asian and part-black. So the term has varying and evolving meanings.

55. One scholar estimates that over 58,000 Japanese journeyed overseas in the first three decades of the seventeenth century. See Jansen, 1992, 19.

56. Among the known half-Japanese, half-Siamese, a man named Oin, son of Yamada Nagamasa (1590-1630) and his wife, a Siamese princess, stand out. Yamada settled in the Nihonmachi in Ayutthaya and came to head the (perhaps 3000-strong) Japanese community. He obtained a high post at court and a governorship inherited by his son who, forced to flee to Cambodia in the wake of a succession dispute, placed himself at the disposal of the Khmer court as head of a samurai force, dying in battle in their service.

57. There were a few exceptions. About 500 traders and envoys from the domain of Tsushima were allowed by the Korean court to reside in a walled compound (the "Japan House" or *Waegwan*; in Japanese, *Wakan*) in what is today Pusan. They were generally forbidden contact with Korean women and some were punished for smuggling prostitutes into the compound. Even so there are references to "Wae bastards" in Korean records. See Lewis, 2003, 194-197.

58. There were Japanese women as well as Japanese men in the Nihonmachi in Ayutthaya, the Siamese capital. Whole families had left Japan due to the persecution of Christians. A distinctly Japanese community endured into the eighteenth century and even in the late nineteenth century there were "Japanese guards" in the service of the Siamese court, who were descendants of samurai settlers.

59. The view that Japanese are a "pure race," still widely held in Japan, assumes that the people of the islands evolving in isolation have never absorbed significant outside DNA. This view, which dovetails with right-wing nationalist ideology, is simply untrue. The first hapa in the broadest sense of half-Europeans, half-Asians may have appeared as early Roman times when Romans traded and settled in India and visited China. There were certainly half-European, half-Mongol and half-Chinese at the Mongol court of Khan Bhalig in the thirteenth century.

60. "Yayoi" technically refers to the material culture of the people whose artifacts were first excavated in the Tokyo neighborhood of Yayoi. But the term *Yayoijin* is commonly used by Japanese scholars to refer to the people who created this culture themselves.

61. "Jōmon" refers to the "cord pattern" pottery produced by these people. Some DNA evidence links the Jōmon to the Buryat of Siberia, while physical anthropological (dental) evidence suggests an Austronesian connection. See Matsumura 1999; Hammer et al., 2006.

62. "The modern Japanese population is recognizably the product of intermarriage between Korean emigrants and Jōmon Japanese natives... The new way of life that arose in Japan from this flowing together of emigrant Korean and in situ Japanese peoples and cultures is called Yayoi." (Aikens, 2012, 61).

63. Aikens, *Ibid.*, pp. 64-65. Soon after 662, when the kingdom of Paekche fell to the rival Korean kingdom of Silla, much of the Paekche nobility relocated to the Japanese (Yamato) court where they were welcomed into the ranks of the Japanese aristocracy.

64. Miller, 1974, 190. See also Tsunoda, de Bary, and Keene, 1958, 112. The issue of ancestry is complicated by the fact that among the Korean clans present at the Yamato court were some, such as the Hata and Aya, who engaged in silk textile weaving, who claimed to be originally descended from Chinese. Into the early modern period the term *Kara* was applied to Koreans, or both

Koreans and Chinese, or sometimes even to the Dutch as a generic term for foreigners.

65. Nagasaki Shiyakusho, eds., 1925, 30. There was also intermarriage with Koreans on the island of Tsushima.

66. The conversation took place in written Chinese, the *lingua franca* of East and Southeast Asia.

67. Tsunoda et al., 1958, 309.

68. The Japanese borrowed their characters for "barbarian" from the Chinese, but employed the term somewhat differently. To the Chinese, who built walls to keep out "uncivilized" steppe peoples, "barbarians" were mainly Central Asian tribes inclined to invade and raid the peaceful agrarian empire. In Japan—where there were few walls designed to keep people out and rather a keen interest in, and hospitality showed towards, outsiders—the term was used for anyone not plainly from one of the Three Countries. The Portuguese (and other Europeans including Spaniards, Dutchmen, and Englishmen) were *banjin* of some sort, if only because they were unable to communicate in written Chinese. But they also had some connection to (civilized) India. According to information available to the Japanese, the people of southern India were darker skinned than those of the north. It was thus natural to suppose that the dark-skinned slaves and servants brought by the Portuguese aboard their ships—men from Angola or Mozambique who with their full lips, crinkly hair and dark faces reminded Japanese of blackened bronze Buddhist images—were in fact people from the land of the Buddha and to treat them with particular respect.

69. The lord was the *daimyō* of Hakata and Bungo. (Katz, 1989, 279).

70. See Elison, 1988, 33f.

71. Genesis 9:18-10:32. Here Noah curses Ham, declaring his progeny will be the "slaves" of his brothers. Thus biblical religion seemed to validate a natural hierarchy of bloodlines ("races") and, especially for white slave owners in the U.S. south, supported arguments for black African inferiority. See Wood, 1990, pp. 84-111.

72. Cooper, 1965, 60.

73. Ibid., pp. 46-47.

74. Lach, 1968, 685.

75.  Sansom, 1977, 174.

76.  Lach, 1968, 696.

77.  See Leupp, 2003, 22f.

78.  Valignano compared Japanese to Indian Christians, actually stating that "there really is no room for comparison between them" since the Christians in India were "blacks, and of small sense" while the Japanese, "since they are white and of good understanding and behavior ... become very good Christians." (Boxer, 1951, 94).

79.  Lach, 1968, 656.

80.  Cooper, 1965, pp. 39-40.

81.  The belief that Japanese were descended from the Babylonians or lost tribes of Israel was still expressed in the nineteenth century. See Leupp, 2003, pp. 76-77, 129.

82.  Arima, 1962, 634. The Portuguese left the country with the girl for Macao but returned the following year with her as well as a gunsmith able to properly instruct Yasuita. The dating of the *Yasuita-shi Kiyosada ichiryū no keizu* is unclear. Arima places it in the 1570s, but one source places it as late as 1808. For the difficulties, see Lidin, 2002, pp. 8-14.

83.  Lidin, Ibid., pp. 8, 11-12.

84.  See Kaempfer, 1906, 157. Kaempfer was not Dutch but from Northern Westphalia in Germany. He volunteered to join the VOC in Japan largely to pursue his studies of botany.

85.  Boxer, 1979, 43. This was before the expulsion of Portuguese in 1636.

86.  Elison, 1988, 98.

87.  Murdoch and Yamagata, 1903, 79.

88.  Quoted in Ibid., 245.

89.  Boxer, 1951, 299. "China" in the early modern Japanese imagination was not confined to the Ming or Qing Empire's borders. It embraced the surrounding countries, such as Korea, the Ryūkyū Kingdom and Annam, which were governed by Confucian elites, employed the Chinese written language for official and scholarly purposes, and paid tribute to the Chinese court. The word *Kara* (derived from *Korai*, Korea) was used

by Japanese to refer to either Chinese or Koreans during the centuries of seclusion (1635-1859) and even sometimes applied to Europeans! (See, for example, the testimony of English merchant John Saris [1613] in Cooper, 1965, 288.) It became a general term for non-Japanese ethnic other.

90. Cooper, Ibid., pp. 64-65.

91. Uemura, 1929, pp. 269-270.

92. The Brazilian historian Gilberto Freyre argued that Portugal's unique history of intermarriage between Celts, Germanic peoples, Jews, Arabs, Berbers and others caused Portuguese to be particularly inclined to intermarry with native American and black women in Brazil; Africans in Guinea, Angola and Mozambique; Chinese in Macao; etc. "As to miscibility," wrote Freyre, "no colonizing people in modern times has exceeded or so much as equaled the Portuguese in this regard" (Freyre, 1946, pp. 11-12).

93. Hidemasa, 1971, 61. See Leupp, 1992, pp. 17-18.

94. Murdoch, 1903/1964, 243. See also Boxer, 1979, pp. 45-46. Some of the Europeans acquired partners for lifetime terms through outright purchase. In 1590, the warlord Hideyoshi, having reunited Japan under his rule, banned the purchase and sale of human beings. Before and after his edict, foreign men bought women in Japan, including Koreans forced to settle in Kyushu during the Japanese invasion of the peninsula (1592-98). Even the servants and slaves of the Portuguese (Gujaratis, Javanese, black Africans) did so. A Jesuit reported in 1598 that "the very lascars [south Asian sailors] and scullions of the Portuguese purchase and carry [Japanese or Korean] slaves away" to Macao, while "Kaffirs and negroes of the Portuguese...give a scandalous example by living in debauchery with the girls they have bought, and whom some of them introduce into their cabins on the passage to Macao." On the intermarriage of Japanese and Africans in Macao by the late sixteenth century, see Snow, 1988, pp. 16-21.

95. Pagés, 1869-70, pp. 744, 769.

96. Papinot, 1909/1972, 777.

97. Pagés, Ibid., pp. 394, 477; Papinot, Ibid., 773; Profillet, 1895-97, pp. 147, 184; Boxer, 1951, 345.

98. Kaempfer, 1906, vol. 2, 163.

99. A handful of Dutchmen and one Englishman first arrived in 1600.

100. Games, 2008, 106.

101. Ibid., 107.

102. Cieslik, 1974.

103. Boxer, 1951, 439-40; Japanese text in Tokutomi, 1924, 289; Iwao, 1974, 331.

104. Cieslik, 1974, 30. The *Taiheiki* is a fourteenth century epic describing the fall of the Kamakura shogunate and subsequent brief restoration of direct imperial rule.

105. Elison, 1988, pp. 190-91, 208-211; Cieslik, Ibid., pp. 16-22, 37-38.

106. Cieslik, Ibid., pp. 19-20, 22.

107. Cieslik, Ibid., 22; Turnbull, 2000, 4.

108. Cieslik, Ibid., 53.

109. Ibid., 23.

110. Ibid., 30.

111. Ibid., 24.

112. Turnbull, 2000, 48

113. Jennes, 1959, pp. 176-177.

114. Boxer, 1951, 391.

115. Murdoch (1926), vol. 2, pt. .2, 689; Iwao, 1974, 332.

116. Murakami, 358.

117. Villiers, xi.

118. Murakami, 359. Presumably many of these women were originally Roman Catholic. Not all Dutchmen cohabiting with Japanese women in Batavia "legitimatized" their relationships in these ceremonies but it was normal (one such wedding every two years), whereas Dutch-Javanese formal marriage was rare. See Stoler, 1991.

119. He had in any case become engaged to a Dutch noblewoman on his trip!

120. Villiers, lxvi. The very concept of a "stain" of illegitimacy that troubled men like Caron was unknown to the Japanese. See Hayami, 1980.

121. Part of southern Taiwan was colonized by the Dutch between the 1630s and early 1660s but their holdings were lost to Chinese forces led by the half-Chinese, half-Japanese general Koxinga in 1662. While the Dutch controlled parts of Taiwan, the Dutch Reformed Church seriously undertook the conversion of the natives.

122. Smith and Mikami, 1914, 135.

123. Boxer, 1971, 148-149.

124. A letter from her dated January 1624 expresses concern about the safety of the two, referring to the boy as Uriemon, and mentions a daughter and son in Japan.

125. Massarella, 1990, pp. 321-322; Games, 2008, 290; Itoh, 2001, 17.

126. Iwao, 1985, 153. The original Latin, referring to "doctissimus juvenis D. Petrus Hartsingius, Japonensis," can be found in Smith and Mikami, Ibid., 133. This very dated account fails to discuss Pieter's early years and depicts him as 100% Japanese.

127. Iwao, 1985, 157.

128. Murakami, 1939, 358.

129. Iwao Seiichi concluded that the Oharu letter was at least based on a real letter, if embellished by the Japanese geographer Nishikawa Joken in 1714. See Cobbing, 1999, 341; Iwao, 1966, 360.

130. Cobbing, 1999, 38. A rare collection of these *Jagarata-fumi* or "Letters from Djakarta" is held by the Hirado Kankō Museum in Ōkubo-chō, Hirado. Despite the ban on overseas travel, there is at least one possible instance of a Japanese woman leaving the country almost two centuries after Oharu. In 1842, a letter arrived in Nagasaki with a Dutch ship and was forwarded to Osaka, where a magistrate had it copied while conducting a ten-month investigation. While the letter itself does not include the sender's name, it was identified by the magistrate as written by a "Fumi, daughter of one Horiya Shinbei from Tanimachi in Osaka," who had entered service in a teahouse in Osaka before transferring to Nagasaki's Maruyama in 1820 and "eventually became the wife of a Dutchman." The contents of the letter, addressed to Fumi's mother and sister, indicate that she was smuggled out of Nagasaki in 1825 and after seven months arrived

in Holland, where she settled happily with her husband's family and gave birth to a son around 1833. She writes that every morning "at daybreak, when it is the seventh hour in the daytime in Japan," she and her son "look southeast together" praying to meet them both. Little is known about this woman, and her Dutch husband (whom she refers to as *Teruyuu*) has not been identified. There are some implausible elements to the story. Still, it was taken seriously by an Osaka magistrate, and must have been kept in some archive whence it was fetched for inclusion in a compilation of historical documents published in 1900. It, along with the archive, was likely destroyed in World War II. While the original, and any official copy of it have been lost, two other versions of it dating back to the 1840s have been discovered in Iwate and Saga Prefectures. These incline the leading scholar on the document to assert its legitimacy. See Cobbing, 2001, 52; Cobbing, 2000; Cobbing, 1999, pp. 35-37, 42. Cobbing also writes of "a Dutchman who claims descent from a Japanese woman in the early 19th century. The evidence is a record ... his grandfather made out by the Nazis on their occupation of Holland in the 1940s, which specifies that he was 1/8th of Japanese origin" (personal correspondence with the author, November 23, 2012).

131. This mission undertaken at the command of the abdicated shogun Ieyasu was supposed to facilitate trade with New Spain and Europe. But it produced few results since the latter died in 1616 and anti-Christian sentiment soared thereafter. For a psychological examination of "Christian" versus "Japanese" identity in the minds of the envoys, see Endō Shūsaku's insightful novel *Samurai*.

132. Ryoichi Awamura, "Spain's Japon clan has reunion to trace its 17th century roots," *Japan Times*, December 11, 2003, 3.

133. Reyes and Palacios, 2011, pp. 191-237.

134. It is also possible she was a descendent of Yamada Nagamasa.

135. Smith, 2011, pp. 118-121.

136. Ibid., 121.

137. Hamilton, 1744, 175. The French East India Co. owed the Phaulkons money, and Maria and a daughter-in-law pursued the matter through agents in the French court system. In 1717, the Council of State in France issued a decree in Maria's favor, and provided her with a maintenance allowance.

138. Pelras, 1998, 168.

139. Blussé, 1986, 251.

140. Following such reports, doubtlessly obtained from the Dutch, the English East India Company dispatched ships to Japan in 1682 requesting the resumption of trading ties. The English were treated politely but their request refused. See Cocks, 1883, xlvii.

141. Massarrella, 1990, 112.

142. Paske-Smith, 1968, 54.

143. Rogers, 1956, 117; Paske-Smith, Ibid., 55.

144. Rogers, Ibid., 93. We can only speculate about what mix of religious ideas were discussed in the Adams' household. They were no doubt raised to believe in the Christian God, while realizing the need to be thoroughly discreet about such beliefs in the growing anti-Catholic climate.

145. Paske-Smith, 1968, 55.

146. Lewis, 2010, 292.

147. We have noted Kaempfer and Thunberg's surprise that women having served Dutchmen as prostitutes could marry well after leaving the profession, and Furukawa Koshōkoen's reference to women who "volunteer" to go to Dejima.

148. Vos, 1971, 616.

149. Christopher Fryke, The Book of Travel (1700), quoted in Paske-Smith, 1968, 124.

150. Teruoka and Higashi, 1971, 298.

151. See for example a woodblock print by Hosoda Eishi (1750-1829) in Leupp, 2003, 107.

152. Van Opstall, 1985. Recall the christening of English merchant Henry Smith's son in 1621. Presumably any specifically Christian content of these rites was concealed from the Japanese.

153. The Mon are a people who apparently migrated from western China into what are now Myanmar and Thailand over a thousand years ago.

154. Takekoshi, 1930, 148. The Chinese population in Nagasaki was around 2,000 by 1618; see Jansen, 1992, 9. It grew rapidly

thereafter, but became divided into the merchants and sailors confined to the *Tōjin Yashiki* and naturalized Japanese able to move about freely. See Morris-Suzuki, 1998, 83.

155. This is assuming that the small number of black servants and slaves on Dejima were not allowed access to prostitutes. Such contact was in fact forbidden by law and there is at least one incident on record in 1752 when four men described as "Blacks" (*kuronbō*), having snuck across the bridge, were arrested in a brothel in the town. See Leupp, 1995, pp. 4-6; Harada, 1994, 102; Fujita, 1987, 249; Vos, 1971, 630.

156. Furukawa, 1980, pp. 145-146.

157. Shiba, 1986, 629; Harada, 1994, 103.

158. Thunberg mentions this in 1775, adding, "I cannot believe the Japanese to be inhuman enough" to commit the act. See Vos, 1971, 621.

159. The term used for foreigner in the edict was *Tōjin*, which incorporating the character for the Tang dynasty, had originally meant a person from China. But by this period it was used broadly to include Europeans as well. See Suzuki, 2007, 83f.

160. Nagasaki Shiyakusho, 1925, pp. 20-24, 73-75. See also Stanley, 2012, pp. 94-95. There seems some doubt as to whether *Tōjin* at this time meant foreigners in general, or only Chinese. In any case the edict was applied to the Dutchmen.

161. Vos, 1971, pp. 629-630.

162. Ibid., 627.

163. Boxer, 1979, 93.

164. Quoted in Vos, 1971, 621.

165. This is a paraphrase of Doeff's report found in von Siebold et al., 1973, 29.

166. Vos, 1971, pp. 629-630.

167. Keene, 1969, pp. 1-2.

168. Leupp, 2003, pp. 87-89.

169. Keene, 1969, 170.

170. Vos, 1971, 629.

171. Ibid., 630.

172. Harada, 1994, 106.

173. Screech, 1999, 282.

174. Titsingh, 1990, 73; quoted in Blussé, 1999, 79.

175. Hildreth, 1907, 165.

176. Screech, 1999, 286.

177. Ogawa, 1989, 349. Mrs. Blomhoff and her Javanese maid are the only foreign women known to have resided (briefly) on Dejima during the period, and they were shipped off by Japanese demand at the earliest opportunity.

178. Cortazzi, 1987, 280.

179. Uemura, 1929, 370.

180. Cortazzi, 1987, 179.

181. The title was reported in the U.S. at the time as a curiosity. See "Sir Edwin Arnold's Marriage: The Bride is a Lady of Japan," *Hartford Courant* (Hartford, Connecticut, Oct. 20, 1897) and "Lady Arnold: Only Japanese Woman Bearing an English Title," *Chicago Daily Tribune* (June 20, 1898).

182. On the importance of the appearance of the retinues of public figures in this period, see Leupp, 1992, pp. 45-46.

183. Furukawa Koshōken reported in 1783 that Nagasaki women playing with their children on the bridge to Dejima would shout out in Dutch, "I love you!" See Plutschow, 2006, 99.

184. Nagasaki may have had a population of 60,000 by the mid-nineteenth century.

185. Screech, 1996, 15. These would include those confined to the Chinese compound in the city, but the great majority of part-Chinese were not subject to such confinement and treated as Japanese.

186. Andaya, 1999, 7.

187. Even U.S. seamen visited Nagasaki, handling the Dutch trade from 1799 to 1801 during the Napoleonic War. Dutch fear of British naval attacks in the waters between Java and Japan caused the VOC to hire Massachusetts-based ships to carry

cargo to Nagasaki from Batavia. Japanese officials were aware that these merchants were American, not Dutch but did not protest the temporary arrangement and indeed treated the U.S. merchants with courtesy. See Dulles, 1965, pp. 6-7.

## CHAPTER THREE

188. Boxer, 1951, pp. 91-136.

189. Koga 1968, vol.1, pp. 2-3.

190. Domingo Fernandez Navarette, *An Account of the Empire of China, Historical, Political, Moral and Religious* (Madrid, 1676). Cited in Koga, 1968, vol.1, pp. 5-6.

191. Koba, 2007, 41.

192. Nagasaki Shishi Nenpyō Hensan Iinkai, 1981, 43.

193. Jansen, 1992, pp. 29-30.

194. In 1865, French priests had just completed a Catholic church in the Nagasaki Foreign Settlement when Japanese peasants appeared at the door and revealed their faith. The discovery of the underground Japanese Christians, after more than two centuries of hiding, caused a sensation in Europe and provoked a final wave of persecutions by Japanese authorities.

195. Kaempfer, 1906, vol.2, pp. 83-84.

196. Thunberg, 1796, vol.3, pp. 74-75.

197. Ibid., pp.76-77.

198. Wang, 1876. I thank Jamie Berger for this information.

199. Translated from Chinese by Jamie Berger.

200. Koga, 1968, vol.2, pp. 137-141. The surname "Michitomi" is composed of two ideographs that are pronounced "Dōfu" in the *onyomi* or Chinese reading and thus simulate the pronunciation of "Doeff."

201. Tilley, 1861, 66.

202. Ibid., 60.

203. Koga, 1968, vol.2, 282.

204. For example, see Tracy, 1892, pp. 8-9.

205. Loti, 1888.

206. The short story *Madame Butterfly* published by American author John Luther Long in 1898 borrowed heavily from Pierre Loti's travelogue but added the birth of a child as well as the dramatic return of the "lieutenant" to Nagasaki. The stage play produced by American impresario David Belasco caught the attention of the Italian composer Giacomo Puccini, who transformed it into the now world famous opera in 1905.

207. *The Nagasaki Press*, January 14, 1901.

208. *The Nagasaki Press*, February 16, 1904.

209. Hayashida and Kittleson, 1977.

210. Wada, 1973, vol.2, p.110. Copies of *Volya* are preserved today at the Historiographical Institute, Tokyo University, Meiji Newspaper Collection, Tokyo, Japan.

211. Burke-Gaffney, 1997.

212. *The Nagasaki Press*, July 8, 1906.

213. From documents preserved today at the Mitsubishi Heavy Industries Ltd. Nagasaki Shipyard and Engine Works. I thank Hatsuho Naitō for this information.

214. Robert Walker Jr. died in Nagasaki in 1958 and was buried at Sakamoto International Cemetery. His descendants continue to live in Nagasaki today, still cutting an unusual figure with their Japanese citizenship and English names.

215. Ōizumi kokuseki zenshū was re-published by Midori Shobō (Tokyo) in 1988.

216. Ōizumi Kokuseki, *Mizuoto* Vol.33-34, June 1955. Translated from Japanese by the author.

## CHAPTER FOUR

217. This is a slightly modified version of Ellen Nakamura, "Working the Siebold Network: Kusumoto Ine (1827-1903) and Western Learning in Nineteenth-Century Japan," *Japanese Studies* 28 (2), 2008: 197-211. *Japanese Studies* by Taylor & Francis Ltd. Reproduced with permission of Taylor & Francis Ltd. in the format reuse in

a book/textbook via Copyright Clearance Center. This project
was funded by a University of Auckland Early Career Research
Excellence Award. I am grateful to Pauline van der Wiel
for assistance with translations from Dutch, to the Siebold
Memorial Museum, Nagasaki, the Institute for Japanese
History, Faculty of East Asian Studies, Ruhr-Universität
Bochum, and Ōzu Shiritsu Hakubutsukan for permission to
use their collections. I thank Yasuhiro Hoki and Yusaku Iwata
for generous support in Japan, and Tessa Morris-Suzuki, Kate
Wildman Nakai, Shizu Sakai, Robyn Hamilton, the anonymous
reviewers, and many colleagues for their helpful comments.

218. Ine was known by several names during her lifetime. She used
the name Itoku in later life. Her surname too, varied. She
sometimes used Shimoto, which used the same first character
as her father Siebold, before taking on her mother's name
Kusumoto in later life. Following Japanese convention, she will
be referred to here throughout as Ine.

219. See for example Nihon Joishi Hensan Iinkai, 1962, pp. 41-45.

220. Ogino, 1893, 483.

221. Fukui, 2000; Nihon Joishi Hensan Iinkai, 1962; Yoshimura, 1978.

222. Plutschow, 2007, pp. 184-197. Plutschow does not utilise the
Uwajima sources introduced here.

223. The original handwritten notes are preserved in the Nagasaki
Museum of History. I am grateful to Professor Sakai Shizu for
sharing her copy of these notes with me.

224. Personal Narratives Group, 1989, 262.

225. Many of these are held in the Siebold Memorial Museum in
Nagasaki.

226. I am indebted in particular to the work of historian Masafumi
Miyoshi, whose extensive reading of Uwajima Domain sources
has uncovered several important references to Ine.

227. Yoneyama Bunko 15-3-1. Siebold Memorial Museum, Nagasaki.

228. Plutschow, 2007, 195 suggests that women were specifically
prohibited from practising medicine by the 1884 regulations, but
this was not the case. There was no mention of women at all,
something which Ogino Ginko used to her advantage.

229. Kōseisho Imukyoku, 1976, 92.

230. Homei, 2006, pp. 412-413.

231. Kōseisho Imukyoku, 1976, 92.

232. On the modernization of Japanese midwifery see for example, Homei, 2006; Terazawa, 2003.

233. See Homei, 2006 for developments in Japanese obstetrics at this time.

234. Numata, 1989, 245.

235. It has been suggested that Taki (Sonōgi) was not a prostitute before entering Siebold's service, because he was careful to select a virgin for fear of contracting syphilis. See Leupp, 2003, 121. Her family however, was of low class, and her elder sister Tsune also was a "Dutch-going" prostitute.

236. Harada, 1981, pp. 370-371.

237. On Siebold in English see Beukers, 1998; Kouwenhoven and Forrer, 2000; Plutschow, 2007. In Japanese, see Ishiyama, 2003.

238. See for example, Yoshimura, 1978; Plutschow, 2007.

239. Letter in German from Heinrich Bürger to Siebold, dated December 21, 1831. Brandenstein Collection, Microfilm no. 110091.

240. Letter in Dutch, dated November 22, 1832. Bochum Siebold Collection, Dept. East Asian Studies, Ruhr-Universität Bochum. 455/XVII-1-B-6/VI, 12.

241. Shūzō was born in neighbouring Ōzu Domain, but later studied with Keisaku and worked for Uwajima Domain.

242. Miyoshi, 2001, pp. 170-173.

243. According to her résumé of 1884, Yoneyama Bunko 15-3-1. Siebold Memorial Museum, Nagasaki.

244. Maruyama, 1958, 29.

245. Fukui, Miyasaka, and Tokunaga, 2001, 51.

246. Tsukizawa, 1992, 73.

247. Koga, 1924.

248. Ibid.

249. This is apparent from the diary of the doctor Mitsukuri Genpo (1799-1863), who wrote about his meeting with Ine in Nagasaki in 1854. See Kimura, 1991, 408. His letter also corroborates the fact that Tada was born in Okayama. Plutschow suggests that she was born in Nagasaki. See Plutschow, 2007, 190.

250. Hiramatsu, 1999, 166.

251. On Takano Chōei, see Nakamura, 2005.

252. Zōroku had studied Western learning in Ogata Kōan's Tekitekisaijuku in Osaka, where he had been made top student. He came to Uwajima in 1853 at the invitation of Ōno Masasaburō (?-1880), and was employed by the domain for his expertise in Western military science. See Miyoshi, 2001, pp. 98-142.

253. von Siebold, 1981, 82.

254. Parts of some letters have also been translated in Beukers, 1998. The letters used here are from the Bochum Siebold Collection.

255. Plutschow suggests that Ine was upset because Siebold fathered a daughter (called Matsu) by this maid (Plutschow, 2007, 113). He does not connect this Matsu with a letter written by Heinrich von Siebold to his brother Alexander in October 1877, which also refers to the circumstances surrounding a "Matsune" who was living with Ine and Takako in Osaka. (Schmidt, 2000, 312). Curiously, however, there is a photograph held by the Ōzu Shiryōkan, in which Ine, Shūzō, Takako, a male retainer, and a child described as "Kusumoto Matsune" appear, which suggests that the two could refer to the same girl.

256. It is unclear who Ine means here. Perhaps Abe Roan?

257. Letter in Dutch, Bochum Siebold Collection, Dept. East Asian Studies, Ruhr-Universität Bochum. 456/XVII-1-B-6/VI,13.

258. Letter in Dutch, Bochum Siebold Collection, Dept. East Asian Studies, Ruhr-Universität Bochum. 457/XVII-1-B-6/VI,14.

259. Letter in Dutch, Bochum Siebold Collection, Dept. East Asian Studies, Ruhr-Universität Bochum. 445/XVII-1-B-6/VI,7 (1.446.001)

260. A mixture of soap, camphor, and essential oils, used as a liniment.

261. Letter in Dutch, Bochum Siebold Collection, Dept. East Asian Studies, Ruhr-Universität Bochum. 445/XVII-1-B-6/VI,7

(1.446.001)

262. Letter in Dutch, Bochum Siebold Collection, Dept. East Asian Studies, Ruhr-Universität Bochum. 445/XVII-1-B-6/VI,7 (1.446.002)

263. van Meerdervoort, 1860, 91. Pompe does not mention Ine by name, but there is little doubt as to her identity.

264. Wittermans and Bowers, 1970, 42.

265. Bauduin was an experienced medical teacher who had been working in Utrecht. He arrived in Japan in 1862. Mansveld arrived as Bauduin's successor in 1866.

266. von Siebold, 1981, 158.

267. This letter is cited in full in Ogata, 1942a; Ogata, 1942b. All efforts to locate the original have been unsuccessful. At the time of Ogata's article, it was in private hands. Although the author states that the letter was addressed to Keisaku (whose penname was Nyozan), it was actually addressed to Ninomiya Ichizaemon, Keisaku's brother-in-law (who had the similar penname of Nyozui (See Miyoshi, 2001, 179). Keisaku passed away in the third month of 1862, before this letter could have been written.

268. Taka was working in the women's quarters, serving Munenari's wife, Nao.

269. Date Munenari (1818-1892). Munenari retired from office in 1858, but continued to wield power in his domain.

270. Ogata, 1942a, 836.

271. Miyoshi, 2001, 190.

272. Quoted in Ibid., 159.

273. By comparison, when Shūzō was invited to serve Uwajima Domain upon his release from prison in 1866, he received a three-person salary (sanninfuchi). A one-person salary was generally equivalent to five bales of rice per year, and was considered enough to feed an adult man for a year.

274. Miyoshi, 2001, 189.

275. Ibid., 160.

276. Quoted in Cortazzi, 1985, pp. 78-79. The interpreter mentioned was Alexander von Siebold.

277. Miyoshi, 2001, 159. Some of the records have been published as Kindaishi Bunko Uwajima Kenkyūkai, 1978-80. See vol. 2, 364 for the entry concerning Ine.

278. Bowers, 1980, 35.

279. Tokyo Nichiran Gakkai, 1984, 659.

280. Tsukizawa, 1992, 175.

281. His father Ishii Sōken reported the news in a letter to an acquaintance dated 1858 that his daughter in Nagasaki was well and was now eight years old, despite his failure to send any money for her upbringing. Ibid., pp. 124-125.

282. The 1874 diary is reproduced in full in Tsukizawa, 1992.

283. The certificate announcing her employment is held by the Siebold Memorial Museum in Nagasaki. Yoneyama Bunko (1) 13-2-2 (9-2).

284. Kunaichō, 1969, vol. 3, 130.

285. From Ine's résumé. Yoneyama Bunko 15-3-1. Siebold Memorial Museum, Nagasaki.

286. Tsukizawa, 1992, 301.

287. Ibid., 280.

288. Schmidt, 2000, 312.

289. Cited in Tsukizawa, 1992, 316.

290. Koga, 1924. The children were Hajime (a boy who died young) and two girls, Taki and Tane.

291. Cited in Tsukizawa, 1992, 316.

292. Walthall, 1998, pp. 352-353.

293. Patessio, 2004, 5.

294. Walthall, 1998, 185.

295. Wittermans and Bowers, 1970, 42.

# CHAPTER FIVE

296. Jan Cock Blomhoff, the Dutch Director of Trade at Dejima, attempted to challenge this policy in August 1817, by bringing his wife, Titia, a wet-nurse and a maid with him to the island, but the Japanese refused to let them stay and the following month ordered them home on the return voyage to Batavia and the Netherlands. They eventually left with Hendrik Doeff, the previous director, upon his return in December 1817. Titia Blumhoff died in 1821, never again seeing her husband. See Bersma, 2002, 13.

297. Doeff, 2003, pp. 207, 213.

298. Kouwenhoven and Forrer, 2000, pp. 24-25.

299. Rev. Henry Wood to Rev. George Bethune, November 30, 1858, *Records of the Board of Foreign Missions, Japan Mission*, Reformed Church Archives, Rutgers University, New Jersey.

300. Elisha Rice, U.S. Commercial Agent at Hakodate, to U.S. Secretary of State, May 22, 1859, *Despatches from the United States Consuls in Hakodate, Japan, 1856-1878* (Record Group 59), microfilm, National Archives, Washington D.C., 1957.

301. *Report of the Surgeon-General of the Navy for the Year 1883* (Washington DC, 1884), 227.

302. "Register of Citizens of the U.S., August 1890." *Records of the United States Consulate at Nagasaki, Japan, 1859-1941* (Record Group 84) [Hereafter cited as RUSCN], National Archives, Washington D.C. In this document, Edward Lake is recorded as having registered with the U.S. Consulate in Nagasaki in September 1863, but Nagasaki Kenritsu Toshokan, 2002 lists him as residing in Oura in October 1862. His official registration at the consulate may have occurred once he was of legal age.

303. *New York Times*, June 12, 1878.

304. RUSCN, July 7, 1871.

305. Ibid.

306. Ibid.

307. Ibid.

308. *New York Times*, June 12, 1878.

309. *St. Louis Post Dispatch*, September 5, 1883.

310. *New York World*, July 13, 1886.

311. *Independent*, September 3, 1898, as quoted in *Nagasaki Press*, September 17, 1898.

312. John Walsh was born in July 1829 in New York City. At the age of twenty-nine, he came to Nagasaki with his elder brother to establish the trading firm Walsh & Co., which would soon become the largest American merchant firm in town. John Walsh was appointed U.S. Consul to Nagasaki in May 1859. He received no salary from the U.S. Department of State, but was permitted to conduct his own private business. Walsh served as U.S. Consul for more than six years, but his business interests often took him out of town, and eventually he moved his business operations entirely out of Nagasaki. While in Nagasaki, John Walsh began living with a twenty-one year-old Japanese woman named Rin Yamaguchi in 1863. The following year, the couple had a daughter. The family moved to Kobe when the foreign settlement opened there in 1868. John Walsh and Rin Yamaguchi developed a strong, stable twenty-seven year relationship that did not end until Rin's death in 1890 at the age of forty-eight. Walsh died in Kobe in August 1897 at the age of sixty-eight.

313. Jose Loureiro was born in Hong Kong in 1835. By at least May 1861, he was in Nagasaki, where he served as Portuguese Consul. In addition to his consular duties, Loureiro also had business interests centered on the tea trade. According to Nagasaki Kenritsu Toshokan (2002), in early 1863, Loureiro was listed as the father of a three-year old daughter born to a Japanese woman from Yoriai-machi in Nagasaki. He left Nagasaki in 1870. Loureiro later became Portuguese Ambassador to Japan and resided in Tokyo in that capacity in June 1888. After the embassy closed in 1892, Loureiro returned to Hong Kong, where he died of pneumonia in August 1893 at the age of fifty-eight.

314. *Rising Sun and Nagasaki Express*, April 4, 1888.

315. Dr. Mary Suganuma, a native of Ohio, came to Nagasaki with her Japanese husband Motonosuke Suganuma (called Joe Suganuma by the foreign community) in September 1893 and operated a women's hospital there for almost three decades. Mary, who received her medical license from Cleveland Homeopathic Medical College in 1883, went to Osaka in 1891 in order to conduct medical missionary work with the Presbyterian Church. However, in February 1893, at the age of thirty, she married and was thus forced to sever her official relationship with the Presbyterian mission. In August of the same year,

she received a medical license from the Japanese government, enabling her to practice medicine in the country. After coming to Nagasaki in the fall of 1893, in addition to her hospital practice, Mary worked in the dispensary of Kwassui Jo Gakkō, the Methodist women's school in the foreign settlement. In June 1921, fire destroyed both the Suganuma home and Mary's medical practice. While much was lost in the fire, Mary began the struggle to open another hospital out of her new home on the hillside overlooking the harbor at Minamiyamate. Six months later, however, her husband, Motonosuke, died suddenly. In mid-March 1922, Dr. Mary Suganuma decided to return to the United States to live with her adopted Japanese son who was a student at Garrett Biblical Institute.

316. Earns and Burke-Gaffney, 1991, 165.

317. *The Nagasaki Press*, February 19, 1925.

318. Ibid., September 12, 1901 and November 10, 1911.

319. The building, known officially as The Christian Endeavour Home for Seamen, was opened in February 1896. It was a non-alcoholic home for visiting sailors in Nagasaki's foreign settlement that grew out of efforts by seamen from an American man-of-war and resident Protestant missionaries. The Seamen's Home operated on a continual basis in Nagasaki for more than forty years, providing American and European sailors an alternative to the grog shops and tea houses of the city. It offered aid and comfort when needed, and a place to relax and socialize without having to consume alcoholic beverages. James Hatter was born in New York in February 1843. He served in the U.S. Navy from 1869 to 1890. Living on a U.S. government pension of eight dollars a month, Hatter came to Nagasaki in 1896 and soon thereafter opened a small tavern/restaurant business near the Oura River called the Boston Restaurant. His business catered primarily to visiting American and European naval personnel.

320. James Oliver was born in January 1852 in Rochester, New York. He served in the U.S. Army before coming to Nagasaki in 1900. Oliver married Saku Yamaguchi of Urakami in June 1900. Oliver operated the Alahambra American Hotel along the Oura River prior to his death in February 1917 at the age of sixty-five. He was buried in the addition to Sakamoto International Cemetery. His wife, also known as Saku Isabellina Oliver, passed away in October 1936 at the age of seventy-three and was buried next to her husband.

321. Knox, 1970.

322. Earns, 2002, 140.

323. *Naigaijin iinazuke jinmeibo.*

324. *The Nagasaki Press*, January 5, 1910, December 19, 1916 and October 22, 1919.

325. Message from John Denbigh to author dated February 14, 2007. His uncle, John (Ian) Denbigh, met Anne Neale Taylor in a Japanese prisoner of war camp in Shanghai. They married in Shanghai in 1945.

326. Kinoshita, 2008, 204.

327. Cohen, 2001, 3.

328. *Official Correspondence*, November 16, 1895.

329. Earns, 1994, 80.

330. Ibid., 83.

331. Ibid.

332. Ibid., 86.

333. Ibid., pp. 87-89.

334. Ary William Van Ess was born in Rotterdam, The Netherlands, in November 1838 and later became a British citizen. He served in the British Legation Escort at Beijing from November 1869 to November 1874 and then from September 1876 to 1903 he was constable at the British Consulate in Chefoo. Van Ess came to Nagasaki upon his retirement in 1903. He died at his residence on Minamiyamate in October 1913 at the age of seventy-four. Van Ess was survived by his Japanese wife, Mary Anna Kotani Kizue, of Nagasaki (who died in Kobe in January 1961), and a daughter, Amy Van Ess Kotani, plus three children from a previous marriage.

335. According to *Official Correspondence*, May 30, 1899, Carl Paul Heinrich Sciba [Scriba] (30) married Miwa Naitō (19) of Obama.

336. According to *The Nagasaki Press*, August 18, 1925, Carl Scriba went to the United States to study engineering at Pasadena College.

337. Wada, 1973.

338. The ship-chandler and compradore Carlo Fioravante Urso was born in Italy in 1849 and came to Nagasaki in the mid-to-late

1880s, although he did not open his own business until 1895. From this time until his death in 1918, he presented himself as "Compradore for the Italian, Spanish and Austrian Navies." Urso married Take (who was about half his age) in the late 1880s.

## CHAPTER SIX

339. Kamoto, 2001.

340. Recent publications from historians who specialize in the early modern period include Leupp, 2003; Arano, 2004; Matsui 2010; and Yokota, 2011.

341. Okamura, 2013. Iwabuchi eds, 2014.

342. As the Jewish sociologist Georg Simmel, who was active during this period, wrote: "The stranger is fixed within the span of a particular space, or within a span whose boundaries are similar to spatial boundaries, but his position within this space is determined, essentially, by the fact that he has not belonged to it from the beginning, that he brings qualities into it that do not or cannot stem from the space itself." Simmel, 1979, 129.

343. Whitney, 1979, 54.

344. Merton, 1941, 362.

345. Blussé, 1986. Children born of relationships between White men and local women in the Spanish and Portuguese colonies were called *mestizo*. The term varied depending on the context of the times and the ruling state. Blussé's approach in his research is clear. Wives were held to be legally incompetent, and a woman's property would become the property of her husband. For this reason, in one case, a white Dutch man, who had few prospects for advancement in Holland, strategically married Cornelia, a Japanese widow. Blussé's work is a highly thought-provoking one that examines the ways in which intermarriage under colonial rule in the *ancien régime* is based on different assumptions and conditions than international marriages in modern nation-states.

346. Leupp, 1994.

347. Leupp, 2003.

348. Nishikawa, 1966.

349. Hayami, 1993, pp. 135-164.

350. Nagasaki Shiyakusho, 1981, 9.

351. Etō 1972, 124.

352. Yoshida, 1938.

353. Haruta, 1994, 65.

354. Nihon Shiseki Kyōkai, 1967, 4.

355. I am using the now-discriminatory term "illegitimate child" (*shiseiji*) deliberately because the child of a concubine who was recorded in the household registry would be a "legitimate child" (*kōseiji*, literally public child). Until the term "concubine" was removed from the penal code in Meiji 15 (1882), the meaning of "illegitimate child" (*shiseiji*) differed from the modern meaning. The law on illegitimate children was, along with the systematization of the household registry, a law that regulated the treatment of illegitimate children born to two Japanese people.

356. While in the Japanese coastal waters, a Chinese man who had been forced to board a Peruvian ship named the *Maria Luz* could no longer endure being treated as a slave and sought help from a British ship. As the incident took place in Japanese waters, the British entrusted the decision to the Japanese government. This was in 1863, just after President Lincoln had issued the Emancipation Proclamation, and slavery had come symbolize barbarism to the Western world. In response to the Japanese inclination to free the slave, the Peruvian side argued that Japan had a custom of selling human beings in the form of prostitutes, and therefore could not say it had no slavery. The response was a semantic dodge, arguing that prostitution was a domestic issue and that these people were never taken outside of the country. However, the Meiji government realized that it would never be accepted as a civilized nation by the Western powers if it did not emancipate its prostitutes, and issued an emancipation law lamenting that prostitutes had been treated as if they were "horses and oxen" and invalidating all of their debts.

357. McArthur, 2013

358. See the *Naigaijin kekkonbo Meiji 26, Kanbō gaimugakari* issued by Tokyo Kōbunshokan.

359. Hepburn translated this as "social position, station in life" in his *Wa-eigo rinshūsei* (Japanese-English Dictionary) also known as the

*Hebon jisho* (Hepburn Dictionary). This can be accessed from the home page of Meiji Gakuin University, of which Hepburn was a founder. Accessed May 1, 2013: http://www.meijigakuin.ac.jp/mgda/index.html

360. See the *Naigaijin kekkonbo Meiji 26, Kanbō gaimugakari* issued by Tokyo Kōbunshokan.

361. Law Reports Probate Division, XV 1888-1890, London, pp. 76-81.

362. See Gaimushō Gaikō Shiryokan Shozō, *Naigaijin minkan shussei no shijo shūseki toriatsukai zakken*. Also see Kanami, 1996.

363. See Yokohamashi, 1968, 337.

364. See Gaimushō Gaikō Shiryokan Shozō, *Naigaijin minkan shussei no shijo shūseki toriatsukai zakken*.

365. For marriages between two Japanese people, the Outline of the New Criminal Code issued in 1870 defined concubines as second-degree relatives of the husband. In 1875, a directive was issued making it necessary to submit notification of transfer of registry for concubines just as with wives. "Concubines" did not disappear from the laws until the 1881 proclamation and 1883 implementation of the new criminal code.

366. Oguma, 1998, 155.

367. Huang, 2013

368. Kim, 1999, 31.

369. Mizuno, 2001, 2002, and 2008.

370. In recent years, efforts to re-consider colonial law through the relationship between household registries and nationality have flourished. See Asano, 2004, 2008; and Endō, 2010.

371. Takeshita, 2000, 57.

372. Yamamoto, 1994; Yamamoto, 1996.

373. Moriki, 2002, 303.


## CHAPTER SEVEN

374. Jennifer Robertson, "Blood Talks: Eugenic Modernity and the Creation of the New Japanese," *History and Anthropology* 13, no. 3

(2002): 191-216. Copyright by *History and Anthropology* by Taylor & Francis. Reproduced with permission by Taylor & Francis Ltd. in the format reuse in a book/textbook via Copyright Clearance Center. This chapter is part of a section in my forthcoming book, *Robo sapiens japanicus: Robots, Eugenics, and Post-Human Aesthetics* (University of California Press). For their welcome suggestions and helpful advice, I owe special thanks to Celeste Brusati, Veena Das, Gillian Feeley-Harnik, Sabine Frühstück, Caitrin Lynch, Tobie Meyer-Fong, Steffi Richter, and Hoon Song. I also owe thanks to my colleagues at the following institutions where, over the past several years, I have presented different versions of this article: American University in Cairo, University of British Columbia, Chiba University, University of Chicago, Harvard University, Hebrew University, University of Illinois, University of Iowa, Internationales Forschungzentrum Kulturwissenschaften in Vienna, Johns Hopkins University, Leipzig University, Lewis and Clark College, University of Oregon, University of Pennsylvania, University of Pittsburgh, Stanford University, Tokyo University, and University of Vienna. Early drafts of this particular article were presented at the Association for Asian Studies annual meetings (2000) and the Israeli Anthropological Association annual meetings (2000). Funding for my on-going research on "blood ideologies" was provided by the following grants and fellowships: Japan Foundation Fellowship, 2002; Office of the Vice-President for Research, College of Literature, Science, and Arts, and the Life Sciences, Values, and Society Program (University of Michigan), 2001-2002; Faculty Grant, Institute for Research on Women and Gender (University of Michigan), 2000; Center for Japanese Studies Faculty Fellowship (University of Michigan), 1997-1998; Wissenschaftskolleg zu Berlin (Institute for Advanced Study, Berlin), Invited Fellow, 1996-1997; Wenner-Gren Foundation for Anthropological Research, Regular Grant, 1995; and National Endowment for the Humanities Fellowship from the American Council of Learned Societies and the Social Science Research Council Joint International Post-Doctoral Program, Advanced Research Grant, 1995.

375. A more literal translation is, "As for blood, [it] expresses things."

376. The slash in the translated title, while awkward, reflects the fact that *undō* refers to both exercise, as in athletics, and movement, as in activities organized toward a specific political objective. Born in January 1892 in Nikaho Town (Yuri District, Akita Prefecture), Shigenori Ikeda attended college in Tokyo. Following his graduation from Tokyo Foreign Language

University (Tokyo Gaigodai), he was employed by Kōdansha, a prominent publishing house, to edit the magazine *Taikan* (Outlook). He later joined the *Hōchi Shinbun*, a major daily newspaper, and served as a special correspondent to Germany from 1919 to 1924, where he earned doctorates in eugenics and women's history. He was transferred to Moscow in 1925 before returning to Japan and founding the Eugenic Exercise/ Movement Association and a eugenics journal, both of which were aimed to foster among the general public an interest in incorporating hygienic and eugenic practices into everyday life practices. The journal ceased publication in January 1930. Ikeda rekindled his journalism career the following year by assuming the editorship of the *Keijō Nippō* (Seoul Daily News) based in Seoul, Korea. He returned to the *Hōchi Shinbun* as an editor in 1938, and from 1941 through the end of the war worked for Naval Intelligence (Kaigun hōdōbu). After the war he became a prominent "social commentator" (*hyōronka*), known for his entertaining essays on a wide array of topics, from the origins of sushi and Japanese photography, to canine welfare in different cultures and the fate of Japanese *konketsuji* ("mixed-blood children") (Ikeda, 1956; 1957).

377.  "Disciplinary bio-power," as elaborated by Michel Foucault (Foucault, 1978; 1979), refers to a state's or dominant institution's politicization of and control over biology and biological processes, including recreational and procreational sexual practices, as a powerful means of assimilating and claiming people as subjects. Although the applications of bio-power can be both positive or negative, Foucault focuses especially on its the misuses and perversions.

378.  For example, Hayashida, 1976; Dower, 1986; Yoshino, 1997; Frühstück, 2003.

379.  Imperial assimilation policy is productively understood as an application of the technology of "blood" although I do not have the space to elaborate here.

380.  Jennifer Terry makes a similar point about the relationship between science and (homo)sexuality in the United States (Terry, 1999, pp. 11-13).

381.  Beginning in the 1910s and blatantly obvious by 1940 was the prolific use of *kagaku* (science) in the titles of popular magazines, such as *Kagaku Sekai* (Science World), *Kagaku Gahō* (Science Illustrated), *Kodomo no Kagaku* (Science for Children), *Kagaku no Nippon* (Science Japan), and *Shashin Kagaku* (Photography Science), to name but a few magazines.

**435**

382. As Tessa Morris-Suzuki notes, "the imagery of the family was particularly apposite because it created the ideal framework for asserting the paramount place of the emperor in Japanese society" as the head of the family-state. The familial conception of the nation-state profoundly influenced the nascent idea of the uniqueness of the Japanese as a distinct race (Morris-Suzuki, 1998, pp. 84-85).

383. Until 1985, paternal "blood," or patrilineality, was the de jure condition of nationality and citizenship, which in Japan, as in Germany, is jus sanguinus (unlike in the United States, where it is jus solis). That year, maternal "blood" was legally recognized as an agent of nationality and citizenship.

384. Nishida, 1995, pp. 18-19.

385. Historically, in some regions of Japan females were required to spend the period of their menses in a menstrual hut located at some remove from the main house (Segawa, 1963). Many Japanese today are reluctant to acknowledge the equation of blood and symbolic pollution as one factor influencing the widespread corporate practice of allowing (until a few years ago) monthly "menstruation leaves." Today, Shinto priests rationalize as a precautionary measure, the banishment of all females, regardless of celebrity or political rank, from the sumo ring, certain sacred mountains, and road construction sites on account of their polluted and dangerous bodies that can provoke destructive forces.

386. Nishida, 1995, pp. 206-209.

387. Nishida, 1995, pp. 32-35. Note that niku, as in nikumanjū (flesh bun), has been a slang word for female genitals since at least the early seventeenth century (Maeda, 1979, 757). There is no apparent vulgar equivalent for tane.

388. Nishida, 1995, 35. The history of "blood" symbolism in Japan runs contrary to Foucault's eurocentric theory that an "ancien régime of blood" endured as a descent ideology forming the foundation of a modern racialist and racist system of heredity. Moreover, in modern Japan, "blood" symbolism was collapsed with, and not replaced by, sexuality and race (Foucault, 1978, pp. 147-148; see the discussion with respect to Germany in Linke, 1999, pp. 36-37).

389. Nishida, 1995, pp. 18, 65, 76.

390. Lebra, 1993, 125; Van Bremen, 1998. Although Lebra here is

referring in particular to the adoption practices of the modern Japanese nobility (which she presents in terms somewhat timeless), adoption was deployed pragmatically by all classes and status groups since at least the fourth century, when Japan first appears in Chinese dynastic histories. The *ie*, or household, is a corporate group and an economic unit of production that perpetuates itself from generation to generation beyond the life span of any single member of the group. Prior to the postwar constitution, the *ie*, and not the individual, constituted the smallest legal unit of society. The *ie*, which is lead by a househead who is regarded as the caretaker of the group, may vary over time in composition from a childless couple to several generations, although only one married couple per generation may claim membership in an *ie*. As I note in the body of the chapter, succession tends to be on the model of male primogeniture; younger sons form branch *ie* and daughters marry out.

391. Honjō, 1936, 21.

392. Also, wealthy merchants, who controlled the *de facto* monetary economy during the Edo period, could purchase swords that only samurai could, theoretically, own and which, therefore, were akin to sartorial markers of samurai status.

393. Tōgō, 1945, 34.

394. See Otsubo, 1999.

395. Ikeda, 1929, pp. 26-27.

396. Two years earlier, the Association together with the Japanese Red Cross designated November 11 as "the day to emphasize the importance of marriage" (*kekkon kyōchōbi*). As explained by eugenicist Hisomu Nagai, the Chinese characters for the number 11 resemble the character for "soil," itself a metaphor for blood as an organic, generative power (Nagai, 1936, 8; also cited in Otsubo, 1999, 68). Nagai, who had studied at Göttingen University from 1903 to 1906, was very likely familiar with the Germanic idea of kinship originating in the commingling of blood and soil (*Blut und Boden*), later reified by the Nazis, as suggested by his reference to "beautiful flowers growing from [Japanese] soil."

397. For a description of one aspect of the application of eugenics by women's groups, see Otsubo, 1999. Curiously, Otsubo does not seem aware of the relationship between an ideology of pure-bloodedness, discussed here in detail later, and ideas of race

hygiene and fears associated with miscegenation. Consequently, she limits notions of blood purity to the literal (non-allegorical) sense of disease- or pathogen-free hemoglobin. After World War II, Nagai distanced himself from his earlier work as an enthusiastic advocate of negative eugenics (see Frühstück, 2002).

398. Norgren, 2001, pp. 145, 155.

399. The association of eugenics with maternal health has overshadowed its invocation as scientific grounds for the ostracism, exile, and even sterilization of persons suffering from Hansen's disease and other conditions erroneously assumed to be genetic who were thus treated as pariahs.

400. See Lebra, 1995, 125.

401. Early in the Tokugawa period, the Tokugawa shogunate codified a status hierarchy that classified people into four endogamous groups—samurai (*shi*), farmers (*nō*), artisans (*kō*), and merchants (*shō*). Above these groups were the members of the imperial household and the Buddhist and Shinto clergy, and below the four groups were people grouped into two categories of sub-humanity, the "non-people" (*hinin*) and, at rock bottom, the "filthy" (non-) people (*eta*). The *hinin* constituted a heterogeneous group comprised of beggars, prostitutes, itinerant entertainers, fortunetellers, fugitives, and criminals. Among their ranks were also individuals who had fallen out of the "real people" categories for one reason or another. *Eta* is a word of uncertain origin. In the Tokugawa period, it referred to families of outcastes who performed tasks considered to be ritually or symbolically polluting, including the slaughtering of animals and disposal of the dead. The *eta* were "quarantined" in specific, undesirable locations, such as dry river beds, and forced to wear special clothing to mark their outcaste status; in some localities were mandated to wear a patch of leather on their sleeves, whereas in others, they were tatooed, as were some *hinin*. In 1871, as part of its modernization programs, the new Meiji imperial government, whose supporters overthrew the shogunate, passed an edict officially abolishing all status discrimination. The four-part status hierarchy was leveled and reconstituted under the rubric "commoners" (*heimin*)—although aristocrats remained such. The non-people and *eta* were recategorized as "new commoners" (*shinheimin*), whose creation marks the beginning of the *burakumin*, or literally "village people," a Meiji-period name that emphasized their endogamous constitution. Moreover, the prefix "new," in "new commoner," did not eradicate but rather

contemporized the centuries long practice of discriminating against persons historically categorized as subhuman.

402. The blurred semantics of "eugenics" and "race hygiene" also typified debates about "applied biology" in Germany before and during the Third Reich; see Proctor, 1988.

403. *Jinshu* is the Chinese-style (*onyomi*) pronunciation of this compound ideograph; the Japanese-style (*kunyomi*) pronunciation is *hitodane*, or "human seed." My perusal of the early eugenics literature suggests that *hitodane* was the pronunciation used for the English term "germ plasm," as indicated by the frequent inclusion of syllables [*furigana*] printed alongside the ideographs in texts. Also, whereas *jinshu* is used for "race" in the biological (phenotypic) sense, *minzoku* more often denotes social race, or ethnicity.

404. Embree, 1939, pp. 88-89 suggests that consanguineous marriages tended to involve patrilineal parallel-cousins, while adoptions tended to be transacted within matrilineages.

405. For definitive research on the history of sexology in Japan, see Frühstück, 2001 and Frühstück, 2003.

406. Among the most tenacious superstitions is that of the *hinoeuma*, or zodiacal sign of the fiery horse that cycles every sixty years. Females born in the year of the fiery horse are, according to this "superstition," headstrong and predestined to harm males, and thus are eschewed as marriage partners.

407. Wikler, 1999, 192.

408. Pernick, 1997, pp. 1767, 1769.

409. See Ikeda, 1927a; Ikeda, 1927b; and Stocking, 1968, 25.

410. Irizawa, 1939, pp. 17-21, 34, 61.

411. Hayashida, 1976, 24.

412. Having published already on the vicissitudes of the "pure-blood" and "mixed-blood" positions, I will only briefly summarize them here in order to reduce redundancy and to allow more room to explore related phenomena; see Robertson, 2001a.

413. "Marriage" was used as a euphemism for "procreative sexual intercourse."

414. Suzuki, 1983, pp. 32-34, 39.

415. Weiner, 1997, 7 states incorrectly that Takahashi's ideas were shared by Katō.

416. Suzuki, 1983, pp. 35-38; Katō, 1990, pp. 33, 40-47; Fujino, 1998, 385. Incidentally, Baelz himself did not support mixed-blood marriages, and proposed instead a "negative" eugenics approach to race betterment by segregating the fit from the unfit (Fujino, 1998, 388). He did not follow his own advice, however, and married a Japanese woman, Hana, with whom he had two children. Similar arguments about the pros and cons of the pure-blood and mixed-blood positions were waged in China, where one advocate of mixed marriages attempted to strengthen his case by claiming that the Japanese government had sanctioned the practice of intermarriage between "Whites" and "Yellows," which of course was not accurate. For general information about the discourse of race and eugenics in China, see Dikötter, 1992, 88 and Dikötter, 1998. Although aware of their Chinese counterparts, a number of whom visited and studied in Japan, Japanese eugenicists did not cite their work, favoring instead the publications of Europeans and North and South Americans. Doubtless Japanese imperial aggression in China since the Sino-Japanese War (1894-1895) also had a negative effect on scholarly exchanges between Japanese and Chinese nationalists and eugenicists. See also Tanaka, 1993 for an informative analysis of the status of China in Japanese scholarship during the late nineteenth and early twentieth centuries. Ann Stoler's perceptive article on the cultural politics of "mixed bloods" in French Indochina and Netherlands East Indies offers useful comparative material. However, she neither mentions nor addresses the influence of the international discourse eugenics and race hygiene on French and Dutch colonial administrators, and glosses specific and distinctive French and Dutch colonial strategies as "European." Perhaps their eschewal of miscegenation justifies their melding here, but the notion of an internally coherent "Europe" is problematic. Where, for example, do Spain and Portugal fit within the rubric "Europe," two arguably "European" colonial powers that *did* pursue miscegenation as a means of assimilation? The argument against miscegenation made by the Dutch legalist J.A. Nederburgh in 1898 parallels Katō's argument, made twelve years earlier, for preserving the purity of Japanese blood. It would have been interesting to know from what body of literature and contemporary debates Nederburgh was drawing (Stoler, 1995, 138). As an aside, Japanese writers apparently enjoyed musing about the conceptual problems associated with and the fate of "Dutch mixed-bloods. For example. "Daitōaken no bunkateki shomondai," *Kaizō*, 4 (1942): 70-94"; Kitahara,

1943; or Sōichi Ōya, "Jawa no senden katsudō," *Tokyo Shinbun*, November 13-15, 1943.

417. Oka'asa, 1915, 2. One of the main vehicles for popularizing eugenics among the *fin-de-siècle* Japanese public was the journal *Jinsei* (Human Life), founded in 1905 by Yū Fujikawa, an internist and medical historian. It was discontinued in 1919. Fujikawa was among the dozens of Japanese medical students who studied in Germany at the turn of the century and who were keen on applying European ideas about eugenics and race hygiene to the general project of "improving the Japanese race." *Jinsei*, subtitled *Der Mensch* (The Human), was modeled after German eugenicist Alfred Ploetz's *Archiv für Rassen- und Gesellschafts-Biologie* (*Journal for Racial and Social Biology*) founded a year earlier. The contents were divided into sixteen categories which reflected the prevailing synthesis of Darwinian and Lamarckian theories and assumptions: biology, social anthropology, historical anthropology, physical anthropology, legal anthropology, comparative psychology, psychology, national psychology, cultural history of medicine, social hygiene, race hygiene, law, sociology, education and pedagogy, religion, and statistics.

418. Ijichi, 1939, 86. Years earlier, some colonial administrators had considered a similar policy with respect to Korea and Koreans under the tautological rubric *dōbun dōshu no minzoku*, or "people of the same culture and race"—"tautological" because the alleged sameness was proposed by Japanese colonial ideologues who supported assimilation, or *dōka*, literally "same-ization," that is, Japanization. Support for assimilation and pacification through intermarriage waned as Korean hostility toward the occupiers grew more intense, especially after the anti-Japanese uprising of 1919. The very few "mixed marriages" that were officially condoned were those strategically arranged between Japanese and Korean royalty (Duus, 1995, pp. 413-423). Ijichi's views paralleled the dominant position of the state's assimilation policy toward the aboriginal Ainu of Hokkaido, who, since the Meiji Restoration of 1868, had been categorized as "proto-Japanese." Assimilation, it was believed, would accelerate their evolution as "civilized people" (e.g. Takakura, 1942).

419. Tōgō, 1938, pp. 142-144; Tōgō, 1945. Although published in 1945, Tōgō here reiterates a eugenic argument first made in his books on colonial administration published two decades earlier (e.g. Tōgō, 1922; Tōgō, 1925).

420. Yoshida, 1977, pp. 58-60, 87-91; Ishizuka, 1983, pp. 75-77, 112-115.

421. See Kokumin to hansū jogai, *Fujo Shinbun*, January 27, 1935 and

McClintock, 1994.

422. See also Otsubo, 1999; Norgren, 2001.

423. Similar events, such as "better baby contests" were staged in early twentieth-century United States at state fairs and other public forums.

424. See Kenkō yūryōji, *Tokyo Asahi Shinbun*, May 6, 1930, pp. 8-9; and Risō no yūryōji. *Osaka Asahi Shinbun*, June 7, 1931, 11.

425. Nippon ichi no yūryōji no hyōshō. *Yūsei*, 2 (5) 1937: 8-9.

426. Females averaged 11.9 years of age, 156 cm in height, and 45 kg in weight. The respective statistics for males were 11.10 years, 158 cm, and 46.5 kg. See Kenkō yūryōji, *Tokyo Asahi Shinbun*, May 6, 1930, pp. 8-9. Another term used for consanguineous marriage was *kinshin kekkon*, or "marriage between close relatives." See Beardsley, et. al. 1959, 323. Embree, 1939, pp. 24-28, 88-89 suggest that patrilineal parallel cousin marriages were typical, while Hendry, 1981, pp. 124-125 indicates that there was no preference for either parallel or cross cousins noting that first-cousin marriages have been discouraged since the end of World War II. All suggest that consanguineous marriages likely forged easier and closer household ties.

427. Yasui, 1940a: 14; Furuya, 1941, 117.

428. Elderton, 1911, pp. 24-28.

429. Jinkō Mondai Kenkyūkai, 1933-1943.

430. Civisca, 1957.

431. Shinozaki, 1949.

432. Imaizumi, 1988, 235.

433. Embree, 1939, 88.

434. See East and Jones, 1919, pp. 226-244.

435. Taguchi, 1940, pp. 33-35; Mizushima and Miyake, 1942.

436. Elderton, 1911, 38.

437. The Leprosy Prevention Law was formulated and informally activated in 1907, formally adopted in 1953, and abolished in 1996. In the spring of 2001, the Kumamoto District Court ruled that the government should pay 1.82 billion yen in reparations

to the plaintiffs. For various reasons, the government of Prime Minister Koizumi decided not to appeal the ruling, although it remains to be seen how the former exiles will be "repatriated." See Suvendrini Kakuchi, "Rights-Japan: Leprosy patients demand end to isolation," (1998). org/ips2/sept98/05_15_010. html; Satsuki Oba, "Abandoned by heaven," *Time (International edition)* (February 5, 1996); Kay Schriner, "Leprosy court case shakes Japan," September 18, 2001. http:/www.disabilityworld. org/05-06_01/leprosy.

438. Taguchi, 1940, 35. Gresham's Law refers to an observation in economics that "when two coins are equal in debt- paying value but unequal in intrinsic value, the one having the lesser intrinsic value tends to remain in circulation and the other to be hoarded or exported as bullion" See *Webster's Ninth Collegiate Dictionary.* Springfield, MA: Merriam Webster, 1985), 5. A brief word about blood-type is a useful here in connection with overlapping notions of blood and purity. Although today the pseudo-scientific fiction that the Japanese constitute a "blood-type A race" is widely invoked in the mass media, knowledge about specific blood-types was not deployed as a eugenic tool in the discourse of race betterment. There were competing attempts among Japanese scientists to classify the so-called races of the world on the basis of the pattern of distribution of the A, O, B, and AB blood types. However, unlike in Nazi Germany, a specific race was not singled out for isolation and extermination in a diabolical scheme to purify "Japanese blood." By the same token, comparatively few involuntary sterilizations were performed in Japan following the passage of the National Eugenics Law in 1940. Between 1941 and 1945, 15,219 persons (6,399 females and 8,820 males) were targeted for involuntary sterilization, of which 435 persons (243 females and 192 males), or about twenty-nine percent, were actually sterilized, over half of whom were women (Suzuki, 1983, 166; Tanaka, 1994, 164). From 1955 to 1967 in Japan, about 9,500 persons, two-thirds of whom were female, were involuntarily sterilized; about 432,000 persons, 97% percent of whom were female, underwent voluntary sterilization during this time (Health and Welfare Statistics Association, 1987). From 1907 to 1957, over 60,000 persons (more than half females) were sterilized in the United States. One ultranationalist Japanese critic of sterilization argued that the "divine origins" and purity of the "Yamato race" raised serious philosophical doubts about the validity of that procedure: "one must not," he asserted, "equate a divine people with livestock" (Makino, 1938, pp. 18-21; see also Suzuki, 1983, 163, and Takagi, 1993: 46). Moreover, the militarily strategic need to raise the population by one-third in twenty years, from

73 to 100 million persons, together with an emphasis on bigger, taller bodies over enhanced intellectual ability, effectively diminished support for sterilization as a eugenic strategy (Suzuki, 1983, pp. 162-163; Takagi, 1993, 46). Other wartime critics of sterilization, such as sexologist Tokutarō Yasuda, stressed instead the importance of the physical and social environment on human development and also the complexity of human motives to reproduce or not (Suzuki, 1983, pp. 162-163).

439. Fujino, 1998, pp. 140-141.

440. Fujikawa, 1929; Kōseisho Eisei Kekkon Sōdansho, 1941; Fujino, Ibid., pp. 141-142.

441. Ikeda, 1927a; Okada, 1933; Fujino, Ibid., pp. 83-86. Unlike the Wandervogel and Sokol movement that inspired it, the Legs Society was a coed organization from the start. The Wandervogel was later absorbed into the Hitlerjugend.

442. Ikeda, 1925, pp. 31-38, 386.

443. For example, Miwata, 1927; Ikeda, 1929, 19.

444. Quoted in Pearson, 1909, 45.

445. Ikeda, 1927a.

446. Fujino, 1998, 88.

447. See "Yūsei kekkon sōdansho annai," Yūsei 1 (1), 1936: 20; Robertson, 2001a; and Robertson, 2001b.

448. This ideal female body was somewhere between the measurements of the 1931 Miss Nippon and her "average" counterpart. Miss Nippon was nearly 159 cm in height compared to the average female's 148.5 cm, her chest measured 79 cm compared to the average female's 74 cm, and she weighed 52.5 kg, compared to the average female's 46.5 kg (Robertson, 2001a, pp. 23-24).

449. See "Kore kara no kekkon wa kono yō ni," Shashin Shūhō, April 29, 1940, pp. 8-9.

450. "Kore kara no kekkon wa kono yō ni," Shashin Shūhō, April 29, 1940, 8.

451. Mizushima and Miyake, 1942; Satō, 1943.

452. Fujino, 1998, 388.

453. Takada, 1986, pp. 394, 401, 514.

454. Ibid., pp. 395, 403, 514. Takada put class ideology over actuality, for girls and women were the primary workforce in factories and in the new urban service sector.

455. Ibid., 405.

456. Fujino, 1998, 392.

457. Ikeda, 1928, 59.

458. Ibid., 1928, pp. 59-60.

459. Ibid., 1928, 61.

460. "Shimin no junketsu dē ni tassū fujin no sanka," *Yūsei undō*, 3 (12) 1928, 21.

461. "Shinbun ni arawareta yūsei mondai," *Yūsei* 1 (5), 1936, pp. 18-22; 1 (9), 1936, pp. 15-16.

462. Corrigan and Sayer, 1985.

463. The author, Shunpū Sakamoto, was the Akita Prefecture correspondent for the Great Japan Association for the Betterment of Public Customs and Morals.

464. Sakamoto, 1889, 8.

465. Ikeda, 1928, 60.

466. Space precludes me from discussing these here.

467. Matsunaga, 1968, 199.

468. Schull and Neel, 1965, 19.

469. Similarly, Uli Linke argues that in contemporary Germany, "a retrograde archaism of national state culture is continuously repositioned in the present" (Linke, 1999, 239).

## CHAPTER EIGHT

470. Paul D. Barclay, "Cultural Brokerage and Interethnic Marriage in Colonial Taiwan: Japanese Subalterns and Their Aborigine Wives, 1895-1930." *The Journal of Asian Studies* 64, no. 2 (May 2005): 323–360. © 2005 by the Association of Asian Studies, Inc. Reprinted with the permission of Cambridge University

Press. Previous versions of the original article were presented at the fifty-fourth annual meeting of the Association for Asian Studies in April 2002, the Women's History Workshop at Academia Sinica's Institute for Modern History in March 2003, and the Seminar on Globalization in the History of East Asia at Kyoto University in June 2003. The author would like to thank Ann Waltner and the anonymous readers at the *Journal of Asian Studies* for helpful comments. Thanks go to John R. Shepherd and Murray A. Rubinstein for sponsoring and supporting the Association for Asian Studies panel from which this collection of articles originated. Janice Matsumura, Eika Tai, Robert Eskildsen, Antonio C. Tavares, Paul Katz, Linda Gail Arrigo, Melissa Brown, and Tonio Andrade contributed ideas, challenges, and encouragement on earlier drafts. Research was supported by the Japan Society for the Promotion of Science, the Social Science Research Council Japan Program, and Lafayette College. For generous assistance and intellectual guidance in Japan and Taiwan, I thank Ken Arisue, the Ikegami family, Paul Katz, Susumu Fuma, Masaharu Kasahara, Yuji Nakanishi, Victoria Muehleisen, Peite Kang, and Chen Wei-chi. Naoko Ikegami and Wu Haotian deserve praise as able and enthusiastic research assistants.

471. Brooks, 1976, 40.

472. Perdue, 2003, pp. 9-24.

473. Stoler, 2002, pp. 27-29.

474. Peterson 1978; White 1991.

475. Stoler 2002; Wildenthal 1997.

476. Stocking 1968; Thomas 1994.

477. Hirschman 1986; Young 1995; Fabian 1983.

478. Richter, 1988, 41.

479. Thompson 1964, pp. 177-178.

480. Blussé, Everts, and Frech, 1999, 1.

481. Ibid., 29; emphasis added.

482. I have quoted from Thompson's 1964 translation, but have altered the romanization to pinyin and added Chinese equivalents for key terms based on Yu, 1957 [1697]. See Keliher, 2004 for a more recent translation of the complete text.

483. Thompson, 1964, pp. 195-196; Yu, 1957 [1697], 36; see also Inō, 1904, pp. 74-75; Shepherd, 1993, 116; Keliher, 2004, 115.

484. Thompson, Ibid., pp. 197-198; Yu, 1957 [1697], pp. 42-45.

485. The term *shengfan/seiban* has been translated as "wild" (Faure, 2001, 5), "unpolished" (Kang, 1996, 1), "raw," and "unfamiliar" barbarian (Teng, 1999, 461). The referent of this term is not precise and has shifted over time. In general, *shengfan* refers to Aborigines who did not pay taxes to a central government; did not speak Chinese; had not adopted Han modes of dress, cuisine, marriage, or burial; and/or did not reside near Han settlements. As *shengfan*'s binary opposite, the term *shufan/jukuban* has been variously translated as "tame" (Faure, 2001, 5), "polished" (Kang, 1996, 1), "cooked," and "familiar" barbarian (Teng, 1999, 461). The term generally refers to acculturated Aborigines who submitted to Qing authority. Since there were also *shufan* who were acculturated but did not pay taxes and others who paid taxes but remained unacculturated, the category was confusing even at the time of its use. For a detailed and authoritative discussion of the Qing-period usage of *shufan* and *shengfan* and the variations thereupon, see Teng, 1999, pp. 460-461. During the Japanese period, authors often conflated the terms "Peipoban/ Pingpufan," or "Plains Barbarian," and *shufan/jukuban* without much precision. By the Japanese period, the term *jukuban* seemed to refer to Sinophone Aborigines who maintained some modicum of commercial contact to relatively unacculturated Aborigines of the interior, often with the connotation of mixed parentage. The term "Métis," as used in reference to Franco-Indian trading villages, would probably be a good equivalent to the Japanese usage of *jukuban*.

486. Faure, Ibid., 16.

487. Thompson, 1969, 130; Huang, 1957 [1736], 153.

488. Thompson, Ibid., pp. 91-92; Huang, Ibid., pp. 85-93.

489. Richter, 1988.

490. Hall, 2000, 238.

491. Ibid., 241.

492. Ibid., pp. 241-243.

493. Zhang, 1988; Shepherd, 1993.

494. Shepherd, 1993.

495. Ka, 2001, pp. 149-183.

496. Shepherd, 1993.

497. Ka, 2001; Shepherd, 1993.

498. Chen, 2001, 31; Lin, 1999, pp. 208, 254; Faure, 2001, 18.

499. Inō, 1903, pp. 1016-1019.

500. Grierson provides several examples of hostile borders across which trade could be brokered only by females (Grierson, 1903, 58).

501. Sangren, 1985; Gardella, 1999.

502. Teng, 2004, pp. 209-213.

503. Swinhoe, 2001, 66.

504. Pickering, 1993 [1898], 143.

505. Steere, 2002 [1874], 314.

506. Iriye, 1896b, 17.

507. Ibid., pp. 17-18.

508. Mori, 1976a, pp. 176-177.

509. Matsuoka, 2004, pp. 83-84; Junker, 1999.

510. Chang, 2003, pp. 95-101.

511. Fujisaki, 1930, 455.

512. *Tokyo Asahi shinbun*, September 28, 1895.

513. *Tokyo Asahi shinbun*, September 29, 1895.

514. Hashiguchi, 1895a; Hashiguchi, 1895b, pp. 313-318; Inō, 1896, 181; Inō, 1995, 4; *Tokyo Asahi shinbun*, September 29, 1895.

515. Shibayama, 1896, 203.

516. The transformed barbarians were defined by Japanese sources as unacculturated Aborigines who maintained either a tributary or commercial relationship to lowland, Han-dominated society.

517. Kawano, 1895; Shibayama, 1896, pp. 203-205; Taihoku-shū Keimu-bu, 1924, 1; Fujisaki 1930, pp. 544-545.

518. Inō, 1895, 97.

519. Eskildsen, 2002; Yen, 1965.

520. LeGendre, 1874, pp. 408-409; Nihon Shiseki Kyōkai, 1933, 351; Hara 1900; Inō, 1995, pp. 157-158. I am indebted to Robert Eskildsen for providing these sources to me.

521. Inō, 1995, 157; Sagara, 1896.

522. Inō, Ibid., 157.

523. Inō, 1906; Inō, 1995, pp. 157-158.

524. In a similar description of *tongshi*, camphor merchant Kenji Saitō (Saitō, 1899) insisted that they were all *shufan*.

525. Nakajima, 1896, pp. 247-248.

526. Saitō, 1897b, 180.

527. *Yomiuri shinbun*, September 30, 1895.

528. Barclay, 2003a.

529. Inō, 1995, 17.

530. Saitō, 1897b, pp. 178-179.

531. Saitō, 1897a, 146.

532. November 20, 1896.

533. Inō, 1995, 105.

534. Tashiro, 1984, pp. 46-48.

535. Uno, 1981, pp. 88-89; Matsuda, 1998.

536. At the time of this writing, there is no standardized international system for spellings of Atayal names. In this article, I have adopted the spellings used by Deng Xiangyang (Deng, 2001) where possible. In all other cases, I have transcribed the *katakana* used in the sources. The original *katakana* versions of all names used herein can be found in the list of characters. For names ending in *katakana su*, the superfluous (for Atayalic languages) *u* has been dropped.

537. *Hōchi shinbun*, April 5, 1896; Iriye, 1896a, 29; Araki, 1976, 79; Deng, Ibid., 164. Hiyama's successor, Yoshitora Nagano, touched off a more serious round of violence after distributing gifts to Toda

emissaries after a feast at the Puli Bukonsho. On their way back to Toda, the gift recipients were ambushed by jealous Wushe men. In the ensuing battle, Toda suffered fifteen casualties; Wushe absorbed two casualties (*Taiwan nichinichi shinpō*, May 10, 1898).

538. *Taiwan nichinichi shinpō*, December 21, 1930. For Kondō's transcribed and annotated autobiography, which contains a full account of his life as an interpreter and a merchant, see Barclay, 2004.

539. Torii, 1901, 131; Uchiyama, 1905, 66; Inoguchi, 1995, 232.

540. *Taiwan nichinichi shinpō*, December 21, 1930; Ide, 1937, 278.

541. Uchiyama, 1905, pp. 62-63; Fujisaki, 1930, 612.

542. *Taiwan nichinichi shinpō*, December 21, 1930; Fujisaki, 1930, 606.

543. *Taiwan nichinichi shinpō*, December 25, 1930; Uchiyama, 1905; Yamabe, 1971, 509.

544. *Taiwan nichinichi shinpō*, December 25, 1930.

545. *Taiwan nichinichi shinpō*, January 13–14, 1931; Fujisaki, 1930, pp. 614-616.

546. Inō, 1995, pp. 148-149.

547. Asako, 1997, pp. 1-10.

548. Mori, 1976a, 105.

549. Nagata, 2003.

550. Blacker, 1958.

551. Asako, 1997, 11.

552. Nagata, 2003, 291; Garon, 1993.

553. Iriye, 1896a, 29.

554. Araki, 1976, 79.

555. Ide, 1937, 279; Fujisaki, 1930, 614.

556. November 7, 1907.

557. Taiwan Sōtokufu, 1925.

558. 1898, 1: 102; 1899, 6: pp. 76-77.

559. Mori, 1976b, 144.

560. Taiwan Sōtokufu, 1905-34.

561. Taiwan Sōtokufu, 1920.

562. Inō, 1995, pp. 163, 165.

563. January 11, 1901.

564. Suzuki, 1932, 453.

565. Inuzuka, 1996, 403.

566. Simon, 2003, pp. 176-177.

567. Chen, 1998; Kawano, 1895; Miyazaki, 1901, 3; Taihoku-shū Keimu-bu, 1924, 79; *Taiwan minpō*, June 24, 1903; January 20, 1904; *Yomiuri shinbun*, February 24, 1896.

568. In Japanese *kana*, "Iwan," "Iwari," "Yuwan," and "Yuwari" were variations of the spelling that I have rendered "Iwan."

569. *Taiwan nichinichi shinpō*, December 19, 1902.

570. Gao, 1988, 13; Aui, 1985, 20.

571. For a description of the guard line, its staffing, and its movements, see Barclay, 2003b.

572. Inō, 1995, pp. 533-534.

573. Grierson, 1903, pp. 41-54.

574. Kawashima, 1989; Spence, 1996.

575. Perdue, 2003; Peterson, 1978; Richter, 1988; Hagedorn, 1988; White, 1991.

576. Fabian, 2000, 130.

577. An official outline of government-general attempts to teach Aborigine languages in formal settings is found in the compiled records of the Police Bureau and the records of Aborigine Administration. See Inō, 1995, pp. 504-505, 707; Taiwan Sōtokufu Keimukyoku 1986, pp. 923-924.

578. *Taiwan nichinichi shinpō*, February 2, 1931.

579. *Taiwan nichinichi shinpō*, February 3, 1931.

580. *Taiwan nichinichi shinpō*, February 5, 1931; Aui, 1985, 180.

581. Inō, 1995, pp. 638-639.

582. Aui, 1985, pp. 179-180.

583. Taiwan Sōtokufu, 1920; *Taiwan nichinichi shinpō*, February 15, 1931.

584. Igarashi, 1931, pp. 118-121.

585. Yamabe, 1971, 694.

586. *Taiwan nichinichi shinpō*, February 10, 1931.

587. Hashimoto, 1999, pp. 148-149; Yamabe, 1971, 611.

588. *Taiwan nichinichi shinpō*, February 7, 1931.

589. Barclay, 2003b.

590. Hayashi, 2002, pp. 42-45, 103.

591. Yanagimoto, 1996, 39; Hayashi, 2002, pp. 56-57.

592. Hayashi, 2002; Yanagimoto, 1996.

593. Mikami, 1984, pp. 110-111.

594. Hayashi, 2002, 84.

595. Hayashi, 2002; Aui, 1985, 115.

596. Mikami, 1984.

597. Mikami, 1984; Hayashi, 2002.

598. Stoler, 2002.


## CHAPTER NINE

599. Moriyama, 1985, 8 and Ogawa, 1978, pp. 5-6.

600. See Takaki, 1983, pp. 18-19 and Kotani, 1985, 10.

601. To be more precise, the first Gannenmono group was forty-two contract laborers to Guam who left on May 2, 1868, fifteen days before the Scioto left with the 153 Japanese to Hawai'i. One difference between the two groups is that the Guam trip did not result in anyone from the group staying in Guam after the end of the contract; all returned to Japan. See Ushijima, 1978, pp. 14-16.

602. Hazama and Komeiji, 1986, pp. 8-11 and Ushijima, 1978, pp. 3-50.

603. The early Japanese migrants around the world showed a
readiness to marry into the population of their new homes,
as shown not only in Hawai'i or North America, but in places
such as New Zealand and Papua (New Guinea) where five early
Japanese migrants married native Papuan women, where
matrilineal traditions allowed land ownership that would
normally have been denied the Japanese in Western nations
and their colonies. See Tanabe, 1996, pp. 19-30 on New Zealand
and how in 1890, Asajiro Noda ended up working on the Kauri
gum fields in Dargaville. He would later marry a Maori (native
New Zealander) woman, Ngati Mahuta, have five children with
her, and work their family farm trading strawberries. Also see
Iwamoto, 1995, pp. 111-113. The five men to marry local women
were: Heijirō Murakami, Taichirô Tanaka, Shigematsu Tanaka,
Jimmy Koto, and Mabe Tamiya. A trader, Jimmy Koto, was
the first Japanese to arrive on Papua and married Maegar from
Sabari Island and proceeded to father two children, George and
Florence. The second Japanese to arrive on the islands, Mabe
Tamiya, married a native woman called Kalele from Basilaki
Island and worked as a trader, shell-fisher, and boat builder. He
fathered three boys: Tetu, Hagani, and Namari Tamiya.

604. Kuykendall, 1953, pp. 145-146.

605. See Akemi Kikumura Yano, "Issei pioneers: Hawaii and the
mainland 1885-1924 - Part 1." (2011) http://www.discovernikkei.
org/en/journal/2011/1/3/issei-pioneers/ (retrieved Nov. 2, 2014)

606. Ogawa, 1978, pp. 5-6.

607. Hazama and Komeiji, 1986, pp. 10-11.

608. Embree, 1941, 66.

609. Kotani, 1985, pp. 18-19.

610. For more on Robert Walker Irwin and his family, see Moriyama,
1985 and Irwin and Conroy, 1972.

611. For the most comprehensive study of Fred Makino, see
Compilation Committee for the Publication of Kinzaburo
Makino's Biography, 1965.

612. Fooks, 2005, 76.

613. For writing about the Wakamatsu Colony, see Pearce, 2001.

614. For this and other articles about the Wakamatsu Colony in
historical newspapers like the San Francisco Alta Daily News,

see http://www.arconservancy.org/site/c.psKZL3PFLrF/
b.7544683/k.5E3F/Archive_of_Historical_Documents_from_the_
Wakamatsu_Tea_and_Silk_Colony.htm

615. See Stanley Williford, "Descendants in U.S., Negro," Pacific
Citizen, (April 10, 1970): 1. Also, in 2010, the National Japanese
American Historical Society held an award ceremony honoring
these descendants of the Wakamatsu Colony, including
Aaron Gibson, the great-great-great-grandson of Kuninosuke
Masumizu, and Emily Collins, sister-in-law of Masumizu's
grandson.

616. My thanks to Kiyo Endecott at the Oregon Nikkei Legacy Center
and Emily Anderson for their assistance in tracking down
information about the Iwakoshi-McKinnon family. Other
scholars who have noted Miyo Iwakoshi as the first Japanese to
settle in Oregon, include Azuma, 1993-94, 315 and Yasui, 1975.

617. Others included John Milne, the well-known British
seismologist called the "father of modern Japanese seismology"
who married Tone Horikawa, the daughter of a Buddhist
temple priest in Hakodate; Josiah Conder, the British architect
of the Rokumeikan, the Ueno Imperial Museum, and Kano
school painting enthusiast, who married Kume Maenami, and
Edmund Morel, the British expert on railways and the so-called
"father of Japan's railroads," who married a Japanese woman.
Some of the most well known mixed-race individuals from this
period were Toku and Uta von Bälz (the children of the German
Erwin von Bälz and Hatsu [also known as Hana] Arai) and
Kazuo, Iwao, Kiyoshi, and Suzuko Koizumi (the children of the
Greek-Irish Lafcadio Hearn and his wife Setsuko Koizumi). Bälz
was prominent doctor from Germany, who in 1876 accepted the
Japanese government's invitation to teach at the Tokyo Medical
School. Hearn was an English teacher and prolific writer,
introducing Japan to the West through his books. He was also
the first Westerner to take on Japanese citizenship; he also
legally changed his name to Yakumo Koizumi.

618. Asato, 2006, 86.

619. H. C. Merriam report: "The Increase of Japanese Population in
the Hawaiian Islands and What It Means" (May 1918).

620. Sarasohn, 1998, 72.

621. Ichioka notes, "In an almost romantic law, there was to be no
more than 13 years difference between husband and wife to
promote harmonious marriages." Ichioka, 1988, 165.

622. Noguchi would write in an unpublished essay in 1942: "To be hybrid anticipates the future. This is America, the nation of all nationalities. The racial and cultural intermix is the antithesis of all the tenet[s] of the Axis Powers. Because of my peculiar background I felt this war keenly and wished to serve the cause of democracy. A haunting sense of unreality, of not quite belonging, which has always bothered me, made me seek for an answer among the Nisei". This quote can be found in Duus, 2004, 164. Thanks to Lily Anne Yumi Welty Tamai for alerting me to this quote.

623. Lone, 2001, 70.

624. See "Miscegenation: Wedded Bliss Denied to Jap," *Los Angeles Daily Mirror,* March 16, 1910 and "Brown Man and Fiancé Can Not Get Knot Tied," *San Francisco Call,* March 16, 1910, 3.

625. Karthikeyan and Chin, 2002, 14.

626. Ibid., 15. On the complex positioning of Filipinos in these anti-miscegenation laws, see Volpp, 2012.

627. Sims, 2005, 238.

628. See Yu, 2001, pp. 54-63, 68-71, 229-230.

629. On the Aoki couple, see Brenda Aoki Wong's play *Uncle Gunjiro's Girlfriend*. Also see Aoki, 1998.

630. Many thanks to Emily Anderson for bringing the Nakaya-Morton case to my attention.

631. On the marriage, see *Denver Rocky Mountain News,* June 20, 1987, 7 and the *San Francisco Chronicle*, June 20, 1897, 20. Also see Yu, 2001, pp. 54-57.

632. A copy of the serialized piece is available at Stanford University—Major Documents 53, Box 24, PSRR (Papers of the Survey of Race Relations, Hoover Institute). For more on this case, see Yu, 1998, pp. 446-458.

633. The case of the Archdeacon is recounted in Sarasohn, 1993, pp. 128-129.

634. Roy, 2003, 33.

635. This was Case No. 44,797 as found in NYSPCC Annual Report (issued on Dec. 31, 1889). For more on this case, see Lui, 2005, pp. 94-95.

636. See Tamura, 1993, pp. 186-187.

637. Quoted in Heuterman, 1995, 26.

638. MacCaughey, 1919, 44.

639. Matsuoka, 1931, 178.

640. Ibid.

641. Azuma, 2005, pp. 187-188.

642. Lone, 2001, pp. 69-70.

643. Walz, 1998, pp. 89-90.

644. Quoted in Daniels, 1962, 28.

645. Quoted in Roy, 2003, 34.

646. Quoted in Heuterman, 1995, pp. 20-21.

647. Quoted in Snow, 2007, pp. 33-36.

648. Roy, 2003, 32.

649. Snow, 2007, 36.

650. Daniels, 1962, 68.

651. Stoddard, 1922, pp. 297-303.

652. Roy, 2003, 20.

653. Daniels, 1962, 80 and Snow, 2007, pp. 42, 90-91, 99.

654. Quoted in Roy, 2003, 195.

655. Ibid., 307, ftnt 17.

656. Snow, 2007, pp. 48-49.

657. See Robertson, 2002 for the development of eugenics in Japan. For Imamura's comments, see Shimada, 2008, 162.

658. Roy, 2003, 33.

659. See Yoo, 2000, pp. 85-86.

660. On the Ozawa case, see López, 1996, pp. 79-86.

661. Quoted in Ibid., 54.

662. Quoted in Ibid., pp. 62, 67.

663. Kimura, 1988, pp. 15-16. Kimura also notes that a Masakichi Suzuki faced the same situation as Jō Makino.

664. See Knight 171 F.299, 300, 301 (Eastern District New York, 1909); quoted in López, 1996, 59. Also see "Think government can't debar Knight: United States court officials say the alien sailor can win citizenship by appeal–Shutout by Mongol blood." New York Times, July 16, 1909, 4. Thanks to Greg Robinson for alerting me to this newspaper article.

665. The quote above can be found in Williams-León and Nakashima, 2001, 107, and is referenced in López, 1996 (as cited below). My thanks to Cindy Nakashima for alerting me to this legal case.

666. The precedents of "half-breeds" denied citizenship include:
1909 In re Knight case (eastern District New York)—denied (legal precedent) [171 F. 299]

1912 In re Alverto case (eastern District Pennsylvania)—three-quarters Filipino and one-quarter White—denied (legal precedent and congressional intent) [198 F. 688]

1912 In re Young (western District Washington) —half Japanese and half German—denied (legal precedent and common knowledge) [198 F. 715]

1927 In re Fisher (Northern district California) —three-quarters Chinese and one-quarter White—denied (legal precedent) [21 F. 2d 1007]

1938 In re Cruz (eastern District New York)—three-quarters Native American and one-quarter African—denied as not African (legal precedent) [23 F. Supp 774]

For a full list, see López, 1996, pp. 203-208.

667. Kitagawa, 1967, pp. 60-61.

668. For the most comprehensive study of government policies on interracial families and individuals vis-à-vis the incarceration during World War II, see Spickard, 1986.

669. Mitson, 1974, pp. 38-39.

670. Inomata, 2012, pp. 163-180, 195.

671. Ibid., pp. 187-188.

672. Takami, 1998, 61 and Naske, 1983, 129. Takami claims 150 and Naske 120 Alaskans as being affected by this policy.

673. E. L. Bartlett letter to Simon Buckner (Gruening Papers, University of Alaska-Fairbanks Archives).

674. Naske, 1983, 128.

675. Naske, Ibid., 132 and Wegars, 2010, 14.

676. Ten Broek, Barnhart, and Matson, 1949, 126 cited 613 mixed-race families in camp. The WRA census lists 1,192 intermarried Japanese Americans and 287 mixed-race individuals. Paul Spickard provided a detailed account of how to estimate the numbers and proposed his best estimate at 1,400–1,500 intermarried Japanese Americans and 700–900 mixed-race individuals. See Spickard, 1986, pp. 18-19.

677. See the diary of the Buddhist priest, Daishō Tana. Tana, 1976, August 28, 1942 entry.

678. This story in "Topaz" documentary film produced by KUED (University of Utah). Original interview of Mary Kimura can be found Box 5 Folder 5, KUED Topaz (Utah) Residents Photograph Collection, 1987, Utah State Historical Society.

679. Sarasohn 1998, pp. 184, 203.

680. For more on Ginger Masuoka, born in 1931, see the San Francisco Japanese American Internment Project at the San Francisco City Library exhibit from 2007.

681. Quoted in Friday, 2004, 140.

682. Ibid., pp. 140, 145-146 and Mitson, 1974, pp. 33-38.

683. See Katherine Bishop, "Obituary: Elaine Black Yoneda, 81, radical labor activist." *New York Times*, May 30, 1988. http://www.nytimes.com/1988/05/30/obituaries/elaine-black-yoneda-81-radical-labor-activist.html [accessed November 2, 2014]

684. Hirohata and Hirohata, 2004, pp. 32, 213-214.

685. See Wegars, 2010, pp. 167-169. In this situation, Okazaki wrote to the Provost Marshall requested that the family be united in the so-called "family camp" in Crystal City, Texas. His letter can be found in the National Archives (NARA). See Takeshi Okazaki, SFIC "Petition for Repatriation" (June 21, 1943); E466F, Okazaki Takeshi RG 389, NARA II.

686. Spickard, 1986, pp. 6-9.

687. Quote found in Ibid., 7.

688. Ong, 2014, 35. Ong has chronicled quite a few cases of multiethnic and multiracial families in the WRA camps in his recent study.

689. Walls, 1987, pp. 151-153.

690. Of the 101 children who resided at the Children's Village between 1942-45, 19 were of mixed-racial heritage. See Irwin, 2008, 9.

691. Ong, 2014, 45.

692. Irwin, 2008, pp. 258-259.

693. For a lengthy oral history with Ronald Kawamoto, see Ibid., pp. 270-280.

694. Ibid., 261.

695. Ibid., 254.

696. Hatsune Helen Kitaji noted the existence of this diary in an oral history that took place in Salinas, California on September 3, 1986. This excerpt can be found in Nisei Christian Oral History Project, 1991, 105.

697. Westdale, 2009, pp. 74-80.

698. Inomata, 2012, pp. 15-32.

699. Westdale, 2009, pp. 83-91.

700. Ibid., pp. 98-102.

701. Ibid., pp. 98-102.

702. Ibid., pp. 104-204.

703. Ibid., pp. 200-204.

704. See Mike Markrich, "Hapa Soliders," (2011) http://www.100thbattalion.org/history/stories/hapa-soldiers/ (retrieved Nov. 2, 2014)

705. Duus, 1987, 33.

706. Duus, 1983, pp. 147-148.

707. Walls, 1987, pp. 166-170.

708. Fujita, 1993, pp. xii-xiv, 5-9, 16-18, 82.

709. Ibid., pp. xii-xvi, 15, 26.

710. Ibid,, pp. ix, xv-xvi, 47-48, 53, 70-71.

711. Ibid., pp. 88-89.

712. Ibid., pp. 95-96.

713. Ibid., 155.

714. Ibid., pp. 193-194.

715. See Ibid., pp. 79-82 for a reprint of the newspaper article.

716. Ibid., pp. 309-310.

717. On Laffin, see http://www.marauder.org/laffin.htm; http://www.marauder.org/nisei01.htm; http://www.javadc.org/CPT%20William%20Laffin.htm (accessed November 2014).

718. Thornton, 1983, 47.

719. Academic research on Japanese war brides in the United States has a long history. The earliest studies, such as those by Anselm Strauss (on couples in Chicago), John Connor (Sacramento), Yukiko Kimura (Hawai'i), and George DeVos, focused on the sociological and psychological dimensions of interracial and international marriages. In more recent times, the oral histories and historical surveys by Regina Lark and Tomoko Tsuchiya of the Japanese war brides have contributed significantly. See Strauss, 1954; Kimura, 1957; DeVos, 1959; Connor, 1976; Lark, 1999; and Tsuchiya, 2011.

## CHAPTER TEN

720. Le, 2012; Fong and Shinagawa, 1999.

721. Sakamoto, Kim, and Takei, 2011. There have even been occasional predictions of the disappearance of the ethnic community. One anonymous discussion thread from 1999 offers a revealing dialogue among different people about the question: JA Ties Talk, "Interracial marriage," http://members.tripod.com/runker_room/tiestalk/intermge.htm (accessed August 8, 2013).

722. The outstanding historical work on the subject is Spickard, 1989. See also Ono and Berg, 2010.

723. There was a strong gender-based factor in relation to intermarriage, as romances between Asian men and white women were far more taboo than those between white men and Asian women, especially in Asia. Indeed, biracial Chinese Canadian author Onoto Watanna (Winnifred Eaton), made such romances her stock in trade. A curious point concerns the first well-known fictional image of a mixed-race Japanese American, the baby named "Trouble" in John Luther Long's story "Madame Butterfly" and its subsequent theatrical and operatic adaptations. Born in Japan of the union of a white American sailor and the Japanese woman he abandons, Trouble is claimed by the returning father and his new white American wife, who seek to adopt him and take him to the United States. While the result varies, in none of the versions of the story is there any sense that Trouble's mixed ancestry makes him undesirable to his white family or that he would face difficulties once in America.

724. This was not the first occasion in which white journalists and political leaders mobilized fears of intermarriage against Asians. In the 1870s, groups of Chinese immigrants who had previously been employed in building the transcontinental railroad moved throughout the country to search for jobs and housing. They faced rioting and racial violence, and in some cases were driven out of the country entirely. Prominent amid the wave of anti-Chinese propaganda were newspaper articles in New York that heavily publicized the formation of unions between Chinese men and Irish women as threats to the nation's racial composition. See Tchen, 1999; Koshy, 2005.

725. Popular commentator Walter Lippmann deplored the insertion of race-based appeals into an economic argument for exclusion: "The Japanese ask the right to settle in California. Clearly it makes a whole lot of difference whether you conceive the demand as a desire to grow fruit or to marry the white man's daughter" (Lippmann, 1956, 103).

726. Roosevelt, 1923, 478. See also Robinson, 2001, chapter 1, and Robinson, 2013, pp. 27-39. FDR's cousin Laura Delano, who was refused family permission to marry a Japanese suitor with whom she had fallen in love during an Asian voyage in the first years of the twentieth century, remained unmarried as a result. There is a slightly garbled version of the story in Roosevelt and Brough, 1975, 302.

727. The War Relocation Authority of the United States, which was formed in 1942.

728. Ishikawa, 1935.

729. On Hartmann, see Weaver, 1991; and Knox, 1970.

730. "Newest public amusement," *New York Times*, September 14, 1902, 32.

731. Tamagawa, 2007. See in particular the introduction, written collectively by Floyd Cheung, Elena Tajima Creef, Shirley Geok-Lin Lim, and Greg Robinson.

732. Tamagawa, 2007, 157.

733. The best secondary source on Clarke H. Kawakami's early life is Komori, 1987. I am greatly indebted to Takako Day for her careful reading and translating for me of its information on Clarke Kawakami.

734. See Asahi Shimbun, 1934.

735. Jack Stinnett, "A Washington daybook," *Corsicana Daily Sun*, April 28, 1941, 6; "Japanese in Washington catch love on the run," *Chester Times*, August 13, 1941, 3.

736. "Ex-Domei writer to join U.S. Army," *New York Times,* December 15, 1941, 5. There was a note of skepticism in public reaction as to the sincerity of Kawakami's actions. See "The old query: What is national honor?" *San Antonio Press*, December 16, 1941, 9.

737. See, for example, Clarke H. Kawakami, "Asia for Japan? Nippon's conquests—A boomerang," *Washington Post*, July 9, 1942, 9.

738. On Kawakami's wartime military service, see for example McNaughton, 2006, pp. 404, 455-456.

739. Although the work was initially claimed as personal property by General MacArthur and withheld from publication, it was later published as United States Center of Military History, 1966. On its initial suppression, see Forrest and Kawakami, 1952.

740. Milton K. Ozaki obituary, *Chicago Tribune*, November 15, 1989.

741. On Ozaki's career, see Steven G. Doi and Greg Robinson, "Milton Ozaki: Mystery Writer," *Nichi Bei Times,* May 15, 2008, 3.

742. Author telephone interview and correspondence with Marilyn Takahashi Fordney, July 31, 2013. I am obliged to Ms. Fordney

for generously sharing extracts from the unpublished family history written by her mother, Margaret O'Brien Uchiyamada Takahashi.

743. Mary Oyama, "With apologies to 'Ambie'," *Kashu Mainichi*, October 22, 1957; Larry Tajiri, "A Nisei writer, '41," *Nichi Bei Shimbun*, January 1, 1941, 3.

744. Mitsu Yamamoto, letter with attachments to author, September 10, 1999. For the university's exclusion policy, see Robinson, 2000, pp. 38-41.

745. Brockett and Brockett, 1956; Copyright Office, Library of Congress, 1964, Part 3, Drama.

746. Mitsu Yamamoto, "The good news," *The New Yorker*, November 23, 1957, Vol. 33 Issue 40, 128. Mitsu Yamamoto, "In any language," *Redbook*, June 1962, Vol. 119, pp. 38-39; Mitsu Yamamoto, "Miss Kemper comes home in the dark," *Saturday Evening Post*, Spring 1972, Vol. 244, pp. 30-32; Mitsu Yamamoto, "Karen Stixx and her jigsaw puzzle," *Saturday Evening Post*, November 1973, Vol. 245, pp. 77-78. Yamamoto, 1977.

747. Yamamoto, 1974, 1950.

748. Letter, Isamu Noguchi to Carey McWilliams, February 25, 1942; letter, Carey McWilliams to Robert Oppenheimer, February 20, 1942. Box 2, Carey McWilliams Miscellaneous Papers, 1941-1945, Hoover Institution Library, Stanford University.

749. On Saki's early life, see for example "Marion Saki one-quarter Japanese," *Boston Globe*, December 27, 1925, A45. A hapa chorus girl, Ruth Sato, performed in Billy Rose's 1933 revue "Crazy Quilt." For the career of another hapa singer and actor, George Hirose, see Greg Robinson, "The great unknown and the unknown great: Hapa baritone George Hirose's theatrical story," *Nichi Bei Weekly*, November 7, 2013. http://www.nichibei. org/2013/11/the-great-unknown-and-the-unknown-great-hapa-baritone-george-hiroses-theatrical-story/ Another hapa performer was the opera singer and vaudeville artist Haru Onuki [Marion Ohnick].

750. H.T.P. "They still live on Hope Down East," *New York Times*, January 1, 1933, X1.

751. Michael Minn, "Sono Osato." http://michaelminn.net/andros/biographies/osato_sono/.

752. Sono Osato, in "Extravagant crowd: Carl Van Vechten's portraits

of women," http://brbl-archive.library.yale.edu/exhibitions/cvvpw/gallery/osato1.html Retrieved August 20, 2013.

753. Osato was preceded in Hollywood by the hapa actress Lotus Long (Lotus Pearl Shibata), born in New Jersey in 1909 of mixed Japanese and Hawaiian ancestry. On Lotus Long's career, see Worrell, 2004, pp. 21-50. See also Long's unsourced Wikipedia entry: http://en.wikipedia.org/wiki/Lotus_Long, searched August 21, 2103.

754. "Weds a Japanese artist," *Washington Post*, January 13, 1910, 1.

755. Howard Devree, "A reviewer's notebook," *New York Times*, October 10, 1943, X11.

756. Ibid., X6.

757. "A founding father, back on his pedestal," *New York Times*, September 2, 2011, C22.

758. "Show openings around area," *Sarasota Herald Tribune*, March 8 1981, 29. Among Girard Goodenow's book illustrations are Meindert de Jong's *Smoke above the lane* (1951); Laurence Houseman's version of *Stories from the Arabian nights* (1955), Felix Salten's *Bambi* (1956); Albert Payson Terhune's *The heart of a dog* (1959); and Gladys Plemon Conklin's *The bug club book* (1966) and *How insects grow* (1969).

759. Krantz, 1985.

760. The career of Franklin and Robert's elder brother, Elbert Yone Chino, provides an interesting subject for speculation about the workings of mixed-race identity. After working for many years as an aerospace engineer and executive, Elbert retired and devoted himself to producing art of the American West. He legally changed his name to Cheyno and identified himself as "Easy Cheyno," a Cherokee Indian—he insisted the family had Native blood on the maternal line. In part due to of Elbert's denial of his Japanese side, he remained distant from his brothers in later life.

761. Interestingly enough, Mercelia's sister Louise Hicks, was introduced by Frank to another Japanese immigrant, Sidney Tokichi Ohi, who proceeded to settle in Chicago and found work with the Pullman Company. The Ohis married in 1910. They would have three hapa daughters and a son, who grew up close to their Chino cousins. Their eldest daughter, Kuma Elizabeth Ohi, Franklin Chino's contemporary and law school classmate, became, in 1937, the first Nisei woman to be admitted to the

bar in the United States. In later years she changed her name to Elizabeth Owens and worked for the U.S. Labor Department.

762. F. Chino, "We should mind our own business," *Chicago Defender*, April 6, 1940, 14.

763. The principal sources on Toshi Ohta Seeger are Dunaway, 1990, 45 *passim*; and Winkler, 2010; as well as obituaries. See, for example, "Toshi Seeger, wife, muse, and ally of Pete Seeger, dies at 91," *Washington Post*, July 11, 2013. On Takashi Ohta, see also "Pawnshop to aid poor is adventurer's idea," *New York Times*, September 29, 1929, N22.

764. Ohta and Sperry, 1929.

765. Woody Guthrie and Pete Seeger in turn inspired Masa Aiba, a young hapa Nisei who was a JACD member, to take up folk singing. In later years, Dr. Masa Aiba Goetz, a clinical psychologist, founded the Wild Jammin' Women music camp. "Personality sketch," *JACD Newsletter*, March 1946, 4.

766. "On the distaff side," *JACD Newsletter*, June 1942, 4.


## CHAPTER ELEVEN

*I would like to acknowledge and thank the local people of Broome who helped me with this research, especially the main interviewee. I also would like to thank Mr. Derek Wee for editing.*

767. See, for example, Collections Australia Network, Broome Historical Society Museum, http:/www.collectionsaustralia. net/org/1430/about/.

768. Ganter, 2006.

769. See, for example, Ifekwunigwe, 2004; Parker and Song, 2001; Rockquemore et al. 2009; Root, 1992 and 1995; Zack, 1995.

770. See, for example, Root 1992; Spickard 1992.

771. Ropp, 1996

772. Ibid., 14.

773. Rockquemore et al., 2009.

774. Csizmadia et al., 2012, 187. See also Aspinall and Song, 2013; Jones, 2012.

775. Ropp, Ibid.

776. Arocena, 2008.

777. Okamura, 1980 and 1994.

778. Fujikane, 2008; Trask, 2008.

779. Christian, 2000.

780. Bauman, 1999.

781. See, for example, Bain, 1982; Balint, 2005; Black and Sone, 2009; Ganter, 2006; Martinez, 2011; Shnukal, Ramsay, and Nagata, 2004.

782. See, for example, Chi et al., 1991 and 1996; Davies, 1993; Lo 2010.

783. Some Japanese people came not as migratory workers but to do their own business within these Japanese communities. Their numbers significantly decreased after 1901.

784. Kyuhara, 1986; Nagata 1999 and 2004; Sissons, 1979.

785. Suzuki, 1992.

786. Kaino, 2011.

787. *Shinju Matsuri* started in 1970. Its roots are three festivals, conducted separately by Japanese, Chinese, and Malay communities but at roughly the same time. After 2009, the Asian-Aboriginal community in Broome did not officially participate in the *Shinju Matsuri*.

788. Ganter, 2006, 195.

789. Ibid., 192.

790. In this case, "Indigenous" refers to both Aboriginal Australians and Torres Strait Islanders.

791. Dalton, 1986, 1.

792. See, for example, e.g., Ganter, 2006; Yu, 1999.

793. Ganter, Ibid., 195.

794. Ogawa, 1976.

795. Kaino, 2011.

796. Choo, 2009.

797. Compare, for example, Bain, 1982, and Yu, 1999.

798. Dalton, 1964; Nakano, 1986.

799. Ganter, 2006.

800. The cultured pearl industry employed the ex-pearl shell divers to get the mother-of-pearl shell for their pearl farm. This helped some Japanese pearl shell divers stay in Broome. However the rest of the pearl farm workers stayed at the pearl farm, which was about 370 km north of Broome, and rarely spent time in Broome.

801. Nakano, 1986; Similar phenomena are reported about other Asian groups by Dalton, 1964.

802. Nakano, Ibid.

803. Ganter, 2006.

804. Dalton, 1964, 1.

805. Commonwealth Bureau of Census and Statistics, *Census of Population and Housing, 30 June 1971, Commonwealth of Australia, Bulletin 6: Population and Dwellings in Local Government Areas and Urban Centres, Part 5 Western Australia*. Canberra: Commonwealth Bureau of Census and Statistics, 1973, 3.

806. Australian Bureau of Statistics, *Census of Population and Housing, 30 June 1981, Persons and Dwellings in Local Government Areas and Urban Centres, Western Australia*. Canberra: Australian Bureau of Statistics, 1982, 4.

807. Australian Bureau of Statistics, *Census Counts for Small Areas: Western Australia, 1991 Census of Population and Housing*. Canberra: Australian Bureau of Statistics, 1993, 31.

808. Australian Bureau of Statistics, *2001 Census Quickstats: Broome*.

809. Ibid. http://www.censusdata.abs.gov.au/ census_services/getproduct/census/2011/quickstat/ LGA50980?opendocument&navpos=95

810. It does not mean that all the newcomers have bad relationships with the Asians, Aboriginals, and their mixed descendants. Also, it does not necessarily mean that all the white people are considered to be "newcomers." There are some white families who have been in Broome since the pearl shelling days.

811. Sissons, 1979.

812. Jones, 2002.

813. *Broome Advertiser*, September 3, 2009; Shire of Broome, Minutes for the special meeting of council, October 13, 2009.

814. Kaino, 2011.

815. Gardiner-Garden, 2003.

816. Nakano, 1986, 11.

817. Ibid.

818. Nagano, 2011.

819. Trask, 2008; Hokari, 2003.

## CHAPTER TWELVE

820. This is a slightly modified version of Paul R. Spickard, "Injustice Compounded: Amerasians and Non-Japanese Americans in World War II Concentration Camps," *Journal of American Ethnic History*, 5, no. 2 (Spring 1986): 5-22. Copyright by the Immigration and Ethnic History Society. Reprinted by permission.

821. See, for example: Daniels, 1972; Girdner and Loftis, 1969; Grodzins, 1949); Irons, 1983; Leighton, 1945; Myer, 1971; Spicer, et al., 1969; Tateishi, 1984); ten Broek, Barnhart, and Matson, 1954; Thomas, et al., 1952; Thomas and Nishimoto, 1946; Uchida, 1982; United States Commission of Wartime Relocation and Internment of Civilians, 1983.

822. The WRA census listed 1,192 intermarried Japanese Americans and 287 mixed people in the WRA prison camps. However, the dates and manner of taking that census shed some doubt on the accuracy of those numbers. Census schedules (WRA Form 26) were filled out as Japanese American prisoners were transferred from the Wartime Civil Control Administration (an arm of the Army's Western Defense Command) assembly centers to the WRA's prison camps in the summer and fall of 1942. Some individuals were recorded as early as June, others as late as December. All the while, intermarried Japanese Americans and mixed people were being let out without being recorded in the WRA census. My guess—and it is only a guess—is that most of the 141 intermarried Japanese Americans and 433 people of mixed ancestry listed by the WDC as residing on the West Coast when it took a count in early 1943 were released in time

to miss being recorded by the 1942 WRA census (that is, they went straight home from the WCCA assembly centers without ever coming into WRA custody). Thus, I would guess that the WRA census and the early 1943 WDC counts do not overlap very much. There were also other intermarried Japanese Americans and mixed people who would have been missed by both counts because they were released from the assembly centers to points east of the WDC's West Coast jurisdiction. One must also be aware that the WRA's census takers were not consistent in the manner in which they recorded the existence of mixed people. In examining hundreds of census forms, J found all those who were listed as mixed people were in fact of mixed ancestry, but I also found some people of mixed ancestry listed as Japanese or Mexican or Filipino. The upshot of all this is that the WRA totals underestimate the actual numbers of intermarried Japanese Americans and mixed people who were at one time or another in the custody of the WCCA or WRA. My own very rough estimate is that there were 1,400-1,500 intermarried Japanese Americans and 700-900 people of mixed ancestry.

823. The system that allowed certain mixed people and intermarried Japanese Americans to leave the WRA camps was part of a larger leave clearance program aimed at providing workers for the labor-starved farms of the mountain West and granting a limited kind of freedom to those Nisei the government came to regard as adequate security risks. On that program see Thomas, et al., 1952, pp. 91, 615; United States War Relocation Authority, 1946a, pp. 10-18; Myer, 1971, 81; United States War Relocation Authority, 1946b, pp. 51-53; United States War Relocation Authority, n.d., pp. 23, 57; O'Brien, 1949. In the fall of 1942, several thousand Japanese Americans went out on temporary permits to work in the harvest, and a few students went to Eastern and Midwestern colleges to continue their studies. In 1943, some seven thousand Nisei were let out of prison under a program of permanent leave clearances, most to take jobs or continue schooling in the Midwest and East. But in the latter months of 1942, the bulk of the permanent clearances seem to have gone to people of mixed ancestry and their families. See Girdner and Loftis, 1969, pp. 342-354.

824. Wilkie C. Courter, memo to Maj. Ray Ashworth, "Emancipation of Japanese children, issue of mixed marriages," November 13, 1942, Records of the Western Defense Command, United States National Archives and Records Center, Washington, D.C., Military Archives Division, Modern Military Branch, Record Group 338, File Number 291.1: "Mixed Marriage File" (henceforth, WDC). Emphasis added.

825. Maj. Herman P. Goebel, Jr., memo to A. H. Cheney, "Release of mixed-marriage families," July 12, 1942, WDC. Hugh Fullerton shed further light on the WDC's attitudes toward the genetic basis of loyalty when he wrote to the Los Angeles chief of police that Glenn Jiobu and Raymond Oda should be let out of prison because, not only were they of mixed parentage, they were "definitely Caucasian in appearance." Capt. Hugh T. Fullerton, to C. B. Horrall, August 10, 1942, WDC. Goebel appears in WDC documents as the chief administrator of the mixed marriage leave policy. However, Col. Karl R. Bendetsen, director of the WCCA, made most key decisions regarding Japanese Americans in this period. See Daniels, 1972, pp. 45-68.

826. Goebel, memo to Cheney, July 12, 1942; Charles W. Dulles to Lt. Gen. J. L. DeWitt, July 31, 1942, WDC.

827. Goebel, memo to Cheney, July 12, 1942; Maj. Herman P. Goebel, Jr., memo to Capt. Astrup, "Mixed Marriage Policy," July 16, 1942, WDC; J. J. McGovern to Emil Sandquist, WCCA, San Francisco, July 20, 1942, WDC; Maj. Herman P. Goebel, Jr. to Manager, Stockton Assembly Center, July 22, 1942, WDC; Frank E. Davis, Tanforan Assembly Center, to Emil Sandquist, WCCA, San Francisco, July 31, 1942, WDC; Maj. Herman P. Goebel, Jr., to Manager, Portland Assembly Center, August 2, 1942; Goebel to Manager, Tanforan Assembly Center, August 3, 1942, WDC; Maj. Ray Ashworth, memo to Lt. Col. Claude B. Washburne, January 23, 1943, WDC; J. L. DeWitt to John J. McCloy, June 16, 1943, WDC. In enunciating policy here, Goebel may have been conscious of the precedent set by Federal District Judge Lloyd Llewellyn Black, who on April 12, 1942 denied freedom from imprisonment to Mary Asaba Ventura, a Nisei woman married to a Filipino (Daniels, 1972, 131). Despite possible knowledge of the Ventura case, however, Goebel and others in the WDC persisted in describing all non-Japanese marriage partners as "Caucasian." Goebel did not follow Black's formula and instead gave a limited freedom to some Japanese women married to brown- and yellow-skinned, non-Japanese men.

828. Ashworth, memo to Washburne, January 23, 1943; "Persons of Japanese Ancestry Granted Exemption from Evacuation ... Under the Mixed Marriage and Mixed Blood Policy," April 15, 1943, WDC; Col. Karl R. Bendetsen, memo to Commanding General, WDC, "Mixed Marriage and Mixed Blood Categories," June 16, 1943, WDC; Claude B. Washburne, memo to Commanding General, WDC, "Deferments from Evacuation Granted to Japanese," August 26, 1943, WDC; Lt. Col. Albert H. Moffitt, Jr., draft memo to John L. DeWitt, "Mixed Marriage Policy,"

September 24, 1943, WDC; "S.O.P. —Operations Branch, Miscellaneous section, Mixed Marriages," November 26, 1943, WDC. The change may have come as early as the latter part of August 1942, when some Filipino-Japanese couples were allowed to return to the WDC area. Whether they returned as United States Army policy or as exceptions, however, is not clear (cf. Goebel, letter to Manager, Tanforan Assembly Center, August 24, 1942, WDC. WDC policy in this regard was muddled. The citizenship status of Filipinos at this time was complex. Since their homeland was theoretically an American colony (temporarily held by the Japanese Army) they were American nationals. But they did not enjoy all the rights of American citizens, such as the right of free and unlimited entry to the United States. The term "citizen" is here applied to the Philippines in the loosest sense. For a detailed study of Filipino immigrants, their citizenship status, and a host of related issues, see Lasker, 1969.

829. Dillon S. Myer to John J. McCloy, January 15, 1943, WDC; McCloy to J.L. DeWitt, February 11, 1943, WDC; Telephone conversation, Col. Bendetsen/Capt. Hall, May 24, 1943; WDC. Takeyashi is the spelling used by DeWitt in a letter to McCloy on June 16, 1943. Other WDC documents spell her name Takashashi or Takayashi.

830. J.L. DeWitt to J.J. McCloy, February 15, 1943, WDC; DeWitt to McCloy, June 16, 1943; Bendetsen/Hall phone conversation.

831. Myer, 1971, 81; DeWitt to McCloy, June 16, 1943. For DeWitt's racist motivation, see Daniels, 1972, 36.

832. Claude B. Washburne and Lt. Gen. Delos C. Emmons, memo to C.G., W.D.C., October 19, 1943, WDC; "WDC Press Release, Japs Return to Coastal Area," December 13, 1943, WDC. Emmons's stewardship of the WDC was in many respects very different from that of his predecessor.

833. Herman P. Goebel to Manager, Merced Assembly Center, July 19, 1942, WDC; Ashworth, memo to Washburne, January 23, 1943; Goebel, memo to Capt. Astrup, "Mixed Marriage Release," September 6, 1942, WDC; N. L. Bican, Manager, Portland Assembly Center to Herman P. Goebel, August 14, 1942, WDC; Dulles to DeWitt, July 31, 1942; Girdner and Loftis, 1969, pp. 527-533; Thomas, et al., 1952, 91; United States War Relocation Authority, 1946b, pp. 51-53.

834. Thomas, et. al, 1952, 615.

835. "Resume of Mixed Marriage Work," February 18, 1943, WDC;

"Persons of Japanese Ancestry Granted Exemption," April 15, l943; Peter J. Crosby, Jr., memo to Karl R. Bendetsen, "Total Number of Mixed Marriage Families, Mixed-blood and Full-blooded Persons Exempted to Date," June 20, 1943, WDC; Crosby, memo to Bendetsen, September 12, 1943, WDC.

836. Asterisks denote pseudonyms. "Grace Umeko Record. ... Miki I. Funn. ... Florence Koto Asbury. ..." (WDC); Davis, to Sandquist, July 31, 1942, WRA Census Form 26, no. 103835-103836, 214209, 402178, 400954-400955, Japanese American Evacuation and Resettlement Study Archives, Bancroft Library, University of California, Berkeley [henceforth, JERS]; Daniels, 1972, 131; Irons, 1983, pp. 112-114; R.J. Patell to Chester Rowell, San Francisco, April 8, 1942, JERS B2.08.

837. Robert A. Leflar, W.R.A., to Philip M. Glick, W.R.A., Washington, D.C., 13 October 1942, WDC; John Thomas Hayes, Denver, to E. Besig, October 11, 1943, WDC; Dillon S. Myer to Besig, November 17, 1943, WDC.

838. WRA Census Form 26, no. 100042; 206904-206906; 108976, JERS; Chuman, 1976, 191; ten Broek, Barnhart, and Matson, 1954, 236; Korematsu's conviction has recently been overturned, more than forty years after the fact.

839. WRA Census Form 26, no. 206860-206863, 10835-103836, 209331-209332; 217702-217703, 218074-218078; JERS; Whitney, 1948, pp. 65-68; Grace Umeko Record (WDC); and *Pacific Citizen*, June 4, 1942, 8.

840. Karl R. Bendetsen, memo to Commanding General, WDC, "Deferments from Evacuation," February 10, 1943, WDC; Bendetsen, memo to Commanding General, June 15, 1943, WDC; Bendetsen, memo to Commanding General, June 29, 1943, WDC; Bendetsen, memo to Commanding General, August 2, 1943, WDC; Bendetsen, memo to Commanding General, April 28, 1943, WDC; Bendetsen, memo to Commanding General, May 13, 1943, WDC; Bendetsen, memo to Commanding General, May 31, 1943, WDC; Bendetsen, memo to Commanding General, July 12, 1943, WDC; Washburne, memo to Commanding General, September 16, 1943, WDC; Peter J. Crosby, memo to Washburne, November 3, 1943, WDC; Crosby, memo to Washburne, December 3, 1943, WDC.

841. "Families Which Appear to be Eligible for Release ... But Which Have Expressed a Desire to Remain in the Center" (WDC).

842. WRA Census Form 26, no. 106359-106361, 204337-204338, 208984,

209305-209311, 400376, 606761-606762, 700442-700444, 708063-708069, JERS; "Families Which Appear to Be Eligible for Release … But Which Have Expressed a Desire to Remain"; Davis to Sandquist, July 31, 1942; Fullerton to Harrall, August 10, 1942; Girdner and Loftis, 1969, pp. 174, 225.

843. "Relocation Program at Tule Lake," pp. 358-362; Rose Hayashi*, interviewed by Charles Kikuchi, Chicago, 1944, JERS.

844. Elaine Black Yoneda, interviewed by Betty Mitson, San Francisco, March 3, 1974, CSU Fullerton Oral History Tape OH1377a; Yoneda, 1983, pp. 125-149; D.S. Myer to Ray B. Johnston, n.d., WDC; WRA Census Form 26, no. 206909-206911, 707564, 702933-702934, 707557-707558, JERS; Ishigo papers (Japanese American Research Project Archives, Department of Special Collections, University Research Library, UCLA, Boxes 77-80); Ishigo, 1989; "Relocation Program at Tule Lake," pp. 358-362.

845. Peter Ogata (pseud.), interviewed by Charles K. Kukuchi, Chicago, April 10, 1944, JERS, case 5. Naske, 1983; Weglyn, 1976, 57; United States War Relocation Authority, n.d., pp. 183, 190; WRA Census Form 26, no.109751, JERS.

846. See note 21 above; DeWitt to McCloy, June 16, 1943; Bendetsen/Hall phone conversation.

## CHAPTER THIRTEEN

847. Cooper and Stoler, 1997.

848. Salesa, 2011, 2.

849. One can think for example of the importance of age, religion, and education amongst others.

850. See also the introduction in Brah and Coombes, 2000, which underlines the importance of looking at how hybridity is constructed and contested through complex hierarchies of power.

851. The Stichting Pelita is a Dutch welfare foundation that assists former inhabitants of the Dutch East Indies, especially for those bereaved by the war in the Pacific and the post-war conflicts in Indonesia. One of their tasks is to give support to applicants for war relief.

852. Touwen-Bouwsma, 2010.

853. Stoler, 2000.

854. Bosma and Raben, 2008, xiv.

855. Veur, van der 1968, pp. 191-207. Taylor, 1983. Bosma and Raben, 2008.

856. According to the *Indisch Jaarverslag 1940* the number of indigenous men married to European women ranged from 6 in 1929 and 1930 to 43 in 1936.

857. Lijnkamp, 1938 analyzes the background of this law.

858. Shimizu, 1993.

859. Ohnuki-Tierney, 2000 is a good example of research drawing on diaries of Japanese soldiers.

860. The abstracts of the Oral History Collection are available in English in Steijlen, 2002.

861. NIOD archive, Nederlands-Indische dagboeken en egodocumenten, inventory 370, diary C.M. Engel-Bruins.

862. Buchheim, 2013.

863. Personal communication with Sadao Oba and interview with Kaoru Uchiyama.

864. Due to privacy constraints, personal data related to information from the social reports in the Stichting Pelita archives is withheld.

865. Interview with Mrs. E on December 27, 2006; she was born in 1919; see Buchheim, 2010.

866. Interview with Mrs. S on July 28, 2005, she was born in 1928.

867. Stories of intimate relationships with Chinese, Indonesian and British-Indian soldiers can be found in the Oral History Collection at KITLV Leiden, in the Stichting Pelita archives, and in diaries from the NIOD collection.

868. A phenomenon that can be witnessed likewise on fraternization in Europe. Although there was some concern about unions with liberators (Canadians in the Netherlands after World War II) they were not judged as harshly as unions with the enemy (German soldiers in the Netherlands during World War II. A good example is the popular Dutch song 'Trees heeft een Canadees' [Trees has a

Canadian], about the difficulties Dutch women who fraternized with the German enemy in the Netherlands experienced.

869. Goldstein, 2001.

870. See Diederichs, 2006 about the difficulties experienced by Dutch women who fraternized with the German enemy in the Netherlands.

871. See Buchheim 2013. Also see Gieske, 2016.

872. On the multiply illegitimate status of children born out of fraternization see Warring, 2005.

873. Buchheim, 2008.

## CHAPTER FOURTEEN

874. This chapter draws on Walter Hamilton's *Children of the Occupation: Japan's Untold Story* (Sydney: NewSouth, 2012 and New Brunswick: Rutgers University Press, 2013), for which the author gratefully acknowledges the publishers. The expression "enemies in miniature" comes from Joji Tsutsumi. All translations from the Japanese are by Shizue Noguchi-Hamilton to whom the author expresses his appreciation.

875. *Asahi Shinbun*, December 1945, quoted in Wildes, 1954, 328. See also Gayn, 1981 [1948], 51; *Pacific Stars and Stripes*, April 3, 1946.

876. Chōji Takahashi, Kanagawa Prefectural Assembly, Ordinary Session, November 10, 1945, quoted in Kanō, 2007, 217.

877. Gayn, 1948/1981, 179.

878. Supreme Command[er] for the Allied Powers, the common acronym for the U.S.-run Occupation bureaucracy.

879. Berrigan, 1948, pp. 117-118.

880. Takasaki, 1952, 19. The word *konketsuji* literally means "mixed-blood child." Partly by association with the children of the Occupation, the word has acquired a pejorative connotation and is no longer used, for example, in Japanese newspapers. It is retained here for the sake of historical authenticity, with no intention of causing offense.

881. Kalischer, 1952, 16.

882. The Press Code permitted nothing which "might invite mistrust or resentment" of Allied troops (Coughlin, 1952, pp.149-150). After formal controls were lifted in October 1949, publishers exercised self-censorship.

883. Roeder, 1993, 112.

884. Takami, 1965, 265. Takami was not an unthinking critic of the Occupation; he acknowledged that the Americans behaved better than the Japanese had in China.

885. Ōya, 1952, 194; *Fujin Kōron*, September 1953, 48. In equating luxury with dirt, the rhetoric harks back to jingoistic wartime slogans.

886. Ōya, 1952, 194. The expression he used was code, in the censored press, for GIs in jeeps.

887. The subject spawned a vast terminology. See Kanzaki, 1953, 333. The *panpan's* independence was more apparent than real. They formed associations and relied on pimps, moneychangers, and operators of bars, cabarets, and cheap lodgings, who all demanded a cut of the takings.

888. Koyanagi, 1952, 112.

889. A letter sent to General MacArthur in 1950 put it succinctly: "No Japanese, but street girls, want American military forces to stay in Japan" (Sodei, 2001, 91).

890. *Chūgoku Nippō*, May 1, 1952. Tamaki Uemura commented: "Few *panpan* become mothers. This may be because the unnatural sex life of *panpan* extinguishes pregnancies. This is good" ("Baishōfu no Inai Sekai o," *Fujin Kōron*, April 1953, 44.)

891. Quoted in Deverall, 1953, 159.

892. Berrigan, 1948, 117.

893. Coaldrake, 2003, 219.

894. Sawada, 1953, pp. 131-132. The date of the letter is inferred from the context.

895. Iglehart, 1952, 303.

896. Hirohito visited in October 1955 (*Shūkan Shinchō*, March 2, 1989, pp. 37-38); Klein, 2003, pp. 154, 158; Eveland, 1956, 113; Sawada, 1953, 46.

897. Our Lady of Lourdes Baby Home had sent only fifteen children to

the United States by 1955 (Koshiro, 1999, 199).

898. *Sunday Mainichi*, January 8, 1956; Buck, 1963, 63.

899. Miki Sawada, "Minna shiawase ni sodatteiru," *Sunday Mainichi*, January 10, 1960. The number of adoptions given here is 362 (almost all to the United States). In 1963, Sawada said the number had reached 530, but figures used by her and others over the years are impossible to reconcile. It was stated in 1989 by the then head of the Elizabeth Saunders Home that, out of a total of 1,287 "graduates" of the facility, 559 were *konketsuji* (*Shūkan Shinchō*, March 2, 1989, 38). Sawada biographer Elizabeth Hemphill and Pearl Buck both use much higher figures. Robert Fish, a researcher given access to the records of the Home, offers no figure for the total number of mixed-race children raised there. See also *Asahi Shinbun*, June 9, 1956 on adoptions from Sawada's Home and Our Lady of Lourdes Baby Home.

900. Quoted in Nomoto, 1996, 140. According to Sawada, one midwife who brought a child to the Home claimed to have killed twenty-two other children she had delivered (Hemphill, 1980, 89). Horror stories, many traceable to Sawada, dominate the *konketsuji* historiography.

901. Sawada, 1953, pp. 92-93, 159.

902. Hemphill, 1980, pp. 119-120.

903. Letter to Bishop Norman Binsted, quoted in Fish, 2002, 166. Offering another insight into Sawada's mentality is the way she assigned children names such as Suteko Kinoshita ("abandoned under a tree") or Ochitada Kawabata ("neglected at the river edge") ("Konketsuji to tomo ni jyūgonen," *Shūkan Asahi*, January 18, 1963). Even one of her admirers wrote: "I wonder if she could drop the idea that *konketsuji* are born evil and, instead, think about nurturing each soul with more human and natural affection" (Takasaki, 1952, 84).

904. Kubota et al., 1953, 93.

905. Trumbull, 1967, 113.

906. Thompson, 1967, 48.

907. "Roundtable," *Fujin Kōron*, July 1952, 54.

908. *Shūkan Asahi*, January 18, 1963.

909. Sawada, 1953, pp. 200-201. Once the children were adopted

abroad, however, Sawada tended to emphasize their finer qualities.

910. Fish, 2002, 166; Buck, 1963, 47. Sawada's rages were notorious. Sometimes she would take off her shoe to strike a child with. The photographer Kōyō Kageyama, a frequent visitor to the Home, found he had to look away when she disciplined a child (*Shūkan Asahi*, January 18, 1963).

911. Fish, 2002, 167.

912. Ibid., 7. A primary school and a junior high school were built on the estate.

913. Ibid., pp. 144-154 (Fish could find no evidence of organized opposition in Ōiso); *Shūkan Asahi*, March 1, 1953.

914. Hemphill, 1980, 96.

915. Hemphill, Ibid., 97; Fish, 2002, 214.

916. Coaldrake, 2003, 488.

917. For positive contemporary assessments, see Tayama, 1953 and Takasaki, 1952. Sawada received Japanese and international awards for her philanthropic work.

918. It is unclear who came up with the figure "200,000"—Uemura, Sawada, or a Welfare Ministry official—which suggests how widely it was accepted.

919. *New York Herald Tribune*, April 21, 1952. The longer Japanese text is in *Fujin Kōron*, May 1952, 36ff.

920. Like Sawada, Uemura considered female chastity a "noble and sublime" aspect of Japanese feudalism and condemned Occupation reforms to the patriarchal *ie* (household) system. In her letter to Mrs. Ridgway, she wrote: "Do you know of any case in which the American military directed other nationals to successfully effect such a fundamental change in their family or social morality?"

921. As far back as 1947, Japanese officials had wanted to make a survey but were refused permission by SCAP (Berrigan, 1948, 24).

922. Kōseishō, "'Iwayuru konketsujidō' jittai chōsa hōkokusho," Kōseishō Jidōkyoku (February 1953); Graham and Giga, 1953, pp. 51-53; *Asahi Shinbun*, December 24, 1952.

923. Graham and Giga, 1953; Ogawa, 1960, 140.

924. See Kubushiro, 1953, 28, and Hirano, 1969, 231.

925. "Aoi me no ichinensei: Konketsuji no nyūgaku mondai," *Shūkan Asahi*, March 1, 1953.

926. Kanzaki, 1953a, 130. It has been claimed, for instance, that more than eight hundred *konketsuji* are buried at Negishi Foreigners' Cemetery in Yokohama (*Japan Times*, August 25, 1999).

927. *Jiji Shinpō*, June 9, 1952; *Asahi Shinbun*, August 14, 1952. Koya, a medical doctor, contributed to a 1943 Welfare Ministry study which described mixed-race persons, in a colonial setting, as "dependent, obsequious, irresponsible, and weak-willed, with a tendency to be nihilistic and self-destructive" (Kōseishō Kenkyūjo Jinkō Minzoku-bu, 1981, pp. 303-308). See also Koya, 1939, and *Yomiuri Shinbun*, November 2, 1952.

928. "Konketsuji wa dō kaiketsu subeki ka," *Nihon Keizai Shinbun*, February 2, 1953; "Konketsuji monogatari," *Fujin Kōron*, April 1953, pp. 164-169. Notwithstanding Koya's role, the expertise of the other members suggests a greater concern for child welfare than race theory. See Suda, 1952, pp. 31-32, and *Shakai Taimuzu*, February 9, 1953.

929. "Konketsuji monogatari," 165.

930. *Nihon Keizai Shinbun*, February 2, 1953.

931. *Asahi Shinbun*, November 14 and 27, 1952; "Keredomo konketsuji wa sodatte yuku," *Fujin Kōron*, July 1952, pp. 50-57; *Nippon Times*, November 28, 1952; *Mainichi Shinbun*, February 28, 1953 (editorial).

932. *Asahi Shinbun*, July 11, 1960.

933. *Pacific Stars and Stripes*, August 24, 1946 carried a report on the psychological testing of more than three hundred "juvenile vagrants."

934. Kubota et al., 1953, 93.

935. Hanihara, 1965; Kubota et al., 1953, pp. 112-125; Kimura, 1976, 1984.

936. *Tokyo Shinbun*, August 22, 1952.

937. Ibid. For a more careful treatment of the subject, see *Shūkan Asahi*, March 1, 1953.

938. Prominent Socialist member of the House of Councillors, Michiko Fujiwara, in December 1952, quoted in Koshiro, 1999,

pp. 177-178. See also *Yomiuri Shinbun*, November 2, 1952.

939. Ishihara, 1969, pp. 1-7, reproduces IQ test scores he implies were derived from three hundred and fifty *konketsuji*, when the actual sample size (according to the original research paper) was as small as twenty-eight or twenty-nine children (see Kubota et al., 1953).

940. Kubota et al., 1953, 110; Hayashi, 1950, pp. 68-69. Ishihara's follow-up IQ testing on *konketsuji* at the Elizabeth Saunders Home in 1967, from which he concluded that "mixed-blood children were lower in intelligence and academic achievement compared with Japanese," used a doubly unrepresentative sample: not only were all his subjects living in an institution but also they were mainly older individuals who had been unable to be placed in adoptive homes. Berrigan, 1948, 117, criticized the research efforts he witnessed in 1948.

941. *Mainichi Shinbun*, March 20, 1952. Others, such as literary critic Naoko Itagaki, also felt mixed-race children should have been aborted (Itagaki, 1953, 163). See also Aoki, 1952. For more restrained and sanguine commentary, see *Yomiuri Shinbun*, February 19 (editorial) and March 5, 1953, and *Mainichi Shinbun*, February 28, 1953 (editorial).

942. Ōya, 1952, 199; Ōya Sōichi, "'Taiheiyō sensō' o meguru 'chi' no mondai: Puchiburujoa ga deruka," as told to Shigeo Sakaguchi, *Shōsetsu Shinchō*, June 1952, 71.

943. Kanzaki, 1953a, pp. 132, 134.

944. "Kichi Itami," *Fujin Kōron*, December 1953, 181.

945. Mombushō Shotō Chūtō Kyōikukyoku, 1957, 140; Takasaki, 1952, 51; *Shūkan Asahi*, March 1953.

946. *Enka* singer Jero (Jerome Charles White) in an NHK-TV documentary broadcast on March 20, 2009.

947. See, for instance, the image of a black *konketsuji*, photographed in Nagoya in 1952, reproduced in Makino et al. 2006, pp. 42-43.

948. Moser, 1969, 43.

949. *Asahi Shinbun*, February 21, 1953; *Shūkan Asahi*, March 1, 1953.

950. *Asahi Shinbun*, August 3, 1965; Hirano, 1969, 232, says "more than ten."

951. *Mainichi Shinbun* (evening edition), April 6, 1953.

952. *Yomiuri Shinbun* (evening edition), April 6, 1953.

953. *Sunday Mainichi* (magazine), May 31, 1953 reflects this skepticism. See "Konketsuji wo miru seken no me," *Yomiuri Shinbun*, July 6, 1953 for episodes of public ridicule of mothers of *konketsuji*.

954. "Kichi no teisō" ran April 15-25, 1953. U.S. military bases in Japan (excluding Okinawa) then occupied 257,000 acres of land; the 733 facilities included 44 airfields (*Tokyo Evening News*, March 5, 1953).

955. *Tokyo Nichi-Nichi*, April 25, 1953.

956. *Asahi Shinbun*, April 30, 1960. See also *Asahi Shinbun* (evening edition), November 18, 1955.

957. "Pēru Bakku joshi e: Konketsuji o kōfuku na michi e," *Fujin Kōron*, May 1952, 34. Buck responded in the July edition of the same publication: "In most cases, mixed-bloods are superior children. They are cute and clever. Looked after with affection and given abundant opportunities, they will prove a treasure for any country."

958. For a range of contemporary public opinion, see Michiyo Abe, "Konketsuji o dō suru ka," *Fujin Kōron*, April 1953, pp. 170-173.

959. Eveland, 1956, 115, estimated "nearly half" the parents went through a Shinto wedding ceremony. A survey by Kanagawa Children's Clinic found that of 193 mothers who visited the center, and whose backgrounds were known, only 10 percent could be described as *panpan*, while 43 percent worked in jobs directly connected with the Occupation, e.g., maids, PX shop assistants, etc. Less than 4 percent of *panpan*, in a separate survey, admitted to having a mixed-race child (*Shūkan Asahi*, March 1, 1953, 5; Keiō Gijyuku Daigaku Shakaijigyō Kenkyūkai, 1953). Robert Fish estimated that up to a quarter of the women who left children at the Elizabeth Saunders Home early on may have engaged in some form of prostitution (Fish, 2002, pp. 39, 42, 52).

960. Spickard, 1989, 152; Kalischer, 1952, 18; Berrigan, 1948, pp. 24-25, 117.

961. Hirai, 2007, pp. 88, 96; "Roundtable," *Jidō Shinri*, July 1953, 12.

962. *Jidō Shinri*, July 1953, 10. At school, however, black *konketsuji* tended to be less popular than white mixed-bloods (Mombushō Shotō Chūtō Kyōikukyoku, 1957, 126).

963. Among *konketsuji* living outside welfare facilities in 1953, 11 percent were known to have had black fathers, or about the same proportion as that of African Americans in the Occupation (Kōseishō, 1953, 2).

964. Shizue Abe, "Tsumi no nai ko ni muzanna shiren o ataeruna," *Kokumin*, March 1953, 13. A similar view is expressed in *Sunday Mainichi* (magazine), May 31, 1953.

965. *Shūkan Asahi*, March 1, 1953, 11. See also her appeal for society to "relax" about black *konketsuji*—they would "sink into yellow Japanese" within two or three generations and enrich the nation's "racial resources" ("Kokujin konketsu no mondai," *Yomiuri Shinbun* (evening edition), March 5, 1953).

966. *Jidō Shinri*, July 1953, pp. 11-12.

967. "Comment" in Kataoka, 1985, pp. 127-128.

968. See Minoru Miyoshi, "Konketsuji to jinken mondai" in Mombushō, 1960, pp. 7-14.

969. *Ushio*, October 1952, 37.

970. During the war, teachers helped spread an ideology of racial superiority. Thousands resigned in 1946, opening the way for others with liberal or Marxist views to enter the profession.

971. Mombushō Shotō Chūtō Kyōikukyoku, 1954.

972. Mombushō Shotō Chūtō Kyōikukyoku, 1957.

973. Mombushō Shotō Chūtō Kyōikukyoku, 1960, pp. 15-25.

974. Ibid. See also "Konketsuji shidō no shiryō matomaru," *Chūgoku Shinbun*, May 20, 1956.

975. Mombushō Shotō Chūtō Kyōikukyoku, 1960, pp. 44-59.

976. Ibid., 148.

977. Ibid., pp. 51-53.

978. Ibid., pp. 99-108.

979. Archives of ISS America: Social Welfare History Archives, University of Minnesota Libraries, box 34, folio 1; Eveland, 1956, 113.

980. *Mainichi Shinbun*, January 30, 1953. The committee included members from the American Chamber of Commerce in Japan,

the Inter-Board Missionary Field Committee, the Tokyo Union Church, the Christian Children's Fund, the American Legion, and the Veterans of Foreign Wars. A full list is given in Eveland, 1956, 114.

981. Graham, 1954.

982. Ibid.

983. Ibid.

984. Deverall, 1953, 110.

985. Goodman, 1998, 153.

986. Ibid., 155.

987. Hayes and Habu, 2006, pp. 1-2. Adoption was also the only way then for a foreigner to become a Japanese citizen.

988. Goodman, 1998, pp. 150, 155; Hayes and Habu, Ibid., 3.

989. *Tokyo Shinbun*, May 4, 1952.

990. Archives of ISS America, box 34, folio 1 and box 17, folio 4.

991. Laurin Hyde and Virginia P. Hyde, "A Study of Proxy Adoptions," Child Welfare League of America/ International Social Service American Branch, June 1958, 6.

992. Florence Boester, "Summary Report for Period May 1-August 30, 1955," Archives of ISS America, box 34, folio 7. The following group of citations shares the same archive reference.

993. Ruth Larned, "Surveying the International Social Service after 25 Years."

994. Briefing document dated September 1, 1955.

995. Boester to Valk (ISSAm), November 9, 1955; Boester to Kirk (ISSAm), January 31, 1956.

996. Pettiss (ISSAm) to Boester, November 29, 1955; Kirk to Boester, February 8, 1956.

997. Boester to Geerken (U.S. Embassy Tokyo), March 9, 1956.

998. Boester to Valk, November 9, 1955.

999. Boester to Pettiss, May 10, 1956. Boester wrote to Kirk on January 31, 1956, alerting him to a "shocking" plan by the Elizabeth

Saunders Home to send all its 140 children to Brazil. Japanese teachers, she had been told, would only agree to accompany the "feeble-minded" cases if the "normal" children were sent along with them. Miki Sawada had begun actively looking for a "paradise for my children" in Brazil two years earlier, though it was not until 1963 that a small number of young men from the Home went there (Hemphill, 1980, pp. 140-142).

1000. A precise figure is unavailable. According to Seiho Miyano, in Mombushō Shotō Chūtō Kyōikukyoku, 1957, 145, a total of 1,942 visas for "orphans" (mostly *konketsuji*) were issued between January 1952 and the end of January 1957. Foreign Ministry records showed another 618 children went for adoption between June 1957 and November 1958 (Mombusho Shotō Chūtō Kyōikukyoku, 1960, 156).

1001. Boester to Moffit (ISS Australia), May or June 1958, National Archives of Australia (hereafter NAA): A10651, ICR5/1 Part 2.

1002. Wood, 1998, pp. 51-54.

1003. Kubushiro, 1953, 28.

1004. Hamilton, 2012, pp. 130-142.

1005. *Sunday Sun* (Sydney), June 18, 1950.

1006. Memo of February 16, 1956, NAA: A1838, 3103/10/12/1 Part 1.

1007. Briefing note, NAA: A446, 1962/67628.

1008. A two-year-old boy admitted under this rule in 1956 did not receive his naturalization papers until 1962. The adoptive father (no blood relation) was never assessed by social workers. To the author's knowledge, only one *konketsuji* was placed through an adoption agency with a family in Australia. This was in 1965.

1009. Hamilton, 2012, pp. 172-177.

1010. Statement to *The Sun* (Sydney), May 6, 1958. Note how all the children were rendered "illegitimate."

1011. *Commonwealth Parliamentary Debates (New Series)*, House of Representatives, vol. 26, 701.

1012. Hamilton, 2012, 86.

1013. The term "Kure Kids," coined by the author, will be used hereafter for the children born in or around Hiroshima Prefecture between 1946 and 1956, whose fathers were foreign servicemen and mothers Japanese, and who remained in Japan at least until the age of twelve.

1014. Hamilton, 2012, 13.

1015. Author's interview: Nagoya, October 12, 2005.

1016. Author's interview: Canberra, May 3, 2005. Teruko and her husband Bill Blair eventually had three children and settled in Australia. She was one of more than six hundred war brides who went from Japan to Australia.

1017. *Chūgoku Shinbun*, November 23, 1956.

1018. Teru Ōno, "Gunji kichi to kurisuchan," *Nyū Eiji*, February 1953, 46.

1019. *Kure Nippō*, August 22, 1952. The reference to "American" soldiers was tailored to the audience of Teachers' Union members and other anti-base activists.

1020. Kanzaki, 1953b, pp. 196, 204.

1021. For example, see *Chūgoku Shinbun*, July 11, 1952 and *Chūgoku Nippō*, June 26 and July 15, 1953 and January 23, 1954.

1022. Yone Itō, "Actual Situation of Mixed-Blood Children in Kure and Surrounding Areas" (Spring 1960), in ISS Japan branch files viewed at the organization's Tokyo office (hereafter ISSJ).

1023. Hamilton, 2012, pp. 174-178.

1024. Ibid., 216.

1025. For negative portrayals, see Porter, 1958, 155; Moser, 1969, 40; Wagatsuma, 1973b, pp. 261-262 and 1977, pp. 9-17; Takemae, 2002, pp. 80-81.

1026. Based on author's interview, Hiroshima, October 16, 2005, and ISSJ documents. Many more case studies can be found in Hamilton, 2012.

1027. "Individual List" 1965, ISSJ.

1028. Itō, "Actual Situation," ISSJ. The exact number of children left behind by BCOF troops cannot be established, though it was probably several hundred. ISS concentrated on the most needy cases, mainly confined to a small geographical area, whereas BCOF troops visited many parts of Japan, on duty or on leave.

1029. "Mixed-Blood Children Documents," Kure City Social Section.

1030. It was recognized to be a contributing factor in the unpopularity of *konketsuji*. ISSJ advised Australian colleagues not to send clothing ("It's not as if Japan lacks material things"), Tamura to Kelso (ISSA), May 28, 1964, ISSJ.

1031. "Actual Situation," ISSJ.

1032. Compare this with the Freudian views of Seiho Miyano of ISSJ who claimed the mothers typically came from matriarchal families, which explained why they clung to a "harmful illusion" about their happy lives with their partners. He blamed them for the children's unhealthy mental development (Mombushō Shotō Chūtō Kyōikukyoku, 1960, pp. 99-103).

1033. "Actual Situation," ISSJ.

1034. *Chūgoku Shinbun*, July 22, 1956 reported that Kure shops would not employ women who had worked for BCOF/BCFK.

1035. Attitudes fluctuated wildly. For instance, the *Chūgoku Nippō* of June 29, 1957 portrayed the mothers as deceived women whose husbands had failed to overcome racial prejudice in Australia, but the same paper later (December 27, 1959) branded them as bad mothers and the *konketsuji* as "shameful children of destiny."

1036. Formed in 1961 under the patronage of the governor of Hiroshima Prefecture. Kure City Education Board also established a special advisory council that commissioned Hiroshima University researcher Mitsuya Yamauchi to prepare instructional manuals for teachers with *konketsuji* in their classes.

1037. Mayumi's mother was nineteen when she became pregnant. The family suspects she may have been sexually assaulted. Another of the Kure Kids, Kiyotaka Kawasaki, recalls: "My father [an Australian BCOF soldier] said the Occupation army was fairly bad. There were rapes. Older people in Kure remember that" (author's interview: Brisbane, August 19, 2005).

1038. Yone Itō, "Report of ISS Kure Project," October 1977, ISSJ, 12.

1039. The national retention rate in 1962 was 65.2 percent. See Table: "Percentage of Lower Secondary School Graduates Entering Upper Secondary School," in Mombushō, 1965, Appendices. The original Japanese version was published in November 1964.

1040. The Welfare Ministry estimated that less than 10 percent of all *konketsuji* advanced to senior high school (*Asahi Shinbun*, May 9, 1962).

1041. "Activities Report 1963-64," June 15, 1964, ISSJ; Itō, "Report of ISS Kure Project," 14.

1042. Itō to Calman (former ISSJ volunteer), March 23, 1965, ISSJ.

1043. Joji Tsutsumi married at twenty, had three sons, and held down a steady job until retirement. In 2007, he went to Australia for the first time and was able to visit his father's birthplace.

1044. *Melbourne Herald*, April 24, 1964.

1045. "Establishment of Kure ISS Office and Its Activities," January 29, 1964, ISSJ.

1046. Author's interviews: Tokyo, June 2 and November 8, 2005.

1047. Itō et al., 1984, pp. 18-21.

1048. Internal memos, ISSJ.

1049. *Tokyo Shinbun*, April 22, 1960.

1050. The individual concerned was raised in a *burakumin* neighborhood of Kure. This added an extra dimension to the discrimination Itō hoped he could escape. As the youth possessed an exceptionally high IQ, she also tried, unsuccessfully, to send him to Australia for his higher education.

1051. Case report, May 1966, ISSJ.

1052. Author's interview: Kure, June 7, 2005. After the death of Junko's father in 1980, her Australian relatives recognized her and her brother as his legal heirs. Junko was eventually able to marry and has one daughter.

1053. ISSJ newsletter, January 16, 1973, Archives of ISS America, box 34, folio 9.

1054. Itō, "Report of ISS Kure Project," ISSJ. Based on data from the National Institute of Population and Social Research, in their age group, sixty, rather than thirty-six, might be expected to have married by then.

1055. Spickard, 1989, 149; Strong, 1978, 220.

1056. Her husband is a politician: Kunio Hatoyama. Hal Porter made use of the Baird family for a dyspeptic short story in which the daughters were portrayed as "nearly untouchable" outcasts (see Porter, 1970). It is another example of *konketsuji* doom-saying gone astray.

1057. Burkhardt, 1983, 538; Strong, 1978, 194. Similarly, claims of higher rates of juvenile delinquency among *konketsuji* have not been backed up by hard evidence (Wagatsuma, 1973a, 222).

1058. The phrase "damaged goods" was used, independently, by two of the Kure Kids in conversation with the author. A study of *konketsuji* who were adopted to the United States in the 1950s found 7 out of 129 children showed "severe symptoms of trauma" and 26 others "appeared disturbed to a lesser extent" (Graham, 1958). Another researcher rated 3 percent of his sample group as "seriously self-destructive" (Strong, 1978, pp. 194, 222). However, an over-emphasis on clinical cases, exhibiting extreme maladjustment, has distorted academic approaches to the *konketsuji* issue. A frequently cited 1977 study set the tone: "All the children I interviewed gave me an impression that they tended to be emotionally insecure, immature, dependent, passive or even apathetic. Some of them were openly aggressive and harbored strong hatred" (Wagatsuma, 1977, 13).

1059. Itō, "Report of ISS Kure Project."

1060. Susumu Sawakai, "Konketsuji ni tekisetsuna taisaku wo," *Kōmei*, March 1967, 54.

1061. *Newsweek*, February 13, 1967. See also Trumbull, 1967, pp.112-114.

1062. "Konketsu hosutesu sono honpo na yoru no seikatsu", *Asahi Geinō*, September 17, 1967, 108.

1063. "Yokosuka no Koibito," an installment of the documentary series *Kamera wa Mita!* produced by Tokyo Channel 12 and broadcast on April 19, 1967.

1064. Mitsuharu Inoue, *Asahi Grafu*, May 12, 1967, 68.

1065. "Watashi tachi wa Nihonjin da," *Asahi Jyūnaru*, October 22, 1967, pp. 82-91.

1066. Ibid.

1067. *Sayonara*, adapted for the screen by Paul Osborn from the James A. Michener novel (MGM, 1957).

1068. Quoted by Mayumi Kosugi (author's interview).

1069. Spickard, 1989, pp. 115, 150.

1070. Hall, 1980, pp. 74, 125. The author observed the same tendency during his work with the Kure Kids and their children.

1071. Strong, 1978, pp. 50-51, 87, 145, 150, 219.

1072. Ibid., 49-51; Burkhardt, 1983, 535.

1073. Valentine, 1990, 45.

1074. Macdonald, 1995, pp. 265-266.

1075. Fish, 2002, pp. 228-236 makes a similar case.

## CHAPTER FIFTEEN

1076. This essay was made possible through a postdoctoral fellowship with the USC Shinso Ito Center for Japanese Religions and Cultures from 2013-2014. I want to thank Karl Lippincott, who was willing to talk with me about his life history. I extend my appreciation to Paul Spickard and Akemi Johnson for their helpful comments in earlier versions of this chapter.

1077. Karl Lippincott, Oral History Interview with Lily Anne Welty Tamai, Hapa Japan Conference, University of Southern California, Los Angeles, April 5, 2013. This interview was a part of a conference sponsored by the Hapa Japan Database Project, housed at the University of Southern California's Shinso Ito Center for Japanese Religions and Cultures. The video of the interview is archived at the center.

1078. Even these positive images are debated today. See Hefalein, 2012.

1079. Lippincott, Oral History Interview. The term, *konketsuji*, literally "mixed-blood child," was the Japanese term used to described multiracial American Japanese in Japan following World War II. *Konketsuji* replaced the pejorative term, *ainoko*, literally "child of mixture." *Konketsuji* was used during the Occupation era and into the 1960s, but later fell out of favor for the term, *hafu* coming from the English word half, meaning mixed-race ancestry.

1080. Ibid.

1081. Ibid.

1082. For more on the Recreation and Amusement Association see Dower, 1999; Sanders, 2012; Kovner, 2012. Not all women who dated American men were involved in sex work.

1083. Wagatsuma, 1977; Burkhardt, 1983.

1084. This is an estimate of the number of births. Few accurate statistics exist, and the numbers vary wildly ranging from 20,000 to 200,000 babies. The first mixed-race birth was in 1946, and by 1952, obstetricians reported about 5,013 births of children of mixed-race background to the Ministry of Health and Welfare. See Kanzaki 1953, 129; Fish, 2002.

1085. The terminology continued to evolve. See Murphy-Shigematsu, 2001.

1086. Strong, 1978; Hall, 1980; Kich, 1983; Thornton, 1983; Murphy-Shigematsu, 1986; Williams-León, 1989; Wagatsuma, 1977.

1087. Strong, 1978; Hall, 1980; Murphy-Shigematsu, 1986; Williams-León, 1989; Thornton, 1983.

1088. Thompson, 1967; Wagatsuma, 1978; Kōya, 1953.

1089. Sawada, 1953; Hemphill, 1980.

1090. Maeda, 1964; Taga, 1991; Hale, 1988.

1091. Murphy-Shigematsu, 2001, pp. 215-216.

1092. Welty, 2012; Kozeki, 1967. For more on the British Commonwealth Occupation Forces, namely children fathered by Australian Occupation servicemen and Japanese women see Hamilton, 2012.

1093. *Kiku to Isamu* [Kiku and Isamu]. Directed by Tadashi Imai (1959) 116 minutes DVD; Kozawa, 1957, pp. 8-9.

1094. Thompson, 2000, 25. I would like to thank Mira Foster for kindly directing me to this source.

1095. These are considered pejorative terms meaning love child and mixed-blood child respectively, both which are no longer used in modern day parlance.

1096. Dower, 1999; Kovner, 2012; Sanders, 2012. The term, *panpan* or "woman of the night," was used to describe sex workers in post-war Japan. Women who fraternized with American soldiers were assumed to be prostitutes even if they were wives or girlfriends of the G.I.s. Therefore the term, *panpan no ko* was extended to mixed-race people.

1097. Karl Lippincott, email correspondence. September 8, 2014.

1098. Lippincott, Oral History Interview.

1099. Karl Lippincott, telephone interview with Lily Anne Y. Welty

Tamai. July 27, 2008.

1100. Lippincott, Oral History Interview.

1101. Ibid.

1102. Ibid.

1103. Ibid.

1104. Ibid.

1105. Hirano published multiple books in Japanese. In English the titles translate to, *The Lives of the Mixed Bloods* (1954), *Remi is Living* (1959), *Remi Come Outside* (1962), *Remis who were Left Behind* (1964), *Remi is Twenty Years Old: A Multiracial person's Experience of Love and Tears* (1966), *Remis' Mothers* (1967), and *Without A Hometown* (1969).

1106. Pearl Buck in Hirano, 1966.

1107. Hirano, 1967.

1108. Ibid.

1109. Lippincott, Oral History Interview.

1110. The Pearl Buck Foundation opened offices in Korea (1965), Okinawa and Taiwan (1967), the Philippines and Thailand (1968), and Vietnam (1970). Conn, 1996, 359.

1111. For more on Pearl Buck, see Conn, 1996.

1112. Karl Lippincott, telephone interview by the author, August 9, 2009.

1113. Karl Lippincott, telephone interview by the author, November 27, 2011.

1114. Lippincott, Oral History Interview.

1115. Ibid.

1116. Ibid.

1117. Ibid.

1118. Ibid.

1119. Campbell Gibson and Kay Jung. *Historical Census Statistics on Population Totals By Race, 1790 to 1990, and By Hispanic Origin, 1970 to 1990, For The United States, Regions, Divisions, and States*. Working

Paper Series No. 56, Population Division U. S. Census Bureau, Washington, DC 20233 (September, 2002). http://www.census.gov/population/www/documentation/twps0056/tab44.pdf (accessed 4 September 2014).

## CHAPTER SIXTEEN

1120. Many thanks to Aphra Kerr, Sean Ó Riain, Brian Conway, and Laura Grindstaff for thoughtful reading, discussion and comments. Thanks also to the Northwestern University Department of Sociology (John Hagan, Chair) and Library.

1121. Spencer, 2009.

1122. Matthews, 2007.

1123. Ibid., 41.

1124. See Eric Liu, "The new color wheel," *New York Times,* February 13, 2011. http://www.nytimes.com/roomfordebate/2011/02/13

1125. Becker, 2002; Griswold, 2002; Peterson, 1997.

1126. Chin, Feng, and Lee, 2000, pp. 273-274.

1127. Ibid.

1128. Maira, 2000, 361.

1129. Cornell and Hartmann, 2007.

1130. Goldberg, 2002; Omi and Winant, 1994.

1131. Studies such as Wacquant, 2004 also make this connection between the body and the cultural production of race.

1132. For more on mainstream, pyramidal pageants as texts see Banet-Weiser, 1999; Cohen, Wilk, and Stoeltje, 1996; or Riverol, 1992. For more on Japanese American pageants see Yano, 2006.

1133. Kurashige, 2002.

1134. For more on 'retro' femininity see Tasker and Negra, 2007. For more on "hyper" femininity see Espiritu, 1997.

1135. Inglis, 2005, pp. 29-30

1136. Kurashige, 2002.

1137. King-O'Riain, 2006.

1138. Davila, 2008, 17.

1139. Craig, 2002.

1140. Ibid., pp. 14-15.

1141. Yano, 2006.

1142. Craig, 2006, 174.

1143. Peterson, 1997, 225.

1144. King-O'Riain, 2006.

1145. Many of the judges, chaperones and pageant organizers were past queen or court members or family members (brothers) of the queens/princesses.

1146. Potts et al., 2008.

## CHAPTER SEVENTEEN

1147. This is a slightly modified version of Christine C. Iijima Hall, "Please Choose One: Ethnic Identity Choices for Biracial Individuals," In *Racially Mixed People in America*, ed. Maria P.P. Root, 250-264. Newbury Park, CA: Sage Publications, 1992. Reproduced with permission of Sage Publications, Incorporated in the format republish in a book via Copyright Clearance Center.

1148. Teicher, 1968.

1149. Park, 1928.

1150. Stonequist 1937.

1151. Ibid., 8.

1152. Antonovsky, 1956; Gist, 1967; Goldberg, 1941; Green, 1947; Kerckhoff & McCormick, 1955; Wright and Wright, 1972.

1153. Kerckhoff and McCormick, 1955.

1154. Goldberg, 1941.

1155. Ramirez, Castaneda, and Cox, 1977.

1156. Park, 1937, xvii.

1157. Erikson, 1968.

1158. Dien and Vinacke, 1964; Rosenberg, 1965.

1159. Dien and Vinacke, 1964.

1160. Aiken, 1971.

1161. Bogardus, 1925.

1162. Cheek, 1972.

1163. Cross, 1978.

1164. Kitano, 1974; Piskacek and Golub, 1973.

1165. Goodman, 1964.

1166. Cooley, 1902.

1167. Reviewed in Brand, Ruiz, and Padilla, 1974.

1168. Clark, Kaufman, and Pierce, 1976; Matsumoto, Meredith, and Masuda, 1970.

1169. Hall, 1980.

1170. Cheek, 1972; Criswell, 1939.

1171. Sotomayor, 1977; Taylor, Bassilli, and Aboud, 1973; Taylor, Sinard, and Aboud, 1972; Uyeki, 1960.

1172. Clark et al., 1976.

1173. Strong, 1978; Wagatsuma, 1967; Wagatsuma, 1977.

1174. Festinger, 1957.

1175. Cooley, 1902; and Clark and Clark, 1939.

1176. Erikson, 1968.

1177. Hare, 1965.

1178. Bern, 1974.

1179. Stonequist, 1937.

1180. Garmezy, 1978.

1181. See Park, 1937 and the "multicultural people" considered by

Ramirez et al., 1977.

## CHAPTER EIGHTEEN

1182. See King-O'Riain, 2006; Kurashige, 2002; Murphy-Shigematsu, 1986; Robertson, 2002; Spickard, 1989, l996

1183. Anne Milan, Helene Maheux, and Tina Chui, "A Portrait of Couples in Mixed Unions," http://www.statcan.gc.ca/pub/11-008-x/2010001/article/11143-eng.htm (retrieved February 17, 2015).

1184. Lesser, 2007; Masterson, 2004.

1185. Adachi, 2010; Hirabayashi, Kikumura-Yano, and Hirabayashi, 2002.

1186. Tanaka, 1980, 240.

1187. Jon Inouye, "A Major Ethnic Disaster," *Pacific Citizen,* March 25, 1977, 4.

1188. Ibid.

1189. Bill Hosokawa, "The Intermarriage Question," *Pacific Citizen,* April 18, 1977.

1190. Ibid.

1191. Kurashige, 2002; King, 2006.

1192. King-O'Riain, 2001, 2002, and 2006.

1193. King-O'Riain, 2006, 202.

1194. George Yoshinaga, *Kashu Mainichi,* July 19, 1976; cited in Kurashige, 2002, 243.

1195. Linden Nishinaga, Letters to the Editor, *Rafu Shimpo,* August 27, 1982, 3.

1196. King-O'Riain, 2006; Kurashige, 2002.

1197. See Hedy Posey, "Letter to the Editor." *Rafu Shimpo,* September 10, 1982, 2.

1198. Chin, 2012.

1199. http://www.discovernikkei.org/en/nikkeialbum/

albums/176/?view=list (retrieved on February 17, 2015).

1200. Lane Hirabayashi, "Is the JA Community Disappearing? Or is the Choice up to Us?" *Pacific Currents*, 1993, B15-16.

1201. Kurashige, 2002, 185.

1202. Murphy-Shigematsu, 1986.

1203. Yuen, 2003.

1204. Ropp, 2002.

1205. Solomon Moore, "The Courts of Ethnic Identity," Los Angeles Times, July 14, 2000. http://articles.latimes.com/2000/jul/14/news/mn-52993 (retrieved on February 17, 2015).

1206. Mireya Navarro, "Young Japanese-Americans Honor Ethnic Roots," *New York Times*, August 2, 2004, 15.

1207. Gwen Muranaka, "JANM Enters Next Phase," *Rafu Shimpo*, November 5, 2012, 1.

1208. https://www.linkedin.com/company/nikkei-youth-network - retrieved March 22, 2015.

1209. http://v3con.com/category/v3-con/page/4/ - retrieved March 22, 2015.

1210. http://www.ladowntownnews.com/news/new-ceo-shakes-up-japanese-american-national-museum/article_f44cc95a-0430-11e2-bd8e-0019bb2963f4.html - retrieved March 22, 2015.

1211. Appadurai, 1996.

# AUTHOR BIOS

**Paul D. Barclay** is Associate Professor and Chair of the Asian Studies Program at Lafayette College, and General Editor of East Asia Image Collections Digital Archive. He has published articles in *Journal of Asian Studies*, *Japanese Studies*, *Taiwan Genjūmin Kenkyū* (Studies on Indigenous Peoples of Taiwan), *Humanities Research*, and *Social Science Japan Journal*. He is a recipient of awards from the National Endowment for the Humanities, Social Science Research Council, Taiwan Ministry of Foreign Affairs and the Japan Society for the Promotion of Science.

**Eveline Buchheim** studied Cultural Anthropology at the University of Amsterdam and works as a researcher at NIOD: Institute for War, Holocaust and Genocide Studies in Amsterdam. Her research interests include intimate relationships in colonial Indonesia and changing gender relations as a result of the Pacific War. Her research is largely based on unique personal documents from this era, including letters, diaries and oral history interviews. She was awarded a Ph.D. by the University of Amsterdam for her dissertation *Passie en missie: Huwelijken van Europeanen in Nederlands-Indië en Indonesië, 1920-1958* (Passion and Purpose: Marriages of Europeans in the Dutch East Indies and Indonesia, 1920-1958). She has published on women's contributions to empire, Dutch-Japanese fraternization during the Pacific War and its legacies, and heritage tourism.

**Brian Burke-Gaffney** was born in Canada and came to Japan in 1972. A former Zen monk, he is currently Professor of Cultural History at the Nagasaki Institute of Applied Science. He has published several books in both Japanese and English, including *Starcrossed: A Biography of Madame Butterfly* (EastBridge, 2004) and *Nagasaki: The British Experience 1854-1945* (Global Oriental UK, 2009).

**Lane Earns** is Professor of History and Provost and Vice Chancellor of Academic Affairs at the University of Wisconsin Oshkosh. He received his Ph.D. in history from the University of Hawai'i at Manoa in 1987. His research focuses on intercultural relations between Japan and the West, seen primarily through developments at the port city of Nagasaki. Earns is currently working on a manuscript tentatively entitled *Yankees in the Naples of the Orient: A Century of American Culture, Commerce and Catastrophe in Nagasaki.*

**Christine C. Iijima Hall** received her Ph.D. in social psychology from UCLA in 1980. Her dissertation on mixed race identity was the first large study on the topic conducted in the United States. Dr. Hall has authored numerous books chapters and journal articles on multiracial identity, ethnic women and body image, and the need for psychology to diversify its profession in teaching, research and practice. After serving 35 years as a higher education administrator, Dr. Hall's retirement includes coaching mid-level administrators on career advancement and navigating the political waters of higher education.

**Walter Hamilton** is a journalist who reported from Japan for eleven years for the Australian Broadcasting Corporation. He is the author of *Children of the Occupation: Japan's Untold Story* (NewSouth, 2012) and *Serendipity City: Australia, Japan and the Multifunction Polis* (ABC Books, 1991).

**Itsuko Kamoto** is a sociologist and a Professor on the Faculty of the Study of the Contemporary Society of Kyoto Women's University, Japan. Her main research focus has been the emergence and transformation of the relationship between cross-nationality marriage and Japanese society. She is the author of *Kokusai kekkon no tanjō: "Bunmeikoku Nihon" e no michi* (Shinyōsha, 2001) and *Kokusai kekkon ron*, 2 vols. (Hōritsu Bunkasha, 2008).

**Nadia Kanagawa** is currently a doctoral candidate in the history department at the University of Southern California. After earning a BA in History from Yale University in 2006, she spent a year at the Inter-University Center in Yokohama, and then moved to Tokyo and worked for Google Japan for three years before returning to the U.S. and to academia. Her dissertation examines how the Japanese *ritsuryō* state approached the incorporation, assimilation, and configuration of immigrants and their descendants over the Nara and early Heian periods.

**Rebecca Chiyoko King-O'Riain** is a Senior Lecturer in Sociology at Maynooth University in the Republic of Ireland. Her research interests are in emotions, technology and globalization; race/ethnicity and critical race theory; people of mixed descent, beauty, and Japanese Americans. She has published in *Global Networks, Ethnicities, Sociology Compass, Journal of Asian American Studies, Amerasia Journal, Irish Geography* and in many edited books. She is the lead editor of *Global Mixed Race* (New York University Press, 2014). Her book *Pure Beauty: Judging Race in Japanese American Beauty Pageants* (University of Minnesota Press, 2006) examined the use of blood quantum rules in Japanese American beauty pageants. She is currently researching and writing about "The Globalization of Love".

**Gary Leupp** is Professor of History at Tufts University, specializing in the Tokugawa period and issues of class, sexuality and ethnicity in Japanese history. His writings include *Servants, Shophands and Laborers in Tokugawa Japan* (Princeton University Press, 1994); *Male Colors: The Construction of Homosexuality in Early Modern Japan* (University of California Press, 1997); and *Interracial Intimacy: Japanese Women and Western Men, 1543-1900* (Continuum, 2003).

**Ellen Nakamura** is Senior Lecturer in Japanese and History at the University of Auckland, New Zealand. She is interested broadly in the social and medical history of nineteenth-century Japan. Her current research focuses on the Japanese physicians who lived through the transition from Tokugawa to Meiji.

**Cynthia Nakashima** is an independent scholar who has been involved in the study of people of mixed race since the late 1980's. Her publications include the co-edited volume, *The Sum of Our Parts: Mixed-heritage Asian Americans* (Temple University Press, 2001). She lives in the San Francisco Bay Area with her husband and two daughters, Madeline and Charlotte.

**Jennifer Robertson** is a Professor of Anthropology and the History of Art at the University of Michigan. Author of *Native and Newcomer: Making and Remaking a Japanese City* (University of California Press, 1991 & 1994) and *Takarazuka: Sexual Politics and Popular Culture in Modern Japan* (University of California Press, 1998 & 2001), among other books and articles, Robertson is completing a new book on robots, eugenics, and posthuman aesthetics.

**Greg Robinson** is Professor of U.S. History at l'Université du Québec À Montréal, a French-language institution in Montreal, Canada. His books include *By Order of the President: FDR and the Internment of Japanese Americans* (Harvard University Press, 2001) an academic best-seller that uncovers President Franklin Roosevelt's central involvement in the wartime confinement of 120,000 Japanese Americans; *A Tragedy of Democracy: Japanese Confinement in North America* (Columbia University Press, 2009), winner of the 2009 History book prize of the Association for Asian American Studies; and *After Camp: Portraits in Midcentury Japanese American Life and Politics* (University of California Press, 2012), winner of the Caroline Bancroft History Prize in Western U.S. History.

**Paul Spickard** teaches History, Black Studies, and Asian American Studies at the University of California, Santa Barbara. He has taught at fifteen universities in the United States and abroad. He is author or editor of eighteen books and seventy-odd articles on race, migration, and related topics, including: *Race in Mind* (University of Notre Dame Press, 2015); *Global Mixed Race* (NYU Press, 2014); *Japanese Americans* (Twayne Publishers, 1996, Rutgers University Press, 2009); *Almost All Aliens: Immigration, Race and Colonialism in American History and Identity* (Routledge, 2007); *Is Lighter Better? Skin-Tone Discrimination among Asian Americans* (Rowman & Littlefield, 2007); *Race and Nation: Ethnic Systems in the Modern World* (Routledge, 2005); *Racial Thinking in the United States* (University of Notre Dame Press, 2004); and *Mixed Blood: Intermarriage and Ethnic Identity in 20th-Century America* (University of Wisconsin Press, 1989).

**Lily Anne Yumi Welty Tamai** grew up in the agricultural community of Oxnard, California, speaking Japanese and English in a mixed-race household. Her undergraduate studies in Sociology and Biology shaped her research interests and she holds advanced degrees in Biology and History, and a Ph.D. in History from the University of California Santa Barbara. Her dissertation research documents the history of mixed-race American Japanese born after World War II and raised during the post-war period. She has a chapter titled, "Multiraciality and Migration: Mixed Race American Okinawans 1945-1972" in the edited volume *Global Mixed Race* (NYU Press, 2014), and articles in *Pan Japan* and *Southern California Quarterly*. She is currently the history curator at the Japanese American National Museum in Los Angeles.

**Duncan Ryūken Williams** is an Associate Professor of Religion and East Asian Languages and Cultures at the University of Southern California, the Director of the USC Shinso Ito Center for Japanese Religions and Culture, and founder of the Hapa Japan Database Project. He has also served as the Executive Vice-President of Japan House, Los Angeles. He received his Ph.D. from Harvard University and previously held the Shinjo Ito Distinguished Chair of Japanese Buddhism at University of California Berkeley and served as the Director of Berkeley's Center for Japanese Studies. He is the author of *The Other Side of Zen: A Social History of Sōtō Zen Buddhism in Tokugawa Japan* (Princeton, 2005) and *Camp Dharma: Buddhism and the Japanese American Incarceration During World War II* (UC Press, forthcoming). He has also co-edited a number of volumes including *Issei Buddhism in the Americas* (Illinois, 2010); *American Buddhism* (Routledge, 1998); and *Buddhism and Ecology* (Harvard, 1997).

**Yuriko Yamanouchi** is Associate Professor at Tokyo University of Foreign Studies. She received her Ph.D. in Anthropology from the University of Sydney. Her research interests include urban Indigenous Australians, identity and indigeneity, communities, relationship between Indigenous Australians and Japanese migrants.

# INDEX

anti-miscegenation laws, *see* marriage laws

# B

# C

# D

Dejima, 18, 29, 36-40, 47-57, 76, 85-7, 108
  courtesans in, 36, 40, 42, 51-5, 60, 111
  demographics, 37
  hapa children in, 40, 53-4

demographics of Japanese and mixed Japanese populations,
  Australia, 256-7, 259
  Hawai'i, 266
  Japan, iii-iv, 37, 298, 331, 385
  Japanese diasporic community, iv
  U.S., iv, 189, 195, 225, 266-7, 385, 393
  U.S. internment, 226, 271-2, 274

Doeff, Hendrik, 38, 40, 42, 51, 55-7, 86

Dutch East India Company, 22, 26, 29-31, 37-41, 50-5
  in Taiwan, 158

Dutch East Indies (see also Indonesia), 188, 279-91
  Dutch colonial legal classification of Japanese as
  "Europeans", 282
  Indisch (mixed Dutch Indonesians), 279, 281-4, 287
  Japanese internment of Dutch, 280-1, 287
  Japanese invasion of, 219-20, 279-91

Dutch traders, 17-8, 24, 26, 28, 36-40, 42, 45, 47-57, 86-7,
108-9
  colony at Batavia, 18, 29-34
  hapa children of Dutch traders, 30-1, 33,4, 38-40, 42-
  4, see also Kusumoto Ine
  in Taiwan, 153, 158, 160
  see also Dejima and Dutch East India Company

# E

Edict 103 (Meiji Japan), see marriage laws

Edo (see also Tokyo), 47, 53, 76

Edo period, Japan, see Japan (Early Modern)

beauty pageants and, 350, 354-5

International Social Service (ISS), 307-8, 312-23

# J

# U

unequal treaties, 58, 113-4
  end of unequal treaties, 61, 118
  *see also* European imperialism and Opening of Japan

United States,
  anti-Japanese organizations, 202
  attitudes towards Japanese, 195, 197-207 passim, 223,
  225-6, 265-8 passim
  attitudes towards mixed Asians, 199-206, 293, 342-5
  first Issei, 189-95
  idea of Anglo-Protestant America, 199, 205
  immigration laws, 195-8, 203, 205-6, 223, 248
  marriage laws, 105, 195-9, 202, 222-3, 226, 387

United States Military Information Service, hapa
Americans in, 221-2, 231

United States occupation forces
  war brides, 223

United States occupation of Japan, 231, 293-4
  occupation policies, 293-4

United States treatment of Japanese Americans during
WWII, 206-22, 226, 230-1, 235, 265-78, 386
  attitudes of Japanese Americans towards hapa people,
  214-5, 276-7
  criteria for internment, 267-70
  demographics 226, 271-2, 274
  hapa and mixed families, 226, 265-78
  Hawai'i, 207
  internment, 206-222, 265-78
  loss of property, 266, 272
  U.S. Army Western Defense Command (WDC), 265-75
  U.S. Central and East, 214
  U.S. War Relocation Authority (WRA), 207, 209, 226,
  267, 269
  U.S. West Coast, 207